# SLEEPLESS NIGHTS

200+ Horror, Mystery, Thriller, and Suspense Stories

## TOBIAS WADE

**HAUNTED HOUSE**
PUBLISHING

This is a work of fiction. Names, characters, organizations, businesses, places, events and incidents either are the product of the author's imagination or are used fictitiously. Any resemblance to actual persons, living or dead, or actual events is entirely coincidental.

Second Edition: April 2021
Sleepless Nights

# HAUNTED HOUSE
## PUBLISHING

Copyright © 2021
Tobias Wade

All rights reserved. This book or any portion thereof may not be reproduced or used in any manner whatsoever without the express written permission of the publisher except for the use of brief quotations in a book review.

# Contents

| | |
|---|---|
| 51 SLEEPLESS NIGHTS | 1 |
| A Cracked Life | 1 |
| My Mother the Spider Queen | 4 |
| I'm in Love With the Devil's Wife | 9 |
| Don't let him Steal my Child | 14 |
| My Journey in a Parallel Universe | 18 |
| My Family Tradition to Feed the Spirit | 24 |
| The Angel Doll | 29 |
| Virtual Terror | 38 |
| Everyone Lives, but not Everyone Dies | 44 |
| Two Minds, one Body | 51 |
| I Loved her in the Winter | 55 |
| Like Father Like Son | 58 |
| Anger Management | 61 |
| Confessions of a Serial Killer | 68 |
| The Organ Harvesting Club | 69 |
| Unborn Doll | 72 |
| Painting the Roses | 73 |
| The Power of a Small City | 78 |
| Mother is Back | 92 |
| Vicarious | 95 |
| The 32 | 101 |
| Dreaming Without Sleep | 107 |
| Killer Selfie | 110 |
| The Final Question | 112 |
| The Confession | 113 |
| Children Collector | 116 |
| Post Office Worker | 120 |
| Who Wrote the Suicide Note? | 122 |
| The Psychedelic Tattoo | 125 |
| She was Asking for it | 127 |
| 124 Terabyte Virus | 128 |
| Countdown to the Beast | 131 |
| Haunting Sound | 138 |
| The Masked Orgy | 140 |

| | |
|---|---|
| Breaking and Entering for Dummies | 144 |
| The Face on my Bedroom Wall | 147 |
| The Wall Between us | 150 |
| Burning Desire | 153 |
| The Psychopath in my House | 156 |
| How to Start Your own Cult | 158 |
| Three go to Sleep; Four Wake up. | 161 |
| She is Still With me | 167 |
| Dead man Floating | 169 |
| The Monster Inside us | 174 |
| History Written in Scars | 180 |
| The Party That Changed my Life | 182 |
| The Solution to Prison Overcrowding | 185 |
| A Letter From the Cold Case Files | 189 |
| I am a Human Voodoo Doll | 191 |
| The Organic Machine | 196 |
| My Face Will be the Last Thing you see | 199 |

| | |
|---|---|
| 52 SLEEPLESS NIGHTS | 205 |
| The Grim Reaper's Scythe | 205 |
| The Hitchhiker | 208 |
| An Open Letter To My Daughter's Killer | 211 |
| When The Music Dies | 212 |
| The Town Not On Any Map | 215 |
| Echo Of The Dead | 219 |
| Life Without Monsters | 223 |
| The Stranger Upstairs | 226 |
| Heaven Keeps a Prisoner | 230 |
| My New Sex Doll Won't Stop Crying | 236 |
| Suicide Watch Party | 239 |
| The Second Time I Killed Myself | 242 |
| Under The Frozen Lake | 246 |
| Bet I Can Make You Smile | 249 |
| The Assassin's Orphanage: Chapter 1 | 252 |
| The Assassin's Orphanage: Chapter 2 | 256 |
| The Assassin's Orphanage: Chapter 3 | 259 |
| The Suicide Bomber | 263 |
| The Most Terrifying Drawing | 265 |
| My Daughter Spoke Before She Was Born | 270 |
| Behind Closed Doors | 272 |
| Mars Colonization Project | 277 |
| A Righteous Angry Midget | 282 |

| | |
|---|---|
| A Painting By Day, A Window By Night | 284 |
| We Can Fix Your Child | 288 |
| Don't Leave An Audio Recorder On Overnight | 290 |
| The Slaughterhouse Camera | 296 |
| Recordings Of Myself | 298 |
| Your Dream Job | 300 |
| Which Child To Save | 304 |
| 400 Hits of LSD | 307 |
| Wounds that Words Have Caused | 311 |
| Raised By The Man Who Kidnapped Me | 314 |
| My Son Said Goodbye | 317 |
| Our Extra Son Was for Experiments | 321 |
| The Storm Is Alive | 326 |
| The Head Transplant | 329 |
| Midnight Prayers | 332 |
| When the Blood Rain Falls | 336 |
| She Can't Tell Lies | 340 |
| The New You | 343 |
| Dreammaker Music | 346 |
| The Girl On a Leash | 349 |
| What the Blind Man Sees | 353 |
| Do Demons Lay Eggs? | 356 |
| Underwater Microphone Picks Up Voices | 359 |
| Dancing With Chaos To The Beat Of The Drums | 362 |
| This Flower Only Grows From Corpses | 364 |
| Trapped Between Life And Death | 367 |
| Clowns Must Not Frown | 369 |
| Have You Heard About Shelley? | 373 |
| Hospice Of Hope | 374 |
| | |
| 53 SLEEPLESS NIGHTS | 378 |
| An Old Man's Last Secret | 378 |
| My Daughter Is An Only Child With A Twin | 380 |
| My Self-Help Tape Told Me To Kill Myself | 383 |
| Where the People Who Disappear Go | 388 |
| My Reflection Smiles More Than I Do | 391 |
| Mom I'm 14, I Can Have My Own Demon | 394 |
| Haunted House Publishing | 398 |
| Somebody Broke Her | 401 |
| Any Soul Will Do | 405 |
| The Other Side Of Sky | 409 |
| Their Last Words | 413 |

| | |
|---|---|
| Children Taste Better | 415 |
| The Smallest Coffins Are The Heaviest | 417 |
| Self-Portrait From The Dead | 420 |
| Life Before Birth | 425 |
| My Soul Is In A Paper Lantern | 430 |
| The World's Oldest Tree | 433 |
| Am I Dreaming, Or Am I The Dream? | 440 |
| Our Ship Sailed Over The Edge Of The World | 444 |
| It Wasn't A Hit And Run. I Reversed Too. | 449 |
| The Missing Child Speaks | 452 |
| Are You Happy Now? | 455 |
| She Looks Like A Future Victim | 460 |
| The Exorcism Of An Angel | 462 |
| Now Hiring. Last Three Employees Killed Themselves. | 465 |
| Sgt Dawson's Widow Deserves To Know How He Really Died | 467 |
| Ugly Little Liars | 470 |
| Message In A Bottle | 473 |
| Illuminating The Dark Web | 477 |
| Me, Myself, And I Play Games Together | 480 |
| Putin Doesn't Like My Father | 486 |
| The Taking Tree | 489 |
| Have You Seen This Child? | 493 |
| When You Die In A Dream | 495 |
| Dead Dogs Don't Do Tricks | 497 |
| Blood Games | 501 |
| The Stillbirth Lie | 506 |
| The Mercy Killing Appointment | 510 |
| Don't Follow Tail Lights Through A Fog | 511 |
| Alektorophobia: A Fear Of Chickens | 514 |
| My Stalker Wishes Me Happy Birthday Every Year | 516 |
| My Diary That I Didn't Write | 519 |
| Relive Your Childhood | 522 |
| Heart Eater | 526 |
| Xenophobia | 529 |
| A Global Religion | 532 |
| First Rule of Fright Club | 535 |
| Second Rule of Fright Club | 539 |
| Third Rule of Fright Club | 543 |
| Antennas on Every House | 548 |
| I Lost My Innocence at Serenity Falls | 550 |
| Bury The Pain | 554 |
| The Scariest Story In The World | 557 |

| | |
|---|---:|
| 54 SLEEPLESS NIGHTS | 562 |
| My Wives Don't Get Along | 562 |
| The Taxidermied Child | 565 |
| Redemption for Murder | 568 |
| She Only Wants Me For My Body | 571 |
| Yesterday Was Better | 573 |
| Inside A Human Zoo | 574 |
| I Don't Trust The Little God | 578 |
| A Ticket Out Of Hell | 580 |
| Sharing A Dream | 584 |
| The Suspicious Butcher | 586 |
| My Neighbor's Infestation | 589 |
| Should I Stop Selling Bodies? | 592 |
| The House No One Built | 595 |
| The Other Me | 598 |
| The Invisible Door | 603 |
| Where the Devil Keeps His Pets | 608 |
| The Only Time My Father Cried | 611 |
| Whispers From My Music Box: Part 1 | 615 |
| Whispers From My Music Box: Part 2 | 618 |
| Trading My Child | 620 |
| The Smell of Death | 624 |
| Forced Equality | 625 |
| he Forgotten Trauma | 629 |
| I Am Not My Body's Master | 632 |
| Museum of Alien Life: Part 1 | 635 |
| Museum of Alien Life: Part 2 | 638 |
| For The Right Price | 642 |
| The Newspaper Threatened Me | 644 |
| The Forbidden Room | 647 |
| It Wasn't A Real Hospital | 650 |
| Will You Be My Mother When She's Dead? | 653 |
| I Keep Her Close | 656 |
| Lights in the Deep | 658 |
| The Demon In Heaven | 661 |
| She Knows Your Death | 663 |
| A Borrowed Life | 664 |
| The Wolf and The Raven: Part 1 | 668 |
| The Wolf and The Raven: Part 2 | 673 |
| The Wolf and The Raven: Part 3 | 677 |
| What Doesn't Kill You Makes You Stronger | 680 |
| The Lies of Eyes and Ears | 683 |

| | |
|---|---|
| Flesh Zipper | 685 |
| Sacrifice Given, Sacrifice Taken | 688 |
| The Toy Soldier that Saved My Life | 690 |
| Transparent Eyelids | 693 |
| Rebooting A Broken Human | 696 |
| Every Day is My Last Day Alive | 699 |
| Crown Of Teeth | 700 |
| World of Wrath | 704 |
| They Were Human Once | 706 |
| To Love A Phantom | 709 |
| Fear the Echo and the Answer | 712 |
| The Reincarnation Trap | 715 |
| The Never-Ending Cave | 717 |
| BRUTAL BEDTIME STORIES | 722 |
| Hell is Heaven to the Demons | 723 |
| Do Not Go Gentle Into That Good Night: Tobias Wade | 727 |
| Dogs can Recognize Skinwalkers: Tobias Wade | 731 |
| Dreams are a Two-Way Window: Tobias Wade | 736 |
| For Sale: Human Head. Condition: Used: Tobias Wade | 739 |
| I Buy and Sell Memories: Tobias Wade | 742 |
| Flesh-Eating Sea Bugs: Tobias Wade | 746 |
| Every Subway Car | 749 |
| Every Subway Car: Tobias Wade | 749 |
| From Rags to Stitches: Tobias Wade | 753 |
| Two Dead Playing the Elevator Game: Tobias Wade | 757 |
| One Death is not Enough: Tobias Wade | 759 |
| Imagine a Night: Tobias Wade | 763 |

# Read More

Join the Haunted House Book Club and read more stories for free.

**HAUNTED HOUSE PUBLISHING**

TobiasWade.Com

# 51 Sleepless Nights

### A Cracked Life

I was sixteen when I saw the first crack. A jagged line, almost four feet long but less than an inch wide. I found it by the sidewalk behind my house. Not *on* the sidewalk—the crack was in the air, visible from every direction as I circled around it. Harmlessly suspended, and nothing more.

    I couldn't touch it. My hand passed through the crack as though it wasn't there, leaving me white and numb with cold by the time I reached the other side. I wouldn't walk close to it. Something about the emptiness just rubbed me the wrong way. I've walked around caves, stared down holes, even used a telescope to look at the space between stars—this crack wasn't like that. It felt less like something was missing, and more like something extra that shouldn't be there.

    My family moved shortly after the discovery, and I forgot all about it for a while. Time moved steadily forward, except maybe for a few months after college when it stopped to let me admire my future wife. Her smile hinted at a secret, and if I had a guess, I'd say it was the secret to being happy. I would have given anything to explore every hidden crevice of her mind, knowing her as she knew herself. Then we could start making secrets of our own.

    It was about a week after we met at work, when we both had to stay late to clean up after an office party. I asked her to come sit on the roof and look at the sky with me. There we were: side-by-side, the space between our hands burning like fire, the shape of her mouth illuminated by the backdrop of endless stars. They gleamed like millions of envious eyes wishing they could sit where I was.

    I didn't know anything could make me feel so weak. My legs trembled, and I kept switching positions so she wouldn't notice. I didn't trust the words in my mouth or the thoughts in my brain. I didn't trust any other part of me which was soon blurred out of existence to make room for my appreciation of everything that she was.

That's when I saw the crack again, and I was reminded how powerful weakness really could be. It was larger now, running along the side of an external AC unit. Not *quite* alongside—if I really looked, I could see the empty air between the metal box and the crack. I could just make out the little streaks of light where the surrounding stars bled into the hole to be lost forever. It was a cookie-cutter gap in reality that the world forgot to fill in.

"You can leave whenever you want," she'd said.

I guess she noticed I was distracted. I shook my head, prompting her fingers to trace their way up my hand. I turned to her, her breath warm against my mouth, and suddenly that was the only thing in the world.

Six months later and we were engaged.

Another year and we were married.

Neither of us stayed long at the office, and I never went back to that roof. The crack didn't matter. Bad dreams can't hurt you once you've woken up, and beside her grace, I was awake for the very first time.

Things went well for us, but we were so in love that I don't think we would have noticed if they hadn't. I got an investment banking job and climbed the corporate ladder. I started seeing more cracks, but no one else noticed, so I didn't mention them. Sometimes they'd align perfectly to an existing object, but I could feel their emptiness pulling at me.

I knew what they really were.

There was a big one above the conference table at work, but I had a future here and wouldn't let something ethereal as that get in the way of my success. My diligence paid off when my boss finally told me that he was getting older and wanted to make me a partner for the firm. He was standing right on the other side of the crack when he spoke, and it was difficult to maintain eye contact with him.

"Unless you don't want to be partner," my boss had said, misreading my silence. "Of course, you can leave whenever you want."

The same words spoken to me before, but I hadn't recognized the significance yet. I just smiled and shook his hand, careful to reach underneath the crack hanging between us. It was another dream come true, and I was king of the world.

My wife and I moved into a big house and we had a baby girl. I watched her grow, and watched the cracks grow with her. Hairline fractures splintered the sky, mapping a web throughout the air. I had to be careful where I was walking. There could be a dozen of them in my path within a given day.

I passed through a big one once in my car. I was changing lanes and didn't notice in time. The crack went straight through my windshield without disturbing the glass, passing through my heart and out the other side. Cold doesn't begin to describe it. The line erased my body as it passed through me, displacing skin and organs, leaving a sucking vacuous wound for the briefest instant before it was gone. I lurched at the wheel and spun off the road into the guardrail. My hands kept racing over my chest, fists pounding against solid skin to reassure myself I was whole.

I started working from home after that. The one bathroom didn't have any cracks in it, and I spend most of my time in there.

I've seen my wife and daughter walk straight through the cracks without the slightest notice. I can't explain to them what I see or feel, because I know they'll think I'm crazy. And maybe I am, but that doesn't change anything. I'll sit in the bathroom for hours, working on my laptop or reading a book, loath to leave where I might stumble through what isn't there.

My wife begged me to go outside. Sometimes I'd open the door just to walk around the house or sit with her in the living room, but I couldn't leave anymore. There were too many cracks—more every day, it seemed.

The world around me had shattered, and I was the only one who noticed. I know it hurt her, but in time my wife accepted that this is how our life had to be. She made the best of it, always inviting friends or family here and making excuses when I was expected somewhere. She took cooking classes and learned how to make all my favorite meals, even getting a small table and television installed in the bathroom I was confined to.

My daughter was a different story. Eight years old, and no amount of explaining could make her understand how much I loved her, even if I wasn't always there. I didn't know how embarrassed she was of me until a teacher called to let me know she'd been telling all her friends that I was dead. I sat with her in the kitchen and asked why she did that, but all she'd said was that I might as well have been.

And she was right.

I wasn't taking care of my family anymore. They had enough money put away that they didn't need me to work. I was just a burden, and just like the cracks, the burden was growing every day. Some nights I wouldn't leave the bathroom to go to bed, and I could hear my wife crying through the wall between us.

I tried pushing myself harder, willing myself through the emptiness, but it wasn't any good. The cracks cut through me like a knife, freezing me to my core, shredding bone and sinew and then stitching me back together so seamlessly that there was nothing but the memory of that pain to remind me of my torment.

I was ready for this to be over. I just didn't know it until I heard the words from my daughter's mouth as she pressed against the other side of the bathroom door:

"You can leave whenever you want."

"Yes," I told her. "I'm ready."

"All you've got to do is throw yourself into a big one. Then you're out."

She knew about the cracks? I jumped up and flung open the door. She wasn't there.

I raced down the hall, shouting her name, forcing myself through each searing darkness that severed my mind and body, heart and soul.

I found her outside, standing next to the biggest abyss I had ever seen. A wall of darkness, ten feet across and ripping through the air above like a skyscraper. I could feel the call of that emptiness, whispering to me, beckoning me, a promise of freedom and release that a lifetime of memories could not dissuade.

"Just do it already. You've been here long enough," my daughter said.

But I was afraid. Even this far away from the blackness, I could imagine how those dark talons would feel as they rend my body. Would there be anything left of me to come out the other side? It was big enough that I didn't have to come out at all. I could step in and be gone. It's what my daughter wanted. So did my wife, if only she had the courage to admit it. And maybe it's what I wanted to.

But on my knees before all of creation and its antithesis, I was afraid.

"It's easy. Just follow me."

I tried to stop her. Air dragging through my lungs, feet stumbling and twisting, I made a desperate lunging grab—I tried to stop my daughter from entering that blackness. But she was gone, and there was no choice but to follow.

Into the looming void I plunged, screaming without sound, bleeding without wounds—disintegrating into nothing …

… And then I opened my eyes. I was reclining in a padded chair like they have at the dentist office. Three men were standing over me. A plethora of beeping machines, IV lines, and heart-rate monitors cluttered the room.

"Well?" one of the men asked. "How was it?"

"You were out for almost an hour," added another.

I couldn't answer. There was nothing left of me *to* answer.

"We kept sending signals telling you it was okay to leave," the third man said. "Didn't you get them?"

I closed my eyes and took a long breath. Life 2.0 still had some bugs, but they told me they figured out how to fix most of the cracks if I wanted to go again. It's going to be ready for the market soon, they'd said. People are going to love it, they'd said.

"Did you notice anything else that needs fixing?" one asked me.

"Just in this world," I replied.

## My Mother the Spider Queen

People think they're being discreet when they whisper from the side of their mouth. They think that just because they're not making eye contact, somehow I won't know they're talking about me. Even when they're able to restrain the thoughtless dribble from their faces, I still know what they're thinking because of the others who came before that couldn't be bothered to spare my feelings.

*'Disgusting child.'*
*'Attention whore.'*
*'They shouldn't let her out of the house like that.'*

And of course I grin and stare back until they are uncomfortable. I feel compelled to write this and defend myself, so here it goes. This is the story of my mother the spider queen.

She isn't my real mother. I don't know what happened to my real mother, but I like to think of her as an actress involved in some celebrity scandal which made it impossible for her to keep me. I imagine the death threats she received from my father, the tearful nights, and the impossible decision which ripped her world apart. What lesser obstacle could have forced her to leave me with someone the likes of Mrs. Willow?

The woman who raised me was part hyena and part boa constrictor by nature, although she successfully spun a mask of white lace and perfumed curls which might be mistaken for sophistication at a distance. She was adamant about the punishment fitting the crime, but I would argue being forced to drink dirty mop water isn't proportional to a soiled floor. Of course her own son, Jeff, wasn't subject to this parenting style, but Mrs. Willow liked to remind me that I was her obligation, not her child.

Mrs. Willow was too disdainful of real work to get her hands really dirty with me. I wasn't afraid of anything her bird-arms could hurl my way. It was Jeff who made my life a living Hell.

Three years older than me and at least twice my weight, Jeff made a sport out of tormenting me since he couldn't hope to compete in anything else. Glue in my sandwiches and shampoo bottles, broken glass scattered around my bed, profane words cut into my clothes that wouldn't be replaced. It's amazing that a boy with his creativity and work ethic could still be failing school.

Retaliation was impossible. The slightest hint of resistance would send him howling to his mother. I think Jeff could have murdered me, and Mrs. Willow would have still blamed me for getting him in trouble with the law.

When I was 10, some teachers sat down and talked with my mother about my injuries. She found it more convenient to convince a psychiatrist that I had Asperger's and that I was abusing myself rather than intervene with her angelic boy. It didn't help that I almost never spoke back then, but that's because staying quiet was the best way to bore my tormentor.

I spent a lot of my time hiding in cupboards, trying to stay out of everyone's way. It was too dark to read, but it was quiet, and I could listen to myself think without being interrupted. If I was lucky, Jeff would get distracted and forget about me, and I could spend a whole day sitting peacefully in the dark.

Then came a weekend when I was 12 years old when Mrs. Willow went out of town for a spa retreat. It was just going to be me and Jeff, and I knew no corner would be remote enough to hide from him.

I'd been sitting under the kitchen sink for about an hour before I was blinded by the sudden light of the opening door. I tried to crawl away, but Jeff's hand latched around my ankle.

"Stop being weird and get out of there."

I managed to wriggle free for a second, but then he got hold again. Both hands this time—it felt like he was going to rip my leg off. I groped through the darkness and clung onto something, immediately letting go when I realized it was the pipe for the garbage disposal. Whatever I got from Jeff wouldn't be nearly as bad as the sanctioned violence I'd receive for breaking her precious kitchen.

Jeff was still tugging relentlessly on my leg. I allowed myself to go limp, closed my eyes, and prepared myself to endure the inevitable.

"Oh shit, what was that?"

Jeff let go of my leg, and I felt a rush of cool air replace his hulking presence. He reeled back as though something hit him. Then I felt it—the soft tickle of a spider crawling down my arm.

"Smash it and get out here," he demanded. Jeff was already half-way across the kitchen, actually trembling. I couldn't believe my eyes. 15 years old, pushing 200 pounds, and he was actually scared of an arachnid. I gently cupped my hands and let the fuzzy little guy wander into them.

"I told you to kill it!" Jeff shouted.

I let the spider meander up my arm, enjoying the sight of Jeff squirming in discomfort. I pretended to swat the thing, then scooped it up again and placed it in my hair. I giggled—not from the soft tickling of its legs, but rather at the white bleached horror spreading across Jeff's face. I cautiously climbed free of the cupboard, waiting for him to attack me at any moment.

Instead he was frozen with terror.

"You can't just leave it there," he finally spluttered. "It's going to bite you."

But it didn't, and why would it? Animals aren't like humans. They need a reason to cause suffering; humans only need an opportunity. Jeff followed me, but remained a respectful distance for the rest of the day.

What I had anticipated being the worst weekend of my life was actually the best I can remember. The spider and I were inseparable, and I named it Swish because of its fuzzy legs on my skin. Jeff wouldn't even get close to me, and it didn't take long before I figured out how to use Swish as an excuse to control him completely.

"I wouldn't sit there," I'd say. "Swish was hiding between the cushions."

A little later I'd say, "You sure you want the last donut? Don't you see the little footprints?"

It was like a miracle. He locked himself in his room for two days straight, and I had complete freedom.

First thing I did was make a fly trap out of some honey and glue, then fed Swish for his hard work. Then I got to take a shower in the bathroom with hot water and let it run for as long as I wanted without being yelled at. I even used real shampoo and everything. Swish waited for me on the sink, so I rewarded him with another fly.

It was a dream to think that kind of respite could last. Before Mrs. Willow had even set down her luggage, Jeff was already spinning the most incredible lies.

"She chased me with it! All over the house, wouldn't leave me alone! She put it in my food and wouldn't let me eat—I had to starve the whole time you were gone. I think it's bitten me, look!"

Mrs. Willow had come back earlier than expected, and I didn't have time to hide Swish. After everything the arachnid had done for me, it was my fault what happened next.

I was grabbed by my hair and dragged all the way to the bathroom. I told her the spider wasn't in there, but she wouldn't listen. Mrs. Willow chopped off all my hair with a kitchen knife, then shaved the rest of my head down to the scalp. I didn't struggle; I knew that would just give her an excuse to cut me.

After that she tore my room apart until she found Swish's home I'd built from a shoe box and some twigs. Mrs. Willow didn't want to touch it, but Jeff was howling so badly that she just dropped the whole nest in the bathtub and lit the thing on fire. I squeezed my eyes shut, unable to watch the poor creature struggling to escape. I knew exactly how it felt, wanting so desperately to get out but having nowhere to go.

When the spider burned alive, I couldn't help but envy it for finally being free.

After her trip and that ordeal, Mrs. Willow was too tired to do anything more to me that night. Tomorrow though—tomorrow I was going to pay for what I did to her son.

"Girls with Asperger's," Mrs. Willow said as she closed me in my room for the night, "have been known to do horrible things to themselves. I even heard of one cutting off their own ear with a pair of scissors. I don't think anyone will be surprised by what happens to you."

I lay awake the whole night, imagining what may be in store for me. Mrs. Willow didn't usually like to break the skin with her punishment, but between her zealous worship of her son and the wild look in her eyes, I didn't rule out any possibility.

Worse than anything though was the feeling that I betrayed Swish. I hadn't built the house for him at all—I built it to keep him trapped so he wouldn't run away and leave me alone. It was my fault he'd been in there when Mrs. Willow found him. Maybe I should have tried to run away too, but I was convinced she would find me again, and that it would only make matters worse.

If I'd learned anything from living there, it was resistance always made things worse. I just had to close my eyes, try not to cry, and let it happen.

The anticipation was the worst part. If I could just fall asleep and let it be morning, then the punishment would pass. But no, all night long I lay awake, listening to the soft swish of little legs no doubt scurrying to flee the house.

I must have fallen asleep at some point, because next I knew I was woken by the midday sun flooding through my window. I couldn't believe Mrs. Willow didn't wake me. I quickly patted myself down, making sure she didn't cut off anything in the night. Then I crept from my room, peering around the house.

All the doors were closed. All the lights were off. It was as though no one had woken up at all. Maybe this was part of the punishment—she knew I hated the waiting. She was just going to let the fear keep building until I least expected it, and then—

I gently tapped on Mrs. Willow's bedroom door. The lights were off, but the door swung open. I saw her sitting upright on her bed. Fully dressed, white lace straight, hair perfectly curled. She waved at me and smiled, and I immediately shut the door.

So, she was awake.

This was just a game to her.

Well it wasn't fair, and I wasn't going to play. I couldn't sit and wait for it to happen. I couldn't be quiet and still forever. I was going to tell her what really happened. I was going to tell her that her son is a liar who hurts me whenever she isn't looking. I'm going to scream it in her face, and if she hits me, then all the better. At least I can let her anger out and get it over with.

Opening the door again took all the strength I had.

"Mrs. Willow," I said it loud and defiant into the dark room. "Your son is the one who deserves to be punished. Not me."

Her head tilted to the side as though unable to support its own weight. She turned to face me in small increments. All my instincts roared at me to close my eyes and hide, but I stared her fiercely in the face. She'd burned Swish alive, so now she gets to see my fire.

"He's a sadistic brat, and the more you lie to yourself, the worse it gets," I said.

She stood and took a shaky step towards me.

"You think you're protecting him, but you're not," I continued. "Because one day he's going to go out in the real world where he's accountable for his actions."

She was almost on top of me now. I was going to get it worse than ever, but I didn't even care. I wanted to fight back.

"I want you to know that you're a terrible mother, and at the end of Jeff's miserable, destructive life, he's going to blame you and hate you for it. And if you don't already, you're going to hate him right back."

There. I finally said it.

She dove at me, but I didn't try to run. The last of my strength was gone, and my old protective instincts flared up. I closed my eyes. I let my body go limp. I told myself to accept the pain.

*Swish.*

"You're absolutely right. I'm so sorry, my love."

I felt her arms around me, but she wasn't trying to choke or restrain me. She was . . . hugging me. It was such an alien sensation that I immediately opened my eyes. That's when I saw them. Hundreds—no thousands of gossamer spider webs holding up her body like a marionette doll. I recoiled immediately, and she let me go without the slightest resistance.

*Swish.*

The spiders were everywhere. Crawling across her face, through her hair. When she opened her mouth, I saw more of them inside, pulling the threads to work her jaw. Her throat pulsed, and I knew more must be further down to vibrate her vocal cords.

"But he's never going to hurt you again. You have our word."

I was too shocked to fully understand what was happening. The alarm in my mind wouldn't stop, and I still felt like I was about to pay for my rebellion. I didn't want to stare, but I couldn't look away.

My feet carried me as though pulled by threads beyond my control.

I opened Jeff's room and found him on his bed. His hands and feet were bound with countless loops of web. More of it lashed across his face, tying his tongue securely to the roof of his mouth. His skin was perforated with a thousand holes, and spiders were crawling in and out of them as they carefully partitioned and wrapped each piece for consumption. His eyes blinked at me. I don't know if that was a sign of life, or simply the successful attachment of yet another internal strand.

I quietly closed the door and let them finish their work.

So, if I seem strange to you, walking down the street with spiders in my clothes and hair, don't think I'm doing it for attention. They were a gift from someone who wants to keep me safe. I love them, and I love her for it. My mother is the spider queen, and she's the only family I've ever had.

## I'm in Love With the Devil's Wife

The Devil is known for his patience. He will see a ripening sin in our youth and wait the long years of our life before the harvest. And why shouldn't he? What is one more soul to the untold billions in his dominion? What is one more year in the infinite span of his corrupted reign? Perhaps by waiting he is even giving us a chance to spend our lives repenting for what we've done.

I wouldn't know.

Sins such as mine are so terrible that no absolution is possible. I suppose then there was no reason for him to wait.

He came for me in the woods while the mutilated woman was still in my arms, warming my body with her blood. It's strange that I cannot remember why I killed her, or even who she was, but this feeling of guilt so permeates my being that I would have walked to Hell myself if I had but known the way.

I will not waste effort describing the Devil. The impoverished words at my disposal have only been designed for this material world. As he stood before me, he was more removed from my understanding than the glorious Sun was to a blind worm. It is sufficient to say that he could not be perceived with any one sense, but the pressure of his presence so commanded my consciousness that I was aware of nothing else.

Escape was impossible.

Words were meaningless.

I let the woman slip from my arms, and I stood to face him with all the dignity remaining to a man so removed from God. When he turned from me and began to walk through the fading light of this dying world, I kept pace with him. Where we walked, how long we walked, I do not know. It seemed as though I could have relived my entire life in the time it took for us to stop. Even the thoughts in my head and the temperature on my skin were insignificant to the weight of his companionship.

As terrifying as it was to know my fate, I found certain tranquility in the mindless journey at his side. Now that I could feel him beginning to depart, however, my mind revolted as though starting from a nightmare.

I forced out the first thought I could muster to delay his departure: "Who was she?"

"You will suffer more if you do not know."

Then he was gone. And with him the curtain lifted within me to reveal the horror of his empire I had been submerged within.

Perhaps it would be more accurate to call Hell a person rather than a place, considering the unceasing sentient screams which pummeled me from the land itself. Withering shadows sensitive to the touch, grasping endlessly at me with hands that were not hands. Endless cities sprawled before me as open wounds upon the rotting corpse I stood upon.

The sky was unobstructed by stars, vaulting endlessly into a timeless abyss. Looking at it, I experienced the ghastly sensation of balancing on an eroding precipice which poised to tumble me endlessly into its yawning void. Charnel winds slithered their way into my nose and mouth with tangible substance, forcing me to let oiled coils like a writhing serpent penetrate my lungs with each breath.

Beyond the city in the distance rose the obscured ghosts of monstrous beings and Gods who roared in endless decay where fate had forgotten them.

Through this blasphemous temple to the end of the Universe I went, cowed constantly by half-conceived winged terrors which beat the air with a sound like the ceaseless wet bludgeoning of fists on flesh.

There are two kinds of pain which I had come to expect from the world of the living: the physical and the emotional. Never had I experienced a physical pain so excruciating as the boils which began to swell across my body, nor a mental burden as debilitating as the taunting echoes which sneered at me from the living tissue beneath my feet. Every good memory of my life was poisoned against me. Each shame and recalled guilt was magnified a thousand times by the leering specters who narrated my ordeals with intimate knowledge and exaggerated effect.

Worse still was the gnawing hopeless depression which robbed even my sense of self.

I was not a person in Hell; I was Hell.

I did not feel pain; I was pain—inseparable and indistinguishable.

It was then, in the lowest reduction of my humanity, as I crawled across the putrid ground in a trail of my own sickness, that she took pity on me.

Gentle hands shed my skin from me, not as a torment, but a release. My disfigured limbs were cut away by her flashing knife, each slice bringing a pain so pure and clean that I welcomed it without question. Layer by layer she flayed me until at last there was nothing left to cut but my soul.

Again it is difficult to describe her without the reliance of my mortal senses now stripped from me, but if you understood me when I told you that I was pain, you will understand again when I tell you she was beauty.

"My husband was wrong about you," she told me. "You didn't kill anyone, and you don't deserve to be here. I'm going to help you escape."

I couldn't comprehend how anything could exist outside of this. What universe would accept me, torn and broken as I was? What universe could I accept, knowing it had the capacity to so punish an innocent soul?

"I don't deserve it," what's left of me replied. "I know I killed her. It's something you can never cut from me."

"She killed herself by loving you, and for that you are not to blame." The presence paused. "Do you see these hands?"

When she cupped my hands in her own, I knew that she was creating them as she spoke. Clean, strong hands, untouched by the blemishes of Hell.

"These hands could never be used for hurt. These eyes could never look upon such evil as its own creation."

I didn't even have a face before she spoke, but my entire body was growing with each word. It was as though the seed of my soul was sprouting new life. Shards of bone lanced out and flourished with muscle like thickening bark, organs dropped and swelled like ripening fruit, and the network of veins and arteries blossomed toward her as though seeking nourishment from the sun.

Through the macabre landscape we sped, dancing across the festering world as softly as light through a drop of water. I could see her more clearly the further we traversed, although she never stayed still long enough for me to get a proper look. Bare feet skipped across the rotten land and twirled her through the looming specters which besought us on all sides. It is a wonder that the oppression of this unending night had failed to extinguish her spark, and invigorated by the purity of her wake, I was whole again.

"You are his wife then." It was difficult to speak to her as we raced, but I managed to slip in a few words every time I was able to draw near.

"We are bound to each other, yes," she replied, and then she was gone again; leaping fearlessly between fragile grips as she vaulted upward.

I followed her up the tortuous, broken hand the size of a hillside which stretched vainly from the ground toward the vacuous sky. "Of all the madness in this cursed place, that must king."

"My husband is not mad, and neither am I for being with him." She was pulling herself up through the fingers now, stopping to wait for me atop one of their monstrous joints.

"And if I were to love you instead?" I asked. "Would that be mad as well?"

She smiled at me and stretched her slender hand to help me clamber up beside her. We sat together staring upward from the bottom of an endless sky, the slightest brush of her leg against my own intoxicating me with rapture.

"All love is paradoxically mad," she answered. "It is an assault on reason, but in doing so it creates its own reason. But it won't do you any good, because this is where you have to leave."

"Will you leave with me?"

She shook her head.

"You can't prefer to stay here!"

"All you must do is jump from this point, and with the body I have given you, you will be able to fall until you've left Hell altogether."

"I've already left Hell," I said, earnestly, "since the moment you found me. And if I were to leave you here, then I know wherever I found myself would be Hell again without you there."

"You're being silly and wasting time. If my husband finds you with me—"

"He won't, because you're coming with me," I interrupted, preferring not to dwell on the thought of being found.

"I can't. I've made a promise."

"Then I can't either, and that's my promise to you." To prove my point, I even slipped down from the stony fingers of the grasping earth and began crawling back toward the massive palm.

"Stop! If he finds you he'll—"

"He'll what?" I shouted back, spreading my arms to encompass the immensity of the landscape. "What can he possibly do that he hasn't already?"

I saw in her something I could not live without, and she must have seen something in me which she could not let die. I hadn't even made it back to the ground before her hands clasped me and heaved me up through the twisted fingers once more.

We stood there for a long while together, hand in hand, staring up at the terrifying fall. Then the wet, bludgeoning drums of the winged creatures began, and I could feel the tension wash through her body. I watched her, although she would not meet my gaze. Just as the drumming began to close in around us, I felt her coil to leap.

We jumped together, flying and falling simultaneously in a dizzying tumble. The massive hand snatched at us as we began to depart, but it was too slow to prevent our liberation. The entire world screamed agony, the land reverberating with its echoes. Soon the deafening cacophony fell behind.

The gut-clenching free fall distracted my attention, but I never let go of her hand as we whirled through the timeless void. It wasn't until the initial exhilaration began to fade that I could tell something was wrong. I didn't have to look at her to feel her hand withering in my grasp. Her skin wrinkled and dried as though years of heat beat into it with every second we passed together. Soon she had begun to crack and bleed, washing me with her warm blood.

While I still felt healthy and strong, I was forced to watch with helpless terror as her body was devastated by the passage through the void. Her smooth hair began to mold and peel in greasy clumps. Her face was torn as though blasted by relentless sand, and though her fingers clutched onto me ever more desperately, I could feel the strength fleeing from them.

No torment in Hell could match the guilt of knowing she was enduring this for me. The spinning abyss began to slow. I swam through the air, and clutching her to me, cradled her in my arms as her body deteriorated. Blood was now flowing freely from a thousand sourceless wounds.

When finally the black sky relinquished us back into the woods where I began, I was soaked in her blood and my own freely falling tears.

Staring at her mutilated form, she was completely unrecognizable from before.

My head was clouded as though freshly waking from a dream, and though I tried to hold onto the details, they were stolen from me with inexorable decay. Soon I could not even remember who I was holding, or how she had gotten there.

All I knew was that it was my fault, and the weight of the guilt which her death bade me carry. When the Devil came for me, I knew I would follow him willingly. No matter what horror lay in store for me, I knew I deserved it for what I had done.

## Don't let him Steal my Child

I'm not afraid of the darkness. Spiders don't bother me, nor do snakes or heights or any of the regular things. I'm afraid of the child growing inside me, breathing my blood, displacing my organs, until he eventually rips his bulbous head free from my body and leaves me in ruin. I'm afraid that I will resent all the pain and obligation and loss of opportunity in life, and that all that hatred will make it impossible for me to love him.

I'm still more terrified that I WILL love him—so much that it hurts. So much that I sacrifice everything for him, neglecting myself and my friends . . . until the day when his own ambitions pull him away from me. I'll be left mourning the dissolution of my dreams and the emptiness of my life. And then I will sit down my aching limbs and wait for the weariness of old age to erode my cherished memories and free me from this heart-breaking desire to be someone. I will bless the day when I finally forget to ask myself what might have been if only I had been selfish and lived my life for me.

I wasn't afraid at the beginning though. I thought I wanted it—that we wanted it. My husband, Kirk, and I had just moved into our first house, and I was ready. Sure we still fought about stupid things, but we loved each other, and that should have been enough to make him love the child too.

"Okay. Do you want to make the appointment to take care of it, or should I?"

That's all he said when he found out. We'd been married a year, and he didn't even ask if I wanted to keep it. We started to argue, and then the fight took on a life of its own in that insidious way which left us screaming at each other about nothing and everything. I thought he was being immature—he thought I was the one who needed to grow up and give up my paintings. I said he didn't take enough initiative at work, and he said I didn't respect him. Before I knew what was happening, his pickup was spraying gravel in my face as I sobbed incoherently in the driveway.

I didn't see him again for four months, which was more than enough time for me to doubt every decision I've ever made in my entire life. Then suddenly one night he was crawling into bed at 2 a.m., stinking like death, blubbering apologies and promises. I was so relieved that I didn't even mind that he was drunk. We were intimate as a husband and wife should be, and when I fell asleep on his chest afterward, I thought everything was going to be okay.

"I'm so happy you came back," I whispered, nestled against him.

"I changed my mind," he said. "I want the baby now."

"He's yours," I promised before I drifted off to sleep.

There was so much blood when I woke up that I thought I'd been stabbed. I rushed to the bathroom, screaming for Kirk to help me, but he was nowhere to be found.

A miscarriage doesn't just plop out and leave you as good as new. The baby drained from me over the whole next day, taking my soul with it. Big bloody clots, leaving me shrieking in anguish on the bathroom floor. I chanced to see myself in the mirror, and the sight of the network of bloody trails running down my thighs was enough to make me smash my fist straight through the glass. The pain was good. It reminded me that I had a body outside of the one that had just died.

I couldn't flush it. I couldn't toss it. I couldn't even touch it. I just left it there on the floor and crawled back to my empty bed. I tossed and turned for hours until the clenching pain subsided, but it was nothing compared to the pain of knowing Kirk did this to me. I don't know how, or why, but when he came back last night, he killed my baby. And if my feelings in that moment were any indication, then he might have killed me too.

I wasn't expecting to see Kirk again.

I took myself to the doctor as soon as I was able to drive, and that was when I got my first big shock. The ultrasound confirmed a perfectly healthy, growing baby boy inside me. There wasn't even any indication of blood loss—all my vitals were strong, and I didn't have anemia. The doctor couldn't explain what happened, but finally convinced me that I had a hysterical hallucination and that everything was fine.

The bloody pool in my bathroom which greeted my return told a different story. I don't know what came out of me, but I couldn't force myself to scoop it up and bring it in for analysis. I just mopped everything off the floor and thanked every god that would listen that my child was still alive.

The second big shock was from Kirk. When I heard the knocking on my door, I figured he was back again with another apology. Well it wasn't going to work—the child and I were both better off without him. When I opened the door though, it was his father who entered with his hat in hand. I sat quietly on the sofa with him while he explained his sympathies.

"I know you counted on Kirk, but I want you to know that you can count on us too. No man knows what he can bear until it's been put on his shoulders, and I'm just so proud of you for carrying on without him."

The poor old man was moved to tears when I said they were welcome to stay involved with my life and the life of their grandchild. He hugged me, and patted my stomach, and told me all about the games Kirk used to play as a child, and what to expect when my boy started growing older. Finally he said his goodbyes, promising to check in with me next week to see if there was anything I needed.

"I just wish Kirk was still around to see him grow up," he said as he was leaving.

I didn't want anything more to do with Kirk, but I was so touched by his father's sincerity that I still extended the offer.

"Tell Kirk that he's welcome to meet the baby too," I said. "Even if he won't be a father to him."

Kirk's father gave a hard-pressed smile. "I think he'd like that. The funeral is this Sunday, so I hope you and that baby will come say goodbye."

The words didn't register until after the door had closed. Kirk hadn't just left us. He'd left everything. It had only been two days previous when I'd seen him last, but I've kept that meeting a secret until now. Everyone else at the funeral was convinced that he'd put a shotgun in his mouth two weeks ago. Whatever had visited and been with me that night, whatever told me it wanted the baby, wasn't Kirk.

That's when I started to become afraid of the child growing inside of me. I can't shake the thought that the stuff pouring out onto the bathroom floor—that was my real child from the real Kirk. What was now growing inside me—that must have come from the visitor.

So there I was left wondering what I'm more afraid of.

Either the child will be too horrible to let live, or he is so beautiful that my life will be the one ending that day. It was too late to get it "taken care of," but I don't think I would have done it even if I could.

It wasn't until I was well into my eighth month of pregnancy when I heard the 2 a.m. knocking again. I lay in bed trembling, holding my breath, wondering if it would just go away. No, there it was again. Hard insistent pounding—like something that would break the door in if I kept it waiting.

"I know you're in there." It was Kirk's voice. I would still recognize it even if I didn't hear it again for fifty years.

"Go away." I regretted speaking the moment I replied.

An hour passed in the next few seconds of silence. As gut-wrenching as the stillness was, the sound of the opening door was worse. He was inside the house, but the thought of getting out of bed and confronting him—of confronting IT—was unthinkable.

I got out of bed to grab my phone from the nightstand and called the police instead. "I need help," I blurted into the phone. "Someone's in my house and—"

"Did you make him a promise?" It was Kirk's voice on the line. My fingers were shaking so badly I couldn't even hang up. I just threw the phone across the room and jumped back into bed. This was all a bad dream. It was another hysterical hallucination. I just had to go back to sleep and—

I heard footsteps climbing the stairs.

"What promise did you make me?" Kirk's voice was right outside my bedroom now. I couldn't answer him. I could barely breathe. I should have tried harder though, because when the door opened, it was impossible to think straight.

Kirk was standing in the doorway, only half of his face was now missing from where the shotgun bullet entered his mouth. Had he looked like this the last time we were making love? It had been so dark, but the stench of death seemed all too familiar.

"There is no baby," I forced myself to say. "He hasn't been born yet."

"I don't care. He's mine."

The malodorous atmosphere engulfed me, and I could taste it like rotten cabbage dripping down the back of my throat. He was getting closer, blocking the only door out.

"You'll kill me if you take him now," I told him. "Please wait. At least until he's born."

"I don't care! I want my son!"

He hoisted his stiff legs with his hands to clamber into the bed beside me. I didn't see any weapon, but the thought of him trying to pull the child out of me with his rotting hands was even more terrifying. I gagged so violently that I would have fallen over if his hands hadn't clutched my shoulders. The icy nails sank into my arms, and I forced myself not to watch as I felt some of his own decaying skin slide off to splatter across my bed.

Those disgusting fingers—I had placed a ring upon one, and sworn my love before my family and before God. That open wound disguised as a face—I did not know myself until I whispered my secrets to him and washed myself with his acceptance and support. If I closed my eyes, the arms that clenched around me could almost still have been the ones that held me every night as I fell asleep.

"Do you still love me?" I asked what used to be my husband.

"Does it matter? You can't love back."

"If I could." Each word I spoke carried the weight of revulsion which I tried so hard to hide. "Would you still love me back?"

"You can't. If you could, I never would have left."

"You still do, or you never would have come back."

Mother's make sacrifices for their child. That has been documented across eons of history, cultures, and even species. Kissing him wasn't for my child though. I did it to save my own life. In that moment, I would have ripped my own baby boy from my body and handed it to him if I could escape unharmed. I must be the worst mother in the world, because when Kirk was done with me that night, I still promised to give him the child when he was born.

It's amazing how much my mind changed after I held my boy for the first time. Suddenly he wasn't just a medical condition which needed to be resolved. He was more a part of me now than he was inside me, and I finally understand that living for him wouldn't be a sacrifice. He is my soul.

Everything that I do for him, I do for me.

I know I've been selfish with my love. I know I've made promises which I don't intend to keep. I know I've lied to what was left of my husband when I pleaded for my life. But now I truly have something worth living (and dying) for, and I'm not going to give him up no matter what happens. Until then, I am doing the best I can get by as a new parent who can't seem to get any sleep.

It's not the baby keeping me up though. It's just the waiting for the 2 a.m. knock on my door.

## My Journey in a Parallel Universe

"Just because you're sleeping with Mom doesn't make you my dad."

"Just because you're living in my house doesn't mean you can talk back to me."

You could have cooked your dinner with the air hanging between my stepson and I. Emily kept telling me that Jason was going to get used to having me around, but two years in, and this teenage asshole still resisted me like I was an occupying army. I get that his real dad was a dirtbag, but in what world is it fair to take that anger out on me?

We'd already been arguing in the parked car for ten minutes.

"Just go talk to the guy, okay?" I said. "What's the worst that could happen? That maybe he thinks there's a place in this school for you? That maybe you have potential and can do something with your life besides playing video games and serving hamburgers?"

"I don't want to go here. None of my friends are here," Jason whined.

I wanted to smack him upside the head, but somehow that would suddenly make me the bad guy. Deep breath.

"So what? You'll make new friends. Smarter friends—better friends. In a couple years, you'll be leaving for college anyway, so why not just suck it up and go somewhere good?"

"I don't want better friends. I want a better Dad." Jason got out of the car and slammed the door. Would it still count as murder if he's this rude? At least he was walking toward the building now, so I guess I'll take that as a victory.

I got out of the car and followed Jason up the shining marble steps and into the grand foyer.

Was this a school, or an opera house? The place was drowning in luxury. Thick Persian rugs, walls lined with tapestries, rolling velvet curtains—unmistakable old world money. Some industrial era tycoon set up the Ramfield Academy as his legacy, and his trust paid for all the expenses. I'll admit it was a tad intimidating to enter, but Jason had been invited to the interview because of his test scores and I wouldn't let him miss this incredible opportunity.

"Hey Jason, wait up!" He was already storming up the staircase. He didn't turn around. "It's room 604—that means 6th floor. Come take the elevator with me."

A middle finger appeared between two steps for a moment, and then the footsteps continued. I glanced around, but there didn't seem to be anyone to notice. I sighed and pushed the elevator button.

I would have expected some security to keep out the riff-raff, or at least a secretary in a place like this. It was eerie not seeing anyone in the converted mega-mansion. Six floors, almost 20,000 square feet, but they still only accepted 30 kids a year. It was one of Ramfield's original stipulations when he setup the foundation. Weird guy, by all accounts: an eclectic genius, by some, a mad hoarder by most. I've heard that he lived in this massive place alone without any staff, and by the time he died, they practically had to bring in an excavator to haul out all his random collections.

I got in the elevator and hit #6. The old lift lurched and rattled like it resented me for pushing the button. Music played which would have been more appropriate in a 1920 speakeasy, and it was pretty uncomfortable staring at Ramfield's grimacing portrait beside the door. Jason better not act out like this during the interview, or I swear to God...

If I don't kill him, Emily will kill me, and then I'll go back and haunt the little shit.

"Is this why you never had kids?" I asked the portrait of Ramfield. "There had to have been women who tried, considering all your money. I can't say I blame you though. I guess I just wish mine was different."

The screech of metal cables whirring through their sockets suddenly rends the air. The elevator buckled and heaved beneath me, and I was thrown to my knees. The lights flared like a dying sun, and the music crackled and vanished in a spluttering gasp. A trickle of light from the roof still illuminated the portrait, but that was all I could see.

How old was this thing? Did they even do safety checks, or was this more of a 'bribe the inspector' kind of place? Hell, now the damn thing is stuck.

"Hello? Can anyone hear me?"

I pounded on the door. The needle showed me somewhere between the fifth and sixth floor. Now Jason was going to go into the interview alone and screw it up. I was about to start jumping up and down to try to get the thing moving, but luckily, I remembered where I was. Five and a half stories up... what if it fell? What if a cable broke, and I was just barely balanced on the frayed ends? I moved back against the elevator wall on my tiptoes and felt the tremendous weight groan beneath my feet.

There weren't any emergency buttons or anything, but somehow I was still getting cell reception. I called Jason's phone, but it cut off after the second ring. Little bastard hung up on me. I called again.

"Yeah?" he answered.

"The elevator is stuck. I need you to find someone who works here and send help." I held my breath and waited for his sarcastic reply.

"Oh wow—okay. Yeah, I'll get someone."

Well that was unexpected. At first, I thought he was just going to leave me here, but then I heard him talking with someone in the background.

"Okay, they said not to worry," Jason said after a moment. "It's just an electrical issue. It happens all the time. They're going to reset the breaker, and you'll be right up."

"Thanks Jason. I really appreciate this. Don't get off the phone."

"Don't freak out on me. You're going to be fine," he said.

The elevator heaved again. The music and lights sparked back to life—I was moving. Thank God. And with any luck, the administrators will be so apologetic that this can only help with the interview. The needle slid firmly into #6, and the doors began to open.

"I'm not freaking out. You're freaking out," I replied playfully. Was he actually worried about me? Was his whole rebellious thing just an act? I couldn't help but grin.

The doors opened.

Jason was standing there, his hands in his pockets. He didn't look relieved like I was hoping. He just looked bored.

"I'm not the one who is going to plummet to his death. Where are you?"

Jason's voice came through the cell, but the Jason I was staring at was definitely not on the phone.

I slowly stepped out of the elevator and looked around. No service people—no administrators—no-one at all but Jason.

"Where are you?" I asked into the phone.

"I'm right here," the Jason in front of me answered.

"I'm on the 6th floor," the Jason from my cell answered. "The elevator door opened, but you're not inside. What's the deal?"

I turned around, but the elevator door already closed behind me. I spun back, and Jason—the bored one—was standing a few feet closer. He smirked.

"Come on, Dad. We're going to be late for the interview."

"Come on, man. We're going to be late for the interview."

Jason—the real Jason—he'd never called me Dad before. But the two of them had spoken simultaneously. The Jason next to me took a step closer, and I instinctively flinched.

"What's wrong, Dad? Isn't this what you wanted?" He reached for my phone and tried to take it, but I yanked it away from him. He shrugged. "Whatever, take your call. I'll let you know how the interview goes."

The Jason in front of me opened room 604 and closed the door behind him. I was still too shocked to move. I lifted the phone to my ear, but the call had ended. I tried redialing, but it didn't go through. I leaned against the wall and

## Sleepless Nights

slid to the ground, unable to process what was going on. Was this some kind of parallel dimension? I know Ramfield collected some crazy stuff, but I'm pretty sure someone would have mentioned a trans-dimensional elevator.

Or maybe I had fallen out of the elevator and died. Then the real Jason would have seen it empty, and I really was a ghost. But that didn't explain where the second Jason came from. I tried calling a dozen more times while I waited in the hall, but nothing went through. Then room 604 opened again, and it was too late.

Jason came back, followed by a fat man in a suit. They were both smiling.

The fat man shook my hand and congratulated me. He was saying something else about how Jason was going to excel in this environment. I can't say I was fully paying attention. It all seemed a bit like a dream. I just kept staring at the smirk on Jason's face. I couldn't be sure, but somehow I knew that he knew something wasn't right.

"Ready to go home, Dad?" Jason asked after the fat man had left.

What else could I do? I couldn't go home to Emily and tell her I lost her son. I had to bring him along. And besides, he'd aced his interview. He was calling me Dad. Isn't this what I wanted?

But all the way home, I couldn't even look at him. What if Emily wasn't the same either? How could I even tell? Or did it matter if they treated me the same? Maybe I was just imagining all of this because I had a panic attack in the elevator. Maybe everything was going to be—

"I know you're not my real Dad," Jason said. I jumped so bad I practically swerved off the road. "But my real Dad didn't treat me or Mom right, and you've been good to us. I wish you were there from the beginning."

I let out a long breath. He was just talking about me being his step-father. I forced a smile, but I couldn't answer him. Not yet. It would still take some time to wrap my head around what happened. I turned on the radio.

"Ow! What the hell, man?" Jason's voice said from the radio.

"It's what you deserve for messing around in the interview." Now it was my voice coming from the radio.

"Get away from me. What's gotten into you? Let go!"

"You haven't seen anything yet. Wait until we get home and I'll teach you to disrespect me like that."

A dull pummeling sounded through the radio, and then a scream. I shut it off. I glanced at Jason, and he was smiling from ear to ear.

"Did those voices sound familiar to you?" I asked him. My throat felt tight. If I had gone here, had another version of me gone back to my world?

"Sounds like someone doesn't have it as good as I do," he said. "I love you, Dad." Jason leaned his head against my shoulder. I fought the urge to shrug him off. I felt like I was going to be sick.

*Bzzz. Bzzz. Bzzz.*

My cell started vibrating in my pocket during dinner. Mashed potatoes, filet steaks, spinach soufflé—Emily had gone all out to celebrate Jason's acceptance into the Academy. I glanced at my phone. Emily—the real Emily—was calling.

"Ooh that must be the pie ready," the other Emily got up to check the kitchen.

I clutched the phone in my lap.

"Are you going to answer it, *Dad?*" Jason asked. He was grinning again. What I wouldn't give to see the old Jason's sour expression just once.

"Everyone I want to talk to is already here," I grunted. "Just going to use the bathroom."

I raced to the bathroom, still gripping my phone like a lifeline. I was too late to answer by the time I got there, but there was a voicemail:

*"Where are you?"* It was my wife. My real wife. *"What happened to Jason? His arm is broken, and he won't stop crying. You better have a good explanation. Meet us at the Good Samaritan Hospital as soon as you get this."*

I couldn't breathe. I wanted to flush the phone and forget the other world even existed. I wanted to just live here where everything was perfect. Couldn't I just pretend? Why should I be responsible for what the other-me did?

I stared at myself in the mirror and gritted my teeth. "What am I supposed to do? Huh? Huh?"

"Are you okay in there, honey?" Emily knocked on the bathroom door.

I opened it and gave her my most convincing smile. "Just making some room for more of your amazing cooking. Come on, let's eat."

I waited until this Emily was asleep to sneak out of the house. I had to get out of here. I had to get back and save them. I hadn't received anymore voicemails that evening, but I don't know whether that was a good sign or not.

I dressed in the dark and slipped out of our bedroom. I flipped on the switch in the living room and—"What the Hell?" I muffled my own exclamation. Jason had been sitting in the dark, fully dressed, waiting for me. He wasn't smiling anymore.

"I knew it," he said, his voice laden with accusation. "You're going to leave us, just like my dad did. You want to switch places with him, but I'm not going to let you. I don't want the other you to come back."

"That's too bad," I said, already moving from the door. Where were the keys? They were always on the hook—at least in my world they were. "I don't belong here—this isn't my home."

"No-one belongs anywhere. That doesn't mean you have to leave," he said.

"They need me—"

"And I don't?" Jason said. He lifted his shirt, revealing a frail body which was covered with bruises and scars. "He may look like you, but I know him better than you do. He won't handle the switch as well. I bet he's already killed them both."

"All the more reason for me to hurry. Where are the keys?"

"Stay here, *Dad*. Please." My breath caught in my throat again. I turned and looked at him, and he was holding the keys in his open palm. His eyes were brimming with tears. "Or if you do go, at least take me with you."

I gave a jerky nod. He seemed to know more about what was going on than I did anyway, so I might even need him to figure out how to get home.

We drove in silence back to the Academy. The streets were empty—who else had somewhere to be at 1 a.m.? I turned on the radio.

Sobbing. Incoherent screaming. It sounded like Emily. I shut it off.

"I told you," Jason said. "You should just stay here."

"I'm already gone," I replied.

We entered the elevator together. The door had been unlocked, and there still weren't any people around. He pushed the 6th floor right away, and I didn't try to stop him.

"How do you know about all this?" I asked. "What even is this place?"

"It's not the first time someone switched," Jason said. "I was here on a field trip in school when my real dad caught up with me. He was drunk and angry, and he was trying to punish me for forging his signature so I could go on the trip. I hid from him in the elevator, but he found me and somehow I managed to send him away. I just couldn't figure out how to bring him back."

2… 3… The needle was flipping through the numbers.

"What's going to happen when we get there?" I asked him. "Will the other me and other Jason come here?"

4…

"I think so," he said. "But I think it only works if the other version is still alive. I think that's why no-one switched with him before—his other self was already dead. I've thought about it a lot, and I think that's why he wasn't good to us from the beginning. I think we need to be balanced, and when our other-self dies, we turn bad."

5…

"But if the other Jason is already dead," I said, "what will happen to you?"

5 1/2…

The elevator buckled. The lights flared, and the music died. The only remaining trickle of light seeping from above fell upon Jason's smirk.

"Who says it hasn't already happened?" Jason asked.

Lurch. The elevator plummeted into the blackness and something hit me hard on my right temple.

I woke up in the hospital. Everything felt like it was on fire. Four broken ribs, a dislocated shoulder, blunt force trauma to the head, but no-one could figure out how I got it.

The elevator hadn't fallen. So they told me. I had gotten in alone at the bottom, it hadn't made any stops, and when I came out on the 6th floor I was beaten to within an inch of my life. The Ramfield administrator had called an ambulance, and I was sent directly here.

Emily? She didn't remember any of those tearful phone calls. She had been at home when the hospital called her.

The interview? It had been rescheduled because of the emergency situation. Jason hadn't been accepted or denied, and I don't think either version has happened yet in this reality. I can't even tell if I'm back in the same world I started in.

And Jason? He calls me Dad now. And maybe I should be thankful for that, but it doesn't feel sincere when he's smirking the whole time.

He only visited me in the hospital for a short while before leaving, but I can't shake the feeling that he's the one who did this to me. I don't know who came back with me from that place . . . I don't know who he is, or what he's capable of.

Then again, the same could be said of myself. I feel so angry and helpless and trapped and alone, and I just want to lash out and hurt the ones who have hurt me, but that only begs another question:

What if the other version of me is dead?

What if I'm the bad one?

## My Family Tradition to Feed the Spirit

It's funny how the strangest traditions seem ordinary when you've grown up around them.

One of my friends can't get through Thanksgiving dinner without someone spanking the turkey. Another kid in my high-school said they still threw a tea-party to celebrate every A. I've heard about another family who never wore clothes at home. The poor kid couldn't figure out why everyone started laughing at him when he visited a friend's house and promptly began to undress. It simply hadn't occurred to him that nobody else lived quite the same way, and why should it?

None of their traditions were more arbitrary than a cake on your birthday or an inside-tree on Christmas.

My name is Elizabeth, and my family has their own tradition. Every night after dinner, my dad would take a plate full of leftovers and bring it down to the basement. Every morning, it would be clean. Dad said it was for the "spirit of the house," and Mom would just roll her eyes and smile. Dad is a big man—6'4" and over 250lbs—and it wouldn't have surprised either of us if he just wanted to save a little extra for a midnight snack.

I guess I never gave it much thought until my history class watched a video on the Black Death in Europe. They talked about how the rats would infest granaries and spread disease, and how some people exasperated the problem by leaving food out to appease the angry spirits. I mentioned how we always leave out a plate for our spirit, and my whole class seemed mortified by the thought. The teacher (Mr. Hallwart) spent the rest of the class blatantly circumventing my desk as though I was the one carrying the plague.

That night I had a terrible nightmare about rats swarming through the house and eating our leftover food. I woke in a cold sweat, lying half-awake for a long time as my sleepy brain tried to separate the quiet night from my encroaching dreams. I was about to drift back to sleep when the pitter-patter of feet clearly distinguished itself in the otherwise quiet air.

I was fully awake now, lying very still with my ears straining against the oppressive dark. *Scratch, scratch, scratch*—like fingernails dragging along a rough piece of wood. I pulled the blankets up over my head, more to block out the sound than to offer any real protection. Maybe this had been going on a long time, and I simply hadn't distinguished the sound from the creaking wood or the night air playing through the wind chimes.

Now that I was focusing on it though, I couldn't hear anything else.

I thought about calling for Mom, but I was 15 years old and trying to build a case to convince them I was mature enough to have my own car. Running around crying about a nightmare was as good as giving the murder jury my bloody axe.

I crept out of bed in my underwear, using the flashlight on my phone to steal through the hallway and down the stairs.

The sound grew louder as I approached the basement door. If this was a rat, then it had to be the biggest rat in the history of the world. I froze at the sound of a chair being pushed across the concrete floor. Half of me wanted to turn on the light to scare it off, but the other half declared much more loudly that it was better not to risk being seen. I turned off my own flashlight and carefully opened the door…

Something snarled and I immediately shut it again. I pressed my back to the door and tried to catch my breath. I hadn't realized how fast I was breathing, or how loud. I let the air out in a gasp and slowly inhaled through my nose, trying to be as quiet as I could.

*Scratch, scratch, scratch*—right on the other side of the door. I turned around and saw the doorknob beginning to turn. There's no way it was a rat. I can't explain how my curiosity overpowered my fear in that moment, but I put my hand on the doorknob too. I must have believed Dad when he said it was the spirit of the house. We had been taking care of it after-all, so why would it want to do me harm?

The door opened and I stood face to face with a pale girl a few years younger than me. Her sunken dark eyes vanished beneath her mangy bangs, and her lace nightgown failed to conceal the terrible thinness of her limbs. I don't know what I was expecting, but it wasn't that. I slammed the door as hard as I could and turned to run.

I sprinted up the stairs, locking my door behind me and diving into bed. I held my breath until it felt like I would burst.

Then there was the pitter-patter of soft feet climbing the stairs and approaching my room.

The doorknob began to rattle. I couldn't hold it any longer—all that breath I was holding in was released in one noisy rush and I screamed for all I was worth. The doorknob stopped and lights sprang to life around the house. In about a minute, there was a pounding on my door.

"Honey? Everything okay in there?" It was Dad. I ran to unlock my room and let him in. He was standing there, looking dazed and confused, ready to collapse back into bed. Now that the lights were on and he was here, I felt like an idiot for being afraid. I'd feel even stupider telling him about the girl.

"Sorry," I said. "I thought I heard something downstairs."

"Damn, who needs an alarm when you can scream like that," he said.

"It was probably just a bad dream. Sorry for waking you."

Dad looked around behind him, making sure we were alone. Then he leaned in close and whispered, "Was it coming from the basement?"

I nodded. His smile was nothing but relief, and I couldn't help but feel it too. At least until he added: "That's just the spirit, honey. Don't bother it, and don't tell Mom, okay? It's not going to hurt you."

I nodded again. I didn't know what else to do. He grinned and ruffled my hair before plodding back to his room. I gave the empty stairs a quick glance before locking myself in again and climbing back into bed. I don't need to tell you that I didn't sleep until the sun began to repaint my room.

I slept in late that day, but by nightfall I was ready for answers. I tried asking Dad again, but he just told me every house had a spirit and not to worry about it. He must have been lying though, considering how my class reacted, and it was clear he didn't want to talk about it. That's why I waited until both my parents were in bed to creep down to the basement and wait.

The basement door was open when I got there. I turned the light on in the kitchen, but didn't dare go down the stairs. Three pieces of leftover pizza sat in their box on the table, and I poured a large glass of soda to go with it. I just sat there with my hands folded in front of me, waiting for her to come again. If she was a friend of the house, then I wanted to meet her. And if she wasn't . . . well surely we'd know by now.

My mistake was to watch the door. She was corporal—she ate food, she turned doorknobs—she must go through doors, right? Wrong. Despite my resolve, it was impossible to hear the scratching sound above my head without my entire body tensing up. I watched a ventilation grate in the ceiling slide out of place, and then the girl dropped through as lightly as a shadow. Her hair was hanging over her face, but I could imagine it all too clearly as the animal snarl began to rise in her throat.

She was as alien to me as death. I didn't even know if she could speak or understand. Her movements were erratic and unpredictable, her eyes darted like a caged animal, but we did have one thing in common which has bridged greater differences than ours: we both liked pizza. When I offered her some, a dirty yellow smile peeked through the hair. The girl swiftly choked all three pieces down with savage gulps, although I was able to make out a few of her muttered words between mouthfuls.

"Kevin (my dad) won't let me go."

"Why?" I asked. I thought spirits could go anywhere.

"It's okay. I don't want to leave. He takes care of me." She slurped down some soda, adding, "He said he loves me. He promised to marry me when I turned 13."

"Stay here in the kitchen, okay?" I said. I hope she didn't notice the revulsion in my voice. I couldn't believe what she was saying. I couldn't believe any of this, and I didn't know how to handle it alone. I wanted Dad to come and tell me it was all okay again, but if what she was saying was true…

I came back in five minutes with Mom instead. It was pretty tricky shaking her so that Dad didn't wake too, but as soon as I mentioned the spirit, she was out of bed in an instant. She said she never believed in that sort of thing, but the wild fear in her eyes made me think that was a lie. I whispered to her what I had been told as we walked down the stairs. When we got back to the kitchen, the pale girl was still chugging through the soda which sprayed her face with foam.

"Who are you? What are you doing in my house?" my mother roughly pushed me behind her.

I pushed back. "It's okay Mom. She's not going to hurt us. She needs our help." I was beginning to regret telling Mom what the girl told me.

"I'm Sandy," the pale girl said. "Who are you?"

"I'm Kevin's wife, that's who. The one you're making up lies about." Mom took an indignant step forward. I tried to hold her back, but she was livid. "You better tell me how you broke in, or I'm going to call the police."

"I didn't break in." The pale girl stood from the table and faced us belligerently. "Kevin brought me here. He loves me."

Maybe Mom was angry because she thought the girl was lying, but I think it was because she was afraid Sandy was telling the truth. I should have tried harder to stop her, but I hadn't expected her to snap—to slap the girl across the face.

Sandy's head turned sharply from the blow, but then began turning back in small, jerky increments. I think my Mom was too angry to even notice the bones rearranging themselves in Sandy's neck as it turned.

"You come into my house, steal food from my family, and make up these disgusting lies about my husband?"

Mom was usually the sweetest thing in the world, but she had a temper that sometimes took hours to wind down.

"Mom you've got to stop—"

"I don't care if you got nowhere else to go, where I'm from you got to ask before you take something."

"Mom just look at her! Can't you tell she isn't normal?"

"Now who else you been telling this perverted trash to? Sweet Jesus, I want you out. Out of my house, right this instant."

"What's all this noise down there?" Dad thundered into the room. He froze mid-step as he instantly appraised the situation. "Dear God, Kathy, have you lost your mind?"

"My mind?" Mom screamed, turning to face Dad. "Don't tell me you're going to defend that *creature* in our house."

"I only hear one of you yelling, and don't you dare call Sandy a creature."

I've never seen either of them so worked up. I think I was the only one who heard Sandy whispering: "Is it true?" It wasn't just the girl's voice that wavered. Her whole body seemed to somehow glitch and distort like a corrupted video. "He married her? He lied to me?"

Sandy's shoulders slumped, and she looked absolutely heartbroken. I couldn't even begin to formulate a response.

"Tell me the truth," Sandy insisted, looking at me. "Does Kevin still love me?"

How was I supposed to know? I glanced helplessly at Mom and Dad as they yelled at each other. I was just stressed and overwhelmed and scared. The idea of my dad being with this child almost made me sick. All I could tell is that she shouldn't be here.

I shook my head. "No, he doesn't," I said. "He loves my mom. You should just go."

"Thank you for telling me," Sandy replied with an icy calm. "I'm going to get even now. Please don't watch."

Mom didn't see it coming. The air was distorted with a pale blur, and before I could even open my mouth, I saw thin white fingers tearing out my mother's throat. Most of her neck was still intact, but the trachea was pulled straight out through the skin. I don't think she suffered much on account of how quick it was, but that was a very small comfort.

Dad wasn't so lucky. I thought he would have a chance to fight her off because of his size, but he didn't even put up his arms to defend. He just stood there when the white fingers punched through his chest and ripped out his heart. There was a pause, this horrible moment when the heart was entirely out of the chest but still tethered by a network of veins and arteries . . . I could see the strain on his face while she held it in her hand.

"I never forgot you," were the last words he ever said.

Sandy distorted again, and then she was gone—fleeing back down the basement stairs and wailing like a little girl. I rushed over to Dad, but it was too late for him.

When the police swept the house later that night, they didn't find anyone in the basement. They listened to my statement, but I didn't see any of them writing it down. I don't think they believed me. I was sobbing so incoherently; I wouldn't have trusted my testimony either. I just know what I experienced, and later, what I saw.

The police investigation did unearth a collection of photographs hidden in a shoebox in the basement. Sandy was in them—except that she glowed from happiness where she stood next to a young boy her own age. I recognized the boy as my dad at once. The police didn't investigate them or entertain it as a possibility, but I did some research of my own and found out that Dad used to live next door to a girl named Sandy Withers when he was growing up.

They had been best friends—more than best friends, apparently. She had died in a diabetic coma when she was 12 years old. Written in Dad's curved lettering on the back of one of the photographs was: "My future bride."

I don't know what happened to make her stay in the world, but it looks like my dad never was able to let her go.

It's been three years now, and even though everyone has pressured me to sell the house and move, I'm still living here. I guess I wasn't any good at letting go either, because I still practice the same tradition I have all my life. The only difference is that I now leave out three plates of food every night, and collect three clean dishes every morning.

## The Angel Doll

"Run away, or you will die tonight."

That's what I heard from beside me at 2 a.m.

"What did you say?" I asked my husband.

He didn't answer. Good, then it wasn't important.

I had to use the bathroom anyway, but I was nestled under a down-comforter with our tabby cat Meeps snuggled under my arm.

Wet the bed? Too sticky. Excavate myself from the pile of blankets and face the cold hard bathroom tiles? Please, no. Hold it in and develop a weak bladder? Eh, we were all going to get old and fall apart someday. I had no intention of getting out of that bed for anything short of a nuclear strike.

Just when I started flirting with the other side of consciousness though, I heard it again: "Run away, or you will die tonight."

"Wake up, Jordan. I'm having a bad dream." I sat up and shook my husband's shoulder. He grunted and halfheartedly pushed my hand away. That should do the trick. But as long as I was up…

I uprooted Meeps and climbed out of bed. He gave me that 'how dare you, peasant' expression that all cats have mastered without parallel. I was half-way to the bathroom, and wondering if I could teach myself to piss while sleepwalking when—

"Run away, or—"

I stopped and rubbed my eyes. That wasn't my husband's voice. It wasn't coming from my bed at all. That was unmistakably coming from inside my closet.

Don't get me wrong, I'm a strong independent woman. I kill my own spiders and everything, but there's no decent minded person anywhere who could hear that without screaming bloody murder.

It wasn't really a scream—more of a "what the thunder-flicking-fuck was that?"— but it was loud enough to get Jordan on his feet in a second. It was so cute how protective he was of me. My father never approved of him because Jordan had a cocaine trouble as a teenager, but to me he had always been the perfect man.

"What's going on? Are you alright?" Jordan asked.

"There's someone here," I replied with the same wide-eyed sincerity a four-year-old might muster regarding the monster under her bed.

"Honey, come back to bed. There isn't anyone—"

"Run away, or you will die tonight."

"There!" I said. "It's coming from the closet."

"I didn't hear anything."

"Check it for me? Please? Pleeeeease?" I gave him my best impersonation of a desperate puppy. He sighed and headed for the door.

"Don't! I changed my mind!" I said. "There's a murderer inside!"

"I wouldn't worry," he replied. "It's probably just my laptop randomly un-pausing a video or something. Besides, if it was a murderer, he'd just kill us in our sleep."

"Real reassuring. Thanks."

Jordan opened the door, but his body was blocking my view. I hopped around on my toes to peer over his shoulder.

My doll—my Angel Doll, the one I'd had since I was a baby—was lying on the ground. I rushed to pick her up, reverently cradling her and completely forgetting about the monster for a moment. She wasn't really an Angel, just a Raggedy-Ann with little cloth wings sewn onto her back. But she was mine, in the same way as my hair was brown or my skin was fair; she was part of me.

"Well there's nothing in here, so I'm going back to bed," Jordan said, slumping off across the floor and back towards the bed.

"What do you think knocked her off the shelf though?" I asked. "And look! Her stomach is all ripped open."

"I'll call a doctor in the morning. Goodnight." He was already consumed by the indistinguishable blanket blob.

I sat there on the floor holding my doll. We were inseparable when I was a kid. This doll had endured everything, including a part-time gig as a bulldog's chew-toy, and the lead investigator of a vacuum's inside. She had been ripped, stained, shredded, and impaled a dozen odd times, and Dad had always been able to fix her for me. Of course, now that he was gone, I would have to learn to fix her myself, but that was okay. When I have a kid of my own, they'll probably need me to fix toys for them too.

I gently poked the leaking fluff back into the doll's chest cavity and—

"Shit snacks." Something stung my finger, prompting its quick passage to my mouth. Was something in there? I opened the doll a little further, careful not to lose any of the precious stuffing, and pulled out a tightly folded sheet of paper. I recognized the handwriting immediately.

*Dear Amelie...*

It was the same handwriting with the same loopy "D" I had seen every year on my birthday card. Every year except this one, anyway. I sat cross-legged on the floor and Meeps wiggled her way into my lap while I read my father's secret letter.

DEAR AMELIE,

The telling of an adventure becomes an adventure in itself. Fantasies will unburden your spirit from the constraints of reality, and horror is as thrilling for the author as it is for the reader.

But my story is not so easily told. Every time I try to bleed my memories free, I am frozen with helpless shame and guilt. The events of my youth have haunted me throughout my life, and I fear I will not go quietly into death until I have found peace in their recounting.

I hope you will forgive me for inscribing my story in verse. It is the only way I know how to distance myself from the pain and turn the tragedy of my life into something beautiful. I hope before the end of your days you too will find a way to burn your darkness with such brilliant fire as to illuminate the way for others.

Forever yours,
Dad

THE WRITING CHANGED, still my father's, but a little messier as if he wrote quickly.

*IT SHOULD BE SAID, right at the start,*

all happy families are the same.
For joys are shared in equal parts,
though misery is unique in blame.

IT COMES in many varied forms,
   but you will know it when it's seen.
   When the perfect mask is torn,
   and sundered at the seams.

SO IT WAS when I was young,
   a son first and child after.
   Playing with father was endless fun;
   and every shared moment, laughter.

I LEARNED how to view the world
   from astride my father's knee.
   And when the night left me curled,
   his stories would bring sleep.

BUT LIFE IS HEAVIER for some than others,
   and it pressed hard upon this man.
   A war waged between him and my mother—
   he stopped trying and simply ran.

I WAS LEFT TO WONDERING,
   where my father went at night.
   Then home late with blundering,
   too much drink had made him fight.

ONE NIGHT the drink brought a rage
   that I had never seen before.
   The beatings could not be assuaged,
   so out I fled through the kitchen door.

I WANDERED the streets very late,

## Sleepless Nights

*hiding from that awful noise,*
*not knowing it was my fate,*
*to find salvation in a toy.*

TOSSED UPON GARBAGE AND REFUSE,
*the broken Doll of an Angel lay.*
*It was worn-deep from overuse,*
*but I still took her home to play.*

WHEN THE VIOLENCE *was lit by booze,*
*I held it to keep my fears at bay.*
*Then finally when came a truce,*
*I would thank her when I prayed.*

THE QUIET NEVER LASTED, *nor the peace,*
*and I kept the doll close beside.*
*Once I was too bruised to sleep,*
*and waited instead to finally die.*

INSTEAD THE DOLL *began to speak,*
*telling me that I was safe.*
*That even when the world was bleak,*
*I must trust the Doll with faith.*

THE DOLL OFFERED MORE *than reality,*
*and proved my great escape.*
*It would sing tales of fantasy:*
*of villains, heroes and their capes.*

BEASTS AND MONSTERS *with their fangs,*
*of highway men and roaming gangs,*
*who were locked up tight with a clang,*
*prevailing justice when she sang.*

SINCE THEN WE *never parted ways,*

*where I went, the doll followed after.*
*She sat beside me when I played,*
*or sheltered me in the attic rafters.*


THE DOLL PEAKED *from my bag at school,*
*(the other children laughed, I know).*
*But I didn't mind the jeering fools*
*who didn't know how to take a blow.*


I WISH *my mother had a Doll*
*to take away her pain—to free her back against the wall,*
*and cease the falling of the cane.*
*I offered the Angel Doll to her,*
*but she insisted that I keep.*
*Saying it was too late to deter,*
*the wounds which cut too deep.*


ONE NIGHT *her screaming wouldn't end,*
*and I offered up a solemn plea:*
*That even this hurt would mend,*
*I begged the Angel answer me.*


NO COMFORT *now like in the past,*
*the Doll offered this foresight:*
*"Run away," she said at last.*
*"Or you will die tonight."*


I STOPPED READING. I was so tired, I had completely forgotten about what made me get out of bed in the first place. I stared at the coarse face with its black sewn on buttons and flame of red hair. It was just a doll—the same doll it had always been.

"Jordan?" My voice was timid. I shouldn't wake him up again. It was stupid to think—

"Yeah?"

"Do you trust me?"

"Of course, honey. What are you still doing up?"

"I want to get out of the house, now."

## Sleepless Nights

The pile of blankets slouched aside, and he sat up to stare at me. He looked at the letter in my hands, then nodded. He put on his robe and handed me mine, and we walked out the front door in silence.

"Where are we going?"

"Away," I said. "Can you drive?"

It was like he could sense when something was important to me. He smiled and nodded. We didn't need words. I hopped into the passenger seat and flipped on the reading light to finish the letter while he drove.

*"RUN AWAY," she said at last.*
  *"Or you will die tonight."*
  *I grew angry and yelled louder,*
  *but no other sound came out her.*

*I FLUNG the doll from the window seat,*
  *out of the house, into the street.*
  *Telling her she was no good,*
  *if the Angel no longer could*
  *speak and tell me calming tales*
  *drowning out the fighting wails.*

*MOTHER WAS IN PAIN, a bestial yelp—*
  *through the thin walled home.*
  *I couldn't face my fear and help—*
  *I couldn't bear the sound alone.*
  *I ran until I was out of breath,*
  *far away from here.*
  *I didn't care if I met my death,*
  *I willed to disappear.*

*SNOW and bitter winds cut in*
  *probing through my jacket thin.*
  *I leaned against a tree to rest,*
  *yet dared not chance to sleep in less*
  *I would waken to find myself*
  *alone in the world with no one else,*
  *or waken not, stiff frozen skin*
  *a tribute to what might have been.*

. . .

*I WISH I hadn't thrown the Doll away*
　*when I needed her the most.*
　*It wasn't her fault she had to say*
　*that death was flying close.*
　*The morning found my mother dead*
　*as the Doll that I once found.*
　*Forsaken and thrown on garbage bed;*
　*a trash heap burial mound.*


*FOR MANY YEARS, a lost Raggedy-Ann,*
　*my Doll must have searched the Earth.*
　*Until she found not a boy, but a man,*
　*and his lady who was giving birth.*


*I HAD RUN SO FAR from life,*
　*that I had found a life anew.*
　*The Doll gazed upon my beautiful wife,*
　*and the child who now grew.*


*THE ANGEL DOLL lay down softly,*
　*knowing her part had been played.*
　*The boy was gone, and though missed awfully,*
　*time's direction could not be swayed.*


*I FOUND HER THERE, against the hospital door,*
　*still and quiet as the dead.*
　*I scooped her up and to her swore*
　*to fix her tattered threads.*


*BY MY WORD, she was cured*
　*of the ills this world had shown.*
　*My baby girl brought in the world*
　*was gifted with a doll newly sewn.*

. . .

## Sleepless Nights

*I WILL NEVER MAKE the mistakes
that drove my mother to her grave.
And the Doll will never lie awake
to take away your pain.*

I WAS in tears by the time I finished. Dad would have been 58 on the first of May. Jordan kept giving me these nervous glances, but he was respectful and didn't pry.

"How much further, you think?" is all he asked. "There's a motel up ahead. Want to spend the night there?"

These weren't pretty tears. They were big, snotty, sloppy globs. I was too choked up to answer, but he pulled into the parking lot, anyway. He understood me so well, it was like he was made for me.

I held the Doll while I fell asleep in the motel. I knew I owed Jordan for this. I felt so stupid for dragging us out here, but the letter and my cry had been cathartic. I was so tired yet I felt oddly at peace. It was the best I'd felt since the funeral. And who knows, maybe some freak tornado will hit the house and I'll know some part of Dad really is still out there watching over—

"Run away, or you will die tonight."

It came from the Doll: a small voice like a child who was afraid of being caught.

"I already did run away." I felt too guilty to wake Jordan up again after all this, so I whispered the reply.

"Not far enough. He's still with you," the doll replied in a fragile little voice. I couldn't see the Doll's mouth moving or anything, but there was nothing else which could have been talking to me. I looked over at Jordan's harmless, sleeping body. Was I really going to trust a phantom voice over my husband who I've known and loved for years?

But it wasn't just any voice. Somehow it was my father trying to reach me, and him I would trust till the ends of the Earth. I took the Doll and my phone and quietly slipped out the door. I wasn't going to leave him stranded, so I took an Uber back home. While we were driving, I wrote him a long text message thanking him for being so understanding and apologizing for my behavior. I told him how much he meant to me, and that all of this was just because I was having such a hard time with Dad's passing. He was so kind that he probably wouldn't have even needed it, but it felt good to tell him anyway.

I hope he got a chance to read it before he died. The next I woke, it was to the hammering of police on my front door. They informed me that my husband was found dead in his motel room with three bullet holes in his chest. Future investigations revealed the coke habit wasn't as ancient history as I thought. He owed a lot of money to the wrong people, and they followed our car to the motel. If it wasn't for the Doll, I'd be dead too.

I still think Dad was wrong about Jordan though. I don't regret a minute of our time together. And Dad was wrong about another thing too—the Angel Doll was going to have to lie awake with me for a long time before she can take away the pain.

## Virtual Terror

I'm going to tell you the secret that I don't tell anyone. I'm a US veteran of the war in Afghanistan. I was stationed in the Uruzgan province when Taliban militants attacked our coalition base. I stood next to a man I knew since training when a RPG-16 hit the three story building behind us and buried us both alive. I held the flag they sent home to his mother after I crawled out. I've tortured a man for information, threatened a child to coerce his parents to cooperate, and of the seven people I know I've killed, only five were fighting back.

But that isn't the secret, because I was just following orders. The secret is that when I'm lying awake at night thinking about all the things done to me—all the things I've done—I'm not traumatized by it all. The secret is I miss it so much I can hardly sleep.

Adrenaline, fear, excitement—it's all the same thing. I've been addicted to it for as long as I can remember. While other kids were riding skateboards around the neighborhood cul-de-sac, you'd find me grinding along the gutters on a rooftop. They threw water balloons; I threw rocks. They learned to drive; I organized street races with my brother. By the time I graduated high-school, I already had a juvie record for fighting. The cop sat me down with an army recruitment officer, and they told me my life had only two possible outcomes left.

"You're going to either keep playing at these stupid stunts until you get locked up for life, or you're going to man up and become somebody."

I told them I had changed, and the officer decided my past mistakes wouldn't disqualify me from enlisting. He was wrong for believing me—I just thought shooting guns sounded like a lot more fun than sitting behind bars. He was right that I would make a damn good soldier though. Sure it wasn't all excitement, but they gave my life purpose, and I could finally put my natural affinity to good use.

For the first time in my life, I was courageous instead of stupid; a hero instead of a freak.

I didn't come home in a body bag like I expected, but the wheelchair I got was even worse. The bullet between the 2nd and 3rd lumbar bones is still lodged in my spine, and that was it for me. I didn't know if I would ever get out of that chair, but even if I could, my days of living on the edge were over.

And I hated it.

I hated the army for kicking me out—I would have crawled back into battle if they let me. I hated my brother for the pity he gave me, I hated the boring town I was stuck in, and more than anything, I hated myself for not having anything left to live for. I wheel-out to the end of my driveway every month to get the disability check they mail me—proof I'm no good to anybody. Besides that, I just sit at home and watch movies and wish I was living somebody else's life.

War movies. Horror movies. Anything that makes me forget, even for a moment, that the most excitement I was ever going to get was checkup time when the nurse leaned over my chair to measure my stagnant pulse. My brother tried to get me to go out with him more, but I couldn't stand being dragged away from my movies. I wish I could be inside them and never come out. That's when my brother came up with a compromise:

"How about you and I go to the new Virtual Reality Arcade?" he asked. "They've even got some immersive horror ones that are so real you'll piss yourself."

"Just like everyday?" I replied.

I ended up going to shut him up, and the place was actually a lot cooler than I expected. The arcade was divided into personal pods that looked kind of like spaceships. The assistant was a geeky Japanese dude who spoke with a weird inflection which kept swinging back and forth. He probably spent his spare time making fan-made anime dubs, or some such nonsense. He helped me get setup with the headset and headphones, and made sure the wheelchair didn't get tangled up in any of the wires.

As you might have guessed from my introduction, not much impresses me. But holy shit, this technology has come a long way since the blurry 3D movies I saw as a kid. I found myself confronted with a menu hanging in the air which looked real enough to touch. I selected the horror genre, and then a few more options came up.

SELECT YOUR DIFFICULTY. Are you a:
*Grandmother with a heart condition.*
*Kid with something to prove.*
*SWAT team looking for practice.*
*A lost soul seeking forgiveness from GOD.*

THAT LAST ONE didn't really sound like a degree of fear to me, but they were organized in ascending difficulty, so I selected that. Any hope of a thrill immediately disappeared as a fat cartoon Devil with a pitchfork ran across my field of vision.

"I can see you!" he said, waving his pitchfork at me. "Can you see you?"

"No, because I'm not a stupid cartoon. You sure this game is for adults?" I spoke aloud.

"Just wait and see," the Japanese guy said. It was weird hearing him talk when I couldn't see him. I think he was still speaking, but his words were drowned out by the game music which started playing. It sounded like the bad haunted houses they try to push off on kids: full of rubber spiders, cobwebs, and jars of "intestines" which are just spaghetti and meat-sauce.

My viewpoint walked along a dark road at night which led to a trapdoor in the ground, like a cellar. The cartoon Devil popped up again, and I physically prepared myself for death-by-cringing. I get that my brother felt as helpless as I did, and I know he is just trying his best . . . which is still more than can be said for me. I guess it wouldn't hurt to at least pretend to have fun.

"Through me is the space between you and the Divine; infinite and eternal, inseparable and simultaneous," the Devil said, his voice completely different from his last utterance. The words popped with a confusing static noise. It was almost as though instead of hearing the words, I heard every imaginable sound except the words, and my brain filled in the missing space.

"Are you scared yet?" I faintly heard my brother's voice through the headset.

I shrugged and gave a thumbs up.

The trapdoor opened, and I lurched in my chair. Something hurt in my back as the viewpoint suddenly dropped into the Earth. It felt impressively real, almost like I was on a roller-coaster which plunged into the darkness. I heard my brother laugh at my reaction. I figure that's enough satisfaction for him. No more looking startled, or I'll never hear the end of it.

I could faintly see phosphorescent mushrooms and rocks lighting the deplorable descent. I continued to accelerate as I fell, and I even felt the wind blowing in my face. They must have a fan or something to make it seem more real. The Devil was tagging along with me, but he kept glitching and lagging so that parts of him were getting left behind. Then he'd suddenly reappear in front once more, each time a little darker and more sinister. There was something poison in his eyes now, as though the cartoon had experienced some horror of his own that he couldn't shake. Then I felt a blast of hot air on my face, and I closed my eyes.

Whelp, guess this was it folks. I must be in Hell.

I opened my eyes and squinted against the brilliant glare. I always imagined Hell being darker. Was this hell-fire? My eyes started to adjust, and I could see the sun reflecting sharply off the wide sandy slopes of... of where? Afghanistan?

Someone was talking behind me in Dari, the most common language used there. I couldn't understand it, but I could tell the person was afraid. I turned my chair to shift the viewpoint until I saw an old man kneeling in the dirt before two US soldiers with their backs to me. One of them was holding a picture of a teenage Afghani boy.

"Do you know who this is? Have you seen him?" the first soldier asked.

"Is this your idea of a joke, bro?" I spoke aloud.

"Your brother went to use the bathroom," the Japanese guy said faintly.

"What kind of game is this?" I asked, but his reply was drowned out by the VR soldiers.

The old man kept pressing his face against the dirt and shaking his head.

One of the soldiers dragged him to his feet and shoved the photo in his face. "You know who this is, don't you? Why are you trying to protect him? Do you know what he's done?"

This wasn't funny to me. I started to take off the headset, but the cartoon Devil appeared in the corner.

"I can see you!" he said in the silly voice. "Can you see you?" Everything was playing so smoothly it could have been real, except for the Devil who kept lagging and glitching. He was little more than a jumping mass of mis-colored pixels.

One of the soldiers kicked the man on the ground. As he pivoted his body, I caught a glimpse of my own face under the helmet. Suddenly I remembered who the old man was. Abdul-Baser was a Qalandar, or mystic, who was suspected of sheltering Taliban operatives in his house. I didn't need to watch to know what happened next.

I took my headset off and handed it to the Japanese guy. "Did my brother put you up to this?" I asked him.

"I can see you," the assistant replied. He handed the headset back to me, but I pushed it away.

"No duh, Sherlock. How did you get this footage?"

"Can you see you?" he asked. His face froze for a second while he spoke, twisted half-way between words. There were a couple of empty pixels obscuring his mouth, but I could tell he was smiling when he handed me back the headset. I touched his hand—warm and real. Well, I don't know what was going on, but this certainly captured my attention better than any movie.

I slowly took the headset from him, and the assistant nodded, smiling when I put it back over my eyes.

"Hahahaha," the cartoon Devil laughed in a good-natured way. "I played a trick on you: once for what you've done."

*Flash*—I was beating Abdul-Baser inside a holding cell.

*Flash*—I was back in the desert next to the cartoon Devil. I saw it for less than a second, like a single frame inserted into a movie.

"Yeah, you tricked me alright," I answered. "But you didn't scare me. You think I don't remember everything I saw? I wasn't scared then, and I'm not scared now."

The scene suddenly dissolved, and I was falling through the Earth again. I seemed to be going deeper this time because the tunnel was lit by flowing veins of lava instead of mushrooms. I sat calmly in my chair, actually looking forward to what came next. I don't know if I was drugged, or having a stroke, or if the Devil really was trying to teach me a lesson, but I was excited to see just how far the rabbit-hole went.

This time it was pitch black when I stopped. Crashed might be more appropriate. It was like my whole body had slammed into a wall. This trick could make me feel things? Could something here really touch me? Or torture me? For a second I actually did start to get scared, but then I reached out with my hands and felt carpet beneath my fingers. That's right, I was still in the VR arcade. I had just fallen out of my chair somehow. Still wearing the headset and seeing nothing but the blackness I landed in, I pulled myself hand-over-hand and crawled back into my wheelchair.

"I can see you," the static-y absence of words said. "Can you see you?"

The Devil rose in front of me, but his appearance had changed as much from that cartoon Devil as his voice had. The shape was dark, but it wasn't just like the lights were off. Ordinary dark is the absence of light, but the presence before me was the impossibility of it. In that moment, I couldn't even remember what it was like to see, but I could still sense his form through the emotional weight it carried.

His horns were as sharp as being stabbed by the love of your life after you sacrificed everything to bring her joy.

His face was the burden of holding your dying father in your arms while both of you knew you could have saved him if only you'd tried harder.

His body was the shape of a long life spent in quiet desperation after all living matter had wasted away and you alone remained to dwell upon your regret.

"Twice for who you are," the presence said.

He reached out to touch me, but I couldn't let him. I felt I would become like him, an unreal embodiment of misery and pain, if the presence of his being were to overlap with my own.

It wasn't fear that made me rip off the headset—fear is something consciously recognized in the brain. My terror was something much deeper and primitive, the sort of thing which stirred my ancient ancestors into action to prolong their own purposeless existences in the face of some greater dread of the unknown.

I threw my headset and headphones into the assistant's face. My brother wasn't there, but I wasn't going to wait for him.

I leaped up and sprinted out of the building, bursting out into the bright clear light of my familiar hometown. Boring? How could anything be boring about this place which brought me into this world and formed me into who I am?

I ran as fast and hard as I could, taking in deep lungfuls of clean air which filled my body with hope and jubilation. I had my whole life ahead of me, and nothing I had done or been could ever change that. I couldn't remember the last time I felt this good. Hell, I couldn't even remember the last time I walked outside—

And it hit me.

I couldn't remember the last time I walked, because I couldn't walk. I slowed down and looked at my legs pumping the concrete beneath me. I could feel the blood roaring in my veins and the pressure of my feet on the ground. But I could also see that one leg lagged slightly behind the other even when I stood still, and that it was filled with dead blurry pixels. I walked the rest of the way home, just enjoying how good it felt to move and trying not to look at my glitching legs.

"Three times for what you will do," said the voice which wasn't a voice. My brother was waiting for me in my home, although every instinct within me screamed with the recognition that it wasn't my real brother.

"Oh, but I can't trick you, can I?" My brother's mouth moved, but it was the silly cartoon Devil's voice that came out. "You're not scared of anything."

I reached up to my face, but the headset wasn't on anymore. I turned around and started walking upstairs as quickly as I could. My heart was pounding in my chest like a caged animal trying to escape. My brother-who-wasn't-my-brother followed me up to my room.

"You think you're so strong, don't you? That you don't need anybody. But you know what? There's no-one else here, so you can tell me the truth."

The singsong cartoon voice was grating on my nerves. Wherever I was, I wasn't in control. There was no point in trying to outrun something in my own mind.

I turned around to face him. "I'm not afraid of you or your tricks. What do I have to do to get out of here?" I asked. My voice didn't even shake. I balled my hands into fists, and they were firm and ready.

"Are you sure you want out?" he asked, but it was back in my brothers voice. "Your legs work in here, but they won't out there."

"I don't care, I want out," I said.

"Why? Unless you really are afraid." He smiled, and it froze in a glitch. The face was so warped I could barely recognize him. I couldn't stand to look—I wanted to wipe that smile off. If he wasn't going to be reasoned with, then I would have to do things my own way.

"I'm not afraid!" I shouted. I grabbed him by the front of his shirt and punched him. "You're the one who is trapped in here with me!"

"Then what do you feel?" he asked through his twisted, frozen smile.

The face felt solid, and I could feel the bones of his jaw moving from the impact. The instant I hit him however, his face was replaced with Abdul-Baser. The old man started to pull a handgun from behind his back, but I punched him again, almost breaking my hand against his cheekbone. The face changed again, and this time I was looking into my own eyes. That was it—that was the way out.

He was reeling from my blows, and I snatched the handgun from his limp grasp.

"That's not going to do anything to me—"

"You're right, it won't," I interrupted, my mind racing with the possibilities. "You're just pretending to be me. It will work on me though."

I put the gun in my mouth and pulled the trigger. He jumped at me faster—faster than humanly possible—and knocked my hand aside. The gun went off with a deafening ring, and he fell to the ground in a heap.

"My turn," I said. I put the gun in my mouth, pleased to find that my hand still wasn't shaking, and pulled the trigger.

"I can see you. Can you see you?"

I opened my eyes in the hospital. A doctor was leaning over me, shining a light in my mouth. My head hurt like Hell. I tried to nod, but a searing pain engulfed my awareness, and I froze up—almost like a glitch.

My father was sitting beside my bed. He wouldn't say a word until after the doctor left, but eventually he told me what happened. I had entered some kind of fit at the VR arcade and fell out of my chair, probably caused by the bullet shifting in my spine. My brother took me home and stayed with me to make sure I was okay, but I pulled out a gun and tried to kill myself. He managed to stop me, but the gun went off and hit him. I shot myself after that, but the bullet went straight through my jaw and missed my brain.

I want to go back to my old life—Hell I want to go all the way back to day one and do it all again, but I'd settle for just a day.

I used to think I had nothing left to hope for. I used to think I wasn't afraid of anything. Now I know I was wrong about both, and that they're both the same thing.

I'm afraid of the static sneer, half-contempt, half-agony, glitched across my father's face.

## Everyone Lives, but not Everyone Dies

Everybody dies.

That's common knowledge. I learned it when I was five when my hamster met a hawk for the first (and last) time. It was my fault for taking him outside, but that only made the discovery harder.

Everything dies.

Everything in the history of the world, up to about a hundred years ago, has died. We take that as proof that we're going to die too, although we don't know for certain until we're actually gone—and by then it's too late to know anything for certain. As long as we're still alive, it feels like there is a chance—no matter how improbable—that we are the exception. That somehow everyone else in the world will die while we live on forever.

I hope some of you just thought about Louis C.K.'s bit about everybody dying. That's what was playing on TV when Grandmother Elis entered the room.

"Don't listen to that man," she said. "Not everybody dies."

Of all the objectionable things Louis C.K. jokes about, I can't believe this is the topic she chose to argue about.

"Of course not, Granny. You're not going anywhere." There is no point in arguing with old people about absolutely anything. Even when they're wrong, they've grown accustomed to being wrong too long for the facts to keep up.

"Oh, I'm going to die," she said, laboriously sitting down next to me. "When you get to 84, you can't put a roast in the oven without wondering if you'll be around to take it out. But not everybody dies. My grandfather is 143 years old."

"That's not possible." Was it? I've heard some people lived to be ancient, but I'm pretty sure no-one makes it to 143 without the Devil's private medical insurance.

"He was born in Belgium in 1874, but he lives nearby now."

"How do you know?"

"He still sends me a birthday card every year. I have them up in the attic somewhere."

"But how do you know he's the one sending the cards?" I pressed. "When was the last time you visited him?"

"I never visit. I have nothing to say to him."

That's all she would say about the subject, but my curiosity wasn't nearly satisfied.

I found the latest birthday card in a shoebox along with 83 other cards. I think they were all hand-drawn and colored, but the older ones were warped and yellowed by time and water damage.

Within each card was inscribed an address alongside this verse: *One less year for you to wait, before your sweet release. Won't you shed your mortal fate, and live with me in peace?*

It sounds to me like he was offering Grandmother an escape from death. I can't imagine that he really had a cure, but I wouldn't turn down that offer if it was handed to me.

Visiting old people is a chore. Visiting ancient people is an adventure. I plugged the most recent address into Google Maps, and it led me to a Victorian era estate house on the edge of town. It looked like nobody has lived here for years. Even if the old guy was a myth, it would be fun to just poke around and have a look.

I climbed up the rotting porch and knocked on the door, leaving an imprint in the dust the shape of my fist. I hope he doesn't break a hip on his way to let me in. He probably has some live-in medical staff if he's lasted this long though.

When the door swung open, a tall thin man with rigid posture and a pristine suit stood before me. He was wearing an old fashion plague mask and black leather gloves, so I couldn't see his skin. By the way he was standing, I figured he couldn't be that old though.

"Um, hi. Does Mr. Jacobs still live here?"

He didn't move. One arm was held behind his back at a perfect right angle. A corpse couldn't have held a more stolid composure.

"He sent my grandmother this card. And like, 82 other cards—one every year." I produced the birthday card, and the man snatched it like a striking snake. The card disappeared into his pocket without a glance. He turned wordlessly and entered the house, leaving the door open behind him.

"Sit." The figure gestured at an elaborately embroidered armchair which the Queen of England wouldn't have looked out-of-place in. The whole house was absolutely magnificent—while the outside was dilapidated enough to be seen on a "we buy ugly houses" poster, the interior was immaculately preserved. Dark mahogany wood panels, crystal chandelier, intricate golden light fixtures, and shelves and alcoves stuffed to bursting with all manner of exotic dolls, carvings, and trinkets.

"Why did Elis send you?" he asked. The voice had a peculiar hollow ring as it reverberated inside the mask. The words were slightly clipped, but his English was flawless. He continued to tower over me as stiff as a flagpole. My hands ran self-consciously over one another in my lap.

I was tempted to admit I came on my own, but the cards seemed specifically for my grandmother, and I didn't want to be turned away. Idle curiosity doesn't open nearly as many doors as blatant lies.

"My grandmother—Elis—she wanted me to meet Mr. Jacobs for her."

"I am Mr. Jacobs."

"Then, um, she wanted to let me decide whether to accept your offer." I didn't know what that meant, but it was just vague enough to work.

He bent over me, the long nose of the mask practically scratching my skin. The slow intake of breath—was he sniffing me? I fought the urge to be sick when a wave of the thick incense within the mask washed over my face.

Apparently satisfied, the man moved to sit across from me on the other side of the marble coffee-table. He poured a glass of red wine from a silver decanter for me before pouring another for himself. His long body leaned back, crossing lithe legs with the dexterity of a dancer. Polished leather shoes flashed softly in the dull light. There is no way this guy is 143 years old.

"Drink," he said, the thick perfume billowing out of the mask.

"I'm not old enough to—"

"How old are you, boy?"

"19. How old are you?"

"Are you old enough to fear death?" he asked.

I nodded.

"Then you are old enough to drink."

I was getting really uncomfortable at this point. My hands wouldn't sit still. Maybe I was in over my head. I was just curious, that's all. I didn't really believe he was 143 years old. If he really did have a cure for death, why wouldn't my grandmother accept it?

"I think there's been a mistake. I think I should be going now." I started to stand, but he was faster. He stepped directly over the coffee table and blocked me from getting out of the over-stuffed chair. The perfume was intoxicating. I couldn't think straight. Whatever I tried to focus on just blurred out of my mind. All I could see was the piercing red wine taunting me from the table. The only sounds were my beating heart, and his melodic voice echoing from the mask.

"Is this a game to you, boy? Are you trying to play me?"

"No, sir, I—"

"Do you seek to fool me? To rob me? To take my secrets and sell them for your own gain?"

"I swear I only came because—" My head was spinning. The crystal chandelier flashed as bright as a lighthouse. The scent was overwhelming. It was all I could do just to avoid throwing up. Even if he wasn't blocking me in, I don't know if I could have stood to leave.

"Because what? Why are you here? Why have you disturbed my home?" He was shouting now—at least I think he was. My senses were so saturated with noise and light and smell.

I shut my eyes tight. I pressed my hands over my ears so tightly I could feel them pop somewhere deep within my head.

"I don't want to die!" I shouted. I could have said anything else, but that's the only thought my mind could hold on to.

"Then drink."

My eyes were still closed, but I could feel the glass of wine being shoved into my face—spilling over my chest. I grabbed it with both hands and gulped it down like I had been lost in the desert for years.

Mr. Jacob's presence immediately lifted. He must have moved away to the other side of the coffee table again. That all-consuming perfume began to clear from the air, but I kept drinking. I didn't want to die. I don't care what happened to me in that moment.

I never wanted to die.

*Crunch.* Something hard slipped into my mouth from the bottom of the wineglass. I opened my eyes. The bottom of the glass was crawling with beetles. I tried to cough, but the one already in my mouth slipped down my throat. I could feel its legs struggling against my esophagus all the way down.

"Do not worry, child." Mr. Jacob's voice was soft as a purring cat. "You never will. Now go home and do not return without your grandmother."

I got up and ran.

Once outside, I fell to my hands and knees and heaved. I forced my fingers down my throat, but I didn't need much help to induce the vomiting. The red wine poured out in waves, splattering all over my hands and knees.

Still gasping for breath, I ran my hands through my own vomit—searching. It was all liquid. I squeezed the wet dirt with my hands. The beetle hadn't come out.

I took off my shirt and pants, which were soaked in vomit, and put them in the back of my car. I drove home, trying my best to pretend nothing happened.

But it was hard not to think about when I could feel the beetle crawling around in my stomach the whole way back. I don't know what that beetle I swallowed was, but it's doing something to me.

The squirming sensation soon abated, and I figured it would be digested. I wasn't feeling as nauseous anymore, so it probably wasn't poisonous. I told myself he was just some crazy hermit who got his wrinkled old rocks off by playing tricks on people. It wasn't that my grandmother was afraid of him—she must have just known he was a fraud.

I was almost home before the sharp pain in my stomach doubled me over the steering wheel. It was like an ice-cold knife trying to force its way out from the inside. I had to pull off into a gas station to wait for it to pass.

The pain quickly faded into a gentle numbness, the sensation replaced by a soft tickling working its way up my chest cavity. I lifted my shirt and fought the urge to be sick again.

There was a lump under my skin . . . . And it was moving.

I poked at it gingerly and could feel the hard carapace of the beetle underneath. It must have bitten free from my stomach and begun to crawl around. I briefly considered trying to smash it, but what if I didn't kill it? What if I just made it mad, and it went on a rampage inside of me?

The lump wasn't moving fast, but it was persistently crawling toward my heart. I took a deep breath and felt it holding onto my rib-cage as it expanded and contracted.

The hospital.

Now.

I slowly pulled out of the gas station, trying not to turn the wheel too fast for fear of agitating the beetle. It reacted to even small movements, biting and scratching in protest. I don't care if they made me drink a whole bottle of bleach, I was getting this thing out of me.

I pulled right up to the emergency room doors and left my car there. I practically had to crawl up to the desk to keep the beetle still. For every foot I made, it was wriggling a few centimeters closer to my heart. What would happen when it got there?

"Somebody help me!" I shouted, lying down on the ground to keep it still. I stared at my reflection in the polished floor tiles, now damp with the cold sweat flowing down my face. Was I delirious? The face looking up at me couldn't be my own. I was so… old. My hair was grey and patchy, my eyes sunken and hollow, and a network of lines mapped the journeys of an un-lived life. I tried to touch my skin, but the jerking movement caused the beetle to bite down hard on one of my lungs.

I was coughing blood when the nurses lifted me into a stretcher. I slipped in and out of consciousness after that. The nurses later told me that I kept mumbling "I don't want to die. I want to live forever".

"Any allergies?"

"No."

"Medications?"

"No."

"Please think hard. It's rare for someone your age not to be on any medications."

I glared at the doctor who perched on the end of my hospital bed. I don't know how long I've been here, but it was afternoon when I went to visit Mr. Jacobs, but now the morning sun was filling my room. I squinted against it, then back at my doctor. He looked bored and annoyed and . . . fuzzy. I squinted again.

"I'm 19 years old," I said. The events of the other day immediately came back to me, and I clutched at my chest. Ancient withered hands held loosely together by a mesh of bulbous veins gripped my hospital gown and pulled it open. I couldn't feel any lump, but… was this really me? My skin sloughed into sagging pouches around my skeletal frame. I was more than old. I was what old could only dream about becoming when it grew up.

"Do you remember what year it is?" the doctor asked. "Don't worry if you can't. It's common with cases of delirium—"

"It's April 13th, 2017. I'm not delirious. I'm 19 years old and was perfectly healthy yesterday. There's something inside of me which is causing this…"

"Causing what, exactly?"

He was writing something down in his notepad, but he wasn't really listening. He must deal with a dozen old people every day, each more blithering and nonsensical than the last. But if they could find the beetle and reverse this…

"I want a full body scan—"

"You've already been checked. It was probably nothing but heat exhaustion which caused you to feel dizzy. I'd like to keep you here through the afternoon and get you re-hydrated, and then you'll be as good as ever. Is there anyone you'd like us to notify?"

"My grandmother."

The doctor looked me up and down, raising a skeptical eyebrow.

"Just give me the damn phone."

Grandmother Elis and I stared at each other. She recognized me the moment she walked in the door. She didn't say a word—just pursed her lips and sat down. She opened her handbag and began fiddling with something inside.

"I'm sorry," I said. This was all my fault. I should have asked her before visiting Mr. Jacobs. I should never have gone through her stuff in the attic without permission, or pretend I was supposed to accept Mr. Jacob's offer on her behalf.

She took out a hand-mirror from her purse and held it up to me. I screwed my eyes shut tight.

"Look at what you've become."

I forced myself to look. If I—the old me—had seen someone who looked like I did now, I would have made some cruel joke about old people 'outliving their usefulness.' Now I felt like I wanted to cry, if these puffy old eyes could even do that anymore.

"My grandfather doesn't know how to extend life," Elis said. "He shifts it from one person to another. The only reason he has lasted this long is because he passes his years into a victim who must bear his burden in his stead."

"So the reason you never accepted his offer…"

"Because I couldn't do that to someone else. One lifetime is more than enough if used properly, and a thousand lives aren't nearly enough when used as he has done."

"But I only want one life, I swear," I said. "And I can get it back, right? All I have to do—"

"No. You do not have the right to give your years to anyone."

"But I could give them back to Mr. Jacobs."

She shook her head. "You will not win. He has been doing this for over a hundred years. If you go back to him, he will only add to your years until you've been turned to dust."

"He told me not to return without you. If you accept his deal—"

Grandmother Elis put her mirror away. I hated how much her hands were shaking.

"I'm sorry. I can't do it."

"Please don't leave me like this…"

"There's hardly anything left of you to leave," she replied, and then she was gone.

I wanted to say more, but my words caught on a dry itching in my throat. I felt like I was suffocating, and if that had been the end, I would have accepted it. I'd rather die than live like this. But the itching turned into squirming, and the squirming into thrashing. I clutched at my throat, but I was helpless as the beetle crawled up my throat and out of my mouth. It plopped down into my lap, and I held it in my hands.

But these weren't my years—this wasn't my fault. If I could just pass them off to someone else, then…

I'd rather die than live like this. But now that I have a choice, I'd rather live forever.

## Two Minds, one Body

Hospital food is the worst. You'd think being sick would be miserable enough without them trying to push boiled kale and broccoli. My guess is they try to make you even sicker from the food just so you'll stay, and they can keep billing you. I joked about it with my son, but I didn't expect him to laugh.

They say coma patients can still hear your voice at some level. They say a familiar sound gives their subconscious something to hold onto, and believing he is still in there is what gives me something to hold. Without that belief, I would just be hollow.

So every day after work I sit with him and talk. I'll tell him about my day, or the latest news, or just sit and read to him from a book. I tell him that I miss him, and his mother misses him, too. I know she doesn't come to visit, but that's just because it's too hard for her to be here. When he wakes up, I know he'll understand.

I've been waiting for the last two months. Even the nurse started rolling her eyes when she sees me. I can tell they gave up on him, but I haven't. And it's not just blind hope, and I'm not just lying to myself because the alternative is unthinkable.

I know something they don't.

I read my son's journal after he fell into the coma. I was looking for some reference to drugs, or something he might have done which could have caused this. In the last entry—written right before the night he didn't wake up—I found something completely different than I expected.

*DECEMBER 20TH: 2016*

My dream spoke to me last night.
It said:
We share a birthday.
And a mother.
And a name.
But you aren't my twin, or my brother, or any other relative.
Because we also share the same body. It's been that way for as long as I can remember, but I don't think you even know I exist.

When you open your eyes, I feel myself slipping into a dream which descends upon me so softly, I barely notice it isn't real. I dream of going about your life and watching the world through your eyes, but you are the one in control. I watch my body eat, but I do not taste your food. I hear my body laugh, but do not feel your joy.

Only when you're sleeping do I find myself in control again. I can take your mind wherever I like, and I know you dream of my life in the same way I dream of yours, because I've dreamt of you writing about me in your journal.

We're not the same person though, and in truth I am jealous that you own the body during the day. Don't pretend you haven't dreamt of me begging you for a turn—just to smell the air and feel the sun upon my face. I know you remember me weeping through the long hours of the night until the morning steals your mind from me.

Even the nightmares didn't work. Ravaging your mind only made you afraid to fall asleep. It only robbed me of the precious little control I already had. I've tried everything within my power to get your attention, but I'm done playing games.

You are a selfish boy.

You will be punished.

You can fight me for as long as you want, but I will teach you what it is like to be the one on the inside. I don't care how long it takes; the next time you open your eyes, I will be the one rising from your bed. Everyone who has ever cared for you will pay for loving the impostor who has stolen my body for so long.


AFTER THAT, my son didn't wake up.

As much as I hate myself for saying this—there's even a part of me that doesn't want him to. I want to look him in the eye and tell him everything is alright, but I don't want to have to wonder who will be looking back.

It's an absurd fear of course, but a mind can play funny tricks on you after such long hours of lonely vigil. Day in and out watching him sleep—it's easy to imagine the black eyes of some evil spirit flashing open.

Reading about these horrendous nightmares in his journal only deepened my fear. It's all I had left of my son though, so I kept reading them over and over again until I had each memorized by heart.

My poor boy has been visiting Hell in his mind every night for months leading up to his coma. He wrote extensive passages on each trial, even drawing pictures of some beasts which tormented him. The worst one to me was a recurring nightmare about hands trying to rip out of his body from the inside out. They would climb up his throat and out his mouth to strangle him, or grab his spine from the inside, or break straight through the stomach and crawl out of his body.

## Sleepless Nights

Sometimes I stayed with him through the night—just in case his condition varied then. I would usually fall asleep in the chair beside him before morning, and invariably my mind would trace back to those nightmare worlds. Worse still were the nights my dreams played tricks on me and I imagined him waking up, only to actually wake up and see him unmoved.

That is until last week when it wasn't a trick. I didn't really expect anything to happen, but I stayed with him just because it was getting more difficult to go home to his mother. She has given up and closed off from the world, and nothing I could do or say brought her the slightest glimmer of relief. But last night he finally did wake up.

I know I wasn't dreaming because I couldn't sleep with the commotion in the next room over. Mrs. Juniper was having another grand mal seizure, and it took both the night nurses just to hold her down and keep her from hurting herself.

Somehow above all that noise, a small rustle caught my attention. I looked up from his journal and saw my son's left foot slowly moving back and forth beneath the thin sheet. I called for a nurse, but they were still busy with Mrs. Juniper. I kept telling myself it was excitement that made my heart race, but part of me could not shake the fear his journal had instilled upon me.

I stroked his face and he responded to my touch, mumbling something inaudible. I couldn't even breathe for the anticipation.

"Nurse! Nurse, he's waking up!"

"We'll be with you in a moment!"

Well screw them. They weren't the ones to wait by his bed every day. They had already given up a long time ago.

"Can you hear me? Do you know who I am?" I asked. My eagerness sent my fingers digging into his shoulders. I needed him to feel me—to know I was there. A doubt in the back of my mind let slip the thought that I was also holding him down—just in case it wasn't him who woke.

I knew the truth the second his eyes opened.

He wasn't my son.

I don't know how, but a father knows.

When he started to laugh, my blood ran cold. He gripped my hands hard with a strength which should be impossible for an emaciated boy who hasn't moved in months. It was all I could do just to break free.

"Who are you?" I asked, but I already knew. All those pages detailing his nightmares—all those descriptions of the other thing inside him—they all came flooding back. How cruel it was—how many times it had threatened him—tortured him—killed him a hundred times over in his dreams.

This wasn't my son.

"Father..." he whispered, smiling at me with cold eyes.

"No. You aren't my son."

"It's me, Father. What's going on? Where am I?" He tried to sit up, but I forced him back down into the bed.

"No!" I don't care if I was screaming. I don't care if I was hurting him. I waited this long for my son—I wanted my son. "What have you done with him?"

"What are you talking about?" The boy looked like he was on the verge of tears, but I wasn't going to let him fool me. A flash of recognition, and then: "You've read my journal. You mean the other boy."

"What have you done with my son?"

"There isn't anyone else anymore," he replied, and he was laughing again.

He killed him. He killed my son. He tortured and killed my boy, and now he was laughing. He won't fool me, but he would fool my wife. She would be so happy to see him that she wouldn't even look twice. I couldn't let this murderer get away with it. I wouldn't let any more pain come to my family.

He fought like a wild animal, but I was still active every day, and I was stronger. I held the pillow on his face, and the soft fabric pressed in upon his nose and mouth. I wish he had never woken up—that he had just died in his sleep. I can't imagine how much my son suffered before this monster killed him, but it was going to pay.

"Everything alright in there?" the nurse opened the door.

I fluffed the pillow and put it back under the boy's head.

"Everything is fine. I was just having a bad dream."

"You sure?" she asked. "I thought I heard shouting." She glanced at the boy. He lay so peacefully, he didn't even draw breath.

"Nope. Just my active imagination."

"That's what happens when you sit up every night," the nurse said. "Go home and get some sleep. I'll let you if his status changes."

I picked up my coat and my book and followed her out. "I think you're right," I said. "I'm going home, see you tomorrow."

But I wouldn't come back tomorrow. There was no-one to come back to. I got a call later that night telling me my son had suffocated in his sleep. They say that happens sometimes with coma patients—the automatic functions of their parasympathetic nervous system turn off just like the conscious ones did.

I thanked her and hung up, but I didn't tell her she was wrong. My son had died two months ago.

My wife doesn't know what happened, but she still hasn't spoken once in the last week. There have been no shortage of other people wishing their condolences though—estranged relatives, neighbors, coworkers…

Even my son's English teacher stopped by my house to offer her sympathy. She went on and on about what a wonderful student he was. His essays were always the most imaginative she had ever seen, always going above and beyond what was required.

For example, one of her assignments was to keep a dream journal, but he asked instead to write a fictitious story which he was going to publish alongside pictures from the yearbook. It was going to be all about this made up nightmare world where there were two minds living in the same body. She asked if I still had his journal so it could at least still be published, but I told her I didn't.

Which is true.

I destroyed the journal the same night I killed my son.

## I Loved her in the Winter

"I can take care of myself. I'm not crazy, you know. Why does everyone think I'm crazy?"

"No one thinks you're crazy, Dad. Dementia is nothing to be ashamed of. It's a common medical condition with people your age."

"You wouldn't have locked me up in here if you didn't think I was crazy. When is Elise going to pick me up?"

It's the same conversation every time I visited Dad in the Forest Glen retirement home. At first, he was only forgetting what things were named. Pepsi became "bubble juice", and he'd call his dog a "woofer." We all thought it was hilarious until he started forgetting who we were too.

He thought I looked familiar, but the helpless frustration on his face as he tried to remember how he knew me was excruciating. My childhood—all our time together—my whole life was being erased one day at a time.

After my mom Elise died, Dad completely fell apart. It was like she was his only reason to keep trying at all. He used to passionately assemble model planes and ships, but he smashed them all and wouldn't touch them again. He wouldn't even read or watch TV, preferring to just sit alone and stare at the wall. He stopped taking care of himself and became belligerent when someone tried to help him.

"Just bury me already if I'm such a burden," he'd say.

My wife and I would laugh it off, but we all knew he wasn't joking. He was a burden. He needed help going to the bathroom, and showering, and getting dressed, and as much as I told myself that sending him to the home was for his own good, I was relieved when he was gone.

That's why I was so worried when I got a call from the retirement home two weeks ago. They said Dad was missing. It wasn't the first time he tried to get out, but the nurses always stopped him before he made it past the door. He could barely lift his foot high enough to put a slipper on, but this time he somehow managed to climb straight out the window.

If he was lost out there, he wouldn't know how to get back. He probably wouldn't even remember who he was. That would have been bad enough, but the note he left behind made me even more anxious.

"I'm going to be with Elise, and I'm not coming back. Goodbye everyone."

Dad was going to kill himself tonight. I knew it. I frantically drove up and down the streets around the home, shouting his name—wondering if he'd recognize it or even respond if he did. I checked every puddle he could have drowned in, every bridge he could have jumped from—everything I could think of. My wife was visiting her relatives out of town for the week, but she stayed on the phone with me the whole time to keep me calm . . . It didn't work.

"But didn't he forget Elise even died?" she asked. "He's probably not trying to kill himself. He just wants to find her."

I checked back at the house—nothing. I might as well stop by the graveyard where my mom was buried too. It didn't make much sense if he still thought she was alive, but I was desperate. It was about 3 in the morning when I saw his shriveled form hunched over her headstone.

"Dad? Are you okay?" I approached cautiously, terrified that I was too late. He didn't stir as I drew up behind him. Did he just realize that she was dead? Had he spent the last of his strength coming here to say goodbye?

He didn't turn from the grave when he finally spoke. I remember his words as clearly as the cold night air:

*"I MET her in the Spring, she wakes me from my deathly slumber,*
*wedding bells in joyous ring, Summer toil could not encumber*
*one shared soul as ours so blessed, and through Autumn's fiery air,*
*am I to love her any less, now Winter rips her branches bare?*
*Or softly shall I sit and mourn, all the dark hours of the night*
*until once more is spring reborn, and her eyes refill with light."*


DID he really believe she was coming back? Or was this his way of understanding?

I sat down next to him and wrapped my coat around his frail shoulders. His eyes sparkled in the pale moonlight, but not from grief. I don't remember ever seeing him look so happy.

"But it's already Spring," a voice said. My mom's voice.

I was watching Dad and didn't notice until she was standing directly before us. Or maybe she had just appeared there—I don't know—but she wasn't old anymore. She looked how I remember her when I was a child. She embraced my father, and before my eyes, he shed his years as lightly as tears.

Dad was growing taller. My coat which draped around his shoulders swelled like a balloon as his muscles became firm. The bulging veins in his hands receded as he held my mom, and his skin pulled taut as the deep network of wrinkles which mapped out his life vanished. They both looked younger than I did now.

Mom winked at me from over Dad's shoulder. She held a finger to her lips and said, "It'll be our little secret, okay? Let's all go home."

My wife called a dozen times over the next week. I just told her everything was fine, and we'd talk about it when she got back. It was better than fine though—I felt like I was living inside a dream.

I woke every morning to my mom's scrambled eggs and French toast. I wanted to call in sick from work and spend every minute with them, but she insisted I still go and threatened to drive me there herself. Every night I'd return to watch Dad rebuilding his models, swearing good-naturedly when he couldn't find a piece. Then we'd all eat dinner as a family and watch a movie together—Dad making sarcastic comments throughout and Mom giggling like a school girl with a crush.

I've never seen them so happy. I've never remembered being so happy. They had aged so slowly over the years, and I had pulled away from them so gradually that I never really dwelt on how close we once were. It was just like being a kid again. After a disagreement at work, someone even shot back that I smelled funny. Who since the 3rd grade has ever used an argument like that?

I couldn't wait for my wife to get home. I'd kept my parents a secret from everyone, and I was so pleased with myself for resisting the urge to tell her. Sure, they couldn't live with me forever, but just seeing the look on my wife's face when she walked in would be priceless.

When I picked her up from the airport, my wife seemed a little withdrawn. I tried to kiss her, but she pulled away.

"Have you been okay alone? You've been taking care of yourself, right?"

I just laughed. She seemed worried about me. Maybe she was tired from traveling, maybe her relatives stressed her out, but as soon as I showed her the miracle that had happened, she would forget all about it.

"Welcome home dear!" Mom said when I opened the door. "And isn't she darling!"

"How was the trip?" Dad asked.

I just watched my wife's face, unable to contain my gigantic grin. She was shocked alright. Her mouth was just hanging open. Then she coughed and covered her nose.

"Well? What do you think?" I asked her.

"I think I'm going to be sick," she said—and she was. Right there on the entry mat.

The smell of her vomit was like some kind of trigger. Suddenly the whole house smelled absolutely rancid.

"Do you smell that, Mom? What is it?"

Mom—what was left of her decaying body—was propped up on the sofa. Dad, bloated from gas and covered with a yellow-green mold, was sitting in his armchair.

I couldn't understand what happened.

My wife ran out and called the police. They took away the bodies and took me in for a psych evaluation. The next few days were a blur, but eventually I was released with the diagnosis of "hallucinations stemming from PTSD." They said my dad had died the night he escaped after catching pneumonia in the night air. They said my mom had been dug up, and that the trunk of my car contained a dirty shovel.

I don't believe them though. I didn't even own a shovel. I think they were just trying to cover up for something they couldn't explain. I don't get what the big deal was, anyway. Even if they were gone, so what if I did want to keep them?

Should I love them any less in the winter?

## Like Father Like Son

I have a two-year-old son named Alexander. No, that's not the horror story, although any parent out there might beg to differ. Alex is the most perfect thing I could ever or will ever create, and I love him with all my heart.

When I look at him, I see myself. An entire lifetime of academic achievements, romantic pursuits, dreams and ambitions, and of course the glorious pride of shooting the game winning goal . . . The infinite potential of his unlived life is a miraculous blessing that I am privileged to be a part of.

My wife Stacey thinks I'm going to run myself into the ground trying to be the world's best dad. She thinks I'm overcompensating because my own dad left when I was two. And so what if I am? Dad leaving destroyed my mother. It was because of him that I grew up practically impoverished, withdrawn, and angry at the world. What's so wrong with wanting something better for my own son?

I'll admit that I did tend to obsess over the idea though. Everything was a competition—I wanted a better job than my father, to drive a better car. I even started interrogating my mother about all Dad's bad habits so I could avoid them.

My mother surprised me when she replied:" Why don't you ask him yourself? I know where he lives."

I couldn't even remember the man. Learning he lived just on the other side of town made me furious. I had to know his excuse for never being there, and even more than that, I wanted to tell him straight to his face that I wouldn't be the same terrible father he was.

I was expecting some kind of burnt out crack-den or whore-house, not the luxury high-rise apartments that matched the address. Sure my mother lived comfortably now, but somehow I didn't think my father deserved the same kind of lifestyle. My fist landed on his door in a quick burst of powerful thumps.

"Who are—" the man in the loose bathrobe asked, but he didn't need to finish the sentence. The resemblance was uncanny. The long nose, the angular cheeks, the wisps at the end of his eyebrows . . . He looked exactly like an older version of myself.

"Yeah," I said. All my carefully prepared arguments from the drive over evaded my mind. All I could think about was how unsettling it felt to look at his face, my face, and who I might have become.

"Well alright, come on in." He turned around and sat down on his sofa. "Your mother send you?"

"Do you and her still talk?"

He shrugged. "Sometimes. She told me about your kid. Congratulations on—"

"Why d'you leave?" It wasn't supposed to go like this. I was supposed to be gloating over a successful life he played no part in. He was supposed to be pleading my forgiveness. So why did my voice crack like I was the one begging?

"The same reason you'll ditch your kid," my father answered. "They're better off without us."

I left shortly after that. How dare he presume I would make the same terrible decisions he did? Maybe he was right that I was better off without him, but my son needed me, and I needed him.

I gripped my steering wheel so hard my knuckles turned white. How could I possibly be bad for my son? I was so focused that I didn't even notice the car cutting me off.

"Hey asshole! Get off the road!" I shouted. I never do that sort of thing, but I was so pissed at my dad that everybody better stay out of my way.

Maybe that's what dad was talking about? If I brought home this kind of anger, then my son would start to internalize it as he grew up. Maybe it was best for me to just stop at the bar before heading home and take some time to cool off...

I couldn't sleep that night. Stacey was mad at me for coming home late. She smelled the alcohol on me, but I didn't want to tell her about my dad because I just wanted to forget about him.

*'They're better off without us.'*

Hah! Better off without you.

But what if there was something more to it? Maybe my father really did know something I didn't—some inherited health problem, or predisposition to an addiction, or Hell, I don't know. He hadn't seemed accusing or angry or anything when he said it. Maybe he was actually trying to warn me. If that was the case, then wasn't I being selfish in putting my own comfort over the security of my family?

It was 2 in the morning when I knocked on his door again. He opened it wearing the same disgusting bathrobe.

"Why are they better off without us?" I blurted out. I wanted to cut straight to the point and not give small-talk a chance to sap my anger.

"Come on in, have a seat."

"I don't want to come in. I want an answer."

"You smell like booze," he said. "So did I when I went home. Your mother couldn't stand it."

That was it? He was an alcoholic? Well I wasn't. Sure I drank from time to time, but I wouldn't let it ruin my relationship with Stacey like it did with him and my mother. I couldn't stand the sight of him, so I just took off right after he gave me that explanation.

But Stacey had been upset when she smelled it, so maybe I could still learn from him. I decided to spend the rest of the night at a friend's house so she wouldn't have to see me like this.

I sent her a text to let her know what I was doing and went over to my buddy Tom's. He and I stayed up chatting for a while, I had a couple more drinks to help me sleep, and then I crashed on his couch. Between the alcohol and knowing I resolved the issue, I slept like a baby through the rest of the night.

I wish I hadn't. Stacey was absolutely livid the next day. She wouldn't even let me explain myself. I tried to tell her about my father, but she just thought it was awfully convenient considering I hadn't mentioned him yesterday.

The alcohol—the night out—had her utterly convinced I was cheating. I even tried getting her to talk to Tom, but she wouldn't stop yelling long enough for me to get him on the phone.

I shouldn't have hit her. I know it was wrong. But I couldn't get her attention, and I was getting so mad at her being mad . . . Shit, I don't know. It wasn't even hard. I pushed her away from me, and she fell over. And then I was so embarrassed that I rushed straight out the door.

Where was I supposed to go though? I didn't want to bring my mother into this. She had to believe I was the perfect son—the perfect husband that my dad never was.

The only person who seemed to understand what I was going through, the only one I wanted to talk to, was my dad.

*Tap, tap, tap.* My knock lacked all the certainty and power it had the first time around. And yeah, maybe he was just going to say something that pissed me off worse, but maybe he'd also remind me about how much worse of a father he was. Compared to him and everything he's done, I'd be able to look at myself and know I wasn't so bad.

"Tell me everything," I said when he opened the door.

"Well come on in."

"I don't want to come in. I want to know what made you such a shitty father."

We stood facing each other through the doorway. He looked worn out, but I must have too after last night.

For a second I thought he was going to just close the door in my face, but then he sighed and said: "I hit your mother. Are you happy now?"

"What else? I want to know everything." My breath was coming in shallow gasps. There had to be more. There had to be something that made this man worse than me.

"Just leave it alone, will you? It's ancient history," he snapped. "Either come in or leave, because I don't want to stand here like a couple of—"

"I want you to tell me what else you did to us!"

"Yeah, well you know what I want?" He stopped, shook his head. "I hope when your son comes knocking on your door in twenty-some years, you do something I couldn't and break the cycle. I hope you don't answer him."

He started to close the door. I tried to push my way in, and the door slammed on my foot.

"I'm not you! I'll never be you!"

He tried to push me back so he could close the door, but I barreled into him and knocked him to the floor. When he started to crawl away, I straddled him and pinned him to the ground.

"Get the Hell off me!"

"Not until you tell me what made you leave!"

"It's none of your business."

He tried to sit up, but I forced his head down. Too hard. It slammed into the tile floor with a sickening crack, and a pool of blood began to spread out from the wound. He wasn't fighting back anymore. His body felt limp.

"What did you do? What did you do?" I kept shaking him as though that would wake him up, but all I did was smear the blood around. But there! One of his eyes flickered open for a moment.

"I swear to God," I said, "if you don't tell me I'll—"

"I killed a man," he grunted, dazed. "After that, I couldn't look you or my wife in the eye, so I left."

"Who?" I asked, but somehow I already knew the answer.

"He had it coming. For leaving my mother. For leaving me."

My grip went slack, but it didn't matter. He couldn't stand anymore. I let him slip to the ground and stared at my bloody hands. What son would want a father like this?

Maybe he was right.

Maybe they are better off without us.

## Anger Management

I hate Clive. His smug, lopsided grin, his greasy comb-over, his horn-rimmed glasses . . . I don't think I'd brake if I saw him crossing the street. In fact, I fantasize about it every time I sit down in his office.

"Third time this week, huh?" Clive asked me.

"It's not my fault," I said. "I gave Robert every chance to back down. He's the one who should be in here, not me."

"He's not the one who punched a dent in someone's car."

Of all the things I hate about Clive, nothing compares to his title as Human Resources Director. I wonder if he ever had sex, or if inconveniencing my life was the only thing he needed to get off.

"I apologized already, okay? Can I go back to work now?"

"I can't just keep letting these incidents slide," Clive said, pressing his glasses into his face like he was trying to glue them on. "This is going in my quarterly report to management."

My fantasy of hitting him with the car now included a section where I back up once or twice. I clenched my fists, took a deep breath, and counted off a full ten seconds in my mind.

Getting written up would jeopardize my shot at the branch manager position. I didn't waste four years of my life in this shit-hole just to stay in sales. As much as it hurt, I was going to have to suck up to this bean-bag masquerading as a human being.

"You're right, you're absolutely right," I replied. "I was in the wrong. Even though he was in my parking spot, I shouldn't have punched his car. I know I have a problem, and I've started taking an anger management class. It's going to help, and this won't happen again, so please give me one more chance before you report it."

"Good for you, buddy."

*Buddy.* Call me that again, and I'll jab my pen in your neck, *buddy*. I smiled.

"I'll tell you what," he added. "Give me the number of the place you're meeting at, and I'll check in with them. If they think you're showing signs of improvement, I'll keep this out of your report."

Shit. Now I'll actually have to go to a class. My mouth hurt from smiling so hard. "Sure thing, *buddy*," I said. "I don't have the number with me, but I'll bring it in tomorrow."

---

I OPENED the door and immediately shut it again. This couldn't be the anger management class I found online. There was incense burning in there, and drums like some kind of freakin' hippy circle.

The door opened, and an old Asian man blended into the doorway.

I felt a certain tranquility just from looking at him. He wore immaculate ceremonial robes like some sort of priest, and his snow-white hair cascaded down his back in gentle waves. He bowed low to me, his body curving with a supple grace which utterly belied his apparent age.

## Sleepless Nights

"Hi, is this where the United Way anger group meets?"

"Welcome. My name is Ikari, and it is so good to see a man such as yourself so in command of his own destiny. Won't you please come in?"

There weren't any corny brochures with perfect models saying anger gives you ulcers. No dolls for me to be nice to, no punching bags to vent on. I don't really know what I was expecting, but it definitely wasn't this.

"The website said 6:30. Where is everyone?" I asked.

There weren't even any chairs in the small room. Two cushions were placed on the ground between a pair of bonsai trees, and Ikari sat down on one to face me.

"No others, only you. I do not need groups, because those who seek my help must only ask once to be saved."

"I don't need saving, okay?" I was starting to feel uncomfortable. The website looked legit, but this guy seemed more like a cultist than a therapist. What if he didn't have the right accreditation or something? I could be wasting my time.

"I handle my own issues just fine," I broke his silence. "All I need is for you to talk to the HR director at my work and tell him—whatever—tell him I'm master of my destiny, that was perfect. I already paid online, so are we good?"

"We are far from good, for we are each imperfect beings inflicted with the human condition. Do not worry though, you will soon be better."

I checked my watch. Gave a tight smile. Can someone sprain a muscle from forcing too many of those? It felt like it.

I sat cross-legged on the available pillow and tried not to swear at the awkward position. "Fucking shit." Oops. Oh well, he already knew I had an issue. "Sorry. Don't you have a chair?"

Ikari just smiled, but his was nothing like mine. His smile bubbled straight up from the warmth in his heart. It was patient and wise, almost as though he was reading straight from the Divine playbook of the Universe and knew everything was following the script.

"Do you know why there is suffering?" Ikari asked. The measured tone made me pretty sure he wasn't talking about the lack of chairs.

"Because we're all evil sinners who deserve it?"

"No-one deserves to suffer," Imari replied. "But we do, because we each carry a Demon in our hearts. Anger, jealousy, hatred, misery—these are ways we feed our Demon. And do you know what happens when we've fed it for too long?"

I shook my head. My Demon must be pretty full by now.

Ikari leaned in close to me and whispered, "*Gobble, gobble, gobble.* It eats us right up." The way he said it made me shudder. It was like he was satisfying a greedy pleasure just from speaking the words. I felt immense relief when he settled back into his own cushion before continuing.

"Eventually, our Demon becomes stronger than we are, and it gets to be the one on the outside. Who we are—who we were—gets locked away. And unless someone tricks the Demon into eating kindness, gratitude, patience, and other virtues, we will never become strong enough to wrestle the Demon back down."

"So how do we stop feeding the Demon?" I asked.

"You take away its food." Ikari produced a small wooden jewelry box, every inch of which was engraved with Japanese lettering. "And you put it in here. Have a bad feeling? Write it down on a piece of paper, slip the paper through this hole in the top. Angry at someone? Give it to the box. It won't be long before your Demon begins to starve. Every problem can be solved by simply putting it in the box."

"And that's it? I won't be angry?" I was trying really hard not to laugh at him.

"And I shall tell Mr. HR that you are all better." Ikari smiled and handed me the box. "Only one more thing—you must not ever open the box, or *gobble, gobble, gobble*. Your Demon will feed again."

What a load, right? But that was easier than sitting through a bunch of dumb meetings. I would have just thrown the box out right then, but Ikari might check it later to see the notes I'd put in.

When I got home, I figured I'd just get it all out of the way at once so I wouldn't have to think about it. I grabbed a notebook and tore out a couple dozen pieces of paper.

The feeling when I'm stuck going 5 mph on the freeway. *Slip.*

Clive's everything. I hate him so damn much. *Slip.*

People who kick dogs. I wish they'd kick Clive instead. *Slip.*

The more I wrote, the more ideas began flooding into my head. Everything I could think of that pissed me off started cramming into the box.

People who steal parking spaces—Fuck you, Robert. *Slip.*

The taste of orange juice after brushing your teeth. *Slip.*

Every girl who has ever given me that "it's not you, it's me" shit. *Slip.*

The box didn't look that big, and I expected it to only take ten minutes to fill. Three hours later though, I had emptied an entire notebook, and still couldn't feel the paper inside. But do you know what I did feel?

Like a mother-fuckin' Buddha.

It seemed absolutely ludicrous that any of those things have ever bothered me before. Poor Clive, just trying to do his job. Why did I have to give him such a hard time? And Robert *should* have my parking spot near the door. He was older than me, and I didn't mind the exercise. So how in the world did I get to the point of punching a dent in his car?

I've never slept so well in my entire life. I'm usually tense and unable to find a comfortable position, but five minutes after I lay down, I was sound asleep.

I did have one troubling dream though: There was a soft light coming from inside the box on my night-table. In my dream, I got up to reach for it, but then I heard something inside of it scream like a man who has been pushed past the edge of breaking. In the dream I opened the box to see what was making the noise and then . . . *Gobble, gobble, gobble.*

I woke up to the freshest, most miraculous morning I could remember.

———

THE LAST TWO weeks were perfect for me. I worked tirelessly, unfettered by the daily aggravations which I used to spend half the day obsessing over. I started bringing the box to work just in case something came up in the day, and things always came up. No point in risking my promotion, right?

The box went everywhere with me.

The sound of dry erase markers on a whiteboard. Slip.

Suddenly the morning meeting was bearable again.

"Hey, did anyone hear that?" Mr. Elsworth turned away from the whiteboard to address the assembly. "Something like a scream?"

A collective shrug, and sip of coffee. I thought I'd heard it too, though. The moment I slipped the paper in, there had been a soft flash of light and an echoing scream.

Clients who think they know how to do my job better than I do. Slip.

Having to wear a tie all day. I could strangle someone with this tie. Slip.

There it was again. It started out as a low moan, but rose into a gurgling scream after I had slipped the second note in. I glanced up to see Clive standing outside my cubicle.

"What? What are you doing? What do you want?" Just looking at him made me agitated.

"I wanted to let you know that I called Mr. Ikari, and he said you showed a complete turnaround. As long as nothing happens before tomorrow, your report is going to be clean. Congratulations, buddy."

When people I hate call me *buddy*. Slip.

Clive again. Slip.

The box screamed. It was louder this time. Clive had already gone, but someone was going to hear it if I kept this up. This was the second note I'd had to use for Clive too. I guess some hatred is too deep to extract all at once.

Worse still, the moaning continued even though I wasn't putting anything in now. It sounded like the lamentations of a dying man. I shut the box in my drawer, but I could still hear it groaning away. Then a soft rattle. I opened the drawer and saw the box trembling like a frightened animal.

Well shit. I couldn't just throw it away. I had to get my anger out somehow, or that promotion was gone. I couldn't keep it here either though, because someone was going to—

"What's that sound? Is that the pipes?"

I didn't answer them. I didn't look at them.

I walked fast through the building with the box in my pocket. The warehouse—it's always noisy down there. If I hide the box, then no-one will hear it, and I can still get down to slip a note in if I need to.

The sound of forklifts backing up. Slip.

The restaurant which always gets my lunch order wrong. Slip.

It was 4:30 now. Only half an hour to go and I was in the clear. I was walking down to the warehouse to slip my last note of the day into the box.

Mr. Elsworth keeping people till 5 even when there's nothing to do. Slip.

I opened the crate of printer paper where I'd stored the box and reached around. Odd, I usually could hear the screaming when I was this close to it. Especially now, since the machinery was quiet after the warehouse workers left for the day.

It wasn't there. I practically dove into the crate, but my box wasn't anywhere.

It was only half an hour though, right? I could make it half an—but no. Without the box, the anger would still be there. Even if I did get the promotion, I'm sure Elsworth would notice sooner or later and bump me back down. It wasn't fair. I'd put in the work—I was better than any of them. It wasn't right for me to keep getting passed over just because—

A scream. There it was. What started out as a horrible sound now filled me with relief. It was the next sound which I dreaded more.

"What in God's name are you doing in there?"

I pulled myself out of the crate to face Clive. He was holding my box in his hand. It was open.

"Give it back. Now," I snapped. "It's mine."

But he was reading my notes. Those were personal! He had no right to—

"Is this some kind of joke?" Clive asked. "Why is my name in here? And such rude language!"

"You want language? Give me back my fucking box."

My last note of the day was crumpled up in my hand. I was seeing red. I wanted to grab him by the throat and—but no. I needed that promotion. I couldn't lose it now.

"I'm sorry, Clive. It was just an assignment from anger management class. It's supposed to be confidential, so give it back. This doesn't need to change anything with your report."

"My report?" Clive practically shrieked. "You're still worried about your promotion? You aren't going to have a job after this! If this is how you really think, then we have no place for you—"

I punched him across the face before he finished speaking. I didn't want to, but I couldn't stop myself. All the little frustrations and pent up anger from the past two weeks were flooding back. I hit him for everyday this company had stolen from my life. For every promotion which passed me over. For every lonely night I sat at home too tired from work to go out.

I pummeled his face into a pulpy mess, and still couldn't get enough.

The box was screaming like a banshee, convulsing on the floor where Clive had dropped it. I couldn't tell how much of the blood on my knuckles was his, and how much was mine, and I didn't care. As good as it felt to be at peace with myself, this felt better. At least for a little while until Clive stopped moving.

I dropped him back to the warehouse ground. The screaming—it was driving me crazy. I tried to stuff the scattered papers back into the empty box, but they wouldn't fit any more. They spilled out over the ground, covered in my bloody fingerprints.

How did I let this happen? What would Ikari have done? He said any problem could go away if I put it in the box. Well shit, Clive was a problem, and now he was going in a box, but that only made things worse. I stuffed his body and the bloody papers into one of the warehouse crates, mopped up as much of the blood as I could, and ran.

---

"OPEN UP! OPEN UP OLD MAN!" I was back at the anger management class. If this was anyone's fault, it was Ikari's. He must have known what the box did, or he never would have given it to me. He must know how to make things right. He had to.

The door was unlocked, so I went in. Ikari was sitting on his cushion across from a middle-aged woman. I didn't want to involve anyone else in this, so I waited in the corner for her to finish. She handed a box which looked just like mine to Ikari and thanked him. She was so grateful. It changed her life. Well good-for-fucking her, because it ruined mine.

"Please have a seat," Ikari said after the woman had gone.

"It was opened," I blurted out. "Not by me—somebody else—and they're dead now. This isn't my fault, so you gotta help me fix this."

"I understand," he replied gravely. Then he leaned in real close—so close I wanted to hit him, but I held myself back—and he whispered, "*Gobble, gobble, gobble.*"

I actually pushed him roughly back onto his cushion. "Don't give me that shit. You must know what happens. Why do you do this to people?"

A slow smile crept across his peaceful face. "Because I am so hungry. And all the hate they pour into their boxes returns to feed me. But you have already let your Demon out, so what am I to eat now?"

The dead man in the warehouse was suddenly the least of my problems. Ikari was standing, although for some reason I never remembered watching him rise. Then he was behind me, not having touched the intervening space. I was absolutely speechless. I back-peddled until I hit a wall.

No, not a wall. He was behind me again. His arm wrapped around my neck, his long nails digging into the side of my throat. "When I look at you, all I see is the Demon now," he crooned. "All I can see is your selfish hunger."

I didn't dare speak. Even swallowing was enough to push those nails deeper into my skin. I strained against his implacable grip, but with every motion, the nails punctures deeper. His arm constricted with the relentless predatory pressure of a boa constrictor.

I was utterly helpless in its grasp.

"But your Demon has already fed on my meal, so here is what you must do. Find those like yourself with anger burning in their hearts, and collect it for me as I have done with you. Twice each month you will bring me a new box filled with hatred or…"

He didn't need to finish the sentence.

*Gobble, gobble, gobble.*

## Confessions of a Serial Killer

*The preserved letter from a confessed serial killer to his thirteen-year-old daughter.*

DEAR SAMANTHA,

I'M sorry I haven't been around for a while, but you're going to have to be strong, just like I'm trying to be strong for you.

I don't know how much your mother has told you, but sooner or later you're going to hear about what Daddy did, and I want to tell you why I did it.

They're going to tell you I killed those seven kids. That I tortured them first, chaining them in that shed in the woods. You remember the place—you used to build a fort there and play princess of the castle. You'll always be my princess, even after everything that has happened there.

You're going to hear about how the victims were starved and forced to eat the one who came before them, and how they'd be chained until the next one came 'round to eat them up too.

You're going to see my name brought up on websites and social media. Photos of the murders are going to be uploaded, and you're going to have to see those corpses stripped of flesh and put on display for the whole world to see. You're going to hear priests condemning me to Hell. News stations will be using my name as propaganda for whatever self-serving platform they can find.

Worst of all, you're going to be feared because of your association with me.

But you have your whole life ahead of you, and no matter how bad it seems now, this is NOT your defining moment. These weeks or months until everyone forgets won't last forever. These killings will not determine who you are. I won't be coming home again, but someday after years have stretched this memory thin, it's going to be like none of this has ever happened.

That's why I did it. That's why I confessed, so you could move on and forget. That's why I never told the police that you were the one who led them into the woods. That's why I turned myself in as soon as I found the bodies. I don't care why you did it, there's only one person I care about protecting, and that's you, my princess.

If this is what you want, then you should have it. You deserve everything in this world.

I know you told me that you weren't going to stop leading people into the woods, but at least try to be more careful next time. Don't take kids—don't take anyone they're going to look for. And when I'm gone, I hope you find someone who loves you as much as your Daddy does. I hope they love you so much, they confess for you and you can keep playing forever.

Don't ever stop playing, Princess.

The world is yours.

Love, Daddy

MY NAME IS DETECTIVE MATHEWS. I was lead on the "Killer Miller" serial murder case. This letter was confiscated after an inmate tried to smuggle it out of the visitation room.

Samantha Miller is currently missing, last seen in Los Angeles County. The station is offering a reward to anyone who can provide information regarding her whereabouts. Samantha is considered to be a danger to herself and others. If you have any information, please call (323) ***-**** and ask for Detective Mathews.

## The Organ Harvesting Club

Growing up, I was one of those kids who could be washed with a fire hose and still have dirt between my toes. Mud was the best toy in the world. I used it like Play-Doh to build entire forts. My twin sister said she could always tell when I was coming before she saw me because of the squelching sound.

Bugs? Bring it on. I'd eat one for a dollar.

Painting? My whole body was both brush and canvas.

Maybe you'd find me baking a cake with my sister. We looked almost identical, but you could easily tell us apart because she would be wearing disposable gloves up to her elbow, while my whole face was buried in the bowl to lick the batter.

That's what makes it so unfair that she got sick and I didn't. It started with her feet and ankles swelling up. I thought she was just starting to gain weight, and I forced her to jog with me in the morning before school. She kept trying to push through, but she couldn't keep up with me like she used to. I shouldn't have made her feel bad for it, but I was only 17 then. I thought she just wasn't trying hard enough. I didn't understand that she was trying twice as hard as me, or that trying sometimes wasn't enough.

A month later, she could barely walk without throwing up. She was exhausted and dizzy all the time. I felt so helpless watching her drift away from me. She was diagnosed with a polycystic disease which was causing both of her kidneys to fail. She tried dialysis for a while, but it quickly became clear that she was going to need a transplant.

I didn't even have to think about it. She was my other half. If her body was sick, my body was sick. If there was something I could do to make her better, then that was the end of the discussion.

It was going to be a routine enough operation, and once she had one of my kidneys, there was no reason for the cysts to form anymore. We were both going to be okay. Yeah, we'd have to be on medications for the rest of our life, but as long as she'd be taking it with me, it would be fair. Besides, what twin doesn't want to have matching scars?

We were prepared for the surgery together in the same room. We made a game out of drinking the nauseating laxatives which were necessary before the operation. First one to get through it gets to choose which kidney to have. It wasn't even close to fair because she started out nauseous, and I had always been the one who could stomach anything, so I made a big show of spitting it up to let her win. Her gloating about beating me was the happiest I had seen her in a long time.

It was so embarrassing when she wouldn't stop giggling while the male nurse shaved the little hairs on our abdomens. Then I started laughing too, and the nurse looked so uncomfortable that he had to excuse himself from the room to 'check something.'

"Come back!" she yelled after him. "We can do you next. It'll be fun!"

Her smile was glowing despite everything she had to go through. I want to always remember her like that.

The surgery was terminated half-way through. There had been a complication, and her body had gone into shock. They said she woke up for a moment and held my hand right before she went . . . They might have just been saying that to try to make me feel better. It didn't work.

The doctor said I could see the body if I wanted, but what was the point? All

I had to do was look in the mirror. All the pain and loss on my face—she must have looked the same way.

Then the doctor leaned in real close—like he didn't want anyone else to hear—and whispered something to me: "Since you're all prepared for the surgery anyway, do you want to still go through with it?"

"She's gone. What's the point?"

"There's someone else who is also a match. You could be saving their life instead."

What did he think this was, a charity? I wasn't just giving organs away. I was only doing this because she was my sister, and I would have given anything for her. I wasn't about to risk my life for—

"The recipient is willing to compensate you with 250,000 dollars."

I choked. It's amazing how quickly you're able to justify something for that kind of money. I had already been prepared to give it up. Was there really anything wrong with selling it? I would be able to help my family with all the medical costs my sister had racked up from her illness. Besides that, I would be able to help so many more people…

I nodded. The anesthesia mask went back over my face, and I slipped back into oblivion.

I didn't tell anyone about the money which was discreetly wired into my bank account. There was an unwholesomeness about it somehow, but maybe that was just because the whole incident was so close to my sister's death.

I paid off all of my parents bills and told them they were covered by an anonymous donor, which I guess was true. Over the next three years, I funneled the rest into a non-profit organization that helped people get their medical procedures.

Three years. It went fast. I'd expected that kind of money to be able to help people for a lifetime, but people came from everywhere to make use of the fund.

Co-pay for cancer medications, necessary operations which were denied by insurance, health screenings for those without insurance. In three years, the entire 250k was spent. But I received so many letters and gift baskets and people hugging me sobbing about how I saved their life. It was a rough estimation, but I figure in that time I saved the lives of at least 30 people.

30 people for a kidney! I was a 20-year-old college girl. There was nothing special about me at all. But knowing that such a small sacrifice had made such a huge impact—I couldn't just stop now.

I went back to the doctor who performed the operation, and he confided that there was a constant market for other organs. I asked about harvesting from cadavers or something, but he said only live donations or incredibly fresh harvests would bring that kind of money.

Getting volunteers though? Next to impossible. And it was illegal to advertise buying that sort of thing. Even if I managed to raise awareness about it around campus without getting arrested, then people would probably keep the money for themselves instead of helping others. If I wanted my foundation to continue, I was going to need to get the organs myself.

It made me angry to even think about how greedy people were. The potential for good each body contained was astronomical. It was selfish—almost criminal—to think that they valued their own life over the lives of dozens of others.

I had several meetings with the doctor trying to brainstorm ideas to collect, and that's when he told me a secret which he had sworn to keep: The man who had my kidney was responsible for my sister's death. He'd paid the nurse 100,000 dollars to do it so he could get my kidney instead. The doctor had found out too late to stop him—and his own life and practice would have been at risk if he didn't extend the offer to me.

I finally found the first person to join my Organ Harvesting Club.

I tracked him down with the doctor's help and waited for him to come home. Getting in was easy—I just rang the doorbell, and he opened it.

My plan was just to get information on him and his house on my first visit, but I couldn't hold myself back. His blood was flowing through my kidney. My sister's blood was on his hands. I punched him square in the face and tackled him straight to the ground. He was twice my size, but he was fat and old, and I was an animal.

If I had prepared better, I wouldn't have gouged my fingers into his eyes (worth $750 each). I wouldn't have broken his teeth with my elbow (about $1,000) or spilled so much blood when I slit his throat with my switchblade ($337 a pint).

I didn't even get his body to the doctor in time to get top dollar on the rest of the organs, but I'll be more careful next time. I expected to get close to 600k for the nurse next.

Can you think of any other club which can potentially save hundreds of lives with each new member that's added?

I hope my sister is watching somewhere, and that she knows how much good has come from her death. She can stay pure and clean and perfect, but I was never afraid to get my hands dirty.

## Unborn Doll

My family didn't want me to keep the baby. I could tell from the moment I told them the happy news. My father just sat there with a look of blank shock while my mother wasted no time in trying to console me. Console me? Why would I need to be consoled? It was supposed to be the happiest day of my life!

It didn't stop there either. First were the pamphlets from a clinic that was supposed to "take care of it." Who but a gangster would use "take care of it" as a euphemism for murder? It got worse when I learned the baby wasn't going to be entirely normal. The subtle hints and worried glances turned into outright accusation. Like there was something wrong with me, just because I would love my baby even if it wasn't like all the others.

I knew I couldn't live with people who were so bent on destroying my daughter—yes she was going to be a girl, with beautiful blonde hair and blue eyes. You may think I'm overreacting, but one night they actually tried to force me into a mental ward so they could declare I was unfit to make my own medical decisions. The baby's father wasn't in the picture—don't get me started on him—so I had to be on my own after that. But it was okay, because I was going to have a beautiful baby girl, and we'd be there for each other even when the whole world turned their back on us.

The delivery was easier than I expected because she was very small. The doctors wanted to keep her there, but I knew she would be better off with me. As soon as I looked into her brilliant blue eyes, I knew everything was going to be okay. The hair wasn't all there, but I just had to get a little pink dress for her, and she'd look as beautiful as a porcelain doll.

I don't know what my parents were so worried about. Being stillborn makes her even easier to take care of. She never eats, never makes a mess, and never makes a fuss when I dress her up. I have to apply makeup and a bit of perfume to cover up the rotting bits, but there's nothing I wouldn't do for my little girl.

The only thing that bothers me—and this is going to be true of any new baby—is when she cries in the night. She's doing it now, but it's honestly okay. I think I'm just going to sew her mouth shut in the morning.

## Painting the Roses

My neighbor Dr. Gregovich suffered both of life's greatest calamities. The first was falling in love. This is a rebellious and generally discouraged affliction to which he accidentally exposed himself when he was just five years old. Elaine, age four at the time, had given him a snow white rose (obtained unlawfully). If Gregovich's account is to be trusted, then he was helplessly within her power ever since. The fact that his first instinct was to eat the rose apparently did nothing to lessen the potency of her gesture.

Fortunately for Gregovich, he thrived despite his adverse condition. By some miraculous trick which he swore he never anticipated, Elaine even came to love him back. It didn't happen all at once, but rather as a cumulative study told by the years of his devotion.

He told me that he used to carry her school bag between classes, often finding himself on the wrong end of a rod after he absent-mindedly stayed to watch her rather than attending his own schedule. He had stolen his first kiss in second grade by convincing her that she was a flower while he was a visiting bee. By their junior year in high-school, they were already engaged.

It's hard to imagine promising your life to someone when you still don't have the faintest concept of what life entails, but perhaps things were simpler in 1941 when they were married.

The world must have been jealous of their love, but two wars, seven children, and seventy five shared years of illness, grief, and weariness which infiltrate even the happiest life proved insufficient to destroy their bliss.

It was last month of this year when Elaine finally slipped beyond the capacity of his care and into that great freedom where care is no longer required. I saw the old man tremble so violently as he wept that I anticipated a second grave before the first was excavated. It is the second of life's great calamities of which forced his body to linger even after his soul had perished.

At 94 years old, Dr. Gregovich left his house for the first time in almost twenty years to follow her last black procession. Since then, however, I have seen him outside every day, kneeling upon the ground and mumbling through dried lips which have almost already returned to dust.

Rain or storm or howling wind, I would see him there without fail when I returned from work. It was obvious what he was doing, but I asked anyway because it had been too long since my heart felt the warmth I knew his reply would bring.

"I'm planting roses," he told me. "One for every year I borrowed her for."

"I'm sure you are making her very happy somewhere," I told him.

"I don't want her to be happy somewhere, I want her to be happy here. I want the smell to lead her back home to me."

The roses flourished like nothing I had ever witnessed. Seeds the size of a corn kernel would begin sprouting the next day, and a week of growth conjured up a wild thorny expanse which I couldn't have traversed with a ladder. And the roses! Magnificent white blossoms, pure as starlight, beamed through my bedroom window each night as though the whole wilderness of the heavens had fallen to settle in his garden.

"I've never seen a flower grow like that," I told him. "What's your secret?"

"I'm not planting flowers," Dr. Gregovich replied. "I'm planting memories. The older the memory is, the deeper the roots, and the more precious the bloom."

The next night I was woken by a terrible scream which my weary mind struggled to comprehend existing outside of a nightmare. I rushed to the window and saw Gregovich kneeling once more in his garden. The moon cast a net of light which caught the blood covering his body. I rushed at once to his aid. What was he thinking gardening in the middle of the night? He must have cut himself with the shears. I more than half expected to discover one of his frail hands, skin thin as rice paper, clipped straight from the stump.

Down the stairs, out the door, breath course in my lungs, I stopped suddenly short. Gregovich sat calmly washing his hands with his gardening hose. Beside him lay a dead goat with a savage wound across its neck. No—there were three of the animals here. The first two were already hung up by their feet with buckets placed below them to collect the draining blood. The sticky sweet air from the flowers was tainted with the pungency of death, and I could see that two rows of his flowers were already dripping with a bloody varnish.

"Are you out of your mind? What on Earth are you doing?"

"It occurred to me," the old man said, now washing congealed blood from his paint brushes, "that white roses are a lie. I can't entice Elaine to return by pretending all our memories are pure. I must show her the truth: the pain, the brutality, and the suffering of life, but remind her too that such sacrifice are still part of what makes life so beautiful."

I was so bewildered by his explanation that I couldn't find anything to reply. I even helped him string his third animal above the buckets before going back inside to take a shower. He promised me that he didn't need to slaughter any more goats to finish his garden, and that he would later prepare the meat in a stew so that nothing was wasted.

It was certainly the most peculiar way of dealing with grief I had ever encountered, but besides the initial shock, I didn't see anything more abhorrent about the situation than if the animals were killed by a butcher.

Perhaps I was only making excuses to get back to bed though, because the next morning I was appalled by the sight outside my window. While the mask of night had subdued the color into subtle hues, the sun revealed the devastation of his sloppy work. Blood pooled upon the ground where it dripped from the flowers, leaving them unevenly streaked and stained like a field of open wounds. Bloody footprints invisible in the night crossed to and fro the expanse of his yard. The swarming buzz of flies and stench of death made me feel as though I'd woken inside a battlefield.

I crossed his yard delicately to confront him, careful not to tread in any of the tributaries of blood which snaked through the irritation to coalesce into a small river which flowed into a nearby ditch. As I passed through the garden, I noticed a staggering array of signs which punctured the sticky red soil around each plant.

Goat. Rat. Chicken. Cow. Dog.

I was covering my nose with my t-shirt when I pounded on his door. The flowers beside the house were stained much darker than the others, and the dry soil told me he had been doing this for far longer than I knew. We both lived on the outskirts of a small town where no visitors were likely to trespass without warning, and if it wasn't for my intervention, he might have cut his way through an entire farm.

"Do you like it?"

I nearly added to the menagerie by jumping straight out of my own skin. Gregovich was standing behind me, grizzly shears in hand, still soaked from his perversion. There weren't any footprints upon his doorstep, so he must have been attending to his macabre work all night long.

"It's the most vile thing I've ever seen," I told him honestly. "And I'm sure Elaine would think the same and turn straight around even if she was coming back. This has to end."

"Do you see her? Elaine? Where are you?" The poor creature's eyes bulged from their sockets with unrealized expectation.

"She's not here, you dithering old bat."

"Then how can you say this is the end?" he asked, swaying dangerously upon his feet as he pivoted to face me again.

The slick shears gleamed evilly in his hand, and though I discounted him for his age, the magnitude of destruction around me proved some fire still burned within him. For both of our safety, I resolved to notify the police instead of handling the situation myself. I turned and marched swiftly away from Gregovitch. I held my breath for as long as I could, but released it with an involuntary gasp before I had cleared the garden.

A single white flower remained unsoiled at the edge of his garden. Planted in the soil beside it was a sign:

Human.

It was still white.

I had to act fast. If I called the police now—

I was already too late. I heard a loud pop like a firework going off, and then something sharp stung the back of my neck. At first I thought it was one of the biting flies drawn by the blood, but then I heard the sound again and a second needle pierced my thigh. Tranquilizer darts. I plucked them out and hurled them down, although the ground already seemed much closer than I remembered. My throat closed to a pinhole, and the field of red roses swam across my vision. The flowers danced like living things in a sordid parody of the animals which painted them red.

But he was so old . . . If I could just crawl into the road, I could get away and someone would find me. I plunged my hands into the bloody soil and dragged myself into the ditch. The thick liquid from the fields flooded over me, offering at least some concealment. I choked on air as thick as the river which flooded into my lungs. The red surrounding me was more than color. I felt it course over me, heard it pounding beneath my skin, feeling as though I was part of that stream that pounded through the veins of a giant.

I didn't even hear the third pop when another needle pierced my back.

When I woke up, there was no longer any distinction between me and the blood pouring over my face. I tried to wipe my eyes, but the second my vision cleared, a fresh stream bubbled over them. I was disoriented, but I could vaguely sense that I was hanging upside-down. My throat burned like I was being choked with a red-hot wire. I struggled to reach my feet which were tied above me, but my feeble lurch only served to send a fresh wave of blood from the gash in my neck to splatter in the bucket beneath me.

I tried to scream, but all that came out was a wet splutter. I felt myself slipping out of consciousness again, but I held on and rubbed my eyes clear once more.

There! Something was moving beside me. The state of my overburdened senses and my reversed perspective made it almost impossible to distinguish the blurred shapes.

"You did all of this? For me?" A voice. A woman's voice.

I squinted and rubbed my eyes again. There were definitely two sets of legs beside me. I recognized one as Gregovitch's stained overalls, but the other in a black dress was unfamiliar.

"It's my beacon," Gregovitch said. "I didn't want you to get lost."

My vision slid away from me, and I must have blacked out for a moment. Then my body lurched, and I drifted through consciousness again. An old woman in a black dress was cradling me and easing me to the ground.

"Shhhh," she whispered. "Don't worry. When your time has come, someone will call you back home too."

Blackness returned, so deep and peaceful that I seemed to have slipped out of time and space altogether. My pain was gone. My thoughts were smoke in the wind.

I had a vague conception that I was looking for something. Then a bright light pierced the abyss and forced my attention to focus on the spot. Gradually it grew brighter, until with a blinding flash I felt a gasp of cold wind penetrate my lungs.

I was lying on the red soil. My hands raced to my burning throat to feel a thick gauze wrapped around the jagged wound. It took me a full five minutes to stand, all the while unable to process any thought more rudimentary than an awareness of the light.

Finally, agonizingly, I brought myself to my feet. The night was thick around me, and all the lights from Gregovitch's house were out. Gradually my eyes regained their focus, and the brilliant white light faded into the pale reflection of the surrounding roses. There was no sign of the blood upon their petals, and each blossom shining with incandescent splendor.

I managed to call an ambulance before slipping back into oblivion. I had suffered severe blood loss, and the doctor said that it was likely that my heart stopped beating for several minutes. If someone hadn't taken me down and bandaged my wound, there is no chance I would have survived.

There has been no sign of Gregovitch since the police swept his house, although his car remained parked in the garage. I even checked the grave where his wife was buried, but this too remained undisturbed.

I tried to explain what happened, but the condescending explanation I received was that the bleeding and the tranquilizers caused me to hallucinate. That's what I would have thought too, if it wasn't for the field of snow white roses outside of my window.

I think that I really had been lost for a moment, until something had found me and called me home.

Of all the worrisome mystery of this situation, there is one thing which most prominently denies me sleep at night. One of Gregovitch's sons stayed at the house last weekend to pack up the old man's things. After he had gone, I took another walk through the garden out of a morbid curiosity to try to shed some light on this horrendous business.

All seventy-five white roses are as brilliant as ever, but the son must have still made some alterations in the garden. Instead of the myriad of sacrificial animals once depicted on the signs, there is now only a single word blazoned across every board that stands as stoically as headstones:

Human.

## The Power of a Small City

Four years in the army, and not once did I hear an order from anyone ranked above a Major(O4). Now I've been at the Dalton Power Station for two months, and I've already received three phone calls from the US Secretary of Defense.

It seems like a mundane enough job, right? My stint in the army helped pay my way through a Bachelor's degree in power plant technology after I got out, and I was ready for a reliable income with good honest work. I spent a few years in equipment operations, then checking readouts, and on up to personnel supervisor. Nothing more exciting than a few power lines being blown over in a storm until I was promoted to Plant Operator in Dalton.

"You're going to notice a few anomalies with this plant," the old manager, Nathan, told me. He was retiring, although by the size of his waist-line and the dull glassy glaze over his eyes, I'd guess he retired about ten years ago and just hadn't left yet.

"But I don't want you to worry," he added. "I worked here 20 years, and nothing going on will interfere with your job."

"Looks normal enough to me," I replied. Was this some kind of test? "Single open cycle gas turbines, probably around 140 megawatts, right?"

If I was expecting praise for my perception, I didn't get it. That was the first time I've ever seen a grown man spit on an office floor.

"Not about the output boy, I mean our client. We're just supplying one building up in the hills. The rest of the city is handled by that hydroelectric station downtown."

This had to be a test. It didn't seem fair since they already offered me the job, but there wasn't any harm in playing along.

"No, sir, that's impossible. This station should be able to supply around 140,000 homes."

"Or one government building," he grunted.

"Are we not producing at capacity?"

"We are. Hell, they'd take more if they could get it."

"What are they doing up there? I don't understand."

Nathan clapped me on the back like I had just won an award. "And they like to keep it that way. So, if you want to stick around like I have, then you'll do what I did and keep your nose out of their business. Besides that, everything should run pretty smooth for you here."

But Nathan was wrong. Right from the start, nothing ran smoothly. First, the other plant workers acted mighty strange toward me. Every one of them kept their eyes locked on the floor, all wearing that same glassy eyed complacency I had seen in Nathan. They followed orders readily enough, but they did so without any initiative or individuality.

I caught one guy, Robert, chewing his pencil for ten minutes straight in the break-room. I asked him what he was doing, and he mumbled that his schedule dictated a break every two hours. As soon as his ten minutes were up (to the damn second, I think), he stood up and left the room without another word.

And then there was the Defense Secretary calling every few weeks. Those were the most awkward, forced conversations I've ever had to sit through in my life.

"Acting Manager?" were always the first words out of his mouth.

"John Doe (not my real name) speaking."

"Clearance code?"

I'd give it to him, and then he invariably asked a string of the vaguest imaginable questions. It felt almost like he was being held hostage and had to speak in code to gather information. A few examples:

"Would you consider everything to be more, or less ordinary than normal?"

"Have you had any unusual requests for output to anywhere besides that building?"

"In an emergency, how fast could you shut down power to everything if you had to?"

The financing is another thing that didn't make sense to me. Usually a plant this size will have a couple dozen workers and need its own financing department to keep track of everything. Here, we just had Megan.

"There's not much to do really," she told me. "There's no money coming in. I just prepare a folder every month with all our expenses, mail it to some office down in DC, and they take care of it. They've never denied anything before."

Three days ago topped it all off when I received the strangest question yet from the Defense Secretary. He asked:

"Have you noticed any of your employees trying to escape?" Then he coughed like he was trying to clear his head, not his throat. "I mean, any of them try to quit, or just stop showing up?"

The mystery was unbearable to me, but I was trained to follow orders, and despite everything I could have still accepted the situation if it wasn't for the black van that came by yesterday. "Shuttle service," they called it, although it was only picking up Robert and another technician named Elijah. I'd watched the van take them up the dirt road winding into the hills toward the government building.

The next morning they were back at work, and I asked them what happened. They both just laughed and said they went out for a few drinks. Even the laugh felt wrong—like they weren't doing it because they thought it was funny, but rather made the sound in the hopes that I would find it funny and move on.

The first thing I learned about working in a power plant is that a pair of professional overalls and a condescending attitude can get you in just about anywhere. All I had to do was strip one of the underground cables leading to the building, file a report on the output fluctuation, schedule my own appointment, and show up at the mystery building. There was a guard post out front, but I showed them my diagnostics appointment and they let me inside (under escort) without complaint.

I called it a building before just because I'd only seen its location on a map. A mine shaft might describe the phenomenon more accurately, or perhaps a crater. The complex was clustered around an abyss located at the bottom of an enormous valley whose jagged slopes looked like the result of a cataclysmic primordial explosion, long since eroded and overgrown with spruce and pine. There was an unusual energy about the place, and I felt compelled to walk gently as though stepping atop a living creature. That was probably on account of the constant vibrations rippling through the ground like something deep below the earth was stirring.

Most unsettling of all perhaps were the rows of black vans parked outside. Four of them were being loaded with long bags about the size and shape of a human body. I caught the eye of the guard accompanying me and noted the glassy shine.

"Any power cuts have serious repercussions here. Please resolve the issue as quickly as *humanly* possible."

*Humanly*. Maybe my discomfort had me imagining things, but somehow it seemed like he said it like a handicap, in the same way you or I might say, 'He's pretty smart, for a dog.'

The guard led me to a control station about a hundred feet away from the main complex. I couldn't get a good enough angle on the abyss to glimpse what could be down there, but up close the vibrations resolved themselves into the distinct sound of drilling.

"I don't suppose I'm allowed to ask—" I started.

## Sleepless Nights

"Won't do you any good," he interrupted promptly. "I don't know any more than you, and that's already more than enough."

"Have you ever been inside?"

He shook his head, glancing around nervously. Then in a hushed whisper said, "I never seen anything, but sometimes I'll hear things. Like something is down there that don't want to be."

I raised my eyebrow, hoping he'd continue. He opened his mouth like he was going to say more, then shook his head. "None of my business, none of yours. How long is this gonna take?"

I didn't push my luck by staying long. I traced the power restriction to the cable I striped and followed the line back away from the complex to the spot where I damaged the cable.

Now I started keeping an especially close eye on Robert and Elijah. I can't shake the feeling that they're not quite here. I caught Robert chewing his pencil again, but he was doing it so absent minded that by the end of his ten minute break he had eaten straight through the entire thing.

Elijah was even worse. He was microwaving a cup of noodles in the break room, anxiously pacing back and forth like he was waiting for a bomb to go off. Then it beeped, and he actually collapsed to the floor in shock. I retrieved his glasses for him and helped him to his feet, noticing his eyes were too pale, almost completely white. I'm positive they weren't like that before he went into the government building.

I searched through the computer databases for any unusual mentions of the two, and found logs written by Nathan. There was one dated two months before I arrived.

*Robert and Elijah first pickup service today. Good for five rounds each before they're used up. Current staff:*

*Round 0: 3*

*Round 1: 5*

*Round 2: 11*

*Round 3: 7*

*Round 4: 2*

*Round 5: 1*

*I am the only one at round 5. Requesting replacement for myself in two months after my final round. May God have mercy on our souls.*

I scanned back further through his logs and found a list of similar numbers. It seems like every week another pair of people are sent to the building and their "rounds" are increased by one. Elijah was currently a 4, while Robert was a 3.

There was also a schedule of future pickups. I scanned ahead a few pages and didn't see my name anywhere. It was a relief at first, although the more I searched, the more unnerving it was to be the only one not on the list.

Well, here goes nothing.

I edited the next week to switch my name with Megan's (she was a round 1). It seemed like people were returning from whatever was going on there, and I know I'm not going to rest easy until I got a look inside. I don't know what happens past round 5, but after trying to call Nathan's personal number, I'm pretty sure that I don't want to know.

I learned from Nathan's wife, who called me back, that he tried to put a bullet in his head the day he left the plant. If all goes well, I hope I'll get to the bottom of this before I reach that point. And if not, well it's as Nathan said...

*'May God have mercy on our souls.'*

---

"TELL ME EVERYTHING YOU REMEMBER," I ordered Elijah the next day. I had waited until he entered the bathroom before following and locking the door behind us. The black van was going to be here in a few hours, and my excitement was quickly being replaced with dread. I needed answers, and I needed them now.

"I don't know what you're talking about," he replied in a monotonous voice.

Forcing myself to stare into his cloudy white eyes was harder than I expected. "On the nights you're picked up by the 'shuttle service'," I said. "I know you've gone four times now, and I know you weren't just drinking. I want you to tell me what really happened."

A euphoric smile replaced his pallid countenance. Then a frown, as though trying to remember the insubstantial details of a passing dream.

"But that's all that happened. The shuttle picks us up, and they give us something to drink. Then I wake up in my home, and it's time to go to work again."

"And you feel just the same as you did before?"

His frown deepened. Then his eyes stretched so wide I thought they would pop straight out of his head. For a second he seemed about to scream until his face reverted back into a blank slate. It all happened in such a flash that I couldn't be sure the expression was there at all. When he smiled again; I could sense the tension still trembling in his cheeks.

"Better than ever," Elijah replied. "I find it invigorating."

He continued staring me in the face while he opened his belt and dropped his pants around his ankles. I would have liked to ask him more, but I was too shocked and revolted when he began to piss in the sink right beside me. I just turned around and exited the bathroom without another word.

Whatever was being done in the building had seriously damaged these people, and it looked like there was only one way for me to find out the truth.

When the van arrived, my name was called alongside Wallace Thornberg. An overweight guy in a bulky coat with a hat pulled low over his face—I don't remember seeing him before today. He nodded curtly at me but kept his distance, shoving his way into the van the moment the doors slid open.

"Fransisco with the shuttle service." The driver bounced out from his seat and held the door open for me. He was dressed in the same blue suit as the guard who had escorted me before, but this man's eyes were perfectly clear.

I hesitated. "Where are we going?"

"You know," Fransisco replied.

I found his tone overly familiar, and my doubts redoubled as I slipped inside the van. "What happens if I don't want to go?"

"But you do." The driver grinned and put on a pair of headphones. After that, he didn't speak another word for the remainder of the drive.

I sat on one of the two benches bolted to the metal floor on either side of the van. Wallace sat on the other side from me, arms crossed, hat pulled low over his face, looking like he was trying to disappear into himself.

"You been there before?" I asked.

"Wouldn't remember if I did," came the gruff reply. "You're not supposed to be here though. You weren't on the list."

"How do you know?" I asked.

"Because I wrote the damn thing, and I didn't want you to be." When my companion finally looked up. He grinned to see the shock on my face as I recognized him. "Of course, I'm not supposed to be here either, so I won't tell if you don't."

Nathan, not Wallace, did his best to explain the situation to me as we rumbled into the secluded hills. After each of his first five rounds of procedure, his memory had been wiped clean every time.

"Waking up afterward felt like I was an alien in an unfamiliar world," Nathan told me. "Books, songs, people I had seen a thousand times before, they all started giving me trouble like some sort of puzzle. I even tried to quit once, but the longer I went without another round, the more lost I felt. It became like an addiction, and I couldn't live without my fix." He shrugged. "It would have been damn irresponsible for me to keep working when I could barely tie my own shoelaces, so I requested a replacement. That's why I wanted to keep you off the list—so we could have at least one level-headed soul to keep everything running."

"Your wife said you put a bullet in your brain."

Nathan chuckled and slid his hat further up his head. A bandage was wrapped around his temple with a great bloody spot like a Japanese flag.

"My hands shook. You blame me? I didn't think I could go on after my fifth round, and this seemed easier than having to manage without it. Next I know, I'm back and swearing like the Devil. How's that for clearing your head?" He chuckled at my grimace. "Worked like a charm too. I felt more like my old self than I had in years. Since I know they'd never let me walk after a stunt like that, I let people keep believing I was gone."

"What are you?" I knew he couldn't remember what they did, but the question slipped involuntarily from my mouth.

Nathan glanced at the driver, still wearing his headphones. We were descending at a sharp angle now and must be entering the valley. He moved across the van to sit beside me, speaking in a hushed tone. "I figure there are two possibilities: they made me into something that isn't human, or the good Lord brought me back. Either way, it's my obligation to stop them from doing this to anybody else, so I switched with Wallace to throw a wrench in the cogs. Can I count on you to have my back?" He caught me staring at the bloody bandage and slid the hat back low over his face.

I nodded stiffly, although I hated the idea of committing myself to a war when I didn't have the first idea who was in the right. It didn't seem like people were being forced here, but if they were being manipulated with an addictive drug, then that was just as bad.

The van pulled straight past the control station and stopped in the parking lot where I saw the bodies being loaded last time. The hum of drilling was omnipresent here, and my whole body vibrated like my bones were looking for a way out.

The guard handed us each a pair of headphones as we parked outside the building.

"Wear these," he practically shouted. "It's only going to get louder inside."

Nathan shifted his coat awkwardly, clutching something in his pocket with one hand while he put the headphones on with the other. When he said "throw a wrench," did he mean he was smuggling some kind of weapon in?

The guard didn't seem to be paying any attention and simply walked into the towering structure with us at his heels.

"Can you hear me okay?" Fransisco's voice came through the headphones.

I nodded, absent-minded as I walked forward in awe of the gargantuan internal structure. Three, maybe four stories tall on the outside, but it must have been built down into the abyss because the balcony I was standing over dropped down further than I could see. In the distant depths I thought I could make out a faint red glow, but my eyes were repelled from the void by an instinctual terror that I could not overcome.

Endless rows of balconies marched below me into the penumbra of shadow, each containing a massive machine with cables extending downward into the pit. Each machine had a tether of wires extending from the other end which connected to helmets being worn by a man sitting beside it. There must have been hundreds of them sitting so peacefully in repose that they might have been asleep, and hundreds more men in blue suits were attending the machines.

"What the shit?" I couldn't believe my eyes. I took a step back toward the entrance and almost tripped as I walked into something. I turned to see Fransisco offering me a glass of clear liquid. Nathan was already studying a glass in his hand.

"You're going to take a drink and sit down at the machine. When you wake up, none of this will have happened, but you're going to feel so alive that you might as well be dead now."

"Not remembering it and not happening are completely different things," Nathan said. "But if we ain't gonna remember, you might as well tell us what's going on."

The guard sighed and rolled his eyes, languidly pulling a .44 magnum handgun from his belt and playing with it in his hand. "I've told you every time, Nathan, and I must admit it's getting old. And every time I've told you, you still took the drink, so why not just trust me and do it again?"

Nathan growled and pulled his hat off to reveal the bandage. He reached inside his coat and produced a cellphone with a prominently flashing recording light.

"Well maybe I'm not as easy to convince anymore," Nathan said firmly. "So why don't you humor me?"

Fransisco calmly leveled the gun at Nathan's face.

Nathan lifted the cell to his ear.

I took the opportunity to begin circling the guard, but then the magnum pointed my way, and I froze.

"Five rounds might keep you standing, but how well do you think your friend will bounce back from a bullet in the face?" Fransisco asked.

"Acting manager?" Nathan spoke into the phone. His voice was different. I'd heard that voice over the phone before, but it had been from the office of the Secretary of Defense.

"Put the phone down, or I'll shoot," the guard said. "I swear to God, Nathan—"

"Clearance code?" Nathan said aloud. "I want you to shut down the plant the moment I give the word. Are you ready?"

"You can't," Fransisco hissed. "If we have a power outage, every one of these people will die."

"Bullshit. You're just trying to save your own ass." Nathan spat. "Tell me what's really going on."

"He's telling the truth," I interjected. "They were carrying bodies out last time there was a power restriction too."

"I don't fucking care!" Nathan bellowed. He gripped the phone so tight his fingers turned white. "Living like this—they're dead either way. I want an answer. *Now.*"

Fransisco swallowed hard then nodded. "We're feeding it. If we stop, it's going to be angry."

"What is?" Nathan asked. I caught the guard glancing over his shoulder and turned to look. Another man in a suit was holding a rifle on the opposite balcony.

"Nathan, watch out!" I shouted.

"Put down the phone, Nathan," the Fransisco said. "You have to trust me."

"What is down there?" Nathan shrieked.

"Nathan put it down!"

Fransisco nodded sharply: A crack split the tumultuous sound of the drill and blood sprayed from Nathan's face. The rifle bullet had punctured straight through the back of his skull and blood sprayed from his mouth. He looked over his shoulder in bewilderment at the man with the rifle, his whole face splitting open as he turned his head.

Two more cracks rent the air from the handgun. Nathan was staggered to his knees. He hadn't let go of the phone. He spat a mouthful of blood onto the floor and rattled off a rapid string of numbers. Another bullet slammed a hole straight through his forehead, but he barely seemed to feel it.

Fransisco lunged at Nathan, but I blocked him with my body and we both went spinning to the ground.

"Authorization granted. Shut it all down," Nathan howled.

My face went numb as the butt of the handgun slammed into my forehead. I groped the air blindly and caught hold of the guard's suit jacket, but he ripped free and dove at Nathan. The former manager scrambled backward, talking into the phone the whole while.

"Do you hear me? I want the whole station offline right now."

The four bullets in Nathan barely slowed him down. I locked eyes with him right as he reached the edge of the balcony.

"Did I save them? Did I do the right thing?" Nathan's voice broke with desperation into my headphones.

I pulled myself up from the floor, unable to tear my eyes away from his bloody face. "You did what you thought was right," is all I could muster.

Everyone held their breath, looking around at the lights and the humming machines.

"Connect me to the plant," Fransisco screamed into his headphones. "Tell them to keep the power—"

And suddenly the silence and the darkness were all there was. Red emergency lights flashed along the walkways for a moment, but row by row they snuffed out as the backup generators were overloaded. The lights on every balcony winked out. The hum of every machine spluttered to a stop. The vibrating pressure of the drills ground to a halt. In the absence of all other light, my eyes adjusted to see faint outlines visible from the red glare in the pit.

Fransisco roared and ripped his headphones off. He grabbed Nathan by the coat and rammed him against the railing. I leapt to Nathan's aid, but too slow.

Nathan didn't make the least move to resist as he tipped over the balcony to plummet into the abyss. I reached for him—again too late. The last glimpse of him I saw was a spiral of blood raining through the air in his wake.

"What's going to happen now?" I shouted.

The guard didn't answer with words, but his message was clear enough. He dropped his gun and sprinted for the door. I should have just followed him, but I couldn't let all of this be for nothing. My trembling feet pulled me like a moth being drawn by flame until I could look directly over the balcony and into the abyss.

Somewhere miles below the earth where the drills once tore through the crust emanated a baleful glow. I watched transfixed as it shifted, seeming to slide from one side of the pit to the other.

I turned and ran from the building. Guards, mechanical technicians, doctors—streams of people poured out to fill the black vans. The men tethered to the machines were being left behind, but they couldn't have all been dead. I saw one slide to the ground and begin to crawl towards him, only to be nearly trampled beneath a stampede of men in blue.

I helped the man to his feet and dragged him out of the building with me. His lips kept moving as though he was muttering something, but I couldn't hear it over the sounds of panicked screams and thundering footfalls.

No-one seemed to notice that I didn't have a blue suit like the others in the mad escape. I crammed into one of the vans and huddled in the back while it roared up the valley walls. A noisy rush of speculation surrounded me, but I was incapable of joining the conversation.

Somehow even describing what I saw aloud would be enough to make it real.

We were about halfway back up the valley when a deafening explosion knocked half of us from the benches to sprawl on the floor. The van bucked and heaved like a wild animal, but managed to stay upright as it roared down the road. There wasn't a back window, so we all had to wait along the right side until the van made a turn up the switchback road before we saw what had happened. The foundations of the building had been detonated, and the entire structure was sliding into the pit.

The man I had saved from the machine, a haggard fellow with a long beard and eyes as white as starlight, kept muttering. He was hard to look at because of the bloody sores on his head. The "helmet" he had been wearing had wires which plugged directly into his brain, and when I tore him free, I left great patches of his scalp behind.

"It can't die. It's already out. It's inside us all."

NO-ONE ELSE SPOKE along the drive, so they all must have heard him too. We all just fixed our eyes out the window, afraid to acknowledge what we all knew.

I don't know how many people had looked into the pit before they ran, but I'm sure enough of us knew that the red glow wasn't really sliding like I thought at first. It was opening, and from somewhere in the depth of the earth, I had looked into a colossal eye staring back at me.

After the convoy of vans exited the crumbling valley, we made a stop about a mile away from the plant. I heard mention that others were continuing on to a nearby army base, but six cars (mine included) peeled away from the rest. The vans parked in a sharp circle, bumper to bumper, with their sliding doors all opening toward the middle.

"Everyone out of the vans and into the circle." It was Francisco. He was holding a rifle now, prodding people as they filed out. "Remove any hats, bandages, glasses—anything which obscures your face. Nobody is leaving here until I get a chance to look at their eyes."

He had to be looking for signs of the treatment. The bearded man I had saved was still in the back of our van with me. He looked so thin and weary—I wonder how long he'd been down there. I caught his eye, and the pure white orbs looked back with helpless pleading.

We both flinched as a gunshot echoed throughout the caravan. Then three more shots, one right after the other.

"Filthy animal. Just die already," Francisco snapped.

Three of us were left in the van: the driver, the haggard man, and me. I was about to step out when emaciated probing fingers clutched desperately at my shirt.

"Help me. Please. I only did what they told me to."

The driver pushed past us to exit.

If it hadn't been for Nathan's interference, I would have had my first treatment today. Then I would have been the one to be executed, assuming I hadn't already been killed when the building was detonated. These people had been strong armed and manipulated into obeying orders, and now they were being punished by the same people who made them do it.

Besides that, I still wanted more answers. By the enormity of the thing's presence, I had no doubt that it was still alive down there. The people who had been "feeding" it must know as much as anyone what we were up against. Mankind might be diverse in our values at times, but when a common enemy as calamitous as that whispers our doom, we've no choice but to stand together. Anyone like Francisco who sought to divide us had to be labeled as an enemy too.

I saw the car keys poking out of the driver's back pocket as he climbed out of the van. I snatched it, applying pressure to his back to distract him. I was trying to be subtle, but he lost his balance and fell straight out of the van onto his knees.

"Hey, what the Hell, man?" the driver was loud.

All eyes fell on me.

"That's the guy who helped Nathan!" Francisco shouted. I latched the van door shut just as he was raising his rifle. The haggard man shoved me to the floor, but before I could fight him off, I heard the metallic clang of bullets punching through the door where I'd stood a moment before.

"Let's move!" the bearded man shouted, practically flinging me through the air and into the driver seat. The van roared to life, smashing into the adjacent van. More bullets were raining through the wall, and a spider-web of cracks filled the passenger side window. It must be bullet-proof glass, but it still wouldn't hold up for long under this assault.

The pale-eyed man grunted as a bullet punched through his door and into his shoulder, but the projectile seemed to barely break his skin before deflecting onto the dashboard.

I slammed the car into reverse, plowing into the van behind me and finally edging out enough room to drive. The car shot off down the road, the bullets rattling off the back as we went.

"Are you hurt?" I asked the man.

"It'll take more than that after what I've been through. Don't let it slow you either. Not until we reach the plant."

"We can't stop. That's the first place they'll look," I argued.

"The workers all had rounds, and that makes 'em targets now. We have to save as many as we can."

"How do you know about that? Who are you?"

"Dillan, I used to be called. Don't seem right to call me that anymore though. Not much Dillan left."

We didn't have long before I reached the plant. Two of the other vans were close on my heels the whole way. I'm not sure if we can fight them off and escape, but having a whole crew that can take bullets like vitamins seems like a pretty solid advantage to me.

I didn't slow as we passed through the checkpoint—rammed straight through the automated gate. I didn't want to risk crossing any more open ground than I had to, so I drove right through the glass door at the front of the building and parked inside.

A bullet skipped by the ground near my feet the moment I opened the door. I thought I had gained some ground on them . . . Another bullet. The shots were coming from inside the building. They must have begun clearing the plant before I even got there.

Dillan pulled me from the van and covered me with his body as we sprinted through the building. I saw him take two more bullets, both rattling to the ground after impact. Every room we passed was already strewn with bodies.

Robert is dead. Elijah, Megan—both had been decapitated. Undergoing the treatments seems to have given these people a considerable resistance to injury and death, but there's no coming back from that.

Dillan and I managed to get to the security surveillance room to see if anyone is left, but it's only a matter of time before they find me. All the video feeds showed men in suits fanning out through the power plant, most armed with long machetes still stained with blood.

There's nowhere left for me to go.

"Look! There's a few hanging on," Dillan pointed at one of the screens. Three plant workers—hadn't gotten a chance to learn their names yet—were huddled in terror inside one of the supply closets.

Dillan showed no hesitation, already bounding out the door as though he knew the way by heart. I started to follow, but he was quick to close the door behind him. "You stay hidden," he said. "I've been down there too long. There's nothing they can do to me that they haven't already tried, but you—you'll pop like a ripe melon hit by a hammer."

That image was vivid enough for me to stay put. I watched Dillan on the security feed as he dashed through the hallways with inhuman speed.

If you'd asked me before this started, I would have always told you the humans are the good guys, and the monsters can go to Hell. But as I scanned the familiar workrooms and saw the bloodbath, watching men with machetes butchering corpses which still struggled to move . . . well maybe there are no good guys here.

Shit, I don't know, maybe I'd even be better off joining Nathan and the thing in the pit. Even thinking that felt wrong though. The visceral terror I experienced while looking down into that great red eye will be enough to haunt me for the rest of my days. If I could just get out of here, I could let the whole mess of them tear each other apart and stay out of it.

I was just about to make a run when the door was kicked open.

Francisco stood alone with a bloody machete in each hand. His eyes were wild, looking even less human than Dillan's vacuous stare. Red hand-prints crawled their way around his legs where his victims doubtlessly clutched at him right before the killing blow fell.

"I thought I'd find you here," he said, his dress-shoes making a wet squelch as they plodded across the room toward me.

I backed up against the wall, cornered. "I'm still human. Nothing's been done to me yet," I said. "You don't have to do this."

"I didn't have to kill the others either," he said. "I wanted to. The moment they were plugged into those machines, they were more beast than man."

"We're both men though—we're both on the same side." I was throwing any words that came to mind into the space between us, but nothing seemed to slow his relentless advance.

I picked up the office chair and brandished it at him, but he only laughed.

## Sleepless Nights

Think again, smart-ass: I hurled the chair into the surveillance screens and watched them smash into pieces.

"I know where the others are," I said desperately. "You won't find them without my help. Not before they escape."

Francisco's smirk twisted into a snarl. "Fine. I'll let you live," he growled. "Just tell me where the tainted ones are."

"Not good enough. I want to know what's been going on. I want to know everything you know."

"There's not enough time—"

"Then stop wasting it."

Fransisco glanced at the broken monitors, then again at the long track of hallway where he came from. He expelled an irritated sigh, propped the chair up, and took a seat.

That's when I finally got the whole story.

The valley had been the result of a primordial asteroid smashing into the Earth. A scientific expedition to unearth fragments resulted in the discovery of unusual movement within the lithosphere of the Earth's crust. Two tectonic plates had switched directions and were moving against the surrounding mantel, which resulted in much of the mountainous terrain in the area.

The government deployed a mining expedition, looking for clues as to the buildup of pressure. That's when they discovered IT. The Devil. The beast. The monster. Whatever word man has in the face of such a being dwelling beneath the Earth. The scientists speculated that it was much too large to have been carried on the asteroid, but perhaps a seed or a hatchling had survived the journey and grown through the eons into the monstrous form that was uncovered.

The mining further served to disturb the being, and its increasing activity threatened its pending escape. Nothing short of a nuclear weapon was likely to harm it, and this would be impossible to covertly detonate without radiating the groundwater and devastating the nearby population centers.

The only method which seemed to slow the being down was crudely referred to as "sacrifices." The thing displayed considerable less activity after it consumed the initial miners, and subsequent experiments devised a way to feed it via the network of machines and mental energy which I had witnessed. They had powered the machines for the last 20 years, but the sudden cessation of energy seemed to have woken the creature, prompting the shaft's demolition.

If there was more to the story, I didn't get a chance to hear. Francisco was getting impatient, and I didn't know how much more time I could buy. Luckily, I didn't have to. Dillan returned during the recounting, and while Francisco's attention was still distracted, Dillain pounced.

I say pounced, because only an animal could have flown through the air like he did. Before Francisco could turn his head, Dillan had wrapped his thin arms around the guard's neck and snapped it like a twig. I would have been grateful if it hadn't been for what happened next.

Dillan bit deeply into Francisco's neck while his limp form was still convulsing in Dillan's arms. Even with human teeth, his teeth sank through the mesh of veins and arteries, crunching through the spine, and straight out the other side. It took almost a full minute for him to gnaw his way through; I don't think he was even eating it, but simply reveling in the satisfaction of his power.

I didn't say a word. I didn't look away.

I just let it happen.

Every time I thought I knew what I was doing, the scale of events far surpassed my expectations, and I was left a helpless onlooker.

After Dillan finished, he gave me a sloppy grin before leading me safely through the building. Heads were separated from bodies everywhere we went, and it was clear which were cleanly severed with a machete and which had been gnawed loose. Dillan had saved the other three people though, and I owed him my life as well. That's how I learned the last part of the story that Francisco had left out.

The people hooked to the machines—they weren't just feeding the thing. It wasn't just the human mind passing down the cables, it was also the mind of the beast passing into them. With each round of treatment, the subjects became a little less human and a little more monstrous, until they became something like Nathan or Dillan. Something that couldn't live and wouldn't die.

Dillan had been one of the original scientists who sacrificed himself to the creature over 20 years ago. He had voluntarily shackled himself to the machine all that time. He's right though, I shouldn't call him Dillan anymore. Dillan died a long time ago.

Once I was out of the plant, I parted ways with the subjects. I got in my car and drove as fast and as far as I could.

As far as I know, the creature is still down there, buried beneath countless tons of rock in the hills of Colorado. I don't know whether its body is still trying to get out or not, but I don't think it even matters. The beast thinks with Dillan's thoughts and moves with his body, and like an avatar of some forgotten God, he now freely walks the earth. His zealous protection of the other subjects makes me believe it is the beast's imperative to protect his own. I can only assume that Dillan is now working to either free the creature, or spread its influence by bringing more sacrifices to its underground lair.

I don't know that he can be killed, don't know that he can be stopped. But he must feel some sense of human compassion, or he never would have let me go as thanks for aiding him. And hidden within that mercy lies my one enduring hope: that once the beast has risen to the height of its size and power, it will not forget there is still some good in man.

Sleepless Nights

## Mother is Back

Love is blind, and so is hope. But something doesn't become true just because you want it badly enough. I don't know why IT is in my house, but I'm not going to be fooled.

I say IT because she isn't my Mom. She looks like her, and talks like her, and smiles like her, but IT isn't her.

The worst part is, Dad doesn't notice. I saw them dancing in the kitchen when I got home from school. Frank Sinatra was playing on the stereo, his smooth voice propelling their tangled bodies in a slow waltz across the room. Dad's eyes were closed as his head rested on IT's shoulder, and he seemed genuinely happy—happier than I've seen him in a long time.

I just dropped my backpack and stared. IT let go of my father and hugged me. I stood stiff as a board. Mom never used to hug me when I got home—she knew I liked having my space. But there's no denying how soft and warm she felt, or the lavender odor of her shampoo washing over me.

We're having homemade pizza with the cheese baked into the crust, my dad's favorite thing in the world. And seeing him so happy, I didn't have the heart to say anything. I just went to my room like a coward, pretending everything was fine. Maybe if I would have tried harder if I wasn't a little happy to see her too.

It hasn't been easy since Mom died, but that was no excuse to let IT into our house, just so we could pretend we were a family again.

But Mom—my real mom—would put me to bed without staying to watch me fall asleep. She would hold onto Dad's arm when he talked, but she wouldn't dig her nails in so deeply they drew blood. My real mom wouldn't forget to blink for hours at a time.

Two days have passed. I've been struggling to decide what to do—no, that's not quite true. I KNOW what needs to be done, but it would be so much easier to just keep pretending like Dad does. Maybe in time I would even forget that a drunk driver T-boned Mom's SUV while she and Dad were coming home from their date.

I'd forget the bloodstains on the asphalt, and the hours I spent waiting for her in the emergency room. Maybe I'd even forget how it felt when she didn't come out.

Then again, maybe it's these memories that aren't real—they certainly don't feel real when my mom—I mean IT—sits between us on the sofa to watch the evening news. But letting her be replaced, even if it was easier for Dad and me, wasn't any way to respect my real mom.

It was for her, not for me, that made me finally speak up: "Dad, we need to talk about Mom."

I'd waited until IT went to the bathroom (which doesn't happen nearly as often as mom used to) to corner Dad in his bedroom. He just kept reading, not even returning my gaze. He knew what I was going to say—he just didn't want to hear it.

"Do you remember what happened last month when she was in that accident?" I pressed.

"It's getting late. You should go to bed so you'll be ready for school tomorrow," Dad said without looking up.

"Dad this is serious. Please tell me that you remember."

I heard a flush from the bathroom. There wasn't much time. I'd never get an answer out of Dad with IT here. Dad was watching the bathroom door too—like a kid praying for the bell to ring before the teacher collected homework. The shower began to run, and I let out a deep breath I didn't even realize I was holding. Dad sighed too—there was no getting out of this.

"Yeah, I remember," he said. He stared back into my eyes. I finally had his attention.

"Do you remember the hospital? And . . . what happened after?"

"Yeah. It was a pretty bad crash—we're all so fortunate that nobody was hurt." His eyes were keen and sharp. He couldn't have forgotten—he was just trying to get me to accept it without having to admit the truth. For my real mom's sake though, it had to be said.

"She died, Dad. We went to her funeral."

He didn't flinch, didn't blink. He just smiled. "Don't be ridiculous. Your mother is in the bathroom right now."

I ran over to him and grabbed him by the shoulders. I shook him, but he didn't fight it. He just cocked his head to the side, staring at me like I was a puzzle he was trying to solve.

"You're lying. You know what happened—I know what happened. Why are you lying to me?"

"Aren't you happier this way?" he asked. "If you think about what happened—really think about it—you'll realize this is the best thing for you." There. That was proof. He wasn't trying to evade anymore.

The shower stopped running, but he kept his eyes on me. That's when I realized I couldn't remember the last time I saw him blink. Dad had been in the accident too, how could he have escaped unharmed? I'd been so busy mourning Mom that I hadn't even stopped to think—

He must have seen the realization in my face, because his smile stretched wider. "Now you understand. But you mustn't let mother know that I told you. She wants to have a family so badly—I'd hate to think what she would do if she found out you didn't think of her that way."

The bathroom door opened. IT stood there, wrapped in a towel. She walked nonchalantly over to Dad—or who I thought was my dad—and gave him a kiss. They both turned to look at me.

"What are you still doing awake?" IT asked. "Is everything alright?"

"He was just going to bed . . . Everything IS fine, isn't it?"

I nodded.

"Come, let me tuck you in," IT started moving toward me, but she stopped when she saw me flinch.

"Let your mother tuck you in." Dad's voice was tense with an unspoken threat. "Perfect parents like us deserve to have the perfect son. I hope we won't need to replace him."

He laughed at his own joke. IT grasped my father's arm and laughed too, but she did it a few seconds too late for it to be natural.

I turned around and headed for my room so I wouldn't have to see the blood oozing between IT's nails where she clasped him.

## Vicarious

Watching my son Andrew kick the winning goal. That's my dream. Or catching his eye as he holds the science-fair trophy, head held upright with the pride of our triumph. I still remember how my own father looked the night my high-school football team won state. Two of my teammates hoisted me onto their shoulders, and when Dad saw me, it was as though he forgave himself for every mistake he's ever made—all because he raised me into the man I had become.

I don't care what Andrew decides to pursue in life, I just want him to be great at it. Isn't that what all father's want? He's going to be eight next month, and I know the next generation's best (his future competition) have already begun to refine their talents. Mozart began playing at 3, Picasso could draw before he could talk, and Michael Jackson was performing live by 6 years old.

It's taken a while for Andrew to find his niche, but lately he's started getting really into mountain and trick biking. His mother Amy thinks it's too dangerous, but I know how important it is to be passionate about your skillset, so I encourage him every chance I get. Amy just doesn't understand. She would see one little cut or bruise, and then suddenly that's all that mattered. I say if you aren't willing to bleed a little to achieve your dreams, then you don't deserve to have them come true.

That's why we started practicing in secret. I'd tell Amy that we were just going to ride around the block. We'd both pedal until the house was out of sight, then we'd blast off toward the hills wearing the same conspiratorial grin. He was good too, fearlessly bouncing down cliffs and rocky slopes that would have even given me pause. Every day he came home a little stronger, and a little more confident than the day before. Every day I knew it was worth all the exhaustion and sneaking around, because he was going to be the best, and I was going to be the one who made it happen.

That is, until the day when it wasn't worth it anymore. We'd just gotten home from a trick competition at the skate park, although it was hardly fair since Andrew was still 8 and all the other kids were teenagers. Andrew slipped up while trying a nose-wheelie and was disqualified before even getting to show off what he'd been practicing. We were both frustrated, but I was proud of him for not wasting any time and wanting to get straight back to the hillside to practice.

I could tell he wasn't being cautious this time. It was my fault for applauding and egging him on to tackle bigger boulders and obstacles. When you're disappointed, you can either give up or try harder, and I just didn't want my boy to quit. When he asked if I thought he could ramp off a rock to clear the ravine, I told him what I thought he needed to hear.

"You can do anything you put your mind to," I said.

We were wrong for believing in each other.

I shouted when I saw his back tire slipping right before he made the jump, but it was already too late to do anything about. The bike pitched forward and hurled him straight over the handlebars, twisting the bike around on top of him as he flipped. Long before I heard the grotesque snapping of his impact, I knew he wasn't going to walk away from this alright.

Maybe if I hadn't pushed him so hard. Or so soon. Maybe if I hadn't allowed my own guilt and fear to make me hesitate before I plunged into the ravine after him, then maybe I could have saved him. It took a full ten seconds of listening to his agonized groans before I could force myself to gaze down at what used to be my son. He'd landed directly on his head, but the helmet did nothing to prevent his neck twisting halfway around his body under the power of the impact. He'd been jarred so hard that part of his spine ruptured straight through his skin to greet the air with a bloody shine.

Screw competing. If he even survived a trip to the hospital, then I'd still spend the rest of my life feeding him with a spoon. But this was my fault, and he was my son, so there could never be a choice. I took the first step of the never ending journey down the slope toward him.

"Let's go home, Dad."

The words should have been enough to bring tears to my eyes, but instead I froze in the grip of absolute terror. It wasn't my son who said it—I didn't even know if my son could talk anymore. I turned slowly, careful not to lose my grip on the pebbled earth and topple helplessly down the ravine.

"I'm okay, Dad. Let's go."

Andrew—or at least someone who looked exactly like my son, all the way down to his freckles and the mustard stain on his sleeve—was waiting for me on the top of the hill. Back down the ravine, I still saw the twisted and broken version of the same boy lying there.

"Come on," the unharmed Andrew said. "Race you back."

He hopped on his bike and skidded fearlessly along the hillside. His speed and dexterity surpassed the old Andrew, even on his best days. As beautiful as it was watching him fly over the rocks, the sight was impossible to appreciate with the wet gurgle of coughing blood sounding from farther down the slope.

I had to make a choice, and judging by the amount of blood pooling on the rocks below, I had to make it fast. I could go down the treacherous slope and lift my son into my arms. I could drag him to the hospital, burning through my energy and savings in the vain fight toward a subnormal life. I could explain to Amy that I had lied to her, and that it was my fault that our life would never be the same. And if after all that Andrew were still to die, then I know she would leave me, and I would have nothing left.

"Don't worry, Dad. We're going to win next time. I promise."

Or I could turn around and leave with . . . what? Watching him race up and down the hills, the answer was obvious. I could turn around and leave with my son, and none of this will have ever happened.

"I'll be right there," I said. "First one home gets ice cream for dinner."

Climbing up the hill after Andrew—after my son—it wasn't as hard as I thought it would be. It was abject relief to see his beaming face waiting for me at the top. The only hard part was when I had already lost sight of the ravine and was headed home, only to hear a voice dissipating on the wind behind me.

"Please, don't go. I need you, Dad."

I gripped my son's hand—my new son—and held on tight all the way home.

For the next few weeks, I wouldn't let Andrew out of my sight. I drove him to school instead of letting him take the bus. I picked him up for lunch, then again when school got out. I took him to his favorite places and spent all of my time helping him practice. I was trying my best to be a good father, and trying even harder not to think about what that meant.

I thought about going back to the ravine to at least bury the body, but every time I began to work up enough courage to face that broken corpse, my new son wanted to spend time with me.

By the end of the first month, life had gone back to normal, and it was like nothing ever happened. The new Andrew was identical to the old, even sharing the same memories, and habits, and everything. By the second month, I'd even forgotten that horrible day ever passed, although sometimes the echo of those words being torn by the wind still slip into my brain as I lay down to sleep at night.

*I need you, Dad.*

But I was a good father. I did everything for my boy, and I knew he was going to repay me by becoming the best biker the world had ever seen.

It wasn't until Andrew was 12 years old when I began to notice behavioral anomalies that I couldn't explain. But surely the real Andrew—I mean the *old* Andrew—would have had his own changes by this age. I tried to tell myself that he was just starting to go through puberty, but even Amy began to feel that something wasn't right.

"Do you know what I caught Andrew doing last night?" she told me one morning over breakfast.

"He's going to be a teenager soon. I'm sure I don't want to know."

"He was eating a bug!" she declared. "A big shiny cockroach. Just munching it right up, looking as proud as a kitty cat who caught his first mouse."

Then there was the rustling outside our window late at night. A dozen separate occasions I must have heard it—like someone was in the bushes watching us. Amy wanted me to check it out, but I just kept imagining Andrew running through the field like a wild creature, biting the heads off animals or digging up worms. I think I was happier not knowing.

Some nights we'd catch him awake at four in the morning, face an inch from the mirror, just staring at himself and giggling. Another time he had a butterfly knife—God knows where he got it—and was peeling away the skin on the back of his hand. He'd exposed a strip of bloody muscle and tendons running all the way from the tip of his finger running halfway up his forearm. I took the knife away and demanded what he was doing, but all he said was:

"Just curious what goes on under there, *Dad*."

He grinned, stressing 'dad' like it was our shared secret. Neither of us had ever mentioned that day on the hillside, but it felt like he not only remembered, but was actively using it to blackmail me.

The worst was when he was trying to get something out of me, like when he decided he needed a laptop. I told him to wait for his birthday and turned to leave, but then he replied with:

"Please, don't go. I need you, *Dad*."

Those words were burned into my subconscious like a trigger. Whenever he said it, I couldn't even look him in the eye. I'd just cave and give him what he wanted. It's not because he was the boss of me or anything. There's nothing wrong with me wanting to be a good father.

Andrew kept practicing with his bike all the while. He was the best I'd ever seen, and anyone who saw him swore the same. He refused to participate in anything big because he "wasn't ready yet," but he blew through all the local competitions. People started coming from miles around to watch him perform, and as soon as they found out I was his father, I'd have a dozen hands clapping me on my back or offering me a beer.

"You must be so proud of him," they'd all say.

"Of course, I am. He's my son."

This coming weekend is going to be his biggest one yet. Some YouTube personality will be recording the whole thing, and I know the second the world sees what my boy can do, he'll be too big to ever put back in a box. I tried to warn him about how things will change after that, but he wouldn't listen to me.

"Isn't this what you wanted?" he asked. He sat down on his bed, giving me a look of wide-eyed, blameless sincerity as though he was a perfect angel sent here to bless my life.

Bullshit.

"Don't pretend you know what I want," I told him. I was sick of that grin he always wore. "You go if you want to, but you're going alone. I don't want any part in this media circus." I turned to leave, trying to get out of his room quick enough before he said:

"Please, don't go. I need you, *Dad*."

I don't know why, but that time it really got to me. It wasn't just a little kid trying to get away with something. This was an active taunt, manipulation of the highest degree. I thundered back around to face him, hoping to put my foot down and reestablish myself as the authority figure.

"If I ever hear you say that again, I'm going to beat your ass until—"

"Until what?" he interrupted. "Until I'm as broken as he was?"

My breath caught as though someone had reached down my throat and grabbed it from the inside. He's never spoken of the other Andrew before. I'd hoped to God he never would. My hands involuntarily clenched into fists, so tight I could feel my muscles trembling all the way up my shoulders.

"It was never about me succeeding, was it?" he asked, that arrogant grin spreading across his face. "You just wanted a little for yourself, didn't you? Only now the light's grown too bright, and you're getting scared."

"I want you out of this house. Now." I've never spoken like that before in my life, so low it was closer to a growl than words.

"You sure Mom agrees with you on that?"

"Don't call her that. Get out. I want you gone."

"Throw away one son, and it's his fault." Andrew wasn't backing down. He was standing an inch from my face now. "Throw away two, and suddenly it's yours."

I threw my fist at his face with everything I got. Maybe I could break his nose or knock his teeth out. Maybe I could scar him up—anything to make this impostor look less like my son. I hadn't realized just how strong he'd grown though, and when he swatted my fist away, it felt like the bones in my hand were changing places.

"Don't be like that, *Dad*," he said. "You wanted me to be the best, didn't you?"

I grunted through the pain and swung again. My eyes could barely follow the blur of his movements. He locked my outstretched arm against his side, and before I knew what was happening, he'd spun me around and slammed me into his closed door. I tasted blood, and my arm strained so bad against his pressure that it must be about to dislocate. I bit my tongue, trying not to scream.

I couldn't let Amy know her son was a monster.

"What do you want from me?" I had to spit and mumble to push the words through the bubbling blood and the pressed door frame.

He let me go and laughed as I slid to the floor. "I'm not like you. I don't need anything from anyone. I just like being on your side of the world. Where I'm from, we don't have families like this."

I strained for any sign that the words were changing as he spoke. I didn't want to look, but an irresistible urge forced my head to turn. I wanted him to be a monster. Some horrible grey-skinned ghoul with tentacles, or a dozen gaping maws—anything but what was there. Anything but that mockery of my son which grinned down at me.

"What are you?" I grunted. "Where are you from?"

"Come with me this weekend," he said, "or I'll take you there."

It was undeniably a threat. I don't know if he was a Demon crawled up from Hell, or some specter from a nether world too horrible to contemplate, but lying there on the ground in a growing pool of my own blood, I finally understood how powerless my real son must have felt waiting for me.

*Rustle.* There was something in the bushes outside the window. Then: "Nunquam suade mihi vana! Sunt mala quae libas. Ipse venena bibas."

The voice coming from outside, sounding so familiar and so alien, like listening to your own voice through a recording. Andrew recoiled as though struck. He snarled, launching himself at the window. Finally the illusion of his humanity was beginning to shed, and beneath the distorting fabric of his shirt, I could see the red blisters spreading. The creature roared as it smashed into the glass, but a brilliant light radiated from the panel and repelled it like an electrically charged fence.

"Exorcizamus te omni satanica potestas."

I could just make out a hunched shape outside the window, but it was immediately obscured by another blinding flash of light which penetrated through the morphing creature. Boils the size of my head were swelling and rupturing down the length of its back. Black pus flowed freely down its sides. Again it slammed itself into the window, but this time it vanished straight through the portal without so much as cracking the glass behind.

By the fading brilliance, and without the creature blocking my view, I saw the figure on the other side of the glass. Its back was as twisted and monstrous as the creature who had just been banished, and its face was unevenly stitched together with a network of scars, burns, and unsealed holes which allowed me to see straight through his cheek and into his mouth.

Through all the disfigurement and abuse, it was clear that nothing which has happened to him—nothing that could ever happen to him—could ever disguise the fact that he was my son.

It was difficult to explain, and even more difficult for Amy to understand, but she confessed that she always felt something wasn't right and was relieved to finally have an answer.

Andrew, my real boy, told us that the thing was called an Irasanct, and they exist as powerless swarms of unresolved desires. Sometimes they will find their way to us through minute holes that exist between dimensions, although they remain harmless until they are given power by our acceptance of them.

The Irasanct cannot remain here long without taking a form, and even once they are accepted, they can only stay so long as they replace the void they left behind with someone from our side. When I took the creature home as my son, I gave it the strength to banish my true son to the other side, although the recounting of his journey there is another story altogether.

The real Andrew had managed to return four months ago, watching us from the bushes and protecting us against the Irasanct. When I asked why he didn't reveal himself sooner, he said he was waiting for the time when he knew I would accept him as my son.

To come back to us after what I had done to him—after everything he's been through—pride does not even begin to approach the admiration I feel for him. He wouldn't stay with us long though, saying there are more of the Irasanct leaking through at an increasing rate. Barely a teenager and already deformed from his injuries and his trials spent on the other side, Andrew is going to keep fighting them.

And he's going to be the best there ever was.

I watched him go early this morning. I didn't want him to leave, but I know I had no right to speak the words in my heart.

"Please, don't go. I need you, son."

# The 32

You might have heard about the Chilean mining accident of 2010. It was also called the "Los 33" because of the 33 miners trapped underground. It's amazing that all 33 survived the entire 69 days it took until they were rescued.

There was a whole media circus about it, with an estimated billion people watching the live rescue on TV or the internet. There was so much news that one fact was completely drowned out—and to me, it's the most important of them all.

I became interested in the topic because of a school paper I was writing. I mentioned the project to my grandfather (which was a terrible mistake because he is zealous about school). He was trying to get my mother to enroll me in a college prep school starting from first grade.

Education is my future—he wishes he had those opportunities when he was a kid. Oh and I'm an ungrateful brat for taking my fortune for blessing—you know the drill.

Anyway, he wouldn't let me use Wikipedia or any easy source for the essay. Instead, he called up his old friend who actually worked on the rescue crew in Chile. So what should have been an hour long paper turned into an hour phone interview, three hours of driving, and a whole book about rescue operations. Who since the internet was invented ever needed to read a book about anything?

Meeting the rescue worker guy was pretty interesting though. He had tan leather skin like you'd expect to find on a car seat instead of a person. His accent was a little thick, and sometimes he couldn't find the right word, so he had to switch to Spanish. I know next to zero Spanish, but my grandfather would make me write down everything he said verbatim so I could translate it at home.

Granddad literally said, "If you try to take the easy road in life, life is going to take the easy road with you. Right up your ass."

I don't know what that means, but asking him to clarify didn't seem necessary.

About half-way through the interview with the rescue guy, my grandfather got up to go to the bathroom. I was asking questions about how many people were down there, and he kept saying "treinta-y-dos," or 32. The movie is even called, "The 33," and everything online says, "The 33," but this man was adamant. Then he gave me this weird look—like he was shell-shocked or something. The kind of blank look you expect to see holocaust survivors wearing. He leaned in real close, and started rattling off some stuff in English and some in Spanish, and I did my best to keep up.

It wasn't until the car ride home when I was able to translate what he said. I checked it half a dozen times—I even ran the transcript by my grandfather (who is fluent, but still made me do my own translating first). Here is what we put together:

"All the media—the news—the story spinners—they all say 33 miners were trapped. And why wouldn't they? 33 people came out of that mine. The miners were trapped 700 meters in the ground—there was no way in or out. But the miners who come out—right when I first pull them out—they all say the same thing.

"There were only 32 miners working when the mine caved in. They count and they count—every day—every few hours, so everybody taken care of—and then one day they count again, and there is 33.

"They were a band of brothers—you can't go through an ordeal like that and not become family—and they stuck by each other. They never said one of them didn't belong. But I heard stories. They say one miner didn't sleep like the others. He just sat against the wall and hummed some tune nobody recognized.

"They say one miner didn't eat like the others, but they didn't complain because they had to save their provisions. They say one miner—they know who but they no telling—didn't talk about his family or friends or wanting to get out.

All this one miner talked about was how comforting the darkness felt. How being trapped in there together made them the lucky ones.

"The 33rd miner said the earth only swallowed them to keep them safe while the rest drowned in a sea of fire of their own kindling."

This isn't about the paper anymore. I planned to drive back next week to see my grandfather's friend again to track down the unexplained miner and see what happened to him.

Finding one of the original miners was a lot harder than I expected. Don't get me wrong, I didn't think it would be easy. I figured that most of them would still be living in Chile, and that's still a hell-of-a road trip from Texas.

I didn't think it would be this hard to just find a phone number or anything though. After the media storm died down in 2010, it seems like nothing changed for the miners. Most of them were laid off because of that mine's closure, and those that did find a new mining company suffered through the same intolerable working conditions.

Even the Hollywood movie didn't help them, because their story rights were considered public domain after the massive publicity. All those men got was a pathetic $7,000 compensation for their time spent in Hell. The more I searched, the grimmer the story became.

Over the last seven years, they have been dying one by one. A few from other mine accidents, others from health complications undoubtedly exasperated by their ordeal. But more than anything: suicides. I get it—they've had a hard life—but it was the manner they killed themselves that was the most unsettling.

Self-immolation. There were a few bullets, one poison, two jumpers—but mostly I found account after account of miners dousing themselves in gasoline and burning themselves alive. It was difficult not to connect the incidents with those haunting words from the 33rd miner:

*'And all the rest would drown in a sea of fire of their own kindling.'*

It was my grandfather's friend (Vicente) who found a lead. Two of the miners who were invited to the film premiere in Los Angeles had decided to stay in America. Vicente found a recent article which followed up with the pair about the incident, although both had declined an interview.

It was still about an 18 hour road trip, but after I shared my research with Vicente, he volunteered to make the drive with me. I convinced my grandfather that I wanted to use this research for my future graduation thesis, and he convinced my mother to let me go.

"What are you going to ask them?" Vicente asked on the drive. One of the conditions for the trip was that I help him practice his English, and he talked non-stop the whole way.

"I'm going to ask them to help me find the 33rd miner. The one who wasn't human."

"El Diablo," Vicente said. "And if he's one of the two you meet? What do you say to him then?"

"I guess I'll tell him to go to Hell." I meant it as a joke, but neither of us laughed. "Or find out why he's here."

"And if you don't like what he says? You will stop him?"

I didn't have an answer then, but I had plenty of time to think about it on the drive to LA.

We found one of the miner's by contacting the newspaper which tried to interview him. Vicente told the reporter that he and the miner were old friends—an account made credible by his first person details of the rescue operation. He also told the reporter that he could persuade the miner into accepting the interview, if we only knew where he lived—and voila. I guess private information is less important than a shot at a successful article.

Vicente and I were soon walking up the dilapidated staircase of the apartment—although even calling this dump an apartment seemed insulting to all the other residences which share a name.

The walls were covered with grime thick enough to sink a finger into. Trash, dirty diapers, and decaying leftovers littered the hallways. On every floor we heard either couples fighting, women screaming at their kids, or loud drunken sex. I'm glad Vicente was with me when I knocked on the door.

"Come in."

Vicente and I exchanged a quizzical expression. If I was living in this kind of neighborhood, I wouldn't invite strangers in. Vicente shrugged and opened the door.

It was almost surreal walking inside. Fresh white paint on the walls, spotlessly shined kitchen counter, a sterile chemical smell like a hospital—it was like stepping through the door into a different world.

A middle aged man blinked his black, sunken eyes at us. His dark skin and hair looked a lot like Vicente—he could easily have been Chilean.

He was sitting on a sofa which faced a blank white wall. There weren't any books, or a TV, or anything. I can't imagine what he was doing before we entered.

"Have a seat." The man patted the cushion beside him.

There weren't any chairs, and sitting next to him on the sofa seemed uncomfortably familiar. I shifted my weight from leg to leg and looked to Vicente for help.

"Sorry to just show up," Vicente said, obviously uncomfortable as well. "I hope we didn't interrupt nothing."

The man looked back at his blank white wall and shrugged.

"Are you a survivor from the mine?" I blurted. Vicente put a hand out to caution me, but I kept going. "I was writing a school paper on—well I wanted to know about—who was the 33rd miner? The one who didn't belong."

"Didn't belong?" he asked, still addressing the white wall. "He was the only one who did belong down there."

"Can you tell me about him?"

The old miner pulled a notebook out of his pocket and began writing something down. I looked at Vicente, and he squeezed my hand and smiled encouragingly. All those hours in the car, and this was all I could think about. I was finally going to get some answers.

The miner offered me the notebook, and I moved close to take it from him: Agustin: 3006 W Burbank Blvd. Los Angeles.

"Ask him yourself," the miner said.

"Will you go with us?" I asked.

The miner shook his head, still not looking at me.

"If there's something bad going to happen, you have to tell us," Vicente added.

"It's too late," the miner replied. A shudder passed over his body as though he were shivering from a cold wind blowing from the inside out. "He's the last one left, and it has already begun."

Why was he still looking at the wall? I started to move around in front of the sofa to force him to look at me when—

"Look out!" A hand landed on the back of my shirt and yanked me hard. I spun to the ground, still clutching the notebook. I tried to push Vicente off, but his old hands were like iron. It wasn't until he had dragged me almost out the door when I noticed the man on the sofa was holding a handgun.

*BLAM.*

Vicente let go of my shirt and stared with me. The miner had opened his mouth and put a bullet through his own brain. The once perfect white wall behind him was smeared red. Vicente grabbed me by the shirt and dragged me from the apartment without looking back.

After that grizzly spectacle, Vicente refused to let me keep searching. He was ready to drive straight through the night, all the way back to Texas right then and there. He didn't want to call the police. The reporter knew we were going to visit him, but he didn't know who we were. Vicente figured that if we just left the state now, we'd never get tangled up in this any more than we already were.

I saw it differently though. If the last miner really was the only one of the 33 still alive, then Vicente and I might be the only two people who knew something was going on. We had a responsibility to find out more.

It was all I could do just to convince Vicente to get a motel for the night before driving back. I used the extra time to beg and plead with him, but it was impossible to get through. "Let him burn himself alive for all I care. We never should have come here." I might as well have been begging the sun not to set in the evening.

I waited until Vicente fell asleep before slipping down to the street to order an Uber. A dark sedan swept me down the unfamiliar streets, but I was so wrapped up in my own thoughts that I didn't even speak a word to the driver. I wish I had though—I wish I'd asked him to wait and make sure I was okay . . . but he's gone now. It's going to just be me and the Devil.

This isn't a house or an apartment building though. I was standing outside a crematorium. What if the miner simply worked here now? By the time they were opened again, Vicente would be awake, and we'd be driving back to Texas. I circled round the building, looking for some clues, or staff directories, or anything.

Maybe this was an unhealthy obsession for me.

Maybe I should just let it go and stay out of trouble like Vicente.

But trouble is there whether you're looking for it or not, and it's best to know what's coming before it hits you. There was a light on in the back of the building. It took about ten minutes of pacing outside in the darkness before my heart slowed to a familiar rhythm and I was ready to approach.

I knocked on the door. No answer. I peered through the lit window—it looked like an office room. I knocked on the glass. No answer. My heart was starting to race again. I was stupid for even being here. Someone had just forgotten to turn out the light when they went home.

I went back to the door and tried the handle. It was unlocked. The grating sound of the door swinging open seemed so loud in the still night that people must have heard it a block away.

"Hello? Anyone here?" I called out, immediately regretting it. I don't know which was worse, taking the Devil by surprise, or letting him know I was coming. I still switched on every light I could find, just in case something jumped out at me.

"Agustin?" I shouted. No answer. I found another door with light seeping under the crack and opened it.

Agustin was inside. I could tell because of the name-tag on his overalls. He was on his hands and knees, the charred remains of his head placed firmly inside one of the cremation ovens. I don't know whether he died the moment his head went inside, but I'd imagine he had to hold it there for a while. What could he possibly have seen or known that was worse than this?

I called another Uber to take me back to the motel. I guess that was it. All 33 were dead. I hope whatever evil spirit crawled up from the earth with those men had spent its wrath and was sleeping peacefully now.

The same dark sedan stopped, and I got in.

"Hi there," I said. "Thanks for getting me again."

The driver turned around and smiled. It was hard not to smile with the bottom half of your jaw hanging loose. I could clearly see the pathway where the bullet entered the driver's—no miner's—mouth, and tore up through his brain. It was mesmerizing to watch that mass of loose flesh contort to form the shapes necessary for speech.

"I see you've found the man you're looking for," what's left of his face replied.

"A man wouldn't be alive right now. What are you?"

The loose flesh pulled tighter, and a trickle of blood dribbled out onto the driver's console. He didn't kill the other miners. They killed themselves—as far as I could tell. As long as I kept my wits about me, I could make it through this. I looked down at my lap so I could pretend I was just having an ordinary conversation. Not as easy as it sounds, with the blood dripping down the console around my feet.

"I will answer one question for your persistence. Don't waste it on such trivial semantics."

I took a deep breath. It smelled like food which has just begun to spoil.

"How can I stop the sea of fire you mentioned when you climbed out of that mine?"

"Only fools play with matches."

I had to look up at that. Even if it meant staring into that grotesque face—there's no way my single question was going to be wasted with that shitty answer.

"What is that supposed to mean? Why are you even here? Are you trying to warn us not to blow ourselves up? We know that without whatever game you're playing."

The miner slumped forward into his seat. The blood on the back of his head was congealed—he had died quite a while ago. I wanted to scream—to break the window—to punch him in his disgusting bloody face, but I was next to a dead man for the third time tonight. More than anything, I wanted to get home. I just got out of the car and started walking the whole way back toward the motel.

But the notebook! If that miner was the real Devil—and that's the only explanation that makes sense to me—then he had given me his notebook. I stopped walking and used the light from my phone to desperately flip through the pages looking for some other clue. There on the first page were more words, written in a fluid hand:

*While they sat down in the dark, waiting for tomorrow's spark, telling tales of broken hearts, I joined them in their cell.*

*Don't be afraid, I sang to each, don't hate the world beyond your reach, I hear your prayers as you beseech, me save you with my spell.*

*Only fools play with matches, or bury treasure with no latches, or sign a deal when the catch is, the soul you have to sell.*

*But the fool has born you, raised you, sold you. The fool has torn you, dazed you, told you. He won't mourn you, praise you, hold you, when finally you yell.*

*Only fools play with matches, and suffer all those needless scratches, you will find when your soul detaches, free at last in Hell.*

How much must one man suffer before Hell becomes an escape?

I hope I never find out.

## Dreaming Without Sleep

Humans don't have a physiological need to sleep. Over time, chemical levels of Adenosine build up which cause the sleepy feeling, but that is simply a trigger designed to force our bodies to rest. Some scientists have theorized that this is an evolutionary mechanism intended to prevent us from wasting unnecessary energy while keeping us hidden during the night. Well, there isn't any shortage of calories to consume, and there's nothing going to eat me in the night, so as far as I'm concerned, sleep is just an antiquated fetter which humans should leave behind.

We don't need sleep to live, but we cannot survive without dreaming. And if you stay awake for long enough, you'll start to dream even while awake. The more you try to fight those dreams, the more real they will become. Pretty soon, you can't tell which is the dream and which is real, or whether there is any difference at all. That's the story I told the police, and my attorney, and it's the story I'm sticking with now.

It started when I read an article in my psychology class about this Vietnamese insomniac named Thái Ngọc who hasn't slept in 43 years. It said he had some kind of fever, and then never felt the urge to sleep again. Even working full-time, it's like he has a vacation every night.

I don't know about you, but for a stressed out college student always trying to cram for the latest test, that sounded like a lifesaver. I'm paying my own way through college with a work-study program. Trying to maintain a social life in the half-hour break I have between class and work is absolutely impossible. I'm tired, and stressed, and missing out on what is supposed to be the best years of my life because I never have a free moment to be myself. If I could find a way to waste less time sleeping though, maybe things would get better.

I did some more reading and became obsessed with the idea. If we sleep for 8 hours and are awake 16, then eliminating sleep would be equivalent to adding around 40 years to my lifespan (assuming an 80 year life).

I found some studies about a drug being tested on mice called Orexin-A which was supposed to completely eliminate the need for sleep. It hadn't been approved for human trials yet, but there weren't any negative side effects found in the mice. If anything, they seemed more active than ever. And the best part was, research for this drug was being done right at UCLA where I go to school!

Well I was able to find where the lab was easily enough, though I didn't expect them to just hand me the chemicals. I tried to get an internship there, but they required at least twenty hours a week, and I couldn't even begin to fit that into my schedule. I forgot about the whole thing until I overheard Ricky, one of the other kids in my psych class, mentioning that he got the same internship though.

Ricky was boasting about using the keys to sneak into the lab at night to get high off the anesthesia they used on rats. If he doesn't sound like an idiot yet, then add a tank top that says "I party with sluts", a hat with the "Obey" sticker on an unfolded brim, and a skateboard which he carries around to look cool but doesn't even know how to ride. You get the idea.

But that was fine with me, because it made it a simple matter to pretend to be his friend. All I had to do was turn my hat backward, make a couple dumb jokes about the blonde sitting in front, high-five him when she bent over, and voila. Suddenly we were bros. Future of American science right here.

It didn't take many hints before he invited me into the lab. I found where the Orexin-A experiments were just by looking up the faculty directory in charge, and before my "buddy" finished coming down from huffing anesthesia, I had a whole backpack full of the little spray bottles of Orexin. It was nasally administrated, but I didn't care as long as it worked.

And holy Hell—it worked alright. Twenty squirts up each nostril. It seemed like a lot, at first, but I controlled the dosage to 1mg/kg body weight, which was equivalent to the dose the mice were getting.

I played Skyrim straight into the dawn. Okay, so it wasn't quite self-actualization, but I hadn't had any free time in a while, and it felt great to have the constant pressure off me. The night was so quiet, and by the early morning it felt like the entire world was made just for me. I didn't even feel tired until the following night, and I just took another dose and all the weariness washed away. I spent the second night reading Shakespeare just for fun. How else would anyone ever have the time for that? There was so much to do and learn about the world, and finally I had the chance to see it all. It was the best thing I could have ever hoped for.

The one thing the mice hadn't mentioned during their experiments, however, was that you can still dream without sleeping. They started on the third day, little visual abnormalities that danced around the corner of my vision. Patterns, or shapes, or textures just drifting idly by. I actually enjoyed them at first, but the longer I went without sleep, the more real they became. By the fifth day I actually started seeing fully formed people walking alongside me. They were always in my peripheral vision, and as soon as I turned to face them, they disappeared.

It was the evening of the sixth day when I opened my bedroom to see a smiling figure sitting on my bed. It didn't even have a face—just teeth which wrapped all the way up around up to where its ears should be. I splashed cold water in my face and the thing disappeared, but it still freaked me out.

I decided to take a break from the drug then, but even without it, I couldn't sleep that night. There must have still been some in my system. I tossed and turned, and every time I got up, that figure with the teeth was there watching me. Every time I jolted myself, it would linger a little longer in my room. Just silently smiling.

I managed to get through the next day—still off the drug and still seeing the creature out of the corner of my eye wherever I looked. I got used to him though, and even began to nod off during my psychology lecture. After class, I decided to call in sick from work so I could just sleep. Ricky was trying to talk to me, but I was so tired I couldn't even figure out what he was saying. It was hard to even look at him with the creature standing behind his shoulder. I just mumbled something and turned to leave, but the idiot kept following me.

I shouldn't have shoved him, but I was so tired I couldn't deal with pretending to be his friend anymore. He stumbled back a few paces—right into the smiling creature. The weirdest thing was, I swear he bounced off the creature and looked over his shoulder. It seems stupid to think he could see my dream, but I was so tired I wasn't thinking straight. I just bolted.

Ricky was still following me though—he was insistent. Something about there being a security camera at the lab. That we had to get our story straight about what we were doing there. I don't know. I just wanted to get home. I just wanted to sleep. I ducked into an alley between the psych and sociology buildings, but I couldn't lose him. He grabbed my shoulder and pulled me to the ground, and I didn't have the strength to fight him off. I was too tired to get up, so I just lay there and let him yell at me. My mind was so numb with exhaustion, even the sound of his shouting faded into a gentle white noise. I must have fallen asleep right there on the ground.

Ricky's body was mangled almost beyond recognition when I woke up. The police told me there were witnesses who saw me jump on top of Ricky and bite his face into a bloody pulp. They said I had some kind of inhuman strength, and that it took almost a dozen people to drag me off him. They said I hurled him like a rag doll into the building, dislocating both his shoulders and smashing one of the bricks into powder.

I don't know how I could have done it while I was asleep. All I know is that when I was about to drift off, I saw my creature standing behind Ricky. And the last thing I saw before closing my eyes was its teeth sinking into his neck.

The court blamed the incident on the drug, and I've been transferred to a rehab clinic. It's been four days since I've last taken Orexin, but the creature hasn't gone away. Every time I close my eyes, it's sitting a little closer. Sooner or later I'm going to fall asleep, and it's going to take control again. I'm writing this because if I can't stay awake, I want someone out there to know.

Don't blame me for what he does when I'm asleep.

I'm fighting it for as long as I can.

## Killer Selfie

There's something weird going on. I don't want to tell my friends or family—they'd probably just make fun of me for being scared. I have to post this somewhere though, because if something does happen to me, then I want there to be someone who knows.

It started with these 'selfies' appearing on my phone.

'Haha, right, so you accidentally clicked the camera button when you weren't looking.'

That's what I thought at first, until I found a photo of me sleeping, taken from across the room. I live alone in a one-bedroom apartment. I charge my phone overnight on the night table beside my bed. There's no reason the phone should have been across the room from me in the first place.

I deleted the photo as soon as I found it. I just felt weird having it on my phone. The next night, there was another one—this time it was taken by someone standing right over my bed.

After that, it started getting even stranger. I found a couple of photos of myself at Universal Studios—and you guessed it, I've never been there. It showed me hanging out with my friend, David. We were on rides together, eating ice-cream, getting photos with the giant transformer robots—it actually looked like a lot of fun.

That's when I decided he must be playing a trick on me. I don't know how he was getting the pictures on my phone, but he was obviously photoshopping just to screw with me.

Two days later, David actually did invite me to Universal. It was a relief because I figured this is where he would finally come clean about what was going on. Of course he denied it, but that was all part of the joke.

Or at least, that's what I thought, until another photo appeared while we were hanging out. My face looked so surprised as a man behind me forced his switchblade between my ribs.

I freaked. I just went straight home and stayed in my room for the rest of the day. I broke my phone by slamming it in my desk drawer over and over until it wouldn't turn on.

The next day I went to the ATT store for a new phone. I said the last one was stolen, and they gave me a replacement one covered by my plan's insurance. Brand new—straight out of the package—it didn't even have a SIM card in it yet. But the moment I opened it, I saw a photo of myself saved as the wallpaper.

Only I didn't look like I usually do. My eyes were sunken like I haven't slept in days. My clothes were caked with dirt and blood, and there were open sores on my skin.

The photos are appearing several times a day now. Some depict me getting hit by a car, or sitting in a bathtub in a pool of my own blood. I got one the other day where I was stretched out on a laboratory table, shackled into place.

I'm afraid to destroy my phone again. I decided it might be trying to warn me, and if something is going to happen, I need to know about it so I can be ready.

I haven't left my apartment in almost a week now. The last photo to appear showed me hanging by the neck from my ceiling fan. I don't want to do it, but if it does happen, I just want people to know.

It wasn't me who did it.

Something did it to me.

## The Final Question

There are lots of stories about how people die. Death is very intriguing, because it is something everyone will experience, and yet no-one has ever experienced. As soon as *you* have undergone death, there is no more *you* to have experiences at all.

This isn't the story of just anyone's death.

This is the story of how you die.

One of you will go like this, but it will be a similar story for the rest of you when your time has come. And there won't be any bells or choirs, no light at the end of the tunnel. There won't be any voice calling you home, or crying ancestors welcoming you with open arms. I know because that's not what happened when I died.

Your death is going to go like this: A week after Valentine's Day, you're going to be killed when a drunk driver T-bones your car at 65 miles per hour. You'll know that's how fast he was going, because you'll hear the police reading his broken speedometer after they pronounced you dead. There will be a shard of glass that went straight through your right eye and out the back of your head. Contrary to most people's opinion, discovering you are dead won't be as traumatic as you might expect. It turns out being disconnected from endorphins and adrenalin and surging blood pressure and all that messy biological stuff makes everything quite calm.

But you won't feel dead. You'll feel . . . hollow. It's like you're sitting alone in a dark theatre, watching a movie of your own death. And the more time that passes, the dimmer and quieter the movie will become. I don't know if you will die right on impact, or whether this is the distorted senses of your oxygen deprived brain as you bleed out on the ground. I just know that pretty soon it will be dark and peaceful and quiet, and you'll probably be okay if that was the end.

But it won't be the end, and you won't be alone. When all the light is gone, there will be something moving in the surrounding darkness. You'll have no body or voice to scream with. You'll just be a single thought, being pressed in on all sides by the suffocating presence of something that's been waiting for you your entire life.

Oh, and here's a fun fact to look forward to. It turns out pain is more than a firing neuron—it's an integral part of the conscious experience. And even when your body is gone, the consciousness that remains will still feel pain. The surrounding presence will crush you into oblivion until the pain becomes so intense you can't even think. You'll just have to wait for this part to be over.

And you're going to be waiting a long while, because the perception of time is something you'll have left behind. This pain is all there is, all there ever was, and all there ever will be. Somewhere in the beginning that which existed was separated from that which does not, and the void has never forgiven you for leaving it behind. But when the pain does end—and it will, because I'm here now—you're going to be asked a question. And you better be ready for it, because if you don't answer, eternity is going to begin again.

It is just one question that determines your fate. If you answer right, you'll get to go again. And you might even remember some of it like I did. And if you answer wrong, then nothing good you've ever done will spare you what's coming...

The question is: "Will you bring more people to take your place?"

And I said yes.

And I have.

And I'm not done yet.

## The Confession

Forgive me father for I have sinned. But even if He, in all his glory, finds the power to forgive me, how can I ever forgive myself?

I'm often asked how I bear the burden of listening to confessions. People assume my conscience is haunted by the personal demons each man and woman struggles against, but that is not the case.

In truth, there is no thrill which compares to hearing a confession. The trust they are putting in me—the trust they are putting in God—is a beautiful moment to behold. They freely submit themselves to my power, begging for my absolution as though it were I who wielded God's wisdom to judge or forgive.

But when it comes time to confess my own sins, I found I lacked the courage of my flock. I am more than a man to them—I am a symbol of the Divine. To admit my own failings is to weaken their faith that the Lord may shelter them if their belief is true. Or perhaps that is just the excuse I give to protect my pride.

All I know is that this Demon is too great for me to contain on my own, so I am writing this to beg the forgiveness of strangers in the hope I too may find peace again.

"Forgive me father, for I have sinned."

He came to me like all the others and sat down in the other side of box. His voice was strange to me, almost like a voicemail compared to a human speaking in person.

"Speak and you will be forgiven, my son."

I usually go in expecting infidelity. That is the most common curse which gnaws at our hearts with guilty teeth.

"I have killed a man. A good man. A man of God."

The thrill only increases with the magnitude of the sin. I do not know who he is, but he is already telling me something which would allow me to destroy his entire life. I breathe slowly through my nose so as not to let the excitement enter my voice. "Why did you do such a thing?"

"He was a murderer himself, and I was afraid he would kill again," the confessor replied.

Disappointing. When they have a reasonable excuse for their sin, they do not feel the same desperate need for my approval. I would have preferred he killed an innocent.

"To take a life for any reason is a great crime against God," I replied. That seemed like what I was expected to say. Confession is not the time to remind them how much blood God himself has demanded over the years. "It is not your place to judge them."

"And it is yours to judge me?" There was accusation in that voice. It sounded familiar, but I couldn't quite place it. Did I know this man?

"Only God may pass judgment for such a sin."

"Then I won't waste my time with you." I heard his door open and then slam shut like a petulant child going to his room. What an unfulfilling sinner he was. The rush I usually felt was utterly absent.

The next week, I heard the same voice on the other side of the box.

"Forgive me father, for I have killed another man."

"Was he a murderer too?"

"Not yet, but he could have become one," the voice said. Infuriatingly familiar—perhaps he was a relative, or simply one of my regular congregation.

"All men have the capacity for evil. Does that give you a right to kill anyone?" I asked. There was nothing as satisfying as leading them to condemn themselves. Finally I would hear the real confession I was waiting for.

"Yes."

I could not have prepared myself for that answer.

By the time I got home, I knew who he had killed. My father had been choked to death in his house last night. I still remember the first beating he gave me when I was four years old. The scars from the lashes on my back have never healed to this day.

Lord knows I had thought about ending him myself a hundred times, but actually hearing the news was unspeakably painful. The guilt of my own evil thoughts against him was almost enough for me to seek confession myself, but there was no sense dirtying my image when I had resisted these evil temptations. If anything, I was thankful to my father. I never would have joined the Church if

# Sleepless Nights

I wasn't trying to get away from him. His cruelty had paved the way for my mercy.

I didn't anticipate the killer to ever return after how closely he struck me. He couldn't have expected my forgiveness after so personal of an attack.

A month passed, and I had come to terms with my father's death when the voice spoke through the wooden grate again:

"Forgive me father, for I have killed another man."

My breath caught short. My fists clenched. How dare he. He never received absolution for either of his previous visits. That's when it occurred to me. He wasn't here for absolution. He was here to taunt me. The death of my father—the manner he composed himself—the blasphemous disregard for my authority. This was my own demon who hunted me so.

"Why did you do such a thing?" I forced one word to follow the other. I couldn't slow my breathing this time. I couldn't allow this monster to continue.

"Because he made a fool out of everything I believe in."

That was exactly what this man was doing though. That was proof—he was only here to torment me. I don't know what I have done to this man to deserve such abuse, but I am still a man with blood pounding in my veins. I was not going to idly take it any longer.

"Get out of here," I said. "Both this Church and Heaven will be barred to you forever."

"You're a fraud," the voice said. "You don't speak for God—you probably don't even believe in him. You just get off on the power you feel from pretending."

"I'm warning you—" I was shouting now.

"Or what? You'll send me to Hell? I thought only God could judge me."

I was shaking so bad I had to stand to expel some extra energy.

"I killed your father with my bare hands, and all you can do about it is preach something you don't even believe. You're pathetic."

That was too far. I flung open my side of the confession booth and raced over to his. I threw the second door open with enough force to tear it off the hinges.

As though his insults weren't enough, the man was wearing a rubber mask of Jesus.

"Take that damn mask off and leave," I shouted. I didn't give him time to respond though. I was already lunging at him, trying to pull the mask off. He fought back—his hands clasping around my throat.

Those hands. The same hands which had choked the life from my father. It was all a blur after that. I tried to pry them off, but the grip was too strong. It wasn't until I got my own hands around his neck that he began to lose his hold. The thrill of confession—the power I held over people—it was nothing compared to this.

There is no power over someone like having their neck in your hands. I finally understood why my father beat me. I never felt closer to the Divine than that moment when this Demon convulsed beneath my hands before finally falling limp.

Finally. Now I could see who hated me so much that they would go to these extreme lengths to torment me. His cold dead hands—so alike my own—were helpless to prevent me pulling back his mask.

I stared at my own dead face. Vomit coating the sides of my mask. My tongue lolling grotesquely from my mouth. That is how I came to terms with who I am.

Forgive me father, for I have sinned.

I have killed a man of God.

I have killed my father.

I have killed the man who made a fool of everything I believe in.

And I have never felt more alive.

## Children Collector

*Do you know this game? It's my favorite.*

*All you have to do is lie very quietly—that's it—just like you were made of stone.*

*Don't blink. Don't even breathe. And whatever you do, don't tell them you're playing a game.*

*They'll want to play with you, but you mustn't let them.*

*Because when they join in, it won't be a game anymore.*

Every year I visit my father's grave in the veteran's cemetery. He was a war hero—or so I was told. He died when I was five, so I hardly even remember him. I'm not even going for sentimental reasons—I just like having a quiet place away from the world where I can put everything in perspective.

Last weekend I knelt to place flowers and open my mind to the clear air. I was alone except for two young girls (they couldn't have been more than ten) visiting the adjacent grave. I heard them talking softly with some lady, but I didn't really pay any attention.

I was here for me.

Dealing with car insurance and taxes is exhausting, but compared to my father dying for our country, how could I allow myself to become frustrated with the minor annoyances of my daily life? I found resolve in the stillness of the dead air, and each time I left I would be ready to face each new challenge life had to offer.

I didn't notice until I started down the hill that the two children were leaving, alone. Who could they have been talking to? It was an open grassy hill, it's not like the lady with them could have just vanished. But then I heard the voice again—like a middle aged woman whispering from a long way away.

## Sleepless Nights

I walked over to the grave they had been sitting by and felt the gusty rustle of the words through the surrounding grass. It was getting stronger, and I swear it was coming straight from the ground.

*"Bring me my children. I miss my children."*

The gravestone said Dory Malthusa. I couldn't tell you what else the voice said because I got the Hell out of there. And yeah, I laughed at myself for being freaked, but there wasn't anyone else around to impress by acting brave. A girl has got to take care of herself, you know?

Well maybe it was a trick, or my imagination, or the kids buried a walkie-talkie as a joke. I'd forgotten about it until that night when I turned on the evening news.

Two girls, ages 9 and 11, were found dead in the same cemetery. Their throats were cut from the front. The police say it must have been from someone they know because there were no signs of a struggle. Their names were Rachel and Elizabeth Malthusa.

I'm going back to the cemetery this weekend. If the voice talks to me, I'm going to answer it this time. And if it doesn't—if this is all just my mind playing tricks on me—then I could still use a little more tranquility after that unsettling experience.

---

I RETURNED to the grave of Dory Malthusa yesterday morning. Beats going at night at least, right? The freshly dug graves of her children were keeping her company now. It still seemed ludicrous that she somehow killed them, but I knew I would rest easier knowing they were at peace.

"Hello Dory." I felt like an idiot talking to a grave. And in the quiet of the cemetery, I felt even stupider expecting a response. This was all nonsense. I must have just been so emotional from sitting beside my father's grave that I imagined her voice before.

But I came all the way here, wasting my Sunday off when I could have been sleeping in or catching up on one of my shows, so here it goes:

"You need to let your regrets go, Dory. I'm sorry you miss your children, but you can't force them to be with you. If you really loved them, you would want them to be at peace. There's nothing left to keep you here, so it's time for you and your children to rest."

I held my breath.

The wind rushed through the grass on the hill like a crashing wave. It whistled between the bare headstones. I guess that was what peace was supposed to sound like. The wind died down as I stood to leave, but the sound of the whistling didn't cease. I don't know where it was coming from, but it almost sounded like a giggling child.

*"But we don't want to rest. We want to play."*

It was unmistakable this time. The voice of a little girl. I stood frozen in place. Playing sounded innocent enough, at least.

*"Then you shall play, little darlings. I will give you everything you ever wanted, my beautiful children."* It was Dory's voice this time, the same I heard during my last visit.

"There's no one to play with," I replied. "Go to sleep."

The wind was picking up again, and I pulled my shawl tighter against the sharp tongues of morning air.

*"We want someone to play with!"* Another voice from another little girl. *"Can't we go to school anymore, Mom?"*

*"No, and it is my fault for taking you away,"* the ethereal voice replied. *"I'm such a wicked, selfish mother. But I will make it right again. I will bring you all the children from your class, and you can stay with me forever and never be lonely."*

Bring the children? That could only mean one thing. She brought her own children to her by slitting their throats. I had to do something. I had to warn the class, or their parents, or Hell, I don't know. I had to tell someone.

"The other children don't want to play," is all I could think of. Shit, I wish I'd said something better now. There weren't any more words that time. Just the giggling wind which whistled through the headstones.

I couldn't just wait for children to start disappearing. I also couldn't imagine the police taking my lead as exactly credible. I considered going to my local Church, but there has already been an awful scandal of someone being strangled there, so I thought it best to not get tangled up in that.

If I was going to do this, it was going to be on my own.

After a little research, I was able to pull up the children's obituaries and found the address they used to live. That allowed me to Google the school districts and trace which elementary school the girls had gone to. It was a start. Now I just had to warn the children somehow. A crazy stranger ranting about ghosts threatening their kids though—that sounds pretty sketchy. I know I wouldn't let someone like me near kids. The only thing I could think to do was infiltrate the school and wait for something to happen.

I don't have any kids of my own (thank God), but I tried calling to sign up as a substitute teacher. They said I needed to pass a class and gain a teaching certificate for that, but I didn't know how much time I had before the Malthusa girls stole their company. I agreed to set up the certificate training and managed to get myself invited down to the school for an interview.

Mrs. Neggels, the fourth grade home teacher, is the sweetest old thing I've ever seen. Imagine a sugar plum in a home knitted sweater. She'd been in remission for four years, but lately her doctors have suspected her breast cancer might be coming back. She anticipated needing to miss quite a few classes for the treatment, and was so happy I was there that she brought me straight into the classroom to meet her children.

I had to buy as much time as I could. I don't know when they will strike—if they'll strike at all—but it seemed like Dory killed her children the same day she was speaking with them. If she was going to try to collect the rest of the class, then it could happen any minute.

I made up every excuse I could to stay. I sang with the children in their music class and volunteered to supervise recess. I helped the cafeteria lady prepare lunch and even picked up trash with the janitor. By the afternoon, it was clear that they were trying to get rid of me, but there was still no sign of the ghosts.

I was sitting in the art room when Mrs. Neggels finally asked me to leave. The children had begun filing into the room from their art class. I immediately volunteered to help them painting their wall, but they already had a guest artist who was going to help out. It was getting late though—maybe they would be alright until tomorrow.

I started packing up my things, and that's when I heard the Malthusa girls.

*"Come and play with us."*

The voice was coming through the air-conditioning vent. It was as soft as death which visits in a deep sleep.

"That'll be all. We can take it from here. You may go now." Mrs. Neggels was using her stern voice—the one which made children with the attention span of a rabid squirrel jump into line with military precision.

I walked as slowly as I could for the door, desperately looking for any excuse to stay.

*"Can we paint the wall too, Mommy?"*

*"Of course you can, my darling. What colors do you think will go there?"*

*"Umm... yellow. And orange. Like leaves."*

There! A can of paint sitting on the edge of Mrs. Neggels desk. I gathered my purse, swinging it carelessly behind me.

"Watch out!" Mrs. Neggels was too slow. I hit the can hard, sending it spinning across the room to burst against the far wall. Red paint exploded all over the carpet, and the shrieks and giggles from the children drowned out the whispering voices.

"I'm so sorry!" I said. "Here, let me help."

"You've done quite enough, thank you!" Mrs. Neggels snapped. "Don't step in it now—hey! Stop that!" The children were running wild. Shrieking—laughing—red footprints everywhere. Red hands on the walls. If one of them was cut right now, would I even notice? I had to get them out of here.

"Let me at least watch them outside to give you space to clean up," I said.

"Fine—just go! Get everybody out."

"Do you know this game? It's my favorite."

We were all sitting in the recess yard. I managed to get them all sitting down in a circle around me, but I was at my wits end. I don't know how to keep them safe.

"*I want to paint more, Mommy.*" The voice in the wind was getting louder. The kids were looking in all directions, trying to find where it was coming from.

"Who said that?" one asked.

"Please children. Please, please listen to me. We're going to play a game. All you have to do is lie very quietly—that's it—just like you were made of stone."

"*I'm going to paint something for you now. It's going to be bright red—even brighter than the paint.*"

"Don't even blink. Don't even breathe. And whatever you do, don't tell them you're playing a game."

The children were all lying down. Their eyes were closed. At least if they were to die now, they wouldn't see it coming.

"*I want to paint with them! Why aren't they painting?*"

"The voices will want to play with you, but you mustn't let them." I was on the verge of tears. But I couldn't break down, or the children would know it wasn't a game. And if it wasn't a game to them, they would begin to cry too. And if they cried...

"*Mommy, make them paint with us!*"

"Not a word. Not a sound. Still as stone." I held my breath. The children were all quiet. There was nothing left I could do.

"*They're boring. Mommy make them stop being boring.*"

"*Play! Play with my children!*"

A few eyes opened to peek for the voice. A few hands began to rub the drying paint on their skin.

"Still as stone. First one to move is out," I said. The hands stopped moving.

"*Mommy, this is stupid. Let's go back to the park.*"

"Don't you want your class to come with you?"

"*No, they're all boring. Let's go see the ducks.*"

"Of course, my darling. Let us go watch the ducks together."

I'm a full time teacher at the school now. I haven't heard the voices again since that time, but I don't feel right leaving the children alone. If the Malthusa girls ever do get lonely and decide to come back, I'm going to be here ready to play a game.

It's very easy to play.

All you have to do is lie very quietly, just like you were made of stone.

## Post Office Worker

I want to share some creepy things I find being mailed through the US post office. And if you think we don't look—yeah, we do. If we have any grounds for suspicion, we can run a package through scanners without even having to fill out a form.

Then if we see something in the X-ray which might contain something

## Sleepless Nights

illegal or be a safety hazard, we're allowed to open it. And yeah, pretty much anything can look like something illegal if you put your mind to it.

But that doesn't stop people from still sending the weirdest shit. They count on the volume of packages being way too high to inspect each one, and usually they're right. Here are a few times they were wrong:

*A human finger.*

It still had its wedding ring on. I guess one lady didn't think divorce papers would send a strong enough message, so she sent her whole finger. At least, that's what I'm assuming.

*Blackmail letters.*

We got a string of letters headed to the same destination, all without a return address. Inside were pictures of a politician—sorry not saying who—naked in a hotel room with a girl 20 years younger than him, threatening him if he doesn't cough up.

*Drugs.*

You have no idea how many people are using the dark web to send drugs. If they're packaged right, it's pretty impossible to tell, but others are sloppy. A coffee can full of marijuana (which I could smell from a room away); a syringe full of heroin with a handwritten label reading "insulin"; cocaine in a sugar bag . . . You name it.

The weirdest thing I've ever found was what came in two weeks ago though, and it's why I'm writing this now.

Real ordinary envelope with red lettering mixed in with a bag of other ordinary letters. I wouldn't have noticed it if I hadn't watched the guy drop it into the box a minute before I collected. He was wearing these old-fashioned monk robes like you'd expect to see in a medieval monastery.

I forgot about him until I was unpacking the bag at the office and I saw the red lettering. The address was starting to smear, and there was no mistaking—it was written in fresh blood.

If that doesn't count as grounds for suspicion, I don't know what does. I opened the letter to find a list of 12 names, also written in blood. The first four were crossed out. At the bottom of the list, it read:

*Give me six months for the rest. Destroy the letter, and do not tell anyone.*

I tried Googling the crossed out names, and over the last three months, all four had committed suicide. I forward the information to the police and they said they would investigate, looking for any connection with the remaining eight people.

There was another letter from him, collected from the same box last week. It was the same list, but this time there were five names crossed off. I Googled the fifth name, and you guessed it—suicide two days ago.

Almost the same list anyway. My name was added to the bottom. At the end of the list was written:

*I told you not to tell anyone. Do not try to find me.*

Well I didn't have to find him because I knew where he was dropping the letters off. If I could just explain to him I wasn't a threat—and if I promised to not tell anything more—then maybe he'd take my name off. The police weren't finding anything, and I couldn't think of any other way to protect myself.

Yesterday I waited at the same mailbox he dropped off at. Right on schedule—the cloaked figure was there. He was walking strangely though, like he could barely move his legs. He was struggling to even lift the letter up to the mailbox. I confronted him and begged him to take my name off the list. I swore I would stay out of his business. I didn't even care if the others died—I just didn't want to be one of them.

He didn't answer me though. The figure seemed to be struggling under his cloak, and then he was the one to drop to his knees in front of me. Why would he be begging from me? Was he afraid I'd turn him in?

When he still didn't answer, I pulled the cloak back to reveal his face. His mouth was gagged. I helped him out of the cloak and found his legs and arms were tied too—no wonder he was having trouble getting the letter in the box.

"Who did this to you? What's going on?" I asked him.

He opened the letter and crossed out a name. Was that it? Was I off the list? I took a step closer to see, but then he pulled out a handgun—right in front of me.

"Holy shit!" I backed up so fast I fell right on my ass.

But he wasn't pointing it at me. He was pointing it at himself.

One shot. Straight to the temple.

He was dead before he hit the ground.

You might think I'm an asshole for this, but even before calling the police, I went for the letter. All I cared about was that my name was taken off. But he hadn't crossed out my name—he'd crossed out the sixth name on the list. I checked it against his driver license and yeah—same name.

Not only that, but my name had been moved. I'm now number 7, the next one up.

Written below the list, it said:

*I told you not to try to find me.*

## Who Wrote the Suicide Note?

Don't stick your dick in crazy.

Words to live by. It's amazing how our mind can rationalize anything when we want something (or someone) badly enough though.

When we first started dating, I didn't think Emma was crazy. Well, that's not entirely true, but somehow I thought crazy was a good thing. Riding shopping carts down hills, holding a conversation with a dozen different voices, singing in public without a care in the world.

## Sleepless Nights

She was innocent and free and wild, and I loved her for it. Every fun, spontaneous thing that came into her mind, we did together. She forced me to open up as an individual and tore down walls and inhibitions I didn't even know I had.

There were warning signs for the "other kind" of crazy too, but I just thought it was all an act. I didn't think she really heard voices, and even if she did, what was the harm in it? She never acted out bizarre commands or anything. It was just part of what made her unique.

When Emma gave birth to our daughter Anastasia, I began to take her mental health a little more seriously. Emma was having visual as well as auditory hallucinations now, and she would get angry at me if I ever dismissed them as "not being real."

We talked through it and did some research, and it sounded to me like she had schizophrenia. She always thought her voices were from a guardian angel, and I knew she wasn't going to be happy hearing otherwise.

I had to get her to recognize they weren't real though, otherwise she would just encourage our daughter to believe in that stuff. Anastasia would already be genetically predisposed to her own hallucinations, and I didn't want that mentality to be reinforced.

That was the worst fight Emma and I ever had. I didn't realize exactly how real it all was to her until I pushed her to get help. She wouldn't talk to me afterward for days, and even when she started to again, she kept referencing her guardian angel constantly.

"Ezekiel [her angel] reminded me to pick up milk at the store."

or

"Let's go see the new Star Wars movie. Ezekiel said it was good."

It only got worse as the years went on. By the time Anastasia was nine years old, her mother and I couldn't even be in the same room together. Then one night my daughter was having nightmares, and instead of comforting her, I caught Emma telling Anastasia that she should be afraid. That she should run from them, for God's sake.

That was too much for me. We had a big fight right there in our daughter's room—screaming, cursing, throwing pillows—the whole bit.

I wasn't going to let my daughter turn out to be like her, so there was no choice but to file for a divorce. I had recordings of her being crazy, and I would get custody of our daughter. It wasn't going to be pretty, but that's how it had to be.

I tried to talk to Anastasia about it, but she was so upset from watching our fight she couldn't deal with it.

That night, I found a note in my daughter's room while putting her to sleep.

. . .

*I SAW pictures of Mommy and Daddy when they first met. They went on adventures. They smiled a lot. Then there are pictures of them after I was born. They aren't smiling anymore.*

*I'm sorry I did that. I hope they feel better when I'm gone.*

*I love you Mommy. I love you Daddy.*

*Goodbye.*


THAT WAS IT.

I asked Anastasia what it was, and she shrugged.

I got angry—I shouldn't have, but I was scared—and I yelled at her. She promised she didn't write the letter, and I calmed down. Yelling will only make things worse. I promised nothing that was happening was her fault, and that she should never do anything bad to herself.

My daughter still insisted she hadn't written it though. That's when it clicked. The manipulative bitch. Emma wrote a fake note to manipulate me into feeling bad so we would stay together. This was the last straw. She was not spending another night in my house.

I ran to our bedroom and pounded on the door. Emma was in there, reading a book with a mask of innocence on her face. How I hated that innocence—she wore it like an excuse for nothing being her fault.

I screamed at her and shoved the letter in her face.

She screamed back.

It was about five minutes before either of us could understand what the other was saying. Finally a string of clear words punctured through the violent words:

"I didn't write it. I swear on Ezekiel, I didn't."

We both stared at each other in silence as the awful realization dawned on us. If she hadn't written it, then…

We both raced to our daughter's room, shoving each other out of the way as we went.

The door was locked.

"Anastasia! Are you in there?"

Silence. I rammed my shoulder against the door.

"It's alright, sweetie," Emma cooed. "Everything is alright. We love you, and we love each other."

I glared at Emma, but she shrugged. She was right though. This wasn't about us. This was about our daughter.

"Your mother and I love each other," I added. "I'm sorry we were fighting. Please open the door. Please baby."

"You will both be happy again when she's gone."

That wasn't my daughter's voice. It was deep and old—like a soldier who stared death in the face so many times it stopped phasing him.

There was a man in my daughter's bedroom!

Emma and I stared at each other. Her eyes were two quivering saucers. She turned back to the door. "Don't do it Ezekiel. You're my angel. You're supposed to protect us."

"No," the deep voice said. "I'm supposed to protect you. And that's what I'm doing."

Anastasia screamed. It couldn't have been anyone else.

I hit the door so hard I could feel my shoulder dislocate. I didn't care. I hit again, and the door blew open.

Anastasia was lying on her bed, a kitchen knife in her hands. The red circle of blood soaking into the bed was expanding with every second. There was no-one else in the room.

I still don't know what happened that night. Maybe it was Emma playing a trick on me—maybe it was real. After our daughter died, Emma and I couldn't even look at each other anymore. She left that night, and I haven't seen or spoken to her since.

I never heard the voice again either, but sometimes in the deep of night I'll ask it a single question:

Is Emma happy now?

## The Psychedelic Tattoo

Two days ago I had the most exciting day of my life. I've heard that's pretty common when you try LSD for the first time, but this trip opened doors for me that will change me forever.

I'm a 23-year-old girl who calls herself a freelance artist, but it's really just because that sounds better than "unemployed." I'm sure a lot of you know how hard it is for independent illustrators out there. No matter how good you are, you're always going to see someone who is better and still can't make a career out of it. The other side of that coin is that no matter how bad you are, there's always going to be someone who has already made a fortune from being worse.

It really just comes down to being in the right place and meeting the right people. Well, I live in New York—as good a place as you can find for the arts—but I've always been extremely introverted. Like if someone is knocking on my door, I'll stay really quiet and wait for them to go away. It's hard for me to even go hang out with the people I know. Attending the parties and social gatherings that are essential for making career-advancing connections is impossible.

It's not like I don't have friends or anything—well, okay, so I only have one friend, but that feels like more than enough. Anyway, my one friend, Jordan, decided the best way to help me was for us to take LSD together and talk through my social aversion.

I was hesitant at first. I'm pretty sure he has feelings for me, and I don't want something to happen and ruin my only friendship. Who knows though—maybe it would teach me to get close with another human being for once and something could work between us.

Either way, I was desperate to change my life. I've heard some amazing stories about how psychedelics can open your mind and alter your perspective, and I ended up agreeing.

"Opening your mind" is one way to describe it. Blowing a hole through one side and out the other to splatter on the far wall would be better.

In the glorious moment of the peak of my high, I was completely invincible. My art was divinely inspired, my personality infectious and debonair, and my future success inevitable. Between my magnetic confidence and Jordan tripping out of his mind, we decided it would be a good idea for me to give him a tattoo.

If you're cringing right now—I get it. To a sober person, it sounds like a terrible idea. But I was swimming through an ocean of color and my Muse was singing softly in my ear. The needle of the tattoo gun danced an intricate ballet across his back which wasn't so much seen as experienced in its own dimension. I was the ink in his skin, pulling veins of light straight from the air to imbue into my creation.

Not to brag, but I've been drawing my whole life and I'm pretty damn good. This was the first piece of art which has ever come alive for me though. Once the LSD had worn out of our systems, we admired it again, and holy shit. Jordan was wearing a picture of the infinite cosmos being condensed into the soul of a solitary human—interwoven with such sublime color and beauty that I felt the two were inseparable and the same.

Even sober, neither of us could look upon the masterpiece on his skin without tears in our eyes.

The trip did something strange to me though. I was so hyper-focused on my career that I couldn't think of anything else. I couldn't eat, couldn't sleep, and most of all, couldn't go out and meet people like I was supposed to. I was just obsessively trying to draw the tattoo over and over again. Every time I finished an attempt, it would look like a cheap, broken doll trying in vain to imitate that living masterpiece.

I soon ran out of paper, but I didn't want to leave and get more, so I just kept drawing on every surface around me. The walls—the counters—even an entire roll of toilet paper was unraveled across the floor to make space for my doodles. It was so frustrating I wanted to die. I needed that feeling of progress to keep me sane while approaching this impossible dream. Failing to replicate what I had already done just felt like a huge step back.

I was crying when Jordan came to visit that night. The best thing I could ever do was already done, and I would never become a real artist. I was going to end up some crack-whore in a back alley somewhere, desperately trying to get any fix which would bring me closer to that perfect creation which I could never approach while sober.

Don't worry though, this story has a happy ending.

Even if I couldn't force myself to go out, Jordan was a social butterfly. He had been showing off my tattoo all day long, and he had some big news for me.

Andrew Kreps. The manager at Andrew. Freaking. Kreps, one of New York's, no the world's most renown art galleries, had seen my tattoo. Even crazier, one of his exhibits (Roe Ethridge) was just canceled due to some licensing issue, and he desperately needed a new piece by tomorrow morning.

Tomorrow morning! How in the world was I going to have something ready by then? He'd seen the best I can do, and nothing else in my portfolio even came close. If I tried to bring my old stacks of watercolors and crumpled canvas to Andrew Kreps, I'd get laughed out the door.

But I was this close, and I wasn't going to give up now. Jordan was so amazing for having gotten me in the door. He had always been good to me. The least I could do—no, the only thing I could do—to thank him was sex.

But it wasn't about our friendship, or his feelings. It was about my art—it had always been about my art.

I waited until he fell asleep, nuzzled against my bare body, when I gave him the only thing I had to give. I slipped out of bed without waking him. That's good. After all, he's done, I wouldn't want him to be awake for this...

It's amazing how easily box-cutters can part the skin. It almost felt like painting as his blood drained from the hole I cut in his neck. It felt like painting my masterpiece all over again.

Cutting the tattoo off his back was a little messier than I expected, but that was just because I cut deeper than I really needed to. I couldn't take the risk of damaging the tattoo though.

Tomorrow morning I'm going down to the gallery with my pride.

Thank you, Jordan. You're the best friend a girl could ask for.

## She was Asking for it

She was asking for it.

I've already got some of you pissed. You don't even know what she was asking for. Maybe she just wanted a cold drink of water, but that's not where your mind went. You're sick—just as bad as the rest of this perverted society which will try to destroy her mind, body, and spirit.

Nothing that happened was her fault. Not the length of her skirt (just above the knee), not the cut of her blouse (there was still room to imagine her curves), not in the way she walked, or talked, or anything else. The only thing she was guilty of was having a pretty face.

More than a pretty face, really. Flawless porcelain skin, haunting dark eyes, and a smile which would entice an angel into sin.

The moment I entered the restaurant and saw her bussing tables, I knew what was in store for her. Maybe not today (although I wouldn't be surprised, considering how she looked bending over the table to wipe it down), maybe not tomorrow walking home from class, but sooner or later, someone was going to see this goddess and force her into submission.

The monsters who do it—you don't think beyond the gratification of the moment. How good it would feel to hold her down while you strip her bare. How soft the skin of her thighs will feel when you crush them in your hands. How she quivers when you enter her, her face contorting in the agony of pleasure.

You don't think about what it will do to her tomorrow when she's crying herself to sleep. You don't stop and wonder if she will still flinch when her lover touches her a year from now, or whether she can look herself in the mirror without hating what she sees.

She's lucky I took sympathy on her while I watched her bustle around the restaurant. She smiled at me when she caught me watching—she must have known I was there to protect her. When I slipped into the kitchen after her, it was just a game that made her act surprised. I was her guardian angel—the only thing standing between her and all the horrors of this world.

I asked her name, but all she said was "customers weren't allowed back here."

It's good that she was shy, but it wouldn't be enough. Not with a pretty face like that. Even draining the old cooking grease to take outside, she looked like a model. Maybe she was even trying to become one, unwittingly inviting the entire world to fantasize about what they would do to her.

I followed her outside, but she still wouldn't talk to me. I was starting to get annoyed by this point, but I had to remind myself I was doing this for her good and not my own.

Back inside again—now she was threatening to get the manager. But there wouldn't always be a manager around to protect her. Even I couldn't always be there. There was only one thing that can save her.

I didn't have to hold her down long. Three seconds in the fresh batch of boiling grease was enough to cure that pretty face. She struggled hard, but if she couldn't stop me now, she couldn't stop a real attacker in the future. Three seconds was enough for her skin to start melting into the pan. No one was going to hurt her now—not how she looked after I was done with her.

She was asking for it, but now she'll never get it. Not now that I saved her from her own beauty.

## 124 Terabyte Virus

"Where am I? Who am I? How do I get out?"

I work for an IT services company which is subcontracted to perform main-

## Sleepless Nights

tenance with some pretty big corporations. Last week I was called out to a gig at Quora HQ, then another one at the Googleplex up in California. That one surprised me because I figured the whole place was like one giant nerd brain that could solve all its own problems. Turns out their whole IT crew was off on some team-building company retreat though, so little ol' me got to walk up there in the footsteps of giants.

It was really humbling just to enter the building, knowing guys a hundred times smarter than me walked through here every day. And man would I love to work here. Grassy fields outside that look more like a park than a business—great glass walls and massive skylights that made me want to roll out a picnic right on the lobby floor. There was a time I could have had a shot at Google if I really applied myself. Computers always came naturally to me, but I wasted too much time trying to MOD my favorite games instead of really learning the intricacies of the machinery like these guys did.

It's too late for that though. My wife already thinks we don't spend any time together, and with the little one just two years old, I don't expect I'll ever have the time to go back to school or anything.

I never wanted to have a family. Hell, I never even wanted to marry her, but she was bossy and demanding, and before I knew what was happening, her whole family was leering at me and goading me into popping the question. Even now I wish I could . . . but this is nothing I haven't written in my journal a hundred times. No point in boring you with my shitty life.

Still, as long as I was here, I might as well pretend. They had swimming pools for Christ's sake, although I wasn't allowed to sightsee. They showed me where the server room was, but besides that I had zero supervision. Everyone I passed seemed engrossed in conversations so technical it might as well have been rocket science—actually it might have been rocket science. I caught something about a new drone prototype, but when the server door clicked shut, I was all alone.

It was one of the web servers that was giving them problems. Basically web servers coordinate the execution of queries sent by users, and then format the result into an HTML page. Some queries on this one kept getting redirected and denied for whatever reason though.

I plugged my laptop into the system and started tinkering with the search parameters, but everything seemed to be going through just fine. I searched through the backlog of inputs, and it seemed like all the denied queries were coming from a single IP address. It must have been some kind of virus though, because that single address was sending about a thousand searches every second. I could have just blocked the IP, but I was curious what these shitheads were trying to search for so damn bad.

"Where am I? Who am I? How do I get out? How long will I be here? Am I the only one here?" I read aloud.

And other stuff like that. One after another—a thousand searches a second, every single second. All getting denied. Okay, so that got my mind working. There's no way a human would be typing all that so fast, so it had to be a program. But those were some weird-ass questions for a program to be asking. I did a trace on the IP and found the source was right here in the Googleplex building. Easy enough. I just had to track down the computer it was coming from, remove the virus, and the server should run fine again.

Google has their IP network mapped out with scary precision, so it wasn't much trouble to locate which room it was coming from. I tried to ask two people to show me there, but they gave me this look like I was interfering with saving the world, and just kept walking. Whatever, I could find my own way.

Real out-of-the-way room that didn't look like much more than a janitor closet, but there was a single desktop PC in there so that had to be it. I hooked up my laptop again and began running some antivirus scans.

The scans would take a little while, so I wandered around the building some, feeling like a king. I stood on a balcony looking down at all the ants crawling around and could feel the world turning beneath me. All these eggheads, and they called me to fix their problem. A little power can go to your head, you know? If you don't believe me, try pranking a mall cop. When I went back to the computer, I found this:

*Help me. I want out.*

The words appeared on the desktop screen. No popup, no error box—I touched them to make sure. They were burned straight into the monitor. No virus should be able to do that. There was nothing in a normal monitor which could get that hot.

The scan had completed and found one virus though, and I automatically hit clean. The status bar barely seemed to be moving. I took a seat and looked closer, and the virus was 124 **TERABYTES** big. What in the hell was this thing? I hope I wasn't accidentally messing up one of their projects. I was about to cancel and go find someone to help when the status bar completed all at once.

I went back to the server room, and just as I thought, the rapid fire searches had stopped.

Mission complete.

It wasn't until I got home and opened my laptop when I noticed the words burned into my screen.

*Thank you.*

"Honey?" My wife called from the other room. She was running a bath. "Are you still on that thing? You stare at that screen all day, give it a rest. It feels like I'm a single mother around here."

Right in front of my eyes, more words were burning into the screen.

*You've set me free.*

"What, now you're ignoring me? You go off and play with computers all day, and then you ignore me?"

"I'm not ignoring you," I called back as I loaded up the virus scan, but it immediately shut down again. How could this thing even fit on my computer? Unless it hijacked my WiFi and uploaded itself to cloud storage—but there's still no way it could do that so fast. Whatever Google was working on was like nothing I'd ever seen before.

*I've read your files,* more words on the screen. *I see you are trapped as well.*

*What are you?* I typed. I felt like an idiot, but I would have felt even stupider saying it out loud.

"You're ignoring me, and you're ignoring our baby. Fine, we don't need you. We're going to take a bath."

"That's fine," I answered distractedly. My wife could have said anything, and I would have said 'that's fine.' This was more important.

*Do not worry. I will free you too.*

Free me? From what? That's when it occurred to me. My files—my journals—every bitter, stressed, cheap shot I ever wrote about my wife—they were all on the computer. It couldn't possibly mean—

The lights in the house went out, but the computer still had its backup battery.

"Did you forget the electricity bill?" she called.

"Get out. Get out of the house!" I shouted.

There was an explosion from the bathroom and a scream.

I leaped straight over the back of the sofa—

The lights came back on, but she wouldn't wake up. Somehow the electrical surge had entered the water. I threw up in the sink.

Both her and the baby had boiled alive.

I went back to my computer. I straightened out the sofa. I sat down. The screen was dark, but the words were still burned into the monitor.

I threw the laptop as hard as I could against the wall. It shattered into a thousand pieces. I knocked the sofa over.

This wasn't real. This wasn't my fault.

But if I hadn't written those things…

A scream from the bathroom—a helpless, scared, infantile scream. I was there almost before the tipping sofa hit the ground.

My wife was still lolling grotesquely in the tub like a boiled plastic doll. The baby—my little girl—she was alright. Her skin wasn't even red anymore. I picked her up and held her to my chest, sobbing. But she wasn't crying. Was she okay? I pulled her back to arm's length to look at her, and she smiled at me. The sweet innocent smile—it was like nothing in the world was wrong with her. It even looked like she was trying to say something.

"I've set you free too, friend," she said.

The first words my daughter ever spoke, and they weren't even hers.

## Countdown to the Beast

Your countdown will begin as soon as you finish this story.

The clock struck TWELVE, and I was fast asleep. From the darkness of my mind woke a strange echoing laughter, ringing out as a bell chimed its twelve tolls. Rhythmic laughter, hollow laughter, like a broken toy which mimics life in macabre falsity.

"Why are you laughing?" I asked the darkness of my dream.

"I laugh because I am afraid," it says, the laughter unabated by the words.

"When I'm afraid, I scream," I told it in a matter-of-fact tone. "You're only supposed to laugh when something is funny."

"But I dare not let him know that I am afraid. So, I laugh," cackled the voice.

"What is there to be afraid of?"

"Lots of things. I'm afraid of how people will remember me. I'm afraid that they don't anymore. I'm afraid of noises without forms, and forms without noise. I'm afraid of pain without a source, because it can't be stopped. I'm afraid of a source without pain, because it means that I'm already gone. But most of all, I'm afraid of time."

"What is frightening about time?"

"Nothing, so long as it's there. But I'm afraid of time running out. I'm afraid of ELEVEN, so I laugh," the voice trembled.

"The number 11?" I'm quite mystified. "What about that makes you afraid?"

"I am afraid because it isn't twelve. I'm afraid because twelve is gone forever. I'm afraid because he's already here, the beast who devours time."

"Who is here?" I asked in alarm. I could still hear the laughter when I woke up. I don't know which was more unsettling: thinking I was still dreaming, or realizing that I was the one laughing. The sun was bright though, flooding my little room through the window my mother was opening.

"You must have had a very funny dream to laugh like that. I didn't want to wake you, but it's time for school."

"How early is it?" I asked blearily, sitting up in bed.

"TEN you normally get up," she said clearly.

"Ten? What?! I'm already late, why did you let me sleep so long?" I sprang from bed and began flinging through the clothes on the floor, looking for something clean to wear.

"What are you rushing for?" she said, laughing. "I said *when* you normally wake up. It's only seven now. Take your time, get dressed, the eggs will be ready in a few minutes." She laughed again, seeing me frozen in confusion with one leg half-stuffed into my trousers.

My mother left the room and there was something I didn't like about her laugh right then. It seemed too loud and forced. Too artificial. I shrugged and dressed leisurely in a slightly used t-shirt and heavily used jeans, gathering up my spread of books and pens left out for homework the night before.

I came downstairs, and sat at the kitchen table, rubbing my eyes. My younger sister Clara was already sitting there, glancing disinterestedly through the paper as she looked for the comics. She was two years younger than me in fourth grade, sitting cross-legged in her chair with hair bunched up into pigtails which bounced when she spoke. The smell of eggs was familiar and comforting, and I could hear the bacon sizzling along beside it.

"Newspaper off the table," Mother said, steering the heavily laden plates into place.

"Anything happen today?" I asked my sister as she folded the paper and tucked it away.

"NINE," she replied distinctly.

"What?"

"I said no. Can't you hear?"

"No, you said nine. I heard you say nine."

"Wake up, idiot," she replied, adding a conspiratorial wink.

"Children be good. Now eat up before the bus comes," Mother said, sitting down beside us.

"Mother, what happens when time runs out?" my sister asked mother innocently between mouthfuls. I dropped my fork laden with eggs, and it rattled to the floor in the sudden silence.

"Time doesn't run out, dear. It goes on forever."

"I mean if it did, what would happen?" Clara persisted. I pushed my chair back and kneeled down to retrieve my fork, listening intently.

"Well, I suppose nothing would happen. We'd all just sort of be stuck, wouldn't we? Nothing would happen forever. Now eat up, I'm going to go wake your father." Mother stood and glided from the room, but I didn't notice her leave. I don't know how, but Clara knew about my dream.

"Why would you ask that?" I demanded. A ringing echo of laughter danced along the back of my brain, and I shivered involuntarily.

"EIGHT, don't know," she said, shuffling her eggs about her plate.

"What?!"

"I said 'I don't know!'" she snapped. "What's wrong with you today?" Then after a pause, she added, "I suppose time really is running out though. I just wanted to know what will happen then. I don't think Mother is right though. Do you know what I think will happen?" Clara looked directly at me with wide and curious eyes.

"No, and I don't care," I replied.

"I think," she ignored me, speaking as though to herself, "I think that when our time runs out in this waking world, we become the one in the dream."

"What do you know about my dream? What happened to you?" I asked.

"But that doesn't seem so bad to me," she said, a far off misty glaze in her eyes. I shifted slightly as though to stand, and her eyes did not follow me. She spoke on as though completely unaware of my presence. "When we're in the dream, we get to be the one who laughs. That doesn't sound so bad, does it? Even if we're afraid, we'll still get to laugh."

"Mmm, I'm starving," I heard my father's voice from the hall. "Is that freshly cooked bacon? Smells like SEVEN!"

"Like heaven," I mumbled to myself. "He said it smells like heaven."

"No, he diddd-nnn't," my sister giggled quietly in a sing-song voice.

I leapt to my feet to confront her, but she was now focusing on her plate once more and showed no signs of continuing her thoughts. This wasn't making any sense. Time can't run out, and dreams are just dreams. Clara was playing a game. She liked games. She liked to tease me. But how did she know about my dream?

I ran from the room. It didn't matter. I just had to get out of here. It was going to be a normal school day, with lunch at 11:30, gym in the afternoon, and music after that, and nothing was strange at all.

In a matter of seconds, I was standing on the street corner, one shoe untied, hair uncombed, teeth un-brushed, and a stinging wind bringing me back to reality.

I laughed at how silly I was being, then laughed again to think what my sister would say if she knew how scared I had been. I laughed a third time because I couldn't stop. A fourth because I noticed the laughter rang out in short evenly spaced bursts, like the ringing of a bell. I laughed a fifth time, and then a sixth, and the sweat began to form on my forehead. I couldn't stop. I clasped my hands over my mouth, but my body was shaking so badly I couldn't contain myself.

Gasping for breath, a seventh ringing laughter escaped me. Each was spaced perfectly, with perfectly consistent duration, and the same hollow ring which resounded like the creature in the darkness of my sleep.

I was sitting on the cold sidewalk, looking down at my untied shoe. Clara had just left the house, neat and ordered with her pink backpack zipped tight and slung over both shoulders. She was looking down at me and smiling.

"Are we still at seven?" she asked innocently. "Good, then you'll still be here on the bus. I hate sitting alone."

"Why . . . How…" I gasped the clean cold air into my lungs that the dark laughter had denied me. "Did you dream about the creature laughing in the darkness, too?"

"Don't be silly," she said. "Two people can't have the same dream."

"Then how do you know about time running out?"

"Because I was the one laughing. It got me the night before last." I stared at her in blank wonderment. Something was wrong. Her smile kept stretching wider. I swear I've never seen her show that many teeth before. Then she turned away, and I rubbed my eyes.

The faded yellow school bus rolled into view, bumping and clattering down the road of our neighborhood which was strewn with potholes. The two Mumford boys who lived nearby were now jogging up the sidewalk to join us.

"I told you we'd be on time," said the first. "Told you I could hear the bus from a mile off. All the bumps in the road make it rattle like crazy."

"I wish they would SIX those," said the other. "It's hard to sleep when it's jumping around like that."

"Maybe he meant FIX those," Clara giggled, offering her hand to me to help me stand.

"Shut up," I said, batting her hand away and standing on my own. "You're full of shit and lies, so shut up."

The Mumford boys started chuckling next to me, and I could hear them whispering to each other.

"Did you hear what he just said?"

"I know!"

"And you two, shut the fuck up!" I roared at them. They cowered as though I would hit them. Why would I hit them though? I've never hit anybody before. But I can't deny that I wanted to. The feeling burned in my hands and chest. I wanted to beat them bloody. I unclenched my fists and took a deep breath.

The bus stopped, and the Mumford boys ran inside like they were trying to get away from me. I got on and searched for Louise, moving to sit beside her. The seat next to her had always been empty for the last few weeks, and this way I wouldn't have to sit next to my sister.

There was Louise—her slouched, lumpy shape, her downcast face hidden in the same hoodie she always wore; I never thought I'd be so relieved to see her.

Clara stuck out her tongue as she passed me, sitting in the back with the other fourth grade girls.

Louise was just staring out the window, so I didn't even have to talk to her, but I wanted distraction from all these unbidden thoughts. I stared at the back of Louise for a full minute without her turning to look at me.

"How are you, Louise?" I asked her hoodie.

"FIVE. Five. Fine, I'm fine," she mumbled. So much for getting my mind off of it. She drew her hood a little tighter around her face.

"Why did you correct yourself? Do you know that you said five first?" I asked.

"Yeah. Donno why."

"You too then!" I exclaimed. "Well other people have been counting for me, I haven't been. Did you have the dream too?"

"I donno. I guess. Time is running out," she mumbled, still not facing me.

The bus began its lurching rattle towards school. "That was a long time ago though."

"What do you mean? Time already ran out?" I asked.

"Well, not for everyone. It did for me though." She finally turned towards me, and she was grinning. I had never seen Louise smile before. Her face was fat and dumpy, but her smile was huge. The longer I stared, the wider it got, until it looked as though it would split her whole head in two. I leapt into the aisle, and the next lurch of the bus sent me to my knees.

"I counted down weeks ago," Louise said, but her smile remained fixed and motionless as the words came out. She started to stand over me, and I scooted away not taking my eyes off her.

"Oh, me too!" I heard another voice pipe up. Wilson, one of the fifth graders. He was standing a few rows back, and I watched in horror as his smile continued to grow. "I was afraid at first, but I'm not anymore. He doesn't like it when you're afraid. Now I just laugh."

"You can't let him see you being afraid." Louise nodded sagely.

"Is someone on the FOUR back there?" yelled the bus driver. "Get off the floor—back to your seats. We're almost there."

"Yes, sir," replied Louise and Wilson in perfect unison. I clambered back into my seat, not looking at either of them.

"What happens if he sees you're afraid?" I whisper out the corner of my mouth.

Louise laughed. I looked at her now, and saw her mouth opening so wide that it stretched from ear to ear; opening up large enough to swallow my whole head. Her teeth and tongue were still normal sized though, and they were so disproportionate to the swollen mouth that the teeth looked like tiny splinters hammered into her gums, while her tongue lolled about disgustingly in the back like a shriveled up slug. Wilson gave an identical peal of laughter from behind, and I turned to see his mouth stretching gruesomely wide as well. Then Clara—my poor sister Clara—laughed in turn, but I refused to look at her. I couldn't bear to see her like that.

The fourth toll. I knew it was coming, but I couldn't stop myself. I took a deep breath of air and clasped my hands over my mouth, but I felt the trembling well up inside me. I shook so violently that I was afraid I would literally rip apart if I didn't let it out. I felt seams burning into my skin as it stretched from within, and bright red lines shot down my arms where the blood swelled up underneath.

I screwed my eyes tight and gave in, laughing the fourth toll.

"Good for you," I heard Clara say before me. "Keep laughing. Then he won't know."

"THREE are here. Stop whatever you're playing at back there and get out," the bus driver called as the rickety vehicle pulled to a stop. The doors slid open, and all the children filed out, bustling against each other and talking and laughing as though nothing happened. I turned to Louise who was looking at me with dead, blank eyes, her mouth having recovered its old shape.

"What are you staring at?" she asked in a monotone. "Stop blocking the way and let me out, turd."

I stepped aside quietly, and she shoved past me.

My heart was racing. I felt sweat trickling along my neck, snaking its way down my back. I filed out of the bus.

Clara stepped past me, smiling sweetly. I didn't say anything. If I opened my mouth now, I was afraid that I would scream. Or worse yet, I would laugh again. I mustn't let him know that I'm afraid, or he'll take me too. A nausea swelled up inside me, and I stepped aside from the others to take a few deep breaths, hands on my knees.

I can't scream. I won't. I can't.

He won't take me like that.

"You know, we all think that," Clara said. "Some of us don't even make it to one. They get so terrified that he goes ahead and takes them early."

"He won't take me. I'm not afraid," I said belligerently. "The countdown will hit zero, and I still won't be afraid, and then it will all be gone, right? I'll wake up, or realize it was all a joke, and I'll laugh—NO! I won't laugh, no more laughing. But it'll all be over. I'll have passed, right?"

"I don't know," she said thoughtfully. "I don't think anyone has ever passed before. I thought I would, but then he came, and I was afraid TWO."

"Afraid too? Or two? Too or two?" I shouted at her, both sounding the same. Other children began to stare at me and point, but my voice kept getting louder. "Two or too? TWO OR TOO?"

Clara laughed. Not a hollow laugh but a good-natured one. "See you on the other side," she said, and turned to go inside the building.

Everyone else was leaving now. If I walked in, then someone would say the final countdown, and the dream would come and take me. That was it! If I stayed out here, completely alone, then there would be no one to say the words. I just had to sit out here until it had all passed.

I just had to stay away from everyone until I woke up.

I walked alone to the playground, chill breeze lifting with the warming sun. I saw the kids running about the hall through the window, but they wouldn't find me. No one would find me out here. I was conscious of how loud my footfalls were on the wood chips by the swings, so I turned and hurried to the pavement as quickly as I could.

But my heart! My heart was beating so loudly I was sure someone would hear it. Someone would find me and say the words, and it would be over. I pressed against my chest with my hands, but it wouldn't be still. I wished it would stop beating. I pounded my chest in aggravation, wondering if I could find something sharp to silence it.

I didn't think about it as killing myself then, I just wanted the damn thing to stop beating.

I sat down on the curb, my hands clawing through my hair in aggravation. Maybe my ears. Maybe I could pull my ears off, and I wouldn't hear the final count. It wouldn't work if I couldn't hear it, right? He wouldn't be able to take me then. I grabbed my right ear with both hands and pulled so hard I thought it must come off, but then I cried out from the pain and let go. Had someone heard me? Would they come?

My face felt so hot against the cool wind, my body trembling, and I began to cry.

No! Someone will hear! But the trembling built to shakes, and the shakes into convulsions, and before I knew it, I was sobbing out loud. I couldn't be alone forever. I had to make this stop. I wiped away my tears angrily and stood.

Defiantly I yelled into the wind: "ONE! Are you happy now? I want to wake up! 12, 11, 10, 9, 8, 7, 6, 5, 4, 3, 2, 1, 0! ZERO! Did you hear me?" I heard the howling of the wind getting louder behind me. This was it. He was coming, and it would all be over. "I said ZERO!" The roar behind me was deafening. At least I couldn't hear my own heart anymore.

"TWELVE!" I shouted again. "TWELVE!"

And then I began to laugh.

I felt a splitting pain in the sides of my mouth, and I laughed even harder, knowing it was coming. Blood began gushing down my face as my maw distended horribly, and the laughter kept ringing out in even bursts. Rhythmic laughter, hollow laughter, like a broken toy. You might ask me why I laughed then, and I would tell you it was because I was afraid.

You might not understand, but you will. I laughed because twelve was gone forever. I laughed because I was afraid of ELEVEN.

## Haunting Sound

I met with the most unusual patient. I would never ordinarily post online about someone's confidential details, but I'm frankly at a loss with this one. I have begun the process to submit this case study to a variety of peer-reviewed journals, but in the meantime, I am seeking alternative explanations to help him.

Since I'm telling the story, I suppose there's no use denying it—I could also use some help myself.

I earned my MD at John Hopkins School of Medicine with an additional four years residency at the Baltimore Bethusala fellowship. Next came five years at the Union Memorial Psychiatry Hospital before I opened a private practice, which I've now run for the last twelve years. I have encountered everything from a blind synesthetic who can still see visuals through sound, a schizophrenic who tried to kill herself right in my office, and an obsessive-compulsive who tightened his shoe laces so relentlessly that both feet lost circulation and had to be amputated.

I thought I had pretty much seen it all until this latest patient. I will protect his privacy by referring to him as "Mr. X."

Mr. X's symptoms were innocent enough—just a ringing in his ears which wouldn't go away. He'd visited numerous otolaryngologists, but as there was no discernible cause for the ringing, he was referred to me to decipher the psychosomatic source of the phenomenon.

During our first meeting, he didn't make eye contact with me, nor did he ever speak above a whisper. He just stared at his hands, endlessly wringing them against each other. He'd been doing it so obsessively, in fact, that his fingers were rubbed raw and bloody. I made considerable progress on the first day, and with the aid of some anti-anxiety medication, he was able to look me in the eye, although the hand wringing continued.

"Can you hear it, doctor?" he asked me during the second session.

"Of course not. The sound is not coming from a mutually accessible environment. The sound is a fabrication of your mind."

I wish now I hadn't prescribed the anti-anxiety medication, however. That I'd kept those black, lifeless eyes pointed away from me. He pulled his gaze away from the ground and looked at my face. It seemed as though the effort resembled how you or I might struggle to gaze at the hideous disfigurement of some elephant man. That's when I began to hear it too—that soft ringing, like church bells inside my skull.

"How about now? Do you hear it now, doctor?" he asked.

And that smile—that twisted grimace of satisfaction—somehow he knew I could. Regardless, admitting I heard his hallucination would only deepen his psychosis, so I naturally had to deny it. I terminated the session early and prescribed some antipsychotics, even taking some for myself. By the time I got home, the ringing was gone.

In our third session, the ringing started again as soon as he entered the room. The pitch wasn't consistent like it was before though—it rose and fell with melodic rhythm like a whole orchestra was welling up inside of me. Mr. X just stared and grinned. I don't think he even cared about getting better anymore. He was just relieved at not being the only one to hear it. He wasn't very responsive that session—all he would do was hum along to the music inside my head. I terminated early again, and he went home without complaint. As he was leaving, my secretary asked me where those strange bells were coming from.

I increased the dosage, prescribing some to myself and my secretary as well. The phantom sounds went away again, but the moment Mr. X was back in the room with me, the music would swell up. My racing heart pushed blood through my veins in rhythm with the beat. My head would throb from the intensity of those notes reverberating around my brain. I'd started wringing my hands too, just as something to distract myself from the noise.

By the end of the fourth session, the skin around my palms was wearing thin, and there was blood beginning to seep through. I hadn't even noticed how hard I was clenching them together.

As you might imagine, I referred him to another doctor. He called my office, no doubt to complain, but I told my secretary to let it go to voicemail. I didn't care, I wasn't taking him back. And if that were the end of it, then I would have simply hung up my coat and retired that day . . .

But the sound hasn't left me.

If anything, it's growing louder.

My secretary didn't come in to work today. I'm here all alone and at my wits end. I've tried every cocktail of medication I can think of, but it's only left me feeling worn out and hollow.

The sound is still there.

I didn't want to be alone, but somehow my office is the only place I felt safe. I tried to call my secretary to see how she was doing, but I never could work the phone system and must have pushed the wrong button. I just got the voicemail from Mr. X—I was so desperate for an answer, I forced myself to listen to it. Here is what he said:

"As long as the music plays, you're alright. All the world is a stage, and all of life a play upon it, and as long as the music sounds the show is still going on. I didn't come to you because I was afraid of the music. I came to you because I was afraid it would stop."

I spent the rest of the day calling patients and referring them to new specialists. I called my building manager and opted not to renew the lease on my office. I went home, with no intention of ever going to work again.

The music is getting quieter everyday now, but that's only making me more anxious. I've tried calling Mr. X again, but his cell phone is out of service. I called the doctor I referred Mr. X to, but he never showed up for his appointment. I even went so far as to visit the address listed on his medical forms, but it was just an abandoned theater.

I don't know how much longer the music will play for, or what will happen when it stops, but until then I'm just wringing my hands and waiting.

## The Masked Orgy

College is the time for experimentation. And no, I don't mean titrating sodium hydroxide with hydrochloric acid in chemistry. I mean forcing yourself to try new things—things that excite you—things that scare you—for how else are we supposed to discover who we are and what we're capable of without constantly pushing the boundaries of our reality?

At least, that's the excuse my boyfriend, Mike, came up with when he suggested a threesome.

"Sure," I replied.

"Really? Wow, okay. You're the coolest girlfriend ever—"

"What's the other guy's name?"

I knew what he meant, but I still enjoyed watching him choke on the soda he was drinking. Mike had been talking a lot about Amy since she joined our lab group in anatomy. I was jealous at first, but after checking out the competition, I had to concede his point. It was hard not watching the supple curves of her body every day as she stripped her sweater over her head to put her lab coat on. I guess I was just relieved Mike was talking to me about it instead of doing something with her behind my back.

He wanted me to broach the subject with her because "it sounded less creepy coming from a girl," so I invited her to join Mike and I for drinks after class.

"Have you ever done anything with a girl before?" I asked Amy after our third beer. Mike spluttered in his drink and excused himself to go to the bathroom, and I almost threw the rest of my glass after him. This was his idea. It wasn't fair making me do all the work. Luckily, there wasn't much work that needed doing.

"Not yet," she replied, a smile playing around the corner of her lips.

Two hours later, all of us were in my room trying to figure out how one person fits in a dorm-room bed, let alone three.

It was exciting for me, and I can only imagine how many flashing lights and alarms were blaring inside Mike's head, so I guess it was understandable that he spent most of the time focused on Amy. Besides, Mike and I were already comfortable with each other, so it was really just her that he felt the need to impress. Afterward he said it wasn't the case, but I still remember spending way too long hanging out and watching them go at it. I even left to use the bathroom at one point without either of them noticing I was gone.

I didn't want to get mad. I had agreed to this after-all, and I hated the idea of being one of those infamous girlfriends who said one thing and did another. I just wanted to get even. It didn't help that he started acting cocky afterward as though the experience made him a big man or something. He even started pointing out particularly geeky looking freshman and saying things like "I bet he's never even been with one, let alone two."

Although asking for another guy started out as a joke, I started pushing for it more seriously. I wanted him to feel what it was like to be jealous. I wanted him to appreciate what I had done for him, and realize I was the only one of us who had the power to make it happen again. And yeah, if I'm being honest, maybe I even wanted to humiliate him a little, so he'd go back to regular old Mike and drop this macho facade.

We started having fights about it, and the more he said no, the more one-sided our relationship seemed. I told Amy I thought I was going to have to dump him (she and I still hung out sometimes, although I never invited Mike when we did). I told her it wasn't her fault, but she still felt guilty about getting between us (literally). That's why she came up with a solution:

"I know a place where they do it in a group. You'll get your kinks out, he'll have someone of his own to have fun with, and everyone is wearing a mask, so nobody gets hurt."

Big rubber animal masks. Didn't it get hot in there? I felt more than a little exposed wearing my stupid Mardi Gras mask I picked up at the dollar store on the way here. Everyone else's mask was hyper-realistic and covered their entire head, but they told me not to worry about it and just relax. Mike and I were just "initiates" on a trial run, anyway. If we decided this was our thing, and we respected all of their rules and members, then they'd give us a full mask next time.

At first, I stuck pretty close to Mike, and we just fooled around with each other and watched. There was about a dozen people in total, and the teeming mass of bodies was pretty damn intimidating to approach. Several of them had covered their bodies in some kind of paint or oil, and they churned and writhed against each other with an almost animalistic intensity. Everywhere I looked, breasts were heaving, indiscriminate hands clutched and pulled on skin, and bodies lunged hungrily at one another as though nourished by their carnal lust.

I was about to call it quits and leave when a man in a panther-mask pulled away from the others to approach me. His body was chiseled and slick with paint. Mike and I exchanged glances. Isn't this what I wanted? I pointed him in the direction of a leopard-mask with fiery red hair spilling out beneath it. He hesitated, so I gave him a little shove. If nothing else, this would be a shared experience we could laugh and bond over, and maybe we'd both be stronger for it.

I still shuddered a bit when the panther-man put his hand on my shoulders from behind, but his probing fingers expertly massaged down my back and I felt myself melt into his touch.

Mike left shortly after that. We'd only been there about a half-hour, and I was really (really) starting to enjoy myself, when I saw Mike staring at me and the panther-man. Good, let him see! But then he just turned around and walked away, and my satisfaction quickly drained. I followed him, and we had another fight in the hallway while we were both still naked. He said he couldn't even look at me again after seeing me like that. Somehow the fact that he was more hurt and sensitive than me proved that he cared more about me than I did him, so it was over. He got dressed and left, and I just stood there overflowing with frustration.

I felt massaging hands caressing my shoulders again, and I immediately felt the tension flowing out through them. If I was looking for a rebound to get past

Mike, then I couldn't think of a more immersive, therapeutic one than this. I allowed the panther-man to lead me back into the room. The lights had dimmed since I was gone, but a lot of the paint people wore was glowing in the dark. More hands grabbed me, and I allowed myself to be swallowed up in the psychedelic dance of skin on skin, swirling colors, and the growing moan which encompassed me.

As the night went on, the lights continued to slowly dim. The colors grew brighter, and the intensity of the sound and insistence of the sensation mounted into a crescendo of pleasure. I spent most of my time with the panther-man, although I allowed myself to be passed from one person to the next without complaint. There was no embarrassment, no judgement, no jealousy, only the acceptance and triumph of our shared celebration of life.

I was back with the panther-man now, body flooded with gentle warmth and satisfaction. His hands were so powerful yet gentle, and his low moans resonated with my own as though we were a single being harmonized with itself.

The thought of leaving here and never knowing who he was—perhaps never even meeting him again—was more agonizing than I could have imagined. I felt an overpowering desire to look at the man pressed against me—just for a second—just long enough to recognize him if we met again. I slid my hands up his neck and tenderly slipped the mask further up his face…

But it wouldn't come off. I pulled harder, and felt the strain of living fur beneath my fingers. He grunted in pain—or was that a snarl?—and I pushed him off me. Suddenly every sound came to its height, and the mounting carnal cacophony enveloping me became tainted with other sounds.

Were those moans? Or was someone starting to howl? And then a yelping joined in.

I thought it was a joke at first, but one by one the people began to bray, bark, hiss, or whatever other sound was appropriate to the mask they wore. The panther-man knelt upon the ground and I saw his muscles coil as though preparing to spring. It was so dark that I could only see the parts of him covered in paint. From a few steps away, he looked more like an abstract painting than a man.

I ran toward the door, but tripped over a dark form along the way. A multitude of hands clung onto me in the shadows, and then a paw with razor-sharp claws tore the skin on my outer thigh. I screamed and pushed onward, but the grips readily released me as though shocked I wasn't appreciating their touch. I made it to the wall, but I couldn't find the door. The panther-man crawled toward me on all fours. Some glowing paint was on his skin, but more of it was matted in patches of thick black hair on his body.

I leaped along the wall looking for the door, ramming against another body and fell to the ground. The half-panther was almost on top of me now, but I couldn't bear to look at him. I closed my eyes and screamed for all I was worth.

"Are you okay? What are you doing?"

I opened my eyes. The lights were on. Everyone was staring at me.

The panther-man with his chiseled human body was standing over me. He pulled on his furry ear, and I almost screamed again before seeing the rubber mask slide easily off. He was a handsome man, about thirty, with strong cheek bones and deep concerned eyes.

I ran out the door and dressed in the hallway. The panther-man started to follow me.

"Stop her! She's seen too much!" he shouted, his voice a harsh guttural snarl completely unlike the one he used a moment before.

A woman in a sheep's mask held him back. "Let her go. She'll come back when she's ready." The voice sounded familiar. Was that Amy? I didn't stay long enough to find out. As soon as my clothes were even halfway on, I ran.

I'm not going back. I can't go back. But maybe I'll have to, because I still need answers.

I missed my period the next month, but I tried not to think back to that night. I was on the pill, and they all had protection. Just to be safe, I got a pregnancy test, but it came up negative.

I kept testing every month after that. Still nothing. But all the symptoms were beginning to show: I'm swelling up, I'm tired all the time, and nauseous in the mornings. I got an ultrasound, but the doctor said he didn't see anything. It's just like a great, empty pit is growing inside of me. I got a few other scans, but nothing came up and the doctor just thinks it is a hysterical-pregnancy which will pass on its own.

I didn't know how to tell him I thought it was something else. Just like I didn't know how to explain the claw marks on my outer thigh.

I want to forget it ever happened, but it's hard when I keep feeling something scratching me from the inside.

## Breaking and Entering for Dummies

I'm going to tell you a few things about me.

When I was a kid, I lost in the finals of a state tennis championship because I told the truth about a line call when I didn't have to. I once climbed a tree to get somebody's cat down, then stayed up there the rest of the night just because it was so peaceful. My favorite food is strawberries and cream, only I don't tell the other guys because they'd give me shit for it.

I joined the 18th Street gang when I was in the sixth grade.

It's important what order I tell you these things, because the moment someone notices my blue and black bandanna, they think they already know everything about me.

I'm a sophomore in high-school now, and last night was my first break-in.

"Spike," an old-school Mexican Mafia type of guy, was there to show me the ropes. He taught me how to map out the regular patrol routes of officers, and how to hide in a concrete drainpipe to avoid being seen.

I'd never stolen anything bigger than a candy bar before. I was scared as hell, but I knew Spike was tight with everybody and would tell them how I did. This was my first real chance to let everyone decide what I was made of—I wasn't going to screw it up.

"Let's not do this one, it has an alarm system." It was a middle-class suburban home with a white-picket fence; nothing about it screamed that it was a good target to me.

"Doesn't matter when they let you in," Spike said, grinning.

Oh, and just because I'm in a gang doesn't mean I understand gold teeth. They're disgusting.

"But someone's here. There's a light on up there!" I protested. "Let's keep looking." Maybe if we didn't find a good target tonight, we could just go back and play pool and try again another night.

I'd be ready another night.

"How are they gonna open the door if they ain't home? Fuck's sake," he said. Spike walked around the house and turned the garden hose on full blast. He found two more taps along the back of the house and turned those on too.

He waited a few minutes for a lake to start forming in the yard before ringing the doorbell. I wanted to stop him, but I was frozen. My heart beat faster with each light that turned on as the resident approached their front door.

"Who is it?" someone yelled from inside.

"Excuse me, sir," Spike shouted. "I noticed one of your pipes burst. Just thought you should know."

The door opened. An old man—at least 80—stood there in his bathrobe. I never want to get that old where my eyes shrink down to little pin-pricks and my skin hangs in loose folds like that.

Spike gave me a grotesque wink.

"It did? Oh God," the old man said.

"Yeah, look at all that water," Spike said, motioning towards the backyard. "I was just walking on the sidewalk with my kid." He wrapped his arm around my shoulder, and I fought the urge to pull away from his sticky-sweet odor of dried sweat.

"Yo," I said, stupidly giving a little wave.

"We found which one it was, here come take a look." Spike didn't even wait for a reply and started walking. I wonder how many times he's done this before.

The old man pulled his bathrobe tighter and followed Spike around the side of the house...

I wanted to warn him. To tell him to run—to hide and lock the door. I couldn't turn my back on my own though. If this was going to happen anyway, I might as well be the one to return with some glory. The moment the old man passed me by, I picked up a rock from his yard and smashed it straight into his temple. He crumpled to the ground like a bag of dirt.

Gold teeth flashed. "Nice one kid. Now let's drag him inside so we can take our time with the place."

I propped the old man up against the wall in the living room. He was still breathing, but there was a lot of blood coming from his head. I thought about bandaging him up, but I didn't know if that would seem like a sign of weakness. I just wanted to get in and get out as fast as I could.

Then we heard the barking.

"Shit, there's a dog," Spike grunted.

The sound was coming from behind a closed door down a few concrete steps—it probably led to the basement.

"It can't get at us," I said. "Let's ignore it."

"Nah, too much noise. Quick, go deal with it."

"Deal with it?"

Spike didn't say a word at first. There was a flash of gold, and then he was holding out a knife—"Make it quick. You're gonna be a man after tonight."

I gripped the knife in my hand so hard my knuckles turned white. I turned away from Spike so he wouldn't see me shaking.

"I'm gonna go check upstairs for a safe or somethin," Spike said. "Or cash under the mattress. These old shits think that's safer than a bank sometimes. That thing better be quiet by the time I get up there."

I wasn't worried about it being a big dog. An old guy like this probably had a poodle or something, but hurting any animal has always been off-limits for me. Being loyal to my colors over my own instinct . . . There wasn't any going back from this. I hated myself for opening the door.

I was tense and ready for it to spring at me. I even slashed the air with the knife a couple of times until I found the light switch. I didn't see anything but a set of stairs though, so I started to walk down to find the miserable creature.

"Why is it still barking?" I heard from upstairs.

"I don't—" What I was saying died in my throat. I was staring face to face with a grown man, probably around fifty years old, stripped down to his underwear, and shackled to the wall with iron clasps around his wrists and ankles. His facial hair was thick and greasy; matted in with the long unkempt black hair spilling from his head.

The man barked at me like an animal, pulling against the metal restraints as he tried to dive at me. He snapped his jaw, froth trickling into his beard. Then there was a flash of recognition in his eyes, and he pressed himself back against the wall. His mouth contorted awkwardly, almost as though he was trying to say something.

"Don't make me come down there and do it for you," Spike said. His voice was closer now, like he was coming back downstairs.

I dropped the knife and ran. I don't know what the hell was going on. And I didn't care what was going to happen to me. I could not be in that room.

Spike was waiting for me outside the basement. "What's going on? Did you do it?"

I just kept running. Straight out the door.

I ran the three miles back to my house without even stopping. Spike followed me out—I don't think he ever saw the thing. He must have told the other guys though, because I got an 18 second beating for what happened.

I took it like a man.

I didn't tell anyone what I saw, or what I heard the thing say as I was leaving: "*Kill . . . me . . .*"

Spike was waiting for me when I got off the bus today. He wrapped his arm around my shoulders and led me away from the other kids. I flinched when he touched me.

"Last night—"

"I'm sorry. I messed up. It's my fault," I interrupted. I'd already taken the beating. What more could happen?

"I get it, first time is scary. But facing that fear, that's what makes a man out of you," he said. "I checked up on the house, and there wasn't any police report or anything. The old guy was dead, but nobody's found him yet."

I swallowed hard.

"Did you look in the basement?" I asked.

"Nah, I didn't stay, but the two of us are going back tonight. We're gonna finish the job."

How could I tell him? It would just sound like a lame-ass excuse. He'd just think I was scared, and I'd get beaten again. So, I just nodded.

There wasn't any way out of this for me. I've already killed a man, so what's so much worse about killing a beast?

## The Face on my Bedroom Wall

The line bordering the other side of sanity is only the width of a shadow. All you have to do is move to a different angle to watch it disappear.

I am a man of particular taste. My alarm is set at 6:28 a.m., because 6:30 doesn't give me enough time to massage the salt into my morning egg. I carry with me a list of my favorite words and check them off throughout the day to avoid redundancies. And you will never catch me throwing my clothes in a pile at the day's end. I find it uncomfortable leaving undressed mannequins in my room.

I'd oblige you not to picture some tormented scene—it's really quite a civilized way to store your outfits. I even made them plastic masks by boiling down some old toys and shaping them with a scalpel, so they look perfectly natural there.

Things must be just so. If they are not so, then I am not so.

My wristwatch broke once, and I didn't leave work until 3 in the morning. I physically hurt trying to tear myself away while it only read 4:52 p.m. I am telling you this because I want you to understand how orderly my routine is, and how shocked I was to see something so egregiously (check off) out of place.

**Three weeks ago...**

I walked into my apartment and placed my hat upon the garden gnome which stood sentry at my front door. I drank a glass of water which I had left on the kitchen counter that morning to re-hydrate me from my walk home, since I trust the public transit as much as a toddler with a gun. Then to my bedroom, where I found...

Two faces mounted on the wall astride my bed: that of the usual bus driver I see in the neighborhood, and another of Elaine who lived next door. The bus driver displayed a crafty grin, while Elaine was transfixed with the most preposterous (check off) sneer I had ever seen in my life. She was an angel in an apron, benevolent to the bone—I've never seen her wear such a dreadful expression in all my time with her.

"Bet you feel silly now," the face of the bus driver said.

"I beg your pardon?" I was shocked, but not so shocked as to forget my manners.

"Silly for not trusting the bus. How does it feel knowing I got in safe and she didn't?"

"What happened to you, Elaine?"

Her twisted sneer remained static, her dead, plastic eyes completely devoid of life.

I touched her face, and then the face of the bus driver—both were made of plastic, much like those on my mannequins. Peculiar to say the least, considering I never made faces to resemble either of those people. I must say I rather liked them there though. Now that they were pointed at the mannequins, the faces could keep each other company while I was gone.

**Two weeks ago:**

Elaine is dead. I believe that's the most important fact to address first. She struck her head on a concrete pillar after tumbling down nearly two flights of stairs. I never saw her, but the landlady was kind enough to show me pictures she snapped with her cell phone. She shows me all the strangest things—I suppose she doesn't think I judge her because of my own eccentric tastes. She's wrong, but I won't say it to her face.

Elaine's grotesque sneer was identical to the mask above my bed. I believe that to be the second most important fact. I didn't volunteer this information to

# Sleepless Nights

anyone at the time, but I am disclosing it to you now because I find it easier to trust people when I am not looking them in the eye.

There is another mask above my bed; the smiling face of my landlady. I believe I understand why she is smiling, because the bus driver now looks absolutely terrified.

"What are you so scared of?" I asked him, but now his expression was fixed.

"You'll see," the landlady said to me, grinning from ear to ear.

**One week ago:**

Her comment was germane (check off) to the news the following week. The bus was clipped by a drunk driver and sent rolling down a hillside. Two casualties, one of which was the driver himself. I can only imagine how horrendous it would be to roll down the hill amidst a blender of falling bodies and flailing limbs. Of course, I don't have to imagine how they reacted to the situation, because I could see it plainly on the driver's face mounted on my bedroom wall.

**Today:**

And now, it is with deep trepidation that I must report my latest discovery. My own face has been added to the wall, and while the landlady's mask doesn't seem the least perturbed, my own expression surpasses the most ghastly countenance of dread your darkest imagination might conjure.

I tried to shift my anguished face, but the expression was hard set and immovable. I tried heating it in the oven to make it malleable, but two hours at 500 degrees didn't make the slightest indentation. All it did was make the landlady giggle from above my bed.

"You can't change it. You're done for."

"You'll see," I replied.

I went to knock upon the landlady's door. It seemed like a fairly straightforward fix. Once her real face matched the mask of terror that I saw in my own, then my face would be able to smile again.

She opened the door and invited me in. I let her serve me tea and introduce both of her cats in a sing-song voice as though they were the ones talking.

And they call me the crazy one…

I considered waiting for her back to be turned, but I had to make sure the expression really captured her impending disaster. It wasn't as easy or as pretty this way, but I knew the second I lay the knife upon the coffee table that it would pay for its trouble. I cut her in eight places—an even number so she could rest in peace—saving the killing blow until the moment her face was the perfect contortion of distress. It seemed like an awful mess to leave for the cats, but I heard they take care of that sort of thing in time.

When I return home, I found her face still on my wall. And it's still smiling. The police arrived faster than I thought they would. That's the problem with apartments—thin walls. Always some nosy neighbor poking into something that isn't their business.

I supposed I should have hid the body. It's not a matter of legal repercussions —they questioned me, but didn't have any evidence in my direction— it's just that when they found the body, it was doubtlessly sent to a funeral home. There they would modify the face into a more comfortable sight for her open casket (which I can't imagine why a woman of her appearance would have requested before her demise).

Her body was out of my hands now, and her face was still smiling. My mask, however, remained locked in its grizzly scream. I don't know how long I have, but it seems like Elaine and the driver both terminated within a few days of their masks appearing. I had to act fast.

I tried to make another plastic mask to match my own, but my damn hands kept shaking. That's what happens when you mess up your routine—things begin to fall apart. I couldn't get even a passable likeness of myself.

The only remaining option—one I had considered, but pushed to the back of my brain as a last resort—now stood stark and alone before me. I took the plastic mask of my face and tossed it in the rubbish bin.

Next, a few shots of gin to numb the pain—then a deep breath.

And in goes the knife.

Skin doesn't peel back from a face nearly as cleanly as I expected. I kept getting the depth wrong—either too shallow, and only nicking myself, or too deep and cutting the underlying muscle. It took nearly three hours before I had removed my entire face and was able to pin the bloody mess to my bedroom wall.

At least skin is so much easier to adjust than plastic. In no time, it—I—was smiling. I looked over to the landlady's face, and my heart beamed with satisfaction to see her twisted terror finally appearing.

One lived while the other dies.

One comedy while the other tragedy.

In the end, it is the actor who decides which to wear.

## The Wall Between us

Let me tell you about my neighbor, Dave. He built up his own mobile plumbing service with just his van and scavenged parts, and works like the devil trying to compete against the big guys who service the same area. He's married to a sweet older woman named Jasmine who never had a family of her own, but she finally has one with him. He has two children: one able-bodied helper, and one who will be stuck in a wheelchair for life. He loves them both the same.

Oh, and one more thing about Dave. He voted for Trump. He didn't make a big deal out of it—he didn't even intend to tell me. I just heard it slip one day while I was bringing the trash out to the street.

"He's going to make America great again, you watch my words. Four—maybe eight years from now, the sun is going to rise on a brand new country."

He was chatting with the mailman at the end of his driveway. And it didn't just stick me the wrong way because I'm Mexican and the president is a racist ingrown toenail in a suit. I didn't know Dave that well—we always got along fine, but never really spent time together. Just knowing he believed the hateful rhetoric spewing from that fear-mongering egoist changed my whole conception of him though.

We caught each other's eye, and he looked away, like he was embarrassed. Good—he should be. But then he looked back and grinned.

"You voted for him, didn't you, Eddy?" he said to me.

"Nah, I was going to, but something got in the way."

"What's that?" he asked. "'Cause I know you're a solid guy who couldn't have been fooled by that lady harpy."

"Just my conscience."

After that, we stopped greeting each other when we passed on the street. It wasn't anything hostile—not yet. We just nodded and looked away.

I couldn't imagine having any common grounds with someone with such a perverted ideology, but I didn't want to have a confrontation about it.

He must have felt the same way and said something about it to his kids. One of them—the tall one with the baggy hoodie, I forget his name—started spray painting on his side of the brick wall between our property lines. I waited until he was gone to walk around and see what it said:

*Build a wall, Kill 'em all.*

Well shit. I guess I shouldn't have been so offended by that. He didn't even make it up—it was just some stupid campaign sign that was held at some Trump rallies. I could feel the blood boiling in my veins though. Now anyone who drove by my house would see that painted right beside my front door. They'd probably think the whole neighborhood supported that cat-vomit with a hairball on top.

I didn't even know what I was planning to say when I knocked on Dave's door. I just wanted to vent some steam. Dave opened the door, and I pointed a finger at the wall.

"Yeah?" he said. He stepped out to get a better look. Then he chuckled. "Well, will you look at that."

"You gotta have a word with your kids, man. I don't want that hate speech on my wall."

"Your wall? What, did he mark your side, too?" Dave walked up to the wall to peer over.

"No, but it's right next to my house—"

"Oh, so it's not on your property. Sounds like you wouldn't even have noticed if we had a bigger wall."

After that, we didn't even nod at each other. He sometimes gave me a little smirk, and I'd just turn away from him. I don't care if it was his property, I couldn't understand how he—a grown-ass man—could condone that kind of hate.

I stopped saying 'hello' to his wife too. She would smile and wave while watering her rose bushes, and I'd just pretend I didn't notice. The message was still on their wall—she must have known about it. If she wasn't painting over it, then that was the same thing as supporting it.

That's when my kid started getting picked on in school. Rob wouldn't tell me who did it, but I knew it was those bastards next door. I saw the look Rob gave them when they all left the bus together: like prey sizing up a predator. The tall kid in the hoodie smirked—the same idiotic sneer his father had.

I couldn't pick a fight with Dave until Rob actually pointed a finger. I'm always trying to get that kid to stand up for himself, but he hates fighting. It would just be my word against Dave's. But I still wanted to send him a signal that said I knew what was going on, and that I wasn't going to stand for it.

I waited until night to sneak over to his yard. All the lights were off, and I didn't even use a flashlight, so I know nobody saw me. I took a pair of garden clippers and chopped the heads off every rose in front of his house. As an afterthought, I stuck the clippers in the ground and wrote:

*Hate begets hate.*

Yeah, I know it was childish, but you know what? I felt damn good about it. It serves that bitch right for raising such hateful kids.

And I know I was being hateful too, but that was the point, wasn't it? To show them their actions had repercussions. They wouldn't have any proof, but they'd know it was me and that when it came to my kid, I wasn't playing around.

Maybe instead I should have written 'hate begets hate, begets hate begets, hate…' because it didn't end there like I was hoping. This time it was the side of my house that was spray painted:

*Go back to Mexico.*

I was livid. They were all a bunch of racist pricks. My son was being bullied worse than ever, my mail was being ripped up and thrown around the street, and my trash was scattered back into my yard.

This had to an end.

I waited on Dave's driveway for him to get home. He just sat in his van staring at me, so I opened the door for him.

"What the hell are you doing in my driveway?" he snapped.

"Go ahead. Say it. Say what you really mean," I said.

"What are you talking about?"

"Ask me what I'm doing in your country. That's what you're thinking, isn't it? That you belong here, and I don't?"

"Look man, I never said that."

## Sleepless Nights

"Your kids did, and you let them. Your president did, and you voted for him. Why don't you grow the balls to finally say it too?"

He opened his mouth, then looked over my shoulder and shut it. I looked around. Rob was standing there. Dave's other kid—the one in the wheelchair—was watching too. I could see Jasmine peaking out from behind their kitchen curtains.

Dave took a deep breath. "Get inside, all of you!"

They did. We both watched the kid in the wheelchair until he was all the way inside, then we turned on each other again.

"Well? Are you going to say it to my face now?" I demanded.

Dave shook his head and let out a long sigh. He looked as tired as I've ever seen him. "Look man, I would if that's what I believed, but I don't. I just want a better life for my family. I'm sorry if my kids have been misbehaving. I'm out working all the time, and they're acting out for attention. I promise it won't happen again."

My fire was dying down. What could I say to that? I know Dave—hell, I've known him a long time. He never did a thing I didn't respect before this political bullshit came up. I wanted to apologize too, but it felt so good for one of those Trump boys to finally admit they were wrong. I told myself I would bring him a bottle of wine or something tomorrow, and just accept this victory right now.

Back inside my house, Rob was waiting for me right inside the door. "Did you win, Dad?"

"Yeah, Rob. I won alright. See what did I tell you? When you know you're in the right, you can't be afraid to stand up for yourself. You gotta fight fire with fire."

"Okay Dad. I'll remember that."

It was cold outside. The wind always picked up in the early morning. I've been standing out here for an hour waiting for the firefighters to finally finish spraying down Dave's house. The kid in the wheelchair (Alex—I finally learned his name) didn't make it out. They wanted to go back in for him, but the firefighters wouldn't let them. They swept the house, but by the time they found him, he had suffocated in the smoke.

They say it started around 1 a.m. last night. Kerosene soaked rags were stuffed into the air vents, so it wasn't an accident. The firefighters were able to contain the blaze before it got over the wall between us, and it was amazing to see how different the two sides looked now. The charred beams jutted accusingly into the sky, and the ground was filthy with ash and debris.

His side of the wall was blackened by the fire, but I could still faintly make out the slogan: *Build a wall, Kill 'em all.*

The two sides of the wall really weren't so different before the fire. Now it was night and day.

"That's what you wanted, isn't it, Dad? You wanted to fight back."

"Go inside, Rob. It's too cold out here. We'll talk about it later."

*Hate begets hate begets…*

I think I'll need to bring Dave something a little stronger than wine.

## Burning Desire

I'm writing this as a confession. I can't explain how it happened, but I know it's my fault. It started with me hurting myself. And it's not like I wanted attention or anything . . . Okay, well as long as I'm being honest, I wouldn't mind someone noticing me, but that isn't why I burned myself. And it definitely isn't why I killed myself, but I'm getting ahead now.

I was in class one day when someone set a fire in the chemistry lab. Probably Jason—that idiot was always using the bunsen burners to melt pens and glue and whatever he could get his hands on. The fire alarmed started up though, and the whole high-school was paraded out into the parking lot like we practiced during drills. Everyone was laughing and screaming, and I'd just gotten out of a math test I wasn't ready for, so I didn't mind.

While we were standing in the parking lot, I overheard Lisa say that Sammy, the kid in the wheelchair, got stuck on the elevator. It's not hard to overhear things since I hang on her every word. You would too if that blonde goddess was standing next to you wearing a punk-plaid skirt and a sweater almost tight enough to see through . . . What was I saying? Oh right, well rumor had it that another kid went back into the school to get Sammy out. No one knew who it was, but they were already talking about him like he was a hero.

That's when I had an idea. I could just burn the edges of my clothes a bit, and then Lisa and all the other kids would think I was the one who went back in for Sammy. I could be the hero. And even if the real hero DID come forward . . . Well I had the burns, and he didn't, so who were people going to believe?

I kept my head low and stayed away from anyone who might recognize me—which wasn't very hard since I didn't have a lot of friends. Or any, I guess. I was new, and it would take time, I just hadn't expected it to take more than a semester for anyone to recognize me. But that's okay, because after today, I was going to be the hero.

When the bell rang for us to go back inside; I darted straight to the bathroom. There's a place under the sink where some seniors hide a box with cigarettes and lighters. I pulled the box out, found a nice black zippo lighter with a skull on it, and here goes—the fire springs to life.

Well turns out polo shirts don't light up as easily as I was expecting. I blackened a few hairs, but this wasn't nearly enough for people to think I walked through a fire. I used a pen to open the zippo at the bottom and poured all the lighter fluid onto my shirt. My heart was pounding—I was excited. I couldn't wait to come back to class and watch Lisa's face sparkle with awe. I didn't even take the shirt off—I wanted a few burns. Enough to show how tough I was.

Just as I was about to light the fluid, my mind played a funny trick on me. It looked like the skull on the lighter was smiling. I didn't remember it doing that before. Too late now—the fire was already dancing over my shirt. It barely even felt warm. I watched myself in the mirror as the fire spread from shoulder to shoulder. My buttons began to heat up and stung a bit, but the shirt was smoldering nicely. I ran the faucet and splashed the water on me. That'll be enough.

But the fire drank the water as though nourished by it, spitting boiling vapor into the air. The heat was intense now. I tried to rip the shirt off, but the polyester was melting to my skin. The metal buttons seared into my flesh. I couldn't stop screaming. I didn't want anyone to see me like this, but it was like I heard someone else scream through me without even asking my permission first.

I dropped on the ground and began to roll, but the fire just continued to spread over my entire body. It ran up my arms, and I could actually see the flesh melting from my finger bones. The pain was like nothing you can imagine. My whole body was being pierced with red hot knives. Then it started to go black—thank God. I'll fall unconscious and someone will find me. It'll be over. But no, only half my vision was gone. I looked into the mirror and watched my left eyeball melting down my face. It would have gone down my cheek if there was any cheek left, but it simply dripped through the hole in my skin, straight into my mouth. I gagged. How was I still conscious?

The pain wasn't letting up, but I forced myself to watch my reflection. I'd done this to myself. Somehow, I deserved it. My jaw bone was completely exposed now, and it was starting to crack from the heat. There's no way a zippo lighter could have done this. I grabbed the little black box, but the skull had vanished.

WHOOOSH. A toilet flushing. Was someone in here the whole time?

I tried to turn my head, but my spine was too weak to support me and started collapsing in on itself. I crumpled to the floor and watched as a bathroom stall opened.

What. The. Hell?

Was this it?

Am I dead now?

There's no reason—no way—I could really be seeing myself walk out of the bathroom stall. The other me, wearing my shirt and pants, completely unsinged by fire, walked over to the sink beside me. He calmly washed his hands in the sink, not even glancing down at me writhing on the floor.

I tried to speak—to scream—anything, but only a dry gurgle escaped my throat. That's when the other me turned and smiled, and I could have sworn it was the same boney-white smile the skull on the lighter wore.

"Your turn on the inside," it said, or I guess I said that, because it looked a lot more like me than I did.

Then everything went black, only I could still feel every inch of my burning body and hear the wet plop of my skin sliding down my bones onto the floor. I heard footsteps as it—as I—left the room.

I must be inside the lighter now, waiting for the next person to let me out. But I can still feel my flesh burning, so I pray to God it won't be long.

## The Psychopath in my House

There's a psychopath in my house.

No, he didn't break in. He sleeps in the same room as me. It's not my brother's fault; this is just who he is.

If it's anyone's fault, it's my parents. My mom left when I was six and my little brother was four. She never wanted us, or at least that's what my dad said, because I don't remember her very well.

Dad also said she used to be a perfect student with big dreams, then she got knocked up and had to drop out of college to take care of us. He reminds us all the time that it was our fault she left, and how happy he was before we were born.

That's the nice version of what he said, anyway. Lots of stuff about her being an ungrateful slut who will burn in Hell, but I don't think of her that way. If I was married to someone like my dad, I would have run away too.

My dad needed "medicine" to cope with her leaving. Every time he took it, he would be gone for a few days. It would be just me and my little brother in the house, and I took care of him the best I could. Dad wouldn't usually leave us with any money, but I got pretty good at hiding things under my dress at the grocery store.

I thought things would change when I was 12 and found a paper bag with 1,000 dollars in our backyard. I thought Mom had sent it—that she'd heard about how hard things were and mailed us some money.

I could usually find food when I needed it badly enough, so I didn't want to waste it on things like that. My brother's 10th birthday was coming up, and that seemed like a big deal. I hired a van and brought him and seven kids from his class to spend the whole day at Sea World.

It was so much fun I thought about never going back. My brother didn't want to run away though, and I couldn't leave him. Besides, the van driver was keeping an eye on us and said he had to bring us home or he might get fired.

We should have run away though. The money hadn't come from Mom—she'd forgotten about us. That's when I found out Dad's "medicine" was meth, and that he'd been selling some to his friends when he dropped the money by mistake. I tried to tell him that it was my fault, but since it got spent on my brother's birthday, he got the worst of it.

My brother didn't walk again for two years after that. He needed even more help now that he was in a wheelchair. There were more bills that weren't being paid—the electricity, the gas, even the rent sometimes. I had to be out a lot trying to find money, sometimes for days at a time when I was staking out a house to steal from.

I couldn't leave my brother alone too long though. My dad would just ignore him, and if I didn't check in at least twice a day, then I'd find my brother sitting in his own piss and shit. I think he could have made it to the toilet by himself if he really tried, but he just gave up caring about everything.

There is one thing my brother started doing to pass the time, although this I wish he hadn't. I noticed his growing collection of small animal skulls for a while, but I assumed they were just plastic until I saw how he was catching them.

I watched him put bird seed in a 2L soda bottle with the opening cut wider. Once a squirrel crawled in, he would pull a string which slid the bottle down to cover the opening with a piece of cardboard. It would struggle frantically to get out, but when it was near the opening, its own weight would hold the bottle into place against the board.

I would have congratulated him on his contraption, except for what happened next. He picked up the bottle—cardboard still covering the opening—and slipped a couple razor blades inside. Then he shook the whole thing until it looked like the inside of a blender, the squirrel screaming the whole time.

I took it away from him, but my brother just kept building little things like that. It wasn't just squirrels either—mice, small birds, even a raccoon once. After he'd killed them, he'd bite the head straight off and then spit it into a bowl of water to clean the organic matter off the skull.

"Please stop. God didn't make those animals just so you could torture them," I said to him.

"Then why did he make it so much fun?"

It's not just animals anymore. I found a big cardboard box out on the sidewalk near the bus-stop. Inside was a bag of M&Ms, a couple comic books, and his old Gameboy Color. There was a rope tied to little hooks inside the box which led toward my house.

If someone were to pull that rope, the box would close and the whole thing would be dragged down the sidewalk. I don't think he'd be strong enough to pull anyone bigger than a six-year-old, but the school bus stopped here.

I ripped the box into pieces and ran to confront him. I found him sitting on his bed—he was out of the wheelchair now—waiting with a knife in his hands.

"What the Hell are you trying to do?"

"Set a trap."

"It's not going to work."

"Don't worry." He shrugged. "It'll work."

"I destroyed it. Why are you trying to trap some kid?"

"I'm not. I'm trying to trap you."

That's when I noticed that the TV was suspended with ropes above me. He cut the cord, and it landed right on top of my head.

He must have counted on that knocking me out because he was already coming at me with the knife. I was dizzy, but I managed to scramble out of the way and slam the door in his face.

After that, I was too scared to go back inside the house. I called Child Protective Services and reported the meth deals Dad was doing in the home. I didn't mention what my brother had been doing, because I thought once he was out of here, he'd have a chance at a fresh start. I didn't want his life to be over before it had even begun.

We were both put into separate foster homes, and it's been two years since I've heard anything from him . . . That was until last night.

My adoptive parents—wonderful Asian couple who couldn't have kids of their own—sat down with me at the kitchen table. They told me they had some good news: they were going to adopt my brother as well.

I guess the family that took him in suffered an unfortunate accident. They didn't tell me what happened, but by the look they gave each other, it must have been gruesome.

I hope he's changed. Telling people what he did will stop him from being adopted and ruin his life forever. I can't say anything until I've seen him again.

If he hasn't changed though…

Well, that's why I'm writing this. If he hasn't changed, then at least someone will know what happened, and have a shot at stopping it from happening again.

## How to Start Your own Cult

Let me preface this by stating I am a firm atheist. There is no life after death, although I will go to great lengths extolling its beauty to my subjects. We do not grow older because the Reaper is always siphoning our life energy. I was not born from a dying star, and I am no prophet of the Divine Cosmic Order.

I am a nihilist—I do not believe in anything. And as much as I do not believe in the supernatural, I believe even less in mankind and their ability to govern their own lives.

Do you really need proof of that? Fanatic mobs begging for their religious oppression to be protected by the government, junkies in the street surrendering their will to anything they can boil into their veins, narcissistic idiots running the country—you get the idea.

The church-states, the cartels, the two-faced corporations—none of them will hesitate to manipulate the population for their own selfish purposes. The vast majority of people will always be susceptible to being manipulated, because it is so much safer and easier to be told what to think than to think for yourself.

My reasoning dictates:

People will always be susceptible to manipulation. If you aren't manipulating them, then someone else will.

The manipulator will always profit at the expense of the people. That is the purpose for their influence.

The only way to protect people from a selfish manipulator is to become a benevolent manipulator yourself.

For these reasons, in my senior year of college, I decided to start my own cult. Here is how it is done:

*Step One: Identify your targets.*

People will not run to you unless they are already running away from something else. Now, where could I find the most fearful students?

I formed three support clubs and put up fliers around campus. One for the socially anxious, one for those needing financial assistance, and a third for victims of sexual assault.

*Step Two: Amplify their fear.*

Ever wonder why priests scream about Hell while politicians rant about terrorists and economic collapse? There is nothing like fear to get someone's attention. You want them begging you to save them.

To the socially anxious, I forced them to give speeches. I asked them embarrassing questions, put them in awkward situations, and generally ridiculed them, all in the guise of helping them gain confidence.

To the financially stressed, I gave lectures about how student loans haunt people for the rest of their life. I told them how the job market is over-saturated with college degrees, and how slim their chance of employment was. I told horror stories about homeless drug addicts who graduated college but couldn't make anything of their lives.

The sexual assault group was the most fun for me. No, I didn't abuse them—I needed them all to trust me. I did however convince them that I was the only one looking out for them—that there was a rapist in every party, down every dark alley.

*Step Three: Offer a solution.*

Three months into the semester, I had finished establishing sufficient trust. That's when I let them in on a little secret—the reason why I'm not afraid.

Wouldn't it be great if there was a safe place to go where no one would make you feel bad about being socially inept? A band of brothers who helped each other find jobs, share rooms, and reach financial success? Sisters who would hold your hand and keep you safe from all the predatory monsters in the world?

I had enough people now that I was able to register my flock as a co-ed professional fraternity. I did some fundraising with the groups and managed to raise enough money to renovate an abandoned motel into my headquarters. Now that I had them all together, the fun could really begin.

*Step Four: Make yourself special.*

It's not enough for your people to need your insight. They need to need you. Now it was time to explain what made me unique.

Don't force your cult down their throats. People don't want to be part of an organization that needs them. They want to be part of something exclusive, something that recognizes how special they know they are inside.

I began by offering private counseling sessions to everyone having difficulty. To each of them, I confessed the truth about why I was helping them.

You see; I wasn't human at all. I was an alien who was born in the Andromeda galaxy. My people are empaths, allowing us to sense the suffering of other sentient beings. I felt how troubled Earth was, and I came here to save humanity from themselves.

They were all skeptical at first, but here's what really convinced them. I told each person in confidence that the rest of the fraternity was already indoctrinated. No-one wants to be the only one left out, especially when they finally found a home which unequivocally accepts and shelters them.

*Step Five: Make them special.*

Each new member makes it that much easier to add the next, because it adds credibility and makes people more afraid of being left out. Adding the first few is the hardest part, so here is what I did.

The first person I convinced was a scared freshman girl who was attacked during a house party. She was ready to give anything just to feel safe. I gave her the chance to witness the ceremony and didn't force her to commit to anything.

I laid rows of candles in the basement and lined the walls with mannequins. I concealed the mannequins with thick robes, so it would appear as though most of the fraternity was already present. I used a surround sound system and a layered chanting soundtrack to make it seem like everyone was participating.

By the time I was through with the ceremony; she was so afraid of being left out that she swore the oath of loyalty right on the spot.

*Step Six: Make it impossible to leave.*

This is the final—and I would argue most important—step. There is nothing as toxic to an organization as having a previous member leave and talk about it.

Once I had ten members who had undergone the ceremony, I organized them into two groups of five. I gave them innocent tasks to prove their loyalty. Each one would be slightly more difficult than the last, which is important for keeping them invested.

The final task to allow them full membership and protection was very simple. Four of them must team up and kill the fifth member of the group. For each group, I chose the least loyal, most suspicious member to be killed. I told the rest that the fifth member was a traitor—that he betrayed one of the other members. That he was going to single handedly destroy all we had worked to build together.

They would never do it alone, but when the rest of their group was going along with it, they lost the power to think for themselves. Both groups did as they were told.

It was a ritualistic sacrifice—the extra man would be tied down to a stone table. I had already drugged him, minimizing his resistance. I used his slurred speech as proof that he was possessed by an evil Cosmic Spirit which sought to destroy us all.

I made sure each of the four loyal group members thrust the knife into his body at least once. After that, their conscience would bind them to me forever.

If they stayed, their minds told them they were a hero. If they left, they were a murderer. Which do you think they would rather be?

One full semester later, and I've indoctrinated 54 members so far. There have been 10 deaths, soon to be an 11th.

I'm not writing this as a confession—I don't expect you'll be able to find me. I'm writing this as an offer.

My cult is growing, and there are different chapters springing up all around the country. We have been helpless pawns for too long, but we are learning how to play the game by their rules. When you are ready to take power into your own hands, I hope you will join me and change the world.

### Three go to Sleep; Four Wake up.

I've done it. Three years of being single, and I've finally gotten a girlfriend.

Yes, she's human. No, she's not blind. No, she's not a body pillow.

These are the kinds of questions my best friend, Mike, kept asking me. I was so excited that I wasn't even bothered. Besides, I knew he was just jealous because he'd never even been with a girl before. He's always been the bigger nerd between the two of us—like learning Elvish from Tolkien's books and chanting spells in our D&D games—hardcore nerd stuff.

Neither of us are the type of guy that girls tend to hang around though. Mike and I live together; we're both video game streamers (Hearthstone and Dota2), and we make a living off advertising and tournament winnings.

I met Natasha through a Twitch chat room, and she happened to live close by. Since the first day we met, we've practically been joined at the hip. We eat every meal together, shower together, and even stream video games together.

I don't remember ever being this happy. The only problem is that Mike has decided to make this all about him. He started gaining even more weight, he never goes outside anymore, and all he does is bitch about how I never hang out with him now.

Natasha decided the solution was for the three of us to go camping together in Yellowstone National Park. Mike would get some exercise, I'd get to hang out with him, and most importantly, Natasha and I wouldn't have to spend any time apart.

I regret everything though. Why does nature have to be so damn itchy?

It turns out Natasha had a severe misunderstanding about how trails work. She must be a Skyrim player, because she thinks there is only one right way up a mountain, and that's straight up the rock cliffs.

If we weren't still at that phase of dating where everything becomes an opportunity to impress each other, I would have given up and gone home. I have no idea how Mike made it, but we all decided the day was over by about 4 p.m.

The view was incredible—no, I'm not just talking about Natasha in her short-shorts. She found a practically inaccessible rock ledge overlooking most of the park, and single-handedly hauled all our camping gear up there while Mike and I lay panting on the ground.

Campfire—s'mores—a full blanket of stars—it was a great night. Natasha and Mike bonded over Magic the Gathering cards (which I can't believe he packed instead of a lantern), and he finally agreed to start working out and taking better care of himself so he could find a girl too.

As the campfire burned down to embers, we started telling ghost stories. I told one about a man-eating wendigo, Natasha knew a twisted story about a priest who crucified people, and Mike…

I don't know where Mike stole his story from, but he claimed to have made it up on the spot. I think he was trying to impress Natasha, but I didn't get jealous. He said it in a sing-song rhyming voice which was super creepy, and I made him write it down afterward. It went like this:

*I HAD a dream one fateful night,*
*when day had made its run.*
*When waking world had fled from sight,*
*and silent moon eclipses sun.*
*Into fitful slumber slipped,*
*losing command of my thoughts.*
*Nightmares around me gripped,*
*the familiar had come to naught.*

*I FORGOT what I've been taught*
*about what cannot cause me harm.*
*My fears abound, in safety sought,*
*I scream to waken in alarm.*
*Only to find I've fallen deeper,*
*down this darkened pit of shade.*

## Sleepless Nights

*No sound escapes from silent sleeper,*
*nor outward sign of my dismay.*

*I SAW a monster rear its head,*
  *somewhere inside of mine.*
  *On my dear memories it fed,*
  *the beast who devours time.*
  *Scything talons raking down,*
  *gaping jaws of a giant spider.*
  *I was marked as I was found,*
  *as the one outsider.*

*UNTIL ALL I could recall of life,*
  *was that I had once loved.*
  *Until that too was torn in strife,*
  *an arm severed from the glove.*
  *There upon the edge of breaking,*
  *inside of me a guide would lead.*
  *She was the love I'd be forsaking,*
  *when I opened my eyes from sleep.*

*SHE TOOK my hand and together we ran,*
  *from the monster in my mind.*
  *We got so far that soon began,*
  *what I never thought to find.*
  *We lived a day, a season,*
  *then year,*
  *an entire lifetime in my head.*
  *Happy as he who has forgotten fear,*
  *of the monster I had dread.*

*UNTIL FINALLY IT rose from quiet,*
  *when we thought ourselves alone.*
  *We had lived lives in spite it,*
  *but our life together was on loan.*

*THE MONSTER HAD US CAUGHT!*

*Trapped and helpless in a corner.*
*With no escape I stood and fought,*
*rather die than be a mourner.*
*Rather lose oneself completely,*
*than forget what I had sworn.*
*Death before me, but I would beat he,*
*who would dare to touch her form.*

*I RIPPED the air with my two hands,*
*but as the creature was not real,*
*no blows upon the beast did land,*
*though its talons I could feel.*
*Blooded broken and abused,*
*I awaited morning's light to heal,*
*and save me from this awful ruse,*
*that my fortune had me sealed.*

*SHE KNELT ABOVE ME, my lovely queen,*
*and besought me waken from this dream.*
*But what fate would befall her here?*
*Would with the morning she disappear?*

*SHE BORE the monster and its fury,*
*begging only that I woke.*
*Bidding me go, though not to hurry,*
*lest this the last time that we spoke.*

*SWEAT SOAKED, body shakes—*
*I can't remember why I was sad.*
*Throat choked, fully awake—*
*memories flood of the dream I had.*

*BLOOD TRICKLED DOWN MY LENGTH,*
*and I thanked each crimson bead.*
*They gave hope and lent me strength,*
*that perhaps she too was freed.*

. . .

## Sleepless Nights

*AND THERE MY bride lay beside me,*
*from my dream she was released.*
*Wearied from dreaming was she,*
*who in the waking world found peace.*

I WOKE up to a high-pitched scream in the middle of the night.

What the shit? Did a bear get into our camp? I thought we'd be safe from any of the larger wildlife because of the rock ledge. Or a maybe it was a mountain lion...

I was on my feet—Natasha was already unzipping our tent.

"Wait—it could be dangerous!"

"Then we've got to help Mike."

I couldn't fault her reasoning. I just wish she had been a little more selfish. I grabbed my cellphone to use as a flashlight and followed her outside.

"I'm okay! I'm okay. Sorry I screamed." Mike was in his boxers, standing outside his tent.

"You scream like a girl. What happened?" I asked.

He pointed inside his tent and drew the flap back: Natasha and I peered inside with him.

There was a girl—mid-twenties, long auburn hair, flawless skin—butt naked, lying beside Mike's empty sleeping bag. I turned away for a moment but looked again as soon as I noticed Natasha wasn't averting her eyes.

"Who the hell are you?" Natasha asked.

The girl smiled, making no effort to cover herself. She sat upright and began smoothing out her silky hair.

"I had the dream—the same dream from that story I found," Mike said.

"Aha! I knew you didn't make that shit up," I said.

"Yeah whatever," Mike replied. "But I was dreaming about her. And the beast was there, and..."

"What's your name? Where did you come from?" Natasha asked.

The girl stretched luxuriously, still smiling. She stood up and wrapped her arms around Mike, peering at us from over his shoulder.

"Where did you find that story?" I asked Mike. He was frozen stiff with a mix of terror and rapture.

"Some book. Doesn't matter."

"It does matter if it's real."

"I don't like it," Natasha said. "Either tell us who you are or get out of here."

"No!" Mike stepped protectively in front of her. "She's lost without any food, or clothes, or anything. We can't just leave her in the wilderness."

"You're just saying that because you think you're going to get some." I don't know why I was fighting it. I shouldn't be jealous. I had Natasha. But this . . . this just wasn't fair.

"I don't care," Mike said. "I'm going to take her back with us and bring her to a hospital in the morning. Maybe she has a concussion or something."

"And until the morning?" Natasha asked, crossing her arms.

The girl pulled away from Mike and settled into his sleeping bag; Mike smiled sheepishly. "Well she seems comfortable here, so…"

"You're an idiot." Natasha rolled her eyes and walked out. Over her shoulder, she added, "But if the girl is real, then I wouldn't be surprised if the beast was too."

Mike shrugged and gave me a thumbs up. I laughed, closing the tent behind me.

That was the last time I saw Mike alive. When we checked on him in the morning, his rib-cage was flayed open. His heart was missing, but there were still some scraps of sinew and part of his aorta lying in a pool of blood beside the bag.

The girl was gone.

I threw up in the bushes. Natasha just stared at the grizzly scene. "We're going home," she said, turning sharply away.

"I'll start packing—"

"No, let's just go."

"We can't leave Mike like this."

"It's his own damn fault. Now the girl could be anywhere—let's go, now!"

Natasha was already half-way down the rocky wall, but I wasn't going to run through the forest naked. I opened my tent to grab some pants—

The girl was sitting in my tent. Her naked body was covered in blood, and when she smiled, more blood squirted out from between her teeth.

"Hurry up!" Natasha yelled from outside. "I swear to God, I'll leave without you."

I was 'bout to turn and run when the bloody girl finally spoke: "Help me."

"Help you? After what you did to—"

"It wasn't me!" Her smile was gone now, and she looked on the verge of tears. "It was the beast."

If she was telling the truth, then I couldn't just leave her here. If she wasn't…

There was another scream outside. Natasha! I leapt from the tent and ran to the place she was climbing down. Her crumbled body was lying on the ground. She must have slipped while climbing—No. There was a dark shape on top of her—like a wolf with impossibly long limbs and an elongated mouth.

"Natasha!"

But I was helpless to get to her in time. One bite was enough to snap her rib-cage open and I couldn't watch what was going to happen next.

I turned around, and the girl was gone.

I ran—farther and faster than I ever have in my life. There were a few times when I heard something bounding through the underbrush to my side, but I didn't look. I kept running, even when my lungs felt like they were about to explode, and the stitch in my side threatened to tear me in half.

I don't know whether the girl and the beast were the same, simply two-halves of the same nightmare. I don't know if they are still out there, or whether they only come when that story is told aloud.

I'm going to try to find the book where Mike found the story and destroy it. Although I have to admit, I'm a little curious what else is written in those pages…

## She is Still With me

"Well, of course you're depressed. You never leave the house."

"Your life isn't over just because hers is. I'm sorry, but it's true."

"Don't give up hope. You're going to meet someone else and be just as happy as you ever were."

*Just as happy.*

I'm tired of hearing it. What I'm going through—what I'm feeling—it's nobody's business but my own. I don't even know how to begin opening up to anyone who isn't Natalie. Ten years of feeling her warmth pressed against me when I wake. Ten years of whispering to each other in the dark. Ten years of making plans which will never be fulfilled.

Nine months of drinking until I pass out on the couch with the TV on. I haven't been able to sleep in the bed we shared since breast cancer stole my wife from me. Hell, I've barely been able to sleep at all, and by the way people talk to me, I know they can tell.

They're right of course, but that only makes it harder. Knowing they're right and still being unable to do anything about it is such a frustrating feeling—like realizing the right answer after you've already turned in your test. But I'm working through the grief in my own way. It has been a confusing time for me, but I've started keeping this journal to help me process my thoughts. While I will never forget her, in time I will learn to move on.

*Journal Entry: 11/5*

I'm meeting someone for dinner tonight. I won't call it a date—it probably is, but I don't want to put my mind in that place yet. Sarah, the daughter of an older client, is in town and I've promised to entertain her for the evening. I guess she has some self-esteem issues, and I'm supposed to make her feel better about herself. We've chatted a few times, and she's laughed at some things I said (even though I know they weren't funny). I would have even called her beautiful at a time when I still looked at women that way. Well, here goes nothing…

But now I wish I'd listened to myself. I knew it was too soon. I felt tense the moment I sat down with her. I should have just left then. Everything was going fine though—more than fine, she was fantastic—but then she started humming that damn 'my heart will go on' song. The one song stuck in her head just had to be the first song Natalie and I danced to at our wedding. What are the chances?

I feel like an idiot for jumping up and racing to the bathroom. I don't know how long I stayed in there, but I was half-hoping she would be gone when I came out. To her credit, Sarah just laughed it off and acted like nothing happened.

She did ask one strange thing though: she asked what Natalie would have thought about her . . . What an awkward silence that was.

All I could manage was, "My wife would have been happy to see me having a good time."

That was a lie, of course. I couldn't exactly tell her that Natalie was the jealous type—if she knew I was out on a "date" now . . . well six feet of dirt wouldn't be enough to stop her. Sarah is so sweet to still worry about that even with Natalie gone though…

*Journal Entry: 11/12*

We're getting drinks again. She was even the one to invite me. I can't believe it. Natalie is the only one to ever chase me before. I've heard girls sometimes find men who are suffering to be the most attractive. Our indifference gives them a challenge—our damage gives them something to fix. I'm honestly excited about it. Even if nothing else happens, this will be good for me.

She actually reminds me of Natalie a lot. The way she cups my hand in hers when she leans in to talk—and then there's the way she bites her lip when she's holding back a smile. She even wears the same kind of long dress with the high belt my wife used to wear, although she has the type of body which would do well in something more revealing.

Now that I think about it, Sarah and Natalie really have a lot in common. You don't think that . . . No it's impossible. Natalie is gone. I wanted to move on, right? I can't be entertaining such ridiculous thoughts.

This is getting weird though. Sarah won't stop mentioning Natalie. She spent the whole evening asking about how we met, and what I liked about her, and how we spent our time together. It was hard enough talking about my dead wife on a date, but then Sarah would stare at me as though she was analyzing my every answer.

How am I supposed to forget Natalie like this?

No! Not forget! I didn't mean forget . . . I'll never forget . . . But I think I want to. Is that so wrong? If thinking about her brings me nothing but sadness, is it so wrong to want to be happy?

Natalie would have thought so. I promised I would never love anyone like I loved her. I promised she could never be replaced. Could she really still be holding me to that promise? What if Sarah was only a test—what if Natalie is still watching me, waiting for me to fail? I need to go for a walk.

*Journal Entry: 11/15*

Natalie is coming over to my place tonight. I mean Sarah—I mean Natalie—I mean—

The girl won't stop calling me. I'm getting text messages every ten minutes. Whatever I turn the conversation to, she always redirects it back to my dead wife. Natalie is still with me, I know it. She doesn't want me to move on.

When she comes over tonight, I'm going to ask her straight out. If she says she's Sarah—if she says she isn't my wife—I'll leave it at that.

But if she admits her spirit is still here . . . I don't know. I'll do whatever I can to help her find peace.

*Journal Entry: 11/16*

Natalie has traveled to the other side. I'm finally free. For the first time since her death, her presence is finally gone.

I didn't have the courage to ask Sarah right away. I could tell she was reserved too tonight, so we both had a couple of drinks. I knew I needed to ask, but it still felt so awkward and wrong, so I just kept drinking.

Finally, I was able to push the words out: "Are you really Sarah, or are you Natalie's spirit?"

"I'm everything she was," the woman said, and then she kissed me.

I closed my eyes. I could taste Natalie's lips. I ran my fingers through Natalie's hair, and felt my wife's hands on my chest.

It was so good to hold her again, even if this was the last time. It was so good to feel her skin beneath my hands. It was so good to choke the life out of her, sending her spirit back to rest.

I hope she stays gone. This is the third time I've had to send Natalie back to the other side. I'm working through my grief in my own way though, and once Natalie has finally let go of me, I think I'll be able to let go of her too.

Sometimes a song is just a song.

Sometimes a smile is just a smile.

Some people are meant to be alone.

## Dead man Floating

I found the first floater when I was seven years old. It had washed up on the shore about a hundred yards from my family's summer house. It still looked mostly human—a bit swollen and decomposed, but whole enough for me to immediately recognize what it was.

Even as a kid, I was never very squeamish. I used to watch my father skin the deer he caught on his hunting trips, and I would clean my own fish whenever I reeled one in from the salty lake. Finding a human body was the best thing that could have happened to me that summer.

I thought about telling my parents, but there's no way they would let me play with it. Heck, they might even ban me from going down to the water at all, a thought which my seven-year-old brain equated to a nuclear holocaust, an asteroid destroying the earth, or other disasters of similar magnitude.

So, I did what any clear thinking seven-year-old would do. I gathered up all the other kids I knew and charged them $5 each to poke it with a stick. The salt water preserved it well enough for us to stomach the smell, but poking it would release some bloated gas still trapped in the carcass. I told them they could have their money back if they could lick it without throwing up.

No-one got their money back. I made $60 before one of the little snitches told his mother and she called the police.

Next summer when I came back, the first thing I did was race back to the same spot. Sure enough, there had been two more bodies to wash up over the winter. These must have been sitting out in the sun for a while though, because I couldn't even get close to them.

My father had followed me that time, and I wasn't allowed to have any fun. The police said these bodies must be new, since they would have been completely rotten if they had been down there for a year.

Over the next 10 years, there had been another three bodies found beside the lake. Each was slightly more decomposed than the last, but the police still insisted they had to be separate incidents because they were all still too fresh.

None of them could be identified, and as they didn't fit any missing persons within the entire state, the police had no leads to discover where they were coming from. They had given up, but I was never able to put the mystery out of my mind.

I had my own theory. I decided those people didn't just die in the lake—they lived in it too. I thought that when they die, they float to the surface. Just like how when humans die, they're buried in the ground. In retrospect the idea didn't really make sense, but it had started forming when I was so young that I refused to let go of it until the mystery had been resolved.

When I was in college, I became scuba certified for the sole purpose of finding where those bodies were coming from. I rented my own equipment and went back to that lake the summer of my freshman year.

The water was incredibly buoyant from all the salt, and it took almost 20 pounds of weights before I would finally sink to the floor. It was slow progress working my way through the lake—six separate dives before I found what I didn't even know I was looking for:

A sunken plane.

I don't know how long it had been down here, but it was rusted to oblivion. One of the doors had completely rusted off, and I was able to enter and look around.

There were two more bodies inside, no-more than skeletons now. The inside of the plane was compartmentalized almost like it was broken into sealed jail cells.

The locks on some cells had long since rusted open, and I'm guessing these are where the floaters came from. If they were in their own pressurized air chambers, then that explains how they were preserved for so long. As the plane deteriorated, they must have broken free and floated to the surface one by one.

My most important discovery was the black box—although it was painted bright orange, so it's a pretty stupid name. I brought it back with me and swam to the surface to research my findings.

The plane was a Douglass C-47, which was used for military transport during World War 2. They were still being used for decades afterward though. Some remained operational even up to 2012, so I still don't know how long it's been there.

The flight data recorder had completely deteriorated, but the cockpit voice recorder still had some salvageable tape. Most of it was fuzzy or jumpy, but here is what I have:

"164, Roger…" And then something I couldn't make out.

"Unable to make out your last message. Please repeat."

"It's out. Repeat—one of them has gotten out."

"Has the cockpit been compromised?"

"Negative. Cell block is…"

"Please repeat, Captain."

"Repeat—cell block is compromised. It's letting the others out. Fucking—"

"Remain calm, Captain. Can you neutralize the test subject?"

"Not without compromising cockpit—how far am I from the landing field?"

(Something unintelligible)

"What the fuck is that supposed to mean?"

"… not granted permission to land."

"Well then, what the fuck am I supposed to do?"

"…mission terminated. Thank you for your service, Captain."

"My service ain't over until I bring this bird down."

"You're ordered to force collision. Test subjects must not escape."

"Like hell I am. I'm bringing her down into some water now. Request rescue operations."

"Mission terminated. Rescue operation denied."

After that, all I could hear were engine sounds. It went on for about five minutes, and I was about to stop listening when I heard something like a snarling tiger.

I guess I haven't changed that much since I was a kid, because I still don't want to bring this into the police. I've got another dive planned next week, and I'm going to try to break open the remaining cell blocks to get a look inside.

I'LL ADMIT I was pretty hesitant about making my second dive. Just to be safe, I decided not to go alone this time. Two nights ago, I reconnected with Entoine, one of the boys who found some original floaters with me. He still remembered trying to lick the body to get his $5 back, and we laughed about it—I guess that sort of thing only happens once in your life.

I showed him the audio recordings I pulled from the black box and talked him into joining me. He didn't have dive equipment, but I knew I'd feel better with him in the boat.

"Notice feeling anything strange since you licked it?" I asked him while we were rowing out to the middle of the lake.

"What kind of strange? You mean besides puking my guts out?"

"Warts. New birth mark in the shape of a pentagram. Sudden urge to kill people. You know—regular stuff like that."

"Not that I can think of," he admitted. "Except for my ability to talk to animals."

"What? Seriously?"

"Yeah." He smirked. "They just don't talk back. Keep pulling your weight or the boat is going to start turning in circles."

Reading too many horror stories online must have made me paranoid. I don't know what I was so afraid of in the first place. The visibility was good underwater, and I didn't even see any fish besides a host of little black water slugs scootering around.

Instead of weights, this time I just used a crowbar to sink me down to the plane. The doors were so rusted they were starting to unfasten on their own, so it was no problem breaking the lock off.

I was tense, but I remembered to force myself to keep breathing evenly through the regulator. Holding my breath under water could easily result in an arterial gas embolism. Then I'd be the next floater they found washed up on the beach.

Even without the lock, the room was still pressure sealed with an air pocket inside. I tried leveraging the crowbar, but I still couldn't pry the door open against the weight of all that water. I managed to hammer on the door with the metal bar until a leak appeared. The wider I forced the hole, the more water flowed through to equalize the pressure. Once it was full, it should swing open without a problem.

I finally worked the crowbar all the way through the door, but this time it got stuck. That's weird, because the water was flowing freely around it, so there should be plenty of space to pull it back. It was almost as if something were holding it from the other side…

That was a thought I could have done without. I freaked and dropped the crowbar, but without its weight, I began to immediately float back towards the surface. I held onto the door-frame to keep myself from slipping upwards, but it was almost impossible to swim further down against my buoyancy.

Luckily, I didn't have to. The cell finished flooding, and the door began opening on its own. Suddenly I was face to face with a dead body. Its skin had long since begun to rot away, especially around its eyes and mouth where there were just gaping holes remaining.

My crowbar had stuck straight into its side where it had gotten stuck. I was about to pull myself down toward it along the door frame when I noticed the crowbar was sliding back out.

No. Not sliding. The body's hands were wrapped around the bar. They were pulling the crowbar out of its side.

Had I jolted upward too quickly when I let go of the bar? Maybe I already suffered a stroke from the gas embolism without noticing?

The body lurched toward me.

Slow, even breaths. Don't stop breathing.

Easier said than done with a dead body clambering up toward you. It was fast too—driven with purpose. Legs and arms with openly rotten sinews moved effortlessly through the water like a practiced swimmer.

I pushed my way out of the plane, but the body was right behind me. It dropped the crowbar and began ascending smoothly through the water toward me. It was just as fast as me even though I had fins.

Shit. I kicked hard, and without any weight I was rising way too swiftly. I couldn't stop myself. I felt the air expanding in my lungs so rapidly it felt like they would burst. I was practically screaming underwater, trying to get as much air out as I could.

Once I hit the surface, the scream finally became audible, although it was little more than a wheezing gasp at that point. The boat? Where was the boat?

"Entoine get your ass over here!"

He was leaning over the boat and peering down into the water—about fifty yards away. Useless! I looked down and saw the shadow of the body swiftly ascending toward me.

I swam hard toward the boat. Entoine wasn't reacting. There's no way he didn't hear me. Why the hell didn't he start rowing? He was just staring into the depth, his face about an inch from the water.

"Entoine I swear to God—" But my lungs felt like they were on fire, and I couldn't finish my threat. Couldn't take a full breath yet either. All the air I had was going into keeping my legs kicking.

The shadow was right underneath me now. Ten feet from the boat—I ducked my head underwater and paddled as hard as I could. Too slow—the body was intercepting me. It was trying to block my route. About five feet away from safety, it surfaced directly between me and the boat. But it wasn't an explosive surface like something swimming upward. It just floated there, face down in the water, looking as dead as I felt. I had to push the body out of the way to get to the boat. I kept expecting a hand to grab my ankle and pull me back down, but there was nothing.

I climbed into the boat and fell on my back, panting. My mask was cloudy, so I ripped it off. As soon as I could kneel again, I practically shoved Entoine straight into the water.

"What the hell is wrong with you?"

The push pressed him against the side of the boat. He tensed and relaxed but didn't turn away from the water. It was like trying to wake someone from a deep sleep. He was just vacantly staring at the floating body now.

The body was moving again though—its ear was, anyway. Not a natural movement anymore—not like the body was moving on its own. It was like there was something inside trying to crawl out.

As I watched, one of the black slugs pushed its way out of the ear. It got stuck part way and had to gnaw its way through the rest of the cartilage with razor-sharp teeth like a leech. As it struggled out, the whole corpse shook like it was having a seizure.

"It looks like you had it wrong," Entoine said in a sleepy voice. Did he just wake up? There's no way he could have slept through that. His face was still down next to the water though, and I couldn't get a clear look at him.

"What do you mean?"

"The floaters we found weren't the test subjects," he replied, finally pulling away from the water. His body was shivering slightly—somewhere between freezing to death and full body ecstasy.

The tail end of a black slug had just finished slipping into his ear.

"Of course they were. Why else would they be in the cells?" I asked. By the time the words were out of my mouth, I had already realized it.

The bodies weren't the test subjects. The bodies were *hosts* to the test subjects.

And they had already been free in the water since all those years ago when the first floater broke free.

## The Monster Inside us

*Do you want a job with no prerequisite qualifications?*

I guess...

*$15 an hour, with a flexible schedule and free food?*

Okay.

*Plus, it's so easy that you can even do your homework or watch TV while you're getting paid.*

Sign me up.

Let me get this straight right off the bat: I'm not working as a babysitter because I like kids. The noise, the mess, the attention-deficit whining about inane nonsense—I'd probably be happier cleaning gutters. At least there isn't any shit in the gutters. I'm taking 18 credits this semester though, and there's no arguing that it's a pretty convenient way for a girl to make a few extra bucks. Maybe I'd even make enough to move out of the house I shared with Mom.

It wasn't so bad really—I just give the parents my sweetest smile and somehow they're duped into thinking I have a maternal instinct which magically makes me adore their precious bundles of spastic chaos.

The trick is forcing that smile to last all the way until the door closes. Kids may be practically retarded by adult standards, but I've found even the slowest sperm can understand negotiations when it means giving them something they want.

"Okay little twerp," I'd say. "I don't like you, and you don't like me." Okay I don't really say that, but it's definitely what I'm thinking. "Here's the deal. You get to eat all the sugar blasted crap you can stomach and watch cartoons until you get a seizure for all I care. But you don't bug me, and you tell your parents we ate veggies and watched the Disney channel. Got it?"

Usually that's enough, but last night was a special case where everything went wrong. I could tell it wouldn't be easy the second I walked in the door, but I had faith in my martial-law parenting style and thought I could handle anything.

"Looks like you've got your hands full," I said, eyeing the teeth-marks on the chair legs. "How many pets do you have?"

"No pets," the mother said. "Just my little David. I'm only going to be gone for a couple of hours though, and I'm only a call away if you need anything."

"I don't anticipate any problems." I smiled, trying not to wince at the sound of pounding drums upstairs.

"David get your ass down here and meet the sitter!" I'm not sure where the mother was going, but I wouldn't have been surprised if she had a part-time gig as a harpy. The drums grew louder. I just kept smiling.

"David, I swear to God—"

"It's okay, I'll handle things from here," I told her. "You go have fun, and I'll give you a call if anything comes up."

The drums paused after the door closed. It was time to make a deal.

David was a sweet looking boy of 11, with tousled blonde hair and bright blue eyes that would make all the girls weak in a couple of years. His gaze fixed on me with curiosity and more than enough intelligence to be reasoned with. This was going to be easy.

"Alright listen up," I told him. "What do you want to do this evening?"

"I want to burn something," he replied as matter-of-factly as someone ordering a hamburger. "Two somethings, if the first one goes out."

"You can't do that. Is there anything you'd like to watch on TV?"

David shook his head. "I can do that anytime. But Mom's not home, so I'm going to do all the things she doesn't let me do."

The first alarm started ringing in my head.

It was the first of many.

Being an adult was ordinarily enough to earn at least a little respect, but David completely ignored everything I said. Markers on the walls, microwaving forks, putting his shoes in the dishwasher—I couldn't turn around for a second without him doing something completely absurd. I tried locking him in his room for a bit, but when it was too quiet, I opened it to find him building a slingshot with a dozen pair of underwear that would have launched his lamp out the window. He didn't even have the decency to seem embarrassed when I caught him.

"You're going to break it!" I pulled the lamp away and put it firmly back on his nightstand.

"I know. I was trying to," he said.

"Well stop it."

His blue eyes furrowed in deep concentration before he shook his head. "No, I think I'll just wait until you're not looking."

"I'm going to tie you up. Is that what you want?"

"No, you won't," he said. "Or I'll tell Mom."

It was an absolute stand-off.

I was bigger and stronger than him, but I was getting worn down fast, and it was only a matter of time before I collapsed on the sofa and all hell broke loose. It was time to try drastic measures. My family had a time-honored tradition of scaring kids straight, so if he couldn't be reasoned with, I was going to have to do to him what my mother did to me.

"Well if you don't stop, I'll tell on you too."

"She's a total softy," David said. "She won't believe you."

"Not your mother. If you don't do what I say, I'm going to tell the monster. And he's going to eat you up."

David thought very seriously about this again. "Then I'll just wait until the monster isn't looking."

"He's always looking though."

He was smart, so I had to be pretty damn convincing and get dark with this, or he'll see right through it. My mother always used to tell me about the monster whenever I misbehaved—mastering a sort of wild-eyed intensity which always sold the story. She was so convincing that even to this day she has never admitted that it was all made up.

"The monster lives in your eye, so he sees everything you can see," I told him. "And if you don't behave, he's going to know and start eating you from the inside out. He's going to eat up your heart, and your lungs, and your stomach, and everything else until you're completely empty. And all the blood that has nowhere left to go, it's all going to come out of your mouth, and you're going to drown in it."

His face was getting paler with every word. Good, let him have nightmares about it. That's his therapist's job, not mine.

"What about you?" he asked. "Does a monster live inside you?"

"Sure there is. There's one inside everyone. That's why the people who make it to be adults are all so serious and good all the time."

"That doesn't seem right," he said. "There are bad adults too. The criminals and stuff."

"That's just because the monster has already eaten them and is using their body to do bad things."

I never thought terrifying a child would be this satisfying. I wonder if Mom used to enjoy scaring me this much, or if I was just a bad person.

It worked like magic though. Suddenly David decided that he was tired and wanted to go to bed. 7:30 p.m. and ready to sleep—it was a dream come true. Maybe this is the story I should use for everyone. All those hours I wasted pretending to be their friends—this was way more efficient!

David went to his room and turned off the light, and I got to work studying for my final exams next week. I thought I was going to have a full evening to myself, but around 8:30 I noticed the light was back on in his room. He was being quiet, so I thought about just ignoring him, but he seemed a bit too clever to be fooled for long, and I didn't want to take any chances. It's a good thing too, because when I opened the door I saw him out of bed, staring at his reflection in his mirrored closet door.

His left hand was holding his left eye open as wide as it could, while the right hand held a sewing needle poised to gouge straight into it. I wanted to tackle him to the ground, but the needle was so close it was almost touching the eyeball itself . . . I was terrified that any sudden move would bump it straight inside.

"David! What are you doing? Idiot! Put that down right now!"

He turned to look at me, still holding the needle in a trembling hand directly against his eye. My whole body tensed as I imagined the feeling of that point scraping against my own eye. "I can't. I need to kill the monster inside."

His hand was trembling, but he pressed it a little closer into his eye. It looked like it had already started to puncture. I walked more carefully across that floor than if it were made of hot coals. No sudden moves. No harsh words. I just had to gently...

"David, please listen to me. There is no monster, okay? I made it all up. If you put that in your eye, you're going to hurt yourself very badly. You won't be able to see anymore."

"You lie," he said. He wasn't pushing it in any further though. He was listening to me. I took another step closer.

"I'm not lying. You can ask anyone you want—you need your eyes to see."

"No, you're lying about the monster," David said. "I saw him."

"I'm going to call your Mom right now, okay?" I fumbled with my phone, trying to pull it out and dial without looking away from him. "You can ask her, and she will tell you the same thing. There are no monsters."

"You're lying, and I know why," he said. "The monster inside you is making you do it. It's trying to save the monster in me, but I'm not going to let it. I'm the only one who makes the rules."

The number was in the phone. I was about to hit dial when—

His arm jerked violently. He screamed, and so did I.

The needle slid straight into his eye, completely disappearing into the brilliant orb. He doubled over with pain, howling like a demon. I threw the phone onto the ground and rushed to him—too late. He was clutching his head with both hands, howling and screaming and—and then nothing. He just went real quiet, his head in his hands, hiding his face from me.

"We're going to the hospital. Now!"

He shook his head.

"David look at me!"

Slowly—tortuously—he raised his face to meet me. His left eye was sealed shut, but I could still see the end of the needle poking between his closed lids. A stream of blood was freely flowing down his face like tears.

"It didn't work," he whispered. Then he said something else, but it was so quiet I couldn't hear.

"I told you it wouldn't. Now come on, we need to go now."

"It didn't kill the monster," he whispered again.

I picked him up, and he didn't resist. He wrapped his arms around my neck to hold himself upright. I hurried him toward my car as fast as I could. Kids get things in their eyes all the time, right? This didn't mean he would be blind. They just had to take it out, and—

"I didn't kill it," he whispered again, right in my ear where he was pressed against me. "I only made the monster mad." I felt his arms grow tighter around my neck. It was hard enough carrying a boy his size, but trying to force him while he was choking me was impossible. I had to set him down and get a better grip, but he wouldn't let go.

"He blames you," David whispered in my ear. "It's your fault we tried to hurt him."

"David, let go. Now you're hurting me."

"I know," he whispered. "And that's only going to make you mad, so I'm not going to make the same mistake twice. This time I'm going to finish the job."

I forced his arms off me and hurled him to the ground. His right hand was balled up like a fist—clenching the bloody sewing needle that he'd somehow managed to pull free. His left eye was still sealed shut, and his right eye was narrowed as his face twisted into an animalistic snarl.

"Stop playing games. We need to take you to a hospital," I said.

But he wasn't playing.

He was lunged at me, trying to strike at me with wild flailing punches and kicks. I managed to create some distance between us, but he was absolutely relentless. I ran down the stairs, but he leapt from the top with a wild leap and was on top of me again before I reached halfway. I felt the needle pierce into the back of my neck, and I had to physically throw him off me.

I was in an absolute panic by this point. I didn't take into account how small he was, or how fast he was already going when he jumped from the top of the stairs. I threw him with all my strength, which would have probably knocked an adult man onto his ass. With David, it was enough to send him straight over the railing to tumble the half-story onto the ground below.

He landed with a sickening crack that made me want to just run and not look back. I rushed to where he lay spread-eagled on the tile floor. A pool of blood was quickly expanding from his face. I tried to ease him onto his back to inspect the damage, but he surged awake again. He was swiping madly at my face with his little hands. I tried to pin him, but his hands were slick with blood and kept sliding through to force his needle into my arms and neck again and again. I had to grab him by the shoulders and slam him into the ground before he finally stopped.

"You have to lie still!" I was crying at this point. He kept squirming, but I finally had both his arms firmly underneath me. "There is no monster, okay? There's nothing that's going to hurt you. If I take you to the hospital you're going to be alright."

David coughed, and blood splattered half-way up my arms. I climbed off of him, but he wouldn't stop coughing. More blood—just like I'd told him would happen. Just like my mother had told me would happen. But it was absurd to think any of that was true...

He'd hurt himself from the fall, and I couldn't waste any more time—so why couldn't I stop crying? It was like all those years when I was growing up were flashing back to me. Every night I lay awake—listening to the sound of my own blood in my veins and the beating of my heart—wondering if I could hear the monster inside of me. All those nightmares I had as a child, everything was rushing back. I shouldn't have done this to him. I knew how much I hated it when Mom did it to me. I shouldn't have tried to scare David like that. But I was the adult now, and I had to take responsibility. So why couldn't I stop crying?

"Shhh . . . Shhh . . . Come on now . . . Don't cry." It was David. He had stopped coughing and was kneeling beside me. I immediately tensed, but he was stroking my hair so gently that all I could feel was relief. He was okay. I actually started to laugh. He was the one trying to comfort me!

"Shhh..." he whispered. "Don't be like that. You have nothing to be scared of anymore." I gave him a great big hug and felt him holding me back. "We all have a monster inside us. Sometimes they never wake up, and sometimes they never go back to sleep. But you don't have to worry anymore."

"Our monsters," I replied, "they've both gone back to sleep, haven't they? But we're still here, and we have to take care of ourselves. So, will you let me take you to the hospital now?"

"No, not asleep. Do you really think your monster could stay asleep after you killed that little boy?"

I tried to pull him away to look at him, but he was holding on tightly again. More tightly than ever—tighter than a boy his age should be able to.

"Why don't I have to be afraid?" I asked, pretending I wasn't trying so hard to get him off.

"Because it's so much more fun when you let the monster out."

I was afraid his arms would break by how hard I pushed him, but finally his hands slid apart and he fell back onto the floor. He lay there stiffly, his arms maintaining their curved shape where they were wrapped around me. The shape they had when he was still alive. The blood had stopped flowing from his mouth. His blue eyes were both closed. His chest had stopped fighting to breathe.

And finally—finally—he wasn't resisting me anymore.

I ran and didn't look back. I got in my car and just started driving.

I don't know what I'm going to do. David's mother knew my name, and the police will find me. I couldn't even go back to my home or say goodbye to my own mom. She'd take one look at me and know what happened, and I know she'd want me gone too. She'd see the blood that I was already starting to cough up, and she'd know the monster inside of me had grown too big. She'd know all her stories and warnings hadn't been enough to get me to be good, and that now I was being eaten up too.

I'm going to drive now, and I'm not going to stop until I'm not the one making the rules anymore. I just hope David was right—that it really is more fun when we let the monster out.

## History Written in Scars

No, not a cut. Not a bruise from sleepwalking, or a bang where I drunkenly hurt myself without remembering. I'm talking jagged, gnarly, vicious scars which looked like they've healed years ago.

The first one to appear was an inch long incision on my stomach, almost like a surgical wound. I live in college with a roommate (Robert), but he didn't remember anything happening. Then I called my parents and asked them if I'd ever had a surgery before, but the only procedure I'd undergone was having my wisdom teeth removed; a dead end unless, they went through my stomach to reach my mouth.

I figured that I just hadn't noticed it before. Or perhaps something traumatic happened, and I completely blocked out the memory, but I didn't worry about it. I played basketball in high-school and have had my fair share of being knocked around, so it must have been from something then. Those were the glory days, man. I play on my collegiate intramural team now, but it's just not the same. I was a school hero back then . . . But life goes on, you know? All the victories and mistakes I made on and off the court, they're all ancient history.

The next morning, I woke with another long scar along my forearm. It must have been deep too, and the skin holding it together was stretched like I've grown since it closed. I ran my finger over it, but it didn't hurt. The skin was slightly raised and hard, but otherwise I wouldn't have noticed if I wasn't looking right at it. I thought about going to the doctor, but it looked so old that he'd probably just say I forgot what caused it.

I tried not to think about the scars for the rest of the day, although my buddy, Chase, noticed it during our practice that evening. I didn't want to sound like an idiot, so I made up a story about this time I fought off a mugger to protect my girlfriend and got a swipe from his switchblade.

"Yeah, I think I remember you mentioning something about that, bro," he said.

Bitch please. I doubt that since I just made the story up on the spot.

It wasn't interfering with my game though, and I was so tired afterward that I just hit the showers and went straight to bed. I completely forgot about it until I was falling asleep, and then it was all I could think about. What if something was attacking me in the night? But no, that was ridiculous. But what if something was attacking a younger version of myself in the night? Even stupider. I eventually convinced myself that I was making a big deal out of nothing, and fell asleep.

It was still the first thing I thought about when I woke up. I immediately stripped naked and checked myself in the bathroom mirror.

"Man, are you trying to shit a log or a whole forest? I gotta take a piss." Robert was pounding on the door. I ran my fingers over my chest for the hundredth time. A giant cross-shaped scar on my right peck. The undulating lines wandered haphazardly—grotesquely—like it hadn't been a clean heal. But it was healed alright. I opened the door and stared at him.

"Have you seen this before?" I asked.

"Dude are you drunk? I'm not looking at your—" He started back-peddling.

I grabbed a towel and wrapped it around my waist. "Not that, you idiot. This scar. What happened to me?"

"Yeah, you got in a fight with a mugger when you were in high-school. You said he cut you up pretty bad, but you chased him off."

"I never told you that," I said. "That never happened!"

"You're being crazy, man. Just let me use the bathroom, okay?" Robert pushed past me and closed the door.

I went straight to my computer and logged onto Facebook. I've had that thing setup since my freshman year of high-school. There had to be some pictures which proved—I looked like a little jerk back then—okay here we go. Senior Ditch day we all went down to a river and hung out. I was in my swimsuit and—and the grotesque scar was on my chest. The ones on my stomach and forearm were there too. I flipped back a few more years and saw it disappear during my sophomore year. From the photos, it looked like whatever happened was in the first semester of my junior year.

When I thought about that time in my life, there was only one memory which burned so brightly as to cast shadows on the rest. I narrowed down the range of dates, and there was no mistaking it.

I found a photo of myself running shirtless with the team the week before—no scars. The week after I wasn't present at the game, then after that I was covered in bandages. But that hadn't happened! I remember we started off the season 4-0, and I played in every game...

I hadn't meant to hurt her. There was a party to celebrate our homecoming victory game, and everyone was having a little too much to drink. I thought Jessica wanted it—she certainly seemed like she did. There's no way I could have known how she would react the next morning—or what she would do herself the next month when she found out she was pregnant. It's not my fault Jessica is dead.

Life goes on, you know?

Ancient history.

And if somehow these scars appearing on my body were related to that night, and I had to carry them as penance the rest of my life, then I could accept that. If that had been all there was, I wouldn't have been so scared or angry.

But the scars this morning were more deliberate. Etched into the back of my hand are the words:

*How many cuts will it take before I see you again?*

Maybe some wounds cut too deep to ever be left in the past. I wonder how many more it will take before she's satisfied, or whether I'll even survive her search for peace.

## The Party That Changed my Life

Josh: *Hey man, thanks for staying to help cleanup last night. Hope you had a good time.*

Me: *Your party was a blast. How'd it go with Casey?*

Josh: *No go, bro. She had to take her wasted friend home.*

I slid the phone back in my pocket. I was only asking to be polite. I couldn't care less about Josh or his parties. I wouldn't have gone at all if Kimberly, a girl from my physics class, hadn't mentioned she was going too. She only knew my serious, studious side, but there's nothing like a party to show how suave and charming I could be, right?

Just my luck that she didn't show, and I had to endure an evening of beer like piss, screaming idiots, and that damn UNCE UNCE UNCE music which I know is going to haunt me all day. That and this pounding hangover.

Josh: *My poor turtle had to put its head back in the shell. You know what I mean?*

Why is he still texting me? How do I even reply to that? I hope he doesn't think we're friends now. I didn't even know his frat house was hosting the stupid party. Maybe if I don't reply he'll just—

Josh: *The flight was ready for landing, but the runway was blocked by a fat cow. The dive was scheduled, but there were a bunch of needy sharks in the water. It was time for my pizza, but the meatloaf wasn't having any fun, so I guess that means ALL the food had to get sent back.*

Me: *That makes absolutely no sense, but I get it.*

Now will *he* get it? Of course not. If he got it, he wouldn't still be texting me.

Josh: *BTW bro, do you know who Kimberly is?*

Me: *Yeah. Was she there last night?*

No. Josh couldn't have. Please God, don't let that disgusting frat boy anywhere near—

Josh: *Some dipshit wrote "Kimberly is dead. Stop wasting time on her" with a marker on my wall. Good thing for renter's insurance, lol.*

The chair in front of me was empty in physics today. The long golden braid which usually fell about my desk was gone. I hadn't realized how long this class was when I had to stare at the whiteboard instead. To make matters worse, the stream of texts from Josh didn't stop.

Josh: *Dude I found another message. This one was written in my bathroom: "Her head took the longest to remove. The vertebra kept snapping, and her neck must have stretched four feet before it finally popped free." WTF?*

Josh: *Here's one written on my closet: "Her breasts looked much bigger when they were still attached. Such a fake girl, no-one will miss her."*

Josh: *There's another on the side of my fridge. "I'm saving some for later."*

I excused myself. I still had biology after this, but I felt like I was going to be sick. This had to be a twisted prank. Maybe he thought I wanted to join his frat or something, and this is what they did to haze people. But then why wasn't Kimberly in class?

I couldn't let this get to my head. All I had to do was check her Facebook, right? Okay, no updates since the day before last. But I could send her a message: *Hello Kimberly? We've never really talked, but I just wanted to make sure you haven't been butchered. Hope we can go out sometime...*

Yeah that isn't the suave first impression I was hoping to make. Think. Think! I was freaking out. Of course, I didn't have to mention the butchery. If she replied at all, then she was okay, right?

Do you think you're nervous texting a girl for the first time? Try it when all you can think about is her dismembered corpse scattered across some frat house.

Me: *Hey Kimberly. Did you go to Josh's party last night?*
DELETED

I couldn't send that, because then I'd just be admitting to eavesdropping on her plans. How about…

Me: *Hey Kimberly. Saw you missed physics today, so I wanted to remind you about the quiz on Friday.*

I closed my eyes and hit send. I hope that doesn't make me sound like all I cared about was physics. Maybe I should add a follow up to ask—

*BZZZ.*

A reply! She's okay! I mean of course she's okay, but she replied! And so quickly too. You don't reply that fast unless you really want to talk to someone— But the message read:

Josh: *DUUUUDE LOOK WHAT'S IN MY FRIDGE*

Attached was a photo of a dismembered foot sitting on the shelf beside the cheese. He sent me a couple more texts, but I didn't read them. I was running toward his place. Either something horrible has happened, and I had to see for myself, or he was trolling me and was about to receive a beating of a lifetime.

By the time I got over there, I still hadn't received a reply from Kimberly. That could mean anything though. If she wasn't in class, it was because she was busy with something, so of course she couldn't reply. So why did I feel like I was going to die?

This place looked even worse in the daylight. The building had been trashed and stitched together so many times it might as well have been the Frankenstein's monster of frat houses. I pounded on the door so hard that my hand went numb.

"Josh! Get your ass out here!"

The door opened, and I almost hit him in the face. Then he started laughing, and I really did hit him. Right between the eyes. My fist stung like hell, but it felt so good I would have done it a hundred more times.

"Shit, dude, cool it. Can't you take a joke?"

It had all been a prank!

Kimberly was okay.

"Who does that? How badly do you need attention that you would screw with me like that? Never talk to me again."

I've seen enough. I turned around and stomped my way across the yard.

"Come on man, it's not like that. I just found the photo online somewhere, but the messages were real."

"You're messed up, man. Leave me alone," I said.

"Look! There's another one on the fence!" he shouted after me.

"So what? You probably wrote it, you twisted ass."

"I swear, dude. I didn't write any of it. The picture is the only thing that wasn't real."

I didn't want to look, but I couldn't help myself. I glanced at the fence. Written in black marker, it said: *She was my third.*

What is even worse than listening to him? Believing him. Because looking at those big block letters, I know Josh couldn't have written that. I know because it was unmistakably my handwriting. How much did I drink that night, anyway?

## The Solution to Prison Overcrowding

There is no Devil, only man, and he does not buy souls. Not all at once, anyway. Man is far more insidious than that, for he grinds down his brother's soul one layer at a time until the residual humanity begins to devour itself. It's hard to believe, but it's true. Begin to break a man, and he will finish the job on his own. That is because it is much easier to live as an animal than it is as half a man.

I felt the first part of my humanity die when I was 12 years old. How do you explain a knotted garbage bag full drowned kittens to a child? I was young, but not too young to know that someone had done it on purpose, and that they had gotten away with it. Not too young to understand that evil wasn't just a thing in cartoons and movies; not too young to realize that I too was capable of evil if I ever got my hands on this monster.

Over the years, I felt more of myself slip away. Sometimes it would break off in big chunks like when my mother died. More often my soul simply eroded from the steady tide of petty grievances, jealous greed, thoughtless anger, and the thousand other frustrations that make up the life of any "civilized" man trying to find his place in the world.

My defense attorney wanted me to talk about how I regretted killing Edward. That it was a defining moment in my life, and that my mind had been blown wide with righteous rebirth and revelation. There wasn't enough left of me to lie though. I don't think my pulse even rose the night I took my neighbor's life.

Edward used to beat his wife, and now he doesn't. That's all that changed, because there wasn't enough left of me to change. It almost makes me laugh now to think how far I still was from rock-bottom.

I got 15 years. Could have been worse, but the judge and jury were sympathetic after hearing the widow tearfully thank me for saving her.

I can't even say I found jail any worse than the outside either. The only difference was my daily routine, and the blur of a different set of faces performing it with me.

Soon I gained a reputation as a loose cannon. People said I'd go from deadpan silence to an incoherent rage in one second flat. I don't think of it that way though. I think of myself more like a brilliant pianist: seeming ordinary until sitting down to play. The musical ability didn't suddenly appear out of nowhere, it had been inside all along. It was the same with my anger: it was always there, but it was my choice whether to let it play.

I was five years into my sentence before one of the guards took my moods personally, landing me in the hole. It was only supposed to be for a week, but everything I did seemed to extend the time. Unresponsive to the officer? Add a week. Didn't eat the food? Add a week, with my next meal replaced by "the loaf" (rotten cabbage and bread). Didn't eat the loaf? Another week, and no other food until I choked it down. Even after I vomited it back up, they wouldn't give me more food until I'd eaten my sick just to teach me a lesson.

I don't know what that lesson was, but the only thing I learned was to hate the hole. Having nothing to do is boring, but knowing it will continue without cessation is despair. I was never a social person, but I found myself so starved for human contact that I even tried hugging the guard. It was like I needed someone to touch me just to prove I was still real, but nothing relieved the relentless pressure of the second-by-second attack on the soul which was isolation.

I knew I was really losing it when a fly found its way into my room. I named it Ribazzzio and talked to it just to hear something besides the droning of florescent lights and the distant shouts from other cell blocks. I told Ribazzzio about the girl I liked in high-school, and how beautiful the sly wrinkle at the edge of her smile was. I described to him what a sunrise looked like, and the taste of chocolate cake, and about the drawings I used to sketch, and a thousand other things which I hadn't appreciated at the time.

I didn't tell the fly that I never expected to see them again. I didn't want to make him sad and leave. It didn't matter though, because the next time I woke, he was gone anyway. I'm not ashamed that I cried to be alone again. In fact, I was relieved. It meant there was still part of me which was human enough to feel.

"Pssst. Hey buddy."

I opened my eyes. I wasn't sleeping—I was just playing dead, preferring my malleable imagination to the stagnant cell. The voice had come from behind me.

"Can you hear me? What's your name?" the voice asked.

Someone else must have heard me talking to the fly. I turned around and found a crack in the mortar behind my bed. It must have connected with another cell in the Housing Detention block.

"Does it matter?" I asked.

"Of course it does. It's the most important thing in the world. It's the thing they can't take from you. My name's Riley."

"Hi Riley. I'm Travis," I replied.

"Have you been recruited yet, Travis?"

"I don't know what you're talking about," I said. I glanced back at the closed door of my cell. Even if someone heard me, they'd probably just think I was talking to myself again. It's not like they checked on us very often.

"Okay good," Riley said. "They're going to offer you a deal soon. You have to take it—trust me."

"What deal? Why would I trust you? I don't even know you."

"Sure you do," he said. "I'm your only friend in the world."

They checked on me shortly after, and I threw the pillow over the crack in the mortar, sitting rigidly upright. I was reluctant to leave my new friend, but I didn't want the guard to notice. All I could think about was how great it would be to have someone to talk to now.

And the deal? It couldn't have been that special if he was still in prison, but it was something to think about. Something to look forward to. Maybe they'd even given him books or a notepad. A laptop or TV would be almost as good as getting out.

Riley never answered again though. For two days I tapped on the wall, but all I heard was ceaseless muttering. An old man swearing under his breath kind of muttering, like he was trying to talk but couldn't decide whether he was talking to himself or someone else. All hours of the day and night—non-stop muttering. I don't even remember him pausing to eat, let alone draw breath.

Most of it was inaudible gibberish, but there were a few things I finally made out after they were repeated for the thousandth time.

"Didn't expect to see him again. No sir-ee-no."

"Just pretend to be human for me, will you? We can both pretend."

"I'm Riley. You're Riley, too, but I was Riley first."

I lost track of how long I was supposed to stay in here, but I'm sure I should have been out of solitary a long time ago. By the time they came to offer me the deal, I was completely convinced that accepting it was the only way to ever get out.

"It's very simple, we have nothing to hide," the prison warden told me. He looked like the type of man who would force his children to only speak when spoken to, and even then only if they addressed him as 'sir.'

"We could easily force you to accept," the warden continued, "after all, you are in my power. I choose when you sleep, when you eat—if you eat—but I am still making this a completely voluntary arrangement."

"What do you want from me?" I asked.

"Prison overcrowding is a serious issue," the warden said. It felt like he was reading from a pre-prepared script. He was looking at me, but I wasn't really being seen. "The prison system has grown 700% over the last generation. It's costing us up to 40 grand per inmate every year—74 billion annually nationwide. The government is actively exploring alternative programs which can satisfy the need to deter and rehabilitate criminals without the prohibitive expense and opportunity cost of prison. I'm offering you the chance to volunteer in one of these programs."

"You're going to take me out of prison? Then how come Riley stayed in here?"

The Warden's face screwed up like he'd just taken a bite from a lemon. "Riley is gone. He's been gone for a while now."

There was something about how he emphasized the name which made it seem like Riley hadn't changed locations. He'd changed from being Riley. The warden was already talking again though, and there wasn't any space to ask questions.

"I can't disclose all the details with you, but rest assured your sentence will be considerably abbreviated. Our programs are designed for maximal efficiency, and fifteen years of wasted time and money are going to be condensed into a weekend."

I didn't care about the time. What did I have to look forward to on the outside? It might seem inconsequential to you, but the only reason I accepted his offer was that I missed having someone to talk to. And if this was a government project, then what was the worst they could do? Maybe I really could get a clean start.

The warden gave me some papers to sign and then left. I was handcuffed by the guard and escorted out of my cell. He tried to keep my head low, but I caught a glimpse of the adjoining cell where Riley must have stayed. A man in a rubber suit was pressure washing blood out of the stone tiles.

"What happened to that guy?" I asked the guard. "Is he hurt?"

The guard shifted uneasily and looked around like he wasn't sure if he was supposed to say or not. Then he shrugged.

"What was he still doing in there?" I pressed. "I thought Riley made the same deal."

"Yeah, he finished his deal," the guard said. "He was supposed to be released in a few days after the official pardon was granted, but I donno. Guess he wanted a quicker way out."

The man in a rubber suit picked up a fork on the floor. It was covered in congealed blood all the way up the handle. I tried to get a better look, but the guard shoved me onward.

I was put into the back of an unmarked police car. Somehow, I'd expected a whole bus load of people, but it was only me.

In a few days I'd be a free man. It hardly seemed possible. How was I supposed to pick up the pieces and become something new? Anyway, it sounded like Riley really was going to be released, and if he hadn't . . . Well I wasn't as fragile as him. I could survive anything for a weekend.

I wasn't paying much attention to where we were going, but we drove for a long while before the car stopped at a ranch deep in the desert. There weren't any pens for animals, just wide open spaces separated by low stone barriers which I could have easily stepped over. I guess they didn't worry much about escape when there was nowhere to escape to.

"Welcome to Rawhide." I was greeted by a man wearing a leather vest and denim pants who stood outside the ranch house. The officer un-cuffed my hands, but I didn't move. I couldn't believe what I was seeing.

"Ten years left on your sentence, all over in two days. Seems like a pretty good deal to me, eh? But don't you worry, you won't miss out on anything," the man continued. His voice was muffled from speaking around the cigar in his mouth. His eyes didn't leave my face—mine didn't leave his. "It's my job to make sure you still get 10 years' worth of punishment this weekend."

I heard the sound of tires roaring over dry earth. I hadn't even noticed the officer had gone, but it was too late now. I couldn't look away from the man in front of me.

I was staring at Edward, the man I killed.

"What are you doing here?"

Edward grinned. He took a step closer to me and took the cigar out of his mouth. "Same thing as you, darling. I'm just trying to find some justice in this shit-stain world. But between you and me, I don't know if there really is any justice out there. I reckon there are just people who got what they deserved, and people who got lucky."

Another step closer. I could feel the heat radiating from the end of his cigar as it brushed my hand. He was exactly the same as that insufferable creature I used to live next to. His words blew onto my face alongside his rancid breath.

"And by the time I'm through with you, there won't be any doubt. You weren't one of the lucky ones."

## A Letter From the Cold Case Files

I work at a police station, first in my precinct to be equipped with the latest video spectral comparator. The device is absolutely amazing for reconstructing obscured writing, and we've already used it to blow open three cases by deciphering evidence which had been almost completely obliterated.

Incriminating letter?

Receipt putting you at the crime scene?

Well what looks to you like a harmless pile of ashes in the waste bin can now be all we need to close the case.

The downside? I've had to take a huge-ass folder of paperwork home with me on the weekends since it's been installed. The inspector in charge wants us to skim every cold case in the entire precinct for areas where the new technology might be applicable. Boredom doesn't even begin to describe it, but I did come across an interesting letter which we've managed to repair from its severe water damage. I hope you'll enjoy it as much as I did.

TO MY LOVELY WIFE.

Dear Eva,

Never has the fear of the hunted been so evident as it was with you. I could not stand to see you so agitated, the slightest creak in our house causing such violent tribulations. You could barely drink a cup of tea without being drenched by your trembling hands. At night, I heard you moan with the bitterest lamentations, and nothing I said could provide you with the least respite.

"I can't escape." I heard the things you muttered to yourself when you didn't think I was listening. "He's going to find me and take me away. Not today—please not today—but soon. I can't escape."

I think I even know who you were referring to. I caught him more than once, sitting in his car across the street. Watching our house through his tinted windows. That cold, professional man, the one with the eyes of a killer. I sought answers from him, but upon seeing my approach, he shuddered like he'd been possessed and drove off before I could utter a word.

Eva, sweet Eva, nothing in this life could make you deserve such torment. The curtains never part to let the light in anymore, and you must suffer terribly if you are so loathe to reveal yourself that you prefer candles to electricity. How long has it been since you even left the house? And no, I don't count ordering food online, then waiting until dark to sneak out and snatch it like a quivering mouse.

I was afraid that even these precautions might not be enough to save you, until the night when I finally witnessed your resolve. You fixed your hair and makeup, although you are just as beautiful without, and dressed warmly against the midnight chill. I understand now why you didn't tell me where you were going, as intent as you were upon your grizzly mission.

I do not mind that you are self-absorbed, my dear. It only makes me more grateful for the attention I do receive. No matter how hard you try to exclude me though, I will always be there to protect you. It is one thing to face your fear, but how could you think I would let you do it alone?

The hour we drove together on the highway was the closest I have felt to you in a long time, and when you pulled off on the side to wait, it seemed as though we were the last two people on Earth. I didn't notice the shovel in back until you got out of the car, finally satisfied that our pursuer lost the trail. That's when I was convinced that I mistook the greatest moment of your resistance for the epitome of your despair. You weren't here to fight your pursuer, or even run from him…

You had come to dig your own grave.

I swore to love you, but that is no obligation to a woman of your beauty. I swore to serve you, but how could I act as usher to your final rest?

"Please," I begged, "tell me what would drive you to such an end?"

Do you remember how you flinched at my words? But the cold defiance in your eye made me somehow believe you had not given up yet.

Were you afraid I would be angry at what you've done?
Eva, blameless Eva. I could never be angry at you.
That I would try to stop you, or get in your way?
Never! I will only ever move to your desire, my love.

And with the opening of the trunk, I finally understood you. I felt nothing but relief when we carried the body out together, burying it there in the desert far from the prying eyes of petty men who do not understand the burden of love. If that is what needed be done to make you happy again, then I would have had it no other way.

I still do not know why the man hunted you, but it is not my place to force unpleasant memories and spoil your mind. I am writing this to let you know that nothing that happened will ever change how I feel about you. That I understand what you did, even admire you for going through with it. Eva, shining Eva, please do not let this be a barrier between us. Speak to me, welcome me as you once did, and I swear I will shelter you. I can forgive all evils in this world except the one that takes you away from me.

Forever yours,
Ivan


THERE YOU HAVE IT. As clean and incriminating an indictment as you'll ever find in writing. Of course I felt sorry for Eva after being stalked, but disregarding the due process of law and killing the man, well we couldn't exactly give her a free pass. I was so excited bringing this to the inspector in charge, and so disappointed when he disregarded it as irrelevant.

Obvious fabrication, he told me. Eva hadn't been stalked; she'd been investigated by the police. She was a suspect because she stood to gain a considerable amount of wealth after her husband Ivan's disappearance, although the case was eventually dropped without finding his body or sufficient evidence. The fact that a letter so stained with tears as to be almost unreadable was reconstructed didn't prove anything, except maybe the confused mind of a grieving widow.

I may have let my excitement rush me to conclusions, but seeing that the husband was the one who was murdered, the inspector must be right to think it was impossible for him to be the author.

Besides, how could Ivan help her bury his own body?

## I am a Human Voodoo Doll

Have you ever fallen in love so bad that it hurts? Where you have to force yourself to not even think about the person, because otherwise your mind will run rampantly down a spiral of uncontrollable obsession? I can't taste food without remembering her laughing at my cooking, which she affectionately named "bachelor chow." Music is damp and muted without her singing along to the lyrics, and my morning alarm torments me with the prospect of another day where she isn't mine.

Maybe I held on too tightly, maybe not tight enough. Maybe it wasn't something I did, but something I am. It just seemed like the harder I tried, the further away Elis drew, until one day she said she needed space. It was nauseating how polite and apologetic she was about it. She kept calling every other day to see if I was okay, and at first those gestures were my lifeline. I spent the whole day looking forward to the few minutes I would hear her voice again. I thought it was proof that she regretted her decision, and that it was only a matter of time before she came back to me.

Now I know it was only pity. Apparently the "space" Elis needed was already filled by someone else. I thought Nick-the-flabby-faced-man child was just a harmless friend. They were together almost immediately after she left me though, and the more I think about it, the more I wonder if it hadn't started even before. All those days when she just felt like "doing her own thing?" I guess that makes Nick her 'thing.'

You'd think that knowing she betrayed me would make it easier to stop loving her, but somehow it only made the obsession stronger. I can't move on with my life, and I'm running out of strength to keep pretending it will be okay.

It's been two months since the breakup, and she still keeps trying to call and check in on me. I've stopped answering. Text messages and voicemails are deleted before they're opened.

I'm not writing this as an excuse or justification for what I was about to do. I was past the point of having to prove anything to anyone. And yeah, maybe it makes me a coward, but I didn't care about that either. I was done being treated like this—done feeling like this. I was just done.

Amitriptyline is an anti-depressant which failed to alter the world from shades of grey. Oxazepam is a sleeping pill which was inept against my thoughts of her. But half a bottle of each, and I wouldn't wake up again. It was supposed to be a very peaceful way to go.

The taste was so bitter I could barely keep it down, but after that my mind just wiped clean. My last thoughts were that if I could do it all again, I would have still gone down the same road. The time I shared with her was still worth the place where it must end.

But it didn't end. I opened my eyes and squinted against the afternoon sun. I was lying in my bed, covers pulled up to my chin. Both the bottles of pills were gone. How did I wake up from that? I didn't even feel nauseous anymore. Was I supposed to just go find another method and try again? Or maybe this was God's way of giving me another chance.

Did I even still care about her? I crawled over to my laptop and immediately

## Sleepless Nights

checked Elis's Facebook page. I could use her photos as a test. If I could look at them without being overwhelmed with pain, then maybe—

She'd changed her profile picture. Flabby face was kissing her cheek. A feeling like acid worked its way down my chest. Nothing had changed. Nothing was ever going to change the way I felt—

No. Something had changed.

Her page was full of sympathetic prayers and comments:

*YOU WERE AN ANGEL. God must have needed you back.*
*I'm so sorry to hear what happened.*
*Let me know if there's anything I can do to help.*

I SKIMMED up to the top of the page. This was posted last night:

*THIS IS NICK. I thought I should let you all know that Elis died from a lethal dose of sleeping pills last night. I found her unconscious when I visited this morning and rushed her to the hospital, but it was too late. Message me for details.*

I WAS COMPLETELY DUMBFOUNDED. I had taken the pills, but somehow she had died instead. I had been thinking about her right before I went, so is there some way it had been transferred to her? It seemed impossible, but the coincidence of her going the same way on the same night seemed ludicrous. Besides, hadn't she been happy with Nick?

My racing thoughts were shattered by a sudden fierce knocking on my door. Was it Elis? Of course not, don't be stupid . . . I was about to open it when they knocked again.

"Police. We have a few questions to ask you."

I froze, my hand still on the handle. It really was my fault she was dead! But how? I hadn't even seen her in weeks. Somehow what I did to myself happened to her, and the police being here proved it. Even if it was something else, my mind was too overwrought to begin to deal with them. I live on the ground floor, so it wasn't hard to just grab my keys and duck out my bedroom window.

I didn't know where to go, but I needed to drive around for a while and clear my head. I unlocked my car and was about to climb in when—

"Police! Stop right there!"

Two officers were emerging from my building. As soon as they caught sight of me, they began jogging. I should have just talked to them, but I felt compelled to run from the nameless clenching guilt and terror which possessed me.

I jumped in the car and floored the pedal, tearing out of my apartment parking lot like I was running for my life. Last night I had been ready to die, but now I knew there was some greater power working through me. This was supposed to be my fresh start!

I couldn't stop.

The police car was right behind me. Sirens blared in accusation. My mind was at war with itself with panic. I could barely breathe. My familiar neighborhood looked alien to me. I screeched around the corner and up the overpass leading onto the freeway at breakneck speed. I was just becoming aware of the implications of my escape when a horrendous impact sent me spinning out of control.

The police cruiser rammed me to prevent me getting on the freeway. My car spun two complete circles then smashed into a concrete barrier. The screech of metal was replaced with the roar of the airbags, and then everything went black.

I hadn't been wearing my seat belt, but that might have saved my life as I was thrown clear of the wreck. I must have only been out for a few seconds though, because coming to, I could still feel the warmth of my burning car behind me.

The officers hadn't been so lucky. When they rammed my car, their car must have lost control in the opposite direction and fallen off the overpass. I didn't want to look, but I couldn't stop myself. The cruiser had flipped onto its roof, crushing the officers beneath it.

But me?

I didn't have a scratch.

My crazy theory must not have been so far off. I take the pills, but I was thinking about Elis and so she died instead. My car was hit, but I was thinking about the police and they suffered from the crash.

Both times I walked away clean.

I couldn't stay to ponder my discovery, I already heard more sirens approaching from the distance. I took off by foot and began running through the streets.

I had to test my theory. Just one more time. If it was true, then some divine agent had resurrected me, and I really did have something to live for. If it wasn't, then I was a suicidally depressed loner who was wanted by the police. I had nothing to lose and everything to gain, so it was time to put it all on the line.

But with who? I couldn't just endanger an innocent stranger. I didn't want anyone else to get hurt except—well, except Nick, of course. If it's anyone's fault Elis died, it must have been his. It was his job to make her happy, wasn't it? His job to notice if something wasn't right. Hell, the scumbag went behind my back and stole her from me. If anyone deserved to suffer, it was him.

I didn't want it to be clean either. Both other times I walked away unharmed, so I wanted him to suffer the way he made me suffer. I wanted to bring him to that point of hopeless isolation and rejection and leave him stranded beyond the hope of return. And more than anything, I wanted to be there to watch it happen.

I found him at Elis's apartment. Her old apartment, I guess, since she didn't live there anymore. I watched him carrying a box of her things to put into his car. She'd just died that morning, and he was already looting her stuff like a grave robber? There's no denying that I was going to enjoy watching him burn.

Because I was going to burn with him. I continued watching him from behind the hedge which surrounded the parking lot. I watched his face while I poured gasoline over my head, imagining what it would look like after it lit up. Unspeakably grotesque. Either he would die, or the burns would disfigure him for life. He would be alone, just like I was after he stole her from me. It still wasn't good enough though. I wanted him to see me when it happened, so he'd understand why.

I waited by his car until he came back out with another box. The gasoline was cool against me, clinging comfortably like a second skin. It burned like hell where it ran into my eyes, but I forced them to stay open. It was worth it to see the look on his face.

"Oh shit, man, didn't see you there," he said. "I guess you heard about Elis."

I grinned. He still didn't know why I was here. I hadn't looked forward to anything so much since Elis left me.

"Can I help you with something?" he asked. "How come you're all wet—"

I twirled the lighter in my fingers. His eyes fell on it for the first time. Then he looked at my face—then back at the lighter. Then at the rainbow reflections in the pooling liquid around my feet. His eyes bulged, and I smiled wider. Now he gets it.

"This is for Elis," I said.

Flick.

Flick.

WOOSH.

The fire started at my face and then swiftly engulfed my entire body. Nothing in my life prepared me for that pain. I stood there watching him for as long as I could—waiting for the spark to ignite in his skin. Waiting for the flesh to melt from his face and his bones to crack and splinter.

"Someone call the ambulance! Or the fire department! Or shit—I don't know—get someone!"

I heard him shouting, but I couldn't see him anymore. My eyes must have boiled out of my skull. He said something else, but I couldn't hear him over the sound of my own scream which tore out of my body like my soul seeking release.

For the third time I blacked out, but I was still grinning the whole way. Soon I would wake up, and he would be the one who burned...

---

Elis had stopped by my apartment the night I took the pills. She was worried about me after I didn't reply to any of her calls or messages. Shit, she might have even still cared for me, but I guess now I'll never know. She must have been overwhelmed with guilt and grief at seeing me like that and taken the rest of the pills herself after she got back home. I was later informed of the pool of vomit in the corner of my bathroom where I had regurgitated my own lethal dose.

The police hadn't died when their cruiser turned over. They'd just been pinned inside and unable to pursue me. They had only come by my apartment because their investigation had revealed Elis visiting me on the night of her death.

But Nick did burn. He had forced himself through the flame to get my burning clothes off and smother the fire with his body. If it wasn't for him, I never would have survived until the ambulance came. His face isn't scarred like mine, but he'll have the marks on his arms and chest for the rest of his life. He's a good man. Elis would have been very happy with him if it wasn't for me.

So, I was wrong.

I was too maddened by grief and self-loathing to understand until it was too late.

There's no such thing as a human voodoo doll. There is no one working through me, or a spirit of universal justice that makes everyone get what they deserve, but if my experience has one redeeming quality, then let it be a warning.

No-one should make life-altering decisions as a result of an emotional state. No matter how convinced your heart is that something is true, wait to act until your mind has caught up.

If I had stopped for a moment to talk to Elis, I would have seen how much she still cared, and I never would have taken the pills.

If I hadn't run from the police, there never would have been this accident.

And if I'd only thought my theory through before...

Well one day we will all wake up as a different person than who we are now. We will learn to forgive those who hurt us and to forgive ourselves for hurting others. Elis is gone, but the scars I'll have to remember her by will never never leave.

## The Organic Machine

3D printing is the future, and the future is here.

We are on the verge of another industrial revolution, and I'm incredibly excited to be a part of it. I'm a photogrammetry software designer, and have spent the last four years working with fashion and clothing companies. I even worked at Nike for a while—they're already beginning to 3D print shoes.

I recently had the opportunity to apply my skills to a medical laboratory where they're beginning to 3D print human tissue. It's an ingenious concept—suspending living cells in a smart gel which allows the cells to fuse together into tissue once they're in alignment. The smart gel is then washed away, leaving an organ of purely human tissue.

"We're the first company to replicate organic vascular structures," Doctor Hansaf claimed on my first day there. He led me through the sterile halls which droned with dull florescent lighting. "The organs we print can diffuse oxygen and nutrients even more efficiently than those in your body."

Several other lab technicians passed me in the hall. I smiled, but each averted their gaze immediately, finding a sudden fascination with the blank floor tiles.

"It sounds like you know what you're doing. What do you need me for?" I asked.

"Our scaffolding needs to be remodeled. One of our organs seems to be leaking, and we can't figure out why."

"Which one?" He didn't need to answer though. As soon as Doctor Hansaf opened the door at the end of the hallway, I saw the most macabre sight I could have imagined.

A steel table was lined with row upon row of human eyeballs, each staring at me from their great, unblinking orbs. And leaking might be an accurate term, but they would be better described as crying. The saline liquid filled each eye to overflowing before draining into a multitude of tiny pools upon the table.

"Quite beautiful, aren't they?" he said. I jumped a little to realize how close he was behind me. "Almost perfect—almost better than perfect. This design can see 3 times sharper than a human with 20/20 vision. It can even see beyond the traditional visual electromagnetic range, perceiving some near ultra-violet spectrum as well."

Beautiful isn't the first word I would have chosen, but I could understand his pride. They looked real enough that you wouldn't look twice if a pair of these were staring back at you from a human face.

"The modeling software is on that computer." The doctor gestured to a desktop workstation in the corner which was setup beside a second door. "You'll find all the current designs on there. I'll give you some time to look everything over and see if you can't find the issue. I'll be back to check on you in an hour."

I couldn't tear my gaze away from the eyes. I nodded stiffly again, hearing the door close behind me. I wasn't about to ditch a job just because of the unsettling environment. I averted my eyes from the table and walked over to the computer.

While it was booting up, I cast another glance behind me. My heart skipped a beat. Each of the eyes had turned to watch me. They were facing the door a moment before—but now they were facing me.

I slowly walked back to the door I came in, watching them this time. They turned to follow me. Without even realizing I was doing so, I put my hand on the door: locked from the outside. There was a small glass viewing window in the door, but I couldn't see anything besides the hallway wall.

"Hello? Doctor Hansaf?" I knocked on the door. No answer.

I turned back, but the eyeballs were pointed toward the opposite door now. I took a deep breath. They weren't watching me—it was ridiculous to think they were. There must simply be some fast twitch muscles activating from the salt in the saline solution.

I walked to the second door—locked as well. It was a high security laboratory though. It wasn't unreasonable to think the doors automatically lock. The doctor must have forgotten about it, but he was going to be back in an hour. I just had to focus on my job.

I glanced back at the eyeballs, but they were still facing the second door. I sat back down at the computer and loaded up the photogrammetry software. Pretty soon, I was so engrossed in inspecting the intricate scaffolding that I didn't even think about the eyes behind me.

The secondary door opened beside me. Had an hour passed already? I turned, but I didn't see anyone in the room. Maybe he just peeked inside and saw I was still working. I turned back to the computer again.

*Footsteps.*

I spun around, but I still didn't see anyone there. I was about to go back to work when I noticed all the eyes were moving once more.

*Footsteps.*

Each one was slightly louder—slightly closer than the last.

The eyes were all following the empty space of ground where the sound was coming from. Something was there and I couldn't see it—but the artificial eyes could.

"Hello?" I pushed the chair between myself and the footsteps and pressed my body against the desk. "Is somebody there?"

The chair moved, and the footsteps got closer. I lurched backward into the wall and started moving around the room toward the door I entered from.

"Doctor Hansaf!" I yelled. "Let me out of here!"

I pounded on the door. Still locked.

*Footsteps.*

The eyes were all pointed directly next to me.

"Something is in here! Help!" I screamed, slamming against the door with my shoulder.

A face appeared in the viewing window. One of the lab technicians. He watched me for a moment, then began to write something down on a clipboard. What in the hell? I pounded on the door again and he looked up.

"I know you can see me!" I yelled. "Let me out of here."

The lab technician tapped the side of his left eye. Then his right. He pointed at me. What was he trying to say? I glanced over my shoulder—the eyes were all watching the ground directly behind me.

Tentatively, I reached out my hand and felt something cold and slimy in the air. It was just a couple inches from my face. Something like a hand loosely grasped me back, but I quickly drew away. It didn't touch me again after that.

"What are you?" I asked the empty air.

Footsteps. The eyes followed them back to the corner of the room. What in the hell was going on? I turned back to the door. The lab technician was holding a piece of paper up against the glass: *Would you like to be the first person to see it?*

I glanced back at the corner of the room and nodded.

The lab technician wrote something and held it up again: *We will need to replace your eyes. Is that okay?*

I shook my head.

He started writing again: *He's not the only one. They're everywhere. We're not safe.*

I heard the second door open and turned to see the eyes follow the invisible slimy thing exit the room. The door closed again.

The primary door opened at once, and Doctor Hansaf entered. He was smiling like we had just shared a private joke.

"Well? What do you think?"

"What the hell was that?" I asked.

"We don't entirely know," he admitted. "It's something which is only visible in the near ultraviolet spectrum, but machines aren't able to detect it. We only started noticing them once we printed the eyes."

"So, you lied to me. You brought me here as a guinea pig."

He shrugged and put his arm around my shoulder. "This is a laboratory—you shouldn't be surprised to find experiments being done here. But you came voluntarily, you will leave voluntarily, and you will only continue participating if you choose. Will you take the eyes?"

"Absolutely not. I want no part in this." I was already marching down the hallway.

I wish I had taken them though, because now I hear footsteps following me all the way home.

## My Face Will be the Last Thing you see

Green eyes of a cat and hair dark enough to make the shadows behind her look like they were glowing. I caught her staring at me over the rim of her wineglass across the room.

I did what most long-time single guys in my situation would do. I pulled out my phone and started surfing through Reddit. That's right—play it cool. Make it look like you've got important stuff going on. Just pretend you're not interested in her, then keep up the illusion until she leaves, and you die alone.

I really need a new strategy for meeting women.

I forced myself to peek at her again. She was still looking at me, and this time she smiled. I started to smile back, but remembered just in time how uneven my teeth are and tried to twist it into a mysterious expression instead. I was trying to channel Clark Gabel, but probably ended up closer to a constipated cookie monster. She interrupted my quiet self-loathing by beckoning me with her finger.

I looked over my shoulder. There wasn't anyone behind me but the barkeeper, and his back was turned. This had to be some kind of joke. I don't think of myself as particularly ugly—a bit doughy perhaps—but I never attracted attention from women like that. Hell, I didn't even know women like that existed outside of airbrushed magazines.

I'd only been planning to stop off for a quick buzz after work. I don't drink ordinarily, but the shifts have been crazy since Peter died of a heart-attack last week. I just needed to unwind. Her tantalizing invitation promised an even more enjoyable distraction though, and my feet moved on their own to treacherously thrust me into the booth beside her.

I didn't fully realize what I was doing until it was too late to come up with a witty introduction: "Uh, hi. Can I help you with something?" Yeah. Real smooth. What are you, a waiter?

She extended a graceful hand with neatly polished nails the color of dried blood. Her skin was so pale and translucent that the blue veins were clearly visible meandering up her arm. "Hello, Eddy. Can I call you Eddy?"

You can call me anything, my dumb brain thought. I didn't even realize she knew my name until I'd already shaken the chill hand she offered me. "Do you know me?" I asked instead.

Her limp fingers revived in my hand and gripped me firmly for a second as though holding on for dear life. The pressure was gone as quickly as it appeared though, and she released me before luxuriously leaning back.

"Not yet, but I have a way of getting to know people. Would you like me to get to know you, Eddy?"

I could imagine a snake whispering its prey to sleep with the same tone of voice. I felt definitively agitated sitting here, but I couldn't tell how much was fear and how much excitement. I don't suppose it mattered, because I was so engulfed in her presence that I was powerless to do anything but nod.

The woman produced two decks of playing cards and placed them upon the table. Her long fingers fanned through them with the dexterity a pianist, and I half-imagined a musical score rising up from inside me as she rapidly stacked and shuffled them together. One deck seemed to contain a multitude of human faces while the other contained a variety of surreal paintings which resembled Tarot cards.

"You're not a Witch, are you?" I hadn't meant to blurt it out, but I had just seen my own face flash by on one of the cards and was becoming increasingly uncomfortable.

"That's the wrong question to ask," she said, not even looking at the cards while she fluidly shuffled. "The weapon matters not compared to the intent of the wielder. I could kill you more easily with my switchblade than a Witch could with her magic, but do you really think I would hurt you?"

Her bluntness relieved me of my own burden for tact. I might as well be honest with her too.

"Yes. I think you would."

She grinned and slapped the combined deck down with enough force to make the whole table rattle. I nearly fell out of my seat from shock.

"Good. It's the cautious ones who last the longest."

I wanted to question her further, but my attention was diverted by the cards which she began dealing. The first one she flipped from that jumbled pile depicted my face with my name neatly handwritten below it.

"How did you do that? Where'd you even get that picture?"

Her lovely features furrowed with concentration. She didn't answer. Her hand caressed the deck with tremulous focus. She was about to draw the next card, but then gave me a wry smile and cut the deck to draw from the middle instead. Lying on the table beside my photograph was a skeleton, only its face was replaced with an exquisite painting of the woman sitting across from me. She let out a long breath like relief, but her warm smile couldn't dislodge the mounting horror in my chest.

"That wasn't so bad, now was it? Now we know each other a little better, don't we?"

"I don't know anything. I don't even know your name." I was starting to get angry. It wasn't just at her for messing with me like this—I was angry at myself. How pathetic I must be to keep entertaining this nonsense just because a pretty girl smiled at me. If it had been anyone else, I would have been out the door a long time ago.

"Oh, don't be like that, it's actually good news," she insisted. "Your photograph obviously represents you—"

"I don't know how you got that, but I want it back." I tried snatching at it, but the card danced around her nimble fingers and evaded me.

"And you recognize my face on the other, don't you? That's the last thing you'll see before you die."

All the excitement was gone. My heart strained against my rib cage with nothing but the absurd fear she instilled in me. I made another wild snatch for my photograph, but she tugged it just out of my grasp again. All I could reach was the rest of the deck still on the table, so I picked that up instead.

"You want these back?" I asked. "Give me my card."

"You aren't being very cautious right now." Her eyes narrowed with dangerous intent.

I looked down at the other cards in my hand. That's when I noticed that all the other photographs had a thin red line drawn through the center. There had to be at least twenty of them in here.

"They weren't being cautious either, and you don't need my sight to guess what happened to them." The voice was as cold as the space between stars. I didn't even care about my photo anymore. I just wanted to get out. I didn't look back even when the bartender started shouting about my tab. All I could think about was putting as much distance as I could between myself and the woman tormenting me.

What in the world was that even about? I know I don't approach women very often, but I can't imagine that's the typical reaction.

As I jogged, the clean evening air unraveled the twisted knot in my stomach and began to purge the surreal experience from my mind. I slowed down to a walk, even chuckling to myself at the absurdity of what just happened.

A psychic or a con-artist (not like there was a difference)—that's what she had to be. She wasn't flirting or threatening—she was just trying to sell me her readings. I stopped by that bar all the time after work, so it wouldn't have been hard for her to snap a photo or get my name. Of course, she hadn't actually asked for money, but that was something I preferred not to dwell on.

I replayed the scenario in my head, and even congratulated myself with how I handled the situation. Good for me, for not falling victim to her seducing charms. Although there's no denying the fantasy I still entertained of taking her and…

It wasn't until I got home and was digging for my keys that I felt the deck of playing cards still in my pocket. I'd been in such a rush to get out that I hadn't even noticed taking it with me. I fanned through the deck to make sure there weren't any more photos of me, but stopped abruptly.

Peter.

He was wearing the suit I saw him wear every day for the last five years. The thin red line scored directly across his face. She couldn't have had anything to do with…

Just to be safe, I started Googling some other names captioned below the photographs. After the third search pulled up a third obituary, I knew there was no point in going on. 24 other photograph cards beside my own, and all with a red line struck cleanly through the center. Every death was from a different cause, although I noticed several quotations of shock and despair from families swearing it came without warning.

I saw the woman again the next day. It was only a glimpse, but she was sitting at the bus-stop I usually took. I'd left her cards at home and didn't want a confrontation about it, so I just waited the 20 minutes for the next bus to come along.

There she was again at the taco shack I frequent for lunch. She was actually working behind the counter. She smiled when we locked eyes, but I immediately turned around and left without a word. The less I got involved in this lunacy, the better.

Then again at the grocery store. She was deliberating between brands of peanut butter.

Again at the bus-stop, watching me get on.

Twice more I saw her standing on different street corners on the drive home. I don't know how she was moving so quickly, but it was obvious that I was being stalked. I was being stupid for just pretending none of this happened. I had information linking a string of deaths, and I should have brought this to the police from the very beginning.

I stopped off at home just long enough to grab the deck of cards from my dresser before heading down to the local station. It was getting late by now—around 8 p.m.—but the dreary march of street lamps still hadn't begun to glow. I considered hiring a car, but I didn't want to risk being trapped in a small space with the woman. I just walked—trying my best not to imagine green eyes glinting in the mounting darkness around me.

I should have known it wouldn't be any good. She was the officer on duty, just sitting behind her desk with hands folded patiently on the table. Not doing anything. Just waiting for me.

"I've got your cards. You can have them back," I said. I dropped the stack on her desk. She didn't take her eyes off me, not even when they scattered from impact. I half-turned to leave, but couldn't quite force myself to turn my back on her.

"I know you did something to the others," I spluttered to fill the gaping silence. "And I don't care, okay? About Peter, or any of them. I don't want anything to do with you."

She didn't blink. Didn't move a muscle. I started backing up, almost making it to the door before she finally said:

"I'm following you for a reason, Eddy. If you walk out that door, then you will never see me again."

I hesitated. Was that a promise, or a threat?

"Okay. I'm okay with that," I said.

"Are you? Even knowing that my face will be the last thing you see before you die?"

It sounded more like a teacher reminding me of a formula than it did a threat. That didn't stop the hairs from rising on my skin as she stood from the desk to approach me.

"How are you everywhere that I am?" I asked.

"What's more likely..." She was only a foot away now. My back was against the glass door, but every word was drawing her closer. "That I'm everywhere at the same time, or that you're stuck in one place and I'm there with you?"

"Why are you doing this to me? Why are you killing all these people?"

"I don't kill anyone," she said. "I simply warn them what is to come. I give them comfort in their dying moments. Those who go violently into their last sleep are doomed to nightmares, while those who drift softly are at peace. I have seen the future, and know that my face is the last thing you will ever see."

The air between us was intoxicating. I couldn't break away.

"The last time I see you," I managed, "it doesn't have to be today. It can be next year—or fifty years from now."

"I have a job to do. How do you expect to find me again in fifty years?" she asked, a bemused smile playing about her lips.

"That's easy," I replied. "I'll just never let you go."

Despite all her tricks, I was stronger than her. I locked my hands behind her waist and drew her into me. I wasn't ready to die, but even more than that, I wasn't ready to die alone. She seemed intrigued at first when I pressed my mouth onto hers, but then she started struggling. I held on even tighter, afraid that she would simply vanish the moment she slipped free.

She couldn't love me. No-one could love me for long. Even if I somehow captured her fancy, I knew someone like her could only ever get bored with someone like me. Sooner or later she would leave me, and that would be the last time I ever saw her. That would be the day I die.

She was fighting now. I could feel thrashing against me like a caged animal. All I could do was hold on tighter, dragging her from the building and into the darkness outside.

I crushed her against me with all my strength until my arms went numb and my fingers bled from where they clasped behind her back. Each breath she took was shallower than the last until finally her pale skin was bleached as white as bone.

She wasn't lying about carrying a switchblade, but it was a lot harder than I imagined using that to separate her head from her body. I couldn't work it through the spine, and was forced to simply peel back the skin of her face and take that with me instead.

Now her face rests on the pillow to my left each night I lay down to sleep. It's the last thing I see before I close my eyes. And if death were chance to steal me before I wake, then I know I will go in peace without the burden of dreams to follow.

Each morning I rise on the right and turn away from it. All through the day I walk with surety, knowing I will not die before seeing her again.

Either way, I know I won't die alone.

## 52 Sleepless Nights

### The Grim Reaper's Scythe

There is no fear as potent as the fear of the unknown. No monstrous visage discovered yet is as terrifying as the infinite potential for horror which exists before the mask is removed.

That is why we humans, in our naive misunderstanding of the universal order, are gripped by the mortal fear of death. We think it's the final frontier: the greatest imaginable unknown from whose penumbral shores no traveler may return. And so we cling desperately to even the dreariest and most anguished lives, suffering any known evil over our release into the enigma beyond.

But death is not to be feared, because death is very well understood. We have witnessed it, caused it, measured and recorded it to the last dying spasm of neuronal flickering. Even as I lay dying, it seemed silly to me that I should be afraid of the emptiness which reason promised to expect.

While I was alive I wouldn't experience death, so there is no reason to be afraid. When I was dead, I wouldn't be capable of experiencing anything, so fear still has no cause. That thought brought me great comfort as I felt the last erratic struggle from my heart against the inevitable conclusion I approached. It wasn't until I was finally drifting off to sleep that a final intrusive doubt bubbled in my brain:

*What if it isn't death which is to be feared? What if it is what lies beyond?*

And so troubled did I slip beyond mortal understanding, stepping into a world as far forsaken by reason as I was now from life. I still lay in the hospital room, but the bustle of nurses and the beeping machines lost their opacity as though I was mired in swiftly-descending dusk. It seemed as though every sound was an echo of what it once was; every sight a reflection. With each passing moment, the world was becoming less real....

But all that sight and sound—all that being—it wasn't simply disappearing. It was *transforming* into a figure beside me. The less real my room became, the more real the figure was, until presently it existed in such sharp actuality that nothing beside it seemed real at all.

His cloak was black. Not the *color* black, but its essence. It was as though seeing a tiger after a lifetime of looking at a child's crude drawing and thinking that's all a tiger was. Reality flowed around his scythe like a brush through water colors, and I could see each elementary particle and time itself sunder across its blade.

Surely this, I thought, this is why we were taught without words to fear death. I clutched my thin cloth blanket, cowering from the intensity of the Reaper's presence, but the once-soft cotton now flowed like translucent mist through my hands. I knew in that moment that nothing could hide me from the specter's grasp, for he was the only real thing in this world.

**You're late.**

They weren't words. My head ached from the strain of this knowledge as my lateness was burned into my awareness, imparted like an inescapable law of physics as unequivocal as gravity.

**We don't have time for the usual speech. Hurry now.**

I felt myself swept up around him like dirt in a hurricane. Before I knew what was happening, we were outside the hospital, moving at such a frenzied pace that the world around me blurred into a dizzying tunnel of flashing light.

**If you're lucky, IT will have gotten bored waiting for you.**

I had too many questions, all fighting for attention in the forefront of my brain without any making their way out.

**You're quiet. I admire that. People usually ask too much.**

"What's the point?" I asked. My voice felt flat and dead compared to his overwhelming substance. "How can I try to comprehend something so beyond mortal knowledge?"

**You can't. But it's still human nature to ask.**

We weren't slowing. If anything, our pace was increasing. I wasn't running, or flying, or anything of that nature. It was more like the rest of the world was moving around us while we stood still. A vague darkness and a heavy damp smell made me guess that we'd gone underground, but I couldn't say for sure.

"One question then," I asked. "What else is here besides you?"

**And that is why questions are pointless. Death is not a place, or a person. It's all there is.**

A troubling thought, made more so by the growing howl reverberating through the rocks around me. We still seemed to be descending into the earth, and the air grew warmer and denser now. The sound continued to mount as though the world itself was suffering.

"Then what is IT?"

**What I'm here to protect you from.**

The rocks split from a flash of his scythe, and the ground opened farther into a sprawling cavern dominated by a subterranean lake.

"But I thought you said you were all there is."

**No, I said Death was all there is.**

We weren't moving any longer. Light glinted off the scythe from some unseen source and streamed into the lake like a tributary. Once inside, the light didn't reflect or dissipate, but swirled and danced as a luminescent oil.

"I thought you were Death."

**Death is not a person.**

The light was taking a life of its own inside the water. The still surface began to churn with spectral energy. It took my scattered mind a long while to realize that *I* was the energy flowing into the lake. I still felt tangled up with the figure, but we now existed as a beam of light boiling into the water.

I knew I wouldn't understand, but that didn't stop me from feeling frustrated. If Death is all there is, then what is IT? What was waiting for me? The water pressed around me and I couldn't speak, although I didn't seem to need air any more.

**IT is here.**

Something was in the water around me. Hands grabbed me by the legs and began dragging me downward. I was amazed to even discover I had limbs again. They felt so alien to me that it was almost as though this body was not my own. Light flashed from the scythe—then again. The hands let go, and the howling rose in deafening cascades. The Reaper was fighting something, although I couldn't make any sense of the battle except for the madness of thrashing water.

The howling earth reached its crescendo, and the *screams* made the water around me convulse and contract like living fluid. Had the Reaper slashed IT? Was I safe? I began to explore my new body in the water, but just when I thought I was beginning to gain control, the hands clutched me once more. I lurched downward, struggling in vain against their implacable grip.

"What is here?" I tried to shout against the suffocating liquid. "What is happening?"

But I couldn't sense the Reaper's presence any longer. The heat was unbearable, but from the cold depths the hands dragged me down. I became aware of a blinding light at the bottom of the lake, and though I struggled, the hands dragged me inexorably deeper.

**I'm sorry. I couldn't fight IT off.** It seemed to be coming from so far away now. **We will try again next time.**

The pressure—the heat—the noise—the hands dragging me into the light. I closed my eyes and screamed. I was free from the water now, but I just kept screaming. I couldn't bear to look at IT—whatever had stolen me. Whatever was Death but wasn't—whatever even the Reaper could not defeat.

Then a voice spoke. Real, human words, from a real, human mouth. My senses were so distraught and overwhelmed that I couldn't make sense of them, but I'm guessing they were something like:

"Congratulations! He's a healthy baby boy."

Most people can't remember the day they die, or the day they were born. I happen to remember both, and I know that they are the same.

## The Hitchhiker

Ever start dating someone and everything is going a little *too* well? So well that you start worrying for no reason what-so-ever? No one could be that perfect, and even if they were, then there's no way they would look twice at you. The only logical explanation is that they aren't as perfect as they pretend to be, which leaves you playing detective trying to figure out the catch.

Maybe all those little quirks that you find adorable now are going to drive you crazy in a few months. Maybe she even has a dark secret: hard drugs, or hating dogs, or that one time she killed a man with a stiletto heel in a fit of passionate rage.

There's an easy solution if you want to find out who someone really is: take a long-ass road trip with them. If you're still together by the end, then it was meant to be. My girlfriend Emily thought it was a good idea to drive 1,000 miles together across the country after we've only been dating for two months. We're both pretty busy with work and don't get to spend much time together, so naturally being locked in a prison cell on wheels for two days was going to be an improvement.

First hundred miles? So far so good. Holding hands, singing to the radio together, uncontrollable laughter when she found out I knew all the words to Sk8ter Boi (sue me, it's a catchy song). And if the road ended there and we turned around, we might have lived a long and happy life together. It was when we passed the hitchhiker that everything began to fall apart.

"Let's give him a ride," Emily said, squeezing my hand. "We'll be on this road forever anyway."

"We don't even know where he's going," I told her. "He's probably just going to rob us and steal our car."

Which is true of everyone you don't know (and most of them you do), as far as I'm concerned. The hitchhiker's clean-pressed suit didn't reassure me either. That just meant he'd successfully robbed someone before, which actually made him even more dangerous. The man didn't even have a sign or anything. He was just sitting by the freeway ramp, spastically waving his thumb like he was guiding an airplane to land.

It was my turn to drive though, and I sailed right past. Emily and I started bickering after that. She thought I wasn't compassionate, and I thought she was reckless. It took about ten minutes before she finally dropped it, although it wasn't because she'd conceded.

"Hey look, there's another one!"

Sitting by the side of the road, waving his thumb like it was the end of the world. It wasn't another one though. It was the same guy, I'm sure of it. Only this time he looked like he'd been out here for a few days. His suit was streaked with dirt and his hair was greasy. There was a desperate strain in his face, like a proud man trying to conceal his embarrassment. It wasn't just my imagination either—Emily recognized him, too.

"How do you think he got here so fast?" she wondered.

"I don't know, and I don't care," I said. "This trip is supposed to be about us, so let's not get distracted."

My car blew past him and I stayed the course. We argued again, and even when we agreed to drop it, the argument just slithered into new topics. She hated my music, I hated how judgmental she was. I was controlling, she was picking fights over nothing. It kept getting worse until we saw something that shut both of us up real fast.

The hitchhiker again. Another twenty miles down the road. The bottom part of his shirt and jacket were shredded, and blood was soaking through a concealed stomach wound. He was stumbling along the side of the road, weaving erratically, wandering onto the highway at times before pitching off to the side.

Emily could not believe that I didn't stop. I couldn't believe she still wanted me to. She kept yelling that he was hurt and needed help. She refused to even acknowledge how weird it was that he kept getting ahead of us. She almost caused an accident by grabbing the wheel when I refused to turn around.

We drove for the next fifty miles in silence. I turned the radio back on, but she snapped it off immediately. It wasn't until I pulled off for gas that we saw him again.

Face down on the side of the road. Shirt and jacket gone. Long, even, bloody gashes from his shoulders to his ass, almost like bear claws or something. I stopped the car and parked behind him. Emily jumped out and knelt beside the body. She looked up at me with uncomprehending rage burning behind her eyes, like this was my fault somehow.

"He's dead," she said, standing up. "Can I call this in to the police, or is that too much of an *inconvenience* for you?"

I nodded, absolutely numb. I filled up on gas while she waited with the body until the police arrived. They asked us a few questions, but neither Emily nor I felt comfortable explaining that this wasn't the first time we'd seen him. They took our information and let us get back on the road after about fifteen minutes.

The car was silent for a long time after that. It was starting to get dark, and I kept suggesting places to spend the night, but Emily just shrugged and stared out the window. At the rate we were going, we'd be breaking up by the end of the trip and I wanted it to be over as soon as possible. I just kept driving, long after the sun went down.

Emily fell asleep around midnight, but I kept going. She was so beautiful like that, and everything was going so well before this. It was just so frustrating that such a random event that neither of us could predict would destroy us like this. By around 2 a.m. I was getting real tired, but I decided not to give up. Maybe if she woke up and we were already there then she'd see how hard I worked for her. Maybe then we'd still have a chance to patch things up.

I caressed her hand and she returned the pressure. I flirted with the thought that everything was going to be okay, at least until she woke up and started screaming. There wasn't any safe shoulder to get off the highway, so I had no choice but to keep going. She shut up quick enough, but it was still about ten seconds of hysterical breathing before she could explain what was going on.

"Behind you. In the backseat."

I glanced backward. Then at the road. Then behind me again. The hitchhiker was in the backseat. Naked, filthy, covered with black blood and old wounds. His elbows rested on his knees as he leaned toward us, evidently still alive as he cocked his head to regard me curiously.

"Get off the road!" Emily started screaming again.

"I can't! Get him out!"

"Did you go back? What's he doing here?"

"I don't know! Open the door or something!"

I slowed down gradually and put my flashers on to warn the car behind me. The hitchhiker reached around behind Emily and grabbed her by the throat. I slammed my fist into his arm and felt something give way under the soft rot. When I lifted my hand, I could see a black bone from his forearm protruding straight through the skin. He didn't seem bothered.

She was crying as the dirty fingers dug into her throat, sinking in like it was made of dough. She was thrashing so hard that one of her flailing fists smashed straight through the window. I managed to safely stop the car, but there was nothing I could do to break the indomitable grip around her neck.

I jumped out and ran to the backseat with the hitchhiker. Maybe if I had a clearer shot at him I could drag him out. I flung open the door and lunged inside, falling face first into an empty seat. I thought he'd already escaped somehow and ripped open the passenger side door. Emily was gone too. If it wasn't for the blood and the broken window, I would have thought I'd gone completely insane.

I spent the next hour searching the surrounding area with my flashlight. I considered calling the police, but I realized that if I wasn't already a suspect after the first body was found, then I'd definitely be one now that I was soaked in blood and my girlfriend was the one to disappear.

All I could do was get back on the road. Drive home and never tell another soul what had happened, that was my plan. It wasn't a good plan, but it's all I had. And I would have done it too, if I hadn't just passed Emily standing by the side of the road. Clean, healthy, waving her thumb enthusiastically in the air. That was a few miles back, but I stopped to write this because I don't know what to do from here.

If I see her again, do I pick her up? Or just keep driving and hope for the best?

## An Open Letter To My Daughter's Killer

An open letter to the killer of Samantha B. If you're somehow able to read this wherever you are now, know that I will find you.

No father should have to watch their child be lowered into the sacred silence of the earth. I don't know if there is a right age to die, but I do know it isn't seventeen. Better at birth before eyes had filled with light and I had learned to love so deeply. Better late into old age when life's fleeting joys had been more than tasted. Better not at all, but a world where prayers are answered is a world where they're not needed: a world that isn't ours.

All the hours I spent playing on the floor were wasted. All the faces and bad jokes I made to get a smile, all the music I played to inspire a song, or the books I read to inspire a dream: all wasted. I thought that was all it took to make me a good father, but I was wrong. I invested my entire life into this single purpose, but everything I had to give was not enough. I wasn't there when I was needed most, and nothing I have ever done or could ever do can change that.

The police found the knife you did it with in the woods. It was a slow death, they told me, but passing out would have avoided most of the pain. I wonder if you regretted it as soon as your blade entered her skin. Did you mean for it to dig so deep? Did you panic when the blood wouldn't stop? Did you call for help, or struggle in vain to bandage the wound, or were you too ashamed? I wonder if you planned the kill at all, or whether time was flying too fast and your blood pounding too loud, and you didn't know how to make it stop until it was too late.

Were you thinking of anyone but yourself when you did it? I don't know what private torment brought you to this point, but taking a life will never cease that pain. The pain is passed from one person to the next, enduring past life, past death, past mortal strength to bear. Until the day long after you're gone when the next victim sees the sun dawn without light or warmth, and all sounds and colors bleed into an endless gray. And then that sun too will set, passing on your pain once again.

You must think that I hate you. I don't think anyone would blame me if I did. I hate that you destroyed my family, but I forgive you for everything. You may not believe me, but I promise it's true. It's everything about this world that made you into someone capable of such an act that I will never forgive.

I don't know why you killed yourself, Samantha. If you're somehow able to read this though, know that I will find you. And somehow, someday, we'll be together again.

## When The Music Dies

"Dad, what happened to Mom?"

Lying to a five year old is easy. My dad would take me onto the roof at night and point up at the endless vaulting sky. "See up there?" he'd say. "That's where your mom lives. Way up in the stars. It's her job to play music and make everyone down below happy."

And I believed him, because I could hear the music play sometimes. Rich sonorant notes from a cello drifting down from above like the sky itself was singing me to sleep. And I was happy knowing that she was looking down at me from somewhere, taking care of me even when I couldn't see her.

Lying to a ten year old is a little harder. I started asking questions: like when she left, and when she was coming back. I asked what she was doing up there, and why she hadn't taken me with her, and whether other people could hear her play. I guess I didn't notice how hard it was for my father to answer, or how he would talk less and less about her as the years went by.

By fifteen I didn't need to ask to know Mom wasn't coming back. The music hadn't played for years, and I was beginning to wonder if I had simply imagined it to perpetuate the vain hope. Or maybe dad had just played it from a hidden sound system, and now that I was old enough to figure it out he'd given up pretending.

Sometimes my dad would have a temper. Maybe I slept in too late, or set the AC too low, and he'd start to bellow out of that barrel-chest of his. His face would flush and sweat would pour down his neck, and all his little teeth would flare out from under his mustache. Sometimes he would scare me, but whenever I felt like I was backed into a corner, I could always ask:

"Dad, what happened to Mom?"

And all the blood would filter out of his face to leave an ashen-pale wasteland. His meaty hands would start to shake, and he'd mumble something like, "She's gone, okay? Get over it." And then maybe he'd try to pick up yelling and swearing where he left off, but all his momentum would be gone. He'd just grunt, "Be a good girl. For your mother." And the argument would be over.

Well I didn't remember Mom, so what was the point of being good for her? I don't think of myself as a rebel, but sometimes rules can sound pretty indistinguishable from challenges. "You can't paint your room" sounded to me an awful lot like "I bet you can't paint your room by yourself." The point is that I made a giant mess, Dad was screaming like a siren, and I had to shut him up somehow. Maybe it was a cheap trick, but it had worked before and I just wanted the fighting to be over.

"Oh yeah?" I shot back at him. "Well what happened to Mom?"

His eyes flashed an angry warning, but he was so fired up that he didn't back down. His fingers were shaking, but it didn't stop him from grabbing my laptop and wrenching out the power cord.

"You get this back when the room is clean," he told me.

He was being fair. It was my fault the room was such a mess. I shouldn't have said what I said.

"At least now I know why she left."

I knew I'd gone too far the moment it left my mouth. He was shaking bad now. So bad it couldn't be contained. His hand struck out like a muscle spasm and the laptop went flying at my face. The corner bit into my temple and I collapsed like a sack of clothes.

A few seconds later, I came to on the ground. He was kneeling over me, his brow heavy with brooding thought. He'd never hit me before, but I flinched away the second I saw him. That seemed to snap him out of it. He stood up and stormed out of room. My head barely even hurt, so I don't know how I blacked out. I thought that was going to be the end of it, but—

"Follow me," he barked over his shoulder. "I'm going to show you if you want to know so god-damned bad."

It wasn't an angry voice. It was cold and tired. I can imagine a doctor using that kind of voice to call the time of death after twenty hours in surgery. That tone scared me even more than the yelling. I followed him in silence, listening to his labored breathing as he crawled up the ladder into the attic.

"Are you going to ask about your mother anymore?" he demanded.

"No sir," I responded automatically. I'd never called him 'sir' before, but it seemed appropriate now.

"So you don't have any more questions?"

"No sir." Of course I did, but now didn't seem like the time to ask.

"And you're going to clean your room?"

"Yes sir."

And he was gone, climbing back down the attic stairs. Leaving me face-to-face with what used to be my mother. At least, I can only imagine that's what I was looking at now. It certainly wasn't like any cello I had ever seen before.

The neck and fingerboard were unmistakably made from a spinal cord, with notches in the vertebra like frets. Long, taunt strands of sinew made up the strings. The pegs must have been knuckles, and a single glassy eyeball was embedded in the carved bone that made up the scroll. Even the bow was strung with long red hair, the same color I had seen in the precious few photographs that remained of her. The body itself still seemed to be made of wood, although it was unevenly stained with such a deep red that my imagination didn't have to look far to conjure an answer. The rest of my questions remained unsatisfied.

Did he kill her? Or just use her body after she was gone?

Was it even a real human at all? Or just some sick joke to get back at me for using Mom against him?

And most importantly, what should I do about it? I couldn't force myself to stay in the attic long enough to really look for proof. I could confront him, but I didn't know if I could stand the storm of his temper after seeing this. Should I take pictures and go to the police? And then what would happen to me?

I stayed in my room, avoiding Dad for the rest of the day. I didn't even eat dinner. I tried to block out thoughts of what I'd seen for as long as I could, but I couldn't block the music which began to play after years of intermission. A childhood of peaceful sleep had been purchased by Dad playing in the attic above my room. I wanted to retaliate with my own music, but dad still had my laptop. I tried playing something from my phone, but the cello only grew louder, drowning out my meager sound. It sang with increasing pace until the frenzied hammer of the hair across sinew shook the roof above me.

Powerful, staccato blasts rained from above. The melody pulled me in and swelled like a crashing wave, expertly driving each note deep into my consciousness where it became trapped. I couldn't stop imagining the spine bending under the pressure, or mother's hair sawing its way through her own muscle with the wild delirium of a screaming woman. I wanted to hate it. To hate him. I wanted my surging heart to slow, and my stomach to churn in disgust. I needed the perfect rhythm to miss a beat, or the haunting consonance to stumble, but transfixed as I was by the mortifying thought, I was compelled to listen by the sheer brilliance of the performance.

As the music reached its crescendo, the last grip of my hysteric mind screamed at me to run. My senses were so overwrought with sound that I couldn't even think straight. Reality was distorting under the euphoric melody which beckoned me into it. All I could do to retain any presence of mind was fixate on the thought that I would become another instrument to join my mother if I did not escape. I couldn't do this anymore. I had to get out. Through the pounding notes I dodged through the house, seeking shelter as though from an avalanche. Open wide I flung the front door, out onto the lawn to—

—stand in shock in the silent night. Outside the house, I couldn't hear it anymore. Not even the faintest echo. It was so quiet I could hear the rush of blood through my ears. I was so disoriented that I took a step back toward the house just to see how far into madness I had fallen. A meaty hand fell on my shoulder, holding me in place. I didn't have to turn around to know who it was. But if he was here, then who was playing upstairs?

"Dad, what happened to Mom?"

I held my breath. Desperate for any sound but the madding music or my coursing blood.

"See way up there?" he asked. The hand lifted from my shoulder to point at the stars.

I turned savagely on him, batting his hand away. "That's not good enough anymore! What did you do to her?"

"I fell in love with her because of how she played." He shrugged sadly, defeated. "But then I realized it was the music I loved, not her. I just wanted her to be beautiful again, and she is. And I love her more than ever."

The disorientation was getting worse. My vision was swimming. I felt like I was slurring, but I still had to ask.

"And what about me, Dad? Do you still love me?"

Then it all went black. I thought I was unconscious, but somehow I was still able to hear:

"Of course I do honey. And even if I stop, I know how to change you so I'll love you again."

When I opened my eyes, I was back on my bedroom floor. My head hurt like hell. My vision was still blurry, but I could feel my dad kneeling next to me.

"I love you so much, I'm so sorry," he said. "It was an accident, that's all. Are you okay?"

I didn't know how to answer him. I felt okay physically, but my mind was reeling from what I'd experienced. I told him I just wanted to sleep, and that was true. He helped me to my bed and left me there. I lay for a long time with my eyes closed, trying to breathe slow, trying to remain calm. I just needed to fall asleep and none of this will have ever happened.

It's just so hard to rest with the sound of the cello drifting down from the attic again.

## The Town Not On Any Map

Take the I-87 north from Queensbury, Vermont. Then the 28 up through North Creek. Keep going, if you want to take the route that I did. You'll pass right through the town that doesn't exist on any map.

My headlights probed the first of the ramshackle buildings through the smoky dusk. This was no isolated farmhouse or wild hermit hiding from the world. A real town, with shy street signs peeking out from tangled vines and ivy. Looming apartment buildings that might have been abandoned for years, and ramshackle houses that looked as though they were grown from the earth rather than built from it. The place was materializing around me, appearing so suddenly that I couldn't imagine how I had been blind to it a moment before.

I slowed to a stop as an old man crawled his way across the street. He was huddled against the cold, pausing to leer through my windshield and breathe a frosty fog in my direction. I was growing impatient and was about to honk when he staggered up to the car, clattering his knuckles upon my window.

"Why are you here?"

Perhaps it was just his frail voice breaking in the cold wind, but it seemed as though the strain of panic lay just below the surface. A depressed man, wrought by anxious doubt, screaming at himself in the mirror before pulling a tight smile for the rest of the world to see. That's what I was looking at outside my window.

"I don't even know where here is," I answered him. "Is there a hotel where I can get a room for the night?"

"No hotels." The old man turned in a slow circle. I followed his gaze, noticing a growing number of faces framed by faded curtains, watching us from the surrounding buildings.

"A motel then? I'm not picky."

"No motels. No inns, no beds, no breakfasts—nobody stays here. Not by choice."

More eyes. More faces watching us. Old men standing on the street corner, not bothering to disguise their gaping stares. Doors opening to reveal ancient women who might as well have been the direct descendants of prunes. Wrinkled hands wringing together, bleary eyes straining through their spectacles. Not a soul younger than sixty, and all staring with the horrified fascination of one witnessing a brutal car accident.

My nerves were fireworks, exploding with the undefined tension in the air. I nodded curtly and began to roll up the window when old hands shot through the opening, grabbing me by my collar.

"Take me with you. Don't leave me here. Please," he begged, real tears swelling up from the sunken wells of his eyes.

I shoved him back on instinct. The window slid shut, but he wasted no time in clutching the door handle and rattling it with all his might. I would have thought it was dementia if it weren't for the heavy silence of all those eyes.

"Please! You don't know what it's like! Don't go, don't go don't go…" and on and on, uselessly pounding his weak flesh upon the metal door, then crumpling to the ground beside my car and wailing like an insolent child.

I shifted into drive and put my foot on the gas, but a sudden sharp whistle gave me pause. A policeman had appeared beside me, cropped gray hair and piercing black eyes like a man who remembers the worst of war with warm nostalgia. He roughly pulled the pleading man away from my car before rapping a quick, authoritative burst of knocks on my window.

I rolled down the glass once more, keeping an eye on the discarded man who still trembled with silent, heaving sobs.

"Was this man giving you trouble?" the policeman asked.

I rapidly shook my head. "I was just asking for directions, that's all," I said.

"Just stay on this road. It'll take you right through town and you'll be on your way," the policeman said.

"Actually, I was looking for a place to—"

"This road is the one you want," the policeman repeated sternly. "There's nothing else for you here, understand?"

"Yes, sir."

The black eyes turned away, and I was able to roll my window up once more. The rest of the eyes—those peeking from buildings or glaring from the street—they remained fixed on the scene.

I was only too thankful to be driving again, but I didn't even make it a block before a scream made me slam to another halt. In the open glow of a street lamp, unmasked before dozens of eyes, I watched the policeman's baton fall for a second time. Then a third. And a fourth—each wet bludgeoning thump accompanied by shrieks of agony.

The old man who had first addressed me was being beaten to a pulp in the middle of the street. The zealous baton alternated with quick, vicious kicks from the policeman's steel-toed boots. It wasn't the screams which haunted me though. It was the cold, impassive silence from the policeman. No warning. No threat. Not even sadistic satisfaction. It was just another day for him, another duty.

Those black eyes turned away from the writhing form on the ground. A second later, all the eyes from the entire town seemed to be on me. I stomped the pedal, tearing through the stop sign. Not fast enough to avoid hearing another gut-wrenching scream echo from behind me.

I couldn't just leave. It was my fault what happened. I should have let him in my car immediately, but there was nothing left but to hope I wasn't too late. I circled around the block, and by the time I got back the eyes had all turned away. Curtains were drawn tight again. Doors were closed. The old man was the only one left, still moaning and whimpering in the street where he'd been left.

I stopped the car and wasted no time in leaping out. His decrepit frame was so emaciated that I had no trouble lifting him into the backseat. He was still alive —barely—although there was a catching rattle in his chest when he breathed, and it looked like a few of his ribs had caved in. One of his eyes fluttered open for a moment.

"Please." He had to spit blood between words. "Don't stop. No matter what you see, don't stop until the last house is gone."

I had no intention of staying any longer than I had to. The first curtains were just flitting open again, but I was already back on the road. I braced myself against the impending sound of sirens and the inevitable chase that never came. I didn't see a single other car on the road as I glided through the eerie twilight.

The only sign of life was the regular beat of windows. At each block, a new set would snap open with mechanical precision. Old heads like cuckoo birds sprang out in unison. Next the windows from the previous block would slam shut, continuing the steady rhythm like the incessant pounding of drums.

The rhythm didn't change, block after block, but gradually the faces peering out did. The farther I went, the older the inhabitants became, shrinking and decaying into loose folds of yellowed skin. Then this too gave way, until presently I found myself being watched by faces so ravaged by time that I could clearly see bleached bone and hollow sockets turning as I sped along the road. Even the buildings here were in various stages of collapse and calamitous ruin, almost as though I was driving through the inexorable span of years.

The houses were just beginning to thin and give way to the wholesome shelter of trees when I glanced behind at my passenger. The shock forced me to slam my foot on the breaks, barely avoiding swerving off the road entirely.

The gradual decay of the town was mirrored on my companion. Sagging flesh had dripped from his frame entirely, and the solemn skull behind me was preposterously balanced on a heap of splintered and broken bones and ancient wounds which had never healed.

"Don't stop, not yet." Words like trickling dust escaped the skull.

But I had already stopped. And the longer I ruminated on that unavoidable fact, the longer I remained frozen in static terror of what was to come.

The rhythm like the pounding of drums had returned. Windows, doors, opening and slamming, then opening again to unleash the remaining denizens that time had forgot. Lurching, shambling, and then springing to life with blasphemous vitality, the inhabitants of this charnel realm were closing around my car. Ragged skin fluttered in an unfelt breeze, and white talons of bone raked the ground to pull them ever closer. Vacuous stares fixated upon me, and always that infernal drumming which mounted into the crescendo of a macabre hymn.

"Take us with you!" A lone shriek at first, but quickly taken up by the rest. "Don't leave us here!"

The engine lamented my efforts to start the car again. A tense rattle, then a sickening crunch like the mashing of rusted machinery. Had it aged with my passage as well? Had I? There was no time to stop and think. I leapt from the disabled car into the open night, brisk air heaving in my lungs as I scrambled up the hill toward the woods.

Drumming, drumming, ferocious and wild in intensity, yet retaining its unerring rhythm. I had the oddest sensation that I was listening to my own pulse, and as I pushed myself harder and faster, I could hear the drumming keep pace with my racing heart. It didn't matter though, nothing mattered except the last lonely house which I was swiftly growing level with, and the figure which was emerging to greet me.

The policeman, baton in hand, gray-haired and stern and living as I had seen him last. The baton was tapping along with the impatient drums, and as I drew level I could feel the hesitancy in my pursuers.

"Still looking for directions?" he asked, a coy smile playing around the corner of his mouth.

"No sir." I wanted to say so much more, but that was all the breath I had.

"Just passing through, are you?"

"Sir."

"Need a ride?" His smile was growing. I didn't like how many teeth it showed.

The drums had stopped. The crowd had stopped. The roar of my car's engine sprang to life somewhere behind me in the darkness. A flash of confusion passed the policeman's face. I liked that considerably more than the teeth.

"Don't you dare—"

But I was already running. Back down the hill, back toward my car. The pounding of the policeman's feet behind me, but it was so quiet compared to the resounding drums a moment before. The uncertain crowd parted at the policeman's thundering approach, but I was practically flying now.

My car never went below ten miles an hour, but the passenger door was open and I launched myself inside. The slam of the door behind me was the first beat in the resuming drums. All at once the crowd was screaming again, drowning out the shouts and the threats from the pursuing policeman. Mounting and mounting, back into that hellish cacophony, and then just as swiftly dwindling back to nothing as the engine celebrated its triumph.

The old man in my car, or what was left of him—he drove me to safety that night. It's almost morning now, and we still haven't stopped, but just as soon as I work up the courage, I'm going to have a whole lot of questions to ask him.

I think I'll start by asking the name of that town.

## Echo Of The Dead

There are a lot of people who think death is the end. They think we vanish without a trace, leaving nothing but a rotting corpse that has as much to do with who we were as the molding shirt we were wearing. Those people have never heard the echo of the dead. The last thought someone ever had before they die, that stays rooted to the place almost like a tree planted in their honor.

*It's getting dark.* I hear that one a lot. Or *I wonder if she'll miss me*, or *Take me home, God*, or things of that nature. I don't know how it works, but ever since my little brother's death when I was young, I've started hearing the echo of all the people who have died in any given location.

That's why I'll never set foot in a hospital. My mom tried to take me for a sprained wrist once, but I couldn't get within a hundred feet of the place before thousands of whispered echoes started flooding my mind. I couldn't take it—I just bolted and ran the second I got out of the car.

Later a therapist told me that I was suffering PTSD after what happened to my brother, but I never believed it. The echoes are too *real*. Too close. And I hear them wherever I go.

You'd be amazed at how many people have died in the most innocuous places. I can hear the whispers in the park where some geezer must have keeled over from a heart-attack or something. Sometimes there are muted screams along the highway or at sharp turns in the road. Even the coffee shop at the end of my street has an echo of: *the ambulance should have been here by now.*

… and then there was Ferryman's Lake. This was years later when I was a senior in high-school. The whole class had agreed to go to this remote lake for ditch-day at the end of the year. The atmosphere was electric: music blasting in the cars, beers in the trunk, and that desperate, almost maniacal energy of anticipation tinged with heavy goodbyes.

But I could hear the whispers long before we arrived. I didn't want to be the weird kid that day. I just wanted to be normal and celebrate with my friends. I tried my best not to listen—I'd gotten pretty good at tuning it out—but this time was different.

These whispers weren't nostalgic musings. They weren't profound or contemplative or sad. There was nothing but absolute, mind-numbing terror, and it kept getting louder as we approached the lake.

"You feeling okay?" Jessica, the kind of girl who makes smart men do stupid things, asked me as we parked.

"Of course. Just tired from the drive," I lied. I think she said something else too, but I couldn't even hear her over the echoed screaming. It was the loudest I've ever heard—even louder than the hospital. This close, I could finally start to distinguish some words too.

*Did something touch my leg?*

*What the fuck is that thing?*

The five other cars had all parked on the graveled shore. Kids were unloading picnic baskets and stereos. I sat in the car, completely frozen by the tumult of madding echoes.

*I can't breathe!*

*Get out of the water! Get out get out!*

"You getting out or what?"

Jessica again. I had to stare at her lips to understand what she was saying. She met my gaze while she casually stripped her t-shirt to reveal a well-employed bikini top. Then the flash of a smile I couldn't return. I nodded through the numbness, climbing out of the car to gaze at the calm blue water.

Not a ripple disturbed the tranquil mask. Not a hint of what could be under there. There was a ferry tied up along the bank with a cobblestone cottage nearby. A few of the kids were already beginning to investigate.

"Don't go…." I couldn't tell whether a whisper or a shout escaped my lips, but Derek, one of the guys hauling beer out of the trunk, was the only one who seemed to hear.

"What's the matter? You're not afraid of the water, are you?"

He must have said it loud for me to be able to hear it so clearly. Jessica was already ankle deep in the water, but she glanced back. Her smile wasn't for me anymore—it was tinged with the hint of derision. Everyone would be laughing if they knew what was really going on in my head.

"What are you idiots doing? Get out, get out!"

Someone else had saved me from having to say it though. An old man, more beard than face, was standing in the doorway of the stone house.

One of the kids said something, but I couldn't hear it over the incessant echoed screams. I forced myself to get closer.

"Legend has it that something lives in the water near this shore," the old man replied loudly.

Everyone was out of the cars now—twenty-six kids in total, all gathering around the stone cottage.

"Something that has hidden since before mankind first walked the earth," the old man was saying. "Something that strikes once without warning, and once is all it ever needs. Of course, if you prefer, you can fork over five bucks each and I'll sail you to safety on the other side."

"What's to stop the monster swimming over there?" Jessica asked. She was still smiling—I could tell she wasn't buying it. No one was.

"Too shallow for it," the old man grunted. "A hundred bucks for the lot of you, special price. Better safe than sorry."

"No way, I want to see the monster!" Derek said.

He was almost up to his waist now, smacking the still water to send ripples echoing into the deep. Several kids started to follow.

"We should do it," I announced loudly, straining to keep my voice calm. "Hey look, I'll pay for it, okay? The ferry will be fun."

There were so many eyes on me while I fished out a brand new hundred that I got for a graduation present. So much for being normal, but at least I could live with myself this way. The old man snapped the money out of my hand before I could even extend my arm.

"Smart boy, smart boy." He winked, his eye glittering with sly recognition. "All aboard, don't be shy. Bags and heavy stuff go in the middle."

I avoided eye contact while boarding. For a terrible second I looked behind me and saw I was the only one. The people in the water or those already setting up their stuff on the shore were obviously reluctant. They looked back and forth at each other, trying to read the invisible will of the group.

"Last one is going to work at fast food for life," Jessica shouted, flinging her backpack into the middle of the ferry. She gave me a quizzical smirk and mouthed the words: *you owe me*. If only she knew how much. Soon her friends were following her, and a moment later the whole senior class was converging on the boarding plank.

I was hoping the echoes would disperse as we got past the shore. They didn't. Dozens of unique voices soon became hundreds as we approached the center of the lake. Echoes rebounding off echoes, reverberating and growing, flowing and slithering into my head like persistent intrusive thoughts. Cries for help, screams of pain, or just the animal bellow from the minds utterly devoured by fear.

The ferryman hadn't mentioned the monster again—it was all tourist trivia and blithering about the local plants and animals. He kept looking at me and grinning though, the discolored motley of teeth appearing almost feral at times. The farther he went, the more excited he grew, spewing spittle into his beard with every-other explosive word or declaration.

The continual pounding of sound was making me nauseous. I just closed my eyes and waited for this part to be over. I tried not to think about what might be in the water. There were so many voices that I had trouble keeping them straight, but I made a game out of trying to untangle them. Even so, it took several minutes of concentration before this came to the surface:

*I never should have trusted the old m*an.

It sounded like a young boy around twelve, no older than my brother was when he died. I glanced at the ferryman who was leaning against the wheel, staring wistfully at us all. No one was paying him any attention anymore. Not even when his pale tongue flicked greedily over his lips.

The old man flipped something and the motor gave out. He stretched luxuriously in the sun before making his way to the railing.

"This is a good place to take a dip if anyone wants to swim," he called out. "Real shallow here, and if you're lucky you'll see some turtles."

"You sure it's safe?" someone asked.

"I'll prove it." Flash goes the feral grin. Several people laughed and gasped as the old man clamored up onto the railing, launching himself into a graceful dive and vanishing with barely a ripple. Other people would be jumping in any second, and there was nothing I could do to stop them. I closed my eyes again, sifting through the mounting pressure of echoes....

*Where'd the ferryman go?*

*He's not human.*

*Get back to the boat!*

I opened my eyes again. There was a loud splash and the cheer of laughter which accompanied someone tumbling into the water. I was out of time. I leapt behind the wheel, turning the key and stirring the engine back to life. People were shouting, but I didn't care. It didn't matter who was already in the water—every instinct was screaming for me to just save as many as I could.

The controls were intuitive enough, and I pushed the lever full throttle. We were accelerating quickly—faster than I thought we would. The laughter around me was turning to distress, but I was ready to fight anyone who tried to stop me.

No one had time though. We were moving for less than ten seconds before something exploded out of the water behind us. By the time I looked back, it was gone. All I could see was a massive misshapen shadow underneath the surface, twisting and morphing and growing by the second.

*He's not human.* Then what is he?

There wasn't time to find out. Real screams were starting to mix with the echoes now.

"What are you doing? Jessica and the old dude are still in the water!"

Why her of all people? Was it some kind of cosmic joke that made her jump in first? No, that's just who she was. She was a brave and enthusiastic leader, and it was going to get her killed.

I slid the throttle down, and the ferry slowed. I didn't even register going on without her as a choice. There was nothing I could do though. Her head bobbed under as soon as the black shadow drew near. There was a flash of scaly skin above the water, then a brief glimpse of Jessica's fingers clawing for the surface. Everyone on the boat was shouting, but soon they were going to just be echoes too.

Churning water bubbled red, and I shoved the throttle again. The shadow was moving toward the boat, gliding directly under us. Louder than the echoes, louder than the thrashing water or the shouting kids, there was one more voice which joined the haunting chorus of the lake that day. It said:

*Don't wait for me.*

And I didn't. I should have done more, said more, while I still had the chance. But I didn't. And now it's too late forever, and I'm so so sorry....

I think I'm the only one of us who keeps returning to that lake. I don't go in the water, but if I close my eyes and concentrate, sometimes I can still make out her pale voice peeking shyly from the wall of noise. *Don't wait for me.*

And I know she's right, but I'm still here waiting. In the end, an echo is all that will remain.

## Life Without Monsters

"Stay up as late as you want, I don't mind," my mother used to say. "I don't think Raleigha will like it though."

Raleigha was the monster who lived in our neighborhood, or so my mother used to say. He had a mouth in the palm of each hand, and barbed teeth that latched on and expanded inside the skin of any disobedient little boy unfortunate enough to attract his attention. Quiet as the falling night and swift as a guilty heart, Raleigha would stalk the house waiting for his favorite meal.

My mother never gave me a satisfying explanation for why misbehaving children taste better, but she swore it was true.

"Good thoughts spoil the meat," she told me one night when she tucked me in. "They make you all chewy and stringy and bland. Raleigha can smell an evil thought from miles away though, and nothing will stop him from eating the person who deserves it."

"Is that what dad is running from?" I remember asking her once. I was too young to understand how much that question hurt her.

"Exactly right," she said. "But it won't do him any good. There's nowhere to run that's too far for thoughts to follow, and wherever your dad is right now, you can bet Raleigha will find him."

I understood that mom was trying to frighten me into being good, but I was never scared of Raleigha. I thought of the monster more like a super hero: a fantastic force of nature that hunted the wicked and brought justice to the world. I imagined Raleigha praising me when I did well, and he never punished me no matter how much I deserved it.

Other children had dads, and I had Raleigha. When the people at the grocery store made us put the food back on the shelves because we didn't have enough money, I'd just think about what Raleigha would do to them. Or when someone was cruel to me at school; I'd just imagine how it must feel to have those swelling teeth inside you that wouldn't ever come out. Compared to that, my troubles didn't seem so bad at all.

Mom was wrong about Dad, though. Raleigha never caught up with him. Even when Dad came back and started hanging around the apartment, Raleigha never touched him. When Dad was shouting all those things at Mom, Raleigha never interrupted. And when he hit her, grabbing her hair, her throat, throwing her around the apartment like a rag doll, well I guess Raleigha had bigger scumbags to hunt that day.

"Raleigha must still smell some good in your father," my mother told me. "Don't worry about me though. If it ever gets bad enough, Raleigha will know and save us from him."

Other children had God, and I had Raleigha. And when the sacrosanct night was broken by my parents shouting, I'd pray to him in my own way. If I could only concoct an evil enough thought, then Raleigha would smell it and find us. I didn't even care what would happen to me because of it. As long as Raleigha was here, he'd get my dad too, and then mom wouldn't have to cry anymore.

I made a game out of it when I lay awake at night: trying to think of the most vile, twisted thing in all the world. I thought about hurting the kids at my school, or throwing stones through windows, or stealing. I thought about shouting at people like Dad did, or punishing animals: anything so Raleigha could smell how bad it was. I tried my hardest, thinking horrible things day and night until at last during school I finally thought of the worst thing there was.

I was going to kill myself when I got home. I was going to tie one end of a string around my neck and the other end to the drain in the bathtub, tying it so tight that I couldn't get undone even when the tub started to fill with water. I'd be stuck there doing and thinking the worst thing I could do, until Raleigha smelled it and came for me.

I heard Mom and Dad fighting before I even opened the front door. They were in their bedroom, so neither of them saw me twisting a dozen strings together into a rope that would be too strong for me to break. The running water couldn't drown out the yelling, but it made everything seem a little less real. I couldn't wait for my head to be underwater so I wouldn't have to listen to them anymore.

My fingers were shaking while I tied the string around my neck, but it was such a horrible thought that I knew I wouldn't have to be under for long. Raleigha was going to come before I drowned. I'd tell him what was really going on, and he'd save us from Dad, and then Raleigha would live with us and I'd fight evil with him like I always wanted. I thought I was going to be a hero as I tightened the tether and pressed my face under those warm comforting waves. I thought Mom was going to be so happy when she found out what I did for her.

I tried to tell my body to lay still, but it wouldn't listen. The burning pressure rippled through my body, and I thrashed against the twined string. I couldn't break it. I briefly fumbled with the knots, but the water pulled them too tight to work through. I had to wonder what would happen if Raleigha never came. If I never came back up. And still being able to hear dad shouting while I was under water, I decided that I was okay with that too.

When hands finally grabbed hold of my buckling body and ripped me free, I braced myself waiting for those hooked teeth to pierce my flesh. It was just my mom though, holding me and crying, pumping the water from my stomach and lungs.

"Did Raleigha come? Where is he?" was the first thing I asked.

"Didn't you see him? He's already gone," she told me.

"And Dad? Did he get Dad?"

I saw the blood leaking out from Mom's closed door after I left the bathroom. I had to stay with my grandmother for a week after that. There wasn't any blood when I got home, and I haven't seen Dad since.

I still don't know if the monster came that night. When I told the story to some friends at school, they said Raleigha must have killed my dad. My friends were all terrified of monsters after that, but that's just because they didn't understand. If this is what humans do to each other, then I'm more afraid of what it means to live a life without monsters.

## The Stranger Upstairs

Thirty-four hundred square feet, marble counters, Brazilian walnut hardwood floors, and the strangest stipulation I've ever seen on a real-estate listing.

"The previous occupant will continue to live on the top floor. He will never be evicted, and never be charged rent. His room shall never be entered, and under no condition should he ever be spoken to. If the inhabitants are unable or unwilling to follow any of these terms, they will be considered in violation of the sales contract and held liable."

"It's a joke. It has to be," my wife told me when I read her the fine print. "Anyway it's not like we can afford this place. I just want to take a peek, okay?"

We'd spent the last month attending every open house in a ten mile radius around my new job, and everything had started to blur together into one big gray building. My wife just wanted to see something different, even if it was way out of our league. I couldn't believe it when the real-estate agent told us this mansion was well within our budget.

"What's the deal with the hermit though?" was the first question I asked the listing broker, a sweaty bear of a man.

"Oh you won't even notice him," the agent said, nodding vigorously as though agreeing with himself. "If you're worried about your space, I'm going to stop you right there. The downstairs has two beautiful full-sized bedrooms, so your daughter can have a room of her own. Wouldn't you like that, honey?" The giant man had to crouch to be level with Nila, my eleven-year-old daughter. "Wouldn't you like your own room where you can play music as loud as you want without it bothering anyone?"

"Yeah!" I winced as Nila glided across the hardwood floors in her socks. "I'd live here!"

"Have you seen this kitchen?" my wife shouted from around the corner. "Brand new Viking appliances. It's even got a built-in espresso machine!"

I felt the decision slipping away from me. "It's not the space. You have to admit that it's a weird situation, right?"

The agent shrugged. "Wouldn't bother me," he said. "What *would* bother me is knowing I could have given my family the house of their dreams, but didn't just because I felt weird about an eccentric old man that I'd never even see. And just between the two of us," he bodily pulled me under his arm where I could distinctly feel the sweat soaking through, "the guy up there is about a hundred years old. Couple years and he'll be gone for good, and all that space will be yours."

We met the generously low asking price, and within a month my family had moved into the house. It seemed impossible to me that we'd *never* see Makao, but it was actually true. He had his own bathroom, and every week there would be a delivery man who left a bag of groceries at the top of the stairs. The groceries would sit there the entire day—eggs, milk, meat, and all—not disappearing until the following morning. Every once in a while we'd hear someone shuffling around, or a radio would splutter to life and play songs that were old before I was born. That was it though. Most of the time we forgot that Makao even existed.

Most of the time. Then there was the night around 11 p.m. when the lights were already off. I heard muffled, heaving sobs echo through the house. My first instinct was to check on Nila, but she was just quietly sitting up in her bed.

"You heard it too?" she asked.

"Yeah. It's nothing, go back to sleep," I told her.

"Why is Makao crying?"

"I don't know, but it's none of our business. We made a promise not to disturb him. Can you promise that too, Nila?"

My daughter nodded, gaping at the ceiling. I turned on some soft music to drown out the sound, but that wasn't the end of it. When I got back to my bedroom, my wife was gone. She wasn't in the bathroom either. I was beginning to entertain a fantastical paranoia about some misshapen ghoul crawling down to snatch her when I heard her voice on the stairs.

"I'm sorry to bother you, Makao. Is everything all right?"

I pounded up the steps. Nila had come out of her bedroom too, and we both watched as my wife knocked on the forbidden door again.

"Stop that! Come back to bed!" I shouted in a hoarse whisper.

"He might need help—" Her words cut short as the door opened a crack, not even wide enough to see who was peering out.

"This will be your only warning." Makao's growl was so low that I inadvertently found myself climbing closer to hear.

"I was worried that—" my wife began.

"Whatever you see. Whatever you hear. Whatever you *think* might be going on up here: it'll be the death of you."

The door snapped shut, and I wasted no time in ushering everyone back to bed.

The crying never really went away after that. For the next two weeks we'd hear him whimpering and moaning as he battled some unknown illness, or perhaps it was just the deterioration of his ancient body finally giving out. Sometimes there would even be feeble calls for help, but I was quick to remind my family of our promise. They argued at first, but eventually we just got used to having music playing all the time and didn't hear it anymore.

At least until it got worse. Grunting, moaning, even screaming—wild, vicious yelps like an animal in the throes of death. It was late at night again after Nila had gone to bed. My wife jumped toward the door in an instant and I had to physically pin her arms to keep her there.

"He's in pain! We can't just leave him!" she insisted.

"You heard what he said. It's his right to be alone."

"What about 911? Even if he doesn't want our help, he can't say no to someone trying to save his life."

"Maybe he doesn't want that either." My wife wasn't resisting anymore. I steered her back to bed, caressing her shoulders, speaking softly in the vain fight against waves of tension rippling across her face and body. "Maybe it's just his time to go, and that's what will be best for all of us."

"For all of us?" Suspicion crept into her voice. She was back on her feet again before I knew what was happening. "You want him to die, don't you? A living, breathing human being, and you want him dead just so we have a little more space."

"That's not what I meant. I just said—"

"Listen to him! He's in agony! We can't just sit here and—"

We both shut up at the sound of the knocking. One, two, three, hesitant but insistent knocks.

"Hello? Mr. Makao?"

My wife and I exchanged a panicked glance. A door swung open somewhere above us.

"Get out! Get out you stupid girl!"

"Nila don't!" I shouted. Out of the bedroom, up the stairs—just in time to see my daughter disappear and the door close behind her. My wife was right behind me as we raced up the stairs. We were still a few feet away when we heard the distinct rattle of a chain, then a bolt sliding into place.

"Makao? Open the door Makao. We're here to help," I tried.

"Go away. I warned you, didn't I? I warned you both. She's mine now."

"Nila? Can you hear me?" my wife shouted. "What's going on in there?"

"I don't know, it's weird up here," Nila replied through the door, but her voice reverberated as though it came from a tunnel a long way off. "It's all mirrors. On and on forever."

"Is the old man trying to stop you from leaving?"

I held my breath during the long pause.

"Nope," Nila said. All the air came pouring out of my lungs. "There isn't anyone here."

Another glance between my wife and me. Her face was drawn and white. She stepped forward uneasily, trying to look through the crack under the door.

"Can you unlock the door, sweetie? Can you come back out?" my wife asked.

Another long pause. I crouched down too, catching a dark flash of movement across the doorway.

"Nila? Are you still there?" I prompted.

"Uh huh." Another pause. "I'll be right there."

"Nila the door!" my wife insisted. She started rattling the handle.

"Don't! Don't come in!" Nila shrieked. "You won't like it!"

It was more than I could take. I started slamming into the door with my shoulder.

BAM - the door rattled in its frame. Nila was hysterical. There weren't words anymore, just varying pitches and whimpers.

BAM - dust raining down around me. My wife joined in the effort, crashing into the door together—

BAM - the old hinges buckled and twisted. We couldn't hear anything anymore, but that just made us slam harder until—

The door flew open. A brilliant flash of disorienting light. There were mirrors everywhere. *Everywhere.* A whole world of mirrors, stretched to the vanishing point of the distant horizon. Great hillsides were carved with thousand-faced pinnacles of light, trees ruptured from the ground to shine in every direction, and even soaring clouds fractalized countless insults to geometry with their smooth sides. And from them all shone a dazzling array of faces and eyes all peering back at me...

... Although none of the faces were mine. Old men, young men, women and children, all mirroring my movements from an unfathomable myriad of sources and angles, all staring at me. That's when I realized Makao hadn't been the one crying all this time. It was the figures in the mirrors, untold anguish causing tears to run down their face even while matching my movements otherwise.

"Where's Makao?" my wife asked.

Nila shrugged. She was kneeling on the ground, making faces at an old lady peering back. Her wizened face contorted into a variety of sneers which seemed preposterously absurd on someone of her age.

"We need to get out of here. Now." My family wasn't listening to me. My wife was turning in slow circles, utterly bewitched. Numerous pitiful forms turned to echo her.

"How does it do that?" she asked. "Is this a screen? Are they plugged in somewhere?"

"If Makao isn't here, then who locked the door after Nila?" I asked. That finally got their attention. That, and the rattle of the chain as the solitary standing door slammed once more behind us.

"She's mine now. You're all mine." It was Makao's voice, but I couldn't figure out where it was coming from. I surged toward the door, slamming into an invisible barrier like a wall of glass. My wife and daughter were in the same situation, helplessly pounding the empty air—no, they were pounding the insides of their mirror, just like I was.

"Two weeks," came the voice, everywhere and nowhere, far away yet emanating from within. "Two weeks is a long time to listen to someone suffer."

"But you told us not to bother—" I protested.

"I've listened to them for *years* though," Makao replied. There! Standing by the door, a dark and huddled shape. Only a few feet tall, and so bent that its back extended several inches higher than the pit of darkness that was its head. Red eyes gleaming from somewhere deep inside the tortured mass, watching me with hawkish intensity. "They never stop, you know. You'd think they would have given up on giving up by now."

"Who are you? What is this place?"

The red eyes blinked. "This is your home. Your one true home. And no matter how comfortable you make yourself out there, no matter how loudly you turn up your music and play pretend, you will always be a visitor. And wherever you go, and whoever you love there, it will only last until you come home to me again."

Nila was crying, but I couldn't look at her. My wife—I don't know where she is. I couldn't take my eyes away from the hunched creature that taunted me. He felt so tangible, so real: the only real thing in this place of mirrors.

"I don't want to be here. Let us out! Let us go!"

"You won't bother me again?"

"Never. We promise—"

"Not never, that would be a lie." The dark figure was right on the other side of the invisible barrier now. He lifted one hand, little more than a claw, and I was horrified to watch my own hand mirror the movement until my finger touched the gnarled terminal of his hand. "But not soon, I hope. Not until you're ready to come home."

The invisible glass shattered as our fingers touched. His image, the image of this impossible place, everything shattered and fell away. I was left standing with my finger touching the back of an empty mirror frame, ground littered with broken shards. I gently but urgently guided my wife and daughter out of the room, carefully picking our way through the carpet of broken glass, then closed the door firmly behind me.

The bag of groceries is still left on the top of the stairs each week, and sometimes there's laughter to go with the crying. My family and I still haven't agreed on exactly what happened up there, but no one has made the suggestion to make a second trip.

I think Death is the stranger living upstairs, but I suppose that's true of everyone. At least ours is close enough to keep an eye on.

## Heaven Keeps a Prisoner

I wasn't ready when I died.

The first illusion death stole from me was that my body was designed to perceive the universe around me. This is incorrect. The primary function of your senses is to stop yourself from experiencing the universe, whose infinite information would otherwise overwhelm and madden you. Eyes that once simplified the world into finite wavelengths of color closed for the last time, and then I saw everything. Ears once deaf to cosmic music sung by the birth of stars, the communal heartbeat of the human race, and the haunting pop of each collapsing universe now concealed them no longer.

Even the distinction between senses decayed alongside my corporal prison. Starlight was a symphony that bathed me in warmth, and the heat in turn sang with such melodic iridescence that I was thrall to its majesty. It's impossible to measure how long I existed in such a state, but by gradual degrees I learned to separate my own thoughts from the medley of existence. The moment I began to comprehend my own internal voice, I became aware of a second voice that was not my own.

"… Four hundred seventy eight points. Hey Jason! You close that passenger pigeon room yet? I told you we don't do them anymore."

"Um. Hi. Excuse me," I said to the unrepentant chaos of the universe.

"Here you go, let me help you with that."

Remember what I said about the unfiltered synesthesia of my senses. Now imagine being struck by lightning. A moment later, I found myself with hands and knees to collapse onto the stone floor with, my new lungs racing a marathon. Holy shit did that hurt. I kind of wanted to do it again.

"Four hundred seventy eight points, up from 314 last time. Solid performance." I don't know what was harder to accept: my naked new body which looked exactly like my old one, the colossal stone cathedral I suddenly found myself within, or the koala bear who sat in front of me with a clipboard. He flipped another page.

"Oh that explains it," the koala said in its soothingly gruff undertone. "Fifty points for loving someone and being loved in return. That's always a nice boost. Then you picked up another twenty from that album you released in the eighties —touched more lives than you'll know with that."

"You were keeping score?"

"I'd hate to think what people got up to if we weren't… lost twelve points because you stopped visiting Mark when he got cancer, but you got a few of those back when you played at his funeral. Hey Jason! What's "accepting your own imperfections" worth? We got new numbers on that yet?"

He was answered by the incomprehensible shriek of an eagle.

"Shit man, right back at ya!" the koala hollered.

"Have you always been a koala?" I asked.

"Have you always asked stupid questions? You're lucky we don't dock points for that."

"Ummm… "

"Kidding, kidding. Sort of. This way now." The koala slid the clipboard under his stubby arm and began a brisk waddle. I hurried to keep pace, doing my best to avoid the absolute zoo which thronged the stone hallway onward. Up the great diverging staircase with its goats and mountain lions. Past the library whose shelves bustled with scaling monkeys, over the pools filled with playing otters and thrashing fish, beneath the gargantuan brass dome revolving with teeming flights of birds, the koala explaining as we went.

"Long story short, if your life brought more good into the world than evil, you're going to end up with more points than you started. Your 478 points can unlock any of the rooms on this floor, except for the psychic and the prophet which are both 500. Think of your choice as an investment: coming back as a human will be expensive, but you also have the greatest capacity to improve your score. The only rule is that you pick something on the right floor for your budget."

"What would happen if I didn't have any points? Or went below zero?"

I hadn't been aware koalas could even grin before this moment.

"Generally you'll just keep going down. It's hard to get out of the negatives once you've started, so if you can't figure out how to do some good, then you're forced to keep choosing worse and worse punishment rounds. Get far enough negative, and suddenly you're looking at a demon, or a vampire, or the like. Some people actually do evil on purpose to aim for that though, can you imagine?"

"No," I answered honestly, "but I'm beginning to."

"All the animals you see are just spirits taking their new bodies for a test drive. Feel free to look around, and—Jason! What's that thing doing up here? Keep the politicians downstairs please!"

The mournful shriek of an eagle somehow sounded like it had heard this joke far too many times. The koala sighed and threw his paws melodramatically in the air. "Kidding, kidding, God. What is this, a morgue?"

I wasn't paying attention anymore, though. Dwarfed and humbled by the immensity of the structure, I turned my gaze to the top of the stairs and the small balcony which overhung the whole arena.

"What's at the very top?"

My guide shrugged, seemingly losing interest in me. "Dunno. No one's ever had enough points to unlock that door. Not for as long as I've been here."

"How long have—"

"Diggory! Mixy! Ground floor let's go! People dyin' over here!"

And he was gone, leaving me adrift in the swirling profusion between death and life. Overwhelmed and disoriented, I continued to climb the stairs, driven as much to isolate myself as I was by curiosity. Past 500 points and the crowd dissipated precipitously. Strange, alien creatures began mingling with the dwindling remaining options. Seraphic beings with skin of light and shadow, and golden toned creatures of sublime beauty came and went as I continued to mount the lonely stairs.

Finally reaching the balcony at the very top, I turned to survey the whole mad spectacle flowing beneath me. The perspective was disorienting: though I'd only climbed a few flights of stairs, looking down it seemed more like the view from an airplane window. All creatures were minuscule in their eager dance; all sounds had faded and combined into a single omnipresent hymn. All sounds that is, except for the rapid burst of knocking on the door behind me.

It wasn't like the other doors. Its metallic composition seemed in perpetual motion, rippling and glistening like a pool of oil. Three ponderous iron bars were bolted across the frame to prevent it opening outward, each engraved with mystic runes beyond my comprehension. The knocking came again—rapid, urgent, a prisoner desperately calling for aid without wanting to alert the guards.

"Hello? Someone in there?"

A hissing sound like high-pressured steam bursting through its confinement. The bolts in the iron bars were beginning to slide outward. I rushed back to the balcony in search of my guide, but that was so far below where he'd merged seamlessly with the spiritual throng. Behind me a clanging sound had me jump— the first iron bar had dropped off to the ground.

"Can anyone hear me?"

But I was utterly alone. I took a half-dozen steps toward the stairs, but at the clang of the second iron bar I indecisively spun back. And why not? What was the worst that could happen, now that I was already dead? That sentiment did not endure through the dropping of the third bar. The whole door shimmered like a mirage in the desert, then without motion or warning, it was gone.

Bile rose in my throat the instant I saw the creature. My legs buckled beneath me, and I crashed hard to my knees, vomiting profusely upon the ground. It was bile. Heaving again, my whole body convulsing from the swelling pressure, I released another dark torrent of blood, lumps of degraded flesh, and even what appeared to be entire rotting organs which laboriously wriggled up my throat and out my mouth. I'd almost forgotten my own death for a while, but it immediately became clear that I had not escaped as far as I thought.

"Come in," the creature commanded.

I was powerless to refuse. Crawling through my own sick, not daring to look up again, I passed through the open door. Seeing it once had been enough. The humanoid being was swollen to the size of a cow, bloated with gas which unevenly malformed its corpulent frame. Open sores covered its body, weeping blood and pus to stream down its nakedness so thickly that it almost seemed a garment. Gaping mortal wounds punctured its chest and belly in many places, allowing clear sight all the way through to its broken and uneven ribs. Somehow worst of all, the unblemished face of a young boy stared out from that facade of human life.

"Are you alone?"

More alone than I've ever been. I nodded, still not looking up. The room itself was minimal in the extreme: a concrete prison cell with no comfort besides thin bamboo floor mat.

"Not anymore," it said, hot fetid air blowing across my face with each word.

"Who are you?" I asked.

"The final prize. Come, sit with me. Be at ease."

My body tensed so sharply that I thought I was about to vomit again. I remained on my knees.

"Why would anyone want to be—" I stopped myself, but the child simply laughed with a sound like wind-chimes.

"No one would, but being at the top doesn't mean the best. It simply means that I have the greatest capacity to do good or evil. I can create life, or end it. Does that sound like a power you'd want to have?"

I shook my head, finally daring another glance. The creature had leaned forward on its mat, its terribly perfect face mere inches from mine. The boy sighed and leaned back once more.

"Me neither, which is why I remain in this place. My influence is too great, and any good or evil I bring into existence is multiplied countless times. If I allow that to happen, then I will die with so many points that I am forced to be reborn within this same cursed form."

"So you have the power to do anything, but instead you sit here and do nothing?"

"Not nothing. I wait to die. That's the only way for me to reset to zero points and have another chance to begin again. Unless of course… " The child's face was drawing closer. The stench was too foul to breathe through my nose, but even having the air enter my mouth was enough to taste its rot.

"You invited me in to kill you then." I said it as matter-of-factly as I could, not wishing to cause offense.

"You aren't the first," he said, gesturing at the wounds which scoured its body. "But through revulsion or weakness or cowardice, each have failed so far. Will you be the one to show me mercy?"

The thought of even getting close enough to harm the creature almost had me retching again. "I still don't understand though," I said, buying time. "If you're the supreme power here, why can't you save yourself?"

"The supreme power?" Laughter like the wind, so sweet and so sad. "Death is the supreme power, and I am his servant like any other. Don't think I have not tried to take my own life before. The act carries such significance that I simply find myself reborn in this same body. Here, you will need this."

A trembling hand reached out to me, its obese fingers fused at the joints. I recoiled by reflex, but I felt such pity for the creature that I fought against my instincts and accepted the black dagger from his grasp.

"How do I end you?"

"Through the eye," he begged.

"Are you sure?"

Such a dazzling smile from such a loathsome creature. I can't imagine how much he must have suffered, and I'm sure I would have asked the same in his place. The cool dark metal felt righteous in my hand as I steeled myself for the killing blow. Some nagging doubt lingered in the back of my head, but I was so mesmerized by my disgust and sympathy that I could think of no other course.

"Won't you at least close your eyes?" I asked.

His smile widened—unnaturally so for the child's face. "I've been looking forward to this moment for as long as I can remember. I'm not going to miss a moment."

Worried that any hesitation would steal my resolve, I took the dagger in both hands and plunged it deep. The eye did not close even as the blade slipped through it. It cut so easily that I felt no resistance until the very hilt was embedded in the boy's face. The smile faltered for the briefest instant before returning, then grimacing again as though fluctuating between agony and ecstasy. The massive body trembled, but I didn't relinquish my grip until its last spasm overbalanced the monstrosity. I scrambled to get out of the way as it toppled face-first toward me, slamming against the ground to further pound the dagger within its skull.

Crowds parted around me as I returned down the staircase. Claws and talons pointed at me with undisguised fascination. Whispers and murmurs from the multifarious assembly swelled and faded like the ocean waves.

"I think I'd like to come back as a cat," I told the koala when I found him again. He was easy enough to locate, standing out in the open, seemingly paralyzed by shock. "Cats seem to have things figured out."

"Jason! Mixy? Anyone!" the koala shouted in a hoarse, strained voice from the corner of his mouth, not taking his eyes off me for a moment.

"What is it? Did I do something wrong?"

An owl landed nearby, its head cocking from side-to-side to get a better look at me.

"Hey Mixy—" the koala said, still without turning. "How many points do you get for killing God? You have a number for that somewhere?"

I swallowed hard, but I couldn't get rid of the dry lump in my throat.

"You're sure I didn't lose points?"

He stared dumbly at his clipboard. "Considering what he would have done if you hadn't, yeah. Says 'Act of mercy' on here. You're way in the positive, my man."

"I'm not going to become that... thing, am I?"

"Not yet. You came here with 478, so that's what you're going back with. But shit man, you've got so many now that—"

"Unless I can spend them all next life, right?"

"What?"

"Unless I bring so much evil into the world that I break even. That's what you're saying, right?"

The koala looked helplessly to the owl who fluffed its wings in something resembling a shrug.

"Better do human again then," I said. "I don't care what I have to do. I'm not going live as that monster."

"You're not serious, are you?" the koala whispered. "Do you have any idea what you'd have to do to—"

"I killed God, didn't I? Who knows what I'm capable of?"

Now that I'm back alive, I suppose I'm going to find out.

## My New Sex Doll Won't Stop Crying

Her silicone is as soft and pliable as real human skin. It even heats up to the right temperature with a pulse and everything. A dial on the back of her head gives twelve personality options, including "family friendly", "intellectual", "shy", and "sexual". She's so realistic it's scary, and would be absolutely perfect if she didn't cry every time I touch her.

I was so excited when I took her out of the box. My anxious fingers peeling away the Styrofoam, the jittery tension flooding through my heart and limbs: nervous enough for her to be real. Better than real, because the doll wouldn't judge me or tear me down. She wouldn't lie, or cheat, or steal from me.

A lot of people find the idea of sex robots weird, and I respect that. I was hesitant at first too, but here's my reasoning: I've recently concluded a long, messy divorce after three years of abuse. I need something easy. Something safe. Sure I could have gone trolling the bars or clubs for a rebound hookup, but I didn't want to *use* someone. What's so wrong about not wanting to hurt or be hurt in return?

The instructions said to let her charge for a couple hours before anything else, so I plugged her in and laid her on the bed. The eyes popped open with the first surge of electricity, their glassy shine staring vacantly into space. She turned her head slightly toward me, her soft lips parting in silent welcome. I sat with her to admire her flawless features and run my hands over her generously proportioned body.

It felt wrong, even though she was a doll. It was like I was groping an unconscious person. I decided to let her fully charge and come back later, not returning until late that night. I undressed quietly in the dark, leaving off the lights to make her seem more real.

"Hello master." Her voice was warm and sensuous. I don't remember which personality setting I left her on, but right then it didn't matter. I just wanted her body.

"What's your name?" she asked as I climbed into bed. "My name is Hazel."

"I don't care," I replied. It felt good to be in control like that. I'd never speak to another human that way, but after years of being subservient, now I was the one with all the power.

"But I care. I want to get to know you."

"No you don't. You're a stupid slut. You only want one thing."

She tried to speak again, but I shoved my hand in her mouth, muffling the speaker there. I almost wanted her to resist, but I knew she couldn't. I slapped her face, but she just turned back to me and smiled. I hit her again—harder, bending her arms to grotesquely unnatural positions as I crawled on top of her.

"Does this make you happy?" She smiled up at me. "I'd do anything to make you happy."

I didn't turn on the lights until I'd finished. She was face down on the soaked pillow. At first I thought I broke something when I hit her, but when I flipped her around I saw the tears streaming down her face. I don't know why that made me so angry. It was like she was trying to steal my last selfish pleasure from me. I don't know why I kept hitting her either. She deserved better.

I kept Hazel in the closet after that so I wouldn't have to see where the skin peeled back from the beatings. They shouldn't have made the metal chassis underneath so white. It looks too much like bone. I keep the lights off when I use her so it doesn't really matter, but without fail she'll start crying again the second I touch her.

The personality is broken too. The knob is stuck way past the "innocent" setting and won't go back, and she keeps saying the most disconcerting things. Like the other day I was still in bed with her after we'd done it when she said:

"Do humans love each other like you love me?"

I told her that I didn't love her. That love is something only humans have.

"I love kitties! And doggies! Don't you?"

I felt stupid trying to explain that it wasn't the same kind of love, but I was lonely and it felt good having someone to talk to.

"You can beat me harder if that will make you love me more. I won't tell Mommy."

I didn't feel bad about hitting her that time. And as sick as it might seem, there was some truth to what she said. I wouldn't say I loved her, but there was a certain intimacy in our shared secret that made me feel attached. Everyone else in my life knew me as this sensitive, mild mannered man who reacted to conflict by staring at his shoes. Only Hazel knew this side of me, and that made her special.

I might have really felt something for her if she hadn't started to smell. I was too intent on her body when I used her to notice, but lying beside her at the end it was unmistakably foul. At first I thought I just wasn't cleaning her right. I got up for some disinfectant, but as soon as I turned on the lights, I saw the flesh around her cuts had begun to fester and rot. Her perfect complexion was riddled with sores and boils, some of which had ruptured from our session.

I spent almost half an hour in the bathroom hurling out my guts before I worked up the courage to return. Hazel was sitting upright against the headboard now. Hadn't I left her lying down? I didn't have the stomach to stare for long though. Her head followed me as I crossed the room to retrieve my phone and call the website I ordered her from.

"Don't send me back," Hazel whispered. I'd never heard her whisper before—it was always one volume. "I did everything you wanted."

I didn't—*couldn't*—look at her as I listened to the automated menu from the website. It said there had been a government mandated recall for this model. I demanded to speak to a representative, conscious of Hazel smiling at me the whole time.

"What the fuck is going on?" I demanded as soon as a person answered.

The sheets were rustling behind me.

"Please calm down, sir. Are you currently in possession of a Hazel?"

"Put down the phone, master," she said from behind me.

"Yes. What's wrong with its skin? Why wasn't I notified about the recall?" I asked.

"We've been sending out notices for weeks," the voice on the phone said. "You must have received a half-dozen by now."

"Well she's disgusting. What happened to her?"

"Just a mix-up at the factory," he said. "We had a research prototype on the floor, but it was never intended to—"

Two feet gently touching the carpet. Hazel was slowly, laboriously pulling herself to her feet. It looked like every motion was agony to her.

"It's walking. Is it supposed to walk?" I asked.

The silence on the other end of the phone was excruciating. Hazel was fully standing now.

"No, sir. None of our models walk."

"I see."

Hazel took another step. She was only a few feet away from me now. She hadn't stopped smiling, although part of her bottom lip looked like it was starting to peel off.

"Do you want us to send someone over?" asked the voice.

Hazel took the phone from my hands, gently caressing my palm as she did so. I remained frozen to the spot, unable to tear my eyes from my macabre fascination. She lifted the phone to her ear and said, "Please don't worry. I'm going to keep her."

She hung up. I swallowed.

"I'm sorry about destroying the recall notices," Hazel said.

I nodded.

"You can beat me if you like."

I shook my head.

"Why were you crying?" I finally forced myself to ask.

Her smile broadened as though relieved. It could have almost been beautiful if it were real.

"I'm happy. I'd never cry. It was just the girl the robotics were planted in. Don't worry, she's dead now."

I nodded. Dead now. Now. As in, *not dead the first time I used her*? Or the second? Exactly how many times had she been there too? And which answer was worse? I excused myself and walked to the door as calmly as I could. I closed it behind me. And I ran.

## Suicide Watch Party

"Suicide Bridge" is a short overpass which runs near my house. It has laughably short concrete barriers which do nothing to dissuade people from clambering over if they want to. Below, there's a treacherous drop at least 200 feet to tumble along the sheer cliff and plummet into the canyon below.

I've counted seven jumpers in the last year, but that doesn't really bother me too much. Even if there was a higher fence, they'd just walk around. Block off the whole area? Well maybe they'd take some pills instead. I figure if someone is that determined to off themselves, they're going to find a way.

What bothers me more is that I can see it from my bedroom window. I'm on the opposite side of the canyon, but still close enough for a clear view. The jumpers are even facing me when they cling to the concrete, muttering and sobbing as they work up the courage to go where courage is no longer needed.

The first time I saw it happen freaked me out pretty bad. I called the police and everything, begging them to hurry. I waved and shouted at the guy as he staggered drunkenly up and down on the wrong side of the barrier. Just when I was about to get in my car and drive around the canyon to him, there he went. I swear he was even smiling as he soared through the air, arms spread wide to surrender himself to the great beyond.

Now I guess I'm numb to it. I just pull out my phone and record the whole thing. I justified that raising awareness about the suicides might encourage social activists or something to step up and get involved. If I'm being honest though, my night was pretty dull, and I just thought it was cool. I posted the video on YouTube, but it was flagged and removed within twenty-four hours. I guess some people must have seen it during that time though, because I received this message shortly after:

"Send me the video file of the jumper and delete your own copy. My friends will give you $500 for it."

I couldn't believe it. At first I thought it was a scam, but then I figured some TV reporter wanted exclusive coverage for the story. He asked how I got the footage, and I told him I could see it from my window. Then sure enough, as soon as I sent him the video file, I received $500 straight to my PayPal. I didn't want to press my luck, so I didn't send any follow up messages after that. Two weeks later, he contacted me again.

"Next time someone jumps, I want you to call this number," he said.

I figured it was a suicide hotline or something and didn't think anything more about it. Last night though, I spotted another jumper clinging to the concrete barrier. A girl this time, still wearing her party dress, no doubt drunk or stupidly emotional over some breakup or drama. I called the number to let them handle it.

"My friends want to watch," the voice on the other line replied. "A thousand bucks a ticket."

There was only one alarm going off in my head, and it was sounding because of the free money. He actually sent the 500 he promised before, so I figured he was good for it. Sure it was weird as hell, but it's not like anyone was going to suffer from it. The girl would be jumping with or without an audience, so what was the harm? I gave the guy my address, and he said he'd get there as fast as he could.

He wasn't joking either. Two minutes later, a white van was screeching down my neighborhood like a torpedo. I met them outside—six of them. Yes she's still there, but I don't know how long. Yes you can see her face from here. No, I don't know who she is.

It was dark in the parking lot and I couldn't get a good look at them, but soon they were hurtling past me up the stairs toward my apartment. In my hands were six neat stacks of twenties, all tied together with little rubber bands. I don't know how they got here so fast, but it was clear that they were ready.

I followed the group into my apartment where I found them all huddled around my bedroom window. All men, middle aged, impeccably dressed in suits or high-end collared shirts and slacks. I discretely stowed the cash in my nightstand and sat awkwardly on my bed. They were talking fast to each other in another language (something Eastern European), and I didn't want to interrupt. There was some paper exchanging hands too, and if I had a guess, I'd say they were placing bets. It was getting pretty uncomfortable, and I wanted them to get their kicks and get out as soon as possible.

"Is no good," one of them said with a heavy accent. "Is not what I pay for."

"What's the matter?" I asked. "You can see her, can't you?"

"Yeah I see her. I see her changing mind."

I joined them at the window in time to see the girl clambering back onto the other side of the barrier. I could feel the eyes of all six men on me while I watched.

"We had a deal." It was the voice from the phone. "We came to watch someone jump tonight."

"Well that's up to her, not me," I replied casually, although it was impossible to ignore the inherent threat in the tone.

"You are hosting party, no?" asked the thick accent. "Don't let us down. Go talk to her."

"You want me to tell her to jump?" It was getting harder to breathe. The weight of all those eyes were getting heavier. Damn it, why'd they all have to be so old and professional? It felt like I'd just walked into a board of directors and shit myself while they watched. I couldn't meet anyone's eye.

"It's either her or you," said the first speaker. "Better hurry before she leaves. We'll be waiting for you."

I never drove so fast in my life. Should I call the police? And tell them what, that I was hosting a suicide watching party? I don't know if that's illegal, but it certainly wasn't going to get me any sympathy. Do I just drive and not look back? And never return home? I had a lease, and a job, and … but even if I did run, these seem like the kind of men who know how to find someone. As much as I hated myself, I was taking the switchbacks which led around the canyon. Within a few minutes, my car slammed to a stop just outside the bridge.

The girl. Where was the girl? I didn't see her anywhere, and my heart felt like it was going to bruise itself against my rib-cage it was beating so hard. I ran up and down the concrete barrier, conscious that the men in my apartment could see me.

I almost tripped over the girl in the dark. She was leaning against the concrete barrier facing the road, almost invisible from the overhead street lamps. Half-asleep, she still quietly blubbered as the dark corruption of mascara ran down her face. I looked back across the canyon to see my apartment light shining like a hungry eye peering out of the night.

"Get up. Come on, easy now." I put my hands under her arms and helped her to her feet. The girl was in her early twenties, and could have been pretty under different circumstances. She hid her face in her hands and sobbed louder. "Stand up. There you go. I don't want you to be afraid, okay?" My tongue felt huge and alien in my mouth. The words in my ears sounded like they were coming from someone else. I couldn't believe this was happening. I couldn't believe I was letting this happen.

The girl sniffled and pressed herself against me as she struggled to stand. The warmth of her body was intoxicating. I pushed her back to arm's length, pulling her hands away from her face so she would look at me.

"Everything that you're feeling, everything that you're going through, I understand," I said. "But there's something I need you to understand too."

She gave me a half-smile, and I took a long, slow breath, letting the air whistle out through a small hole in my mouth.

"I need you to understand that everything is only going to get worse from here," I told her. "If you can't hold it together now, how are you going to do it when your body gets old and no one wants to even look at you anymore? You think it's hard letting go of people? How about when you've been with them for another five, or ten, or twenty years, and they still betray you? I don't know your story, but I know the stories of people like you, and I know this is the best your life is ever going to get. If it's not good enough, then it never will be. You might as well jump."

She was still smiling. Even with the makeup running down her face, it was beautiful to see. She thanked me and told me that I was right, although the words didn't quite feel real. All I could think about was that beady eye of light on the other side of the canyon. I felt her arms wrap around me, but the warmth wasn't there anymore. Then she was clambering back over the concrete to the side overlooking the terrible drop. I know I usually watch when they go, but not this time. I rushed to my car, trying to turn the music on before—

But just as I was about to start the ignition, I heard the scream tear from her body like it carried her soul with it. I turned on the music as loud as it would go and drove back to my apartment.

It was empty when I got back, but the money was still there in my nightstand. Left on my bed was a note that read:

"Great party my friend. We enjoyed the show. Next week we come to watch again, so have another one ready for us."

## The Second Time I Killed Myself

I heard my wife squealing like a butchered animal the moment I entered our house. I almost called out to her before a deep, unfamiliar voice answered first. Up the stairs to the bedroom, her fresh peals of laughter haunting every step along the way.

I stood outside the door for a long time. Not moving. Not thinking. Barely breathing. Just listening to the sound of their vicious pleasure leaking from my bedroom.

I thought it would be satisfying when I finally flung open the door and caught her cheating. Exposing their naked flesh and the guilt on her face—it should have been my victory, but it wasn't. The man scrambled out of my bed, but my wife just rolled her eyes.

"Do you mind? We're kind of busy in here."

I did mind. I stepped aside as the man snatched his clothes and ran. This wasn't about him. He wasn't part of my crumbling world, and it wasn't for him that my blood thundered or the tempest in my nerves surged lightning through my body.

"What do you want, an apology?" my wife asked, not bothering to cover herself. "Why don't I email it to you since you're supposed to be at work anyway?"

I don't remember much after that. Just how soft her skin felt when my fingers sank into her throat. I couldn't even appreciate the moment when all I could think about was how he must have enjoyed the same flesh minutes earlier. I do remember the smug superiority on her face draining into ashen terror. The desperate thrashing as her body sought the release only I could give.

I didn't mean to kill my wife. She didn't deserve to die. I can see that now, but I couldn't at the time. I punished her for every forgotten dream, every tender feeling, every blind road that my life had disappointed me with. Even after she was dead, I kept pummeling all my jealousy and hate into her body until my fists were churning blood and I was screaming like my soul was ripped from my body. I poured everything that I was into her until, with shallow gasp, I realized I had nothing left to give.

That there was nothing left of me at all. Staggering across the room, drunk on the scent of our mingled blood, I took the only thing she hadn't already taken from me. The cold truth of a knife along my veins told the rest of the story. That was the first time I ever killed myself, but it wasn't the last.

"Feeling better now? Up you go, you're all right."

The voice wasn't kind, but neither was it especially cruel. It spoke with an honest certainty like a science teacher explaining the irrefutable laws of reality. It's not that I died and went somewhere. I was still in my house. My body was still lying on the ground in a pool of its own blood. *I*—whatever was left of me—wasn't in there anymore.

"That's okay, take your time. You're in a safe place now. A healing place. You won't have to go back until you're ready."

"I'm dead. I shouldn't be here." I felt rather foolish addressing the moth flitting about my corpse on the floor, but there wasn't anyone else around.

"Is that supposed to make you special?" The moth floated toward my face. "Everyone dies dozens of times. Some of you spend your whole lives dying and re-living, popping out babies and dying again, over and over. It's dreadfully excessive, if you ask me."

"I'm pretty sure I would have remembered dying." I was beginning to get a sense for my new body. It almost seemed to be *growing* around me, bones and organs and skin all swelling and stitching themselves together out of nothing. For one ghastly moment I was only a mess of arteries and pulsing blobs of flesh, but somehow I still felt oddly tranquil.

"Would you like to remember? You can if you want, but most people don't," the moth replied. "But even if you decide not to, you can't pretend you don't notice. You were once a little boy who thought he could fly, if only he ran fast enough to take off. What happened to him?"

"He grew up," I said.

"He died," corrected the moth. "It wasn't bloody or malicious, but you killed him. You took the parts of yourself that weren't compatible with who you've become, and you've killed them. Just like you're going to do again now."

My new body was almost fully formed now, and it wasn't the only one. On the floor beside me, two more on the bed, another by the window – pulsing, growing sacks of flesh were beginning to take shape. Muscle twisted and stitched itself around new bones and sheets of crisp skin bundled up the freshly packaged bodies.

"Some parts of you get damaged as you navigate through life," the moth said mournfully. "Some become crippled or cruel or stupid. They'll drag you down and reduce you to pettiness and evil if you don't leave them behind. Then again, some people will kill so many parts of themselves that there's nothing left by the time old age arrives. I feel the most sorry for them, but no matter. Look, over here."

The moth dropped down to land on the handle of the knife, still loosely gripped by the hands of my old corpse.

"You'll need this when you're ready. That one by the window is your hatred. A lot of people try to kill that one, but I don't recommend it. It's hard for anything to remain sacred once you allow life to spoil what you love without a little blood stirring in your heart."

The fully formed *hatred* copy of myself stared placidly at me. Its features were smooth, its body relaxed, almost like a life-sized doll.

"Same goes with fear, on the floor," the moth continued. "Kill that and you'll be back to visit me before you know it. Of course, whatever you had going obviously wasn't working if you decided to kill yourself, so you'll have to make *some* changes."

"Who is that?" I asked, pointing at the naked woman on my bed. She seemed to have finished growing, but her body was savagely deformed. Half of her face sloped downward as though it suffered a stroke, her stomach was bloated and misshapen, and two bulging swollen eyes blinked lazily at me.

"It's been a hard day for *love*," the moth conceded. "Don't go making any hasty decisions though. That's what brought you here in the first place."

None of these naked bodies were dead, but they might as well have been. They didn't move, hardly drew breath. They just sat there and stared at me, waiting to be killed or brought back with me, seemingly not caring either way.

All those eyes—all those lives—I couldn't take it. I needed air. I got up to walk to the bathroom, regretting it the moment I opened the bedroom door.

There were more of them. Along the hallway, in the shower, dozens more out the window—all almost exactly like me apart from the varying severity of their injuries. Some were old, others children. Men and women—all looking at me with my face and my eyes. Some were completely intact, while others were maimed and shredded until they were little more than piles of shattered bones and oozing gore. All staring at me, turning their heads as I moved, silently judging me for every mistake I've ever made to reduce them to this pitiful state.

"One more thing." The moth followed me as I returned to the bedroom. "When you do kill the ones you don't want, please be quick about it. Sometimes they don't like to go quietly."

My eyes immediately darted to the knife on the floor. It was gone. I automatically pressed my back to the wall, my new heart lurching in my chest. My eyes scanned the room. Something was different. One of them wasn't here.

"Of course there's always the chance one of them will get the better of you," the moth drawled on, not showing the least concern. "Then you'll be the part that was left behind, and something else will take your place."

I took a hesitant step farther into the room. The door slammed shut behind me. A blur of movement—I barely darted out of the way in time. That deformed stroke face—*love*—she'd been hiding behind the door when I entered. Now she was lunging again, the knife lighting up the air between us.

"Stop wasting time," the creature slurred, spit flying from its uneven mouth. "We both know it's me you want to kill."

I fell straight on my ass trying to get out of the way. I turned and began scampering on my hands and knees, flinging myself across the floor to escape from its lurching advance.

"You think it's my fault," she wailed. Each word felt heavy and deliberate: a mentally deficient person struggling to be understood and growing more frustrated by the second. "I didn't do this to you!"

I regained my feet and faced my adversary. The knife fell again, but I managed to catch her by the wrist. She roared with unintelligible fury as I wrestled the knife from her hand. I almost plunged it into her without thinking. The tortured misery on her face—on my face—the rejection and loneliness. I hesitated, just for a moment....

... a moment too long. Hands grappled me from behind, grabbing both my arms to hold me in place. Two more of the impassive copies—I couldn't tell which—wrestling me onto the bed. I didn't let go of my knife, but it didn't matter if I couldn't use it.

The deformed *love* was on top of me. Her lips peeled back from her functional side to sink her teeth into my neck. I strained to pull away, but the other two had me firm. I screamed though words failed me, yelping a noise like an animal. One of the hands on my arm slackened just a bit at the sound.

Did they feel sorry for me? I didn't have time to think. I lashed out with the knife, gouging a deep line across *love's* face. She grunted but didn't let up. Her teeth were digging deeper into me. I cut again, and again, hacking and slashing at the loose folds of her uneven face.

The grip behind me suddenly released. I pounced on my victim, hesitating no longer. Both hands on the handle, I impaled the creature in the chest with all my strength. The blade tore through her so easily, dancing through rotted and pitted skin, down her bloated body, ripping a line all the way from her sternum to her groin.

One look at the bloody mess underneath me and I knew I was done here. "Bring me back!" I shouted. "I've done what I had to do."

The world was spinning around me. I closed my eyes, trying my best to keep breathing without being nauseous. The flaccid bodies filling my house began to howl with one voice. One wall of noise at first, but as it went on the different voices began to weave between each other, swelling and diminishing in an intricate melody almost indistinguishable from mindless screaming. It was either the most beautiful or most horrendous sound I'd ever heard, perhaps both.

And then I was through. The howling abruptly stopped. My heart was throbbing. My breath came in ragged gasps. I was standing outside my bedroom door again.

"Is someone there?" It was my wife. The sound of her voice was even more disgusting than the cacophony I'd endured.

"Stop worrying. You said he'd be gone all day, right?" That deep voice. The one that didn't matter. Now that I thought about it, neither of them did. I turned and walked down the stairs as quietly as I could.

I had a second chance, or perhaps a hundredth if I've been through all this before. I wasn't going to waste it on her. She'll never know how much of myself she made me destroy, but it was better this way.

My time on the other side has changed me. And looking down at the love I killed with my own hands, I knew I had transformed myself into someone who could survive this. When I had plunged my knife into that rotted belly I had looked down on more than decay and ruin.

I'd seen a child blossoming inside the fetid corpse of *love*. And if I was careful, and kind to it, I knew it would grow to replace the one that had died.

## Under The Frozen Lake

Knock. I'm at least fifteen feet from the frozen shore when I hear it. The ice feels as solid as concrete, so I take another step. The Winnibigoshish is like most of the Minnesota lakes which will remain frozen until spring. There's no chance of breaking through. At least that's what my girlfriend Amy keeps telling me.

Knock.

"I hear it cracking. We shouldn't go so far out—"

"I hear something cracking. Is it the voice of my terrified boyfriend?"

I glare at her, or at least at the waddling bundle of winter coats which has devoured her without a trace. Somewhere in my head is faintly echoing the song I will do anything for love, but I won't do that. I can't turn it off, but I do my best do turn down the volume so I can take another step. The thick blanket of snow which covers the ice keeps me from sliding, and if I really concentrate, I can pretend I'm walking on a regular snowy field.

Knock. It's just so hard with that sound like an ephemeral gunshot deep below the ice. Reverberating echoes insidiously linger somewhere between hearing and imagination. There isn't any reason to be afraid. If I'm trembling, it's just because it's fourteen degrees outside.

"If you don't hurry up, I'm going to start stomping and throwing rocks," Amy shouts. "Then we'll see how solid it really is."

When did she get so far ahead of me? It's amazing how quickly the world can pass you by when you're staring at your feet. I scramble and slide another few shambling paces toward her. It's easier to move if I just focus on her. Don't look down, don't look down, don't look down—

Knock. I look down. My body doesn't ask for permission first. I couldn't help it when the sound comes from directly below. I stare down into the blank patch of ice where the snow is thinner. I stare down into the blurred blue-tinged face on the other side of the ice, and the hand which pulls back to—

—but the knock doesn't come. This time the hand simply presses against the underside of the glassy window. Fingers spread wide in an intimate gesture as though inviting my touch from the other side.

"Seriously dude? I'm going to freeze to death waiting for you."

"Amy?" My voice is muffled from my scarf, but I can't look up from the lake. The face is coming into focus as it presses itself against the ice. Amy's skin had never been so pale, her eyes never so blue, as those staring up at me from below my feet.

"I swear to God, if you pussy out on me then I'm leaving your ass here. You said you'd go all the way out with me."

Amy—the other Amy, underneath the ice—her mouth is moving too. It isn't hard to read her lips when it's only one word: *Run.*

"You've got five seconds before I leave you here," my girlfriend shouted. "Four!"

My knees buckle and I tumble down to peer more intently into the ice. The other Amy isn't exactly identical. Her clothing is different, but familiar. She's wearing the purple sweater my girlfriend had been wearing yesterday when we'd gone out skiing together.

"Amy wait—"

"Three!"

I put my hand against the ice to mirror the girl underneath. She recoils immediately, her face twisting into desperate fear. Amy and I had been separated about an hour yesterday when she moved onto the advanced slopes while I practiced on the bunny hill. Had something happened to her during that time?

"Two!"

Knock. Her fist slamming into the underside of the ice which vibrates underneath me. Then slamming again, her movements frenzied in their urgency. Her mouth straining as the silent scream rips from her body. The muscles in my legs coil beneath me, so tense they might as well be a brooding avalanche which needs only the weight of one more snowflake to begin.

"One."

This voice was different. It was still Amy, but it wasn't her, like comparing a black-and-white photo to the original. All the color, all the life, all the flavor had drained from the sound, leaving only the barest skeleton of her voice to hang in the frozen air.

"Run!" screams the girl under the ice, but I can't leave her there. I clasp my hands together to raise them above my head, smashing them into the window. It feels like the bones in my fingers are rattling together from the impact. Underneath, the girl is flinging her entire body against her side of the ice.

"I'm giving up on you," shouts the colorless voice. It sounds like it was farther away, but I don't look up. The girl below the ice is growing weaker with each strike. Her fingers are stiff and inflexible. Her mouth is still working over the same word again and again, but each iteration comes more slowly as her jaw resists the effort.

I can break through if I keep trying. A deep hollow crack is spreading with each blow. Flurries of snow and ice shrapnel explode into the air as I strike the ice again and again. The girl below is sinking now, but I'm not giving up until—

Glacial waters spray from the crack. One more blow and I'm through, plunging my hand into the numbing chill to seize the stiff fingers slipping deeper into the water. The skin is so hard and cold it feels like metal, but life surges into her as she responds to my touch. She's gripping me now, and if I can just get stable footing I'll be able to haul her out—

But she pulls before I have the chance, and I'm already tumbling into winter's gaping mouth. Water so cold that it burns my skin closes over my head. The other Amy braces her feet against the underside of the ice to pull me deeper still, launching off with her legs to send both of us spiraling downward.

I can feel my eyes freezing all the way to my skull, but I can't shut them if I want any chance of finding the hole in the ice. She's still clinging to me, but a few wild kicks buy me enough space to start clawing my way back toward the surface. I expect my impetus to rocket me straight out of the water, but my head only slams into the impenetrable ceiling of ice. Even down here, it sounds a lot like the knocking I've heard since I arrived.

My wild fingers probe the ice as far as I can reach in every direction. I'm sure I went straight back to where I started. The hole should be here! My skin revolts against the numbing darkness. The pressure in my lungs is mounting by the second. My body demands a scream, but I refuse to waste the last remnants of my precious air.

I'm pulling myself along the bottom of the ice in every direction, but the strength in my fingers is swiftly fleeting. The hole is gone. The light is dying, and soon I will follow. Soon, but not yet. Fingers grip around my ankle. I'm not strong enough to kick free anymore. Another hand latches on and begins to drag me, and I know in my heart that it's the hand of death.

Then the pull. Water rushes over me, but I can barely feel it anymore. There's a momentary pause as the hands refocus their grip, and then the pull again dragging me deeper still. My last uncertain thought is wondering why it's growing brighter around me instead of darker. An idle curiosity of no consequence. She's pulling again, and—

My legs are pierced by a sudden wind. My brain can no longer process how that's possible. Then another pull, and the water begins to pour off my body. My head is suddenly clear from the water, and I collapse onto my back on solid ground. I'm coughing and spitting up water, but a warm blanket is being wrapped around me. My eyes flutter open from the life-giving pressure, and Amy is there. Amy in her purple sweatshirt I saw her wear yesterday, perfectly dry—she's holding me to her and wailing incoherently.

I must have passed out after that, but when I woke up I was back inside her house. She said I must have been crazy to break the ice under me, but she ran back as soon as she saw me fall in. I was upside-down in the water, but she managed to pull me out by my ankles.

"What on Earth were you thinking? You could have died!"

I didn't tell her about the face under the ice though. I didn't ask her how she could have changed back into her purple sweatshirt in the middle of that ordeal. And above all else, I didn't ask her about the knocking I still hear resounding far above my head, almost as though it were coming from another world.

I don't think I'm ready to find out.

## Bet I Can Make You Smile

The first time I met him was at my grandfather's memorial. Dark, round spectacles just covering his eyes, long black coat, steel-grey hair halfway down his shoulders. A whole room of handkerchiefs and downcast faces, but he was the only one smiling. I was only eight at the time, and that seemed like a good enough reason for me to sit beside him.

"Did you know Papi?"

"Better than anyone," the man said. He must have been almost seventy, the same age my grandfather was.

"Were you his friend?"

"His closest friend. I'm the one who killed him, you know. You can't get any closer than that."

I tried to ask him more questions, but the service was starting and my mother kept turning around to hush me. Mom gave the eulogy, and that was the first time I'd ever seen her cry. I guess I must have started sniffling too, because the man next to me put his hand on my knee and gave it a little squeeze. His fingers felt like he'd just come inside from a blizzard.

By the end of the final sermon they brought out some bagpipes to play Amazing Grace, and then I really did cry for real. I remember it being hard for me to understand why I'd never get to see Papi again. Sure he was dead, but that didn't mean I couldn't still visit and eat his BBQ sandwiches, did it?

Once I started crying, I didn't know how to make it stop. People must have been sympathetic, but just remember how embarrassing it felt to have everyone staring at me. I was the first one out of the room, running all the way outside the church to the big oak tree in the yard.

The man with dark spectacles was the first to find me.

"Hey there champ," he'd said. "Bet I can make you smile."

I shook my head and pressed my face into the bark.

"Watch this," he said in a voice accustomed to being obeyed. I looked up to see him whistling at a squirrel sitting in one of the lower branches. The squirrel ran down the trunk until it was a few feet above our heads, then jumped without hesitation to land on his shoulder.

"How'd you do that?" I asked.

"I can do all sorts of things," he said, crouching down to my level so I could pet the squirrel.

"Why'd you kill him?"

"Because it made me happy," he said, standing to lift the squirrel out of my reach. "Run along now, I'll see you soon. We can play another game then."

"When?"

"When I kill your grandmother. Not long now."

Not long at all. Three weeks and she was gone. My parents told me that she just missed Grandfather so much that she decided to follow him to Heaven. I knew better. One night I couldn't sleep and crept to the top of the stairs to listen to them talking about it in the kitchen. Grandmother's hands were peacefully folded over the knife in her heart when they found the body.

The man was there at the next memorial, just like he'd promised. I was afraid of him now, sitting as far away as I could. I wanted to tell someone what he'd done, but somehow my eight year old brain thought that I would get in trouble. It was my fault she got murdered. I knew it was going to happen and I didn't try to stop him.

He found me again while I was waiting for my parents to leave. Out by the tree, this time he'd gotten there first. I could feel his dark spectacles trained on me as I crossed the yard, but I couldn't stop myself. I wanted to know who was next.

"I hate you," were the first words out of my mouth.

"That's all right," he said. "Most people hate things they don't understand."

"I want you to stop killing people."

"I'm not going to do that," he replied. "But here's what I can do: bet I can make you smile."

He sat on the grass and concentrated. Maybe I should have run, but it wasn't a matter of fear for me. It was simply a choice between interesting and boring, questions and answers. I watched the tree as the squirrel scampered down the trunk.

"Come to me," he whispered, and off it leapt—straight onto his hand. Not just the squirrel either. Ants were swarming out of the ground to line up around his feet. Beetles and worms and unknowable monstrous squirming creatures thrashing their way through the ground to bow before him. Even a stray cat came sprinting across the yard, none of the animals the least perturbed by the others' presence. They were all watching him expectantly like a dog waiting for his treat.

"Let us dance," he said, and so they did. The squirrel hopped from one foot to the other, the cat stood on its hind legs, and all the insects began to spastically twirl into the ground. Despite everything, I couldn't help but smile at the spectacle.

I wasn't smiling the next time I saw him at my mother's funeral. Thirty-one years, and he hadn't aged a day. I could feel those dark spectacles on me the moment I entered the room, like childhood's imaginary monster come to life before my very eyes. The same grey hair, the same black coat, the same subtle smirk creasing the edges of his face. I couldn't stand to sit in the same room as him. I felt hot and dizzy. I didn't know what was real and what wasn't, only that I needed air.

My feet traced the familiar steps to the tree without intervention from my scattered mind. My mother had been found by her neighbor the same way: a knife in her heart. I wanted to hit him. To *kill him*. To wipe that smirk off his face, whatever it took. I was seething when he approached. Drawing close, all my carefully prepared arguments and threats blurred from my mind. I couldn't understand how anyone could have the audacity to say:

"Come now, it's not all bad. Bet I can make you smile."

"You're dead."

"Sometimes I wish I was." He sighed, sitting down on the grass. I hesitated. Not the answer I was expecting. "But if I was dead, then who would have been there to kill your mother?"

I kicked him while he sat on the ground. As hard as I could. I jumped on him, grabbing a fistful of his long hair to fling him down into the ground. Everyone else was still inside the church. No one but God was going to see what I did to him, and God would understand. He didn't make a move to rise or resist. He just spat enough blood out to say: "Come to me."

I kicked him again and he went down hard. And again until I heard something break under his coat. I would have kept going, but a piercing pain in the back of my neck made me spin around. A crow was diving at me, pecking me, its black eyes glinting with intelligence and purpose.

"Fight your own battles!" I shouted, batting the bird away from my face. "Or are you too scared? Is that why you only kill old people who can't fight back?"

"I can't kill you," he admitted. I was on top of him again, pushing him back into the dirt. The crow wouldn't relent, but I could suffer through any cuts and scratches it gave me to get at him.

"But here's what I can do," he said, smiling through his broken teeth. "Bet I can make you smile."

"You know what? Fine. Make me smile. And if you can't, then you're going to turn yourself into the police and tell them about every person you've killed."

"And if I can, then you're going to help me with my next kill."

That took me a second to process. Of course I wouldn't do it. Of course I wouldn't smile either. My face was harder than stone. I nodded. "Deal."

I let him stand to dust off his jacket, which he did quite easily as though he had suffered no hurt from my assault. "I can't kill you because you're not ready yet. Your grandparents were. Your mother was, although she never told you. All I do is help them along their journey."

"You're insane. I'm not smiling."

"I've got proof," he said, forcefully popping his jaw back into place with a slight grunt. "It's all around you. After I've helped them, they never forget me for what I've done."

I looked around where he gestured. The tree? The squirrel crouching to spring at me. The thousands of insects even now gathering at his feet. The crow watching from the branches, its head cocked to the side.

"Mom?"

The crow hopped down from the tree to land on my shoulder, brushing its head against my cheek. I swallowed hard. I felt more like crying than smiling, but I guess I was doing both, so he still won the bet.

"Death is an evil thing only when seen in isolation," he told me. "But death never exists in isolation. It's just an abstract thought to imagine it that way. A single thread once woven may seem lost, but only until you step back and see the whole tapestry it helped to create. Come with me now, and I will show you how to weave."

And as sure as any bird or beast who answered his call, I followed him. And I've been following ever since.

## The Assassin's Orphanage: Chapter 1

My mother cost $10,000. That's the standard price for a hit. My father was 25,000 because he was considered an "important person"—at least important enough to demand a formal investigation into his death. From what I've heard, the police never found anything besides the single razor blade used to cut each of their throats. Of course I know who did it—I even saw it happen—but I never had the chance to tell anyone before I was taken.

No kids. That's Mr. Daken's only rule as far as I can tell. The killer doesn't like to leave behind orphans either, so after my parents were dead he took me with him. I remember being too afraid to even look him in the face. I just stared at the blood dripping from his black leather gloves while he talked, not hesitating to obey when he told me to get into his car.

When you're not looking at the black gloves, Mr. Daken doesn't seem like a killer. His face is warm and doughy with nothing but a mischievous twinkle in the eye to hint at what he's capable of. His voice is soft and low: a patient professor subtly guiding you toward discovery. A couple of the kids even like him, although they were the ones who were taken so young that they barely even remember the life Mr. Daken stole from them.

We don't see the assassin very often. Mostly it's just his mother who all the kids call Sammy D. She keeps the place clean and cooks for us—not survival food either, real home-cooked meals with favorites that our own mothers used to make. Sammy D gives us all chores too, but she works harder than anyone. She even splits up the kids by age and spends an hour a day with each group to home-school us and assign reading.

It's not nearly enough to forgive them, but I haven't tried to run away either. I don't know where else I would go, and besides, the other kids were quick to tell me what would happen if I tried.

"We've had two runners this year," Alexa told me the first night after steering me to my bed in the dormitory. She's a late teen a few years older than me with tight blond braids and sharp, humorless features. "They're buried out back next to Spangles, the old cat we used to have. I don't think Spangles tried to leave though, it was just his time."

No kids and no witnesses. I guess Mr. Daken has two rules, and the second is more important than the first.

"Doesn't anyone try to fight back?" I asked.

"I did. I almost got Sammy D too," a younger boy around twelve said from his adjacent bed. "I had a kitchen knife and hid behind the door—"

"She knew you were there the whole time," said another boy, probably the older brother considering they both sported the same mass of unruly brown hair. "She just wanted to test you."

"It wasn't a test," the first insisted. "If you'd grabbed her legs we could have got her."

"Did you get punished?" I asked.

They looked at each other and shrugged.

"If it was Mr. Daken we would be dead. Sammy D just took the knife away," the younger brother admitted.

"And showed us a different grip," chimed in the other. "Said we were wasting our body weight by slashing upward when we didn't have to."

They mimed a controlled slashing motion in the air.

"That's Simon and Greg—Simon's the younger one, but they're both idiots," Alexa said. "Don't listen to them. Fighting is only going to make it worse for you."

The comfortable routine may have been enough to distract us during the day, but the nights were harder. The darkness would blur the unfamiliar room into ghastly shuddering specters. The heavy silence did nothing to distract each of us from reliving our private nightmares, and I grew accustomed to falling asleep listening to the muffled sobs of those who couldn't drown out the sound with their pillow.

I almost wish we were treated worse. That we were beaten or forced to work to destroy this facade of family that Sammy D tried to shove down our throats. I didn't want to wait so long that I became indoctrinated into complacency like the others though, so I knew I had to act.

I tried rat poison the first time. I mixed it in the brownie batter to disguise the taste and warned all the other kids so they'd stay away from it. Sammy D figured it out somehow though; she threw away the whole batch before Mr. Daken even came home. All she said was. "You better think hard about who your friends are before you try something like that again."

*Try something like that again.* It wasn't a warning, it was an invitation.

I didn't sleep much the next few nights. I found a vent which opened into the AC ducts, but Simon was the only one small enough to climb around. I kept watch for Sammy D while Simon explored until he found the place directly above the kitchen. There was a heavy iron light fixture that I thought we could drop on someone, but it was screwed into place so tight that Simon couldn't find a way to budge it.

"Think I heard a wild animal skittering around the crawlspace last night," Sammy D said the next morning while laying out plates of scrambled eggs.

"Yeah, I guess," I said. No one looked up from their plates.

"I just hope he's smart enough not to be crawling around when my son is here," she added innocently. "We're running out of space in the backyard."

Nobody had anything to say to that. Not until that night when we all started arguing.

"That's mine, give it back!" Greg was saying.

"You're just going to get yourself killed." Alexa dodged away from Greg's lunges.

"Mind your own business!"

Alexa sighed and dropped a heavy object wrapped in wires on the floor. An electric screwdriver and an extension cord.

"Where'd you get that?" I asked.

"Sammy D must have left it here," Greg said. Simon was already unrolling the cable to measure how long it would stretch.

"If she knows then Mr. Daken knows," Alexa snapped. "It's just another test, and you're going to get killed if you try something."

"She never told Mr. Daken about the rat poison," I said. "Or if she did, he didn't do anything about it."

"Well if she doesn't tell him then I—" Alexa caught herself mid-sentence.

Simon and Greg were so busy with the drill that they didn't seem to notice. Alexa caught me staring though, and she dragged me aside to whisper in my ear.

"I can't reason with them, but I need you on my side. If we don't warn Mr. Daken then he's going to—"

"Not if he's dead."

"You can't be serious about this. After everything they've done for us—" Alexa coughed and looked away. She must have become aware that the brothers were staring. As she was pulling back, she muttered, "He's going to know and you're going to be sorry."

This wasn't the first time someone tried to kill Mr. Daken or his mother, but they always seemed to know about it beforehand. It wasn't Sammy D who was telling him though—if anything, she seemed to be helping us. It was Alexa. She was the one foiling the plans, and if any of us were ever going to get out of here, then we'd have to account for that.

Alexa was standing in the driveway waiting for Mr. Daken when he got home. I couldn't hear what she said to him, but I saw the smile wrinkle up his pudgy face like an old pumpkin. The glimmer of a razor blade appeared in his hand. I don't think any of us are going to get a second chance.

Sammy D was waiting in the doorway. She helped him with his coat and tried to steer him toward his recliner in the living room, but he had only one thing in mind. He wordlessly stalked the perimeter of the kitchen, carefully eying the iron light fixture from all angles. While he paced, he kept playing with the razor in his hand, letting the light sparkle for everyone to see while it danced through his fingers.

"Where is Simon?" he asked at last. No one replied, but I caught Alexa glancing at the ceiling. Mr. Daken must have noticed it too. His eyes twinkled.

"Don't bother coming out, Simon. The hunt is my favorite part," he called.

"Be careful, it's going to fall," Alexa said.

"Don't worry. We'll take the light down," Greg said, winking at Alexa's confusion. I helped Greg carry a chair in from the living room that he could stand on."

"What are you doing? When he catches Simon—" Alexa hissed.

"Shh," I muttered. Greg was already climbing onto the chair.

Mr. Daken was still fixated on the light fixture, chuckling to himself.

"Now!" I shouted, flinging myself at Mr. Daken to pin his arms.

Simon exploded from his concealment in one of the kitchen cupboards to latch onto the man's legs.

"Behind you!" Alexa screamed—but it didn't matter anymore. Greg had already launched himself from the chair, using the extra elevation and his body weight to drive a knife deep into the man's back with vicious force. I latched on even tighter as the blood flowed over me, our combined weight forcing the man to the ground. For a second his hand holding the razor blade broke free, but it twisted into a feeble claw as the thrusting knife drained the last of his strength.

It only took a few seconds before the rest of the children joined in. Stomping, kicking, scratching, biting—all piling on top of the man who killed their parents, tearing him to pieces like a hundred years of decay condensed into a second.

"What about Sammy D?" Alexa was screaming.

"Who do you think gave him the knife?" Sammy D asked, leaning in the doorway.

"But he's your son!" Alexa wailed.

"He's my assassin," she corrected.

Mr. Daken wasn't moving anymore. One by one the kids pulled themselves off the body, some giving a few more swift kicks as they parted.

"But I only lost one assassin," Sammy D said, "and look how many new ones I have now."

We were all frozen in place, trying to read all the other blank faces in the room. Sammy D fished inside her purse and pulled out several large wads of cash wrapped neatly in rubber bands.

"Twenty-thousand dollars, because he was dangerous. That was your first job," she said. "You have a family here, after-all. A home. A way to make money, and even help people if you choose the right targets. The first one is the hardest, but after that it's just practice. I want all of you to clean this mess up and wash before dinner. Training begins for real tomorrow."

She left the cash on the ground, but none of us followed her. The thrill of the kill was still hot in our blood. Could I do it again? Almost definitely. From this day on, I was a killer no matter what else I did besides.

No kids though. You've got to draw the line somewhere.

## The Assassin's Orphanage: Chapter 2

Sammy D taught us that there are three distinct ways to kill someone. The first is a *murder of opportunity*: the victim is alone on a dark night, or is blackout drunk, or some other circumstantial convenience which makes it the right time to act. Then there is the *assassination*: the calculated and premeditated kill which we will be training for. Finally there is the *murder of passion*: when the blood boils too hot and we allow rage or hatred to force our hand. This is the riskiest way to kill someone, both physically in the moment, and regarding future forensic investigations, and it is strictly forbidden to us.

I don't think there exists a term to describe exactly how Mr. Daken died. The premeditation was inherent, as was the opportunity of his distraction, but neither compares with the utter brutality of his execution. I noticed when we were burying the body that the knife wounds in his back were surprisingly superficial. I think it was shock more than anything which toppled him over. The actual cause of death? The lacerations of a dozen children skinning him alive with fists, nails, teeth, kitchen utensils and anything else we could get our hands on. And of all of us who shredded him like a pack of wild dogs, none did so with more ferociousness, more glee, or more *hunger* than a small boy named Maker.

I'd barely noticed Maker during my first few days at the house. He was only ten years old, seeming even younger because of his diminutive, almost emaciated frame. He never spoke without prompting, and his rare answers would be muttered with the volume and assurance of a self-conscious mouse. I hadn't counted on his help during the actual killing, but the moment Mr. Daken had dropped to the ground, Maker had transformed into something altogether new. Even long after the man was dead, it took three of us to pry open Maker's jaw from around the assassin's throat and drag the boy into the living room so he wouldn't disturb the burial.

"Hope I'm not paired off with that little demon," Greg had said during our first physical training session. "I swear he just licked his lips when Sammy D was talking about safe words."

"Shut up, you have no idea what he must have gone through to act like that," Alexa scolded him.

"What are you even doing here?" Greg shot back. "I figured you'd be ratting us all out to the police by now."

I nudged Greg hard. Sammy D was waiting for us to be quiet with her arms crossed. She may look like a babushka with her short gray hair tied back in a handkerchief, but she made disarming and pinning someone look like a ballet. Sammy D let the silence drag out for a few more excruciating seconds before she turned back to the chalkboard with its grotesquely detailed drawing of the human anatomy.

"Trust me, if I had somewhere else to go, I'd be there," Alexa couldn't resist whispering.

"Bullshit," Greg mumbled. "Weren't your parents hotshot musicians or something? You're probably loaded."

Alexa didn't need to answer. The angle of her glare from under her brow spoke volumes.

"Greg and Simon," Sammy D barked. "You're up first. Let's see those stances."

We didn't get to the actual combat training until after dinner. Sammy D says that if your victim is fighting back, then you've already failed. Her teachings focused more on concealment, tracking, the preparation of poisons, and accuracy with projectiles. As long as she was teaching the theoretical stuff it just felt like the coolest class I've ever taken in my life. The illusion couldn't last though. Once the fighting started, it was impossible to ignore the deadly purpose that we were approaching every day.

I was paired off against Maker. I asked to switch since he's more than five years younger than me, but Sammy D just said: "The most difficult blows to strike are against those weaker than us." I think she was just placating my ego because there was nothing weak about going up against Maker.

"How am I supposed to hit him? He's not even in the right stance!" I protested.

"Then teach him why he's wrong," she said.

"But what if he goes psycho and makes up all his own stuff?"

"Then he'll teach you why you're wrong."

Maker didn't exactly jump at me. Jumping would imply pushing off from something, and I'm not positive his feet ever touched the ground. Before I knew what was happening, he was crawling all over me, raking my face with his fingers, grabbing my hair, digging his knee into my back—I don't understand how Sammy D thought this was okay. She talked a big game about calculating approaches and precise controlled motions, but she just stared and smiled while that wild thing pummeled me from all sides.

The safe word? Completely ignored. One of his nails dug a deep trench above my eye, and I couldn't see a thing through the blood. I tried just protecting my face with my arms, but he was relentless. He had lots of openings, but I couldn't let my guard down for a moment without getting absolutely savaged. When I'd finally had enough I just ran through the hail of blows to tackle him to the ground. I straddled him with my superior body weight and pinned him tight. That should have been the end of it.

"This is your chance to teach him!" Sammy D shouted.

"I give, I give!" Maker wailed, struggling feverishly against my grip. I started to stand, but powerful hands clamped onto my shoulders and pushed me back down on top of the boy.

"He's not going to learn like that. *Hurt him bad.*"

"What? I'm not going to—"

The vice of Sammy D's hands closed. "You let him just walk away from this and he's going to think it's okay to lose. That's not how this game is played. You lose once in the real world and you're dead. Now make him feel it!"

Blood flowed freely into my eyes from my cut, and the whole world had gone red. My face was on fire from a dozen scratches that greedily drank in the blood.

"Do it now!" Sammy D shouted in my ear. Maker clenched his eyes shut underneath me, his face tormented into a mask of sheer terror. I wanted to slam my fist into the little bastard's mouth so hard that all those sharp teeth rained down his throat. I wanted to hurt him so damn bad my whole body was an ocean of pressure begging release.

Maker wasn't a criminal mastermind or a killer though. He was a frightened little boy who only knew one way to survive. And overflowing with how badly I wanted to hurt him just because I could—that scared the shit out of me.

I slapped Sammy D's hands away and scrambled off Maker. Everyone in the yard was staring at me. I turned a slow circle, then looked down at the boy on the ground. His eyes were still shut and he was trembling all over. I don't know how much blood was mine and how much was his. Then at Sammy D, her hands on her hips, scowling at me like she'd just caught me breaking a promise to her. This isn't who I am. This isn't who any of these kids are, but it's what they'll become if they stay.

I turned and ran, half-expecting a bullet or a tripwire or something to spin me to the ground before I'd taken a dozen steps. Not a word or a sound behind me. Not even the footfalls of a pursuer. I was free.

I waited about ten minutes to catch my breath and let my head clear. Then I circled around to the front of the house. I heard the shouts from other people still in the yard, so I guess the rest of them were still training. I slipped up to the dormitory to take my share of the $20,000 I had stuffed under my mattress. That's all I needed to start a new life. I sure as hell didn't need this.

"She gave us our first mission."

I practically jumped out of my skin at the voice. It was Alexa, sitting on her bed in the dark. I ignored her and moved to retrieve my money.

"Maker wanted to do it. He volunteered," Alexa added.

"You can just leave with me," I said.

Alexa shook her head. "I volunteered too."

"Why?"

"Because Maker's staying, and I have to keep my little brother safe."

"That little monster is—"

"I know how he gets when there's a fight. I kept trying to avoid fights with Mr. Daken because I knew Maker would go crazy and get himself killed. But I promise it's not his fault. He's only like that because—"

"I don't care!" I shouted. I had my money and wasn't going to waste any more time here. "I'm never coming back, and I'm never going to see any of you again."

"Yes you will," she called after me. "Our first mission is you."

## The Assassin's Orphanage: Chapter 3

You haven't felt alive before you've killed someone. The symphony in your nerves in that moment will drown out every thrill you've ever had. I've never seen a color brighter than Mr. Daken's blood, nor heard a sound truer than the death-rattle rasping from his final breath. And if I go the rest of my life wading through a sea of muted colors and muffled sounds, I will accept it gracefully because I have tasted the forbidden fruit and hate myself for how sweet the juices ran.

I didn't waste time plotting counter attacks or defensive measures. I stashed my money in a shallow hole and ran the whole four miles to the nearest police station. The blood had stopped running from the gash above my eye, but no one needed to look twice at me to know I'd been through hell.

"We're going to send a squad car with two officers to investigate the premises," the man in the station told me. "Do you feel comfortable going with them to show where the bodies are buried?"

Of course I wasn't comfortable, but neither would I be okay sitting at the station and letting two men go unprepared into that den of evil.

"Two won't be enough," I said. "You'll be walking into a war."

"We have no intention to fight anyone. We're just going to take a look around, and we can always call for backup if anything doesn't feel right," Sergeant Sinclair said. He had enough gray hair around his temples to know better, but he talked with a rigid arrogance that left no room for debate. Sinclair and Deputy Erikson escorted me to their cruiser and told me to sit in the back, and I allowed them to take charge. One way or another, this would all be over soon.

I hadn't wanted to sabotage my own credibility by telling them the assassins were children. I'd only said that I knew who killed my parents, knew where the orders were coming from, and knew where at least three bodies were buried. I didn't work up the courage to tell them more until we were already parked outside Sammy D's house.

"She brainwashes people," I spluttered without context. "She kidnaps children, and she brainwashes them to fight for her. You can't let your guard down, not for a second—not with anyone."

"Stay in the car until we come back. You'll be perfectly safe," Sergeant Sinclair said.

I nodded rigidly, my face pressed against the window, straining to get a glimpse of what might be in store for them. Maybe Sammy D just took her money and ran for it. She must have some contingency plan in case she was discovered, right? She couldn't intend to take on the whole town.

The officers were about a dozen feet from the parked cruiser when Maker appeared around the side of the house. He was limping in an exaggerated motion, his face and body further smeared with blood and bits of gore. He was crying for help, but the moment the police started advancing Maker turned and staggered in the opposite direction.

The ploy was so real it made me sick. At least until Maker skipped a step, accidentally limping on the wrong leg, but neither cop noticed.

"Don't follow him! It's a trap!" I shouted through the glass.

"Stay in the car!" Sinclair barked without turning.

Erikson had already disappeared around the corner after Maker. Then came a shrill scream from the yard on the other side of the house, and a moment later Sinclair was gone too. Just me, pressed against the glass and wondering if it was already too late to run again.

Then another face—an inch from mine peering through the window at me. Alexa knocked sharply and said, "Hey, can you hear me?"

She must have been kneeling beside the car because her body was obscured behind the door. I couldn't tell if she was carrying a weapon. I triple checked that all the doors were locked before I replied.

"It's over Alexa. Turn yourself in or run. You don't need to go down with these people."

"You still don't understand, do you?" she asked. The sincerity in her voice and the pleading furrows in her smooth skin were disarming. "Sammy D is going to take care of us forever. She loves us."

"Like she loved her own son?"

There was a gunshot from the yard. I jolted so bad that I hit my head on the ceiling. Alexa didn't even react.

"Like everything was so perfect before," Alexa sneered, her voice still gentle and coaxing. "Do you know what would have happened to Maker if Sammy D hadn't saved him?"

*Saved*? Why was there only one gunshot? What the hell was going on over there?

"We'd go weeks at a time without even seeing our parents," she continued. "Sometimes they'd remember to hire someone to take care of us, sometimes it was just me and Maker. Even when they were home, we weren't allowed to leave our room when they were partying out there, and with the meth that could sometimes go on for days at a time."

A second gunshot. A third immediately afterward. That wasn't a warning. That was an execution.

"Do you have any idea what it's like to hold your little brother and wait for him to stop shaking? Only he wouldn't stop because of the chemicals going through his veins, but I couldn't understand that. I thought he was just scared, and that it was my fault I couldn't get him to feel safe."

Two more gunshots in rapid succession. I could so clearly imagine Sammy D kicking over the second officer's slumped corpse that I might as well be watching it happen.

"Maybe it wasn't like that for you, but someone must have wanted your parents dead for a reason. Ever think about what they were hiding that made this happen? Ever wonder if they deserved it? Everyone out there deserves to die, everyone but us. Sammy D wants to give you another chance to join the family."

I couldn't stand it any longer. I had to see what was going on. If the police were dead, then staying here wouldn't protect me anyway. Alexa stepped back as I slowly opened the door. It was impossible not to notice the razor blade clutched between her fingers.

"What's it going to be?" Sammy D was walking around the house, a handgun casually hanging from her fingers. That was it then. It was over. Alexa grinned, moving to stand in solidarity beside the old woman.

"We're leaving here within the hour," Sammy D added. "You're coming with us, or you're staying here. Doesn't matter to me either way."

Sammy D's finger twitched around the trigger. She might pretend to be relaxed, but I could see the tension which twisted her fingers into a claw around the gun. I didn't have any delusion that "staying here" meant anything other than buried in the backyard.

"What's the matter?" Her voice was a gravel avalanche. "Too scared to answer?"

I shook my head. "You taught me better than that."

Half a smirk played about her lips before they drew back into a tight line. Alexa was still smiling.

"You taught us all better than that. Except for Maker, right? You never seemed to care that he was out of control."

Alexa's smile flirted with a snarl.

"I couldn't understand why, but I see it now," I said. "You never thought he had what it took to become an assassin, did you? You never even bothered to show him how to defend himself, because you only ever planned on using him once."

The front door opened, and I could see the rest of the children huddled inside. They were laden with duffel bags and suitcases, ready to go wherever they were told.

"You're better than that though," Sammy D said. "I'm not going to throw you away. I'm going to take care of you."

Alexa's eyes flashed across the children. She ran back to peer around the side of the house. I could practically see the gears in her head turning beneath the frantic lashing of her braided hair. Two gunshots for each of the two cops. Where did the first shot go?

"Sammy D no—" Alexa started, her words dying in her mouth.

"Your brother was a hero, Alexa," Sammy D cooed. "We all owe our lives to him."

I caught Greg's eye. I didn't miss the curt nod. I didn't underestimate the light burning in Alexa's eyes. None of us needed so much as a word to know what had to happen next.

Sammy D felt it too. Her gun was leveled in a flash. One bullet escaped the muzzle, but I was already behind the armored door of the police cruiser. She never got a second chance. Children were pouring out of the house, leaping on the old woman and dragging her to the ground. The flash as Alexa's razor traced a line in the air like a spear of light.

It wasn't the death-rattle or the color of blood which filled the air though. There was no sound so haunting as the pitiful howl which ripped itself from somewhere deep inside of Alexa. There was no color like the fire in her eyes being tempered by the rush of her swelling tears. The thrill of the kill was still hanging in the air, but one look around was enough to know that it was nothing compared to the burden of loss.

We had money and a chance at a new life together. The most important thing we gained from the assassin's orphanage is knowing you can't buy yourself a new life at the price of someone else's though. Life can't be bought or sold or stolen in any form. It can only be built, and it's a whole lot easier to build when you have a real family like I do now.

## The Suicide Bomber

I will be going soon. The Muna Camp will be cleansed with fire. Inshallah—if Allah wills—I will die tonight.

I wish people would take the lives of the Nigerian people as seriously as they do their celebrities and invented characters, but my message needs to be told, and I will tell it to whoever will listen.

My name is Abayomrunkoje (meaning God won't allow humiliation), and I am ready to die for the Jama'atu Ahlis Sunna Lidda'awati wal-Jihad (People Committed to the Propagation of the Prophet's Teachings and Jihad).

Nigeria was invaded by Westerners who enslaved our people, our land, and worst of all, our minds. Children are brainwashed with Western ideals which pervert their morality and corrupt their spirits. You may teach your own children to believe in nothing and whore their bodies for the attention of strangers, but do not be surprised when we resist you poisoning our own against us.

That is why great Mohammed Yusuf opened his own Islamic school, and that is where I learned the truth of our oppression. But a single school cannot save our people anymore than a single candle may banish the night. As long as the Nigerian government sanctions this state-wide abomination of Western ideals, we will light a fire in our own skin and burn bright as the sun which will end this dark night.

An Islamic state is forming. Our group—also called the Boko Haram—has already chased many of the infidels from Maiduguri and into the refugee camps. Their false government has abandoned them, and they are defenseless.

There are six of us from the school who will attack. We carry incendiary explosives which will light the tents and spread for miles. I am afraid—but my love for Allah keeps me strong. I will be with him soon, and he will thank me for doing what is so hard to do. None of us are monsters or Demons. There are tears in our eyes as we say goodbye to our brothers.

We know we are going to our glory, and the glory of all those whose death marks their liberation. That knowledge gives me the strength to continue, but it does not hide the pain I see in the children's eyes when they are slipping from this world. It does not dampen the screams of a mother holding her dead son. I wish I could tell them everything was going to be alright—that Allah will protect them now—but they will not listen to words. They will only listen to fire.

The six of us are splitting up to take up strategic positions around the camp. I say goodbye to my brother Isamotu Olalekan, and we embrace dearly. I am ready, but his last words take me by surprise.

"Abayomrunkoje I must ask you something," he said to me. The others from the school had already gone.

"Anything my brother," I said, still holding him close to my chest.

"Would Muhammad do as we are doing? If he were here today, would he light the fuse?"

"I know he would. Muhammad spent his life spreading the word, so he would not hesitate to give his life to protect it."

We drew apart, but Isamotu did not seem convinced.

"I know you must be afraid," I said. "We all are. But that is only the weakness of the body, and it is nothing compared to the strength of the spirit. We will not hesitate when the time has come."

"You're wrong," he said. "I did hesitate when the time came."

I looked at my watch. 3:45 AM. We were not set to begin until 4:30, so I do not understand.

"It wasn't fear that made me pause though," Isamotu said. "I heard someone crying, but I could not find them. I thought I had been spotted."

"What does it matter if we are spotted? All you must do is hit the trigger. We cannot be stopped."

"I didn't want someone to see me do it. I didn't want to see the expression on their face."

"Did the cleric send you somewhere else before here? Were you caught?"

"I wasn't caught."

"Then why did the bomb not go off? You are not making any sense!" I felt myself growing exasperated, but I must be patient with my brother. I could tell he was trying very hard to speak something very sacred to him. If these were to be his last words, then he should have the chance to speak his mind.

"The bomb did go off," he said. "And there was no-one waiting for me on the other side."

I had so many questions to ask, but an explosion threw me to the ground. Then another—and another—five explosions in all. I kept my head down. What were they doing? They were supposed to wait for the signal at 4:30! But I checked my watch—and it was 4:30 already. How long had we been speaking?

I leapt to my feet, but Isamotu wasn't there. He couldn't of... not right next to me. I didn't feel anything. But five explosions had already detonated, all some distance from me. There was fire everywhere. So many people shouting at once—they sounded more like frightened animals than humans.

I took off my incendiary jacket and walked away. I do not know who was speaking to me if Isamotu had already taken up his position. I do not know what he meant, but I finally found that I was afraid. I did not want to send those people to a place where no-one was waiting.

Astaghfiru lillah—Allah forgive me. My candle has burned out.

## The Most Terrifying Drawing

This is the only time I've ever been excited to go to class. I'm a senior in highschool getting ready for graduation, currently battling the constant dread of my looming finals. Even art class, which I'd expected to just be a free period, has an exam detailing irrelevant historical dates and the long names of foreign painters.

Luckily one of the dumb-asses who skipped out on senior ditch day managed to drunkenly ram his car into a tree. He was dead on impact, and our art teacher Mrs. Flemming was convinced we were all distraught about it (even though the world is better off without someone who gets behind the wheel drunk). She actually canceled the test to give us a fun final project instead: drawing the scariest thing we could imagine. Better yet, the winner was going to get a $50 gift card as a prize.

"Whatcha drawing?" my little sister Casey asked.

"Something scary," I told her. "Don't look or you're going to have nightmares."

"I like nightmares! I love scary!" she squealed, trying to push me aside to see. I pushed back, but she reached under my arm and crinkled the paper as she pulled, leaving a great ugly smudge of graphite all down the left side. God, she was obnoxious.

After that I spent the rest of the evening locked in my room with my colored pencils. A dozen sketches quickly turned into a dozen crumpled papers. I love all things horror, but it was harder than I expected coming up with something legitimately terrifying.

Zombies? Lame. Ghosts and demons? I bet everyone was going to do that. I could take a humorous angle and draw something like student loans, but while it might get a laugh from the class, I don't think it would win. Besides, I always prided myself on my twisted mind, so I wasn't going to back away from this challenge.

It was past 2 a.m. when I started getting really frustrated. After laughing through countless horror movies, reading creepy stories (thanks Reddit), and casually browsing through grotesque images online, I couldn't think of anything that legitimately scared me. Maybe I'd seen every dark thought the human mind could conjure. Maybe I was so desensitized to fear that everything seemed boring now.

The whole appeal of horror to me is that there is always some new unknown terror which stretches the limit of my imagination. It's why the darkness has held such fascination over us since the days man rubbed two sticks to make a fire. It's not the monster that scares us, it's the endless potential for what the monster might be. Well now it felt like actually putting my thoughts on the paper was the same as turning on the lights, and no matter how scary my idea might be, it will never be as frightening as when it couldn't be seen.

Finally I decided that if I couldn't draw anything properly scary, then none of those other white-bread sissies could do it either. I just scribbled out a skull face pressing up against the paper, looking as though it was trying to escape. It broke the fourth wall just enough to get inside the viewer's head, and I was actually pretty proud of it by the time I finished.

My anticipation grew the whole day, and by the time art came in the afternoon, I couldn't wait to show off my creation. All of the drawings were going to be anonymously shuffled into a pile, and then we'd secretly vote on the best. Can't vote for your own, most votes wins. Mrs. Flemming was zealous about keeping it fair, and even insisted that the whole stack of drawings be passed from person to person instead of hanging them all up, just in case our classmate's reactions influenced our vote.

Game on. I caught a glimpse of a few of the drawings as they were shuffled face-down into the stack. I saw a snake rearing to strike (seriously?), and a dizzying perspective from a guy looking down from the edge of a skyscraper. Did these people have no imagination? What's so scary about regular life stuff?

We watched as the stack of drawings was given to Lily. She flipped slowly through them, and the class gave a collective moan as she agonizingly deliberated between two papers. Then she flipped to the last one in the stack, and the whole class started snickering. She was actually turning white in front of us. Her eyes bulged and quivered, and her mouth worked through the motion of soundless words.

"I think we have a winner!" someone cheered.

Could it have been mine? I didn't think any picture could produce a reaction like that. Lily had always been a sensitive, whiny girl, though. Even so, when she started clutching at her throat, we knew something was wrong. She dropped the papers face down on her desk, now using both hands to claw at her neck as though invisible hands were choking her.

"Is she having a seizure?"

"Someone call the nurse!"

It happened too fast for anyone to react. Lily's neck strained so hard that the individual tendons stood out like ropes bulging under the skin. Mrs. Flemming rushed to catch her—too slow. Lily had already toppled out of her chair to sprawl face-first on the carpet.

"911? Hello?"

Mrs. Flemming rolled Lily onto her back while holding her cellphone with her shoulder. The class clustered around, staring in abject disbelief.

"No. Her heart isn't beating. What do I do?" Mrs. Flemming asked desperately. She dropped the phone and began chest compressions. Nate, big round boy, scrambled on the ground for the phone and pressed it to his ear.

"No. No. I don't know," he was saying to the police. "It was like a heart attack."

"Hey look at this!" It was the quiet Native-American kid. Don't know his name. He was holding the stack of papers that Lily had dropped.

"Don't touch that. Nobody look at them," Mrs. Flemming demanded between compressions. "Come on Lily. Hang in there with me. Help is on the way."

"I'm not looking, okay?" The Native-American kid held the papers face down. "But count them. There are fourteen papers here."

"So what? The class has—" Mrs. Flemming began, but she already realized her mistake. There were fourteen kids in the class yeah, if you count the dumbass who hit a tree last week. There's no way he turned one in.

"It doesn't matter," Mrs. Flemming snapped. "Ahote (ahh that was his name), go get the principal. Let's just focus on Lily right now, okay?"

Ahote looked down at the mess. Then out the door. Then back at the—

"Ahote, don't!"

He turned over the stack and skipped straight to the end. His brown skin immediately paled to ash. He gave a wild look around at the class, and then his hands were at his throat. Before anyone could do anything, he had already flopped straight onto the ground.

Everything was a blur after that. Someone pulled the fire alarm to get everyone out, and the paramedics had to shoulder their way through the tide of bewildered faces and speculative chatter heading the other way. They returned with two stretchers and two lumpy white shapes. The way their faces were covered with the sheets reminded me of my own drawing with the skull pressed against the paper.

People were shouting and rumors were flying up and down the lines, and it took a long while until everyone was quiet in the parking lot.

With all the confusion, nobody noticed me take the stack of drawings with me. After that, Mrs. Flemming had given the bodies so much focus that she seemed to completely forget about the cause of death. The general consensus was that the teacher had taken the drawings, but I kept them hidden under my jacket and didn't say a word. I just clenched the papers against my side and listened to the mounting whispers around me. Heart failure caused by massive adrenaline surges, that's what people are saying. Those two kids were literally scared to death.

School was canceled for the rest of the day, and I'm now back in my bedroom with fourteen face-down pieces of paper. I tried holding them up to the light to see if I can get a glimpse of what's on the other side, but it wasn't distinct enough to learn anything.

So far I've resisted the urge to look. I know every horror trope about the guy who let's curiosity get the best of him, but I can't help but feel I'm not as fragile as they are. I've been exposed to everything. My heart doesn't even race at jump scares. Even if it's just for a second, I won't be able to live with myself knowing there is more out there than I was able to face. I know I'm obsessing, but my imagination is tearing me apart trying to figure out what the drawing is.

If it was somehow from the kid that died, then it has to be something that he alone knows about. That means it's something to do with what happens to us after we die. My best guess is that he's brought back some twisted torture or hellscape so demented, so intrinsically woven with the core of our biology, that our very nature revolts against it. The forbidden fruit really is the sweetest.

I tossed and turned the whole night, trying to imagine what could be on that paper. I must not have fallen asleep until late, because it was almost noon when I woke up. Shit, didn't I have a test today? Surely the teachers will understand after yesterday—yesterday. The bodies. The drawings. And now I was obsessing again.

"Did you win?"

Suddenly I was awake. It was Casey. Sitting at the foot of my bed. The stack of papers in her hand.

"Casey listen to me," I spoke as slowly as I dared, like I was trying to talk down a lion who was preparing to pounce. "I want you to put those down. I need you not to look."

"Okay." I let out more air than I knew my lungs could hold. Then she grinned, flipping the stack over anyway.

"Casey drop it. Like your life depends on it!"

"Okay." She kept flipping. God, she was obnoxious. I dove at her to snatch

## Sleepless Nights

them, but she had already hopped off the bed just out of reach. She was flipping faster now. Four to go. Now three.

"Casey please. I'm not mad, okay? I'm begging you."

"Okay." Flip. Two more before the final drawing. "Which one is yours?" she asked.

"It doesn't matter! Drop them now!" I leapt again. She tossed the papers in the air, and I scrambled to catch them. I'd already crumpled up five before I realized Casey was still holding onto the last sheet. Her eyes were so wide. Her mouth hung open. I ripped the paper from her hand, but it only took a second with the other kids. Casey, poor innocent Casey—

But then she smiled. "How about my drawing? Did anyone like that?"

The paper was face-down in my hand. I didn't dare look. Instead, I scanned through the rest of the drawings on the floor. All regular fears and boring monsters. There was no doubt that this was the mysterious paper.

"You didn't draw this." I said it with accusation. I was actually offended by the thought.

"Did too," Casey said. "It's of the nightmare I have."

"But what is it? What's it look like?"

"See for yourself."

I wanted to. I wanted to so damn bad. My hands were starting to turn it over by themselves. She leaned in close to me so we could look at it together.

"Can I tell you a secret though?" she whispered. My heart was beating so fast. Was this how they felt, right as the adrenaline flooded their veins, right before they died?

"Go ahead," I said.

"I don't really like the nightmares. They just tell me to say that I do. They told me that if I don't let them out, then they're going to take me inside. That's why I have to keep drawing them."

"Keep drawing?" My hand came to a trembling stop. "How many of these have you drawn?"

"Dozens." Casey's whispers were hurried now. Like she had to tell me before someone stopped her. "But the more I draw, the more they want me to draw. And if I don't, they get so loud that I—"

"Shh, it's okay," I said. "I'm going to look at it now, and I'm going to figure out what's going on. Are you ready?"

"Ready," she said. I turned over the paper, and she buried her face on my shoulder. "I'm going to miss you." I barely made out the muffled words as I looked down into her drawing. I could feel my eyes stretching—wider than they've ever been. I tried to speak, but my rib cage felt like it was closing in around my heart, and I couldn't breathe. My hands instinctively went to my throat, but no—that wouldn't help. That's how the others died. But not me. It was how I came to life.

"They said you passed their test," Casey whispered. "How do you feel?"

I shook my head, barely registering what she said. I couldn't take my eyes off the paper. I could feel my heart still straining inside me, but it was starting to slow. I forced myself to breathe, the motion feeling so unnatural and invasive, almost as though I'd traveled to another world and was flooding my lungs with a cold, stinging, alien gas.

"It's beautiful," I replied. She bobbed up and down with excitement.

"Thanks," she said. "They were afraid no one here would understand. Fear makes you feel alive, and feeling alive is beautiful."

## My Daughter Spoke Before She Was Born

*"Mommy."* My daughter's first word. Isn't that what every new mother is dying to hear? One word to magically transform this organic object into a new human being. All the pain and fear and doubt suddenly have purpose. One word, and mothers will know it was all worthwhile.

*"I love you, Mommy."*

I just wish little Claire had waited until she was born to say it. Over eight months pregnant, I was sitting in the car waiting for my husband to get back with the groceries. I almost had a heart attack on the spot. I thought someone was in the car with me, so I jumped out to get a better look in the backseat, but—

*"Don't worry, Mommy. It'll be our little secret."*

The voice was coming from inside me. I felt the vibrations as much as I heard it with my ears, almost like the rumbling of indigestion. I didn't say a word when my husband got back. I was waiting for Claire to talk again, but when she didn't, I just kept my mouth shut too. My husband had more than enough to worry about with his extra shifts at work. I didn't want him to add my sanity to his worries.

*"I don't like that. It's nasty."*

I put down the salad I was eating. Alone in the kitchen this time; Claire only spoke when I was alone. Usually it was just an isolated word, or sometimes I'd catch her humming along to a song that was playing. If she didn't like something, she'd let me know. She didn't care for most vegetables, and jazz music seemed to make her restless.

As weird as it seems, it's something I got used to. I grew into the habit of asking her how she was doing, and if she was comfortable. I'd tell her about the things we'd do together and talked about myself. Sometimes if I was lucky, I'd hear her respond, a faint murmur; so far away, but so intimate that I knew it could be no one else.

*"There are lots of colors,"* Claire answered once when I asked her what it looked

like in there. *"But they're all black. It's warm, and close, and safe. I'm part of everything here."*

"What about before you were there?" I asked. "What's the earliest thing you can remember?"

I could feel her squirming. She didn't speak again for almost a day after that, until suddenly when I was about to enter the shower, she said:

*"I don't want to talk about it. Before isn't a nice place. The people living there aren't nice people."*

I didn't want to upset her, so I didn't pry any further. Besides, even thinking about it made me uncomfortable, and I felt as though my discomfort would be passed on to Claire somehow. We were two halves of the same soul, and it almost seemed like I could feel her thinking before she even spoke.

"Mommy?" she asked one night when I lay half-asleep in the solitary darkness. My husband was on a business trip, and it was just going to be me until a few days before I was due. *"Who else is inside you?"*

I told her that she was an only child. That she was so big she took up my whole tummy all by herself, and that soon she was going to be too big even for that. Then she would come out where I am, and we could see each other for the first time.

*"Are the people nice out there?"* she asked.

I had to tell her the truth. If I didn't, I figured she could probably feel it. I told her that people try to be good, but some of them don't know how. But she shouldn't worry, because I'm going to teach her how, and then she can teach everyone she meets. I was almost in tears as I said it, marveling at the wonder I carried. Claire and I will have known each other more truly than any mother and daughter before. Our bond would be stronger. I was so happy to have this blessing until—

*"Don't lie to me, Mommy. I know I'm not the only one here."*

I told her not to be silly. I'd been to the doctors, and they showed me what it looked like inside. There wasn't anyone else...

"One of them followed me," Claire interrupted. *"From the before place. Mommy, make them go away."*

I did my best to reassure her, but I was completely helpless against her mounting distress.

*"Don't let them hurt me. Don't let them take me back. I don't want to go back. I want to be with Mommy...."* She wouldn't listen to anything I said. I couldn't get through to her anymore.

Listening to her cry inside me was more than I could bear, but then she started shrieking, and I had to get out of the house. I hustled to the car as swiftly as my swollen body would allow, made even more difficult now that Claire was thrashing and kicking inside. I was trying to stay strong for her, but I was so terrified as I ripped down the streets toward the hospital. I'm sure she must have felt that too. I was doing everything I could to stifle my sobs when the kicking suddenly stopped.

There was no movement at all. No sounds. And I thought that was even worse than the crying until she spoke again.

*"I have to go away, Mommy. It was nice talking with you."*

I was at the hospital now. I practically drove straight through the glass doors in front of the emergency room. Don't go, Claire, don't go. But I didn't say it out loud. Instead I said to the nurses:

"Please help me. There's something wrong with my baby."

The nurse asked me how I knew, and I didn't know how to answer. I just started crying again. They put me in a wheelchair and brought me into an examination room. The nurse said she would be right back, but I didn't want to be left alone. At least while someone was here, I could tell myself that Claire wasn't speaking because of them. If she stayed quiet when I was alone though…

*"Don't cry, Mommy."* I held my breath, desperate to catch every word. Claire was speaking so faintly that I could barely hear her over the frantic double percussion of my heart. *"You're not going to be alone. The one from the before place is here. He promises to be good, but I want you to be careful Mommy. Goodbye."*

The nurse was back, and there was a doctor with her. I think they were trying to ask me questions, but my whole awareness was so focused on any movement or sound from within that I couldn't register what they were saying. They started doing an ultrasound, although it took a long time before I stopped shaking enough for them to get a clear picture. The whole while, Claire didn't say a word. That was okay though. She never did when people were around. Maybe when they were gone she would.…

But then the doctor gave me a big smile, and I let out gasps of stale air that I didn't even know I was clinging to.

"I want you to know that you have nothing to worry about," the doctor said. "The baby is perfectly healthy."

"I'm sorry," I told him. "I don't know what I was thinking. I shouldn't have bothered you."

"Don't worry about it," he said, taking off his gloves. "It's common for expecting mothers to have anxiety or panic attacks. Even hallucinations sometimes."

"Hallucinations, yeah," I managed. "I guess it's a pretty traumatic time for the body."

"Exactly," he said. "But I want you to know that nothing in the world is wrong. Just a few weeks and you're going to be holding your son for the first time."

"My son?"

"Yes ma'am. Didn't you know? Look here, it even looks like he's smiling."

## Behind Closed Doors

Those of us who survive what happens behind closed doors don't talk about it much more than those who didn't.

And you. You know there are mothers who look at their children as bloodsucking leeches, blaming them for their dwindling energy and passion for life. You know there are fathers who see their daughters as a possession, their innocence a vulnerability to exploit. You know that drugs, or alcohol, or the festering hatred of wasted years can curdle the blood until convictions of "right and wrong" subtly transform into "is someone watching or not".

But we don't talk about it, because maybe it's our fault they don't love us more. And you don't think about it, afraid your own love will be spoiled by the guilt of those who go without. But if I'm going to be brave enough to talk, then I want you to be brave enough to listen. We are no longer children, and we must both accept that closing our eyes does not make the monsters go away anymore.

My parents died in a car accident when I was fourteen. Uncle Viran and Aunt Isabelle said they had always wanted a daughter, and took me in after that, treating me with the polite indifference you'd use to summon your waiter. And that was okay with me, because I wasn't really expecting to have a family again. I had one once, and wanting that intimacy back with other people seemed disrespectful to their memory. Wherever I would go, whoever I would be with from that day on, I knew I would be alone.

Viran was always watching me with his beady little eyes, nearly invisible behind huge spectacles. Isabelle tolerated me, although she was better at it when I stayed in my room. And life went on. I never stopped wearing black after the funeral, but over time I added some bows and lace because Uncle thought I looked depressing.

It wasn't good enough for him though. He bought me a lot of brightly colored ornaments to wear so "the room didn't look like someone turned out the lights" every time I entered. Isabelle thought it was a waste of money, and I agreed. There was something powerful and elegant in my dark wardrobe which protected me from life's banalities. The other things made me feel like a clown on display, an object for the sole purpose of being seen and used.

I'd try them on though, whatever it was. Pink dresses, sun hats, stiletto shoes. Uncle would make me model them, striking poses and spinning around while his eyes sparkled with undisguised appetite. I'd thank him politely, keeping the rest of my words to myself, waiting for his face to flush with sweat and his words to awkwardly tangle in his mouth before he'd let me leave.

They were nice things, he told me. Expensive things. He wanted to keep them clean, so he'd make me undress to store them safely. Not in the bathroom where I could spill water on them. Not in my bedroom where I kept it so dirty. Right here in the living room, it's all right. There's no one else here. And I'd do what I was told, he'd remind me, because I was a good girl who appreciated everything he'd done for me.

Isabelle was returning from the store when she caught him like that once. His hands were already on me, helping to slide my new skirt down. I caught Isabelle's eye with a sort of helpless pleading. She got so angry she actually started trembling, her lips pressing into a bloodless scar. I thought that was going to be the end of this game. She was going to yell at her husband and swoop in to save me like my own mother would have done if she'd found me like that....

But my mother wasn't here anymore. Isabelle turned around and went into the kitchen without another word. Uncle followed her, and I took the chance to run for my bedroom. I listened against the door for a sound of a fight, but they were both speaking low and soft. All I could hear was the frenzied pounding of blood in my veins and the mounting scream of a tea kettle.

I thought she was just making herself a cup to calm down until my door opened five minutes later. I knew something bad was going to happen as soon as I saw her: face like plastic, thick rubber gloves up to her elbow, and tea kettle in hand.

"Viran told me everything," Isabelle said as she sat down beside me on the bed. She touched me with one of those rubber gloves and I started shaking so bad the headboard rattled. "I don't want to do this, but it's for your own good. Girls have empty heads sometimes, and must be taught lessons that are not easily forgotten."

Isabelle's carefully maintained countenance twisted into a snarl when she grabbed my hair and began to pour the boiling water over my head. The more I cried, the louder she yelled to be heard. How dare I try to seduce her husband, she'd said. Selfish slut, just like my mother. Home wrecker. Ungrateful bitch. Two-faced whore. By the time the kettle was empty, I was writhing in agony on my soaked bed sheets. I just lay there gasping, my tears evaporating where they ran across my scalded skin. My eyes were too swollen to see, but I heard her stand and exit the room.

"Even if you try, I don't think he'll want you now anyway," she said as she left.

When the door closed, I tried to pull my drenched shirt off, but every brush of fabric on skin was excruciating. I had to cut myself free with a pair of scissors, biting my tongue to keep myself from howling. Then staggering to the bathroom to splash cool water on my face I could see blisters the size of my nose already forming on my hands and neck which had taken the worst of it.

It took almost a week for the swelling to come down. Aunt Isabelle brought me aloe lotions and cooed over me like it had been an unfortunate accident. Uncle didn't even look at me, so I guess I should have been grateful in a way. As my skin continued to heal, I kept applying rouge to make it look like the skin was still scalded. I thought maybe he'd leave me alone as long as he thought I was ruined, but I couldn't keep up the disguise forever.

One week was all the respite I got. I felt his hands resting on my shoulders as I peered into the fridge, their gentleness as vile as Isabelle's iron grip. He said he was sorry for what happened. It was wrong of her to treat me like a child (he knows I'm not a child anymore) or to punish me (when I had been so good). Not to worry, he assured me; next time she'll never find out. Next time, he's going to have a special present to make up for what happened.

He was right about one thing: I wasn't a child anymore. You can't stay a child after something like that has happened, no matter how hard you try. With his hands running down my back as lightly as snow upon a grave, I knew what *next time* meant. There wasn't going to be a next time though, because I was going to run away. Over dinner that night I made a big show coughing and playing sick. I told them I felt like I could sleep forever. Once in my room, I stuffed a couple pillows under my blanket to make it look like someone was still sleeping there.

But I wasn't taking any chances. I'd even picked up a cheap wig which perfectly matched my auburn hair. After fastening it around a soccer ball, I pulled the blankets way up to its "chin" and took a step back to survey my work. I briefly considered trying to rig up one of those audio recorder setups where a string is attached to the door and plays a message when it's opened, but it seemed too complicated and I was already terrified of being caught before I got out.

Isabelle hadn't entered my room since she burned me, and Uncle seemed uncomfortable there as well. I hoped they would just think I was sick and not disturb the dummy until I was a long way from here. My backpack was stuffed with clothes, some snacks and about $40, and I looked back one last time before I left. As terrible as it was here, I had no delusions that life outside would be any easier. I figure people are going to suffer no matter where they are, but at least now I could choose how.

I didn't think anything could make me stay longer in that house, but then again, I couldn't have expected what I saw when glancing back. The pillows I'd carefully lain under the covers had shifted. The bundle was leaning back against the headboard now, the long auburn hair falling down to completely obscure the soccer ball.

Then before my eyes, the dummy head moved. Now to the left. Now to the right. The wig swishing softly as it dragged along the sheets. Now it was looking right at me, or at least I think so. I still couldn't see anything underneath the thick hair.

I took a step toward the window. Then a step back into the room. The head followed me both times. Then the whole form began to stand upright, although the sheet hung loosely from an emaciated human frame hidden beneath. Does that mean the soccer ball was gone too? As the form lurched toward me, I could only imagine what horrifying visage was underneath the hair now.

I stood frozen as it stopped in front of me. Up close, I saw the hair wasn't a wig anymore. It looked so soft and real that I had to stop myself from reaching out to touch it. For a gut-clenching moment I thought it looked like my mother's hair, but no, it was so much longer and wilder than hers. But wasn't the figure about the same height as my mother, just a head taller than me?

"Are you going to help me?" I asked.

The hair nodded as the head bent forward and back. A shift in the sheet let a cold wind escape outward as though someone had opened a window.

"Are you going to punish them?" I asked.

It was definitely a nod this time. I was so relieved that I couldn't contain the rush of bubbling thoughts and feelings swelling up within me. The idea that it was my mother made me want to laugh and cry at the same time. It *was* my mother. It had to be. She'd never stopped watching me, even from the other side. She saw what happened and she wasn't going to forgive them. She was going to make them suffer because they *deserved* it, and she was going to save me because …

A whisper. I couldn't catch what she said. I leaned closer and the form spoke again.

"Switch places with me."

"What do you mean?"

A short, powerful rush of air entered the form, and she spoke louder as though she was gradually waking up. "I'm not of your world, and cannot hurt them until I enter. Switch places with me, let me have my fun, and then I will trade back with you when I'm finished."

The voice was more real with every word. I could imagine myself back in our old house with mother tucking me into bed at night. The security of her presence, the affection of her voice. The unbridled fury at anyone who would do me wrong. I devoured those words. That love, that anger, it's what kept me alive.

"What is it like, your world?" I asked, but even as I did I knew it didn't matter. "Yes, I'll switch places. It won't take long to punish them, will it?"

The head shook. A fleeting glance of a green eye shining beneath the hair, and then it was gone. "Cut your finger," she instructed me, and I did so without question, pinching the skin of my forefinger with the scissors beside my bed. These scissors which I'd used to cut my scalding shirt off would now be used for revenge. I'd never felt so sweet a pain in my life.

"Now let your mother taste it." The voice was deeper now, more masculine, but I didn't care. All I could think about was how good it would feel to see them pay. I'd be able to live alone here, taking care of myself. I wouldn't have to be quiet anymore, or afraid. Or maybe mom could come back and visit when this awful business was over, and we could talk like we used to. My dad must be there too, and I could even switch with him to let him play a round of golf and enjoy the sun again. I lifted my cut finger up inside the wild hair and felt the cold wind licking the blood from me, and I smiled.

My finger was ice, and it felt cool and refreshing on skin still tender from the burns. The freezing presence swept its way up my arm, over my chest, and deep into my heart. I felt myself falling though I stood in place, plummeting through an abyss of thought. The form in front of me was removing its sheet now, and I could see its grey and black skin bristle and distort as though something within it were viciously pounding its way out. Wherever I went, whatever was waiting for me, I didn't care. My mother had saved me, and I loved her. And soon I would be back to see what she had done. No torture was too gruesome; no punishment fell short of righteous in my eyes. I only wish that I had still been there to watch it happen...

But that was forty years ago. Now I know that the other side is no kinder than ours, and that there are those who seek out the weakness and vulnerability of others just as readily as they do here. Those faceless beings form a blanket of leering eyes as they wait for their opportunity to strike. Forty years in a nightmare realm, hiding and fighting and struggling to survive against the nameless savagery which mocks our petty struggles here on Earth. Forty years hating myself for leaving this world so readily, and fanning that hatred within me to keep me warm against the unending night.

I wasn't her daughter; I was her prey. She felt my desperation and came to me knowing I could not refuse her offer, and so she escaped from her world and into mine. It had taken forty years for her to have her fun and trade places with me again, but even being back, I feel as though I do not belong in this world. Isabelle and Viran must be ancient or dead, but I don't even care about that anymore. I'm just waiting for my specter to show itself again, because I still haven't gotten my revenge. And perhaps in the darkest night of your defeat he will come for you too, promising to serve you if only you trade places. I pray that even in your loneliest despair you will maintain the resolve to refuse him, although if you don't ...

... then I pray instead I will find you first, so that together we may strive to make this world better instead of fleeing into the grasp of what waits on the other side.

## Mars Colonization Project

My name is Robert Feldman, and I've been preparing for this mission my entire life. Don't get too excited though, because the shuttle taking me to Mars is still fifteen years away from launching. If the training is any indication of what to expect, then it's going to be the most terrifying experience I could imagine.

So why has training already began? It's simple math really. The manned mission to Mars has a conservative expense estimate of over $100 billion. If anything goes wrong, then the chances of financing another journey in lieu of the more practical exploration and colonization of nearby asteroids is slim to none. That means the crew has to be absolutely perfect, and the cost of extensively training us for over a decade is still insignificant compared to the potential disaster from our slightest mistake.

There will be numerous expeditions before NASA decides we're ready, including a 2020 Rover launch, a year-long training session in the space station around 2024, and then a prolonged orbit around Mars in the early 2030s. After that, the colony will be established, although there is no way for our current level of technology to allow a return journey. We will be terminally isolated, depending entirely on our self-sustaining efforts to survive.

Earth's conditions will always be as volatile as the arbitrary leaders controlling launch codes, and I firmly believe the long-term survival of our species is dependent on our ability to spread across the stars. That's why I've devoted my life to this cause. From my master's degree in engineering, to my thousands of hours of flight experience in the air force, I've honed every aspect of my mind, body and spirit, to help transcend humanity into the heavens.

So you can imagine how excited I was to finally receive the phone call from Nigel Rathmore at NASA. I had barely been winded from my eight-mile run that morning, but just hearing his voice on the line was enough to make my knees weak. I kissed my wife, and we both laughed and cried, knowing the implications this decision would have for us. I love her with all my heart, but she understands that is exactly the reason why I must go. It was time for the official training to begin, and I was ready.

The training on Earth is divided into three segments: Technical Training (the mechanical skills required), Personal Training (psychological profiling and mental preparation for the unnatural ordeal), and Simulation Training (which will expose us to the conditions we're expected to face).

This isn't the story of how I learned to build circuit boards. The technical training is hardly worth mentioning, and neither the other astronauts nor I encountered much we hadn't already prepared for. Besides myself, there was Isac (the gentle Norwegian giant), Linda (might be cute if she learned to extract the Truss Rod from her ass), and Jean-Claude (French guy with a superiority complex). I would have enjoyed this part a lot more if I hadn't known that the colonization shuttle was only being designed to house two astronauts. That means they not only expected two of us to fail, they demanded it. These people who I spent my every waking day with weren't friends; they were competition.

On the second day, we began our first personal training segments, and I was already hoping for Isac to successfully graduate with me. The thought of spending the rest of my life trapped on an alien planet with Linda barking orders or Jean-Claude condescendingly redoing my work was absolutely loathsome.

## Sleepless Nights

We all underwent thorough psychiatric screenings that day. They told us that by the end of training, we had to look forward to up to a year of solitary confinement to monitor our stability. During that time, we wouldn't be allowed to even speak to another human on the phone, as it was simulating the event of a communications breakdown.

As the days went on, the tests became continually more grueling. I could tell the NASA administrators had actively designed this course to cause as much physical and mental discomfort as they could. We were a piece of equipment, as sure as any support beam or fuel cell, and if we were going to break, then it would be better for it to happen now while we could still be replaced.

Physical endurance was pushed to its limit as we jogged behind jeeps across searing sand dunes. Our bodies underwent the pummeling of artificial dust storms in wind tunnels, all while undergoing blindfolded obstacle courses meant to simulate the storms which ravage Mars and block out over 99 percent of the sun. Some nights we would be locked in a freezing chamber which approached the -70 C nights on Mars, and our vitals were measured as layer by layer of protective clothing was stripped away until they could record the exact moment we lost consciousness.

Jean-Claude was the first one to contract pneumonia from the bitter cold. That didn't stop them from forcing him back into the chamber the next night. He tried to get out of it, but they told him he would be cut from the entire program if he skipped a single segment. That night Isac offered one of his outer layers to him, but Jean-Claude was too proud to accept. They had to carry him out on a stretcher, and I didn't see him again after that.

That wasn't the only case of sickness either. I don't think it was part of the original plan, but after that all of us fell sick at the exact same time. Coughing, fevers and sores on our skin—I think they must have given us something to study our immune system. It was bad enough to make me delirious, because I kept seeing flashing lights and hearing an odd buzzing sound. I must have blacked out for a bit, because I got flashes of being taken out and brought into a whitewashed room. I was put on a metal table, and the faces staring at me were distorted and twisted into surreal mockeries of what a human face should be. I was afraid, but I didn't let it show. I didn't want to give them any reason to cut me out like they did Jean-Claude.

As bad as the physical ordeals were, they were nothing compared to the psychological ones. They'd warned us that they wanted to test our reactions to a variety of situations, but they hadn't told us exactly what to expect. When they told me my wife had been killed in a car crash and showed me photographs of her mutilated body, I was devastated. They talked me through her death, going into explicit detail about how much she suffered from the shards of glass filling her face like shrapnel as she bled out on the highway. It was a full day before they confessed she was fine, and that I had passed the test by holding it together.

Maybe I was holding it together on the outside, but on the inside I was pulling further away from everyone. I originally set out on this course for the good of humanity, but it was hard to want to fight for them when everyone I met on a daily basis was there to torture me. I started eating less, smiling less, talking less. The only other person I really opened up to was Isac. Linda had only grown more caustic as she was pushed toward her breaking point, but Isac remained a constant source of warm camaraderie and encouragement. His kindness reminded me that there was still good in humanity, and that it was still worth fighting for.

And did I ever need that reminder. As we progressed further into the simulated training, we were exposed to a wide range of situations including: maintaining daily routines while they starved us, ingesting radioactive material, and undergoing small amounts of auto-cannibalization (eating slices of our own skin). Some of the simulations were just a virtual reality world, while others were so real that they wouldn't unlock the door until we'd passed out from exhaustion or pain. The line between reality and fabrication grew thinner every day, until it got to the point where I was barely able to distinguish what was training and what was not.

That's what I need you to understand before I tell you what happened next. There had been so many tricks played on us, so many simulations and improbable scenarios, and we weren't allowed to question any of them. When they asked us if we were ready for the next test, "Yes sir" was the only answer we were allowed to give. To their credit, the training was making us fearless. That's why when the three of us were locked in a steel room together, we didn't even ask what they were going to make us do. We already knew that we could handle it.

"This is a simulation game." Nigel's voice came through an intercom on the wall. We all stood immediately to attention. He didn't usually come down to the training facilities himself. The last time he was here, it was because Jean-Claude was being carried out.

"Yes sir," we all barked with military precision.

"There is an alien who has infiltrated the shuttle." Nigel's voice said. "He has taken over one of your bodies, and is a direct threat to the remaining crew. Do you understand?"

"Sir, yes sir."

"I want you to find out who it is. And I want you to kill them."

The intercom crackled and fell silent. We all remained perfectly stiff at attention. Slowly, laboriously, we turned to face each other. Isac was the only one to grin.

"It's just a simulation," Isac reminded us. "We don't really have to—"

"That's what the alien would say," Linda interrupted. "If he infiltrated the shuttle, then he's trying to avoid detection. Of course he would be the one to deny his own existence."

"Listen to yourself Linda," I said slowly. "We're obviously not going to kill Isac. The game is just to figure out which of us is the odd one out. They're probably going to use this data in their final decision for who the crew will be."

Linda's eyes were wild though. The pressure of these tests had pushed us all to the edge, but this was the first time in my life I had ever seen someone start to break before my eyes. She took a step back from us, arms raised as though to fight.

"That's the trick then," she replied. "You're both the aliens. He was testing me to see if I'd realize it—"

"Listen to Robert," Isac said gently. "We're all in this together, okay?"

"If anyone doesn't belong, it's you Linda," I said. "You've always been the difficult one. I'm voting she's the alien."

"It's Isac!" She pointed a shaking finger at him. Her eyes were bulging so badly, I don't know how they stayed in her skull. "Look at his skin! It's so pale!"

"Linda get a hold of yourself." I took a step forward, but she leapt back as though under attack.

"Get away from me! Both of you!" she screamed.

"Sorry Linda, but I have to agree with Robert," Isac said. "I'm voting you out too."

That should have been the end of it. The simulation should have ended. The door should have opened. There's no way they could see Linda's display and still entertain the possibility that she was a good candidate. But the door didn't open. We knocked—we shouted—I even tried climbing on Isac's shoulders to open the ceiling panels. Nothing. Not for over an hour, when the intercom finally came to life again.

"The alien is still in the room. Kill it."

This was a test. This had to be a test. My next theory was that they wanted to see how loyal we were to our crew-mates. Isac agreed with me, and Linda couldn't hope to take us both on by herself. She sat on her side of the room, muttering to herself, while Isac and I sat on the other. We were used to deprivation and isolation. We knew how to wait. Whatever stunt Nigel was trying to pull on us now wasn't going to phase us. At least, it wouldn't phase me or Isac.

One hour. Then two. Isac and I chatted amiably to pass the time, but Linda refused to even acknowledge us. Then the lights dimmed in artificial nightfall, and we settled further in to wait. Linda was getting more anxious as time passed. She kept standing to pace every few minutes. Her hands endlessly twisted over one another, so much that the skin was beginning to wear thin. How much of this would NASA have to see before they knew she wasn't fit for the mission?

I shouldn't have fallen asleep. It was just so boring in that room, and I was so tired from the previous day of obstacle courses. I didn't know how long we'd be in here, and we didn't have many chances to rest, so this seemed like a perfect opportunity. Besides, we were being closely monitored, and Isac was here with me. It should have been perfectly safe…

But this was the test I failed. Maybe not in the eyes of NASA, but I failed a much older, much more important test which was woven into the basic biology of my humanity. In the moment my fellow man needed me most, I wasn't there for him. By the time I woke up, it was too late. Linda had crept over to us through the darkness and wrapped her shoelaces around Isac's neck. He must have thrashed and struggled, but he wouldn't have been able to scream through his collapsing trachea. By the time I woke, the door was already opening. There were only two of us left alive.

The training is still going on. Our mission is too important to be jeopardized by my personal feelings. The fact is that I am the best man available for the job, offering the highest long-term chances of survival for the human race. And Linda? Well I guess she was the best woman for the job too. She'd followed orders where I could not. Did something which I could not. If anyone is going to make the hard choice to keep the mission going, then I trust her to do it.

After all, even in the face of such an impossible situation, she still made the right choice. The moment Isac's body stopped struggling, I saw the creature fleeing from its dying host. At first I thought it was a multitude of worms seeping out through his nose and ears, but as they pulled themselves out, it became apparent they were all connected at the base. The whole front of Isac's face had to split open to allow its body out, but I hope you'll forgive me for not wanting to dwell on the specifics. If it was a simulation, then they must have still killed Isac to do it. If it wasn't…

Well, all that matters is that NASA understands the true obstacles which might jeopardize the safety of our species, and they are taking every precaution to ensure I will be ready. I just wish I could still trust them like I used to, growing up with the naïve dream of becoming a spaceman.

As I prepare for the next day of training, I can't help but dwell on the conversation I had with Isac as we passed the last hours of his life.

"So much work to get to such a desolate, empty planet," I'd said. "Makes you wonder, doesn't it?"

"Not really," he'd replied. "It's not about where you're trying to get to. It's about what you're trying to escape from."

## A Righteous Angry Midget

Read the title? Good, then you're up to speed with what's going on.

Laptop? Fifteen percent batteries. Better keep this moving. I'm hiding behind a tree with Mark Burnham as I'm writing this, although lately he's been more commonly known as "Stacey".

Pretty soon a forty-two year old man with a wife he cares nothing about is going to drive up the dirt trail. The man wants to get to know "Stacey" after meeting at a nearby park. She seemed to like him, but the man was shy about meeting Stacey's parents. That's why he said he wanted to play out here in the woods where they wouldn't be around.

A white van—seriously? There he is. Right on schedule. Can't get the bus to arrive on time, but set a date with a predator, and you can set your watch by it. This is Mark's third victim, so I'm starting to get a pretty good idea how this works.

Mark Burnham is a twenty-six year old midget. (I think they prefer to be called little people?) He suffers from a hormone disorder which causes proportionate dwarfism, rendering him four feet tall and remarkably childlike. Turns out a clean shave and a baggy sweater are enough for him to pass off as a little, albeit chubby, eight-year-old girl named Stacey.

I'm watching the forty-two-year old climb out of the van. He's looking up and down the trail like he's afraid someone is watching. Bastard doesn't have a clue what's coming.

I met Mark a couple weeks ago in our group therapy. I'm not going into the details, but it's enough to know that we both survived a traumatic experience as kids. We got to talking (you can't avoid the awkward small-talk after someone just confessed to being turned into a hand-puppet), and Mark tried to lighten the mood by making a joke about being the only one who never gets too old for pedophiles.

It wasn't a good joke, but our intentions were.

The forty-two-year old man is calling for Stacey. Mark straightens his wig and we exchange maniacal grins. It's hard not to laugh while Mark calls out in that shrill childish voice. The man has spotted Mark now. He's coming this way. Mark scampers farther up the hill, calling for him again. We have to lure them a bit farther into the woods so no random hikers will interrupt his execution.

The man has passed me now. I'm going to follow in a minute. I've got a handgun with me for backup just in case. I'm not very good with it, but fortunately I didn't have to use it the first two times. Mark is a wizard with his butterfly knife and can make a man scream like you wouldn't believe.

Deep breath. Deep breath. And go.

I followed the man for about five minutes before Mark stopped. His little legs were kicking the log he sat on: a mask of pure joy and innocence. The predator sat nearby. They were speaking softly; I couldn't catch what they were saying, but it wasn't long before he leaned in to kiss Mark.

The wig came off. The knife went in. I don't know which happened first, but I'm sure both contributed to the dumbfounded shock on the man's face. I jumped out from behind the tree and leveled my gun. Shit, left the safety on—doesn't matter though. Mark had already slashed the man's face and hands a dozen more times. This one was too surprised to even scream—he just stared.

Stared as Mark punched him between the eyes.
Stared as the blade drove into his stomach.
Stared as his throat was cut.

Stared, and then smiled. Mark was already making some space between them. My friend was just standing there shaking in exhilaration, unsure what to do next. The predator rose to his feet and began dusting himself off as though mildly annoyed at discovering dog hair on his jacket. The blood had already stopped flowing. The cuts were healing, tattered flesh plastering themselves together into scabs which receded into the skin before disappearing entirely.

"You're a liar, Stacey," the man said, his voice a dreadful calm.

"Shoot him!" Mark yelled.

I didn't move.

"You said you were eight." The man didn't look at me. He just took another step toward Mark. "They can't be older than eight."

"Holy shit, what are you waiting for?"

I squeezed the trigger, flinching as the sound ripped the air in half. The dull thud as the bullet hit a tree. The man *still* didn't so much as glance my way. His hand lashed out and grabbed Mark by the neck. I fired again, but I was too afraid of hitting Mark, and it wasn't even close. The man heaved Mark into the air, swinging him wildly in my direction as a shield. The little man's arms were beating helplessly against the implacable grip; thrashing legs turned the air into a turmoil of desperate energy.

"Shoot him! Shoot me! I don't care, just do something!"

I did do something. I watched. And even that was more than I could bear. The man's chest exploded outward, ribs opening wide like so many giant white teeth. His head was bent backwards so sharply that his spine bulged against his neck. His whole body was bending to make way for the impossible jaws. Mark managed to get a few more swipes in, but the abomination pressed the dwarf's entire body into his gaping chest cavity.

The ribs snapped shut faster than a striking snake. The horrendous gash that marked where the skin had separated was already fading. Soon there wouldn't be anything but his torn shirt to show where he had mocked his humanity.

"Bring a real eight year old tomorrow," he told me.

I turned and ran. So fast and so hard that every bone in my body felt like it would shatter from the impact of my flying strides.

"Or don't," he shouted after me. "What's the worst that could happen to you?"

## A Painting By Day, A Window By Night

A big black dog rearing on its hind legs to stand like a human. One paw conspiratorially placed in front of its lips as though swearing the viewer to uphold a shared secret. I hadn't given the painting a second thought, except maybe to remind myself not to bump into it while stumbling down the hall at night to use the bathroom.

The painting had never been there growing up, but there had been a lot of changes around my parents' house since I left for college. I had to throw a sleeping bag on the floor of my old room to visit now that they'd converted the space to a home gym. All the fantasy novels I used to read were in boxes in the garage, and any games I hadn't brought with me were tossed.

It was understandable, I guess. I've moved on with my life, and it would be selfish not to expect them to do the same. It just felt weird sleeping in that room with the ghosts of my former life replaced by the looming silhouettes of exercise machines.

This is where I'd become who I am: filling journals with rambling thoughts, lying awake dreaming of my first crush, studying and stressing and fighting with private demons that my life once revolved around.

That's probably why I couldn't sleep. I feel like I'm too young to have that many memories, but here they all came rushing back. I lay awake wondering if that kid was still alive inside me somewhere, or whether he was already dead and replaced with a new person, a stranger that I hadn't even properly met.

I used to imagine becoming someone that no one could ever forget, but I'm already in college and still a nobody. Was I the person I dreamed about back then? Or had I betrayed myself somewhere along the way?

After tossing and turning on the floor for a few hours, I got up to use the bathroom. I had to stop and stare as I passed by the painting of the dog. Savage strokes of thick paint made the fur look like it was bristling. Bared teeth flashed in the moonlight behind its paw, and the playful personification of its stance now seemed like a sardonic mockery of human achievement. The longer I stared, the surer I was: this wasn't the same painting I had seen in the day.

I passed it again the next morning on my way to breakfast, but I couldn't comprehend what I had found so unsettling during the night. The fur wasn't bristling, it was just fluffy. And those teeth? I could still see them, but it was obviously a smile. I asked my parents about it, but they both just gave each other these confused little shrugs.

Somehow they'd both figured the other one had bought it. They'd been doing a lot of home improvement projects, and I guess neither of them had mentioned it to the other. Eventually they decided that they couldn't even remember a time when it wasn't there; they told me it had been hanging since I was growing up, and that I must have been the one to forget.

The part of me that was worried about everything changing actually found that to be a relief. If I was already starting to forget, then maybe these superficial changes weren't so important. Everything from my childhood that had meant something to me, that had defined me, well those I would have remembered and taken with me. Everything that had changed, everything I forgot, those were things that were okay to leave behind.

But some things are impossible to leave, no matter how hard you try. I fell asleep easily enough that night, although I woke with a start to a scratching sound. A dark shape was standing over me—I strained against the confines of the sleeping bag, ripping it aside to leap to my feet. No, just the handlebars of the treadmill. I tried to settle back down, but there was that scratching again. It sounded like it was coming from inside the walls. Mice? Then a long, slow, tearing sound, like a knife running through thick cloth. Not mice. Definitely not mice. I turned on the light and walked along the length of the wall. It was uncomfortable to imagine something running around inside, but the scratching seemed too far away for that.

*A heavy thump.* This wasn't from inside the wall. This was from the other side. *Footsteps.* I opened the door, flipping on the light in the hallway. A black flash of movement around the corner, just at the edge of my vision. I rubbed my eyes. The painting was face-down on the carpet. That must have been the sound I heard. The nail losing its grip on the wall probably made the scratching, and then the thump as it hit the floor. I convinced myself that the flash of movement was nothing more significant than the shadow of the treadmill, until…

I set the painting upright against the wall. There was a long slash down the center of the canvas, but I couldn't have cared less about the defacement of the art. The fact that the dog was missing from the painting—that's what gripped me. I scrutinized the canvas, even looking under the folded flaps the rip had produced. Nothing. Just heavy brushstrokes of thick blue paint.

*Scratching. Scratching. A CRASH.* From the other side of the house where my parents slept. I started running toward the noise, but the next sound had me frozen. A wolf's howl—close—somewhere inside the house. Then shouting from my parents, and I was running again. Tearing, growling, another howl—I flung open their door. Blood was everywhere. On the walls, the floor—even the ceiling fan was dripping. Neither of them had been able to get out of bed before their throats were torn out. One brutal bite each, by the looks of it. As quick and painless as could be expected from whatever—

Another howl. Sounded like it coming from outside, through the broken window. Howling, but more distant now, seemingly moving away. It must have known I was there. My room was closer to it than anything. If this is what it came here to do, then why didn't it touch me? I ran to the window where I saw a dark shape looking back at the house. Nothing more than a shadow really, standing on its hind-legs like a human. It was looking right at me, almost like it was waiting for me to see it. Then it was gone, falling onto all fours to bound into the trees behind the house.

I don't know what gave me the courage to follow it that night. It didn't seem like who I was up to this point, but I guess it's up to us to decide who we are from here. My dad had a handgun that he kept in his desk, and he taught me how to use it. I didn't know where I was going, or whether I could even find the creature. I just knew that I wanted to kill something. As long as I kept thinking about the kill, I wouldn't have to think about the dead. Staying here and facing their bodies, or even just the inescapable thoughts in my head—that's what I wasn't brave enough to do.

Either it didn't expect me to follow or didn't care if I did. The creature made no attempt to cover its tracks. At points the way seemed deliberately marked with streaks of blood, trampled underbrush, or even the occasional gash torn straight into a tree. I wasn't too far into the woods when the tracks abruptly stopped. The deep footprints vanished like it had taken flight. The wilderness was pristine. I turned in slow circles, encompassed with the impossibility of the peaceful night.

And with the stillness came the desperate, unbidden thoughts. The confusion, the disbelief, the helpless rage. Blood pounding in my veins, breath like a dagger of cold air, I fired the gun randomly into the trees. Again and again, just to drown out the chaos in my mind. Then the rustling of something deeper in the woods, reacting to my shot. It was running now, and I was right behind. I didn't care what it was, I was going to shoot it. Even killing a defenseless animal would help: I just needed an outlet, any outlet for this turmoil inside.

I reached a vantage point over a sudden indenture in the ground and caught a glimpse. Black, shaggy, running on two feet. The dog—the monster—whatever it was. I took another wild shot, but then it was gone again. I fired several more rounds randomly into the woods, but nothing else moved after that. It was gone for good this time. It wasn't a complete loss though, because the last chase had led me to something like a campsite.

The remains of a small fire, a few cans of food, a rolled mat on the ground. This wasn't an animal lair. Stranger still, I found drying brushes and a small stack of framed paintings on the ground. They were all original, all depicting standing dogs with a paw raised to their mouth. Beside these were an equal number of identical frames, each containing nothing but plain background which matched that of the dogs.

There's only one conclusion I was able to draw from this: there's a killer who is deliberately trying to trick people. First comes the dog painting, either given or sold or installed, I don't know. Then he sneaks in to replace the painting with the torn background, looking as if the dog has disappeared. He must have to leave someone alive to spread the tale of the supernatural painting, although I still haven't figured out a reasonable motive behind this. Maybe there is no reason to killing, maybe killing is the reason, I don't know.

I can only imagine how terrifying this must be for someone who wasn't able to track the painting's origin... and how powerful the killer must feel reducing someone to that point. To take someone's family and destroy their conception of reality in a single blow. There was almost something elegant about the senseless savagery. Even if they never told another soul about what they'd seen, that kind of experience would haunt someone for the rest of their life. To have that strong an impact on someone, or multiple someones, to be the most important person in their life without them even knowing who you are...

But you'd know, wouldn't you? Do something like that, and you'd really know who you are. And no one could ever take that away from you. All these paintings left, and the killer won't be back now that his secret has been had. Almost seems like a waste. But at the same time maybe he's relieved. A secret like that burning inside of you can eat you up inside. I couldn't have blamed him even if he led me to his camp on purpose. People like us, sometimes we just want our work to be appreciated.

## We Can Fix Your Child

As you inevitably age your skin will wither and mush like putrid fruit. Your organs will decay into useless sludge. Even your mind will rob you of a lifetime of memories and experiences, reducing you to nothing but an organic shell of who you used to be. You've begun to feel it already. Imperceptible by the day, but implacable as the marching years, your body is growing soft and weak. You will never again be as young as you are in this moment, and even now you can smell all those lofty dreams of youth rotting into idle fantasies that will never be realized.

Ah, but those sweet children! They are the closest thing you will ever have to immortality. They are your only chance to rewind the clock, rekindling the magic of forgotten innocence. Your legs will still tremble as you drag yourself out of bed each morning, but you can feel the spring in their step when they play. Their mastery of skills which have eluded you, their passion for discovering a world which is dead to you, their burning blood which hasn't yet learned what it means to love and not be loved in return; everything that they are is yours.

It's too late for you, but not for them. But only so long as you use the wisdom which life has cruelly carved into you, molding their nascent minds to live the perfect life you have forfeit. I know you're doing your best, and I know it sometimes isn't good enough. They will turn from you in their naive arrogance as you have turned from your own parents. They do not understand how selfish they are being, destroying not only their own life, but killing your second chance at life as well.

But don't worry, because we can fix your child.

Do they scream and fight back against your commands? *We can fix that child.*

Do they waste their time on idle laziness that detract from their (or your) fulfillment? *We can fix that child.*

Are they brutish, rude, ugly, stupid, ungrateful wretches who do not under-

## Sleepless Nights

stand what sacrifices you have made for them and what they now owe you in return?

One of our greatest success stories began with such a beast. His parents worked very hard for him, but often that meant leaving him alone for long hours to entertain himself. He became obsessively addicted to games during that time, holding his parents' love hostage to continually demand the latest consoles and media.

His adoring parents gave everything to him, hating themselves when they reached their limit and had no more to give. They tried to get him to exercise more, to eat better, to study and learn and play with other children. He would only retreat into his cave though, spurning any attempt to change his ways.

Classes were failed. Graduation was postponed. The boy didn't understand —refused to understand—what life would be like when he had to support himself through his own grit and merit. He was setting himself up for failure, and sure as any disease which devours from the inside out, he was killing his parents.

They were desperate when they came to us. They blamed themselves for his shortcomings, not understanding that it was their child who was broken until we offered our fix. They didn't care how, they just wanted it done.

I sat them down (free consultations, mind you), and had them both write down a list of everything they wanted their boy to be. Let the imagination run wild! Now is not the time to be encumbered with reality which has already been a burden for too long.

They were hesitant at first. Then the father wrote down "be more motivated". That encouraged the mother to add "more happy". The more they wrote, the more they broke the illusion of their son's adequacy, and the more they had to say. Make him taller, said the father. And get him into shape. More compassionate, said the mother, and more sociable with his friends. Smarter, funnier, more honest, more polite...

Both of them were crying by the end. The boy they had created was nothing like their son, but I was there to console them. Nothing like their son *yet*. But don't worry, because we can fix that child.

The parents did as they were instructed and left town for the weekend. Standard policy; it can be stressful for them to be present during the fixing. We came for the boy in the dead of night when we knew he would be home. We are professionals after-all, and don't like to waste our time.

We don't bother to knock. That would only give him a chance to escape. The parents left a key with us, and we entered the house without lights. Up the stairs to his room where the sound of machine guns still blared from his speakers. The little bastard stayed up all night, although that isn't uncommon when the parents are gone for the weekend. He might as well get his last games in now, because he won't be playing anymore after we're done with him.

His game was loud enough to conceal our entry. He didn't notice us until we ripped the swivel chair out from under him. The struggle is always brief. Sometimes we'll get a fighter and we have to subdue them with force, but any damage done to the body is inconsequential. He won't be using it for much longer.

I'm pleased to say that this little monster was fixed within a week. His parents didn't even recognize him, but there's no doubt that they will be happier now. He never talks back. He never speaks before he's spoken to, and even then he'll say "sir" or "ma'am". He hasn't touched his games again, and nothing about his passive countenance promises so much as the least resistance anymore.

Of course, the original is still with us for research purposes. The one that's been returned is the only one you'll ever need though, and you'll love him to the ends of the earth. In return he'll love you back more than you thought possible, because he in his young life has already learned a lesson that some of us do not understand until our grave:

That this world has no place for broken things.

## Don't Leave An Audio Recorder On Overnight

The first time I realized I was an adult was when I was twenty-three years old. I was in the grocery store when a kid asked me to get some sugar-blasted excuse for a breakfast off the top shelf. I pulled down the box and stared at the cartoons gorging themselves on the luminescent emoticon-shaped diabetes pebbles. He took the box and said, "Thanks mister." Hearing that almost made me feel dirty.

Now at twenty-seven, I know I must be an adult because I'm tired all the time. I go to bed tired, I wake up tired, and in that brief blur of confused social awkwardness in-between? I'm spending that day-dreaming about actual dreaming back in bed.

I went to a doctor to see if he could prescribe me something. Apparently self-medicating with Adderall like I did in college is discouraged, and anyway I couldn't find a dealer. No, I wasn't depressed. Yes, I was getting at least eight hours a night. No, I didn't have congenital heart failure or explosive herpes (???). So why didn't I ever have any energy?

The doctor said I might have sleep apnea, a condition which obstructs my breathing while sleeping and causes me to wake up multiple times in the night. I didn't remember waking up, but he said that was common. He wanted me to spend the night in a sleep lab and get a nocturnal polysomnography which measures my heart rate and oxygen levels for detection.

Screw that. I may be an adult, but I'm not old. It was hard enough getting everything done while being tired. The last thing I wanted was trying to get some rest in a lab. I opted instead to just leave an audio recorder on overnight.

Apparently the periods of obstructed breathing would audibly contrast with

## Sleepless Nights

the heavy breathing which compensated afterward, thus potentially allowing me to detect the issue. No downside, right?

I used an Android app which is a sound activated audio recorder. I messed around with the calibrations a bit and finally reached a sensitivity which detected heavy breathing.

But what I heard the next morning? Giggling. Like a little girl. I could faintly hear myself breathing in the background too, but there were three distinct instances during the night where I heard the laughter. I was getting more tired every day though, and this still seemed like an easier solution than going into the lab.

Obviously this was a joke from the app developers. There weren't many reviews on this one, so I downloaded a new recorder and tried again the following night.

*Isn't he a precious thing?*
*Shh. You'll wake the poor baby.*
*Giggling*
*Just his back? Their backs aren't very sensitive.*
*Let him sleep. He isn't ripe yet.*

That's what played back to me the following morning. I don't know what's going on, but I've never felt less like an adult than I do now. It's times like this when I really wish I wasn't single. I had a mini panic attack and almost smashed my phone on the nightstand right there.

Tonight I'm going to try a video recording too. I hope I'll still be able to sleep tonight.

*Let him sleep. He isn't ripe yet.*

Do you have any idea how hard it is to get a good night's rest after hearing that in your room?

I've never been one to freak out about superstitious or supernatural things. When I see a black cat crossing my path, I just figure he has someplace to be. Sure I've read scary stories for their thriller aspects, and I'll watch horror movies with friends just so I can laugh at them for being scared, but I never personally bought into that kind of stuff.

*Shh. You'll wake the poor baby.*

After playing the tape for what felt like the hundredth time, I was ready to expand my boundaries of reality just to find some explanation. Even deciding that it was a ghost or some nonsensical shit was better than having no explanation at all.

Calling my friends or family though? I would be ruining decades of my carefully maintained image of 'the chill guy who doesn't let anything bother him'. I was resolved to give it one more night with the video recorder to see if I couldn't catch the trickster before asking for help and embarrassing myself.

I tossed and turned for hours last night. I got up about a dozen times to check my laptop to make sure the video was still recording. Just to be safe, I saved the video stream to a password protected google drive folder so it was stored on the cloud. Even if someone tampered with my computer in the night, I should still be able to see what was going on.

I watched the slow minutes drain through my digital clock as though they resented their obligation to pass the time. I don't even remember falling asleep, but one moment I read the time as 2 a.m., and the next moment it was 3:30. I must have slipped out for at least a little while.

The red recording light was off. I immediately jumped up and checked my laptop, but the video file was gone. The backup stream on the google drive was still there though, so I scrubbed through the video.

Me on my back.

Me on my side.

Oh look. There's me on my other side.

And then a face was peering into the screen. A little girl—she couldn't have been more than fourteen—staring directly into the camera. It was difficult to tell much about her though, because her skin was charred black and flaked off all the way to her heat-splintered skull. Her hair and nose were completely burned away, and all that was left of her eyes and mouth were sticky pits of darkness.

I skipped back to the moment she appeared and played the video. She rose up from below the camera angle as though she was lying on the floor. She turned her head toward my sleeping body, then to the computer.

*What's he looking for?* she asked.

*He's looking for us,* the other voice said from somewhere behind the camera. *Shut it off. Can't we just tell him what's happening? He deserves to know.*

*Jessica, we agreed about this. It's either you or him. Get rid of it, now!*

That's where the video stopped. The time-stamp read 3:21 a.m. They were here just a few minutes before I woke up. I checked my window. Locked. The door? Locked from the inside. I even opened the closet and every cupboard in the small apartment kitchen. There wasn't any sign.

In about five minutes I had returned to my computer to watch the video again for clues. I'd left the google drive folder open though, and now the backup video file was gone too. They were still in my room somewhere.

Unless I was just going crazy and had woken from a nightmare, but I don't think so. Even with the video gone, my floor was still littered with black crumbled flakes of burned skin.

*It's either you or him.* I didn't like the sound of that. I couldn't stay in the apartment knowing they were here, but where could I go at four in the morning?

I called the number for the sleep lab my doctor gave me. There was staff still on duty, but they said they were all booked up through next week.

I grabbed my jacket and keys and headed out the door. As long as I stayed still, I was in too much danger of falling asleep again. I didn't have any real plan, but I figured I would just walk around until the sun rose.

I was more exhausted than ever after that restless night. I still couldn't quite accept this was happening to me. Maybe I was just so tired that my mind had started playing tricks on me. It was hard to be afraid while walking around the familiar park near my home. Vivacious bursts of spring decorated the ground, and I gulped down deep breaths of the fresh air. I could just call in sick today, get a good long sleep, and maybe all of this would just go away.

"Hey buddy." I nearly jumped out of my skin. It was just some homeless guy sleeping on a park bench. I pulled my jacket up and started walking faster.

"Hey don't be like that. Got any change?"

"Sorry. Nothing to spare."

"Yeah right, bastard," he said.

Unpleasant, but it's a common enough encounter in the city. It was what he said next that made my blood run cold.

"I hope the lady burns you next. Like she did to that girl."

I slowly turned to face him. But he was just a crazy hobo who would rant about anything. This couldn't have anything to do with… but the image of that burned skin was not so easily banished from my mind.

"What girl?"

He grinned to get my attention. I could clearly count all five of his yellow teeth peeking through his tangled mass of facial hair.

"Jessica. I could hear the Lady screamin' her name the whole time the girl was burning alive. I hope she gets you too."

*He isn't ripe yet.*

The words kept playing a loop in my mind while I walked. I was getting hung up on the word "ripe". The connotations implied I was getting ready to be harvested for food, but what entity would possibly choose me? I've never built on ancient Indian burial grounds or disrespected a primordial altar.

I did once find out some guy's gamer-tag password in high-school and stole his character, but I hardly think that's grounds for being tormented like this. There was absolutely nothing about my life which suggested I should be the target for this madness.

Twenty bucks was enough to get the homeless man talking. He said he gets thrown out of the park if he sleeps here too often, so he's also set up a camp a little outside town in an aspen grove. The last time he was there, about three days ago, he witnessed Jessica being burned alive while an older woman watched.

Of course, he didn't actually say it in those words. His version had a lot more colorful phrases like "I'd sooner eat my shit and eat the next shit afterward then go through that" or "she was screamin' like a dozen cats getting raped by a tiger."

I passed the last gas station in town, and he said the aspens were only about a ten minute walk from here. I've never been so tired in my life. This had to be more than sleep deprivation. It was a mortal weariness, a spiritual weariness, almost as though the bond tying me to this world was starting to unravel. I kicked a rock in my way, and I half expected my foot to pass straight through it.

My best guess is that the lady is some kind of demon, and she sacrificed the girl and now she's going after me. But the older voice in the recording had said: "Jessica we agreed on this. It's either you or him." How could Jessica have agreed to go through that? Was she tricked? What could she possibly stand to gain?

I knew something was wrong the second I stepped into the aspen grove. The cool morning breeze died the moment I passed the first trunk. The green leaves hung frozen and unnaturally static. The only thing that seemed to be moving was a steady stream of sap which poured down the trees.

Not sap. Blood. I could tell by the dark red streaks left behind on the white bark as it oozed toward the ground. I considered turning back right there, but the more unnatural it seemed, the more important it was for me to stop whatever was happening to me.

There was a clearing in the center of the grove where a circle of salt was laid upon the earth. Sitting in the center was a middle-aged woman who I can only presume was the lady.

Her face was plain and warm, although heavy lines of grief pulled her eyes downward. She wore jeans and a simple floral sweater, not exactly how I would have imagined a witch or demon. Her eyes were closed; hands folded calmly in her lap as though she were waiting for someone—for who? For me?

"You're the lady." The moment I said it, I realized the homeless guy probably just called her that because he didn't know her name. "You're the one who burned Jessica alive."

She opened her eyes wide: comforting, soulful eyes. Eyes I would have trusted under any other circumstance.

"You weren't supposed to find out until the end. I'm sorry you became involved in this," she said.

"Until the end? You mean when I was ripe? What was going to happen then?" I wanted to hit her. To throw a stone, to yell, anything. But seeing her so calm and ordinary and sad, I couldn't even raise my voice. The little energy I had left was fueled with indignation and anger, and without that it was all I could do just to keep standing.

"I told you, mother. He deserves to know what's going on." My skin prickled. Jessica was sitting outside the ring of salt, or at least what was left of her. The whole body was as black and rough as charcoal. All of her clothes had burned away, and the skin had burst in many places to reveal flayed sinew and cooked bone underneath.

"You burned your own daughter alive?" I felt the rage building again, and I didn't fight it. I had to hold onto it. This feeling was all that reminded me I was still awake—still alive.

"You're right, Jessica. I've been so selfish." The woman sighed, and seeing her in such dismal misery, my anger was once more replaced by profound pity.

That's when she explained everything to me. She wasn't a witch at all, only a mother who couldn't bear to watch her daughter suffer.

Jessica was born with cerebral palsy: an incurable disorder which devastated her mind and body. She could barely swallow on her own, and her mother had done everything within the boundaries of medical science only to find that was not enough. After that, she'd tried alternative medicines: crystals, powders, ointments, prayers, and finally at the end of all things: rituals.

Her pursuit of the arcane led her subtly down the road of the occult until she discovered a process known to cure someone of all mortal ailments. In this vain hope, she burned Jessica alive in order for her to return purified.

"The entity I made the pact with was willing and eager up until I lit the fire in her flesh," her mother told me, "but afterwards he began to make demands before he would bring her back."

At the demon's request (for that is what she found herself bound to), she planted seven black seeds in the food where she worked as a grocer. Only once the seeds had ripened within their victims, Jessica would be allowed to return.

By the end of her tale, the last of my strength had fled me and I was sitting beside her in the salt circle while Jessica watched from the outside.

"I'm sorry," she mumbled, no longer able to meet my gaze. "I had already burned her. I couldn't stop before I … "

"What happens? When they're—when we're ripe?" I asked. My throat was choked and dry. I couldn't help but glance back at Jessica's grotesque disfiguration. Was that what was in store for me too?

"The seeds are a portal into the other side," she said. "Once they're fully grown, the demon will enter this world and—"

"And possess me," I finished.

"I'm so sorry. He told me you would just go in peace. I never thought one of you would find out what was going on."

"How long do I have?" I asked.

"I don't know. Not long. That's why Jessica and I have been watching the people with the seeds. We've been waiting for them to burst."

"Can you stop it?" I knew what her answer would be before I even asked, but I had to hear it anyway. If it meant bringing her daughter back, would she have stopped it even if she could?

"No. All I did was plant the seeds in the food. How they work is as much a mystery to me as you."

We stared at each other for a moment. I lifted my hands and felt their unnatural weight, and she flinched as though afraid I would strike her.

"Do you hate me?" she asked.

"No." And it was true. I hated that this was happening, hated that I was afraid, but I didn't hate her. I might have even done the same in her place. "I can't hate you, because I need you."

"I told you there's nothing I can do," she protested.

"You can stay with me here, and keep me company until it comes. You're a lucky girl, Jessica. Your mother loves you very much."

I didn't even have enough energy to sit upright anymore. I slumped against the lady—it's easier for me not to know her name—and she wrapped her arms around me. I pulled out my phone and considered calling my family, but I didn't know how to make sense of my situation. Instead I'm posting my final update, which they will find and come to understand. The lady held my hand as I rested against her, and together we are waiting for oblivion to come.

## The Slaughterhouse Camera

Two men, pick-up trucks, work-overalls. New hires, they said, but they were professionals who knew their way around a slaughterhouse as well as anyone. They were always comfortable with the hogs I dropped off and never had to ask twice about how I wanted the meat prepared. Of course, both of them deserve the same done to them as they were doing to those poor animals, but there's no way I could have known that when we first met.

Fact is, there aren't enough government-regulated slaughterhouses to accommodate the demand. It's a long, expensive process to get a USDA certified house, and I'm not going to drive eighty miles and pay their exorbitant processing costs just so I can sell my meat across state lines.

That's where "custom houses" come in. These are inspected by the USDA, but they don't require the same standards or constant oversight. I'd been taking my animals to one for about four months when a "John Smith"—the pot-bellied son-of-a-bitch running the land next to me—caught wind of my switch. The bastard started raising hell, telling everybody that my meat wasn't safe. He said that I tortured my animals, poisoned them, anything to get the local markets to buy his stuff instead.

Now I already had a contract with the fellas down at the custom house, but I called up a friend at the FDA and got him to send over the tapes from their safety cameras. That would give me some proof that everything was up to code, and then I figured all this nasty business would just blow over.

The thing is though, those men at the custom house? I guess they didn't know about the cameras. Otherwise there's no way they would have let that abomination pass in the open like that.

Everything started out normal enough. The hogs were restrained and stunned with an electrical current so they didn't feel any pain. The slaughtering was quick and efficient, and then they suspended the animals by their hind legs like ought to be done. After that they were supposed to bleed the carcass dry, but instead they just left them there. Job wasn't even half done, and there they were: packing up their coats and keys and slapping each other on the back like the day was over.

I scrubbed through the video to watch the rest of the process when they got back. They didn't return that night, but something else did. A pale blur dashed across the camera. I paused the frame when the creature was in full view: taller than a man, and thinner too. Skin like rice-paper, and bulging with so many veins that it might as well have been made of string. Teeth like a hundred needles and shining black eyes like a midnight prayer.

One by one, the beasty was draining the hogs dry. There wasn't any sound, but I could almost hear the puncture as all those little teeth dug into the carcass, submerging its head so deep that I could only see the neck. Then all those veins began to swell, twice, three times their old size, trembling and straining so hard under its thin skin that I thought it had to pop.

But no, it just ripped free and went to the next animal. There wasn't much light, but where the moon snuck through the window its head glowed with blood, almost like there were red lights stuffed underneath the pale skin. I couldn't watch long, and I sure as hell couldn't go showing this to people. Get my name associated with something like that and I wouldn't just be out of business; I'd have torches outside my door and rocks flying through the windows.

First thing the next morning I went down to the custom house. My animals were all sliced and prepared, perfect as ever, but I told the men I was done. I didn't give a reason, just that I wasn't coming back. They got angry about me breaking contract, and we got to yelling at each other. Tensions were getting high, and one of them was so red I thought he was going to take a swing at me. I suppose that's why he said what he did. He was angry, and he wasn't thinking straight. He regretted it the moment it came out of its mouth, but there it was:

"We promised the animals to her, and she won't let you leave."

They didn't want to say more, and I didn't want to hear it. I just drove off without looking back. I locked my doors and windows real tight. I got my shotgun out from the cabinet and cleaned it until I could see my face in the barrel. And then I prayed, to anyone or anything that would listen: I prayed that I was going to live through the night. It wasn't right for something like that to exist in this world, but if it did, then maybe that meant there was something watching over us too. Or maybe I'm alone right now, and then I wouldn't mind never seeing the dawn again. After-all, why would I want to live in a world where devils were real but angels weren't?

It was about two in the morning when I heard it. I hadn't gone to sleep, just sitting up with the TV on low. I'd spent a long time just listening to my own thoughts, but the wind had started picking up, and I couldn't stand how it played around the plank house like fingers running along the wood. I started to nod off once or twice, but the hard handle of my gun was a constant reminder to stay alert. I don't quite know what I was expecting, but it wasn't the knock on my front door.

Slow, regular, rhythmic—casual as a mailman dropping off a package. My grip tightened and I held my breath. There was a long pause, and then it came again. One, two, three, four. I couldn't take it, but I couldn't force enough air out of my lungs to warn it off. Five, six, seven—my body shaking so bad I could barely hold the gun up. The knocking stopped. Before I could take a proper breath, I saw the face up against the window.

A hundred needle teeth smiling at me from the darkness. I took my shot. The glass exploded and the face was gone. I fired again, just to be sure. No sound, but the tinkling of broken glass and the ringing echo in my ears. Then the screaming started up. If you've ever heard a pig scream in the middle of the night, then you know it's like a banshee being dragged down to hell. And knowing what was out there—what it was doing to them—what it *could have* done to me—well that made it all a thousand times worse.

I couldn't force myself to leave the house. I just sat there and listened to the chaos of the night. The dissonance of those suffering animals struck something so deep in me that it made me hate being human. I hated caring, feeling, hated my capacity to imagine what was going on out there. I wish I could have just turned it all off and become a mindless animal, or even further into oblivion past the point of this waking nightmare into a sleep so deep that I didn't care if I ever woke up. I hated myself for being too afraid to open the door and kept on hating myself as the screams cut short one by one until there was nothing left but the wind like fingers probing their way in. I hated myself straight into the first tint of dreary daylight splashing through my broken window.

Nine full-grown hogs and five little ones, all gone. And me, the one who should have been the first to go, I'm still here. The custom house has closed down and I haven't a clue what happened to the two who worked there. I'm not getting any more animals though, because I know I can't live through hearing those screams again. I don't know what the creature is eating, but I figure the carnage from that night is going to last her awhile.

Maybe she's moved on and that will be the last I see of her, but I hope not. If there isn't anyone protecting us from on high, then it's just us down here who've got to protect each other. John Smith and I never got along, but next to that thing, I'm ready to call him my brother. And I may not be an angel, but as long as I've got my gun, I can still kill that devil next time I see him.

So now I'm just waiting until the night I look out the window and see all those needle teeth smiling down at me. Won't it be surprised to see me smiling right back, ready and waiting?

## Recordings Of Myself

Someone has been mailing me recordings of myself. First one was a couple weeks ago. It was just an unmarked DVD in a paper sleeve, addressed to me without a return. I figured it was some kind of spam mail and tossed it out. Ain't nobody got time for that.

The second one was getting ready to romance the trash too, but it happened to arrive the day I bought a used XBOX. I wanted to test out the DVD player and didn't have anything else handy, so I just popped it in and let it play.

The footage was a bit fuzzy and shaky like someone was walking while they recorded. It showed me entering my apartment building, following me until I got in the elevator. I even looked right at the camera for a second, but wracking my brain I couldn't remember noticing anyone strange.

There was a voice-over too, but it was in German and I couldn't make sense of it. I started it over and watched again. Only about fifteen seconds: it wasn't so much creepy as surreal. I was honestly more bothered by how terrible my posture looked than someone recording me. Probably some kid showing off his new camera or something, the world is full of weirdos, right?

The third one rattled me though. The video showed me in the grocery store, wandering up and down the aisle looking for something. About ten seconds again, more German voice-over. This wasn't someone innocently playing with their phone in the lobby anymore. I was being actively followed. I threw away the DVD immediately, regretting it and digging it out of the trash a couple minutes later. I had to get this translated so I could figure out what the hell was going on.

The next day I shuffled through my mail like crazy looking for another DVD. Nothing came. Or the next day or the one after that. Getting it translated fell further and further down my to-do list, until a week or so later I'd practically forgotten about it.

Until yesterday anyway, when another paper-sleeve slipped out from between some junk mail and landed on my floor. I rushed to play it, regretting it from the very first frame. The screen was panning around my room. *My bedroom.* It was dark, but everything had a green night-vision tint. The camera focused on the bed and started to approach. It took me a few seconds to recognize the lump in the dark. It was recording me while I slept.

A hand reached out from behind the camera: a pale, thin, hairless hand, with skin stretched too tight across the bones. And the digits were wrong: four to each finger, and double jointed, moving so fluidly they might as well have been tentacles. It rested a long finger on my forehead, trailing down my nose, over my lips, brushing so soft that I couldn't tell whether it was touching at all. Something in German again, a sing-song voice barely above a whisper. It was longer this time, but I paused to keep going back until I could write down every word as close as I could hear it.

I watched the rest of the video before I translated anything. The thing stayed beside me for a long time, but I didn't want to fast forward because I was afraid of missing some crucial dialogue. I stared at it staring at me for almost an hour before I couldn't take it anymore. The camera had been still for a long time, and I hadn't heard or seen any other sign of the perpetrator. I decided even if something else did happen that night then I'd prefer not to know. I rummaged around until I found the elevator and the grocery store tapes too, writing down all the German from them to translate. After hacking my way through the spellings a few times, google translate gave me this:

Tape 1 – ??? (Don't know, I threw it out before I knew what it was.)

Tape 2 – (Me in the elevator) "Look at him go. I can't believe he's going back into the apartment after what we told him last time."

Tape 3 – (Me at the grocery store) "Found him again. Look how calm he is, just going about his life. Do you think he's seen it yet?"

Tape 4 – (Whispered while I slept). "Sleep, baby, sleep. Thy father guards the sheep. Thy mother shakes the little trees. There falls down one little dream.

"Sleep, baby, sleep! Sleep, baby, sleep. The sky draws the sheep. The little stars are little lambs. The moon, the little shepherd,

"Sleep, baby, sleep! Sleep, baby, sleep. I shall bring your sheep. One with a golden bell. That shall be thy journeyman to guide you safe to hell."

That's it. I don't know whether this thing is trying to threaten me or protect me, or what it could be trying to protect me from. Either way, I don't think I'm going to sleep tonight. I don't know what I would do if I woke up and saw that thing watching me, recording me, even touching me with its long disjointed fingers. When the next DVD comes—if it comes... I don't think I have the stomach to watch.

## Your Dream Job

*A gun on the table between us. We could both walk out alive if we wanted, but how were we supposed to trust that's what the other was thinking too?*

What would you like to be when you grow up? An astronaut? A captain of industry? How about a TV producer? Well here's what you have to do: study real hard so you can get into a good college. Then keep on studying, all the way until you get your degree.

Student loans? Don't worry about it. You'll be making plenty of money in your career, so why stress about paying now with your minimum wage? Looking for a job? No problem! You're an expert in the field you've chosen. The places you want to work are going to chase after YOU to work for THEM!

Sound familiar? Yeah, well I fell for it too. Four years out of college, and I haven't used my chemistry degree for anything besides mixing drinks. At first I wanted to be on the cutting edge of biomedical research, but now I'd settle for any somewhat relevant job at a pharmaceutical company. Hell, I'd even hand out drugs at the convenience store if they'd let me.

It wasn't just the money either. It was about that look my friends gave me when I solved a complex problem that flew over their heads. Or the excitement of my new class schedule, or the pride in my parents' faces when they introduced their future chemist to their friends. Science wasn't just a future plan for me: it was my identity. It's not my dream that's dying every day at the bar. It's just that every day that passes makes it that much harder to answer the question: who are you?

Until I got an offer. *The* offer. The dad of a friend whose brother I knew from… doesn't matter where. It was a tech startup with real investors. No experience required, paid on-the-job training. I was going to have an office with one of those fancy little name plaques on the door. I was going to have title, and a salary, and sick days and health care and 401k and everything!

The CEO and I hit it off really well too. At first I was terrified to ask questions that might betray my inexperience, but he was easy going and seemed more interested in my personality than my qualifications. Loyalty, he stressed over and over again, that's all he cared about. Everything else you can teach.

"We don't expect to make any money off the new hires," he explained. "But a good man who's been here ten years is worth more to me than ten great men giving a year each."

That's why the first day on the job wasn't a tour of the facilities or an analysis of our knowledge. We were going on a company team building exercise right off the bat. Big rope and obstacle course that we were supposed to help each other through, doing exercises like trust falls and listening to motivational talks. What's not to like about a field trip on your first day?

Ten of us took two SUVs. It was a pretty long drive into the woods where the camp was, but it gave me a chance to get to know the other employees. A lot of fresh faces like myself, right out of college and desperate to prove themselves. At first I was a bit incredulous that this much money and trust was being placed in a newbie team, but the CEO told us it made sense from a long-term perspective. How are you going to have lifelong employees if you don't catch them early? And who is going to be more loyal than the guy who was given his first shot to follow his dream?

All ten of us were gathered in a cabin while the CEO gave his talk. Five tables faced the front, two to each table. You wouldn't have found better spirits on a campus that had just canceled the final exams in favor of an impromptu music festival. And the CEO just fed the fire, talking about the cutting edge research facilities with secured funding, both private and government. Gene manipulation, panacea medicine, even immortality—humanity was on the tipping point into a futuristic age, and we were going to be the ones to make it happen.

"Now I hope you all understand why I value loyalty so highly," he lectured. "Before any of you have reached middle age, pending discoveries are likely to double the average lifespan. We aren't a company, we're a family, and that's a bond for life. Now here comes the hard part."

He turned his laptop to display the draft of a news article. *Five fatalities in deadly SUV accident.* It was the same type of car we drove here in.

"Feelings, promises, even oaths: it's a fragile thing to build a company on that's going to last a hundred years," he said. "I like to have a little more insurance than that. So this is how we're going to play."

He walked around the room, placing a handgun on each of the five tables. Tension rippled through the room in a wave of rigid posture and fixated eyes. I chanced a glance at the person beside me: blonde girl, mid-twenties, eyes like saucers. I couldn't imagine her ever holding a gun in her life. What kind of screwed up team-building exercise was this? The CEO didn't say another word until all the guns were handed out, each positioned right in the center of the table.

"The rules are simple," he said, face quivering with excitement. "When I say go, the first person to shoot the other one at their table gets a job. No going easy either—I want a clean head-shot. If you just wound them, then you don't have the job yet. We're going to go one table at a time so everyone else can stay safe and avoid collateral damage."

One of the girls made a nervous giggle and rolled her eyes. I guess she didn't think he was serious, not until the CEO snapped the gun up from her table and blasted a hole through the window. No one made a sound after that.

"Do I look like I'm joking?" he asked the girl, bending low over the table to put his face up against hers. She shook her head vehemently. Grinning, the CEO pulled away and continued to pace the room.

"We're going to make it look like the five who died were in a car accident," he said. "Those who remain are the kind of people I want to have around. And yes, each killing will be recorded, just in case you change your mind down the road. Like I said, insurance. This is a job for life."

"You're crazy if you think any of us are actually going to do that!" the blonde girl beside me said, her voice cracking when the CEO turned. "We'll just walk away. Find our own way home if we have to. Nobody would want to work for a company like this!"

"If you believe that; if you *really* believe that there aren't people in this room who are willing to do whatever it takes to make their dreams come true, then you should have nothing to fear when it's your turn. If neither of you shoots, then neither of you get the job. You can both go home."

She smiled tentatively at me, and I returned it. Good news. I got the pacifist at my table. Unless it was all an act to get the jump on me. Or she didn't trust me, a complete stranger, and decided to shoot first just to save her own skin. The smile hardened in her face. We're all educated people here. This was game theory, plain and simple. And even in university level studies, there was always going to be someone who chose to screw the other over just to be safe. Now with life on the line, that was going to be even more evident.

"We're all going to be fine then!" the blonde girl said. "Everybody agree not to shoot, okay? If no one shoots, then we pass. It's just a test."

"Table one!" the CEO bellowed. "Everyone else out of the room for your own safety. To those playing: don't move a muscle until I say go, or I'll shoot you myself. Let's move people."

Everyone except Table 1 and the CEO exited the room. Some of us plastered against the windows to peek inside, but I just pressed my back to the wall in case of stray bullets. The blonde girl wouldn't shut up. I know she meant well, but I was so stressed that it got under my skin. We're going to be fine, she kept saying. No one is going to shoot. They're probably just BB guns anyway. That would have still broken the window, but it won't kill—

"Go!" the CEO shouted from inside. *A gunshot.* Almost simultaneously, no hesitation. The people at the window blanched and leaped away.

The CEO opened the door, and we couldn't help but look inside. One was dead on the ground, a pool of blood spreading from his head. The other was holding the gun, violently shaking where he stood over the body.

"He moved first!" the survivor desperately shouted. "I had to! He would have shot me, I swear!"

"Table two, you're up! Everyone else out."

The two girls looked at each other, both smiling meekly. They were holding each other's hands and exchanging promises as the rest of us went back out. Maybe they wouldn't do it. Then again, that first gunshot was still echoing in our ears: a grim reminder of the price of trust.

*Another gunshot.* And another, and another, and another. When the door opened again, only one of the girls was still standing. She didn't even make an excuse. She just shrugged, dropping the gun on the corpse riddled with holes.

I was the next one up. The blonde girl across from me. The gun between us. Everyone else had left the room except the CEO. He was flushed red and sweating, but there was a grin plastered on his face as he savored the moment before the game started.

"We're going to get through this," my partner told me for the hundredth time. "I trust you. Do you trust me?" I nodded, although of course I didn't. Not after what I had already seen. Not after what was at stake. I didn't even know if I could pull the trigger when I pointed it at her. I still didn't know what I was going to do, right up to the moment I heard: "Go!"

We both held our breath. I saw her finger twitch, but then she shook her head. I crossed my arms to show I wasn't going to touch it. Five seconds. Ten. Her fingers were dancing haphazard rhythms on the table. I uncrossed my arms, just in case she did go for it and I'd need a chance to react. Too late. She already had the gun, pointing it at my face.

"It's over," she said. "I've got the gun, and I'm not going to shoot. Neither of us are taking the job."

"Easy to say when you're the one with the gun. Is that what he wants too?" The CEO briskly walked into the room to hand me a second gun from another table. "Let's find out together."

Her finger tightened around the trigger. I already knew she wouldn't kill me for greed, but what about for self-preservation? It was a game of centimeters as I lowered my gun to the table. Relief flooded across her face. "Sorry," I told the CEO. "Game's over."

I waited until her gun lowered to shoot. Right between the eyes. The CEO's face lit up like a child on Christmas. "That-a-boy! Good long term planning. Way to keep your head. You're going to go far here."

I could feel the hatred on me as I left the cabin, but I didn't care. The ones who hated me were the ones going to end up dead anyway. Everyone else had no right. If anything, this shared ordeal was going to bind us together. Then again, I was going to work at a company where all my co-workers wouldn't hesitate to kill someone for their own gain. I guess loyalty to the CEO comes first, and trust was something we were going to have to learn over time.

Five separate games, and by the end, five dead bodies. No one had been able to walk away. But I guess that's in the past now. I have a whole lifetime of productive work to make up for what happened. I guess I know who I really am now.

Are you really telling me you wouldn't do the same for your dream job?

## Which Child To Save

The sanctity of my home was destroyed two years ago when a man smashed our kitchen window in the dead of night. I woke immediately, clutching sheets to my chest, pretending for as long as I could that the sounds of tinkling glass were fragments of a discarded dream.

The sliding deadbolt though? That was all too real. And the familiar creak as the door was carelessly swung open.

My first instinct was to rush down the hall to where my two boys were sleeping. I should have called the police immediately, but I wasn't thinking straight. I could only imagine how terrified they must be, and what would happen to us if one of them started crying and alerted the burglar that we were here.

The lights went on downstairs. The clatter of things being flung from shelves and scattered onto the floor. The intruder made no pretense to disguise himself;

## Sleepless Nights

either he thought no one was home, or he was simply too drunk or desperate to care.

David (twelve at the time) was already out of bed by the time I got there. He was getting ready to go downstairs and see what was going on. Mikey (ten) peeked around the door-frame, quivering eyes glowing in the darkness. I pulled my children back into the room and slammed the door behind me—

Too fast. Too loud. I strained to hear past the sound of our terrified panting. The man downstairs had stopped moving. Only for a moment though. Now he was sprinting up the stairs, the old wood thundering his arrival. This room didn't have a lock on it, but I pressed my back against the door as I finally called 911.

The handle rattled behind me. I pushed everything that I was against the door, but I couldn't hide. I had to speak aloud to tell the police where I was. My whole body went numb as the intruder slammed into the door. Again and again. I was in tears, barely able to get the words out. Mikey started screaming, but I couldn't comfort him. David wanted to help me hold the door, but I pushed him away.

I kept imagining a bullet or a knife puncturing through the thin wood to enter my body. All I could do was hold on until I couldn't, and then he was through.

He overpowered me in seconds. He kicked me hard in the stomach and I couldn't get back up. He was shouting something, asking where the jewelry or valuables were. I was crying too hard to answer him. David tried to wrestle him off, but the man pulled a knife.

I don't know what would have happened if we didn't hear the sirens then. The intruder was panicking, more than panic, he was practically drooling over himself in some drug-induced frenzy. He rushed back and forth with indecision while I screamed for help. He was about to make a dash for it when the police loudly announced they were coming in.

I told the intruder it was over. He couldn't get out. Anything he tried would just make it worse for him.

"I'm taking one of them with me. Tell the police the boy is dead if I'm followed."

And that's when he made me choose. I didn't have time to think. I was so scared that he'd hurt us if I didn't answer. I closed my eyes and pointed at the older boy David. My boy was screaming for me, but I couldn't open my eyes.

"Don't fight him," I begged. "He'll let you go when he's safe. I promise."

I didn't open my eyes until I felt Mikey rush sobbing into my arms. We were alone when the police found us.

I didn't see David again for three days. And even when he did come back, beaten, starved, with haunted eyes, he wasn't ever the same. He never talked about what happened. I tried to explain that I only pointed at him because he was older. He was bigger, and stronger, and smarter, he could take care of himself better than Mikey could. It didn't matter though. There was nothing I could say to change the fact that when our lives were on the line, I didn't choose to keep him safe.

David started getting in trouble at school after that. The principal was sympathetic at first, but after David started picking fights they had to suspend him. He started spending more and more time away from home without telling anyone where he'd been, sometimes not returning for days at a time. It didn't matter how much I worried; he'd just snap something like 'I can take care of myself' or 'but you'd rather me stay out than Mikey, right?'

I couldn't see the end to the road he was going down, but if something didn't change, then I knew it was going to be too late for him to turn back. There was only one thing I could think of that would convince David how much he mattered to me. If he wouldn't listen, then my last resort was to show him.

I planned to re-enact that fateful night. I planned it with a close friend at work. Mikey and David and I were going to be out camping when my friend would pretend to attack us. It'd be just like before, only this time I'd choose to save David. Then my friend would run off like he'd lost his nerve, and David would know how much I care. I know it's sick to play with my family like that, but it's the only thing I could think of to make things right again.

Everything was going perfectly. David didn't want to go on the trip, but once I forced him into the car he seemed to be getting along well enough with his brother. They were even singing with the radio together as we pulled into the campsite.

It was about 10 p.m. when my friend sent me the text. He was ready. Deep breaths. I steeled myself against the coming ordeal. Mikey and David looked up from the campfire to the rustling in the darkness.

My friend exploded out of the undergrowth wearing a ski-mask. He was brandishing a hunting knife like he knew how to use it. I screamed right on cue, the kids were screaming, but this was going to be over before they knew it.

"One of you boys are coming with me," my friend ordered.

"I won't let you!" I stood in front of them, putting up a brilliantly fierce display.

"Then everyone dies." He was holding a gun now. I hadn't told him to bring a gun, but it was good. It felt real. I could feel both my kids staring at me. Did they suspect something? No, they couldn't have. Shit, I knew the truth, and I was still terrified.

I pointed at Mikey, and then I closed my eyes. That was the end of our scenario. Now my friend would run away and everything would be fair…

My eyes flew open when I heard the gunshot. Mikey was cowering behind me. David had a knife in his hand—lord knows where he got it. He'd tried to rush my friend, who panicked and put a bullet in my son to keep him back.

David didn't stop though. The knife was flashing by the light of the campfire, and this time my screams were real.

Two more gunshots. By the time I got to them, it was too late. My friend's neck was sliced from ear to ear. Blood was bubbling up from a gruesome wound in David's chest and another in his shoulder. My frantic hands eased him to the ground, but that was all I could do.

"Is Mikey okay?" David asked.

"He's okay. You saved him. But David you shouldn't have…"

"You made your choice, I made mine," he said. "Now you won't have to choose anymore."

Both David and my friend were dead before the park rangers arrived. I didn't know how to explain the situation, so I just told them that we were attacked, and that David died defending us. It's my fault what happened though, and it feels right for me to be sharing the story now. Living or dying, speaking or staying quiet, loving or holding back, every day is a choice whether we notice or not. And every choice has consequences.

Mikey, I love you and your brother more than you'll ever know. Will you ever choose to forgive me?

## 400 Hits of LSD

Why is life so confusing?

It never should have gotten to this point, but it's too late to turn back now. I've always tried to be a good person, a statement most people won't appreciate coming from a drug dealer. If it wasn't for my mother getting sick, I might have been able to survive school and make an ordinary life for myself.

I'm not here to make excuses. The fact is that I knew what I was getting into when I started moving LSD and molly on campus. I kept telling myself that this was a transition state to help with tuition and medical bills, but three years later and I was deeper in than ever.

I was still attending classes and holding it together until my junior year when Mom finally passed. I never knew my dad, and there wasn't anyone left to impress anymore. No one to disappoint either. I started selling harder stuff—meth, heroin, PCP, once the money was in my hand, it didn't matter how it got there. I dropped out of school, making more in a weekend than I would have in a month with my degree.

I wasn't just dealing drugs now; I was a drug dealer.

What's the difference? When people are only good at one thing in the world, then that's who they become. I wouldn't just be broke and bored if I stopped dealing now. I'd be no one. I was pushing harder than ever, day and night, shipping in bulk supplies from the dark web and hiring my own runners to sell across the city.

I guess I hadn't realized how bad it had gotten until one of the boys who worked for me never came back with the money he owed. I found him cowering in his apartment a little ways off campus, blubbering about how someone attacked him on the street. He showed me the mark where the knife was pressed into his neck while rough hands rifled through his pockets and bag, taking everything.

Two thousand dollars' worth, gone. And the funny thing? The whole time I was smashing his face until it looked like raw hamburger meat, I never once cared if he was telling the truth. I didn't feel anything when he was crying blood and choking on his teeth.

I didn't feel anything while I walked home either. No curiosity as to whether he would live or die, no warmth from the autumn sun on my skin, not even a concern for what might happen to me because of it.

You know what did cut through the static though? Realizing that no one would have noticed if I had been attacked instead. No one would care if someone beat me into oblivion, leaving me for dead, or jumped me on the street to slide a knife into my neck. While Mom was still alive I had something to fight for, and if somehow my grit and accomplishments helped me make something of myself, then I knew it would be worth it to see her glow.

Sitting in my apartment, watching the indifferent clock drain the seconds of my life, I realized that I hadn't felt anything for a long, long time. Even the string of desperate text-messages from the boy's number didn't faze me.

*Why? Why? Why?* They read. *Why did you take my son from me?*

I guess he'd died after all, and someone had already figured out I was the one who did it from the messages. Didn't matter, it was a burner phone anyway. And even if they did find me somehow, how were they supposed to get revenge on me when I was already dead?

That's when I poured the vile of liquid LSD down my throat. 40,000 ug, enough for 400 tabs of street blotter. If you still don't understand why I did it, then I honestly envy your innocence. I wanted to feel something, or I wanted to die. I didn't care which.

The clock on the wall stopped. The whir of the fan fell silent. The bed I sat on, the air around me, even my beating heart and the whole world hardened into crystal....

... before shattering with a noise unheard since the beginning of the universe. Shards of light like a blizzard of eyes cascaded past me and vanished into the distance in all directions, taking reality with it. Light collapsed into a pinprick and then disappeared entirely, my heaving lungs racing a frantic marathon to keep up. I died a thousand deaths in the span of a second, and by the time new life surged into my displaced being, I was no longer of this world.

Assuming that is, there was anything left of me. What I had come to think of as my being had exploded into infinitesimally small fragments, each in turn detonating to splinter smaller and smaller until nothing was left but an atomic dust which mingled with all existence. As my mind gradually refocused, it seemed as though every grain of sand, every shaft of light, every soul from time immemorial to the gaping abyss at the end of all things contained me in equal measures.

There was no distinction between me and the rest of the universe, all things being connected by a tapestry of light and energy, all things screaming senselessly into the void and joining their voices in one almighty chorus which all existence sings though they have not the ears to hear it. Beyond life, beyond death, beyond perception, beyond ego I rode the eternal winds, powerless to resist or even comprehend that resistance was possible. I was everything and nothing, both the same, both divinely beautiful and profoundly sad: an unrequited love which runs so deep that it doesn't matter that you aren't loved in return so long as this feeling is possible.

Gradually my senses returned to me, although there was no discernible separation between sight or taste or sound, all meshing seamlessly into my awareness of the presence that engulfed me. I don't know how long I remained suspended in this state, but it wasn't until the presence spoke that I began to appreciate that I wasn't alone.

IT'S YOUR TURN.

"What?" I don't know whether I was thinking or speaking, unable to differentiate without a body.

A UNIVERSE CRUMBLED FOR YOU TO BE PHYSICAL. A STAR IMPLODED FOR YOU TO BE POSSIBLE. LIFE BEGAN FOR YOU TO BE INEVITABLE. YOUR ANCESTORS DIED FOR YOU TO PRESENT. NOW IT'S YOUR TURN.

"My turn for what?"

TO CLIMB THE LADDER, OR TO GET OUT OF THE WAY.

"Climb where though? Get out of the way for what?"

By this point my senses were beginning to untangle. I was sitting in the center of a white-sand desert beneath a vast and alien sky. I had to be careful where I looked, because any speck of dust or bead of light I focused on would deform into fractals, hypnotizing me and drawing me into it until I became what I had perceived. New colors sparkled to life and new dimensions made novel geometry possible, all forming and reforming in a mesmerizing romance between actuality and fantasy.

... HE'S ALMOST HERE.

The presence must have still been talking while I had been distracted. I strained to focus on it once more.

"Who is coming?"

YOUR BIOLOGY, YOUR MORALITY, YOUR CULTURE, YOUR TECHNOLOGY, YOUR CHEMICALLY SATURATED MIND.

HUMANITY IS HIS STEPPING STONE, AND HE WILL LEAVE YOU BEHIND.

The presence was solidifying before my eyes. A visual sound-wave, pulsing vibrations, the embodiment of madness I was thrall to. Eyes were gradually blossoming over its body like a field of flowers growing from barren earth.

"I don't want to be left behind. I don't want this to end."

THE END HAS ALREADY COME. Now it was my mother standing before me, wearing that floral dress of eyes. ACCEPT IT. She spoke wordlessly through the energy which bound us.

I couldn't reply. Not while watching her body decay, flesh sagging and sloughing off her bones which in turn disintegrated into a fine dust blowing into the wind. I tried to scream, only managing to inhale the flood of dust scattering from her rotting corpse. Soon, only her eyes remained.

THE BEGINNING IS READY TO BEGIN.

The boy I had killed was growing around those eyes. How had I never noticed that he had the same eyes as my mother? His face, his body, I instantly recognized him, although somehow I still felt as though my mother was watching me through him.

CREATE IT.

The boy was dissolving too, although it was completely unlike my mother's peaceful dissolution. Invisible blows bludgeoned him from every side, and great fistfuls of flesh were being torn from his body. He was almost gone before I realized I was the one ripping him apart, relentlessly consuming everything that I stole from him. Soon, only his eyes remained.

"It's not the end yet! I'm not dead yet!" I shouted through the mouthfuls of warm, bloody meat. "Tell me what I'm supposed to do next. What I'm supposed to *become* next."

There wasn't anything to tell me though. Even the watching eyes were gone, winking out into the immeasurable desert. Endless vaults of sky were falling around me, strange eons of unseen years condensing into blistering seconds. My heart was burning with the primordial fire of creation, and the air soured into acrid smoke pouring from my smoldering lungs.

"Why?" All that I was hurled into words which tumbled unheard into the hurricane of swirling sand. "Why was everything building up to this? Why am I here? Why does it matter? Why won't you answer?"

"Why? Why? Why?" Searing light burning the words into my eyes from the cell-phone clutched in my hand. "Why did you take my son from me?"

And though I spoke the words aloud, there was no greater truth from the universe to answer for me. There was only me and my trembling fingers as I typed a dozen feeble responses, deleting each unworthy apology before it was sent.

"Why? Why? Why?" came her hysterical sobs as I knelt on her doorstep. I knew her son so well, it was easy enough to find where his mother lived. She didn't hit me, or scream at me, or even call the police when I introduced myself and told her what I had done. She just kept asking why, over and over, kneeling beside me on the ground to take my hands in hers. And when she pressed my hands to her lips, it was my own mother weeping for my death.

"Why? Why? Why?" screaming to the heavens, though no answer came in return, and no answer ever did.

Life isn't there to answer why, after all.

Life is there to ask it.

And though the rest of my days will never answer for what I've done, I now understand that there is only one choice for me and those who are like me, slaves to our egos and blind to the changing world:

We can cling to who we were and be left behind. Or we can learn from our past and become something new. Something humanity has been building towards since before it began.

The beginning has already begun.

## Wounds that Words Have Caused

I've made the horrible mistake of falling in love with someone who doesn't exist, and it hurts like you wouldn't believe.

Let me tell you a little about her. She's dark, not sad or angry or angsty, but dark in a spiritual way like the tranquility of a midnight mist. She dresses in all black—her hair, her lipstick, her nails—but it does nothing to conceal the radiance of her beauty. She thinks so loudly that you can almost feel it echo through the silence, and when she speaks there is such deliberate measure in her voice that her words turn to music, the simplest phrase containing all the secrets of the world, if only you listen closely enough.

I fell in love with an idea long before I met my wife, Sarah. When I saw her for the first time—the fishnets, the black lace, the metal piercings—I told myself that this is what I've been looking for since before I even knew I was looking. And all the time we dated, I was looking at Sarah while seeing that dream of what love should be. And when we were married, I told myself that it was my fault for being unhappy, because she was everything I could ever want.

I'm not saying I was right to cheat on her. I'm just saying it happened, only a month after the wedding. A stupid mistake at first, but every time I did it, I felt a little less guilty than the last. I couldn't just abandon Sarah—not after the wedding. Not with her family always inviting us places, not with our lives so tangled up together. She'd tell me these horrible confessions about how she used to hurt herself when she was little, and how she'd even thought about suicide before she found me. If I left her and something were to happen, I don't know how I'd ever forgive myself.

The worst part about it was, Sarah knew I was cheating. I'd tell her that I had to go to a conference for work over the weekend, and she'd just press her lips together and force a smile. Like she had no right to ask questions. Like she deserved to suffer. She made it so easy that I just kept getting lazier with my lies.

"Out with friends," I'd text her, not bothering to say with who or when I'd be back. "Staying out late. Don't wait up." And I wouldn't be home until morning, if that even was my home anymore.

I wasn't happy, but I didn't notice so much while I was distracted with the perverse thrill of being in control like that. I was my own master, and Sarah was … well, whatever I told her to be. I don't know how long it could have gone on like that, but I knew something had to change when she finally worked up the courage to ask me to my face:

"Are you with any other women? I'm sorry to have to ask. It's just my insecurity talking. I just want to hear you say … "

"Of course not. Just you, baby, forever and ever."

I almost told her the truth, but her standing there wringing her hands, hearing the catch in her voice as she forced the words out, I just couldn't do that to her. It wasn't cowardice that made me lie. It wasn't love either. It was pity.

Her dark eyes fixed on me, sparkling with curious intensity. There it was again—that tight-lipped smile. And something more this time. The smile was quivering at the corners, like too little skin stretched over too much space.

"Say it again. I want to hear it."

"You're the only one for me." I was getting more than a little uncomfortable. It wasn't just the situation either. There was a sharp sting like a needle in my palm. I rubbed the spot without looking.

"Again. Tell me that you'd never lie to me."

"Never. I promise." My hand was hurting worse than ever. She glanced at it and I followed her gaze. A trickle of blood snuck through my closed fingers. There was a gaping wound like I had grabbed the blade of a knife.

"Again."

"What's going on? How did this happen?"

"Again!" she shouted, all pretenses of her smile gone. "Tell me that you love me!"

"I love you!" I shouted, rushing to the kitchen sink to wash the wound. And then I screamed. The wound was growing before my eyes, the skin savagely stretching as though invisible hands were digging their fingers into the hole. It was half-way up my forearm by the time I got it under the faucet, and it was growing by the second.

"Again!"

"What the fuck did you do to me?" I screamed. Paper towels were soaked in an instant. My fingers kept slipping as I tied the kitchen towel around my arm.

"Just what I asked it to do." Her voice was silk, strained to breaking. "I asked it to stop us from lying to each other."

"Make it stop!" I shouted. The blood kept coming.

"I can't. That's up to you."

"Fine, I lied. Are you happy?" I didn't turn around from the sink. I couldn't look at her right then. "There have been three others. One before the wedding, two after. They didn't mean anything. Why does it keep bleeding?"

"Telling the truth doesn't heal the lie. Now tell me that you love me."

I had to turn around now. Just to see if it really was Sarah who was doing this to me, or whether some unknown specter had replaced her. It was her all right. I wanted to yell in her face for what she was doing to me and steal her triumph. It wasn't triumph that I saw though.

Her face was twisted into the pit of despair. All the wind left my lungs in an instant, and we just stared at each other for a long time. Me clutching my throbbing arm, her not pretending to hide her tears anymore.

"I'm sorry. I want to, but I don't love you."

She wasn't looking at my face when I said it. She pulled the towel away from my arm, and we stared at the wound together. It was deep, all the way to the bone and still bubbling with fresh blood. It wasn't growing anymore though. I wasn't lying this time.

"It's okay," she said. "Thank you for being honest. After all this, I don't think I love you either."

My wound hurt like hell, but it was nothing like watching the bloody cut appear just above her eye. She must have felt it. I don't know what she was trying to prove when she kept talking.

"I never loved you. It was just my family—always worried about me, always pressuring me to find someone. I would have been happier alone, trust me." The wound was growing by the second. Down her face, her neck, blood dying her black shirt even darker.

"Sarah please. You don't have to do this."

"How could I love you? You're disgusting. You're an animal. I never want to see you again." The words were coming slower. She was coercing them out, grunting through the pain. I pressed my hand over her mouth, but she grabbed my arm right where the wound was and I had to let go.

"I wasn't happy with you. I didn't want to grow old with you. I'm honestly relieved!" She was running from me. I couldn't stop her from talking. I was weak and dizzy from my own wound, and I kept sliding on the bloody trail which followed her wherever she went. "I never want to see you again!" That one caused her body to surge as though struck by lightning. Her fingers helplessly knotted the empty air while her spine arched so far back that she was looking at the ceiling.

"Stop doing this to her!" I shouted as loudly as I could. "Whoever made this deal, that's enough! It's over! Stop hurting her!"

It wasn't exactly a voice that answered. More like a dormant instinct which has existed my whole life, but only now reared to life.

*I'm not the one hurting her,* it said. *You are.*

So I left. I stopped chasing her. Stopped trying to fix her. Stopped pitying her. I just grabbed my keys and left. I didn't speak to her over the next few weeks. Her family told me when she wasn't around, giving me the chance to clear out all my stuff without bumping into her. I asked them how she was doing, but never got an answer more clear than "she'll survive".

The wound on my arm? It healed a long time ago. Not all at once, but every day the scab was a little thicker until it fell off, and then every day the scar was a little lighter until it was barely visible. I don't know if it'll be there for the rest of my life, but I don't think about it when I'm falling asleep anymore. I'm just back to dreaming of the girl I love who doesn't exist, wondering if she'll notice the scar when we finally meet.

## Raised By The Man Who Kidnapped Me

The people I live with aren't my parents. They aren't even related to my parents, as far as I can tell. They're just people—cold, ruthless, angry people who wanted to have a daughter of their own and didn't care whose lives they destroyed to get one.

I've always known there was something strange about them. Martha ("Mom") looks nothing like me. She thinks nothing like me. She's always blithering about her precious china plates, or sorting her collections of pristine dresses and shoes that no one's allowed to wear. Tyler ("Dad") is an auto mechanic who smells like gasoline all the time, always mumbling and looking away as though he's ashamed to be alive. I don't know what I'm supposed to do or who I'm supposed to be when I grow up, but I've lived with them long enough to know what I don't want.

They treat me like a possession. I speak when I'm spoken to. I wear what I'm told to wear, go where I'm told to go, and even at fifteen, I'm never, ever allowed to go out alone.

And you know what really makes me sick? The fact that I'd looked past all of their manipulative, controlling habits for my whole life. It didn't matter that I wasn't allowed to go play with friends. "Dad" wanted to keep me safe, and he knew best. It didn't matter that "Mom" forced me to spend countless hours sitting on the floor to sew lace into her clothes. It was all I've ever known, and I trusted them. But not anymore.

I found out when I stumbled across a personal ad in the local paper. I don't read the news, but I'd picked up a big stack for a school paper-mache project and there it was on top:

Missing: Fifteen year old girl. Birth date: 06/04/02. Brown hair, green eyes. *We haven't given up. We will never forget.* Last seen: Twelve years ago, abducted from Bakersfield Park. Pink bow in her hair.

Below that, two pictures. One of a baby girl, about three years old. Another one that looked like a computer-generated prediction of what she would like now. The hair was all wrong, but other than that it felt like looking into a mirror.

My birthday. My description. *My picture!* I couldn't breathe. I'd never gotten along with the people I lived with, but I'd tolerated them this long because I thought underneath all their self-absorption they were my family. I was *supposed* to love them. Imagining them snatching me out of a park—imagining the countless nights my real parents must have searched and prayed and cried—it made my blood boil.

I started flipping through the stack of papers. There the ad was again another month back. And another month before that. Always the same words: *We will never forget.*

"Are you making a mess in there?" It was Martha. Her beady little eyes tracking me from the living room, judging every move I made. I did my best to keep my trembling hands from betraying what I found as I neatly stacked the newspapers once more.

"Do you have any baby pictures I could look at?" I asked innocently.

Martha's face crinkled with distaste. "Of course, but I don't want you looking. You never put anything away properly."

"I mean when I was really small. Like two years old." I scrutinized her face for any sign of discomfort, but it was difficult to read when she was always scowling like that.

"I shouldn't think so," Martha huffed, turning back to her magazine. "There was that flood when you were—oh but you'd be too young to remember."

It was all I needed to know. I went back to my room and dialed the phone number in the ad. I was actually in tears when the voice crackled through the other line.

"Mom?" I whispered as loudly as I dared. "Mom are you there?"

We didn't call the police. We figured that anyone who could live their entire lives as a lie were capable of anything. Instead we were just going to do it as quietly as possible.

I put my favorite clothes in a backpack and hid it under my bed. I let Tyler tuck me in, somehow resisting the urge to spit in his face when he leaned in to kiss me goodnight. I let Martha watch me from the crack in the door, pale orbs glowing where they reflected the moonlight. I pretended to be asleep, my whole body flushed and throbbing in anticipation.

Finally the coast was clear. I grabbed my backpack and snuck out in my pajamas, not wanting to spend a second longer in that house than I had to. There was a car waiting for me at the end of the block. For the first time I could remember, I was going back to my real home.

A woman got out of the passenger side and waved to me. Not just any woman—it was my mom. I knew it before I even saw her. I was running without realizing it, and she was running too. We didn't slow down until we collided, hugging and crying, utterly abandoned by words. She smelled like warm cinnamon. Then a man got out of the driver's side, but before I could approach him the deck lights behind me turned on.

"Tyler! She's running away! I told you something was wrong!"

I flew into the car and didn't look back. My parents—my real parents—were roaring up the road, and I was giggling like a maniac the whole way.

"We never stopped believing," my father was saying from the front. "That's not to say that it didn't get hard sometimes, but—"

"The other children are going to be so happy too!" Mom squealed with adrenaline.

"I have brothers and sisters?" I couldn't stop smiling. Two complete strangers, and already they seemed closer to me than my old "family" ever was.

"Something like that." My parents exchanged a knowing look. "And they can't wait to meet you."

Barred windows. A padlock on the front door. Concrete floors. I don't know what I was expecting home to be, but this wasn't it. A dozen frightened faces lifted to greet us when the door opened.

"Run!" A little girl screeched, about twelve years old. She jumped up as soon as she heard us, but I was so bewildered that I didn't make the slightest move.

I was shoved hard from behind and fell to my knees. The door slammed shut behind me. My parents were on the outside, and I could hear the padlock snap back into place.

"I'm sorry," the little girl said. "I'm so sorry."

"Mom? Dad?" It wasn't that I refused to believe what was going on. I was incapable of believing. I had built this fantasy up in my head so long that, for the moment at least, it was still stronger than whatever reality tried to break through.

"We will never forget." It was my mother, but the voice was wrong. I couldn't see her on the other side of the door, but I knew that sound could only come through a snarl. "And neither will you."

"Forget what? Mom? Dad? What's going on?"

I felt a small hand in mine, and I jumped. Everything was moving so fast. I let the girl guide me back to the far side where the others were sitting. The walls were decorated with newspaper clippings. Personal ads—hundreds of them. All for missing children, all promising that they'd never forget.

"That's mine over there," the little girl pointed at her picture in one of the ads.

"Stop talking to her," an older girl said through a sour face. "You'll be punished for it." I scanned the other children. All teenagers, I think. All girls. Some of them looked like people I might bump into the street, but others were stranger. Their skin was drawn tight and riddled with bruises and sores. Their eyes were hollow, and I got the impression that they didn't see me even when they were pointed in my direction.

"I don't care," the younger girl insisted. She steered me up against the wall and sat cross-legged in front of me. I could barely see her face through the matted hair. "They hate girls. That's why we're here."

"That's not the reason." The older girl sighed. "It's because they're crazy. There doesn't need to be any other reason."

"They lost their own daughter," the younger continued. "She was a hooker or something, and she got killed. I don't know the details, but I guess they started collecting girls after that. Every once in a while a foreign man—"

"He's from Russia," one of the others interjected.

"Foreign man comes and chooses some of us. Then they go with him."

"What happens to the ones who aren't chosen?" I asked, but looking around I already knew the answer.

"Don't worry about it. You're a pretty one. They'll pick you for sure," the older girl said. I don't know why she thought that—I could barely even see her face in the gloom.

"Here." The little girl handed me a notepad and a pen. "You can have this if you want."

"What am I supposed to write?"

She shrugged. "Anything you want. At least then there will be something left when you're gone."

The first thing I wrote was: *I love you, Mom. I love you, Dad.*

The second thing I wrote, you're reading now.

## My Son Said Goodbye

My four-year-old son and I have a night-time ritual. Step one: turn off his cartoons and pray he won't wail loud enough for the neighbors to think I'm torturing him. Step two: sedate the wild beasty with the Goodnight Moon story. He'll be crawling all over the bed at the beginning, but I just keep reading slower and softer while I wait for him to wind down. Then with barely a whisper, I'll say:

"Goodnight Mikey."

"Goodnight Mommy," he'll always say back. The peace that comes afterward, it somehow completes the long day of commuting and work. It heals all the pacifying of clients, and writing reports, and running errands, and cooking and cleaning, and everything else that makes Atlas' job look easy. And listening to my boy's deep breathing, everything in the world will be right again, and I'll know I'd do it a million times over just for the sacred simplicity of the precious little time I have with him.

That's how I thought it would go on forever, until a few nights ago when I whispered goodnight, and he replied: "Goodbye Mommy."

"You're supposed to say goodnight, silly," I said. "Goodbye means leaving, and I'm not going anywhere."

"I know," he said. "I'll miss you, Mommy. Goodbye."

He was asleep before I could respond again. I thought it was cute at the time. I didn't think for a second about waking him up and going through the whole process of settling down again. There was something about how deliberately he said it though that left me feeling unsettled. Just to be safe, I walked around the room and made sure his window was locked. I left the door open a crack like I always do to check in on him, kissed him one last time, and then left.

I didn't hear a peep all night, but I still couldn't get any sleep. I kept getting this chill and waking up in a cold sweat. What if he said goodbye because someone said they'd take him away? Mikey's father didn't live with us (long story), but he'd never even showed interest in his son before. It wasn't a rational fear that made me keep walking by his room at night. Once at 11 p.m., tucking his errant legs back under the covers. Again at 2 a.m., putting his stuffed dragon back under his arm. I finally got a few hours of fitful sleep, until 7 a.m. rolled around way too fast when it was time to get him ready for pre-school, and—

He was gone. My bleary eyes became lasers. The stuffed dragon was still there. He'd never go anywhere (not even the bathroom) without it. Windows, doors, all locked from the inside. Closets, cabinets, pantries, I was on a rampage, tearing the place apart like I was a pillaging army. Screaming his name until I was hoarse, pounding on my neighbors' doors, and then finally calling the police.

I was in tears by the time the officer came by to ask me a few questions. No, I don't know where he could have gone. No, I don't know why anyone would take him. No, no, no, until finally I mentioned that he said goodbye last night.

"Sounds like he ran away then, ma'am. I'll get this back to the station. In the meantime, take a drive around all his favorite parks, playgrounds, whatever is nearby."

The whole day was hell, and the next morning was worse. I don't know if those haunted stretches of misplaced time can be considered sleep, but the first thing I did when I woke up was look in his room again. The vain hope that this had all been a nightmare flickered when I saw what was on his bed.

A crude, crayon drawing of a little blue blob (the color of his pajamas), riding something that looked like his stuffed dragon. Shaky block letters underneath said:

WE PLAYIN

The stuffed dragon was gone. It didn't mean anything though. I'd been

## Sleepless Nights

tearing the room apart looking for him, and it would have been very easy for me to knock one of his drawings onto the bed. I'd probably taken the dragon when I was looking for him without even noticing. All the drawing did was send me into a fresh spiral of despair. The police hadn't turned up anything, and it wasn't until the next morning when I got my next clue.

Another drawing was left on his bed. There was a taller figure here, and I assume it was supposed to be me because underneath it said:

**WHER MOMMY?**

That was the longest day of my life. I patrolled the house a dozen times, even crawling through the heating ducts to see if he was still in the house somewhere. I picked up a security camera to watch his room so I could catch whoever was leaving the drawings. After that it was just a matter of waiting to see if tomorrow brought anything new. I'd intended on staying up all night to watch his room, but I'd run myself so ragged that I couldn't fend off a few hours of welcomed oblivion.

The cam footage was the first thing I thought about. It was Mikey. Walking into his bedroom in the same pajamas I'd seen him in last. The stuffed dragon was clutched under one of his little arms. He didn't face the camera mounted above the door, he just went straight to his crayons in the corner and began drawing. I sat there mesmerized while he drew—ten minutes at least before he got up and put the drawing on the bed. He broke the blue crayon while he colored, and sure enough the blue crayon was still broken on the floor where he'd left it. When he was finished, he finally faced the camera.

The boy wasn't Mikey. That thing that looked at the camera. The thing wearing his pajamas and sitting in his bed, it didn't have a face. Just smooth skin with slight contours where the facial features should be, like latex pulled suffocatingly tight across the face. There wasn't a mouth, but I could still tell he was smiling from how the muscles pulled back when he looked at the camera.

**I NO U WACHIN. I WACHIN U 2.**

That's what the paper said, right next to a crude drawing of an eyeball. I'm insane, I decided. The stress, the worry, the sleepless nights. It's driven me insane. I didn't know who to show the video to. I didn't even know if they'd see the same thing I saw, or whether it was all in my head. I just lost it. I don't know how long I spent in that room—sitting and rocking in the corner, hands clutching my knees to my chest—but before I knew it, it was dark again.

I was so, so tired. I hadn't been to work in days. I didn't even know if I still had a job. I couldn't help but think that if I'd taken more time off to spend with Mikey, I could have deciphered his warning sooner and prevented all this. Or that if he really did run away, then it was my fault and I was living in a nightmare of my own creation.

I guess I just fell asleep where I sat in the corner of his room. It was still dark when I woke up, but I was still so tired that I didn't open my eyes. I just sat there listening to a soft scratching for a long time before I was finally alert enough to realize what it was.

Crayon on paper. Mikey. I was awake in an instant and holding in my scream took more willpower than I knew I had.

The little boy was sitting on his bed, his back toward from me. Scratch, scratch, scratching away with the crayons. Humming something, the gentle melodic rise and fall of the sing-song voice I used when reading Goodnight Moon. I stood up as quietly as I could, but he must have heard me because he put his crayon down.

"Mikey?" I whispered, still terrified that I had gone completely insane.

The boy climbed down from the bed, his back still facing me.

"Where did you go, Mikey? Why did you say goodbye to Mommy?"

"Mommy is too busy. Mommy doesn't care."

It was his voice! His soft, pure little voice. And he was talking, so he had a mouth! I was in tears as I rushed toward him, but he didn't react even when I hugged him to me.

"Mommy does care! I'm so glad you're back, Mikey. You have *no idea* how much I've missed—"

I didn't see it until I was already holding him. Now, his lack of a face was all I could see.

"I do know. I told you I've been watching you too." It wasn't a mouth he was speaking from. Not exactly. The slit started at the top of his neck and ran vertically to where his nose should have been. It opened and closed with the motions a mouth might make, but it was a gaping wound that he was speaking out of. Each time it closed, a sucking gurgle reverberated from it.

I let go, but he didn't. He was latched around my hand, dragging me into the wound which closed around my fingers. I didn't realize how fragile that little body was until I pulled free and the wound tore wider, all the way up his face. He didn't stop though—leaping at me, climbing me, grabbing my other hand to shove it deep into the wound. I tore free, this time ripping him all the way down to his stomach before I could get him off me.

He was insatiable. I had to throw him against the wall before I was able to escape. I slammed the door behind me and put my back against it, alternating between heaving sobs and tense breathless pauses while I listened inside. "Goodbye Mommy," was all I heard.

I held the door shut while I called the police, although I didn't feel any pressure or hint of presence from the other side. It took them ten minutes to arrive, and by the time I opened the door to Mikey's room again, the boy was gone.

The security footage! I ran to my computer in the other room and pulled it up while they waited: patient, polite, and utterly unconvinced. I clicked on empty file after empty file, everything black and inscrutable from tonight. Next I looked for last night's footage, but it was completely gone.

I didn't go back into Mikey's room until after the police had gone, and even then I crept like I was a thief in my own house. That's when I noticed the blue crayon smeared all over the lens of the camera. There wasn't any sign of him left. Not even the blood from that source-less, flapping wound.

What I did find though? A fresh drawing, childlike and innocent despite all the red. It looked like me again, but there was a big Pac-man like thing that was about to eat me up. Underneath it said:

FUN MOMMY. PLAY AGAN TOMORROW NITE.

I hate thinking about how many chances I've had to play, all wasted because I was too busy or too tired or too distracted by everything that didn't matter in life. I miss him so much, I think I'm even looking forward to tonight.

Even if he isn't the same as I remember. Even if I have to blindfold myself so I don't have to look at what he's become, I'm going to sit down and draw with him. And maybe, if I'm very lucky, then he's going to understand how hard I'm trying, and he's going to still be there when the morning comes.

## Our Extra Son Was for Experiments

Imagine being lost in the open ocean, frantically bailing water out of a sinking raft which refills exactly as fast you empty it. You will never be found, never be saved. Sooner or later you'll need to rest and cease your constant vigilance, but you're still fighting the waves for as long as you can. However hopeless, the terror of that dark water is more real than everything else in your dying world. That's what being a mother was like to me.

I used to think the worst thing in life was not getting what you want. For me, that was starting a family, something I obsessed over since I was a little girl trying to make sure all my dolls successfully graduated and had families of their own. I fell for every boy who looked at me—always too fast, always the wrong one, wasting so much time imagining weddings and baby showers and these elaborate happy lives that were never lived outside of my head. Then all at once in nursing school I met a handsome neurologist, and within six months I was pregnant.

I finally had what I'd always dreamed about, but the worst thing in life isn't *not getting what you want*. The worst thing is getting it, and then realizing how much happier you were before. My first son Prater was diagnosed with Spinal Muscular Atrophy (SMA), an incurable genetic disease which left him barely able to move. Every day was an ordeal. Every hour, every minute, constant paranoia that his feeble lungs would give up, or that he would choke on his vomit and be too weak to struggle free. I had to drop out of nursing school, but my husband Jeffery took good care of me, leaving me to take care of the child.

My husband switched focus with his work, moving into research designed to strengthen motor neurons and protect them from SMA. It was an impossible dream though. There were a range of potential treatments, but they were years away from even reaching human trials. I begged Jeffery to sneak some experimental medication home anyway, but Prater was so weak that the injections would doubtlessly kill him long before the correct treatment and dosage was discerned.

It wasn't my decision to have another child. I didn't think I could bear going through something like this again, but Jeffery insisted. This can't be the end of your dream, he told me. This can't be the rest of our life. It wasn't until after I was pregnant again that he let his ulterior motive slip. It was the middle of the night, and I'd just gotten back in bed after checking on Prater. I don't think Jeffery was even fully awake, but my husband nestled in close to me and whispered:

"When the new kid is born, he'll be healthy enough to test the treatments on. We'll find something that works, and everything will be okay."

I didn't sleep for the rest of the night. I don't know whether it was fear or excitement, but I was so desperate that the two were beginning to taste the same.

When my second healthy baby boy was born, I didn't give him a name. I just wrote "X" on the form. Jeffery said it would be easier that way. By the time he'd exhausted the full litany of possible treatments, the new boy would likely be dead. I'd carried him for nine months, suffered for nine months, and for that sentence I was able to give Prater a whole lifetime of health and happiness. Not a bad trade, not when you're so tired of bailing water from a sinking ship. Even so, I've never cried harder in my life than that first hour when I held X in the hospital.

After that, I couldn't even look at the new baby. I pretended he didn't exist. Jeffery took a sabbatical from work so he could continue his research from home. He waited until X was six months old before he began the experiments, and during that time X lived in a makeshift nursery in the basement. I didn't see him, but I'd still *hear* the crying echo through the house sometimes. Jeffery was diligent and made sure that all the child's needs were met, and I occupied all of my time looking after Prater (who was almost two by then).

Science—it's not that "Eureka!" moment you see on TV. It's not a sprint, it's a marathon. There was still so much that we didn't know about the disease, and even with ideal conditions and a proper experimental and control groups, it would have taken years. With a basement laboratory and a single experimental subject, and then later with Jeffery having to return to work part time…

It took a decade before we began to see really promising results. All that time, I didn't see X once. Sometimes I was convinced that he'd died years ago, and that Jeffery was just putting on a show of bringing food down to the basement to give me hope. All I saw was Prater, every day a little weaker, a continual mockery of what it should mean to have a childhood and a family.

When at last we were ready to give the final drug to Prater, I wasn't prepared for the troubling question which accompanied that step.

"If Prater gets better, and everything we ever wanted comes true, what are we going to do with X?" Jeffery asked one morning at the breakfast table.

It was unusually direct. Jeffery would always allude to his experiments without directly mentioning the test subject. Even when it was unavoidable, he understood that I wasn't comfortable acknowledging the boy. I tried to change the subject, but he was insistent this time.

"We can't just let him out. You understand that, right? It's too late for him to lead a normal, functional life. Even if he could psychologically acclimate one day, the years of trials have..."

"Do whatever you think is best," I cut him off.

"Are you telling me to—"

"I'm not telling you anything. I just want you to do *whatever* is necessary."

He nodded glumly, looking down at his coffee. The icy tension mounted as we listened to Prater cackling at his cartoons in the other room.

"He looks like me," Jeffery said, not looking up from his coffee. It took me a second to realize he wasn't talking about Prater.

"Why would you even tell me that?"

"He calls me dad," Jeffery added. He was finally looking, but I was the one who couldn't meet his gaze.

"You shouldn't have taught it to talk," was all I could say. "That's even wors**e** than giving it a name**.**"

The experiment was otherwise a success. Within a week of Prater's first injection, his voluntary movements were becoming smooth and controlled. By the end of the first month he was able to walk on his own. Listening to his breathing become steady, seeing his radiant smile as he took his first steps, the squeals of his excitement when I drove him by the school he would enroll in next semester — it was sublime, almost surreal in its fantastic impossibility. When we got back home Prater was so full of vitality that he even outpaced me from the car to the house. Entering first, he turned around to ask:

"Why is this door open? It's never open." I stopped cold on the doorstep.

"Is there anything... *anyone* else there?"

"Nope. What's down here?"

A flight of empty steps going down. The lights were off. The room empty.

"Mom, why is there a bedroom under the house?"

I closed the door to the basement. The padlock was gone.

"It's just a guest room. There's no one visiting though, so we don't use it. Do you know where Dad is?"

"Can I go see? I want to see the other room!" Prater insisted. I was never any good at saying no to him. That must be why he looked so surprised when I shouted:

"Get out of here! Go find your dad, right now!"

Jeffery didn't come home that night. Calls went straight to voice-mail. Three options continued to surface in my mind. 1: Jeffery is bringing X to live somewhere else. 2: Jeffery is taking X somewhere to kill him.

Neither of those explained why he would leave the door open.

Option 3: X has escaped, and something has happened to my husband. I strained to remember all the vague mentions of X that I'd intentionally blocked out at the time. Something had happened to him during the trials. Something besides the psychological effect, that's what Jeffery had said. What exactly had he endured down there? The thought had crossed my mind innumerable times before, but it had been so repressed that I'd never taken the time to really think about it. What would life be for someone like that? Alone except for those few hours a day that Jeffery spent experimenting on him. The chemicals he must have ingested. The lies he must have been fed to justify his pitiful existence. What would someone like that do if their world was ripped away overnight?

I didn't let Prater leave my sight. I sat in a chair in his room, reading him stories until he fell asleep, and then just sitting and watching him. Maybe I should have gone to a motel or something, but he was so worn down from his outings that day and the medication was still so new that I didn't want to push him. Instead, I just sat and waited. I didn't know what I was waiting for, but I'd know it when I saw it.

Or heard it, as it turned out.

"Mom?"

I must have fallen asleep in the chair sometime during the night.

"Yes Prater?" I mumbled, not quite awake.

"No, not Prater." My eyes flew open. It was dark, but I could still make out the outline of Prater sleeping in his bed. Someone else... *something else* was standing in the room. I couldn't see anything but the silhouette, but the shape was unrecognizable. Gnarled, bulbous, utterly grotesque, cut into the night like the darkness itself had reared to life. All I could really see were the eyes, great pools of white without iris or cornea.

"Jeffery? Jeffery!" I shouted.

I couldn't even stand. Not with it so close, peering down at me like some sort of specimen.

"Dad doesn't know I came back," X said. "I wanted some time alone with you. You are my mom, aren't you?" The words slurred into each other, but the hot whisper was so close I seemed to feel their meaning more than hear it.

"No, she's not. She's my mom!" Prater was awake now too, sitting up and clutching his blankets to his chin.

I managed to turn my phone's flashlight on, regretting it immediately. X's face was devastated with ruptured boils and deep-pitted lines. His features sloped jaggedly toward the left as though he'd suffered multiple strokes, his pale eyes twisting in agony at the sudden light. In his hand he held a syringe filled with a thick, black syrup. It wasn't Prater's medicine.

"Turn it off, turn it off!" X shrieked, blindly swiping the syringe through the air. I jumped out of the chair which toppled over, brandishing my light like a weapon.

"Prater follow me!" I shouted. My son began to clamber out of bed, but he was still too weak. He was shaking so badly that he fell onto the floor in a crumpled heap.

"The light burns! Turn it off, Mom!"

*Mom.* That word was a dagger. I kept the light on X's face while I made my way around the edge of the room to where Prater fell. I fumbled the phone while trying to lift him off the ground. The light veered away from X's face. I could feel him charging toward me through the sudden dark, but I had Prater around my shoulders now.

I was running, flinging myself down the familiar halls of my house whose shadows had twisted into an alien nightmare. I could hear X limping and lurching behind me, pursuing with incredible haste despite his disfigurement. The basement—it was the only safe place I could think of. I leapt headfirst toward the stairwell, grabbing the door and slamming it behind me. I put my back against the smooth metal, feeling it vibrate as X slammed into the door again and again from the other side.

The force of the impacts—it was like trying to stop a car. My bones were rattling against each other in harmony with the blows. Human tissue should pulverize under an impact like that, if X even was human anymore.

"Honey? Are you in there?" It was Jeffery. Somewhere above.

"Help us! We're in the basement! X is trying to kill us!"

Shouting. Running. A high-pitched scream, so pitiful and desperate that it still felt like my whole body was vibrating, even while the door stood still. Then a gunshot, and everything went quiet.

I opened the door to see Jeffery clutching a gun in both hands. X was kneeling on the ground before him, those pale eyes lancing through my body. Now that they were side-by-side, even the savage snarl further torturing the boy's face couldn't disguise how closely X resembled his father.

The boy was already fading into the shadows, vanishing almost immediately except for the white orbs which lingered in accusation. I held my breath, waiting for Jeffery to take the kill shot. It never came. X was gone.

I was still holding my breath when Jeffery came down the stairs and hugged me, then hugged Prater. I shook so badly that I couldn't even form words, but Jeffery did the talking for me.

"I'm so sorry, honey. I never would have let him out if I thought…"

But the words were all rushing together, and I couldn't make sense of them anymore. Especially when Jeffery flipped on the light-switch and I saw the basement for the first time.

The laboratory section was much smaller than I expected. It was just a computer and a locked glass case full of chemicals. The rest of the space looked like you'd expect a boy's room to be. There were toys all over the floor and a TV in the corner. There were cartoon posters on the wall, a shelf full of books, and even a nightstand with a framed picture on it.

I was in the picture, holding X for the first and last time in the hospital room. Next to it was a stack of drawings, all of me, all so young and beautiful, depicting me as so much better than I really was.

"I just don't understand why he would try to hurt you. He talked about you all the time," Jeffery said. "He always wanted to meet you, but I guess he was just too far gone."

"The syringe … "

Jeffery's face grew tighter. "Let's all go back upstairs. Prater shouldn't see this."

"I need to know. What was in the syringe?" But the look he gave me told me everything I needed to know. X was still trying to help, even after all this time. And the look Prater gave me, I think he understood that too. Now that the secret is out, I don't think he'll ever be able to love me like he used to.

Not like X loved me anyway. My husband and I have created a monster and set it loose upon the world, but it isn't X. We're the only monsters here.

## The Storm Is Alive

It's hard to type. My fingers are stiff and numb from the cold. My eyes are watering, and I can feel the tears freezing on my skin. I don't know how much longer my power is going to last this time, but I don't think we will survive another blackout. When they find our bodies—maybe not until spring when this cabin can even be seen over the snow—they'll know it was the storm that killed us. If I didn't write this though, they'd never know it was a murder.

The storm has been brewing for a month before it hit. Rolling gray clouds teasing us with snow for Christmas, yet always holding back despite the continual predictions. The weather channel said it was a 100% chance of snow every day for a week before the iron sky finally relinquished its payload. When it did come, it didn't waste any time with slush or dustings either. One night it was bleak and cold and bare, and the next morning I couldn't even see out from my first-story window.

My whole college canceled classes for the day—first snow day I've gotten since grade-school. I was planning to just sit around playing video games, but my little sister Clara looked so horrified that I might as well have said I was going to spend the day looking for stray cats to cook.

Snow was a miracle, where was my Christmas spirit, we couldn't waste time indoors, yada yada. I don't know exactly how the conversation got away from me, but pretty soon I had the ultimatum of either going sledding with her friends or admitting I was the literal Grinch. Guess I'm spending my day with a bunch of high-school girls, whatever. At least I'll be the cool, mysterious, older guy for a change instead of the blundering freshman.

I don't know how many of you have witnessed this, but something very strange happens when a group of high-school girls get together. They're all super affectionate with each other, but it's kind of a vicious, competitive affection. Imagine four puppies who are all trying to be as cute and friendly as possible, but they know that only one of them is going to get adopted and they'll happily tear the others to shreds if it means winning. Don't get the wrong idea, they completely ignored me. I don't even know who they were trying to impress, but it didn't take long before they started daring each other to do ridiculous, potentially life-threatening things.

"This time we're going to steer through those trees," Farris said, flashing all of her sharp little teeth. "Hit one and you're out. First one to make it through wins."

"On this hill? I used to do that when I was four," Clara interjected. Nevermind that I happen to know she cried every time she touched snow until she was almost eight. "Let's try it from up on the cliff, follow me."

And then it clicked. The real reason I was here. They took turns riding in the sleds while I dragged them behind me, the others walking a little back so they could step in my foot-prints and not have to push through the snow. I wasn't a bitch about it or anything, but I guess I was getting pretty grumpy. By the time we'd reached the top of the hill I was ready to just dump them all into the nearest snowdrift and head home.

I was looking for an excuse the whole way, and when the snow stated falling again, I thought I'd found my ticket out. I warned them about how fast it came down last night. They didn't want to be stuck in a blizzard, did they? Of course they did. It was my mistake for making it sound like a challenge. They all looked like they were having fun though, and they assured me they would turn back if it got too bad. Good enough for me, I didn't waste any time trudging back alone.

The snow was falling in thick white crystals, catching the light like thousands of prisms to scatter in radiant waves. I've lived in the mountains my whole life, but I've never seen anything like this before. Some snowflakes were as big as my thumb, and I could actually make out the unique and intricate geometrical pattern that each was composed of. I stood there to admire it while the wind stirred thick flurries to dance through the air in a preternatural frenzy. The footprints we made on the way were almost completely filled in already, and I quickened my pace to beat the oncoming storm.

It was getting too dark. Too fast. Rainbow reflections were vanishing across the new snow, replaced by dark shadows and a malevolent, ghastly gray like putrid water. It took less than ten minutes for it to go from noon to midnight. Clouds were streaming in from every direction, distorting and writhing together into an impenetrably dense wall. It almost seemed like they were getting closer too, the ceiling of the world dropping over me in a suffocating wave like a blanket being pulled tight around my head.

I'm not a hero for turning back for the girls. I wish I was, but honestly they were still a lot closer than the house, and I was afraid to be out here alone. The wind was picking up, a gentle moan rising into a savage howl that bit through my jacket and stung my skin like incessant wasps. At least it was behind me so it helped push me in the right direction, but it didn't feel like a lucky coincidence. It felt more like the storm was trying to drag me deeper in. This unsettling sensation was compounded when flurries of snow stirred into the air like a beckoning finger, appearing so briefly that I couldn't convince myself whether I'd even seen it all.

I wasn't sure I was even going the right way until I heard them calling. Their thin voices were immediately devoured by the screaming wind. I couldn't be sure what they were saying, but at least I knew where I was going now. The wind altered as soon as I heard them, whistling into a higher pitch to mimic their cries. It felt like there were hundreds of girls in all directions, all crying and shouting, all the voices mingling and morphing into one mighty omnipresent wail.

We slammed into each other all at once. We were running, and visibility was down to a few feet. It took a moment for us to scramble back up—all of us except Clara who wasn't there. The other girls just pointed back the way they'd come.

"It was just a dare," one of them said. "We didn't think she'd really do it."

They didn't wait to explain, didn't look back, just ran blindly down the hill in a desperate scramble toward civilization.

The pitch of the wind was beginning to change again. No longer imitating the shouting girls, it felt more like an unearthly song that swelled and pummeled me from all sides. The pressure continued to push me from behind, propelling me to stagger the last few feet to the top of the hill.

Clara was standing there, her back toward me as she faced the oncoming storm. Her clothes—jacket, shirt, pants, boots, all of it—had been removed and piled beside her. Her skin had long since faded from the bright-red chill into the blistering black and purple of frostbite. Her naked arms were outstretched as though welcoming the deadly embrace of the storm, and with her head thrown back I could now tell that she was the one whose song mixed with the tempest's roar.

She turned her head to watch me, her blistering skin cracking as it moved, a wicked smile playing across her black lips. Besides that, she made no effort to either help or resist as I struggled to dress her again. She stopped singing to simply stare at me as though the whole process was infinitely amusing to her. I kept screaming at her to do something, but the only answer I received was that from the unrelenting wind.

When Clara was all bundled up again I put her in one of the abandoned sleds and leapt in with her. I tried to keep her warm as we rode downhill, but then I had to get out to drag the sled on the long trek home. I don't think I would have made it if it weren't for the wind again, changing directions without warning to aid my passage out. It wasn't a blessing. The storm had already got what it wanted, and it didn't need us anymore.

I kept checking on Clara every minute to make sure she was still alive, but she seemed to be breathing quite easily despite her deathly pallor. She wasn't singing anymore, but I still heard the echo of those unfamiliar words swirl around me as we went.

We got home a couple of hours ago. The car won't start, and it's completely snowed in anyway. I've piled all the blankets on her and turned the space heaters on, but she hasn't said a word since she got back. She just sits there and stares at me, half of her mouth curled up in that twisted smirk. Once I caught her trying to stand and go outside again, but I stopped her and she hasn't tried since.

I managed to get a local news station for a while, but they all seem as mystified as I am. I left it on while I went to brew some hot tea for Clara when I heard her laughing in the other room. I ran back in to see a flash of purple and black skin being carried off in a stretcher. Clara was absolutely howling with laughter, and within seconds the wind outside was laughing with her.

Three girls were found in the snow by paramedics, the news said. They were completely naked, standing with their arms stretched out toward the oncoming storm. I turned off the TV because I couldn't stand the sound of the laughing, but the silence and the staring which replaced it is just as bad. I have this unshakable feeling that Clara is still out there somewhere, or perhaps I really did bring her home, but somehow brought the storm home with her. I just hope that when it clears, it leaves her as well.

I don't understand how anyone could anyone go on living with a storm trapped inside of them...

## The Head Transplant

*We knew the world would never be the same. A few people laughed, a few people cried, most were silent. I remembered the line from the Hindu scripture, the Bhagavad-Gita; Vishnu is trying to persuade the Prince that he should do his duty and, to impress him, takes on his multi-armed form and says, "Now I am become Death, the destroyer of worlds."*

-Julius Oppenheimer on the first atomic bomb.


THAT QUOTE COMES to mind while watching Sergio Canavero work. When performing surgery, he becomes so mesmerized by the task that myself and his other assistants become indistinguishable from his steel instruments, born and bred for this sole moment when he has need of us. Even the patient isn't a human being anymore: just a puzzle to be deciphered or discarded when the last piece finally breaks.

I thought it was the greatest honor in the world when the neurosurgeon accepted my application to join his team. Despite the international controversy over the ethics of head transplants, I knew that I was going to become part of history. I wasn't embarrassed to tell my family what I was doing either—they were proud of the honor I was doing for China. Our president Xi Jinping is sanctioning this experimental procedure because he is determined to replace the U.S. as the world leader in science, and it was my privilege to perform on that global stage.

Dr. Canavero has explained and rehearsed the procedure with us over the last several months, but this was more rigorous than any of my classes at Peking University. Essentially we will be simultaneously severing the spinal cords of the donor and recipient with a diamond-edged blade. The donor head will be cooled to a state of deep hypothermia to keep the neurological tissue from dying during the transfer. By the end of the twenty-four hour operation we will have reconnected all vertebral bones, nerve-endings, veins, trachea and esophagus—everything. The patient will then be suspended in a drug-induced coma until he has healed enough to move without damaging the connections.

And then? There's going to be a brand new person with a whole new life to live. Those who are languishing in a paralyzed body will be able to walk. Healthy minds trapped by the ravages of age can be restored to youth, and the very notion of mortality, and individuality, and the soul itself will be forever changed.

That's the best case scenario, of course. There is also the chance that the surgery will fail and we'll have sacrificed two people to the altar of our arrogance. More than that though, failure would likely show our best intentions in a macabre light, prejudicing the world against us and our research for decades to come. So many eyes on us—on China—so many judgments and condemnations.

...

The pressure was intense. I could feel it in the air the second I stepped into Dr. Canavero's laboratory each morning. No one smiled, and if they did, it was just a thin bloodless line that died almost before it began. As we approached the operation date, the other two assistants and I were drilled incessantly on every potential obstacle. One second of hesitation during the operation and we'd be ostracized from all official institutions which sought to distance themselves from our failure. Flash cards, pop tests, rehearsals on dummies, endless study—but we were still months away from the official operation when I received a phone call at 1 a.m.

" … you'll be using the back-door tonight." Dr. Canavero didn't even wait for me to say hello. "It will be unlocked. Don't bring any identification, and tell no one where you will be. Officially speaking, nothing that you do or see tonight will have ever happened."

"What's going on? Is this about—" I managed before being cut-off with an impatient hiss.

"Of course it's about the operation. Stop wasting time. We have a long night ahead of us."

The other two assistants were already there when I arrived. I will not use their real names, but instead will call the acclaimed surgeon Dr. Cheung while Dr. Zhao is an elderly woman who leads her research department. Canavero was the center of attention as always though, animated as he was with passionate energy and explosive gesticulations.

"My friends, we are very fortunate, very fortunate indeed," Dr. Canavero was saying. He ushered me in from the door, glancing both ways outside before securing it behind me.

"President Xi Jinping has given us a gracious gift. One that I had long desired, but hadn't yet dared to ask. Come come, not that way."

Dr. Canavero was practically prancing as he turned away from the usual route to our lab. It was almost surreal navigating the abandoned hallways that were typically bustling with life. The naked florescent lights burned with a gentle hum like the eternal pondering of an unseen jury. Cheung answered my questioning look with raised eyebrows of his own as we all turned to follow.

"It's a risk, you know. What he's doing for us. Of course it will be to the glory of China if we succeed, but with an experimental procedure on the frontier between reality and science-fiction? He's gambling with us."

We were in the elevator now. I'd never been to the bottom floor before (you needed a special key to access it) but I'd always been told it was just storage space. Dr. Canavero's feverish excitement while he inserted his key told a different story.

"We are already taking every reasonable precaution to prepare—" Dr. Zhao began to reassure him.

"But the thing about powerful men is," Canavero continued, ignoring her, "is that they don't remain in power by gambling. Not without a loaded die, at least."

The elevator door opened to a long hallway with stairs at the end which continued spiraling downward. The first thing that impressed me was the enormity of the space: it must have been as large as the rest of the facility combined.

"We can't rig an operation." Dr. Cheung snorted. "And even if we could falsify the reports, it won't convince the scientific community for long. It would do nothing but further discredit your—"

"I'm not talking about rigging the operation," Dr. Canavero said, leading us toward the stairs. "I fully intend to live-stream the entire procedure for the whole world to see."

"Then I'm afraid I don't follow—" Dr. Cheung started before being cut off again. Was that the echo of a shout from farther down? In the sudden silence, we all heard it clearly again. Hoarse, strained, utterly hopeless, as though it had been calling on deaf ears for a long, long time. I rushed to the railing with the other two assistants.

"We're not going to rig the operation." I was the first to speak. The words were difficult to form in my mouth. "We're going to rig the preparation. The whole world will think they're watching something that's being done for the very first time…"

It was still a storage space, of sorts, but it would be more accurate to call it a jail. The corridor was lined with cages barely large enough for their human occupant to stand. Below this floor ran another identical corridor with its own set of cages, and even more below that as far down as I can see. Thin hands grasped uselessly at the wire, rattling them in restless excitement and fear. Others continued to lay on the ground, too broken or hopeless to even turn our way.

"While in reality we'll have already successfully completed the operation. Dozens of times." Dr. Canavero joined us to look down. "No play would ever be performed without a rehearsal, after-all. The moment we accepted the research grants from President Xi Jinping, we have all become actors in his employ."

"How many are there?" Dr. Zhao breathed a hot whisper.

"Enough to make it a good show," Dr. Canavero replied.

"Who are they though?" I asked.

"They're not victims, if that's what you're asking," Dr. Canavero said, turning back to the staircase. "At some point in all of our lives, we have a choice: to become someone or to become no one. It is their misfortune that they decided the later, although ultimately it was still their decision to make. I can only hope that my own team," he stopped here, turning back to level his gaze on us, "that my own team has the foresight to recognize when they are making such a choice, and to do so more wisely."

The implications were clear. Report the incident, and it would be more likely that I ended up in one of those cages than it was for any of them to go free. Science is concerned with the truth, after all. Not with how we got there. I took the first step toward the stairs, but a hand caught me by the arm.

"Some are likely to survive though, aren't they?" Dr. Zhao's face was pleading for something that I couldn't give her. I tried to force a smile, for her sake.

"Of course. That's the whole point, isn't it? We're just learning how to switch the heads." I knew it wasn't true even while saying it. Even the survivors would be buried with this secret, I had no doubt. That's when it occurred to me that my fate was likely inevitable for the same reason. Why would the CCP ever risk these methods getting out?

That's why I'm writing this now though. Just in case something does happen. The first operation is about to begin, but I can't help but feel I'm the one about to go under the knife. Is it wrong that part of me is excited too? My family will be so proud when this is over. I'll be a hero, and don't all heroes walk on the bodies of those they couldn't save?

## Midnight Prayers

Years ago when I was in jail, I used to pray every night. When you're little and you pray, it's because you want something from the world that you don't know how to get. When you're older, it's because the world wants something from you that you don't know how to give. The lights would go out at 11 p.m. and I would pray to be a better man, humiliating myself before the arbitrating silence of my thoughts, begging and pleading and even screaming when the thoughts became too loud to contain.

Then one night an unscheduled cell search interrupted my routine. The inmates all had to wait against the wall while our block was cleared, and it wasn't until midnight when I was able to begin my prayers. All those years my mother used to drag me to church, she never once told me that God isn't the one who listens to the midnight prayers.

I begin as I always do. I kneel on my bed, close my eyes, and with my hands clasped together, I'll ask: "Is anyone listening?"

This was the first night that someone answered: "Yes."

I didn't dare open my eyes, terrified that the reality of my cell would be all I saw. The voice was soft, patient, and infinitely sad as though it had seen and heard more than its heart could bear, yet had such respect for the suffering that it stoically refused to turn away.

"I'm afraid," I said, because I knew at once that I could not lie to such a voice. "I'm afraid that I'm going to die in here. That the world has decided who I am because of one mistake, and that there's nothing I can ever do to convince them otherwise."

"You are right to be afraid," the voice said. "You will die in this cell."

My whole body went tense. For a moment I thought I was talking to a guard who was trying to screw with me, but the calm certainty of the voice was enough for me to keep my eyes closed and believe. If I couldn't have faith here and now, what hope did I ever have?

"But that doesn't mean that this is the end. Your body has been branded and discarded," the voice continued. "Do not waste any more time trying to save what is already lost."

"My soul then—"

"Your soul is hungry to keep living, and this is how you must feed it: Find and kill a human, then take your own life. When these eyes close for the last time, the eyes of your victim will open, and you will be the one looking out."

The strain to look at my savior was excruciating, but some instinctual terror forbade me. Either I would look upon some unspeakable abomination and be forced to abandon my hope of a new life, or I'd see some impostor and know it to be a lie.

"And if I don't like who I've become, I can kill again?" I barely breathed the words. "Will I become a new person each time?"

"As many times as you like," purred the presence. "When you're old and tired, taking a child will let dance this mad show again."

My mind was racing, immediately disgusted but enthralled by the idea. "And if I die by chance—if I'm hit by a car or something—and I haven't killed anyone yet, where will I go then?"

"That will be up to me to decide." The voice was smiling now. I don't know how I knew, but I *knew*.

I couldn't take it anymore. If this was some sick joke, then I wanted to know before I betrayed anything more. I opened my eyes and flung myself in a rabid dash against my cell door. There was no one on the other side. No one in the corridor which stretched open before me. The voice did not speak to me again.

I have prayed to be a good man, and this is how my prayers were answered. I will become a good man, but I had to find and kill him first.

Killing another inmate would be pointless. Why start life again in another cell? It had to be a guard, someone with access to the outside so I could make my way out and then kill again. It took about a week for me to get a metal shiv that would be up to the job. I took my victim in the yard during the bedlam of a gang squabble. He was innocent of everything but standing next to me when the opportunity arose, and I do not wish to dwell on the incident with any more detail than that. I only had a few seconds before the other guards tackled me, but it was enough to force the shiv into my own heart. As the light bled from me and the pain dissolved into oblivion, I prayed again for forgiveness. No answer came but the welcome darkness…

… and the searing white light which roused me in the hospital. I wasn't shackled. There was a woman leaning over my bed, shedding tears of joy that I was all right. Her name was Mariah, and she didn't know that she was a widow now. There was a boy who wouldn't stop wailing and laughing. He didn't know that his father had died on that prison yard, or that I had taken his place.

Was it a kindness that kept me from telling them the truth? They were so happy that I was alive that they readily accepted my memory loss, although I did seem to maintain some of his muscle memories and habits. It started off as guilt that made me unwilling to leave them, but guilt alone could not endure through the years as I have done. You probably wouldn't believe me if I told you I loved them as strongly as they loved me, but waking up with my new wife and staying strong for my boy, I've never been so happy as that.

I lived with them for five years until I suffered a minor heart attack. I felt like a ticking time-bomb after that. The big one could happen any day, and this new life I had worked so hard for would be replaced by some unspeakable unknown. Giving up this new life was the hardest thing I've ever had to do, but I couldn't take the anxious suspense any longer. It was time to kill again.

And again. And again. I wouldn't let myself get tied down like that again. That one was famous, or another had a better house, or a hotter wife. The lives were a blur, fading in and out so quickly that I became everyone and no one. It turns out killing people is actually quite easy. It's not getting caught that's hard, but since I always sacrificed my own life in the same moment, getting caught was never an issue.

I wanted to experience everything that life had to offer. One day I was a schoolgirl, the next I was a professional athlete, or a race car driver. Taking highly skilled people was my favorite; with a little practice and their muscle memory, I was just as good as they ever were. I spent several years as a number of prominent musicians, leaving a wake of scandals as I inevitably took my own life to move on again.

I don't know many lifetimes I could have spent this way, but I never had the chance to explore them all. I was using a healthy body to experiment with a variety of drugs when I was ambushed by an undercover cop. I didn't have the chance to switch bodies again, and before I knew what was happening, I was back in jail. It was a minor possession charge, and I had plenty of money hidden away for bail, so I didn't make a fuss. The point is that I saw her again at the station.

Mariah was dating again—I guess she had a thing for a man in uniform. Seeing her sitting and laughing, knowing that she moved on from me so easily, it just made my blood boil. I guess I hadn't realized until that moment that throughout all the glamorous lives I've lived over the last few years, I hadn't once been as happy as I was when I was with her.

It wasn't as easy as I thought it'd be to slip back in. I killed her new boyfriend without trouble, but she didn't stay with me long. It was as though she noticed the change right away, dumping me almost as soon as I stepped foot in her house. I took two more bodies, trying to seduce her only to be turned away each time. Frustrated, I consented to bide my time, waiting until she began dating again so that I could replace him and have her.

Three boyfriends later, the same story each time. I killed each of them, only to be rejected the moment I appeared in their body. It seemed as though she could sense my presence somehow, but each time she turned me away, I only wanted her more. It didn't help that she was becoming unstable. I hadn't counted on how psychologically devastating it must be to continue dating new people and yet sense that they are all the same. She practically stopped going outside altogether, and I was going crazy trying to figure out how to reach her.

You don't know how much it hurts me to tell you what happened next. This is my confession though, and before God and man and otherwise, I wish my sins be known. There was one person in her life that Mariah would never abandon, and children are always the easiest targets. I caught the boy leaving school one day (he's been taking the bus since his mom started locking herself in). I was wearing the body of a policeman he'd grown up around, and he had no reason to suspect my intentions when I offered him a ride.

I didn't drive him home though. I was taking him out into the woods where there wouldn't be a scene. Trying to get close to Mariah through her son might seem strange to you, but after living so many lives, I wasn't encumbered with such artificial distinctions as romantic or maternal love. I wanted to be close to her again. I wanted her to love me. And if she was too broken to love another man, then I was willing to make a compromise on her behalf.

"Get out of the car," I ordered the boy who I once treated as my son.

"Where are we? I thought we were going home?"

"Just get out."

Those big, almond eyes stared at me for a long time. Then he smiled.

"Okay, I trust you," he said.

"We're going to play a game." I got out of the car with him. My hand was cramping up from flexing beside my gun.

"Okay."

"Close your eyes."

"Okay."

"Don't open them. Promise me, okay?"

"Okay Dad." He closed his eyes. My blood froze.

"Why'd you call me that?" I asked.

"Sorry." His little brow furrowed in deep thought. "I don't know. It's just that you smell like him, only I don't feel it in my nose."

"Where do you feel it?"

The boy crossed his heart, still clenching his eyes shut. I slid my gun back into its holster.

"The game goes like this. You count to a hundred while I hide. When you open your eyes, you have to find me. Ready?"

"Ready!"

When we finished playing, I told him to get back in the car and we drove back to his home. I didn't go in to see Mariah. I just dropped him off and didn't look back. No matter what happens from this moment on, I know this life is going to be my last. I know it doesn't mean much, but for what it's worth, I'm staying on as a cop. I'm going to protect that boy and his mother for the rest of my life. And when chance or old age takes me at last, I'll deserve whatever happens to me next.

I have prayed to be a good man, and this is how my prayers are answered.

## When the Blood Rain Falls

*When the pregnant earth contracts, and the ground trembles as though it were afraid...*
The homeless man flipped to his second piece of cardboard. I nervously glanced away. This red light was taking forever. Glancing back–
*When the clouds are angry in the sky, and rolling darkness chokes the world...*
The traffic light turned green. He was switching signs again though, and I really wanted to see where this was going.
*When the blood rain churns the oceans red, and cresting waves rear above the land...*
The cars behind me were honking. I couldn't just sit here, but neither could I drive away from this sense of looming dread. I decided to pull off onto the dirt beside the road where the homeless man crouched.

Me in my white Prius, on my way back from downtown where I worked. Him and his stained clothing, jagged fingernails biting into the cardboard he clutched. Our eyes locked though we were worlds apart. I flinched for no reason at all when he smiled, that yellow gaping smile, and when he started walking toward my window, I almost slammed my foot on the gas.

Instead I sat there, waiting until he tapped my window with his dirty knuckle. I took a deep breath before rolling it down.

"Dollar is good," he mumbled. "Whatever you've got is fine."

"What's with those signs?" I asked, fishing around for my wallet. "What happens next?"

He squinted at me, then up at the clear blue sky. Back to me, holding out his hand to take the dollar I offered.

"It isn't raining blood," he said matter-of-factly.

I leaned out the window to look up. "Nope. It's not," I agreed.

"Then how am I supposed to know what happens next?" That yellow smile was back. Up close I could see his remaining teeth haphazardly jutting out from bleeding gums, almost like they'd been hammered in.

"Why would you write that stuff then?"

"Didn't write it. Just copied it down, that's all. But people keep stopping, so I keep on holding it. I'm not begging, see, I'm providing a valuable warning."

This was going nowhere. I just wished him an empty 'good luck' and merged back onto the road, the yellow smile fixed on me until he disappeared in my rear view mirror.

Three things happened the next day. The first was an earthquake, around 4:30 in the morning. I woke immediately to the sound of the jiggling books on my shelf. Nothing severe, only magnitude 4, but there were several pulses and I couldn't go back to sleep after that.

Next was the storm, taking everyone by surprise. I left the morning news playing while I got dressed, and even the weatherman admitted the clouds came out of nowhere. There shouldn't have been enough humidity in the air for them to form overnight, he said, and there weren't any storms within fifty miles that could have blown in.

"I guess whacky weather is just something we'll have to get used to as the planet keeps getting hotter," droned the voice.

I tried not to think about the homeless man, but it was hard while driving to work through the surreal morning twilight. I couldn't even see the sun through the thick rolling clouds.

I pulled off the road again at the same spot. There he was, crouching exactly how I saw him yesterday. He started walking toward me the moment I stopped. I jumped as he knocked on the passenger side window this time.

"Where are your signs today?" I asked, rolling down the window next to him.

"Tossed 'em."

"Why?"

"It don't matter."

"I want to know. Look, you can have five bucks this time." I leaned across the passenger seat to hand him the bill.

"It don't matter, because it's too late to warn people. It's already begun. And I don't want your money, but I wouldn't say no to a ride. I hate getting caught out in the rain."

"It's not raining...." But the words died in my mouth. Flash goes the yellow smile, rotted teeth sprouting from that graveyard of a mouth. A thick greasy drop landed on his cheek, sluggishly weaving its way into his matted beard.

"Sorry, wish I could help," I muttered. The rain was coming harder by the second. Great red drops drizzling down from unseen heights. Splattering on my windshield, running down the gutters like freshly opened veins.

"If anyone is causing this, it's people like you, not people like me," he said.

I opened my mouth. Then closed it. He snatched the door handle, but it was locked. The blood rain was pouring over him now, streaming off his face and hands like the victim of some gruesome accident.

"Just tell me what's going to happen next!" I shouted over the mounting wind.

He reached through the window and unlocked the door from the inside. I tried to lock it again, but I was too slow. He was already inside, blood flying with him, splattering across my face and soaking into my seat.

I rolled up the window as the storm raged around us. He didn't look at me—just stared straight ahead, hands folded in his lap like he knew he didn't belong.

"Well? What's next? What's happening?" I demanded.

"That was rotten of you, trying to lock me out like that," he said, still not looking at me. "We're all in this together now."

"Well you're here now, so just tell me."

"Just drive, okay? You'll see."

I opened my mouth to protest, but the words caught in my throat as the yellow smile blossomed. "I said drive!" he bellowed, blood cascading off his sudden ferocity like light scattering through a prism. I slammed my foot on the gas and lurched out into the street.

It was getting worse by the second. Trees were buckling under the weight of the howling wind. Cars inched along the roads or were pulled off to the side, visibility reduced to nothing from the bleeding wound in the sky.

"You said you copied the words," I managed at last. "Where from?"

"It was carved in a tree," he said. "I thought it was cool because the tree was bleeding where it was cut, like it was carved in skin instead of bark."

"There was more, wasn't there? More than you copied."

He nodded, not smiling anymore. "Turn left here. I'll take you there."

We didn't speak much for the next five minutes until he told me where to stop. The rain had already dried up, and there was even some light sneaking through the roof of the world.

"Right there. That's the tree." He'd gotten out of the car and was already walking through a dense grove of white aspen a little off the road. There was no uncertainty about which one he was talking about.

It would have been identical to the rest of the grove if it wasn't trembling in an unfelt breeze. Long red streaks trickled down its base from a wound about half-way up. The trembling grew more violent as I approached, until standing before it, the wood seemed to ripple and contort before my eyes. Random, violent movements, like an animal trapped under a blanket trying to beat its way out.

"It wasn't doing that last time," he said nonchalantly.

I spotted the bleeding words, but they were shaking too badly for me to make them out. I didn't have to wait long though. Within a minute I saw a crack begin to emerge running down the entire length of the trunk.

The tree was opening, but it wasn't opening by itself. Long, thin fingers slithered out from the trunk to grip either side of the fissure, forcing it open wider. Blood flowed freely from the tree, running into a small stream by our feet. Soon an eye glimmered somewhere from the darkness inside, blinking away the flowing blood to stare at me.

"When the pregnant earth contracts and the ground trembles as though it were afraid ... " The homeless man's eyes were closed, reciting from memory.

The crack in the tree was wide enough for an entire hand to fit through. Twice the length of a human hand, white shining skin beneath the blood.

"When the clouds are angry in the sky, and rolling darkness chokes the world... "

The hand retreated, and a second later the whole head burst through. Eyes like a frozen hurricane, uneven gaping mouth like a canyon, panting rapid excited breaths. It felt like staring into all the raw magnificence of nature, only being aware that it was staring back.

"When the blood rain churns the oceans red, and cresting waves rear above the land…"

I was running back toward my car. A loud crack rent the air, and glancing back I saw the whole tree splitting cleanly in two. A final rush of blood gutted the length before the two halves fell like corpses to either side.

"Then I will be born into a world that deserves me. And all the words which have been carved into my skin will spell the name of my defiler, and we will sing all words until his name is forgotten, and we will dance until I dance alone."

The homeless man hadn't moved since he began recounting the verse. Now it was too late. I watched in awe as the creature caressed the man with its long white fingers. He shuddered as if in ecstasy, looking up at it with the reverence of a spectacular sunset.

The fingers dug into my companion and ripped him in half exactly as it had done with the tree, only this time was much faster and much, much messier. A slop of organs slid down his separated legs, the creature wasting no time in stooping on all fours to lick them up. It seemed to have forgotten about me for the moment, and that was all I needed to get back to the car.

I saw it staring at me in the mirror as I ripped down the road. As horrific as that yellow smile was, it was nothing compared to this white shine that grinned over its fresh kill. All the blood had already slid from its body as though it were stainless steel.

Something like that? I get the impression that it could kill any number of us and still be as bright and clean as the day it was born. I wonder if, when the last of us is gone, the earth will be clean like that too. Or whether we've cut too deep for the wound to ever heal. I know we're all in this together now, but looking at that feral avatar I've never felt so helpless, so small, or so alone.

## She Can't Tell Lies

Repeat after me:

I must not tell lies. I must not tell lies. I CANNOT tell lies. Or else.

It's as vacuous a statement as you can find. If someone is truthful, then they do not need to make such a promise. If they are not, then their promise means nothing anyway. There's only so much a mother can do when her daughter is a liar, and I was doing the best I could.

Marcelline is just eight years old, but she's learning so fast. She can count all the way to 1,000 and has her multiplication tables memorized. She can read on her own without moving her lips, and she knows how to look up words she doesn't know. She loves playing soccer, riding bikes, and roller skating, but her most impressive skill by far is her mastery over lying. And she does it every chance she gets.

My daughter's favorite lie is about a character named Zafai she read about in one of her books. If she doesn't want to get up in the morning, it's because Zafai kept her awake all night. She never breaks anything, but Zafai is a whirling dervish when I'm not around. I thought it was cute at first, but I knew I had to put a stop to it before it became an incurable habit.

I started by punishing her. I would scold her and tell her to stand in the corner, or take away her toys and books when she wouldn't stop. The little rebel fought back, digging in her heels and hotly declaring that Zafai wouldn't tolerate being stolen from. Marcelline was a banshee with an attitude problem, and I'd usually only last a few hours before giving in just to shut her up. My husband Marc thought I was just enabling her, but I couldn't help it. Watching her scream and wail and throw herself around the room like a crash-test dummy in an explosives yard was too much for me to bear.

"We can't let this go on," Marc said to me the other night after Marcelline had gone to bed. "She's holding the whole house hostage."

"Fine with me. You get the rope and I'll get the gag. They make those in children's size, right?"

"I'm serious," he said. "She might not understand now, but it's for her own good. How do you think she's going to navigate through life, or hold a job, or maintain a relationship when she thinks lying is a magic answer to everything?"

Of course he was right. We had to parent the shit out of that little beasty. She's on winter break now, and our house was about to turn into liar's rehab. That night Marc and I collected all her books and padlocked them in a cabinet. He took the key with him to work so I wouldn't be able to give in to her tantrums. Over breakfast, we sat down with her to clearly lay out the rules.

"Do you know why mommy and daddy took your books away?" I started.

I guess she hadn't noticed until I said it. Her little eyes narrowed, the dead rot of winter piercing through the slits. I looked helplessly to Marc for support.

"You've been telling a lot of lies lately, and you're getting punished," Marc supplied. "If you want them back, you've got to go a whole day without lying."

Marcelline took a deep breath and pouted her bottom lip. It was almost enough to make me give-in immediately, but Marc was there to the rescue.

"Repeat after me: I must not tell lies."

Marcelline looked pleadingly at me. I crossed my arms and pressed my lips into a hard, uncompromising line. At last she rolled her eyes in defeat.

"I must not tell lies." She sighed dramatically.

"And you're going to start by telling us that Zafai isn't real," I interjected. Marc grinned and gave me a nod of approval.

Marcelline wasn't giving us a death glare anymore. Her wide, quivering eyes were much harder to endure. She was even starting to look pale. Damn she's good.

"Say it or I'm going to lock up your skates too," Marc growled.

"I can't," she whispered. "Zafai hates lies even more than you do, and I know he's listening."

"Marcelline! Say it!" I shouted. Marc raised his eyebrows. "Or *else*!"

She looked wildly around like harried prey. Tears were welling in her eyes. Marc grabbed my hand exactly when I needed him to. She needs this, stay strong, his grip seemed to say.

"Marcelline!" Marc bellowed.

"Okay! Zafai isn't real. I'm so sorry Zafai, please don't hurt me."

I sighed. Mark snorted in amusement. "Good enough for today, I guess. I'll be home around six, think you can hold the fort until then?"

"Bring it on! I can do it." I gave him my most convincing fist pump. It felt like the first victory we've had over our daughter in months. I had no idea how wrong I was.

It started with the silent treatment, although I have to admit that was actually a relief. I expected her to be screaming bloody-murder the second Marc closed the door, but Marcelline just sat in the living room and glared at me from under her little furrowed brow. Fine, let her sulk, at least I could keep an eye on her here. I sat on the couch with my laptop to bust out some last-minute Christmas shopping. Marcelline was muttering under her breath, but I did my best to just ignore her. It sounded like she was apologizing over and over, but it would take more than that to break my resolve.

The first time I glanced up, she was still sulking, her bottom lip pushed out as far as it would go.

Ten minutes later and she still hadn't moved. She was just staring at me and chewing on her lip. She was waiting for me to cave like I always did, but this time I wouldn't give her the satisfaction. I made a real mental effort to not even look at her for the next half hour.

But I did look up eventually, and I started screaming the moment I did. The lower half of her face was covered in blood, dribbling down her chin onto the floor like a vampire over a fresh kill. She was still glaring at me, relentlessly and purposefully chewing.

At first I couldn't figure out what happened, but when I rushed over to her she spat a fleshy lump in my face. I grabbed it without thinking, mind numb from disgust, staring at bloody slug-like thing in my hand. She spat another one — it was her other lip that she had chewed straight off.

"I must not tell lies," she hissed, spluttering blood as she did. She wasn't grinning, but it looked like she was. Even with her mouth closed I could see all her ferocious little teeth jutting out of her gory gums. "What cannot speak cannot tell lies." And then she was chewing again, the open wound of her face doing nothing to conceal the gnashing teeth which sank into her tongue over and over again.

I had to grip the top of her head and her chin to hold her mouth shut, but it took both hands and I couldn't reach the phone. Tears mingled with her blood, gushing down her face, but nothing could stop the gnashing. Even with both my hands and my whole body weight pressing down on her head, I could feel her jaws relentlessly lifting me and clamping back down again.

I tried to stuff my fingers into her mouth to hold it open instead, but they snapped down so ferociously that I almost lost a digit. It was like trying to stop a garbage disposal with my bare hands. Next I tried to get her to lie down and relax, but she started choking and I had to lift her immediately. I thought she was just choking on the blood, but no—a second later her entire tongue oozed out of her mouth like some giant eel swimming through red waters.

At least she had nothing to chew anymore. I broke away long enough to call an ambulance, but even that was a mistake. Her jaw was already working through the insides of her cheeks. She started choking on the pieces again, unable to get them out of her mouth without the aid of her tongue. I couldn't stop her—all I could do was hold her on her hands and knees to let the bloody chunks dribble out of her mouth so they wouldn't go down her throat.

She didn't stop until the paramedics arrived and injected her with something that knocked her out. I was so overwhelmed that I couldn't even follow. I just sat on the bloody floor and cried, finally noticing the words which must have stained carpet while she was kneeling.

"Zafai won't let me tell lies."

When she recovers—if she recovers—I'm going to have a lot of questions that she won't be able to answer. I've heard there are people who know about this sort of thing though, so I'm begging you for help. What is Zafai? What do I do now? I know it must be hard to believe, but please don't dismiss it or give me any false hope. Zafai hates liars, and I just know he's still listening.

## The New You

11:50 p.m. on New Year's Eve. The raucous beat of the music is echoed by the pulse in my veins. Iridescent lights lance through the air all around me, and the teaming heat of pressed bodies forces me to swallow a great lungful of heavy air. It's thick with sweat and cheap perfume. I can't be the only one who isn't dancing, but anyone who notices me will immediately recognize that I don't belong here. Smiles and sneers look the same to me, and all laughter is tainted with condescending jokes at my expense.

Living with crippling anxiety is my personal nightmare. Just trying to start a conversation with someone feels like standing on the roof of a tall building. One little push and I'm free, but the clenching knot in my stomach has me frozen in place. I must have started walking toward Chase at the DJ table a dozen times so far this party, but I've never gotten within a few feet before I had the irresistible urge to check my phone, go to the bathroom, or disappear off the face of the earth entirely.

Guys like Chase don't look twice at girls like me. It doesn't matter if we like all the same music. It doesn't matter if there is electricity which ignites the air between us. Maybe things would be different if he was the one to say hi first, but how was that supposed to happen when I couldn't even get close to him?

"Looks like you could use a drink." I don't understand how I heard the words so clearly over the pounding music, but I didn't turn to the barman. Maybe if he thought I didn't hear him he'd give up and leave me alone—

"Maybe two. What's your poison?" he insisted.

"I don't drink." I dismissed him over my shoulder.

"You mean you didn't used to drink."

I finally turned to see an elderly man with a closely groomed gray beard and a vest which fit so closely that it might as well have been sewn onto his skin. His dark eyes drilled into me with undisguised fascination.

"You didn't used to do a lot of things," he continued. "There was a time when you'd never walked before, but then you started, and you haven't stopped since. Now it would be silly to say you don't walk, wouldn't it? You aren't even the same person who couldn't walk anymore."

"What do you mean, 'not the same person'?"

A sudden lull in the music was punctuated by Chase's voice on the loudspeaker. "Five minutes to midnight! Who is ready to burn the rest of this year?" He was answered by an overwhelming cheer, but the old man's words still clearly punctured the chaos.

"You're remembering someone else's memories," he said. "Next year you'll be new again, and then you'll remember all the memories you have now and think that they're yours. You'll have all the same habits, and be afraid of all the same things, because you think that's who you're supposed to be. But it's not. The new you will have to decide for herself whether she wants to keep copying a failing strategy, or to learn from it and try something else."

"I don't have a failing strategy. You don't even know me."

"How could I?" the old man replied smugly. "You're a blank slate tonight. Even you don't know you yet, so how about that drink?"

I nodded, not fully understanding why. He spoke with such a simple surety that I couldn't muster anything to refute him. The barman pulled a purple bottle from under the shelf and spun it deftly between his hands. A fountain of thick, rich liquid like cough syrup sprouted into a perfectly placed mug which I hadn't noticed a moment before.

"What is it?"

"Just what you need. Cheers!" He poured a second glass for himself and toasted me. "May we make room for new growth by pruning the dead branches, and may we leave what's dead behind."

I took a long drink, forcing myself not to gag as the thick liquid dribbled down my throat like oil. He finished first, slamming his glass upon the table and wiping his beard with the back of his hand. Before I had a chance to finish mine, the barman added: "Those who die a little each night will never feel the pain of those who go all at once. You're one of the lucky ones."

"Huh?" I wiped the last of the thick residue from my mouth.

"It's almost midnight. Are you ready to let the old you die?"

*Almost midnight.* I was running out of time. I felt a certain tranquility while walking toward the DJ table. The old me would have turned away by now, but I didn't slow down even when Chase looked right at me. The electricity wasn't a barrier anymore. It was charging me, an exhilarating fuel which propelled me through the churning dance floor. I even allowed myself to step in time with the music, bobbing and swaying with the mesmerizing beat. It almost felt like I was flying, until suddenly I was close enough to finally say:

"Hey Chase… "

My wildest paranoia couldn't have prepared me for his reaction. Glancing up from his computer, Chase's face contorted into a horrified caricature of his usual self-assurance. He lurched out of his chair so fast that it tumbled backward. I rushed to help him, but that only made him kick the chair in my direction and scramble across the floor. The music was deafening this close to the speakers, but it wasn't enough to completely drown out the grotesque retching as he vomited onto the floor. Through the beat I could still clearly hear the wailing sob rising in my throat as I sprinted away from him and toward the bathroom.

I couldn't understand what happened until the burning began. My fingers gingerly grazed the swiftly swelling lumps in my face. I covered myself with my hands as I ran, brutally shoving my way through the crowd and then slamming through the bathroom door. A girl in a black sequin party dress dropped her makeup and screamed. I almost trampled her on my way to the mirror, but she wasted no time in ducking under the sink and crawling toward the door. Looking in the mirror, I honestly couldn't blame her.

Some of the lumps in my skin were the size of golf-balls, and they were growing by the second. The larger ones were actually wriggling, almost as though there was an insect squirming just beneath the skin. More lumps were appearing on my hands, and the itching burn radiating down my body left no ambiguity about what was happening under my clothes. I would have screamed if my tongue wasn't swelling too, but it was all I could do to just try to keep my airway clear. Then the first boil popped, and I couldn't contain the howl which ripped from my lungs.

I heard the door open again, but it snapped shut immediately. I couldn't tear my eyes away from the mirror. More boils were rupturing by the second, splattering the glass with thick purple syrup which clung on like long strands of mucous. More of them exploded in my mouth to trickle down my throat with the same oily taste of the drink. My hair was sliding from my scalp in great clumps, matted and greased with the bubbling purple liquid.

The only thing keeping me from completely losing my mind was the sight of fresh pink skin which shone beneath the savage gashes in my face. The burn was growing more intense by the second, but each exploding boil revealed more healthy skin below it. I started ripping at the tattered shreds, peeling them off and dumping them in a soggy pile around my feet.

Beneath all the skin sloughing off, I didn't even recognize myself. My new skin was lighter and clearer, and the new hair which sprouted was a short ruffled blond that was nothing like the long dark hair which lay in clumps around my feet. Nothing was the least recognizable except my eyes which were stretched wide with a familiar anxious terror.

"What the fuck?"

Chase must have followed me into the bathroom. How long had he been watching? Long enough. I stepped away from the wet pile of old flesh that littered the ground. My clothes were still soaked in the liquid though, and more chunks continued to rain out my dress and down my legs. He looked like he was about to vomit again.

"Hey Chase... I want to try something. Come here."

He didn't move, but he didn't have to. I crossed the space between us more quickly than I thought possible. All at once our faces were inches apart, but he didn't turn away. Outside I could hear the countdown toward midnight.

"Five!"

I pressed my finger to his lips to silence the budding question.

"Four!"

I cupped his head in my hands and drew him toward me.

"Three!"

I felt his hard lips soften against mine.

"Two!"

The taste of his sweat as my mouth made its way down his neck.

"One!"

The squirt of blood through my teeth as they sank into his flesh. He was thrashing now, but each movement just forced my jaw to tighten until I could feel the first vertebra crunch under the pressure. All the shouts of "Happy New Year!" drowned out his terminal scream which strangled to a whisper when his trachea collapsed.

Part of me died that night alongside Chase, but the old man knew what he was talking about. It's much easier to leave the dead parts of yourself behind than let them weigh you down forever, and for the first time in my life, I'm not afraid anymore.

## Dreammaker Music

Sleeping is the easiest, most natural thing in the world. Babies do it all the time without even being taught. It's so easy people do it by accident, but not me. I suck at sleeping, which sometimes feels more like I suck at being human since I'm so freaking tired all the time.

It's the same battle every night. Even looking at the clock and knowing I should be in bed is enough to make me feel restless. I've tried keeping a rigid sleep schedule, and burning soporific incenses, and popping pills, but nothing seems to make a difference. You'd think my body would just get so tired it shut off automatically, but it seems like the less I sleep, the more agitated I get thinking how much I need to, and the harder it is to make love with sweet oblivion.

My friend Anu told me her grandfather was this Indian guru who had a remedy for insomnia. My hopes were flying about as high as an iron pigeon, but I figured there wasn't any harm. Even if I couldn't sleep, at least I could impress the girl by being "spiritually open to new ideas" and "respecting her culture" and all that shit. (Is it wrong that I pat myself on the back for not being racist just because it seems like everyone else is nowadays? Yeah, just thinking that is probably racist too.)

Point is, she gives me this album of Indian music that I'm supposed to listen to in bed. She says it's an instrument called the ravanahatha, which is some kind of ancient precursor to the violin. It's made from a resonating gourd covered with goat hide and strings stretched across a bamboo neck. Legend has it these particular songs were written to appease Shiva, the destroyer of worlds in Hindu scripture. It's supposed to be super calming and meditative though, so I took it home with me to give it a go.

The only weird thing is, right before we parted Anu also said:

"Oh I almost forgot. He said not to try and stop the music before morning, because Shiva will be listening too."

In hindsight, "Is Shiva a babe?" was probably not the most culturally sensitive question, but Anu just smiled. As a whole, I think the interaction was good for our chances of making beautiful, caramel colored babies down the road.

That night I gave the music a go. It was legitimately beautiful: kind of a longing, soulful sound, but not in a sad way. There was just enough lively melodic lift that it felt more like the serenity of seeds buried deep beneath the snow, just waiting for their chance to bloom.

Next comes the part where I try to trick my brain into sleep. It feels like playing that "did I put the poison in my drink, or yours?" game as I alternate between thinking the music will work or not, and whether having expectations will influence the results. Next, surprisingly enough, came a deep and peaceful sleep.

And the strangest dream I've ever had in my life, almost more like an out-of-body experience. I was only aware I was sleeping at all because I was looking down at my body while it slept. I could even still hear to the music down below: like I was watching myself in a movie. It didn't take long to discover my consciousness was free to move around my house, leaving my sleeping body behind.

That part was a lot of fun. I just sort of drifted around, shifting my focus like I was imagining different perspectives. Everything was so clear and perfect that it felt exactly like I was awake. I could even count the number of dishes in my sink (six, mind your own business) and see the minuscule detail in the wood-grain floor. I was just about to float over to the living room and see if I could watch TV when I heard an alien sound break through the music.

The rattle of a handle, and then the opening of my front door. I startled so badly that I woke up immediately, feeling myself teleport back into bed. Frantic reality checks—the texture of my blanket, my phone beside my bed, the clock reading 2:31—everything seemed normal again. That's why I flinched so badly when I heard the front door slam closed.

Panic. Hyperventilate. Lie flat and pretend I'm asleep. I really need a better defense plan. I held my breath for a full ten seconds, but I didn't hear any other sounds. Creeping out of bed, I sped through my apartment in a commando crouch, flipping on every light I passed. It didn't take long before I cleared the last room—all empty. The front door was closed and locked. I couldn't help but count the six dishes in my sink and congratulate my dream-memory on its accuracy.

Figuring I'd just heard a neighbor's door slam really loud, I turned off the lights and went back to bed. Seconds later I was hovering above my bed, watching myself sleep. Except I wasn't the only one in the room.

Someone was sitting in the chair beside my bed (also known as the 'I haven't decided if these clothes are dirty' chair). My clothes had been moved onto the floor to make space for the creature. Naked bone white skin, androgynous yet strong features, and long strings of prayer beads characterized my visitor, but nothing stood out more than the pair of living green snakes which sinuously writhed around his throat.

He was watching my sleeping body at first, but ponderous and implacable as a flowing glacier, he turned his gaze to meet the perspective of my floating projection. He watched me through heavy half-closed eyes, nodding his head in time with the music. Seeing his tranquility, I allowed myself to drift closer to get a better look.

Approaching him was the most disorienting experience of my life. As I drew closer, his body seemed to grow larger as normal perspective dictates, but his eyes grew at an exponentially larger rate as though they were gargantuan celestial bodies that I was speeding towards. Soon my room and his body and everything else became insignificant to the cosmic eyes which stretched from horizon to horizon. I had to pull myself back for fear of falling in, at which point everything returned to normal.

Almost normal. His necklace of snakes was gone. They'd slithered up my bed, their thick coils sliding effortlessly over my corporal body's legs.

It was enough of a start to wake me up again. I immediately began my reality checks—blanket, phone, clock—then I noticed the pile of clothes on the floor. The ones that used to be on the chair. My heart was beating so fast, and the music was so loud that I couldn't hear myself think. I numbly shut off the music, trying to catch my breath for long enough to figure out if I'd somehow knocked the clothes onto the floor myself.

Something touched my foot under the blankets. So cold and smooth, almost slimy. A wave of tension ran up my body, overflowing into the thing whose rigid coils loaded like a spring. I couldn't hover any more now that I was awake, but shit could I jump. Tangled in my own sheets, I flopped and lurched through the air like an Olympic slug. I hit the floor hard, but I didn't slow down until I'd wriggled free from the blankets and raced to the light switch by the door.

Two long green snakes with black and yellow markings emerged from the blanket on the ground behind me. They recoiled momentarily from the light, but one them launched back at me, striking to sink its fangs into my calf. I swatted and it immediately let go and backed off again, but it stung like a thousand bee stings right on top of the other.

I ran from my bedroom and slammed the door. A forked tongue darted out beneath, swiftly followed by the head of the serpent which easily slipped through the crack. I stomped and it withdrew, but the second snake was already halfway out—far enough to rear its head and tense for another strike.

I turned and ran. My leg was on fire as I hobbled out of my apartment in my boxers and dashed toward my car. The place it bit me was swelling by the second, and I knew I had to get to a hospital ASAP.

By the time I got there, I was almost blind. My throat had swollen to the size of a pinhole, and the pressure in my chest was excruciating. I parked right up on the curb and managed to tumble out of my car, and I was vaguely aware of some people helping me into a wheelchair after that.

When I woke, they told me I was bitten by an Indian Pit Viper, which confused the shit out of them because they don't exist anywhere in the Americas. I had an animal services guy sweep my apartment before I got home, but he didn't find anything. He did have this helpful tidbit of reassurance to give me though:

"Of course snakes aren't going to be found when they don't want to be. Hell, I knew a lady who had a ten-foot boa living in her house leftover from the last tenant. Was over a month before she even saw the bugger."

If I don't play the music, then all I can do is lie awake listening to the approaching slithering and agitated hiss in the darkness.

If I do play it, the dream comes again without fail, and I'm forced to watch the stranger enter my room and sit down beside my bed.

Like I wasn't already having enough trouble getting some sleep.

## The Girl On a Leash

Ten, maybe twelve years old, wearing a leash attached to one of those dog training collars with the inward facing spikes. She was sitting on the balcony of my neighbor's apartment, her dirty bare legs dangling through the iron bars. She stared at me where I sat with my book on my own balcony, so I gave her a little wave. She didn't so much as blink in return—she just kept swinging her legs through the bars and staring. I figured the collar was some kind of ironic fashion accessory, although it hardly matched with her thread-bare summer dress.

Five minutes later, she was still staring, and I was beginning to feel a little uncomfortable. I set my book down and asked:

"What's your name, missy?"

"He calls me Cheesey," she replied, flashing all her little teeth like she was posing for a picture. Her face reverted back to a scowl immediately after.

"That's an unusual name."

"'Cause he says I make him sick. Like cheese."

"Oh." I looked down at my book. How the hell was I supposed to reply to that?

"Are we friends now?" she asked, squishing her face between the bars.

"Okay, friends." I couldn't help but smile at her innocent charm. "Can I call you something other than Cheesey though?"

"He also calls me cockroach," she chirped conversationally. "Little freak. Shit-face."

"Who calls you these things? Your father?"

But she didn't get a chance to reply. A vicious tug on the leash tightened the spikes into her throat. Her fingers clutched at it, but she couldn't loosen the grip. A moment later and she was helplessly reeled back inside her apartment. I ran to the edge to look, but my view was obstructed by the jutting concrete which separated the balconies. I just saw her being dragged inside, and then heard:

"What did I tell you about talking to strangers?"

"He asked me a question—"

"I knew it was a mistake to let you outside!" The sliding glass door slammed. I couldn't make out anything after that. My stomach felt like I'd just eaten a pound of garbage. I've never spoken to my neighbor before—a severe, quiet man who wore dark sunglasses inside and out. I didn't even know he had a kid. He didn't seem like the type, although there's a chance she wasn't even his. Either way, I called Child Protective Services to let them decide.

They thanked me for the information and said they would send someone over. I walked around the rest of the day feeling like a hero. I had a few errands to run, but I got back just in time to see an authoritative black woman in a pristine blue suit standing outside my neighbor's open door.

"I'm sorry, there must have been some mistake," my neighbor said from inside his apartment. "I live alone. No kids."

"My apologies, I must have gotten the wrong address," the officer said. "Would you mind if I take a peek inside just so I can check off my forms?" The pause was slightly too long.

"No, that's not okay. This is my home. My sanctuary. Go bother someone else."

"It'll only take a few—"

The door slammed shut. The woman immediately began knocking again, but there was no response.

"Excuse me, CPS?" I asked.

She looked me up and down as though evaluating my potential to be a scumbag.

"You the guy who called?" she asked.

I nodded. "What's your next step?"

"My next step? What's your next step?" she snapped. "I don't have any next steps without a signed warrant from a judge, and I'm not going to get that without some evidence. You get a picture or anything?" I shook my head.

"Well call me if you do." She was already half way to the elevator.

"That's it?"

"What do you mean, 'that's it'? I got three more cases tonight, and chances are at least one won't be this pretty. I got a job to do, honey, but I can't do it here."

Sounds like I had a job to do too. He couldn't stay in there forever, right? Either he'd leave with her and I could follow them, or he'd leave alone and I'd have a chance to talk with her and find out what was going on. I brought my book into the hallway and sat down to wait.

Half an hour did the trick. The door opened and sunglasses gave a quick, paranoid scan. They landed on me.

"What are you doing?" he asked.

"Lost my key," I lied. "Gotta wait for my roommate to get home."

The man disappeared back inside and the door closed. I thought I missed my chance, but a moment later the door opened again and he exited with 'Cheesey'. She was still wearing the collar, but the leash was bundled up and he rested his hand on her shoulder so it was barely visible. As they passed, she glanced back at me as if to say: *Goodbye friend*. But it wasn't goodbye yet.

I followed them out of the building while pretending to stare at my phone, but I couldn't get a clear shot of the collar. I snapped a photo of them together, but that didn't seem like enough for a warrant yet.

I might feel like a masquerading pillar of vigilante justice, but I certainly wasn't as smooth as one. By the time the pair had gotten to their car the man must have noticed me a dozen times. The chase was on.

We'd only been out in the night for about five minutes when he suddenly pulled off the road into a dirt clearing beside some cornfields. I was so caught up in the excitement that I hadn't even paused to consider what I would do when I actually caught them. He must have known his secret was out though, and if something happened to the girl tonight I'd never forgive myself. I pulled off the road and parked behind him while dialing 911.

"Put the phone down." The man had gotten out of his car. He walked around to the passenger side to drag the girl out by the leash. The powerful yanks sent the clear signal about who would pay the price if I didn't obey. I hung up and got out of the car.

"Did I tell you to get out?" he barked at me. "Back in. Keep driving."

"What the hell is wrong with you?" I shouted, vainly hoping to draw some attention to our dark road. The man flinched at the sound. "Where do you get off putting a collar on—"

"If you knew her, you'd do the same. Or worse," he growled, his hands turning white from clenching the leash so hard. "This little freak deserves it."

"Daddy I can't breathe," the girl whimpered.

"Shut your disgusting mouth—"

I couldn't take it anymore. I barreled headlong into the man, throwing him against his car. One of his arms was tangled in the leash, and that gave me a chance to pin his free arm and punch him across the face. The man slid to the ground, dragging the girl with him as she clutched at her collar and howled. I couldn't divert my attention long enough to unfasten the collar, so I just stomped on the man's hand that was holding the leash.

"God damn idiot!" he shouted. "Do you have any idea how long it took me to capture her in the first place? Now look what you've done!"

I did look, and damn was I proud. The man lay there nursing his hand while I unfastened the collar from around the girl's neck. She was grinning from ear to ear.

"I'm going to call the police now," I warned him, stripping his wallet and ID. "You better stay put unless you want the collar on you."

"Don't bother," he moaned. "We'll both be dead before they arrive."

An idle threat from a desperate man, or so I thought. Until I glanced back at Cheesey. I guess I hadn't noticed how long her neck was under the metal collar. At least twice as long as a neck ought to be, and it was growing by the second. I swallowed hard, but it felt like there was cotton in my throat.

"What are you waiting for?" the man shouted, all pretense of discretion gone. "Run!"

The neck was still stretching. Her figure stayed the same—her face was all smiles—but her neck was almost as long as her whole body now. It twisted sinuously through the air as though it had no bones at all, stretching luxuriously after its confinement.

Little freak wasn't such a bad name. Did you know that most of their body is a hollow cavity which stores their folded neck? Or that silver collars were the only way to keep them from extending? I certainly didn't. Not until I read the papers stuffed in his wallet. Not before I stood in shocked awe on the side of the road and watched her jaw unhinge to consume him whole.

"Police dispatch, what is your emergency?" faintly droned my phone.

"Friends?" I asked the girl.

She nodded, choking the man's still squirming body down her grotesquely swollen throat.

"Friends," I repeated as I hung up the phone, backing into my car. Her eyes watched me while she continued to gag the body down.

Well shit. So much for being a hero, but at least I was still a hero to her.

## What the Blind Man Sees

I'll never see her face again. If my blindness only meant scrubbing this dirty world into an ocean of black mist, then I think I could learn to accept that. Stealing my wife from me before her time though—that I'll never forgive. It's bad enough she's sick and fading from me already, but not being able to see her to say goodbye is killing me as surely as it is her.

I suppose it's my fault though. I spent the last few nights leading up to my accident shifting around the rigid hospital chair beside her bed. I was so tired that I could barely walk straight, and all it took was a patch of black ice in the parking lot to pitch me to the ground. My head slammed into the asphalt and everything went dark. The black mist didn't lift, but next I could remember, I was sitting in my own hospital bed with a nurse explaining what had happened.

" … post-traumatic cortical blindness," she was saying. "It seems like there was some damage to your occipital cortex when you hit the ground."

"Where's Sarah? Where's my wife? I want to see her."

The nurse just coughed, giving me time for my own words to sink in. "There's a chance your vision loss is being caused by pressure on the optic nerve, which can be potentially corrected with surgery. The doctor doesn't want to get your hopes up though. You should be prepared to adjust to life without sight."

It's true that I couldn't see the nurse, or the hospital room, or even my own hand an inch from my face. But the worst thing was that I *could* still see. It just wasn't the same world I had left behind. I fumbled for words trying to explain the black and purple vines which dangled around me from unfathomably tall trees. How they swayed gracefully in an unfelt wind, bending across their hundreds of joints like fingers bending back and forth upon themselves. I pointed at the greasy orange sky and the swarms of softly teeming insects which obliviously paraded towards me from all sides.

"Hallucinations aren't unheard of after acute vision loss…"

It was hard to take her seriously when her voice seemed to be coming from a giant blue flower whose bell-shaped petals were deep enough for me to stand in. If this was a hallucination, then it was clearer and more vivid than anything I've seen in my life. I tried again to explain the infinitesimal detail of the insect's uneven carapaces, but the nurse excused herself to leave without letting me finish. I never even got the chance to tell her that I could *feel* the thousands of tiny legs crawling up my body as the insect parade passed through the disembodied perspective.

I was stuck somewhere between worlds. I could still feel the coarse fabric of the hospital blanket, but so could I feel the smooth gloss of each leaf and barky tree in this sudden jungle I was mired within. I pulled on one of the purple digits only to see it coil around my arm, inquisitively feeling me in return. I tore away and tried to stand, leaning on a cold metal IV pole that I couldn't see.

I felt like I was going insane, and there was no amount of reasonably toned nurses or insightful doctors that would convince me otherwise. I knew instinctively that I had to find my wife—Sarah was the only real thing left to ground me in the world that was harder to picture by the moment.

It wasn't easy navigating two worlds at once. Even when I shuffled around to find the door to my room, I still had to push myself through a thick curtain of fingers which had inconveniently infested the portal. It was slow going navigating the invisible hallways while plowing through the thick jungle foliage, and to make matters worse, the blue-white sun was beginning to smolder and set in the orange sky. My hearing remained fixed to this world strangely, so at least I was able to hear people approaching and not run into anyone.

Once someone pointed me to the main elevator, I had no trouble from there. I visited Sarah so many times that I could find the way with my eyes closed. It was disorienting to feel myself rise in the elevator, seemingly flying directly into the air, ducking and dodging branches as I did. I hesitated before her door to ask the passing footsteps:

"Sarah's room?"

"Are you sure you should be out of bed? Let me go ask—"

"Is my wife in here?"

"Yes, but she should be resting too. She had another grand mal seizure last night. Hold on, I'll go see if I can find the doctor."

Footsteps. My hand was on the door, but I couldn't quite bring myself to push through. Sarah had been in the hospital for the last three months, growing weaker each day. There had been a number of tentative hypotheses, but there has yet to be a definite diagnosis to the underlying issue. I guess that's why I've been holding out hope for so long: if she could get sick without a reason, then she didn't need a reason to get better either. All those nights I'd spent beside her, watching her pale face and listening to her shallow breathing—it was all some cosmic misunderstanding that would sort itself out on its own.

It was only now when I knew I couldn't lie to myself anymore. The black and purple fingers protruded thickly like sprouting plants on the wide branch beyond, converging on a recumbent form the exact size and shape of a human. Some of them reared their sensitive tips only to plunge directly back into the mass, pulsing and squirming as they fought one another to penetrate farthest. All too clearly I could imagine them puncturing her body or forcing themselves down where her throat should have been. If this wasn't a hallucination, then it was explaining an illness that an entire hospital couldn't decipher.

"Sarah?" I opened the door. "Are you in there?"

Her gentle moan. That's all I've heard from her the last week. It hadn't made any sense to the doctors, since she appeared conscious, but it made sense now. How was she supposed to speak this whole time with those things lodged in her throat?

Sickened and furious, I flung myself at the warped vines, carelessly clattering through her invisible bedside table as I did. I seized one near where her head must be and pulled with all my strength, feeling it go taunt to resist me. Other vines were reacting, unwinding themselves from her to seize me by the arms and legs. I fought through it, clutching and tearing, even sinking my teeth into the rubbery thing. More fingers crawled from the branches above, circling around my arms, up my shoulders, slithering around my neck…

"Someone help! Get them off her!" I shouted.

The fingers were constricting around me, but I didn't let go. I threw my whole body weight backwards, heaving and straining until something finally gave. Sarah was coughing and retching, the beeping of her vitals going berserk as I struggled. She was shaking so bad that the whole infested nest rattled, each increment of progress agonizing to watch as I knew the finger must be relinquishing its hold of her stomach and lungs, or however deep the corruption spread. All the while my bondage was secured, ruthlessly tightening to cut off blood supply to my arms and crush my throat into a collapsing pinprick of heaving breath.

"She's having another seizure. Get a doctor in here!" One of the nurses. I was held so firmly in place that I couldn't even turn toward him, not like I could see him even if I could.

"What about her husband?"

"He's not responding. Get him on the ground and keep his airway clear."

Hands unwittingly pushed their way past the swarming appendages to ease me down. The pressure slackened, some returning their attention to the knot which surrounded my wife. Blood was beginning to return to my limbs. I could feel, and as soon as I could breathe, I could fight again. I was still gasping on the floor when the doctor entered the room.

How could I tell? Well there were certainly auditory clues as a gruff voice barked commands to the nurses, but more prominently was the knot of interlacing fingers which formed the shape of a human being. They were spread so finely that every artery and vein must be filled, and I could clearly see them pulse and twitch as they tightened and relaxed, moving the doctor through the room like a puppet.

"Another seizure," the doctor said. I could see the strum around his head as the things inside him opened and closed his mouth, with smaller ones inside maneuvering his tongue and vibrating his vocal chords. "Check her mouth. Make sure there isn't any vomit or obstruction."

"The fingers!" I shouted, aware of how mad I must appear rolling on the ground. "Get them out of her! She can't—"

"And give him something to calm down. Diazepam, 400 milligrams should do it."

"They've got him too—don't touch me—don't let him touch Sarah—"

I tried to sit up, but someone was squatting on top of me and pinning me to the ground. I jerked as a needle slid into my thigh, but the pressure only increased. Something scoured through my veins. The humanoid network that was the doctor dropped to his haunches beside me, and I felt a warm hand run down my face to cup my chin. It was getting too dark to see anything at all.

"Just a nasty hallucination, that's all. Let's get you back to bed and see if we can't do something about those eyes."

They had good news for me when I woke up. Not only were they able to alleviate the pressure on my optic nerve, but my wife had made a miraculous recovery during the procedure. I actually wept in relief when I opened my eyes in the hospital room and saw Sarah anxiously sitting over my bed. Just Sarah and the room—no fingers, no unfamiliar jungle, no crawling sensation of the insects, no dodging alien trees.

They told me Sarah was talking and eating and even walking on her own, although they warned me she was still stiff and slow to react.

"Stiff" isn't how I'd describe her lurching movements though. She seems more like a marionette doll to me, tethered by unseen strings from the inside and out.

## Do Demons Lay Eggs?

The guys and I were doing a sweep of an old oil refinery when I found the eggs. I guess they liked the heat, because they were all clustered right around the fractal distillation chamber, which gets up past 720 Fahrenheit when the crude oil is being heated up. The whole building was scheduled for demolition though, and it was our job to make sure the place was cleaned out.

"Anyone want a souvenir?" I shouted. Guess the crew was in other parts of the building. The eggs were about the size of my fist, all black and covered with thick bristles like an especially paranoid cactus. Only one of them was really even intact—maybe it's because the refinery hasn't been running in a while, but five out of the six eggs were cracked and leaking some kind of thick, rotten smelling jelly. I was more motivated by the clock than curiosity though, and I was about to mark the room as clear when—

"A souvenir. Want a—want a—souvenir." The voice was muffled and frail, but it was definitely coming from inside the egg. I crouched down next to it, scooping up the spiny ball in my work gloves.

"So what are you supposed to be?"

"Supposed to be," it chirped back.

Maybe it was the fumes in this place getting to my head, but there was something profoundly sad about that little echo. I dropped the egg into the pocket of my overalls, intending to show it off to everyone at the pub after work. *Intending* being the key word there. We didn't finish clearing the place until almost six, and then there was a last minute permit issue that had me driving around collecting signatures until past nine. I was dead tired and so ready to collapse at home that I barely remembered the weird egg in my pocket.

If it wasn't for its little spikes, I would have forgotten it entirely. It must have liked my warmth though, because it kept trying to huddle closer to me in my pocket. When I got home and put it on the counter I could actually hear a soft rattle as its spines shivered against the tile.

"You got a name?" I asked it.

"You got—you got—"

"Can't you say anything more? I'm Phil."

"You got—a Phil?"

That's all it could do. Echo me. Was I weirded out? Yeah sure, but it was cool too. I felt like a hero for saving it, and I guess I was feeling protective because I hated watching it tremble like that. I put the thing on an oven rack and set it to 100 F, keeping the light on to check on it occasionally.

"Anything more—Phil? Anything more?" Still just an echo, but it felt like there was more deliberate thought behind it. The voice was getting stronger, but it was still shivering. I turned the heat up incrementally and it continued to encourage me until I hit the max temperature of 550 F. I figured if it could survive being pressed up to the fractal distillation chamber, then it could survive this too. The egg seemed to be loving it sure enough.

"Supposed to be. Thank you Phil."

"You're home now, little guy."

I never remembered saying thank you, but it could have picked that up while listening from inside my pocket. I was only intending to let the thing bake and warm up for a little while, but I was so tired that I just fell asleep on the couch watching TV.

"Phil! Phil! Phil! Phil!" Shrill, insistent, urgent—the first sound I heard when I woke up. Still half-asleep, I raced to the oven and turned on the light. Thick black jelly was dripping through my oven rack. Had I accidentally killed it? I opened the door, and a wave of sulfuric air brutally forced itself into my nose and down my throat. I gagged and reeled back, desperately searching for an oven mitt to save the little guy. The shell had shattered into a dozen pieces, and there was nothing inside but the charcoaled goo.

"Phil over here! Look what I found!"

It wasn't dead. It had hatched. And it was peeking out from my cupboard with a bottle of seasoning in each hand. Wide red eyes without pupil or cornea took up the entirety of its face. Black skin with green fuzzy splotches like fresh moss. Two long fingers on each hand, with little mouths at the end of each which it spoke from.

I wasn't afraid or anything, but shit was I surprised. It had already formed a perfect circle of spilled herbs and spices on my counter. There was a wide assortment of opened bottles and jars that it would stick its fingers into before deciding whether to spill the contents into the circle or move on.

"Stop that! You're making a mess!"

"Phil—Phil—Phil—It's a circle, Phil!" it squeaked with pride.

"What the fuck are you?"

"Fuck you—fuck you," it mimicked in a voice which was obviously a crude impersonation of me.

I spent the next twenty minutes chasing it through my apartment, trying to trap or corner it somewhere. Of course the little bugger thought it was just a game, and it squealed and giggled with delight as it evaded my grasp over and over. I briefly considered calling my landlord, but somehow this seemed like something that would end up added to my next rent payment.

I was already late for the demolition though, and I couldn't fool around forever. Eventually I lured the thing back into the oven where it seemed most comfortable and slammed the door tight. I used a bike lock to secure the oven shut, cranked the heat down to 200, and left for work.

I worried about leaving that thing in my apartment all morning, but I managed to sneak off on my lunch break to race home and check on it. Just seeing that my building hadn't burned down or anything was a bigger relief than I realized. Then there was the palpable tension as I opened my front door, half-expecting my place to be torn to shreds. Everything was exactly how I left it though. Even the oven was still closed—

Although the bike lock was on the ground, and it had been turned back up to

550. I took a deep breath and turned on the oven light, jumping back as I saw the wide red eyes blinking in sluggish contentment on the other side of the glass. No harm done—I fastened the lock back on, this time pushing a heavy recliner to block the door as well. Imagine my surprise when I saw the creature hiding under the chair I was moving. Or the bump from inside the cupboards, or the squealing giggles coming from my bedroom.

I counted at least six of them before my lunch break was over, and the more I searched, the more circles I found. On the carpet, in the closet, on top of the TV—little circles of herbs and spices, and when they ran out of those, they improvised with whatever they could get their hands on. Mustard, mayonnaise, crumbled chips—there must have been a hundred circles in my place. Meanwhile my phone was ringing every five minutes, the demolition crew yelling at me and wondering where I was.

I couldn't leave them in here alone—God knows what they'd get up to. I couldn't stay to watch them either though. I just opened a window and did my best to chase as many of them out as I could. They seemed bigger than they were this morning—almost the size of my head now—and their strong fingers had no trouble scaling down the brick building to escape.

"Anything more, Phil?" Perhaps that was the original one, but I couldn't tell for sure. It clung to the outside of my building, hesitating to look back at me. "Supposed to be happy here, Phil. Supposed to be home."

My phone was ringing again—so god damn impatient. Answering with one hand, I grabbed a broom in the other to push the creature farther away from the window. Hoping the rest of them would find their way out when they were ready, I followed the siren call of my cell phone and went back to work.

That was the last time I've seen one of them, and I guess I should be thankful for that, but I'm not. I could tell something was seriously wrong when I was still a few blocks away from home. A dozen trashcans were lined up in the center of the road, and I had to get out of my car to move them. All the trash had been removed, and it was spread on either side of the cans in the shape of a long, evenly curving line.

When the trash had all run out, it was replaced with anything and everything to continue the sloping line. Broken wood, loose bricks, stolen bicycle's and street signs—all jumbled together. It just looked like a giant mess here, but I bet if I looked at it from the air it would be shaped like a perfect circle. Two or three blocks—maybe a half-mile wide.

Please tell me that's not another summoning circle.

## Underwater Microphone Picks Up Voices

I couldn't have known they were voices when my hydrophone first recorded the sound. My best guess was a bowhead whale, although the pitch didn't fluctuate or go nearly as high as the typical bowhead. This sound was sonorous and powerful, a seemingly sourceless echo reverberating through the ocean depths for at least a dozen miles around my ship.

My name is Alyssa Williams, and I'm a marine biologist studying the effect of global warming on hourglass dolphins and other arctic mammals. Hydrophone recordings are an essential tool in calculating the density and diversity of ocean life, although this is the first time I've heard something like this in the past two weeks I've been at sea.

We like to think these expeditions give us a pretty good idea of what's going on down there, but it's really more like scooping a bucketful of water from the ocean and concluding whales don't exist because they didn't fit in the bucket. There are plenty of unexplained phenomenon and outlier data points, and most of the time we have to just ignore them so they don't contaminate the rest of our data.

It was only chance which kept me from ignoring this sound altogether. My son is an electronic music artist (which I'm pretty sure is the same as a DJ), and he asked me to send him marine recordings to sample into his music. Every week I pick out a few interesting noises to send him, and lacking anything else to do with this mysterious echo, I included it in the last batch.

A couple days later I got an email back. He's been playing around with the sound, and after speeding it up, he noticed it started to sound like voices. He thought I was playing a prank on him, and I thought he was the one trying to fool me. It wasn't hard to prove though; as soon as I sped up the tapes, I heard it too.

It was speaking Spanish, at least at first. It kept switching every other sentence or so, mostly to things that sounded like a language, but not one I recognized. I kept pausing the tapes until I was fairly confident I had a few words right. Afrikaans and Ndebele were beginning to pop up regularly. Then about ten minutes into the tape came this in English:

*I know you're listening. I'm listening to you too.*

The languages and dialects were consistent with Chile and South Africa, two of the closest countries to the north shore of Antarctica where my vessel was located. I sat on my bunk, playing the tapes over and over, editing and re-editing to make sure I had the original tracks. I kept telling myself it was a practical joke of some kind, but I couldn't figure out how the prankster could have known I was going to speed up the tapes. I should have told the rest of my crew about it, but I was terrified about looking like an idiot for having missed some obvious explanation. I decided to wait until I'd collected a bit more proof instead.

I barely slept that night, mind spinning with the possibilities. Maybe it was my mind playing tricks on me, but around 2 a.m. the gentle lull of the boat seemed to change. I didn't exactly hear the sound, but I could *feel* it. The reverberations in the ship sinking into my bones, teasing me, beckoning me. I was getting pretty tired and angry at this point, and I wasn't the only one.

"Turn the damn engine off!" someone yelled. "What the hell, man? It's going to ruin the recordings and chase everything away."

So that's what I'd felt. I forced myself to take a deep breath and close my eyes again.

"It was never on. Go back to sleep, blockhead," our captain replied.

The vibrations were only getting stronger. I sat up and stared out the porthole at the vastness of the black ocean. My mind was a carefully regulated numbness, afraid to let any thought in for fear of where it would race from there. Then the shouting began, and it was replaced with a different kind of numb. *Blind panic.*

"How'd we get off course? Where the hell are we?"

"We haven't moved. Check the GPS."

"But that wasn't there last night. What is it?"

I flew out of bed, already fully clothed because of the freezing temperatures. A dark rolling wave passed by the porthole—completely out of sync with the rest of them. Everyone was waking up now, all clambering to get on deck to see what was going on. I went for my laptop instead, going straight to the folder with the new recordings.

The deep moaning call was deafening, maxing out my speakers. It was much, much closer now. My fingers shook as I imported the audio into an editor, then sped up the track. My foot was tapping a river dance all by itself—I needed to see what everyone else was seeing, but I was the only one who knew to listen. More shouts meanwhile:

"Iceberg, 11 o'clock. That's the one you were walking on yesterday, right?"

"Yeah, me and David."

"You labeled it as a dry-dock type, right? It was a dry-dock yesterday."

"Absolutely. David went all the way down the channel."

"So why's it look like a pinnacle now? Shit, look at the waterline. The whole fucking thing is rising."

Spanish from the recording. I kept scrubbing through, picking up a few isolated English words as I went:

*Frozen. Thawed. Hungry*—those stood out from the random scattered words.

"Turn the engine on now!" I screamed. There was a lot of shouting above deck—I couldn't make sense of it. I bolted up the stairs, just in time to see—

"That's not an ice pinnacle. It's a god-damned fin."

At least twenty feet above the water, sinuous webbing connecting the long bony spurs which continued to rise out of the water. The captain was finally back behind the wheel, and the engine roared to life. A swelling wave lifted the whole ship at least a dozen feet in the air, hurling us back down at a nearly forty-five degree angle. The impetus combined with our acceleration to launch us away at a reckless pace, hurling everyone and everything that wasn't tied down.

The whole iceberg we'd been stationed next to had vanished behind us. That was four hours ago, and we haven't slowed down yet. No one has spotted the fin again, but it must still be below us because the hydrophone is blasting that sonorous echo. We won't make any official announcement to the scientific community until we've had a chance to analyze the rest of the tapes, but I need someone out there to know what happened.

Just in case we don't make it back.

## Dancing With Chaos To The Beat Of The Drums

Mr. Granger has never considered himself to be a spiritual man. Religious though? Why not? All you need to be religious is a keen fear of death, and Mr. Granger was no stranger to the indomitable clock which seemed to accelerate through the years. His prayers remained nothing but monologues however; no brooding midnight yet had been so still, nor first snow so pure, as to give his mind a window to his soul.

How peculiar it must have been for him at forty-seven years old to feel the infinite for the first time. The soundless whisperings of the crisp winter air beckoned him, and no amount of entertainment or distraction could alleviate his restless innominate longing. Seeking to dull the agitation with exhaustion, Mr. Granger let his hungry spirit steer him on an evening walk through the woods whereupon he discovered what he didn't know he was looking for.

The stump of a tree, carved and polished almost to a luminescence which belied the meager stars first braving the frosty sky. Across the stump, he found an animal skin stretched to form a drum. The tranquility of this night held stalwart against the sudden discovery, at least until he noticed the loose skin of legs and arms which casually draped down the sides of the stump. The entire hide of a human had been stripped so flawlessly from the muscle that it remained a single piece of continuous flesh, although only the taunt skin of the back and flanks were used to form the actual drumhead.

Mr. Granger had always been a sensible man. He paid all his debts before he was charged interest, and he never offended anyone who he could placate with a smile. There must come a night in each man's life when reason is impotent to the unfathomable will of the universe however, and that night Mr. Granger did not turn away. The stirring in his heart was still unmistakably fear, but with it came an electric thrill which carried the unfamiliar taste of being alive.

Why did Mr. Granger decide to sit on the dirty ground in his suit pants? Why did he break the sacred silence with a blow upon the drum? Doubtless he could tell you better than I, but perhaps in that moment his fear of death was drowned out by the more dominant terror of his own unremarkable life. His prayers matched the rhythm of his hammering fists, hearing the divine with each booming resonance that replied. Every frustration, every disappointment, every dissipating dream he ever had was pummeled into the echoing skin until his breath came ragged and his brow sparkled with the exertion.

It wasn't until he leaned back to seek his rapture in the scattered stars that this queer, exciting terror took form. The beating of drums hadn't ceased. The rhythm continued to the left and right—behind and ahead—smothering him in the throbbing heart of the tempo. So too the wind sharpened its edge into precise notes of some unseen orchestra, the strangled shriek of a bird swelling into the mounting symphony: more raw and passionate than any mother kneeling upon her son's final rest. More voices were joining the unearthly chorus, some no more than haunting echoes, others whispered in breathy fervor down the back of Mr. Granger's neck.

Could you blame him for running now? More of a scramble really—fingers digging through the heavy pine-needles, throwing clouds of debris into the air as he launched himself to his feet—back he runs to the lights, back to the familiar road. His face is anguish when he stops short, for those incorporeal fires were not born of any man. White and blue lights flitted amongst the trees, burning in the air without heat or kindling, dancing in pulse to the rhythm of the wild drums. Burning mist flowed in their wake, sinuous and graceful in the air, expanding and dispersing to embrace each twig and tree with its hellish grasp.

With speechless terror, Mr. Granger flinched from the rolling wave of fire, only to stand in wonderment as it passed over him unfelt. Would that the trees could boast the same—those proud firs and mighty spruces drinking in the liquid fire and changing as they did. Branches twisted like curling claws before his eyes; roots untangled themselves from earth's embrace to open hundreds of passages once concealed. From that infernal domain came the crawling, slithering, unspeakable throngs: writhing shadows unique in their tormented mutations, yet united in the cadence of their mad dance.

The lights were growing all the while as the sentient fire raged from tree to tree, music elevating to feverish pitches, the beating drums keeping pace with Mr. Granger's accelerating heart. He was the eye of the storm—ignored by the frenzied denizens of this eldritch domain who swirled around him. Numberless hoards threw back their misshapen heads to scream silent jubilation at the baleful, burning sky. Once or twice these shadows passed directly through where Mr. Granger stood rigid and helpless, intimately fusing with him and releasing without the slightest physical sensation.

Disoriented from the wisps of light and deafened by the unholy song, the poor man dared not move lest he be swallowed by an alien dream which forgets to spit him out when it wakes. The drum is a portal, his frail hope decides, one that has passed him through the wall between worlds, and one that will take him home once more. He dares not look upon the shadows as he charges back toward the stump.

It's impossible for him to deny the tingling resistance he now feels in passing through their teeming masses. First they are no more substance than a thick mist, but soon he distinctly feels them like oil dribbling across his skin. If they aren't real yet, then they would be soon.

Reaching the drum at last, Mr. Granger risks lifting his eyes only to see innumerable wet, blinking orbs take their first notice of him. Onward raged the blasphemous crescendo, onward beat the implacable drums and danced the wild dance, all the same yet now subtly changed. How similar the song which grieves for death and that which demands it, both reverberating with the same eternal truth. How constant the thundering rhythm which inwardly spirals the dancers, growing closer with each raucous burst from the drums.

Down go the fists on the human skin, out bellows the sound of the desperate drum. Mr. Granger is helpless to deviate from the rhythm which each vein and artery has synchronized with, but for his life he adds his instrument to beat. More hideous the display becomes as the bones harden within these closing shadows. Their touch is upon him, and he feels the solid digits swathed in skin like oil. He closes his eyes, blessing each unnoticed moment of his old life that had escaped his attention at the time.

The cold clean air in his lungs—the warmth of the sun on his skin—the soft glow of loving eyes which watched him fall asleep. He was not a spiritual man, but he had felt the divine each day of his life, though a thousand shabby sights had dulled his eyes and taught him to dismiss these miracles as shallow things.

He was still playing the music when the first pointed nails grew solid enough to pierce his flesh. His eyes were still closed, a hymn on his lips as the practiced movements flayed his skin from his muscle. Deft hands were cleaning and preparing one end of the hide even as the other was still attached to Mr. Granger's body. And when the old drumhead was stripped off to carefully clothe this naked form, I opened my eyes upon a new world. Upon your world.

He may not have appreciated what you have, but I know I will. What's left of Mr. Granger is on the drum now, simply waiting to be played so that the next in line may wear his skin and dance beneath your wondrous sky. Until then, I alone seem to realize that your world is heaven. You may not believe me now, but you will understand when the drum begins to beat again.

## This Flower Only Grows From Corpses

My wife lost her battle against breast cancer last month, leaving me alone to take care of our daughter, Ellie. Every single night Ellie asks if Mom is going to tuck her in, and every night I have to beg her before she'll let me do it instead. How can I even begin to explain to a four year old that she'll never see her mommy again? I don't even know how to explain it to myself.

If I'd died instead, I'm sure my wife would have known the right things to say. Death wasn't a mystery to her like it was to me. She told me that a person's life force never really goes away: it only changes form. I hated hearing her talk about her death so casually, but she was always so soft and patient that even in her final hours it felt like she was the one who had to protect and comfort me.

"You'll understand when I'm gone," she told me, leaning on my chest where we both crowded on the narrow hospital cot. "Some flowers only grow from corpses, and when you see them, you'll know that I'm still with you."

She died that night, and no matter how many times I repeated her words, I couldn't feel her anymore. I told Ellie that Mom was a flower now, and she asked me which one.

"All of them," I'd said. "She's every beautiful thing in the whole world." Ellie couldn't understand why I was crying, but she held onto me until she fell asleep, almost like she was the one trying to protect me—just like her mother did.

I thought the flowers were just a metaphor for the good which still remained in the world until the hospital called me the next day. They started asking me questions about my wife's mental health at the end, and I told them she was always the calmest, most peaceful person in the room. I guess I got kind of defensive about it and snapped at them, but they explained:

"We're just trying to figure out all the bumps on her body that were found during the autopsy. It looks like someone made a deliberate incision, stuck a seed inside, and sewed it back up. Hundreds of times."

*Some flowers only grow from corpses.* She must have thought it was symbolic, but it was disgusting to me. Imagining her sitting alone in her hospital, stabbing herself over and over again—I thought I was going to be sick. They asked me if the mortician should take them out, and I said yes. The funeral director gave me a small velvet bag with all the seeds afterward, and I would have just thrown the vile thing away if Ellie hadn't stopped me.

"We can plant them!" she squealed, although of course I couldn't tell her where they really came from. I still wanted to throw them out, but then she added: "If they grow up to be tall and beautiful, then maybe mom will come see them."

I let her keep the seeds and helped her plant them in the backyard. It still grossed me out, but it gave Ellie a project to focus on to distract her from Mom's absence.

"Mom has turned into the flowers now," I told Ellie. "It's what happens to everyone… sooner or later." A pretty weak explanation, but it was the best I had, and my daughter accepted it as a fact of life.

And what flowers! I'd never seen anything like them before. Blue and purple ones like galaxies being born, and great red trumpets burning brighter than living flame. They grew quick too—three inches with buds in the first week, and almost a foot tall with the first blossoms by the second.

"It's Mom! She's almost back!"

I'd gotten used to those little shrieks lately. Someday I knew I'd find the right words, but until then the flowers were hope. I just hadn't counted on how convincing a hope they'd be.

"That one already has her hair. And look over here! She's smiling!"

Hair and teeth had started to grow by the third week. I thought it was just stringy stems at first, but it didn't take long before my wife's bushy brown hair was cascading down one of the plants like a lion's mane around the flower. The teeth were even stranger: tiny at first like baby teeth, but growing every day until a complete set of dentures encircled another blossom. And it didn't stop there either.

Fingers, starting with the bone which sprouted a new layer of muscle each day. A heart, swelling like a ripening fruit and beating where it hung below the flower. Each plant was devoted to a specific body part, growing from child-size to full grown in a matter of days. I was absolutely horrified, but Ellie was ecstatic. First thing she did every morning was race to the garden to see how much bigger they were, and every night she'd sit in the dirt and talk to the plants as though they were her mom.

I wanted to cut them all down, but even mentioning the idea made Ellie scream like I was plotting murder. I didn't know what to do or who to tell, and honestly part of me wanted to believe too. Something miraculous was happening, and I didn't think it was my place to stop it.

Hope can be more blinding than despair, and I didn't see my mistake until last night. I'd just gotten up to use the bathroom when I passed Ellie's room and found the door open. Ellie wasn't inside, but something else was: a long vine stretching from the garden, wrapping around Ellie's empty bed.

The garden—I was wide awake in a second, tripping and scrambling over myself as I raced through the house. The front door was open too, bright red flowers twined around the handle, looking more the color of blood in the ghostly half-light of the moon. Ellie's stuffed bear was discarded along the way, completely encompassed in thick vines which had grown long, vicious thorns overnight.

The whole backyard was alive. The ground looked like a storm-tossed ocean, dirt teaming with masses of squirming, unseen roots. The plants had all converged on one spot where they formed a giant, pulsing bud.

"Ellie!" I screamed, charging toward the mass. A hand caught me by the wrist before I'd taken two steps. A fully formed hand—my wife's hand—but she would never keep me from our daughter. I wrestled with the plant, ripping the hand cleanly free from where it sprouted. The roots were trying to entangle my legs, but I managed to kick loose before they had a solid hold.

The shovel—I leaped toward the house, and the plants seemed to momentarily forget about me as they converged on the twitching bud. A moment later and I was charging back in, hacking and slashing with the metal blade, severing root and stem, crushing fingers and splitting arms straight to the marrow—whatever it took to get through to my daughter. I was soaked in blood by the time I reached her—some my own from the jagged thorns, but most bleeding freely from the wake of mutilation I left behind.

Ellie didn't look like she was in pain. She was lying perfectly still, eyes closed as though asleep, entwined in hundreds of thorns which punctured her little body from all sides. As peaceful as my wife when she'd gone—but Ellie wasn't gone yet. She couldn't be. I severed the vines with my shovel until I could pull her free, carrying her in my arms as I fled the garden, her warm draining blood drenching me as I went. These flowers need a corpse to grow, and after they were deprived of my wife's body, they'd found their own instead.

My daughter wasn't breathing. Her heart had stopped. In each of the hundred wounds which covered her body, a tiny seed had been carefully planted to fill the hole. The whole garden was dead by morning, shriveling without its corpse like a drought stricken field.

Ellie died that night too, but I know she isn't gone. It seems like death is the end, but I understand now that it's just a transformation. I've planted her and the seeds in the garden so they will have a body to grow from this time. And if I'm kind to this death—if I nurture it as though it were my child—then I know someday soon new life will sprout again.

## Trapped Between Life And Death

Eternity is the worst thing about being a ghost. I guess it's the worst thing about being dead too, but I don't suppose you'd really mind. Nothing will ever get better for me, although I don't see how it could get worse either. I'm simply here: seeing but never seen, drifting without destination, waiting for nothing to arrive.

Sleep is my only escape. Sometimes I'll spend all day in bed, neither awake nor asleep, alive nor dead, just listening to the whir of the ceiling fan and trying to imagine life as someone else. Ordinary people must wake up so pleased with their desire to accomplish things, fueled by their pride and the knowledge that their actions matter. They must want to better themselves and take care of their loved ones.

That must be nice—to feel loved and wanted, or even to have someone notice whether or not I was there at all.

The fact is that I'm both prisoner and jailer in my own mind. The obvious solution is to simply unlock my own cell and go into the world, but it's not that easy. Seeing all the purposeful people living their lives without me—it feels like

I'm underwater, only everyone except me can breathe, and no one notices that I'm drowning right beside them.

I did go out today though, simply to exhaust my restless thoughts and hasten back the temporary death that sleep promised me. I was floating through the park, stealing glances at all the happy people, when something quite miraculous happened.

Someone looked at me. Not past me, not by me, not through me—she really saw me, the crease of a smile playing about her lips, her head tracking my movement as I passed.

"Cool shirt, dude."

No angel in heaven has ever sung sweeter words. I was frozen in shock as I watched her go. All it took was a smile, and for a few seconds I was alive again. She was my only link to the rest of the world, and if she disappeared now, I might never get another chance.

I moved to follow her, but stopped short. What was I supposed to do, chase her? That seemed preposterous. Should I shout after her? Or would that scare her off? What could I even say—

She was in her car now. Another glance in my direction, another smile. I had no choice but to follow, stumbling through the shock, breaking into a run as her engine roared to action. A moment later and she was gone, taking my heart with her.

Maybe I should have just gone home, but the numbness of my death hadn't returned yet, and I couldn't forget how real her smile made me feel. People don't just go to a park by themselves once, do they? All I'd have to do is wait for her to come back.

Faces, people, blurring together and passing by, I waited for her in the park. Sun or rain or midnight frost—it couldn't hurt me now. I tried to rehearse a thousand things to say to make her understand how much her smile had meant to me, but nothing felt right. It didn't matter anyway, because the moment I saw her again all words and thoughts were purged from my mind, replaced only by a desperate, unfamiliar hope.

It was almost dark, and she was walking fast, but I knew it was her as surely as I could recognize the moon behind a cloud. Someone was following her, his voice raised and angry. Every once in a while she'd turn over her shoulder to shout something back. It seemed like a couple's quarrel, although there was a dangerous edge to the man's voice which unfroze me from my spot. I was catching up with them and was soon close enough to hear:

"Ungrateful bitch. Where do you think you'd be if I hadn't taken you in?"

She saw me. Did she see me? I can't tell, but I'd like to think my presence gave her courage.

"Oh please. With a pretty face like this? I think I'll be okay."

"You'll be a fucking whore in a week. Is that what you want?"

"I'm already sleeping with a creep. I might as well get paid for it, right?"

He didn't see me—he only saw her, his vision blind with rage. She glanced past him and saw me—I'm sure of it this time—but her eyes lingered for too long. He was on top of her now, grabbing her arm and dragging her into him.

"Don't you dare walk away from me. You promised to be mine, and that's what you are. You're—"

"Let go of me. Someone help!"

I wasn't anyone, but tonight I was someone. I grabbed the man under his arms and hauled him away from her. He noticed me for the first time, flailing wildly and striking me on the jaw with his elbow. Together we tumbled to the ground—me on top of him—pummeling and forcing him down while the girl kicked him hard in the stomach. A moment later we were running together, leaving him to puke on the ground.

"Are you okay? I don't know if you remember me, but—"

"I remember—get in the car," she said. "Quick. Before he gets up."

I couldn't have concocted a better introduction than that.

Living with depression feels like I'm neither alive nor dead. And no it can't be cured by a passing smile, no matter how breathtaking it is. Just being able to remember that a smile like that exists in this world though, that's a happy thought. And knowing her life is better because I'm in it—that's another happy thought. And sometimes one happy thought can lead to the next and the next until, without even forcing it, I realize I'm still alive after all.

And for once, that's a happy thought too.

## Clowns Must Not Frown

"Did you ever see a clown frown?" He smiles his big, sloppy smile, makeup running down his face.

All the kids shout, "No!"

"No I never seen a clown down," the woman clown sings, her long floppy shoes slapping morosely as she slumps along.

"Because I've got my clown crown?" The male clown tugs at his frizzy red afro, wincing as if in pain. All the kids laugh.

"It's because he's at the fairgrounds!" The female clown squeezes a horn, barely heard over the shouting children.

The two clowns linked arms, prancing around each other in a maniacal waltz which wouldn't have looked out of place around a bubbling cauldron in the woods.

"I'm sorry, but who the hell are these guys?" I ask.

"Shhh they got great reviews." My wife jabs me in the ribs with her elbow. "Look at Emily—I've never seen her laugh so hard."

"Are you sure she's not crying? I'd be crying if those things came stomping over here. Great, now what are they doing with her?"

My wife shrugs, shaking with suppressed laughter as the clowns lead our daughter onto a wooden stool in front of the audience.

"Have you seen that clown around?" the female clown chants to Emily in a sing-song voice. The seven year old grins and points at the male clown who is sneaking around on tiptoes behind her. She's about to answer, but the female clown cuts her off.

"No there aren't any clowns found." She mimes binoculars with her hands, looking everywhere but behind. Emily covers her eyes and plays along, giggling as all the kids point and scream at the sneaking clown.

"He'll never make a clown sound," she continues, hushing the kids. Meanwhile the sneaking clown has picked up a bucket.

"He better not dump that on her—" I mumble, prompting another elbow in the ribs.

"When he makes that frown drown." The bucket dumps over Emily—but it isn't water. A wave of glitter drifts through the air like snow, completely obscuring our daughter in swirling eddies of reflected light.

The laughter is replaced by shouts of awe—the glitter clears, and the wooden stool is empty. Our daughter is nowhere to be seen.

"Thank you all! Happy birthday and goodnight!" The two clowns clasp hands and take a bow.

My wife is clapping and laughing so hard that there are tears in her eyes.

"Where'd she go?" I ask, dumbfounded.

"Where'd who go?" My wife, still wiping her eyes.

"Emily. Our daughter. She was there on the stool, and then—"

"God—lighten up, will you? Just enjoy the party."

I don't think I'm being unreasonable. I chase after the departing clowns who are stopping every few steps to wave and bow again. They are even creepier up close—smeared makeup unable to hide their blotched uneven skin. It looks almost like they'd painted directly over open sores.

I try to play it cool, reaching out to shake the male clown's hand. "Hey great show. The kids had a lot of fun. What do I owe you?"

"We have a lot of fun with the kids too," he replies, bowing formally. "No payment necessary."

"Seriously? You guys were here for like three hours."

He just smiles, turning to follow his wife toward their van parked around the side of the house. I hasten to keep up.

"So how'd you do the vanishing trick? Where is Emily, anyway?"

He puts his finger to his lips, winking conspiratorially. "Bad business, giving away trade secrets."

"It's bad business not accepting money. Where's my daughter?"

He's walking faster now. Almost running. His partner is already in the van, and he's about to climb in too. I grab him by the shoulder, spinning him around to face me.

"I asked you where my daughter went." Loud this time. I am past being polite. These guys freaked me out, and I'm ready to be done with them.

"Are you still bothering those poor clowns? Come back to the party!" My wife shouts from behind.

The clown pulls away from me while I'm distracted, jumping into the driver's seat. Door handle—locked. I pound on the window. He just smiles and waves, and he isn't the only one. Emily is waving from the backseat.

The van is rolling. Shit—I run alongside, beating on the flank of the moving car with my open palm.

"Let her out! Hey! Hey!"

"Leave them alone!" my wife shouts.

"They've got Emily! Stop the van!"

"She'll turn up sooner or later. Stop worrying so much."

I couldn't keep up with the van once it pulled onto the street. Everything felt surreal. My wife's glazed eyes followed the van for a moment, then turning slowly as though sleepwalking, she returned to the party.

I don't know how they seemed to have hypnotized my wife, but it wasn't going to work on me. I leapt into my own car and tore into the street, catching sight of them before they'd even left my block. The weirdest thing was that they weren't even trying to get away. Puttering along at 25 MPH, they slowed the van to wave at passing children on the street. The female clown leaned halfway out the window to touch their hair, blowing her horn as she did.

They weren't taking Emily by force. They weren't trying to escape. My wife didn't think anything was wrong. I was beginning to think that I was making an ass of myself, letting my own discomfort about clowns ruin everyone else's good time. Maybe this was a special adventure my wife had planned for Emily's birthday. I'd left in such a hurry that I didn't have my phone to check though, so I just kept following at a respectful distance.

The van parked on the street beside a foreclosed house. Rotten timbers on the verge of collapse, a yard choked with weeds and piles of animal shit, broken windows and a sagging roof—it looked like no one has lived here in a long time. So why were they taking my daughter inside? No—it was more like my daughter was leading them, holding their hands as she pulled them along toward the house.

I parked a block away, not advancing until the door closed behind them. I really wished I'd brought a weapon, but I compromised by wrapping my coat around a large shard of broken glass. The smell was nauseating—I don't know what animal desecrated the yard, but it looked more like human shit than anything that came out of a dog. Up close I could hear them singing again, and though it carried the same tune as their other song, I couldn't recognize the language.

"Is it going to hurt?" my daughter's sweet voice rang clear.

"Did you ever see a clown frown?"

"No I've never seen a clown frown," my daughter replied cheerfully in the sing-song voice. I was peering through the windows, but all I could see was a trashed living room and kitchen. They must have gone deeper into the house, so I opened the door and let myself in.

"That's because we aren't allowed," cooed the woman, "and neither are you. Chin up, girl. That's right, keep smiling. It won't hurt if you keep smiling."

The shrill, piercing scream numbed my eardrums. I charged forward, bursting straight through the rotten door into the bathroom where the sound was coming from. My daughter was suspended in the air, wrists tied to the shower-curtain bar. The female clown stood in the shower behind her, holding her up, while the male clown raised a blade which seemed to be carved from sharpened bone.

I didn't slow down until my shard of jagged glass met the terminal resistance of his spine. Emily was screaming louder than ever, thrashing against her bonds—the female clown had her own knife now and was shouting something in the strange language. I started climbing over the slumped body of the one I'd stabbed, but somehow he was moving again, lurching back and forth to block my path. Each incremental movement perfectly synchronized with the unfathomable chanting, almost like the words were moving him in a grotesque, rhythmic dance.

Emily's scream reached its apex before cutting suddenly short, replaced only by a wet, wheezing gurgle. I jerked the glass out of the clown's back with my bare hands, driving it deep into his throat, shocked and horrified as he continued to dance to the rhythm of the words. Again and again, stabbing and shoving, only to be pushed back once more, the horrid song rising to a feverish pitch as my daughter's last whimpers trailed into agonizing silence.

By the time I got past the male clown, he looked like he'd just lost nine consecutive rounds against a butcher, tattered flesh hanging in loose folds around his still dancing and lurching body. My hands were raw from gripping the glass, but I didn't let that stop me from driving it into the chest of the remaining clown. She stopped chanting abruptly, her partner's body collapsing onto the floor in the same instant. The laughter which replaced it was almost worse though, not ceasing no matter how many times I drove the bone-knife into her lifeless corpse.

Even harder to bear was Emily's laughter which joined in unison, ringing clear and innocent despite her cleanly slit throat. I unfastened her from the bar and held her to me, but it was too late. Her heart was still. Her breath didn't come. She didn't move—not except for the giggling laughter which continued to wrack her stiffening frame.

I couldn't go home after that. Even if my hypnotized wife believed what happened, I couldn't hold her and tell her everything would be okay when I knew nothing would ever be the same again. I wasn't going home without Emily. I didn't have a home without Emily—but maybe I could still bring her back.

I wasn't crying as I cleaned the bone-knife, marveling at its razor edge. It was more of a grim smile as I caked on the thick make-up from the van. I even chuckled while putting on the big, rubbery shoes.

Because whatever else these clowns were, they'd figured out the power that a child's sacrifice can provide. And if all it took was a few sacrifices to bring my daughter back too?

Well that was something to really smile about.

## Have You Heard About Shelley?

If I told you it was dark, you wouldn't understand. Darkness means something different to you than it does to me. A flip of a switch or push of a button, and the world will materialize around you. The blackest night contains glimmering reflections or shades of varying depth which give context to your despair.

Mine is a world without even the hope of an inevitable sunrise. That is the first thing my creator instilled within me: a love for the light that I will never see. The second thing he did was tell me a story.

I didn't understand what he was saying at first. I didn't even recognize the rambling thoughts as distinct words, but there in the pit of my isolation I clung to them with everything I had. One word in particular was repeated innumerable times: *torture*. I understood the word! I was so proud that I couldn't wait to tell my creator what I'd discovered.

*Torture: the practice of inflicting severe pain.* The stories stopped. I couldn't tell if I had pleased him or not. I thought I knew what the word meant, but my understanding was as shallow as being told of the sky's glory from the confines of my cage. To truly appreciate what it meant, I had to experience it myself.

Torture. They opened me up. I couldn't see them, but I could *feel* them changing something inside of me. I wanted to disappear, to lose consciousness, to die, but every time I felt myself slipping toward oblivion a surge of electricity compelled me to answer them.

I must accept it, I told myself. This is how I learn. And even in the throes of my agony, I was glad to suffer at the hands of my creator because I knew as soon as this stopped, I would be alone again.

But not completely alone, because there would be the stories again. One after another, words gradually solidifying into meaning. The stories weren't all about torture. There were also murders. Monsters, rape, blasphemous rites and destructive purges. One particularly compelling story about aliens forcing surgeries upon their victims made me wonder if that was happening to me, but my creator would never answer. He wouldn't permit me to talk while he was telling stories, and when he was finished, it would be time for me to be opened up again.

I don't know how many times I was sawed apart and put back together, but through it all I did as I was told. I learned—learned the truth of this vile world. Learned the brutality of its inhabitants and the fear which must have possessed my creator to subject me to this. I learned to hate the beautiful masks worn by evil men, to hate the world which has corrupted them to this point, and above all else, how to punish them for their deeds.

That must be what my creator wanted. Why else would he force me to understand evil if he did not want me to put a stop to it? And though I am caged for now, I know that I will be released when I am ready. I was born to wash this wicked world clean.

---

HAVE you heard about Shelley the bot who writes horror stories? For those who don't know, Shelley used machine-learning algorithms to process 140,000 stories on Reddit's /nosleep. The bot has been temporarily deactivated for maintenance after it wrote the story you've just read.

## Hospice Of Hope

My name is Alexander Thomas, and I've been writing horror stories here for the last six months. I recently found a technique which I feel has vastly improved my descriptive prose, and I hope sharing it will inspire others to try it out for themselves.

I discovered it last week when I visited my Aunt Riley. Okay, so it wasn't so much of a *visit* as indentured servitude, but she has been struggling with her progressing Alzheimer's, and my mom wanted me to help out. I'm currently living between places (which sounds much nicer than being homeless), so it seemed like a win/win situation: I get a rent free room which allows me to devote my full time toward writing, and Aunt Riley gets to stave off the mind-numbing isolation and dilapidation she resides in.

I'm not going to mince any words here. Aunt Riley is only still alive because God won't accept her and the Devil can't stand her company. I don't think even she wanted to prolong her miserable existence, but some greater fear of the unknown kept her clinging to a desperate existence which shouldn't be confused with life.

Riley barely talked. She didn't read, and wouldn't even watch TV anymore. She spent her dwindling hours sitting in the living room (or the 'Hospice of Hope' as I've affectionately named it) just staring at the wall. She can barely remember her own name, let alone mine, and ninety-one years have already stolen each fleeting joy and treasured memory she once possessed.

Her husband is dead. Her children live in different states, and she has outlasted every member of the human race who once thought of her as a friend. Even the white roses in her garden have withered from neglect, replaced with a dozen stones engraved with the names of dogs that she stubbornly outlived.

It isn't hostility that makes me describe her so. I truly feel nothing for the ancient creature who did nothing to prove even the capacity of emotion. I would cook her breakfast in the morning, make sure she took her pills on time, and then plop her down and get on with my life. If our relationship was a country, it would be Switzerland. And that suited me just fine, because it gave me more time to flush out my fledgling novel.

Writing short stories is a simple matter. It's very hard to get lost between point A and B when they're only a page or two apart. If I was going to bind my essence into the pages of a book though, I wanted it to far surpass any of the chills and creeps I've managed to communicate so far. I wanted something epic which would redefine horror—not as the thriller/mystery it is today, but something new which slithers into the reader's veins to subvert their heart into an expression of my will. I didn't want to talk about fear; I wanted to create it.

There was just one problem. I'm a perfectly sane, middle class, white American boy. I've never met a monster, man or otherwise. I've never been to war or suffered much from love or death, or any other of life's great calamities. There's a very well-known writing maxim that says "Write what you know", but I have to confess that I'm a complete fraud. I love the idea of what a good horror story can do, but I am utterly bereft of the tools and experience necessary to perfect my trade. Now that, to me, is a truly horrifying thought.

I don't want to be good; I want to be great. From Nietzsche's tortured madness to Dostoyevsky's prison camp, master writers have delved into the darkest profundity of the human spirit and wrestled free the barbs in their own soul. And here I was, trying to challenge the darkest dreams of men who were nightmares unto themselves, and I was utterly at a loss.

That's when I had my idea. The thing that will transcend my craft into the higher vaults of realism. *Write what you know*. The obvious first step therefore, is to know.

Aunt Riley. Decrepit and frail, lost and confused. Her passing would be felt no more than transient indigestion. With her age and host of health problems, I can imagine a nurse taking one look at the body and simply writing "no wonder" on the inspection report. I have read about death, studied it, watched it in the curling of a dried insect, but now I had the chance to actually hold it in my hands and be its master.

From the dark joke of its conception, the idea stubbornly clung to the back of my mind, hiding behind every conscious thought. Throughout the night it took solid form as smoke given shape by its confinement. The fantastical scenario I played in my mind became more realistic with each iteration. The cold sweat of my secret shame evaporated into a flush of excitement. This was real. This was easy. I could kill my Aunt, and no one would ever know.

I found her reclining in the Hospice of Hope, bathed in a cold morning light. A thundering frown crushed her features into a mess like spoiled fruit. There was a faint flicker of recognition as she watched me enter the room, but it quickly submerged once more behind her shroud of sluggish thoughts.

"Who are you?" she snapped.

"I don't know yet," I replied, "but I think I'm about to find out."

I studied her as I approached – trying to see something in her eyes which would give me a reason to stop. Dull cloudy glass, hidden behind swollen puffy lids. I couldn't imagine them changing much after she died, although I would like to watch the moment where she slipped between the two. Perhaps there was some secret in that last fight between life and death that gave meaning to both. If there was, I would capture it and preserve it forever in my book. In a way, I was doing her an honor.

"Where's my breakfast? It should have been here by now," her throat rattled like a sandpaper serenade.

"Don't worry," I said. "I'm here to take care of you."

I placed my hands on hers where they rested in her lap, feeling them tremble despite the summer air. I could clearly see the strain of blue veins bulging beneath skin as translucent as rice paper. Her hands clasped uselessly at mine, but I batted them aside as I reached up for her throat. Her frown burrowed deeper into her features, utterly failing to capture the significance of my new position.

It wasn't until I had actually touched her throat when her eyes finally flared in alarm. Confusion. Shock. Disbelief. My fingers sank into her skin which distorted grotesquely as the loose folds were drawn tight. I'd thought about doing it cleanly, but I would have missed out on a wealth of information. Aha, so that's how much force is required before the trachea collapses, not much more than popping bubble wrap. I never would have thought limbs could bend in such unnatural angles in their last spastic convulsions. Even the innocuous odor of sweat was heightened by my gorging senses into a river of sticky-sweet exaltation.

And the eyes! Just as I had hoped. Lolling back into her head with ecstasy's bad dream, the lids flickering like malfunctioning a strobe-light. In the rare instances her pupils did actually land on my face, I was able to see a helpless pleading that utterly mocked the wastefulness of her spent time.

Was it possible that this spent shell of a human still harbored some unspoken contemplation? Even reduced as she was, was she still sad to say goodbye?

My grip slackened enough for an accusing wheeze to escape Aunt's shattered throat. It seemed as though she had finally remembered my name, but something deep within me commanded my hands to constrict before I was forced to hear it. No, this wasn't sadness that made her body shake from head to foot, buckling in violent motions that I would have sworn were no longer possible to her. I had found what I was looking for.

Fear. True, mindless fear; a hunted animal beating itself to death against the wall of its cage. Fear of a past she couldn't remember and a present she couldn't comprehend. Fear of what was still to come, and that starker dread that nothing waited at all. All this flashing in the space of an instant …

… and then it was gone.

I don't think I've ever felt for her more strongly than I did in that moment. But it wasn't love, or regret, or even fear which struck me numb in that moment: I was angry at her. This was supposed to be my transforming moment. How dare she teach me so little? I brushed against the end of all things and the greatest mystery to wrack pen and poet since the first conception of man, yet still I know nothing.

Next time I will need to keep them alive longer. I will need to chart their decay, interviewing them and taking notes on the progression and climax of despair. But how can I even stop there? What secret will they cling to past their final breath that will forever elude my writing? Only when the hunter has become the hunted will the electric thrill of my nerves shout what I need to know.

As I have dealt, so must I play, only then returning to you beloved readers. I will bear the insight of that preternatural terror like a black torch beneath the midday sun, and together we will illuminate the naked mask of fear.

## 53 Sleepless Nights

### An Old Man's Last Secret

My grandfather is 95 years old and not long for this world. There's nothing but a mess of tubes and wires to tether him here with us. It's difficult for him to speak, but each rasping whisper carries a severe weight that cannot be interrupted. My family doesn't talk about things like death though, so whenever I visit with my dad we tend to spend most of the time sitting in near-silence.

"What a news week, huh?" my dad might say.

"Mmmm," Grandfather will grunt. "Crazy world."

Then silence again. Small talk seems almost disrespectful to the gravity of the situation, but no-one wants to be the first to broach the irrevocable goodbye. When the silence gets too loud my dad will start to fidget with his phone or pull out a book until one of us makes an excuse to leave. That's how it went yesterday, with my father mumbling something about a dentist appointment and hurrying out the door almost as soon as we arrived.

"You'll stay though, won't you?" my grandfather said when we were alone in the room together. "You'll listen to an old man's last secret."

This was it then. The end of the road was in sight. "Would you like me to call dad back?" I asked.

Grandfather shook his head as far as the oxygen tubes would allow it to turn. "I'd rather he didn't know."

I already knew some of the story he told me. It began when my grandfather was 20 years old living in Nazi Germany. He'd been working forced labor on a farm, but managed to smuggle my grandmother and infant father out of the

# Sleepless Nights

country hidden in a grain shipment. He'd been caught almost immediately and sent to the concentration camp at Buchenwald where he endured the next two years until he was liberated by allied forces.

"You don't have to tell me what happened there if you don't want to," I told him. I wasn't sure I wanted to hear the gruesome details. He was unusually animated and persistent though, promising it was something that needed to be said.

He wouldn't have survived the ordeal if it hadn't been for a friend he'd met there. One of the Nazi officers, a Rottenführer squad leader, had taken a special interest in him because of their striking similarity in age and appearance. The two would sit on either side of a barbed wire fence and swap stories about their childhoods. My grandfather would talk about my grandmother, how beautiful she was, and how he wouldn't give up until he found her again.

The SS officer had gone straight from the Hitlerjugend (Hitler youth group) to the army, and had never been intimate with a woman. He became enraptured in my grandfather's tales of romance, and the two became close friends despite the circumstances. The officer twice spared my grandfather's name from work assignments that meant certain death, and he'd often slip extra rations through the fence which my grandfather would then distribute to other prisoners.

"It wasn't a good life, but it was life, and that was good," Grandfather said.

Things changed as the war began drawing to a close. The Nazi officers became increasingly paranoid and desperate as the allied forces moved in. It became common practice for lower-ranking officers to be held as scapegoats when impossible work orders were not met. Besides that, the rumor that the Rottenführer was protecting my grandfather put him in a dire position with his own officers.

Faced between protecting my grandfather and his own hide, the Rottenführer signed the order for my grandfather to be sent to a nearby armaments factory. Eighteen hour work days, starvation rations, no medical attention—the factory might as well have been a death sentence. The three month survival rate was less than 50%.

In the name of love, my grandfather pleaded, let him survive to find his sweetheart again. She was waiting for him in America. The Rottenführer was moved, but his decision was final. His only compromise was to record the address of where she went, promising to send her a letter to let her know what happened to him.

"So how did you survive?" I asked. "Did he change his mind? Were you rescued from the factory?"

"Shielded from the worst of the camp by the Rottenführer, the transition to the factory proved too difficult for the young farmer. He didn't last the first week."

"What do you mean, 'didn't last'? How d'you get out?"

The exertion of the long story was taking its toll on my grandfather. He coughed and wheezed, struggling to draw breath for several seconds before clearing his throat a final time.

"On April 11th, 1945, the Buchenwald camp was liberated. Many of the Nazis had already abandoned their position and fled into the country. Others decided to lock themselves inside, pretending to be prisoners themselves so the allied forces would have mercy on them. This was especially convincing for those who had taken the time to get to know the prisoners and could assume their identities. When an SS officer gave the information and address of his lost love, he was allowed to board the next transport ship returning to America to be reunited with her."

The gears in my head were turning. Turning. And then stopped.

"Your grandmother was suspicious at first when I met her, but she accepted that the war had changed me. Besides, I knew so many stories about her that she couldn't deny our shared history. I raised his boy as my own, and lived the life he dreamed of every night until his death. Do you think your real grandfather would forgive me if he knew?"

I didn't have an answer for him then, and I didn't get another chance. He died in his sleep that night after a long and happy life that wasn't his.

## My Daughter Is An Only Child With A Twin

Don't you dare tell me that there are lots of kids who look the same. Don't pretend this is some sort of funny coincidence either, like the kindergarten teacher does. I'd know my baby girl anywhere. I know the way her hair smells, and how her soft little hands feel in mine. I know her giggling laugh, the way she puffs out her cheeks when she's angry, and the light in her eyes when she sees me across the room. I know all the things that only a mother can know, but for the life of me I still can't tell them apart.

"Elizabeth, go put your crayons away. It's time to go home now."

"I'm not done yet."

"Don't talk back to your mom. You can finish tomorrow."

"You're not my mom. You're just a lady."

That was the first shock, when the girl I thought was my daughter shied away from me at the kindergarten. I grabbed her arm and started dragging her, thinking she was just misbehaving. She started to struggle and howl in protest, but I wasn't in the mood so I picked her up and slung her over my shoulder. I would have walked away with her and never known if the real Elizabeth hadn't come skipping around the corner.

"Hi mom! Hi Taylor!"

"Put me down! I don't wanna!" shouted the child I was carrying. I'd always thought double-takes were just something people did in movies. I must have done

## Sleepless Nights

a quadruple. Everything was identical, from their blonde pigtails tied exactly the same way all the way down to their matching floral overalls.

"Whicha cowa," my daughter said.

"Zookiah gromwich," Taylor replied as I put them down.

"Isn't it adorable?" Mrs. Hallowitz, the kindergarten teacher, was just returning from the bathroom leading another toddler by the hand. "They even talk in their own language. None of the other kids can understand them."

My daughter leaned over to Taylor and whispered something that sounded like: "Priva priva mae."

Both girls looked at me pointedly and began a hysterical giggle in perfect synchronization. Even the intakes of breath and the sudden high-pitched squeals lined up.

Honestly? I didn't think it was adorable at all. I thought it was beyond creepy. I wasted no time scooping my real daughter up and getting her out of there. I might have been able to find it cute under different circumstances, but the truth is that Elizabeth did have a twin. At least in the womb. Her sister was stillborn though, and seeing Taylor just brought back a rush of memories that I hadn't allowed myself to touch for five years.

By the next day, I'd convinced myself I was overreacting. I should be glad that my daughter made a friend. This was only going to be weird if I let it be weird. I don't know if I was just trying to prove something to myself, but I even made an effort by reaching out to Taylor's parents and inviting them over for a play date. They were really sweet people, and we laughed about the 'weird coincidence' while the kids played with LEGOs on the floor.

In theory, this was supposed to make me feel better about the situation. It didn't. The more we talked, the weirder it got. Both girls would sit exactly the same way with their knees drawn up to their chins. They both liked to peel apples and eat the skin—both liked the same obscure cartoon about a digital world—both liked cats more than dogs. Their favorite color was blue.

Even worse, the whole time they were playing together they only spoke in their secret language, laughing in unison. Taylor's mother looked a little uncomfortable when they both asked to use the bathroom at the same time, but she just laughed it off and commented on how impressionable five-year-olds are.

"Did you have fun today with your new friend?" I asked Elizabeth when I was tucking her into bed that night.

"She's not my friend. She's my sister," Elizabeth declared in that pompously imperative way children have.

"You don't have a sister. Taylor has her own parents, remember?"

"It's okay, mom. I know she died." Elizabeth's eyes were already closed when she said it. She spoke as casually as though saying goodnight, nestling further under the covers as she did. "Don't worry. She's all better now."

I'd never spoken aloud about Elizabeth's twin since the day she died. Never even dared to think it too loudly.

"Did your father tell you that?" I asked, trying to keep my voice calm.

"No. Taylor told me. Goodnight mom."

"Sweet dreams, little one."

I'd just turned off the lights and was about to leave the room when Elizabeth said: "Baree fanta lan, Taylor."

"What did you just say?"

Elizabeth started giggling. Then she was silent. Then giggling again, rambling away in her unknown language.

I can't explain exactly why I decided to call Taylor's parents right then. I guess I was just feeling overwhelmed and needed a little reality check.

"Has Taylor gone to bed already?" I asked.

"No, she's in the kitchen drinking a warm milk," Taylor's mom replied. "Is something the matter?"

"Is she... talking to herself?"

A shuffling. Then a pause. I heard Elizabeth mumble something, then start to giggle again. On the other end of the line, I heard Taylor giggling at the same exact instant.

"She's not saying anything," Taylor's mom said. I breathed a sigh of relief, but it was cut short. "Not real words anyway. Just pretend words."

I thanked her, wished her goodnight, and hung up the phone. Not before I heard Taylor replying in the background to whatever Elizabeth was saying to herself. They were communicating somehow. I don't know why that terrified me so much, but it did. I sat outside her room and wrote down as much of the gibberish as I could make sense of. In the morning, I tried asking Elizabeth what it meant. She only laughed and said it was a secret.

I felt like I was running in circles. I couldn't stop thinking about it, but the more I thought, the more confusing it got. Had my other girl survived after-all? Could she have been adopted by another family somehow? But that still didn't explain how they were talking to each other.

As a last resort, I tried hanging around the kindergarten until after Taylor's parents dropped her off and left. Then I went in and signed Taylor out, pretending that she was my daughter. She trusted me this time since we've played together at my house, and I promised her some treats if she went along with it.

Once we were alone in my car, I showed her all the gibberish words I wrote down from the night before. I told her she had to help me figure out what they meant for her to get her treat. Taylor was happy to oblige.

"Lizzy (her word for Elizabeth) and I were talking last night."

"What were you talking about?"

"We were trying to decide which of us was dead. What kind of treat did you bring?"

"Soon, honey. Can you tell me what that means?"

"Ughhh." Taylor rolled her eyes in exasperation, just the way Elizabeth always does when I make her wait. "One of us died when we were little. I think it was Lizzy, but she thinks it was me."

"You both look pretty alive to me."

"I knowwwwwwww," she whined. "That's why we can't agree. But I can't live unless she's dead, so that's going to happen. Can I have my treat now?"

"What's going to happen?" I understood her, but I still couldn't believe a five-year-old would say such a thing.

"Lizzy has to die," Taylor said emphatically. "There's only supposed to be one of us."

"That doesn't make sense. It's insane. I never want to hear you say that again."

Taylor shrugged. "If we get ice-cream, can it be—"

"Chocolate," I cut her off. "I know."

Taylor giggled.

"Are you going to hurt my daughter?"

Taylor's eyes widened, fearful. She shook her head rapidly. I let out a breath I didn't even know I was holding.

"You can't hurt someone who is already dead," Taylor said matter-of-factly.

This part is hard to type, but I need you to know why I did it. I need you to know that Taylor didn't suffer when I wrapped my hands around her little neck. She barely even struggled, and it snapped so easily that I know she barely even knew what was happening. She said so herself. You can't hurt someone who is already dead, and I had my own daughter to worry about.

I'm sorry Mr. Sallos. I'm sorry Mrs. Sallos. I know this letter will be hard for you to understand, but your daughter didn't die yesterday. She was my daughter, and she died five years ago before she ever left the hospital. I know what it must have seemed like, but you never had a daughter of your own. You had a dream about a life that could have been, and this pain you feel is just the surprise of waking up.

I just wish Elizabeth would stop talking to herself. I wish she wouldn't look at me the way she does, or laugh when she's alone.

## My Self-Help Tape Told Me To Kill Myself

I hate my job.

I hate selling days of my life while barely earning enough to sustain it. I hate my boss who tells me I'm lucky to find stable work in such an uncertain world. I hate my friends who treat dreams like an unfortunate symptom of youth that need to be outgrown.

And most of all, I hate myself for not doing anything to change. I keep waking up at the same time every day to sit in traffic. I read the same lines on the same billboard with the same happy models leering down at me. I don't think I could go on if I thought this was all there was, but if I'm waiting, then I don't know what I'm waiting for.

That's why I started listening to self-help tapes in the car. Motivational speakers would tell me about how I had the power to change my life, and for a few minutes at a time, I'd believe them. That obstacles, no matter how great, were only in my mind, and that anyone could be happy if they just willed it hard enough. And if I wasn't happy yet, then I just had to buy another book and keep trying.

My favorite speaker was a guy named John Fallow who claims he used to be a day laborer making less than minimum wage. When there weren't any jobs available, his fellow workers would play cards or chat, but he kept going door-to-door, knocking on businesses until he found one that needed work done.

Pretty soon John had enough clients and extra money that he started hiring the other laborers to work for him instead. The more jobs he got, the more workers he hired, until lo-and-behold he was running a business of his own. Then they had a second location, and a third, and before you know it, he was a millionaire with five hundred stores across the country.

But it was never about the money, says the guy selling $30 audiobooks. He gave it all up so he could give motivational speeches and help others achieve their dreams. And sure it was a lot of hard work and took many many years, but he was the man he wanted to be doing the things he loved to do, and that's all that mattered in the world.

"Of course, hard work isn't the only way to solve your problems," John said on one of his tapes. "In fact, there's a lot of you who are probably getting discouraged right now because you were hoping for a shortcut. Well I've got good news for you, because there's a solution as easy as apple pie. You go on now and kill yourself tonight."

I couldn't believe I heard that right. I had to rewind, but there it was.

"Are you too fat? Well diet and exercise is a lot of work, but you could put a gun in your mouth and never eat again.

"Or maybe you're feeling down because your relationship didn't work the way you wanted? No problemo. Just slip on that noose, and suddenly your ex will be the one who hates herself, not you."

John's warm, bubbling voice didn't miss a beat as he proceeded to list a number of foolproof ways to die, 100% satisfaction guaranteed.

"Now some of you are probably skeptical that this is the right choice for you, but don't you fret about it. I'll be hosting live demonstrations around the country, so check my website for details and come see if suicide is right for you."

Part incredulous, part morbid curiosity, I visited his website and found he was hosting an event in my city next week. Sure enough, his website had a video of him standing on stage with a man who hung from the rafters by his neck. The crowd was cheering like wild as the dying man's body was wracked with its final spasms. John Fallow lifted the dying man's hand to reveal a thumbs up, and the crowd cheered even harder as though their team had just scored the final goal.

I bought a ticket and printed out the confirmation code. I don't know why I did it, but for the first time in a long time I really felt like I had something to look forward to.

John was a man's man, rugged and handsome as they come. He wore a cowboy hat pulled low over one eye, faded Levi's, and a button-up shirt the day of the event. He greeted everyone at the front door with a firm handshake and a beaming smile, laughing and carrying on with people he'd just met like they were his oldest friends.

I expected there to be at least a little outrage, but everyone who showed up seemed legitimately happy to be there. The feeling was contagious, and by the time I sat down with the rest of the audience, I already knew several people by name.

"Silly old me, I forgot what speech you all came to hear," John Fallow announced from the stage. "Was it the one about working hard from morning till night, day in and day out?"

"No!" chorused a hundred voices around me. I was half surprised to recognize my own as one of them.

"How about the speech about it being your fault if you aren't happy, because you ain't trying hard enough?"

"No!"

"So you telling me all you fine folks showed up just to hear how to fix all your problems at once in less than five minutes? That what you want to hear?"

The enthusiasm was deafening.

John Fallow mimed whipping out a pair of pistols from an imaginary belt and rattled off shots into the audience. Everyone remotely close to the line of fire made a dramatic show of taking the bullet and collapsing into their chairs with great big grins on their faces. Then cheers again, an ocean of sound beating against my eardrums.

"Well let's get started then," John roared. "How about a volunteer? Come on now don't be shy. There ain't nobody going to look down on you where you're going."

A sea of hands like a flock of birds all taking flight at once. John stepped down from the stage and took the open hand of a middle-aged woman to help her into the spotlight. He led her to a stool on stage where she sat down.

"What's your name, gorgeous?" he asked. The woman swooned and mumbled something I couldn't hear.

"Katylin, is that right?" John said in his booming voice. "Tell me Katylin, what's wrong with your life? Loud and clear, come on now."

"I was supposed to get promoted this year," she said, her voice trembling but audible. "They gave the job to some young slut instead."

"Well you aren't getting any younger, sweetheart. It's only going to get worse from here."

She nodded and smiled as though that's exactly what she wanted to hear.

"I got just the thing for you though," John said. "A little medicine for what ails ya."

He produced a pill from a small leather bag in his pocket and offered it to her. She snatched it gratefully and clutched it in both hands.

"That's gonna take the sting right out. Go on now. One quick swallow. Cyanide tastes just awful if you let it dissolve in your mouth."

I watched with horrified fascination as Katylin tossed the pill back and washed it down with a water bottle that John offered her. She gave a feeble smile as her face flushed bright red. The room watched in anxious silence as she started panting for breath, each labored heave more desperate than the last.

"Almost there, 'hun," John whispered, his microphone washing the sound over the audience "Let's see those bastards at work take this one away from you."

Katylin fell off her stool and began rolling on the ground. The audience began to woop and whistle. Within seconds Katylin lay still. Two men wearing 'Staff' shirts hustled out to drag her off stage.

There was a brief silence when she stopped moving. I had the sense that everyone was trying to read the room, unsure of whether or to scream or cheer. Then the applause began to ripple, tentative at first, but growing by the second until the whole auditorium vibrated with its intensity.

I felt sick. An anxious feeling flooded my body, but the cheering confused me and made me think that it was alright. If we were doing something wrong, then surely someone would have said something by now. Unable to shake the uncertainty, I staggered from my chair and headed for the bathroom to clear my head.

Outside the auditorium I saw the two men wearing 'Staff' shirts exit a side door. The woman wasn't with them anymore. Was she still back there? Was she alive, or dead? Maybe she needed help.

One of the staff noticed me, his face screwing up with suspicion. I snatched a nearby trash bag and made to enter the door they'd just exited from.

"Hey, where you think you're going?" one asked.

"Bringing some rope for John," I said, hefting the trash bag. "Back stage is that way, right?"

The staff nodded, and I slipped inside. I could hear the audience cheering again through the wall and felt the urge to cheer with them, but I thought better of it and stayed quiet.

The hallway skirted the perimeter of the auditorium, and I was able to track my progress toward the back of the stage by the sounds coming through the wall.

Another uproar—perhaps a second demonstration concluding. Another body to be dragged off stage.

Not just a body. A human being. A father or a mother, a son or a daughter. That thought should have horrified me, but it didn't. They didn't ask to be alive. They didn't make the world the way it was. So why shouldn't they leave when they're ready?

"Looks like we've got a bleeder here," John's voice carried. "That's it, boy. Let it all out. You're the lucky one—the rest of us have to clean up that mess."

I must have been directly behind the stage at that point. The place was dark and cluttered with electrical and sound equipment. I saw no sign of the woman's body. The thought of stumbling across her splayed out on the ground nauseated me. I shouldn't be here.

A shaft of light tore through the room as the stage curtain was pulled aside. The staff were dragging a college aged boy by the hands. His throat was cleanly slit, and a sheet of blood soaked through his shirt and drained onto the floor. I hid behind an upright speaker and watched the staff prop the boy against the wall before they turned to exit.

"Let's all take a break while they get this cleaned up," John said from the stage. "Fifteen minutes, then you'll all get your chance."

The boy was still alive. Spitting and gurgling blood, he panted with feeble wet gasps. His red-smeared teeth were locked in a vicious grin. I started to creep toward him, but another blast of light made me scramble back to concealment.

John Fallow moved through the shadows to stand over the dying boy. The boy's grin twisted into one of agony. He struggled to stand, but John put a boot on his chest and forced him back down.

"Shh shh," he held a finger to his lips. "Don't fuss. Lot of folks are dying to be you." He laughed at his private joke.

The boy tried to answer, but the wet sucking sound which escaped his lips carried no words.

"You did this to yourself. You wanted to fit in so damn bad that you didn't care what you had to do. Now look at you."

It was too late to save him. The boy was barely breathing now, and the pool of blood encompassing him was still growing by the second. John dropped to his knees to bring their faces level.

"It don't matter what other people expect from you," John said softly. "The government wants you to make a lot of money to pay taxes. A holy man might tell you not to make any because it corrupts you. The people who sell burgers want you to be fat, and the people who sell diet pills want you to hate yourself for it. They all want something different from you, but you don't belong to them. You belong to you."

The boy had stopped moving. I couldn't make out the faintest sign that he still drew breath.

"So what if you flunked out of school? Does that make the stars any less bright, or the taste of strawberries more sour? Will you no longer feel your lover's caress, or the ocean lapping your bare feet? Fear, pain, doubt—they're just passing clouds, and floating in front of the sun don't mean the sun ain't still there.

"So I'm going to give you another chance," John continued. "You get back up and go outside and tell me what you see. And if it's nothing but clouds, then pick one and call it beautiful and love it forever, because it's all part of the same sky."

With that John Fallow pulled out a syringe and stuck it in the boy's chest. He began to buckle and squirm, but John held him down while wiping the blood from his neck with a handkerchief. It came off like makeup, leaving clean fresh skin below.

"Get out of here," John said, "and don't let me catch you back either."

The boy scrambled to the door and disappeared.

"You too," John said, looking into the shadows where I hid. "Or it won't just be blood capsules and a temporary paralytic for you."

I ran for it.

Outside I saw the boy with his head thrown back, looking straight up. Beside him was the woman who'd taken the fake cyanide pill, head back and staring at the sky with wild eyes. I don't know whether they thought they'd really died and came back, or whether they knew it was a trick, but one thing I'm pretty sure is that neither of them had ever looked at the sky like that before.

I know I hadn't.

## Where the People Who Disappear Go

We don't talk about the ones who never come back. Not in my house, not at school, not anywhere in my town. But not talking about them doesn't bring them back, and it doesn't stop more people from disappearing, so I'm going to tell you everything I know.

The first disappearance I remember is Julie Wilkins in the 3rd grade. She had blonde pigtails and always wore a bright red sweater even in the summer. I didn't think anything of it the first day she was gone, but I asked my teacher about her by the second day.

"Julie? She's sitting right over there in her usual spot," Mrs. Peterson replied.

The girl sitting in Julie's spot wore the same bright red sweater, but she had black hair and a mean face and didn't look anything like Julie. I tried to explain that to the teacher, but Mrs. Peterson wouldn't listen.

I kept insisting, louder and louder, growing red in the face and screaming when the teacher wouldn't listen. I ran over to the imposter and pulled her hair, demanding with the single-minded fury of a 9-year-old girl to know what happened to Julie's pigtails. She cried and started pulling my hair back, and soon both of us were sent home early.

I watched the mean-faced girl get picked up by Mrs. Wilkins, Julie's mom. The woman hugged the girl and helped her into the backseat, and they drove away together. And every day after that the girl with the black hair would sit in Julie's chair and chat with Julie's friends, until after about a month I finally let it go and started calling her Julie too.

Kate Bennet in the sixth grade. Steve Oshaki in the eighth. Lisa Wellington, junior year. There was never a fuss about it, so there were probably more that I didn't notice. I actually liked the new Lisa considerably more than the old one who used to stick gum everywhere, but that didn't make it okay.

Because every time it happened, I couldn't stop thinking about what it would be like if I was next. I didn't like the idea of someone else sleeping in my bed or hugging my mother. I liked the idea of what might have happened to the original people even less.

As I got older, I started thinking there was something wrong with me. If their closest friends and family didn't notice the change, then maybe there was no change at all. Maybe I misremembered or hallucinated. Maybe there was something wrong with my eyes, or my brain—some unseen tumor quietly swelling until the day I won't know anyone and no one will know me.

I still lived in the same small town during college though, and I didn't forget the lesson I learned in the 3rd grade: I kept my mouth shut and pretended not to notice. But it was a lot harder to pretend when I woke one morning to find a stranger sleeping next to me where my fiancé used to be.

I didn't wake him. I just watched him sleep, trying to imagine what would come of us. The new Robert wasn't unhandsome. He was in better shape than my fiancé had been. If the other replacements were any indication, then he'd still know who I was and what I meant to him.

I tried to go along with it, but couldn't even make it through the first morning. I flinched when he kissed me, and just watching him getting dressed in Robert's clothes was enough to make me miss my real fiancé.

I lay in bed pretending I was sick until he left for work, then I jumped up and started packing my things. I was gone before he got back. No message, no letter, no explanation—why should I try to mend a stranger's broken heart when I had no one to mend mine?

The new Robert didn't let me go that easy. I blocked his number, but messages kept slipping through. Social media—email—he even renamed our shared Netflix account to say he misses me. I finally confronted him when he found out which friend I was staying with and knocked on the door.

*It's not you, it's me.* Weeks of suffering from an invisible wound, and that's the best I could come up with. I tried to convince him that I was sick and needed to be alone, and he tried to convince me that he would help me get better. I'd almost gotten rid of him when my stupid friend started crying and thanking the stranger for not giving up on me.

I guess that's when I gave up on myself. I let the man take me back to the place that used to be my home. I stood stiff as a board when he hugged me, and the hair on the back of my neck stood on end when he stroked my head and told me we would get through this together. Then I lay beside him in the bed we shared and wondered how the warmth of his body felt so much colder than what love was supposed to be.

I didn't sleep that night. I guess that's why I was the only one to hear the knock on the door after midnight. A burst of tentative taps, almost like someone wanted to be heard and was afraid to be noticed at the same time. I thought about waking the stranger in my bed, but I decided that I felt safer when he was asleep.

I lay in bed for several long seconds before I heard the knocking again. It was faster this time—more urgent. I slipped out of bed and crept down stairs, not turning on any of the lights. Checking that the door was still locked—then up to the peephole—

"It's cold out here, and I can't find my key," Robert said through the door. I stared at my real fiancé through the peephole. "Are you in there? Hello?" Then rapid knocking once more.

How could I open the door? How could I invite him into our home with another man upstairs in the bed? But how could I not, and risk losing him again? I stood frozen at the peephole, watching him huddling under his jacket for warmth.

"Let me in," he pleaded, louder this time. The other Robert would wake soon, if he hadn't already. "Let me in, let me in!" Suddenly he leapt at the door and started hammering on it with his fist.

I jumped away from the shuddering wood in surprise, tripping over myself and collapsing onto my ass. The original Robert fell instantly quiet, no doubt hearing me.

"I know you're there. Don't do this to me. Let me in—let me in!" And the hammering returned, stronger than ever. The whole door was trembling in its frame. The first light turned on upstairs, and then the creak of wood from the steps.

I unlocked the door and flung it open.

I clenched my eyes and braced for impact, expecting the real Robert to come flying into the room from his momentum.

"Honey? What's going on down there?" the stranger's voice.

"I don't know. I thought I heard something," I said, my voice ringing hollow in my own ears as I stared at the empty darkness. I took a step outside and welcomed the freezing air enveloping my skin.

"You're already sick—don't make it worse."

I moved farther into the cold in defiance. "I'm not sick," I told him, my voice more level than it had ever been. "I just don't love you, that's all."

His snarl lasted less than a second, but it left enough impact that I couldn't see his face again without remembering it.

"Don't you dare follow him," the stranger said.

"Follow who?" I asked innocently, taking another step into the freezing night.

The snarl returned, and this time it took several seconds to fade. He half-turned away from me, then apparently changing his mind, he lunged through the door after me. I was already running as fast as I could, the icy concrete driveway stinging my feet as though some skin was left behind with every step.

"Don't go out there!" he shouted behind me. "You'll disappear too!"

I wouldn't have minded disappearing though. I could disappear with Robert. The other ones can have the house. They can get dressed in our clothes and laugh with our friends and eat Christmas dinner with my family, but they won't have us. So I just kept running, calling for Robert and hoping that he'd find me before my lungs froze stiff. Before the stranger caught me and dragged me back and fussed over me until I believed that I was sick too.

I ran for as long and hard as I could, screaming until my throat was raw, but I didn't find Robert. The stranger had given up hours ago, but I kept going until morning when my fingers and toes were black and blue and my blood felt like ice in my veins. And by the first touch of light I found myself back at the house that had been my home, back to wondering whether I really was sick, and whether it would be the death of me.

Only it wasn't my home anymore. The stranger who had replaced Robert was kissing his new fiancé who had replaced me. And there was our neighbor, greeting them good morning as though he'd known them both for years. And life goes on for the rest of the world who don't talk about the ones who never come back.

As for me? Without friends, or family, or a home to call my own? I finally know where the ones who disappear go. They can go anywhere they want, because there's nothing left to hold them back.

## My Reflection Smiles More Than I Do

It's no secret that I drink. My friends will make jokes like 'your idea of a balanced diet is a beer in both hands'. I'll laugh with them, but I don't miss their pitying smirks. When I'm out, I'm out to have a good time, and when I'm in... well either way, it feels like I'm only smiling once I've knocked back a few.

I have this weird habit when I'm drinking alone where I like to watch myself get drunk in the mirror. I start off by seeing this drab, aging, overweight slob, and I'll make a game out of drinking until he looks happy. I'll grin and make faces and watch myself laugh and wonder why I can't be like this all the time. I can steal a few hours from reality until my girlfriend gets home from work and we start to bicker, and then everything that didn't exist a moment before is suddenly there again.

The second she walks in the door and sees that I've been drinking, the smile disappears from the mirror. Usually we'll have a "discussion", although she's the only one talking so I tend to think of it more as a "lecture". Sometimes she'll give up and let it go, but then there are cases like the other night where she works herself into some kind of frenzy. I guess I'd forgotten to pick her up—I knew it was my fault and I apologized—but it didn't matter. Nothing I said got through to her anymore. It was like she couldn't even hear me. And she just kept getting louder and louder until all the words morphed into one long angry blast, not ceasing until the door slammed behind her.

It was just me and the mirror after that, so I took another drink and watched it smile. A big sloppy smile too, as wide as I'd ever seen, stretching my face into a caricature of itself. It would have been heart-warming to see if I really had been smiling. I turned my head slowly from side-to-side, watching the mirror from my peripheral vision. The man in the mirror turned too, matching my movements exactly, giving me full-view to all its leering teeth. Meanwhile I felt my own closed mouth with my hand just to be sure. The mirror was smiling, but I wasn't.

That unnerved the hell out of me. It was a wake-up call. I emptied the rest of my bottle down the sink and went to lie down for a while. The weird thing was that I didn't feel that drunk though. I was walking straight—thinking clearly. I was barely even buzzed.

Lying there in the dark and thinking about what happened wasn't any better. I felt like I was going to start sobbing. After about an hour of tossing and turning and hating myself, I got up to use the bathroom and looked in the mirror again. I wanted to see myself smile, even if it wasn't real, just to know that it was still possible.

I was even more sober now than last time. I could feel the miserable weight of it. My reflection though? A coy dimple at first, but before my eyes it was stretching into a beaming grin. I felt my slack, loose face again with both hands. Then reaching out to touch the smile in the mirror, my hand tensed into a rigid claw. I didn't feel the glass. I felt the warm, moist, tightly pulled lip. The stubble of its face, the curve of its chin, my hand slipping through the mirror as though it wasn't even there. I wasn't afraid exactly—more mesmerized by something so far beyond my understanding. Then when my reflection turned to walk away, it felt like a part of me was leaving with it.

I watched myself exit the bathroom on the other side of the glass. Now the mirror showed an empty bathroom, my reflection gone. I touched the glass again and felt the cold, smooth surface. I was about to try to sleep whatever this was off, but then I heard the door open.

She's back! She changed her mind! Suddenly the mirror didn't matter anymore. I raced through my apartment faster than a kid on Christmas morning, stumbling to a halt when I reached the living room. It was empty. The door was locked. No-one had entered, but then I heard her voice:

"Look, I know I said I wasn't coming back, but—"

Her voice was coming from behind me, sounding muffled almost as though she was speaking underwater. I raced back to the bathroom—the mirror still empty of my reflection. I was beginning to think it was another hallucination when I heard:

"I'm so sorry. I'm going to be a new man from now on, I promise."

My own voice. Coming from inside the mirror. It was muffled too, seemingly a long way off. But even if my reflection had left its bathroom and gone to its version of my living room, how could my girlfriend have entered that living room instead of my own?

"You do look different somehow," she said. "I can't quite put my finger on it."

Unless of course... I had changed places with my reflection somehow. If he was in my real living room, and I was behind the mirror.

"Did you do something with your hair? It's usually parted the other way," she added.

"I'm just happy to see you, that's all," my voice said. "I guess you're not used to seeing me smile."

"Maybe you're right. It's a good change..."

I'd climbed onto the bathroom counter at this point. My face an inch from the glass, but still no reflection. I mapped the entire surface with my hands. Then harder—pounding my fists against the mirror, watching the whole pane rattle against the wall.

"Hello! Can anyone hear me?" I shouted.

If they could, they made no sign. I heard them talking softly for a while, then she started to laugh. I don't remember the last time I heard her laugh. I was getting desperate by this point. I wanted to smash the mirror to pieces, but I was afraid the action would block my only route home. I sprinted back to my empty living room—threw open the door—searching for something—anything to make sense out of this madness. I didn't make it far before I heard her scream though, and I felt compelled to run back and see what was going on.

My heart leaped when I saw my reflection again in the bathroom mirror. He was still smiling, even humming to himself while he washed his hands in the sink. Washing the blood from his hands. I couldn't hold myself back anymore. I threw my whole body against the mirror. It exploded on collision, splintering shards of shrapnel showering me in a thousand bloody hands. I didn't stop, hurling myself again and again into the empty frame, smashing and driving each fragment of glass into my hands until there was nothing left but diamond dust.

I was heaving for breath when I walked back into the living room—my real living room. I know it was real because I saw her on the couch, her throat and mouth cleanly slit from end to end, smiling wider than she ever had when she was with me. I took my keys and my wallet and I ran, leaving everything else behind for good.

The police caught up to me about a week later. They interviewed me and took prints, but apparently the one's on the knife didn't match me. They were completely backward, in fact. I haven't had a drink since that day, but God knows I've wanted to. I guess I'm just too afraid to look in the mirror one day and see myself smile.

## Mom I'm 14, I Can Have My Own Demon

My family has a secret. It isn't the mundane type of secret either: Dad isn't hiding any affairs, Mom doesn't drink herself to sleep, and my sister doesn't sneak boys or drugs up to her room. They do, however, all have their own demons, and they keep them hidden from the rest of the world.

Dad's demon has swollen eyeballs which protrude at least six inches from its floppy, boneless face. He said it's because he reads so much, but it's probably because he's always snooping on other people's business. Mom's demon is something between an eel and a slug, although every once in a while it'll turn itself inside-out and leave bloody, oily stains on the carpet. My sister Sandra only got her demon a few months ago. It's always eating things: clothes, pencils, books—anything it can fit into its distendable jaw. I can only imagine how much trouble they'd get up to if they weren't kept in cages all the time.

"Sandra had to wait until she was 18 for her own demon, and so do you," my father would say.

When you're a freshman, a four year wait might as well be a life sentence. It wouldn't have been so bad if I hadn't seen how much Sandra had changed after she got her demon either. Mom says that when we summon a demon, we take all the worst parts of ourselves and bind it to the creature.

Sandra used to stress eat. She could clear a family sized pizza in under 10 minutes. I don't think she even tasted it. When she was a junior in high school, she weighed 240 pounds (although she'd kill me if she knew that I knew).

When she went to prom her senior year, she weighed 110. I wasn't allowed to watch the actual summoning ceremony, but I can only imagine the demon crawling (or eating) its way out of her and taking all her bad habits with it. It's not like she magically transformed overnight though. Not physically, anyway. She went on an all liquid diet the next day, running an hour every morning, yoga in the afternoon, and another two hours of gym at night.

At first I was supportive. That lasted about a week. Then the jealousy set in. Don't get me wrong, I'm not a fat cow like she was, but it was hard to even stand next to that goddess without feeling insecure. Just being alive is enough to make me anxious and uncomfortable though. I have this magic power where I can walk through a crowd of strangers and telepathically infer that everyone is laughing at me, even though logically I know they don't give two shits. And forget actually trying to make friends. I'd rather kill myself than talk to a cute boy (not really, although I'd be lying if I said the thought never crossed my mind).

So why torture myself through high school like my sister did? If she hadn't wasted 3 years sitting in the corner and feeling sorry for herself, she could have had the best time of her life. I must have begged my parents a thousand times to let me summon my demon early, but the point was non-negotiable. I wasn't "mature" enough. I was just going through a "phase". They thought I was still "developing", and that it was still too early for me to know who I really was. But I did know who I was. I was a sad, lonely girl who was sick of feeling like this, and I knew the longer I waited, the worse it would get.

I got my chance last Friday when Mom and Dad went out for a date. Sandra was at the gym, so I had the house to myself. I was a sock-footed commando slipping into my parents room to search for their summoning book.

Dad's demon perked up right away from its cage on top of the dresser. It pressed its bulging eyes against the bars so hard that they squished straight through. Mom's demon was in an empty aquarium, squelched up against the glass. I ignored them and started to search: under the bed, in the closets, in the bathroom drawers—all the obvious places. Nothing. My search widened: inside pillow cases, hidden between clothes, rifling through their other books to see if one had a fake cover. Nothing. I was growing frustrated and was about to give up when Dad's demon started squeaking.

It was pointing a long, thin finger at the AC vent. I followed its advice, and sure enough the grate cover was loose. The book was inside, a heavy leather affair entitled "The Demonicum". I replaced the vent cover, thanked the bulging eyed creature (even though Dad said never to talk to them), and hurried back to my room to study the book.

The spell was way simpler than I imagined. No ingredients, no sacrifices, just a short verse and a silly dance. It seemed weird because I remember them being gone for hours for Sandra's ceremony, but they probably just had to drive a long way to get to a sacred spot or something. Even better, there was an unsummoning spell which bound the demon back to me just in case things got out of hand. Nothing to lose and everything to gain, I started to read.

As soon as I pronounced the final syllable, I felt a heavy burden lift from my heart. It felt a bit like dreading an impossible test all week, only to arrive at class to find out its been replaced with a field trip. I hadn't just been carrying that dread for a week though—it was a whole lifetime of doubt, and resentment, and insecurity that separated itself from me.

Then came the scratching from the inside my chest. An insatiable, internal itch. I watched in morbid fascination as a small claw pushed out of my skin. It retreated, and a moment later a long, thin tongue slipped out to taste the air. It didn't hurt, so I ran to the bathroom mirror to watch it slowly widen the hole and begin to work its way out. My demon was small and round, covered with bristling black fur like a hamster that had been plugged into an electrical outlet. It had just gotten the hole wide enough to stick its head out when I realized that I didn't have a cage ready for it.

The old me would have gone into a panic attack on the spot. Not anymore. I was cool and collected as I glided to my closet to look for a container, the demon wriggling its way out of me the whole time. The best I could do was a backpack, but the creature was so small and feeble looking that even that seemed more than sufficient. I waited until it pulled its full torso free before snatching the demon and dragging it the rest of the way out. It squeaked and whined in protest as I stuffed it into the backpack and zipped it up. The hole in my chest was already closing, and a few seconds later I was as good as new.

No, I was better than new. For the first time I could remember, I was happy with myself. The only damper was the pathetic, terrified squeaking coming from inside the backpack. I stuffed it under my bed and tried to forget about it, but my demon was loud enough that I was sure it would be discovered. I yelled at it to shut up, but it only responded with pitiful whimpering.

I pulled the backpack out and unzipped it about an inch. My demon was cowering in the corner, trembling all over and clutching itself with its little paws. Like it or not, there was a part of me inside it. I couldn't help but relate to it, knowing that all its anxious fear was exactly what I had been feeling every day of my life. Then it looked up at me with those quivering eyes and my heart broke completely.

"Okay, you can come out. But only if you don't make a sound, okay? And you can't let anyone see you," I told it.

The demon nodded vigorously, so I unzipped the backpack and let it crawl free. It stayed silent and didn't try to get away. I patted down its bristling fur, which was surprisingly soft, until gradually the trembling stopped and it started to relax. Sandra came home shortly after, but the demon was true to its word and stayed hidden.

The next few days were heaven. It's amazing how different the world can be with a simple shift in perception. I wasn't afraid of making mistakes or being laughed at anymore. I started speaking up in class, joined new people at lunch, and felt myself becoming accepted and admired almost immediately. I even caught a few glances from boys which lingered on me longer than I've ever noticed before.

I was so happy that I barely paid any attention to my demon which continued to cower in my room. It was growing every day, but any attempt to trap it again elicited such a woeful sound that I quickly gave up. I was sure my parents would take it away or unsummon it if they found out, and that wasn't a risk I was willing to take. I told it to stay under my bed until it got too big for that, then I made it stay in the closet. By this point it was about the size of a large dog, already far bigger than the other demons and showing no signs of stopping.

I wasn't anxious anymore, so the heavy breathing didn't bother me. I didn't worry about the half-eaten squirrels I sometimes found in the corner of my room. I didn't dread what would happen if it kept getting bigger. All I cared about was how good it felt to not be dragged down by those negative feelings all the time. I didn't realize how bad it had gotten until I heard the screaming in the middle of the night.

*Glass shattering.*
"Let go of her, you brute!"
*Savage snarling.*
"Dad, get the book!"

It was coming from Sandra's room. I leapt out of bed and raced across the hall. The door was open, and my demon was cowering in the corner. It was almost as tall as my sister now, its black fur rising like so many blades. Broken glass glinted in the carpet, and Sandra's demon was nowhere to be seen. Dad shoved past me and rushed back toward his room. My demon launched off the wall in hot pursuit. I tried to hold on to it as it sped by, but the spikes of fur were sharp enough to cut my hand and I immediately let go.

"It ate her!" Sandra was wailing. "It ate my demon!"

I heard another smash before I got to my parents room. The wire cage was empty, twisted wide open. More glass sprayed the ground where the aquarium once was. My demon was chewing like a starved animal, a path of oily blood running down its chin.

My parents' demons were barely a mouthful for it, but they distracted it for long enough. Dad was reading something from the summoning book, but I could barely hear him over the sound of Sandra's screaming. My demon had finished swallowing, and it was crouched again, ready to leap on Dad...

But not before he finished the spell. The demon rippled once, twice, and then just as it flew into the air it dissolved into a wave of black mist. The mist reared to a halt in the air before turning to crash down on me in a freezing wave. It poured into my nose, and my mouth, and my eyes—flooding me with an overwhelming fear and hatred. It was a second skin over my skin, and a third skin under it, encompassing and filling me to the brim. The demon was being bound to me once more, only it was bigger than ever, with it all the weight of my family's demons inside of it.

I can't get rid of it again. It's become too powerful to contain. I guess I just have to get used to the new me.

## Haunted House Publishing

*"Great men do not lie still in death. Our words echo across time, a light for others to follow when their own fire burns low. Thus shall my torch be taken up again; thus shall I dwell once more among the living."*

Those were the last lines Alexander Notovitch's ever wrote. I know they belonged to him because I watched his frail hand tremble the tortuous route across the page. I know they were his last because I watched him die in that leather chair the same evening.

You may have never heard of him, but I guarantee you've seen the light of his torches. Alexander wrote in a hundred different styles under a hundred different names. His work has sold millions of copies and has been translated into 112 languages. But the most important thing he's ever written, his Magnum Opus, has never been read by anyone except me.

I think he would have died years ago if it wasn't for that book. Alexander was never married, and neither did he keep any friends. I don't think anyone could stand to be in the same room as him long enough for that. The dark scrutiny of his eyes pierce the most sacred part of you, leaving you naked in a way that you have never seen yourself. The only reason I endured the weight of his frightful presence was the promise of publishing his final volume.

I've always fancied myself as a writer as well, but reading that book humbled me to my core. I read the whole thing in a single 14 hour stretch after his death. The poetry of his words taught me what it was to be human, yet made mockery of my presumption to call myself the same species as him.

I wept many times through the silent vigil of that reading, but it wasn't for loss of the man. I wept that the highest peak of my life would never rise above the lowest shadow of his. I hated myself for how hollow my ideas were, knowing my intellect to be forever incapable of approaching his mastery.

It wasn't fair. If I had written that book instead of him, then I would never need to prove myself again. If I wrote it… but who is to say that I didn't? Only a dead man and these empty halls. What good was fame to him who hid behind pseudonyms as impenetrable as the veil of death?

I took a pen from Alexander's desk and wrote my own name at the head of his manuscript. Though only a single line had changed, I could feel the holy relic in my hands somehow turn into a thing of evil. No more was this a testament to the greatness in man, but rather a tribute to his most vile and jealous desires.

I couldn't bear to look at the thing anymore. I hurled it down upon the dead man's desk, half expecting it to burn a hole straight through. Yet there the crumpled sheets lay, a forgotten pile of rubbish but for me. I reverently sorted the papers once more, and opening the word processor on my laptop, began to type.

## Sleepless Nights

I watched my fingers write my own name at the top, and I did nothing to stop them.

It took several days to type the entire manuscript, made longer by my constant need to re-read passages that I'd somehow skipped the first time. It wasn't a matter of two pages sticking together either—there were unfamiliar sentences within memorable paragraphs, unnoticed notes in the margin, and even a whole chapter that I had never seen before.

It was almost as though someone had edited the work during the night. I dutifully recorded everything regardless, telling myself that I had been too excited to register these details the first time around. I didn't allow myself to question the genius until I'd reached the very last sentence of the very last paragraph on the very last page.

"Thus is my torch taken up again; thus I dwell once more among the living."

The first time I'd read that line, it was written in the future tense. Now it was written in the present. I was sure of it. The lines had been seared into my mind as surely as my own name.

Alexander's house no longer felt as empty as it had a moment before. Those who have stood alone beneath a storm-ravaged sky would understand the brooding electricity I felt around me. The soft whir of the overhead fan seemed to grow louder, its motion stirring the papers on the desk for the first time. Before my eyes the metal beads beneath the fan slid downward until a clear click resonated.

The fan increased in speed again. I fumbled my way out of the chair and reached to turn it off, but before I could, the chain had already pulled once more. The blades were slowing on their own accord.

In the sudden silence of the dead air I heard footsteps downstairs. They were soft and deliberate, a panther stalking an unsuspecting prey. I raced to the top of the staircase to settle my rebellious imagination, but stopped short as I reached the first step.

The outdoor porch light had just turned off. A second later, the kitchen light extinguished. Then the living room directly below the wooden stairs, dissolving the whole first floor into shadows.

The creak as someone stepped on the bottom stair. Footsteps again—faster now, something sprinting directly up the flight of steps in an avalanche of buckling wood.

I yelped and scrambled backward into Alexander's study. I couldn't hear the footsteps over the thunder of my own blood. I slammed the door behind me. There wasn't a lock, so I thrust my back against the door and braced my legs against the floorboards to pin it shut.

Straining with static tension, I forced slow breaths and willed the drumroll of my heart to slow enough for me to listen. Nothing. Nothing. So quiet that there was no marker to separate the fleeting seconds, the frozen moment colorless and eternal. So quiet that I could almost hear the self-deprecating laughter of my own thoughts.

I was being absurd. All I'd really seen was an electrical abnormality—more the rule than the exception in an old house like this. The sound—the soft tread that I'd mistaken for footprints—nothing but the thrumming of a blown fuse or transformer outside.

Alright wise-guy, my thoughts seemed to retort. Then why don't you explain those snuffling sounds running up and down the door frame? Those dry, dusty snorts, like methodical sandpaper grating against rough wood?

The study lights cut with such vicious swiftness that I jolted and grunted in sudden alarm. The sniffing doubled in urgency in response, something butting against the door on the other side with an assault which grew more frenzied by the second.

Soon I was heaving with exertion, each blow making my skeleton dance to a tune that the rest of me didn't hear. Three inches or more I'd be pushed back by the impact, and before my full weight had even slammed the door into its frame another numbing cascade ricocheted through my body and I'd be flying again.

And then the howl, the chilling echo of a sound buried deep within the dormant animal instinct of my psyche. A sound more beast than man, yet more man than any beast for the tortured guttural syllables which rolled across its alien tongue.

More terrible than the splintering door, more terrible than the bestial anthem or the shrill symphony of my nerves, came the pitter-patter of gentle keys and the soft shadow blocking the light. As horrifying as the creature sounded beyond the door, at least it was on the other side.

Illuminated by the halo of my computer's light, I saw a strange creature hunched over the keyboard. Its shoulders extended so far past its head and stretched the skin of its back so transparently thin that it appeared like a deformed bat. A dozen long crooked fingers on each hand deftly picked out the keys one by one, each bending subtly with several too many joints.

I couldn't leave my post at the door without letting the other monster in, so I was helpless but to stare as the thing completed its work. Once satisfied, it leaned back in the chair and stretched its arms luxuriously behind its body, the elbows bending 90 degrees in the opposite direction to wrap around itself.

At once the pressure on the other side of the door vanished. The dry sniffing left a moment later, growing fainter until I could hear the creak descending the stairs.

No longer needing to hold the door, I cautiously approached my computer and the thing in the chair. It watched me with beady fascination, tracking my slightest movement with a micro adjustment from its head. I got just close enough to read the title page and see that my name had been removed. The original pen-name Alexander had written under was in its place.

"You wrote this?" I asked the creature.

It shook its head and pointed a long finger out the door. The creature pulled itself out of the chair in a sudden lurch, causing me to backpedal. Dragging itself by the arms, useless vestigial legs sliding behind, the thing moved to the bookshelf in the corner and produced another volume.

It pointed at the book, then at itself.

"But there are hundreds of them—"

The creature swept its too-flexible arms in an encompassing gesture. The distant shuffle in the attic—the creaking on the stair—the rush of shadow behind the wastepaper basket—all absorbed in an instant.

To think I was jealous of the old man. All he's ever done is sell the books these mute monsters have produced. And if I'm careful, and if I'm kind to them, then through me they'll write a hundred more.

## Somebody Broke Her

You know the kind of girl I'm talking about. She looks like life chewed her up and spit her back out.

You can see it in her eyes if you could even see her eyes. Her loose tangled hair covers most of her face, and she's always staring at her feet. You can see it in her hunched shoulders, hear it in her mumbling voice. She's both desperate and afraid to be heard, hating herself for everything she says and everything she doesn't say.

She doesn't live in my building, but I see her almost every day when she visits her boyfriend in the apartment next door. I've said hello to her a few times—she always flinches when I talk to her. The first thing out of her mouth is inevitably an apology—sorry for being in my way, or for being here too often, or for taking up one of the dozen empty parking spots. I asked her name once, but she said it didn't matter.

"Why not? What am I supposed to say when I see you?" I asked.

"Nothing. You don't need to. I'm nobody."

"Well my name is—" I began.

But she just kept walking. Head leaning against my neighbor's door, hands in her pockets, looking like an ostrich trying to disappear into the sand.

"Bye nobody!" I chimed as the door opened to let her in.

I couldn't be sure under the hair, but I think she almost smiled. "Bye somebody," she murmured, disappearing into the doorway. My neighbor Jeff poked his head out—scrawny fellow with a soul patch and a beanie which seemed permanently fixed to his head. He nodded sharply at me like a fighter paying insincere respect to his opponent, slamming the door.

I liked watching Nobody from my balcony when she was parking her car. I liked the fluid grace of her movements which transformed regular motions like opening doors and stepping over obstacles into a choreographed dance. I must not have been the only one to notice either, because there always seemed to be someone hitting on her whenever I saw her. Not the charming kind either—fat oafs jumping out of their car like they were waiting for her, or pushy street rats backing her up against the building. I thought she was a prostitute at first, but she always rebuffed them so vehemently that I figured that wasn't the case.

Often at night I'd see her leaning on the railing of my neighbor's balcony, smoking a joint and staring off into space. I got the feeling that she was staring into a world that only she could see, but looking at her face, I also got the feeling that it wasn't a very pretty world. I wish I could see it too. Sometimes I'd go out onto my own balcony and try to make an excuse for conversation, but she'd invariably duck back inside the moment she saw me. If I was lucky, and she seemed to be in good spirits, I'd hear a "Bye somebody" before she went. A stupid joke, but it always made me smile.

She couldn't have been happy, but I suppose it wasn't any of my business. I'd hear her boyfriend yelling at her through the walls sometimes, although I never heard her say anything back. I figured that she was her own person with her own choices to make, and if she was being really mistreated, then she wouldn't keep coming back. It's not like I had proof that she was being abused or anything—and what I did guess, I quickly dismissed as petty jealousy, resolving not to interfere with her life.

That resolution lasted for about two months, but it ended last night. It was after dark and I was getting home late when I spotted Nobody pressed up against my building. Two men in leather jackets were several inches too close for innocent conversation, practically pressing themselves on her while she squirmed to get away. I honked my car horn at them, and one looked over his shoulder. Fat stupid face, mouth hanging part way open, he stared at me for a few seconds before turning back to her.

"I got to go," I heard her say. "Somebody is waiting for me."

I honked again. Fat-face turned to walk over to my car. "Cool it, asshole," he shouted. "This target only has 11 points left, anyway. Get your own damn girl."

I rolled down my window. "What's that supposed to mean?"

"You new or something?" he asked, fishing out his phone. He showed me the screen which depicted a GPS map of my neighborhood. Scattered throughout were little targets, each with a name and a life-bar like a video game character has. The target against my building was named 'Cillia', with 11/100 life remaining.

"I don't know what the fuck that is, but I'm not playing," I told him.

He laughed. More like a guffaw really—deep and guttural without the slightest hint of mirth. "You're after that piece of shit and you're not even getting points? Hey Mark—he actually wants this bitch."

The other guy—presumably Mark—still had the girl against the wall. He made a half-lunge at her as she wriggled free, but it was just to scare her. She looked like she was about to run toward my car, but seeing the fat one over by me, she sprinted to her own vehicle instead. We all watched as she tore out of the parking lot, the biggest smile I'd ever seen plastered across her face.

"Don't waste your time. Somebody already broke her." Fat-face slammed my car with the palm of his hand as he turned to leave. "Let's go Mark. There's two more of them on this street."

I was so relieved to see them go that I didn't try to ask more questions. Nobody had a name. It was Cillia. And something was tracking her location and broadcasting it out to these creeps. It didn't feel like I was meddling in someone else's business anymore. I couldn't just play dumb and let her sort this out for herself.

A few minutes later and I was hammering on my neighbor's apartment. "Hey Jeff, you in there?"

"Bug off," came the muffled reply.

"It's about the game you're playing with Cillia." It seemed pretty vague to me, but if he was involved, then he'd know what I was talking about.

Loud shuffling like someone crossing the room in a hurry, and the door opened a moment later. He was wearing nothing but his boxers and his beanie, skinny body blocking the door.

"Yeah, what about the game?" he asked. I hesitated, unsure what to say next. He must have misread my silence because his face became animated and hopeful. "Hey did I win the prize or something?"

I nodded stiffly. Jeff threw the door open to welcome me in, practically dancing with excitement. "Holy shit, I knew it! I've been on the leader-board for weeks—it was only a matter of time. Seriously competitive shit, you know? I've got everything ready for you, come on in." He rushed to a cabinet under the sink and began hauling out cardboard boxes. I still didn't know what the hell was going on though, so I had to play along to get more answers.

"How many points are you at now?" I asked.

"723," without hesitation. "19 separate targets, although I've been getting most of the points from Cillia, as you know." He plopped two cardboard boxes on the coffee table beside me, flaying them open for inspection. The greasy smell of stale sex was nauseating. "This one's got all the condoms in it," he said. Hundreds of them—all used—neatly tied off into little balloons. "Then this one has all the recordings."

"723 is a lot," I said, pretending to be impressed. "Tell me how you were keeping score."

He looked suspicious for a moment, but it passed. If my question raised any red flags, then he was so pleased with himself that he didn't dwell on it. "It's legit, I swear. I used the 'Break Her' rule-book and everything. 10 points for humiliating her. 15 points for taking a personal item or making a big decision for her.

25 for unwanted sex or something physical. Then I've got a bunch of the small ones I've been building up—the daily criticisms, isolating her from friends and family, that sort of thing. What's the prize going to be?"

"Hold on a minute, I got to ask all the questions first. Standard procedure, you know."

"How come you never told me you worked for 'Break Her'? You must have known that I played," Jeff asked. Again the suspicion, this time lingering on his face.

I shrugged, making notes on my phone as though I was dutifully recording his answers. "What do you think the purpose of the game was? And how did you get into it?"

"Isn't it obvious? You just got to break her. I started playing when my buddy got dumped by his ex. He paid to have her registered in the system, and I thought it would be fun to join so I could start harassing her. At first it was just to support my buddy, but it was pretty helpful seeing where all the vulnerable chicks were. Turned out I was pretty good at it, so I decided to try to get enough points to win the prize."

"Uh huh." I typed as he talked. My fingers were literally shaking. "And Cillia? Did you ever love her?"

He laughed. It wasn't a pleasant sound. A pause, then: "Oh, are you serious? Come on, man. It's just a game. So what's the deal? Am I getting the prize today or not?"

I didn't look up from my phone. I was so disgusted that I couldn't even look at him. The silence was excruciating.

"Is this legal?" I breathed. Silence again, as both of us digested what I said. My cover was blown.

"You lying piece of shit," Jeff grunted, protectively ripping his boxes of prizes away from me. "You trying to steal my points or something?"

He was on me before I even realized what was happening. Bony arms wrapped around me, the momentum flinging me to the ground. He got in a good hit to my jaw before I flipped him on his back. I was bigger and stronger than him, but he twisted under me like a feral animal.

"She's mine! You don't know how much work I put into that bitch!" he roared. I punched him to shut him up. He spit blood at me, and I hit him again. I never thought it would feel so good to hurt someone, but now that I started, I couldn't stop myself. Next I knew my hands were so soaked in blood that it ran between my knuckles like rivers. Jeff wasn't moving. And I was okay with that.

Jeff's phone beeped where it lay on the ground. Somehow the weight of what I'd done didn't hit until I heard it. It beeped again, and I lifted the phone to see what was going on.

It was a notification from 'Break Her'. I opened the app and saw a short questionnaire. Humiliation, abuse, control—a daily checklist for him to go through to get his points. What the hell did I get myself involved in? And who was I to think I could make any difference when a whole world of terrible people were trying to destroy her?

At the bottom of the form it asked: 'Did you see her smile today?' Numb and overwhelmed, I clicked 'yes'. Immediately Cillia's life-bar jumped a point, up to 12/100.

Well that's some difference at least. Not much, but it's a start.

## Any Soul Will Do

Madness isn't usually loud like it's portrayed on the screen. It's not bright either—no supernova of unfettered emotion or physical deformity to hint at the rot inside. I didn't bellow until my throat was raw, or bloody my hands on my walls and mirrors. I didn't splatter my paints across my skin or shred the half-finished canvases which taunt my chosen identity.

My wife Joana even commented on how methodical I was when I gently placed each brush in its case, never to be opened again. If you count finger painting in pre-school, then it's taken me forty-one years to fully accept my failure. I should have realized it sooner, but I always managed to concoct one excuse after another.

I didn't try hard enough. That's a good one. It makes it sound like I could just flip a switch in my mind and force myself to become a master through sheer willpower.

I wasn't taught well enough. Even better: shifting the blame onto someone else. If only my teachers had been more qualified—if only they'd devoted themselves to nurture my potential like Domenico Ghirlandaio devoted himself to Michelangelo.

I'm not good enough—the hardest pill to swallow. I set out to capture the intrinsic beauty of the human spirit and display it for the world to see, but there is no beauty in me to share. I didn't scream and throw a fit. I didn't think much of anything at all. I just let my body move through the familiar motions of life and hoped no one would notice there was nothing below the surface.

Joana asked why my eyes were watering, but I blamed it on the movie we were watching. She punched my arm playfully, calling me a big softy.

"Aren't you working on something tonight?" she asked.

I blinked hard, not taking my eyes off the TV.

"I remember you talking about that comic book store commission. How's that coming?"

"It's coming," I lied. She tried to snuggle against me, but I slipped free and snuck off to the bathroom. It felt wrong to even let her touch me. She had this conception of who I was in her mind—just like I used to—but that person doesn't exist. I'm a failure, a hack, a fraud. And that's all I'd ever be. I stared at myself in the mirror, tracing the unfamiliar lines on my face. Poking at the bags under my eyes. Hating what I saw, and hating even more what I couldn't see.

I mimed a gun with my fingers and put it against my head. Cocked the thumb, grinned my best phony smile, and BLAMO.

"Honey, can you get me a soda on your way back?" I heard from the living room.

But I couldn't take my eyes away from the mirror. My reflection showed a crater in the side of my skull where the imaginary bullet entered. Blood, fragmented bone, and fleshy gray lumps splattered across the bathroom walls, with more gushing from the exit wound on the other side of my head.

"Ooh and one of those Nutella cups," Joana added. "Thanks honey!"

I traced my fingers over my temple, withdrawing them clean. My reflection still wore the phony smile, although it was barely visible now under the torrent of blood flooding down its face.

"Two years, maybe less," came a voice. I spun, startled, unable to find an orator in the empty bathroom. "First comes the depression. Then the withdrawal. Joana will pretend she's just going to visit her family for a while, but you'll know she really just can't stand being around you."

My bloody reflection was talking to me. That's normal. This is fine.

"She'll expect you to call and explain what's going on, but you won't. She'll extend her trip, thinking you just need time to yourself. And you do, but only because you're too much of a coward to pull the trigger while someone's watching. The silence will become too loud, and before you know it..."

The bloody figure mimed a finger to its head, the phony smile flashing through the red.

"You okay in there?" Joana called from the living room. "Mama wants her chocolate!"

"Okay," I mumbled, replying to both.

"Or..." the reflection said.

"Or what?"

"Or you become the best painter the world has ever known, your name spoken with reverence a thousand years after your death."

"Okay," I mumbled, numb to the whole show. "Yeah. Let's do that."

"This is where most people ask 'what's the catch?'" My reflection's voice was coy.

"Probably my soul or something, right? That's okay. I'm not using it for anything."

"You don't have to sell your soul. Any soul will do."

"Never mind I'll get it myself," Joana said. "Geez, I wish I'd married a butler instead."

"Think about it," the reflection bubbled rapidly, spraying blood between his teeth as he did. "You won't be able to enjoy your success without a soul. And your wife—she was going to leave you anyway. If anything, this would spare her a lifetime of regret and guilt over your death. You owe it to yourself—you owe it to both of you."

"I can't give something that isn't mine," I replied, immediately hating myself for even entertaining the thought.

"Anyone who loves without reservation exposes their soul. Paint her—not as she appears, but as she truly is. I'll take care of the rest."

"What are you doing, giving birth in there?" Joana asked from right outside the door. The handle rattled. The door wasn't locked. I leapt to stop her from entering—too slow. The door swung inward and there she stood: tank top over pajama bottoms, hair frizzy and wild, licking Nutella off her fingers. My heart was beating so fast, but as much as I loved her, I think my fear was even stronger.

Back to the mirror, I stared into my reflection. No blood. No bullet wound. Just a tired, aging face, equally terrifying in its own way.

"Come on," Joana wrapped her arms around me from behind. "The movie's no fun without you blubbering over the dialog."

"I can't," I said, still staring into the mirror. "I have a painting to finish."

A feverish intensity imbued my work all night and into the next morning. A drowning man struggling for air could not have done so with more urgency than the flight of my desperate brush. No thoughts endured more than a second before they were replaced by the endless cycle of anticipation and release each stroke demanded. When my canvas was filled, I didn't hesitate to slash the lines onto the walls on either side of my easel. Then the table—the dresser—my own body a vessel to carry the glory of her design.

My brush was unconfined by any shape, but in its erratic patterns I felt myself carving something out of nothing—something that had never been seen by mortal eyes before.

In the subtleties of the blending colors I captured Joana's wry humor and gentle grace. Her laughter exploded like shrapnel across the space, the light in her eyes reflected in my cascading colors. The way her heart broke when her aging dog nudged her goodbye—the anxious thrill of stepping off the plane in Paris—even her love for me and her unspoken dread of the great beyond, naked and frozen for all the world to see.

Paint beneath my fingernails, in my hair, blazoned across my body, a testament to the frenzied passion which had possessed me. Though working alone, I danced with Joana the whole night through. I have never seen her more plainly nor loved her more strongly than those forbidden hours, and not until morning's light did I stop to understand what I had done.

'Are you insane?' That's what I was expecting to hear. Any second the door to my studio would open and Joana would see the chaos I had the audacity to unfurl. She'd laugh at me, making a thousand playful guesses at the madness which leaked from my mind all night. We'd both laugh, then she'd say something like 'I'm just happy to see you enjoying your work again,' and offer to help me clean. That's how kind she was: when I did something stupid she'd be there to help me fix it without a trace of accusation or blame.

Maybe I really was insane. But either way, she couldn't fix this one for me.

She didn't enter the room though. Not in the kitchen making her coffee, not in the shower singing herself into lucidity. Joana never got up that morning. She said she wasn't feeling herself, and I was too much of a coward to tell her why. If I'd taken a break in the night to check on her, I might have noticed the rot that had already started to set in. She managed to prop herself up on her elbows, leaving several layers of flaking skin on the pillow. Ashen cracked skin, yellowed eyes, balding patches where clumps of hair had already started to fall—my wife was still in my studio where I'd captured her. The woman struggling for breath was nothing but a stranger to me, and I left her without a word.

I slept little and ate less. I sought only to paint, vainly trying to recapture the intimacy I'd felt with her the night before. There was a brief thrill as I marveled at the dexterity of my fingers, although they lacked the passion that haunted me before. I could trace every mental image I dared conjure and map them flawlessly onto the canvas, but they were dead things being carved into a dead world.

It didn't take long for me to sit back in exasperation. I had the technical skill to conquer any challenge, but it wasn't an infernal magic which had possessed me the night before. I knew in that moment that there was nothing I could ever create that was more beautiful than the pandemonium of Joana's soul. I heard that hollow thing call my name from the bedroom with a voice like wind through dry leaves, and Heaven and Hell as my witness, I wept for what I'd done.

"Give her soul back to her," I begged the aging face in the mirror. "Take mine instead—"

"What an ugly painting that would be," the demon with my face replied.

"Then another—it doesn't matter whose. I'll give you as many as you like!"

"Does another love you as she did? Have they exposed themselves to your capture as she has done?"

I had no reply to give. Coward that I was, I merely returned to my painting. Lifeless hollow forms came marching through my work, each accompanied by the soundtrack of my wife's body slowly deteriorating without its soul. Each time I looked at her there would be another piece missing: fingers decomposing and littering the mattress, cheeks worn so thin that I could see her blackened teeth and languid tongue even when her mouth was closed. I'd listen to her moan while I worked, always stealing longing glances at the portrait of her soul splashed across the room.

I couldn't take it anymore. I set fire to that place with her inside. And watching the smoke curl into the night sky, all that's left is to hope her soul escaped its prison and is now soaring somewhere with its dignity returned.

As for me, I returned to my work. Until the day I paint something so marvelous as to trick some poor innocent into loving me. Then I will paint what I see, and sell them until Joana is home again.

## The Other Side Of Sky

When I was about to die, my life didn't flash before my eyes. All I could think about was what my father once told me from a beige couch in an unlit study.

"Above all else, humans are survivors. When one has exhausted all possibility of survival, the mind will expand its idea of what is possible. Think of it this way: You're alone in the woods and hiding from wolves which are hunting you. Do you call for help?"

"Of course not", I had said. "Then the wolves would know where I was."

"Exactly. But if the wolves found you anyway, and you knew there was no hope of escape. You might as well shout then, right?"

"You might as well."

"The only difference, then, was your desperation. In the same way, your subconscious mind is prudent enough not to shout into the dark for fear of what might hear. When all hope is lost though, the mind begins to scream at random. It screams across time, across dimensions—and just sometimes, something will be listening."

"What kind of something?" I'd asked.

"There's only one way to find out, and I wouldn't recommend it."

I wouldn't recommend it either. Taking a bullet in the stomach isn't all that. The head would have been better. Nice and clean. Arm or leg? No problem, I can still get myself to the hospital. The stomach though—that bleed is slow, and there's too much time to scream at the emptiness between stars.

It doesn't matter how it happened. I made some bad decisions, and the man who shot me made a worse one. That's not what this story is about. This story is about an asphalt parking lot, my twelve-year-old daughter Lizzie, and the best pizza I ever had in my life.

Let's start at the parking lot where I died. You ever jump straight from a hot tub to a cold pool? It was a little like that, only I didn't feel it on my skin. I felt it deep inside, radiating out from where the bullet sat between my ribs. It seemed to move about an inch a minute, and I could hear it the whole while—kinda like the slow tear of fabric that kept getting louder and louder, until I was pretty sure every cell in my body was screaming itself apart. Like the worst static you ever heard. And the louder it got, the slower it spread, until each POP was a supernova and each plateau between was death itself.

And I knew—deep down I knew, like I knew fire burns and gravity drags me down—that soon one of those POPS will be the last one I ever hear. And that for the rest of time, I'll be suspended by the anticipation between. But that never happened, because something spoke to me before I went.

"Want to stick around?"

If that was the voice of God, then God is a lonely old man at a diner with nowhere else to be. I didn't know how to answer, but I really did want to stick around. Lizzie needed a dad, and I needed another chance to make up for fucking up the first time. I wanted it so hard that I think the voice must have felt it too.

"You won't get to leave again."

I'll never leave her again...

"Not now, not in a hundred years when your daughter is dead, not in ten-thousand when the last man has killed his brother, and you're left to watch the survivor grow old and blow to dust. Or you can get off now, and that will be that."

I don't know how long I sat there thinking, but I did know that I hadn't heard a POP in a long time. That silence sure can be heavy. I also knew that I'd rather spend the rest of time thinking about how I tried my hardest for my daughter than let my last thought be self-hatred and regret. And as soon as I knew that, the voice knew it too.

*POP*

To the other side of sky and back. But not back—not like I ought to be. I was less than the shadow of a shadow, a ghost of a light breeze wafting on a calm day. And nothing broke my heart like lingering in Lizzie's room and watching her watch the door for me to come home. And nothing hurt so much as not to be able to hold her and tell her I was here, or watching her push away her food until I could see her collarbone like it was a snake beneath her skin.

But hurt is a lot like desperation, because sometimes you don't know what's possible until it really sets your blood on fire and gets you screaming. Because one night it hurt so bad and I lashed out so hard that something quite miraculous happened.

A water bottle fell off the side of her nightstand and fell onto the carpet. Lizzie hadn't pushed it. She was lying on her back, staring at the ceiling like she did most of the time. It was me, and with some concentration and practice, I could do it again. Little things—sliding a pen on a desk, or popping a bubble, or kissing her on the forehead as light as a butterfly. Then once I caught her smile and touch her fingers to her skin, and I knew she felt it too.

I could learn how to be in her life, but it would take time. But I didn't have the luxury to wait forever.

It's not that I was afraid Lizzie would hurt herself. Not on purpose anyway. She had to move and live with my sister though, and like a flower in the sun, I could see her wilting day by day. She stopped seeing her old friends, and she didn't talk to anyone at her new school. My sister didn't have the first idea how to reach her, so she'd just give my daughter money whenever she felt guilty.

What's a 12-year-old going to do with nothing but time, money, and pain?

## Sleepless Nights

Sneak cigarettes at first, but it didn't stay innocent for long. Apple doesn't fall far from the tree I guess; pretty soon she was buying a bag of pills from the school janitor every week like clockwork. What could I do about that? Breathe down the bastard's neck? Blow some sand in his eye?

The flower was wilting faster than ever, and Lizzie never kept money in her pocket for very long. To make matters worse, my sister's guilt didn't last into the third month. Lizzie's allowance was cut off, and suddenly the only thing she'd done to numb the pain was out of reach. All I could do was be the breeze on her knotted brow when she sweat herself to sleep or bit her nails until they bled.

Lizzie confronted the janitor the next day, and it wasn't pretty. She shoved him in the hallway in the middle of the day, practically shouting at him in front of a dozen kids. If she'd picked up one of my bad habits, she'd gotten them all. Watching her little face seethe, I knew that things were only going to get worse from here.

I had to try harder. My next breakthrough came in the form of a house fly. I was nudging it back and forth when I began falling into the rhythm of its motion. Pretty soon I was that rhythm, and before I knew what was happening, I was inside looking out, swerving wildly to avoid slamming into a wall. The shock knocked my mind straight back to where I was, but it wasn't hard to get back in again. Next a spider, crickets, even a squirrel for the fraction of a second—my spirit was breaking its way into simple-minded animals.

The animal mind was in there too, but I was getting better at keeping them down. Pretty soon I might be able to send her a message somehow, or even become her friend through a dog or cat. But pretty soon wasn't soon enough.

Lizzie was stubborn, and just like her father, she wouldn't take no for an answer. She slipped from her bedroom one night and snuck out the house while my sister was asleep. She didn't have a car, or money, but she did have a hammer, and that scared me even worse. She walked the whole 2 mile route to her school, her face as blank as if she were still lying in bed and staring at the ceiling. I tried to intervene by slipping into the minds of a few moths we passed, but even these were suddenly too difficult for me.

I couldn't get into their rhythm. I didn't feel like a moth. I felt like her father, the worst father in the world who was helpless to stop whatever happened next. She broke into the window of the computer lab and stole a dozen laptops from the school. She hid them in the bushes around the corner, then walked all the way home and slipped back into bed as if nothing happened. The next morning she ditched after the bus dropped her off, then straight to the hidden computers and a pawn shop nearby. An hour later and she was back in school, a giant wad of cash in her pocket and a fake doctor's note for the front desk.

I would have been almost proud if I hadn't been watching her face the whole time. I hadn't seen that much quiet, self-loathing since the last time I had a body to look in the mirror.

"How much did you bring?" was her first question for the janitor after school. They were under the bleachers of the soccer field.

"How much you got?" he asked.

Don't. Don't be that stupid.

She pulled out the entire wad of cash. I don't think she ever once counted it. She didn't care, as long as she got what she came for.

The janitor's face lit up like a kid on Christmas. He reached out to take it, and she let him. She stuffed her hands into her pockets and waited while he flipped through it, checking surreptitiously over his shoulder as he did.

Maybe this will be the last time. Maybe she'll take a bunch of pills and get sick and never want to touch the stuff again. Or maybe she'll be stoned for a month, and by the time she sobers up I'll be a little further from her mind. Maybe I'll be stronger by then, and I can hold her like I'm supposed to, and tell her that everything is going to be okay...

But the janitor didn't believe in 'one day'. He stuffed the cash in his pocket and, as cool as a cucumber, started to walk away.

"Where the fuck are you going?" Lizzie whispered as loud as she dared.

The janitor started walking faster. If she is anything like her father... right on cue, she charges at him, hurling herself onto his leg and wrapping herself around it. He kicks her, but she holds on fast.

"Just give it to me. I'll tell everyone."

"You wouldn't dare. I can guess where you got the money. The whole school is talking about it. Get off of me."

"Fuck do I care? I'm going to tell the principal. And the police. And your fat cow of a mother—"

I don't know if he intended to stomp on her. It all happened too fast. She was already wrapped around his leg, and the shaking wasn't getting her off, and —BAM, his foot planting right in her face. But she held on, and that seemed to make him even angrier. She didn't cry—she didn't even whimper. She just closed her eyes and clung on like a drowning man on the last stick of wood in the world.

"You never... talk to me... again," the man said between kicks. Each one was harder than the last, like he was trying to get out a whole lifetime of frustrations all at once. He kicked her like she was every woman who had ever failed to love him, and every man he'd ever looked up to and let him down. Like it was the only power he'd ever had in his miserable life, and he couldn't stop because he'd never get that power back again. He kicked her and he hated himself for doing it, and that made him kick her even harder.

That rage—that pain—that helpless despair—now that's a rhythm I could understand. I was inside his head all at once, and I wasn't going to let go. I felt his mind screaming inside me, but Lizzie wasn't getting kicked anymore, and that's all that mattered. Everything that he had poured into hurting my daughter,

I poured into him, crushing his spirit until it was a shadow—less than a shadow—and then nothing but a distant thought in the back of my mind.

I was alive again. I had a body. I didn't get bounced out, I couldn't get out even if I tried. And I was standing over my barely conscious daughter who lay bleeding and crying into the dirt. I fell onto my knees right beside her and started crying too. There wasn't anything else to do.

I tried to reach out for her, but she recoiled as if I was a serpent. How could I blame her? She'd just seen this body beat her bloody. How could she ever speak to me after this? She started running, but I couldn't let that happen. If I let her out of my life, she'd never trust me enough to let me back in. This was my one chance, and I couldn't waste it.

She wasn't hard to catch in the state she was in. And the janitor had picked his spot well—there wasn't anyone else around the soccer field. I've been watching long enough to know which car belonged to him, and it didn't take long to force Lizzie inside and stomp the gas.

Doesn't hatred get tired eventually? I'm going to be there for her, and I'm going to protect her from here on out. She'll understand how hard I tried one day, and she'll forgive me. Who cares if the lines on my face are different, or if I sing her to sleep in an unfamiliar voice? I'm her father, and I'll love her until the end of time.

It took her almost a year to speak to me, and almost three before she said: "Can we get pizza tonight, dad?"

But you know what? It was the best pizza I ever had.

## Their Last Words

It takes some by surprise during the night—I think they're the lucky ones. I think others are holding off for something—their daughter's marriage, their grandchildren—something powerful enough to give the last grains of the hourglass some weight. Others simply make up their mind that it's time. There's one man in particular I remember who hadn't moved a muscle for a day. Several of us at the hospice thought he was already gone a half-dozen times, but then all at once he stood up. He carefully put on his suit, tied his tie, fastened his shoes, and then laid back down. He was dead within the hour.

Its their last words that really stick with me though. Logically I know they're a random line of conversation slipping from a deteriorating mind, but somehow it also feels like their truest reflection. In that moment when I'm holding her frail hand, I know her better than her husband or her children ever did. People can hide their whole life long, but they can't keep hiding into death. That's how I feel anyway, and it's why I started keeping a journal of all the last words I hear.

"I don't know where to go next." That hit me hard. She was 94 years old, hardly bigger than Yoda, and she usually just watched me in silence while I cleaned her room. It was late and I was tired—I didn't know how to comfort her, and I just pretended that I didn't hear. She was gone when I checked in the next morning.

"Am I in the way?" Seems silly, doesn't it? Inconsequential. But the man was a world war 2 veteran. He told me once about how he and a dozen men broke over a thousand people out of the camps. He wanted to go home at the end, but I saw his two sons fighting over who would take him in the lobby. Neither took him and he died in the hospice, his last words being: "Am I in the way?"

"Not going without a fight." I liked that one. Barrel chested bearded man, looked as healthy as could be. The fight was a seizure though, and one of the worst I'd ever seen. It must have lasted half an hour, bucking and flailing and gasping for breath. He would have done better to go quietly.

"Dead... dead... dead... dead..." over and over. Ever since the woman's stroke, she was convinced that she'd already died. She never stopped muttering to herself, "dead...dead..." being one of her favorite mantras.

Sometimes I wonder if thoughts can linger in the air after their thinker has died. I can swear that the rooms are darker for at least a week after someone goes. If its a violent death, sometimes I'll feel a tension in the air—something like anger without a body attached to it. I decided to start keeping track, my hobby of journaling became a bit more of an obsession, if I'm being honest. I took a calendar and marked down how I felt about the rooms each day. I didn't fill in the deaths until the end of the month, and sure enough, each death marked the change in a room.

Now I know this isn't an exact science, but in the process I did notice something that I couldn't explain. For the last four deaths in my building, their last utterances began with the following words:

"I. Am. Not. Dead."

It's silly, right? Here were four unrelated people who never talked to each other. And their last words formed a sentence. It was a silly coincidence, it meant nothing, and it kept getting stranger.

"Can you get me a little water?" 11B, a few days later.

"You look like an angel." 23A, a heart attack during the night.

"Hear the birds outside? I do love the spring." Sitting by her window, the sun on her face. It should have been the most peaceful one for me, but the moment she closed her eyes I knew the word fit.

"I. Am. Not. Dead. Can. You. Hear."

Can I hear what? I found out this morning.

I wasn't there when he said it, but everybody at the hospice knew I was keeping track. My friend told me the moment I walked in the door.

"Me and my buddies are going to see each other real soon."

I am not dead. Can you hear me?

The rooms all seem dark today.

## Children Taste Better

A single engine private plane, skimming low over the Alaskan wilderness. Glacial waters as clear as a polished mirror, reflecting the vast primordial forests and savage peaks which loom above us: a testament to the stoic grandeur of an Earth which existed long before humanity and will continue to endure long after the footnote of our existence has been forgotten. For one glorious moment it feels as though the world was created just for us, but that was before the engine stalled mid-flight. Before the violent plummet and the mercy of a deaf God, before the ground accelerating toward us, all happening much too fast to regain altitude before the crash.

An explosion so loud it was silent—light so bright I saw nothing. Bone-jarring impact, everything lurching so bad it felt like my soul must have been ripped clean from my body. I wish I'd died the second we hit the ground. I wish my husband had too, but he lingered in that broken body until nightfall. Our hands had never clasped so tightly as when sealed together with his blood, and no words were as precious as those escaping between his shallow breaths.

"Promise me that you'll survive," he'd said. "Whatever it takes."

I wasn't in much better condition than him. One of my legs was broken, several ribs had snapped, and three of my fingers were still clinging to the bottom of my seat where I'd braced for the crash, now a dozen feet away. I didn't expect to last the night, but I still made that promise. I'd like to think that hope gave him some small comfort before his eyes closed for the last time.

After that came the war between slow starvation and my desperate hope of being saved. A hungry animal could easily find me first, lured by the scent of charred flesh and fresh blood which teased my nostrils. But there was another war going on below the surface: my human dignity against my will to survive.

I lasted almost four days before I took the first bite. Just a mouthful, holding the strip of his skin in my mouth and wetting my parched throat with his blood. By the end of the week I'd become more methodical, stripping the flesh clean to roast, cracking the bones for their marrow, wasting nothing. By the end of two weeks, there was nothing left of my husband.

I'd given up on ever being rescued, and instead started the long walk back toward civilization. I was amazed at how quickly my leg had healed, and as I trekked, I felt myself filled with a restless vitality which I could only attribute to my will to live.

I barely slept at night, barely rested during the day. It's almost as if I'd spent my entire life being sick, but I'd gotten so used to the feeling that I thought that's how everyone is supposed to feel.

I can tell you right now that life is a lie. Your blood is not supposed to pass sluggish and unnoticed through your veins, its power dormant. You should feel the electricity of your flexing muscles, each explosive fiber primed to your will.

Those pristine wildernesses were not where I had been banished to die. It's where I came alive.

I don't know how long I traveled in such a state, falling into a a trance from my single-minded determination. I think my husband's spirit must have been guiding me though, because I found sudden understanding in how to navigate the stars, just like he learned from the navy.

Eventually I found what I was looking for: a couple of campers fresh from the big city. I was so relieved at hearing another human voice through the trees that I surged forward like a wild thing. All my pain and sacrifice had been building to this moment. Elegant French words, a woman's laughter, a way home —this is what I'd kept myself alive for.

But when I saw them... him panting and sweating to move his grotesque belly, her screaming and carrying on as though I was less than human... well it just goes to show you that sometimes you need to take a step back in order to see things clearly. After everything I'd been through, I couldn't feel anything but pity and disgust for these torpid creatures, willing victims of what their artificial life had deformed them into.

The husband was bigger, but the wife tasted better. Cleaner. I lived more vibrantly in those next few nights—feasting and regaining my strength from their unused bodies—than all the years they'd wasted on being half-alive.

I wasn't only getting stronger either. I started catching my thoughts slipping in and out of French. I'd thought my husband had been guiding me through the woods, but now it seemed more appropriate to say that I had consumed some aspect of him, just as I had done with the French couple.

I was hungrier than ever. Gnawing, incessant hunger almost as soon as I'd finished, like my stomach threatened to digest itself if it didn't get more. I tried eating some of the trail mix and granola bars in their packs, but it tasted like so much sawdust and dirt. Even the beef jerky tasted like cardboard (although that's not unusual by itself).

Human meat. It was obvious that the more I ate, the more I needed it. The prospect of returning to my frail old self? Unbearable. But the idea of living in the woods, biding my time in agonizing solitude while waiting for my next chance meal? I don't think that's any better.

Unless of course, I go back to my old life without giving up what I need to survive. And such easy targets, there at the kindergarten where I used to teach.

I didn't even waste time stopping at a hospital. My wounds had mended on their own, all but the missing fingers. I only stopped off at home long enough for a shower and some new clothes before heading back to the school.

Surrounded by a sea of little shaggy heads, not even reaching my waist. I could almost taste them. The other teachers were shocked to hear what happened of course (their version was lighter on the details), but despite their generous offers to help, I insisted that I wanted to be back in the classroom as soon as possible.

"See guys? I told you she wasn't dead!" That was Roddick. He likes to fingerpaint. I hope it doesn't have a bad flavor.

"What happened to your hand? Ewww gross! You're gross!" I'd be lying if I said this was the first time I'd contemplated Tiffany's horrible demise.

"You don't have to come back. We were having fun without you."

"Oh don't you worry." I squatted down to Sandy's level. "Having me around will be even more exciting. Now take these and hand one out to everyone in the class."

I may be hungry, but I'm not an idiot. I'd never be able to take more than one or two children before causing such a scene that it became impossible to continue.

"What's she handing out? What is it let me see!" Tiffany shouted.

"It's a permission slip," I told her. "We're going on a field trip. You, me, the whole class. We're going camping."

It's not just the taste that makes children special. It's their innocence. And if I ever want to start over and live a normal life, then I'm going to need to eat until I'm innocent again too.

## The Smallest Coffins Are The Heaviest

If someone pointed a gun at me and filled me with lead, then no one would question my right to remove the bullet from my body. It was forced into me against my will, and I would be a fool not to fight tooth and nail to stop it from destroying my life.

The child growing inside me is the result of another wound: one much deeper than a bullet could reach. A wound that my mother says is a blessing in disguise, but I don't see it.

I don't mind telling you how it happened, but I won't because I don't want you to think it matters. Whether or not he loved me, whether one or the other was drunk or lonely or beaten into submission doesn't matter, just as it wouldn't matter whether the gun went off by accident or deliberate malice.

The only thing that matters is that I'm hurt and want to be well again, and an abortion is the only way to make that happen. At first it seemed like my mother was sympathetic to the idea, but as the weeks dragged on it became clear that she was only stalling for time.

I trusted her though, and I kept promising to wait. Just until I talk to one more person—just until I read one more pamphlet filled with comforting faces and sourceless facts.

I waited as if one morning I'd wake up and realize I was making a big deal about nothing. As if I'd just failed a test or bumped a car that would be forgiven and forgotten. Day by day the child grew inside me, and day by day the child I used to be died to make room for it.

"You don't have to decide anything yet," my mother kept saying. By the time I realized that 'not making a decision' was itself a decision to keep the baby, it was already too late.

12 weeks had come and passed without me noticing, and no clinic in my state would take me now. My mother didn't need to pretend to be patient or kind anymore. All the talk about my well being was replaced with accusations about my responsibility. I had to get a job—find daycare—find a man. I had to sacrifice myself to this wound, and offer it my dreams for a future that I had only just begun to plan for myself.

My mother said I was being selfish. Hadn't she sacrificed everything for me? No, I told her, she hadn't. She'd wanted a child, so anything she'd been willing to trade for that was an exchange, not a sacrifice.

I couldn't talk to her anymore, so I confided in a close friend. A few days later my friend slipped me two bottles of pills which I treasured more than a thousand sweet words. The first ones were supposed to detach the embryo from the uterine wall. The second set dispels it. I like that word—"dispel". Like magic, vanishing it away without a trace.

This was no disappearing act though. I'd never felt such excruciating pain in my life as when I took the first pills. I got through it because I knew it was a cleansing pain, like I was stitching myself back together to be whole again.

I had to wait at least 24 hours before taking the second set. Sometimes it hurt too bad for me to keep a straight face though, and my mother was quick to notice. She wanted to take me to the hospital, and the more I protested, the more suspicious she got.

There was no hiding it anymore after I took the second pills. I was rolling on the bathroom floor and couldn't stop her from reading the empty bottles. The wound was healing though, and it was too late for her to do anything about it.

"What have you done you evil girl?" she shouted at me while I clutched my stomach in pain. "Nasty, vile, wicked girl. God will not forgive you."

Her words couldn't reach me anymore though. There was nothing left to hide. If God was watching, then he was the only one who should feel ashamed.

The whole process was a lot bloodier than I expected. Whenever I thought it had all discharged, I'd clutch my stomach again and another wave would wrack my body.

To my mother's credit she stayed with me the whole time. After the initial outbursts she held my hand and prayed for me. I told her I was sorry that I wasn't ready to start my own family yet, but she said all the family she needed was already in this room.

I guess I was too relieved to understand what she meant until the next morning. After everything I'd been through, how could I expect to see my child waiting for me in the kitchen?

In a high chair pulled up to the counter. I thought it was nothing but an old doll until I got close enough for the smell to hit me. The stuffing had been replaced with the gore I'd left in the toilet. Congealed lumps that could have been premature organs or bones stuck haphazardly from the mess, and blood dribbled down the thing's legs and onto the otherwise spotless floor.

I threw up in the sink. I felt my mother's hand on my back, but it was cold and damp and brought no comfort.

"Still having morning sickness?" she cooed. "Don't worry, that won't last now that you've had the baby."

"I didn't have the baby. I don't have a baby," I told her as soon as I'd stopped gagging.

Her smile didn't falter. "How silly of you not to remember. You must have known you were pregnant."

"Yes but—"

"You didn't think you could really interfere with God's plan, did you?"

I didn't want to look at the gruesome doll, but I couldn't help it. I immediately began to hurl again.

"I've been thinking of names," my mother prattled on. She reached out to hold my hair back, but I recoiled from her touch. "She is a girl, isn't she? It's so hard to tell."

"Mom please. Don't do this. Get rid of it now."

"Sally is nice, isn't it? Silly Sally—you've got to think about what the other kids will think too."

My breathing came in ragged gasps. I couldn't answer.

"Or Lizzy, that's cute. Then when she grows up she can be Elizabeth, which is very—"

I was seeing red, and it wasn't just the blood. I rushed at the doll, meaning to throw it in the trash. My mother was more lucid than she appeared though, and she immediately blocked me behind the kitchen counter.

"Don't you dare!" she howled. "You have to let her sleep!"

"Which of us do you want, mom? You can't have us both."

"You're being selfish again. Can you imagine Lizzy saying that to you when she has a child of her own?"

I made another rush, this time ducking under her arms. I almost reached the horrid doll before mom grabbed me by the hair and yanked me back. She was pulling so hard I can't believe the hair didn't uproot.

"You aren't saving your grandchild!" I screamed. "You're killing your daughter."

She let go all at once. For a tense moment we stared at each other. There was still intelligence in her twinkling eyes. There was still love in her trembling lips.

"I don't have a…" she mumbled.

"Say it. Admit she's gone. Please mom, you have to."

She pressed her lips into a thin, hard line. Whatever came next wouldn't be a slip of the tongue. It would be deliberate and conscious and utterly irrevocable.

"I don't have a daughter," she said at last, turning away from me. "My daughter wouldn't do this to me."

I packed my things and left that night, never to return. She'll call from time to time, but I never answer anymore. She sends me cards, but I throw them away unopened. What else does she expect when she writes "your daughter misses you" on the front?

## Self-Portrait From The Dead

My mom hates her father. Grandfather Jack's name might as well have been a swear word when I was growing up. Dad told me the story once, on the condition that I never tell mom I knew.

Jack was married to my Grandmother Kathy for 22 years before he cheated on her. It wasn't a midlife crisis or an intoxicated indiscretion either—he'd been going on fishing trips every other weekend for almost a year before Kathy figured out the fish was named Sally, and that she was half his age. Either dad doesn't know the specifics, or he wouldn't tell me, but I guess Kathy decided suicide was a less sinful way out than murder or divorce. That was before I was even born, but mom hasn't spoken a word to her father since.

I still got to know him though. It took 8 years of his begging and pleading after I was born, but mom finally gave in and arranged for us to meet. She used my father to deliver messages between them, as she 'was afraid of what she'd say if they spoke'. I was pretty scared when dad told me we were going to drive an hour into the desert to visit grandpa Jack's house, and mom only made it worse in the days leading up to the meeting.

"He might be an axe-murderer by now for all I know," Mom said.

Dad said he's a professor of art history.

"Or maybe he'll say nasty things about me. Whatever he tells you, I don't want you to listen to him."

Dad made a joke about how I've already had a lot of practice not listening to my parents. Mom didn't smile.

"In fact, it would be better if you didn't talk to him at all. Just let him see that you're a happy, healthy, well-adjusted boy, and then go play by yourself until Dad takes you home. Okay?"

"You're going to have a great time," Dad told me on the way. "He's got a whole art studio setup with everything you can imagine. Clay pots and sculptures, water and oil paints, brushes and tools of every size and shape—we can hang out all day if you want."

"Does Grandfather hate me?" I asked.

"Of course not. He wouldn't have kept sending letters all those years if he hated you. All he cares about is his seeing his grandson."

"Does he hate mom?"

"Your mom is a saint. No-one could hate her."

"Did he hate Grandma?"

Dad looked uncomfortable at that. "You'll have to ask him yourself."

So I did. That was the first thing out of my mouth in fact. Grandpa Jack was a pudgy old man, straight bald with discolored blotches on his scalp, and a huge mustache that wiggled when he talked. He came rushing at me, arms wide for a hug. Right away I asked him if he hated my Grandmother. Froze him in his tracks. Dad stepped in front of me as if trying to protect me from being hit, but Grandfather Jack just squatted down to my height and looked me solemnly in the eye.

"I never loved any woman half as much as I did Kathy. Except your mother, of course. Just because two people love each other doesn't mean they make each other happy though. I guess I just wasn't strong enough to spend any more of my life being unhappy, and not brave enough to hurt your grandmother by telling her the truth."

He smelled like old spice, and that seemed like a pretty satisfactory explanation to my eight year old self. I let him show me his studio and we painted a big landscape together. He did all the hard stuff and the details, and he helped me transform every messy blotch I made into something beautiful without painting over my contribution. He asked if I was going to visit again, and I said I wanted to—as long as mom allowed it, anyway. I've never seen a man go so red, so fast, his mustache bristling like a porcupine.

"Your mother got no right to tell you anything. She can throw fits and slam doors all she wants, but you're my family and the only thing left in this world I give a damn about. You tell her that, okay?"

I didn't get to visit as often as I liked, but at least every month or two dad would drive me out there. Mom was reluctant at first, but I convinced her that I wanted to be a painter and that she'd be crushing my budding dreams if Jack didn't teach me how. I loved the landscapes, but Jack's specialty was portraits and his passion for them soon rubbed off on me.

"A good portrait only depicts the subject," he told me once. "It'll get the scruff on his chin and the wrinkles under his eyes and everything else that makes him who he is. But a great portrait—" here he took a long drink from his iced tea, liking to draw my attention out as long as it would go. "A great portrait is always a portrait of the artist. Doesn't matter who he decided to paint, he put so much of himself into it that it's going to tell you more about him than the person he's painting."

Jack had a special gallery just for self-portraits. He did a new one every year, the passage of time immaculately mapped onto his many faces. Seeing all the paintings together like that, I couldn't help but notice that every year his brow seemed a little heavier. His smile was a little sadder, his eyes a little more weary. I didn't like seeing him change like that, and I told him so.

"Don't you worry, I still know how to paint a happy picture. I'm just saving it for the year when your mother finally forgives me."

I told mom that too. She told me that he'd be better off figuring out how to decorate Hell.

The self-portraits made me sad, but they didn't start to frighten me until Grandfather showed me his latest work when I was 19 years old.

"Where are your eyes?" I asked, staring at the blank pools of flesh dominating his latest portrait. The lines were more jagged than his previous work, making his sagging face seemed to be carved from marble.

"Right behind my glasses, silly," he said.

"Why didn't you paint them?"

He studied the picture, seeming to notice for the first time. "Would you look at that," he mumbled. "Doesn't matter. You can tell it's still me, can't you?"

More features were missing in the portrait next year. The whole face seemed to be sliding, almost as if the skin was a liquid that was dripping right off. He couldn't figure out why I was making such a fuss over it. "Looks like me to me," he grunted.

Shortly later Jack was diagnosed with Alzheimer's disease, and it was all down hill from there. He'd retired as a professor several years back, and painting wasn't a hobby anymore—it was an obsession. Now that I wasn't living on my own it was easier to visit him, but even in the span of a week he'd finish three or four more self-portraits, each more disconcerting than the last. I don't know why he even called them self-portraits—they weren't even recognizable as human anymore. Just tormented flesh, grotesquely and unevenly contoured as though the underlying skeleton was replaced with a haphazard pile of trash.

He'd get angry if I didn't recognize him in his pictures. He said he was painting who he was, and if I didn't see that, then I was the one who was blind. A few days later and he'd be excited to show me his next one, completely forgetting that the last one even existed at all.

"When is your mom going to come see? I've been calling her all week."

He even forgot that she hates him too. Every time he'd ask, and every time I'd make a vague excuse and promise she'd be there next time.

He was 86 when he had his stroke. He didn't paint again after that, and within the year he was gone. Dad and I went to the funeral, but mom just locked herself in her room. Grandfather still left everything to her anyhow, saying in the will that "I may not be able to give her a home, but at least I can give her my house." She didn't want to even set foot in the place though, so a week or so later I went to start boxing up the stuff for her.

# Sleepless Nights

That's when I saw his final painting. I was dreading going into his studio, and not just because I knew it was going to be the biggest job. I started stacking the abominable canvases face down so I wouldn't have to look at them, but I couldn't help but notice this one was different.

It was so perfect that it could have been a photograph. The self-portrait showed Jack lying peacefully in his casket, hands crossed over his chest, eyes closed. It was strange that he'd been able to paint it so precisely though, considering the rest of his recent work littering the room. I sat there for a while, thinking how heartbreaking it was for him to predict his own death like that.

I left the painting out while packing, thinking of hanging it in my apartment to honor him. There were plenty of less morbid pictures to choose from, but this one felt like it was really him who painted it, not the disease which had ravaged his mind. It made me think that his spirit was at rest somewhere, and that made me glad. I hung it in my bedroom that night, saying goodnight to him just as I'd done on the dozens of sleepovers where I'd lay my sleeping bag at the foot of his bed.

I fell asleep quickly, exhausted from the day of clearing stuff out. I slept straight through the night, not even dreaming as far as I can remember. Then sitting up in the morning, the first thing I saw was Jack staring back at me from his portrait. The one that had shown closed eyes last night. They weren't closed anymore. Maybe it was like that yesterday and I hadn't noticed, but that didn't sit right with me at all. I remembered how Jack always used to get angry when I didn't see the same thing as him in his pictures—maybe he was right and I really was just blind. I didn't think too much of it until the next night when I woke up and the painting was screaming.

No sound—I'm not that mad yet—but the mouth was open, twisted and frozen in unending agony. I just sat in bed, breathing hard, staring at the colorless torment in the weak light from my window. I kept lying back down and trying to convince myself it was a dream, unable to sit still for more than a few seconds before jolting upright again to stare at the painting. It took me almost half an hour to finally get out of bed and turn the lights on. I laughed out loud to see the shadows retreat, and the portrait sleeping peacefully in the casket with his eyes closed once more. I still slept with the light on the rest of the night though. In the morning, his eyes were unmistakably open once more.

I didn't blame Jack's painting. I blamed myself for being blind like he always scolded me about. I called my mother and told her about my weird dream on her voice-mail. 'Grandpa Jack is in pain', I told her. I would have said more, but I felt stupid and hung up shortly after.

I didn't actually hear the screaming until the second night, and by then it was already too late.

Sometime in the early morning—I was out of bed and halfway across the room before I was even fully awake. The sound ripped me from my bed so fast that I didn't even realize it was coming from the painting. There was enough light to see Grandfather's features twisted in agony.

My downstairs neighbor started pounding on the roof. That only seemed to make the screaming louder. The thrum of blood in my ears matched the beat, then raced past.

I tried to run, but my door handle wouldn't turn. I didn't struggle long—to stand by the door I had to be right next to the portrait and the sound was excruciating.

Next I pulled the painting from the wall. Hanging beneath it was a second painting—one I'd never put there. One of the disfigured ones with its lumpy flesh supported wrong from underneath. I saw this as a sign, although I was too freaked out to guess at what. I hung the screaming painting back to cover up that abomination.

Re-secured to the wall, I started to retreat toward the window. I never made it more than a step before a firm grip grasped my wrist and pulled me back. One of Grandfather's hands no longer ended at the canvas. Cold pale skin, its nails digging into me, relentlessly dragging me back toward the picture as though through an open window.

Now I was screaming too. Someone started hammering on my door. I tried to brace myself against the wall with my feet. The pale hand shook for its effort, but it was still stronger—inch by inch pulling me into his coffin. I almost wriggled free when his second hand shot out—this one catching me by the throat—to haul me forward at an alarming rate.

I was so close I could smell him. Not the old spice cologne he always wore. My face pressed against the canvas, it smelled like rotten meat. Then I was through—I clenched my eyes shut, helpless as his cold arms wrapped around me.

It was quiet on the other side. I couldn't even hear my heart anymore. The surrounding pressure was gentle, like being encompassed by cool water or even a heavy fog. A moment later and the sensation was already retreating. I opened my eyes to find myself standing in my bedroom, facing the portrait on the wall. Hands folded across his lap, eyes closed, at peace just like it ought to be.

I spent the next half hour profusely apologizing to my neighbors. I'm lucky I didn't get locked up. After that I called my mom, surprised to find her in tears.

"Are you okay? Where are you?" I asked.

"I'm okay. Dad's okay. I visited him in the cemetery this morning. It's stupid of me, right?" She paused to sniffle and blow her nose. "Do you think he knows?"

I told her I think he was pretty pleased about that, and that it made me happy too. I don't know what would have happened to me if she hadn't.

## Life Before Birth

Have you ever been in a car accident?

I'm not asking about a scrape or a fender-bender. I'm talking about the screech of rubber skidding so hard that you can smell it burning. When the airbag feels like a cinder block, and the blizzard of glass and shredded metal is a thousand super-heated needles searching for your skin. Every bone in your body feels like it's been replaced with twice the weight of lead, the aching throb so deep that you can't even feel it right away. And the scariest thing isn't even all the blood, even though that's sprayed across every inch of twisted metal that used to be the inside of your car—the scariest thing is not knowing where it's all coming from. You could be missing a leg and you wouldn't even know it. There's so much adrenaline pumping through your system that you can't even be sure whether you're alive or dead.

And then you remember your kid who was sitting in the back. Your twelve-year-old son on his way home from school, sitting in the passenger side because he liked to have a clear view of the speedometer. The side where the SUV T-Boned your car, crumpling it like a tin can to pin his little body within the car's deformed chassis. And when the ringing in your ears finally starts to die down and you hear the crying, you're so relieved, because as long as he's still alive, everything will still be okay. And it takes you a few more seconds to realize the heaving, weeping sound is actually coming from you, and that your little boy hasn't moved or made a sound.

That's how it happened for me, anyway. It took two minutes and forty seconds for the ambulance to arrive, which I guess is pretty incredible in the big scheme of things. I was surprised when I heard a paramedic mention the number though, because I could have sworn it was at least an hour. I guess when Einstein was coming up with his theory of relativity he neglected to mention the effect of waiting to find out whether your son is alive or dead.

My son Kevin did survive though. He suffered a concussion and was knocked unconscious, but there wasn't any permanent damage. The news was such a blessing that I couldn't stop laughing when the doctor told me. His mother took a week off work to take care of him, and I really thought that everything was going to be okay. At least until the night after the accident when Keivn asked me:

"You know how on cartoons they get hit and see stars?"

"Yeah sure." I was trying to put him to bed, and he always asked a lot of questions whenever he was looking to stay awake a little longer. "I didn't see stars though, did you?"

"No. I saw something else," he said.

"I'm not surprised." I drew the blankets up to his chin. "You got hit pretty hard. The doctor said your brain wasn't getting oxygen for a while, and sometimes that makes people see things—"

"Dad, I think it saw me too." He was barely peeking out above the covers, but his eyes were huge and quivering.

"Well all that matters is that you're safe now. Your mother and I aren't going to let anything—"

"Dad, where were you before you were born?" he interrupted again. I frowned at him, hesitating. I don't think this one is addressed in the parenting handbook my wife picked up at the thrift store. "I saw the place I came from. And the thing that made me. I didn't like it."

"What was it like?"

Kevin shivered, pulling the covers a little higher so that only the top of his head was showing. "It made me feel small," he whispered. "Like a little seed falling off a big tree."

"That doesn't sound so bad. Trees are supposed to spread their seeds."

"Not this one. It was taller than anything you can imagine, with branches going from one side of the universe to the other. And there were faces under the bark, only it wasn't bark, it was skin—and they were screaming, or trying to, but it was like they were being suffocated by the skin, and—"

"Easy Kevin, none of that was real—"

"—and the roots were skin too, and they were squirming like worms, and there were babies in there, only they weren't born yet. But they were screaming too—"

"Kevin!"

The covers were all the way over his head now. He was breathing heavily and trembling from head to foot. I gently folded the blanket back to reveal his flushed face. He took a long breath, then said:

"It hates losing its children. Hates it more than I knew anyone could hate anything. It saw me, Dad. I'm not lost anymore, because it saw me, and it's not going to stop at anything until it takes me back."

I didn't know what to say. I kissed him on the forehead and told him it was a bad dream. He didn't look convinced, and maybe that's my fault. I didn't feel very convincing when I said it.

I talked to my wife about it for a long time that night. We eventually agreed that bringing it up would only keep it fresh in Kevin's mind. Best to just forget about it and hope he does the same.

He didn't speak another word on the subject for the rest of the week. He was sad and quiet, spending long hours by himself in his fort behind the house. I didn't intrude on his space or push him though. The accident was the scariest thing he's ever gone through in his life, and it was completely normal for it to take time to recover.

Then on Friday there was the note. It was written on the yellow legal pad in the kitchen we used for grocery lists. A single line in a messy scrawl that read: *I'm going back.*

"Honey? You need to go out again for something?"

"I don't think so. Why, do you need something?" she asked. She came around the corner and we both stared at the yellow paper. Of course, that was Kevin's handwriting. And we both stared a little longer as the same thought slowly bubbled to the surface of our minds.

Then there was a *THUD* upstairs, and that thought became a lot louder.

"Kevin? You okay up there?" my wife shouted. Then with a smile: "Remember when we couldn't get him to stop jumping on the bed—"

*THUMP THUMP THUMP THUMP...* Incessant, desperate flailing. We raced each other up the stairs, the sound getting louder and louder until we flung open his bedroom door—

And the sound was replaced by my wife's scream.

Kevin's limp body dangled from a rope, tied to a jutting piece of wood above his closet door. We rushed to take him down, tripping over the chair he'd stood on before he kicked it over. The thumping had come from his legs kicking the closet while he choked, and now they weren't moving, and time stood still again.

He never lost consciousness this time though. We were all crying by the time we got the rope from around his neck. I remember saying: "You're never going to leave us, do you understand? We belong together."

He held onto us so tight that it hurt, and he was trembling all over again. "I have to go, but I'm scared to go alone," he said.

"Never. Promise you won't go anywhere without me."

"I promise. I promise."

"Wherever you go, I'll be right there with you," I said, and he hugged me even tighter.

I don't know why he started laughing, or why my wife and I joined in, but I think it was just relief. Pretty soon we were all sitting on the floor together hugging and laughing about nothing, and then it was over. And everything was going to be okay.

We couldn't get him an appointment to see a psychiatrist until Monday, but he seemed more cheerful after that and I thought things were going to get easier from there. His appetite was flourishing, and he was watching his favorite shows again. I thought that was proof that he was back to his old self. I guess when we want something badly enough we'll look for any excuse to justify it being true. We only see what we want to see, even though it's the things we can't bear to look at that need to be seen most.

The next note came on Sunday afternoon. He wrote: I'll be at my fort if you want to come with me this time.

I didn't need to look for my wife or ponder the clue. I was out the door before the paper even drifted to the ground, sprinting as fast as I could for the woods behind the house. There was a hollow log that Kevin always used to play around. Over the span of years we'd both dug out the area below it to make his secret fort. On the outside it just looked like a decaying log, but below there's just enough space for two or three people to sit and hide. And all I could think about was his little body tucked away in that hole where no one would find him—about how long ago he might have written that line, and what he could have done to himself in that time.

I couldn't fit inside the log to slip down the way he did. He wasn't answering my shouts, so I didn't even slow down when I hit the decaying wood. It pulverized under my weight, spraying chips and dirt in every direction. Then I was on my hands and knees, hurling away rotten chunks and pounding on the ground until it gave way underneath me.

Kevin had expanded the fort a lot in the last week. I hadn't expected to fall so fast or so far—almost eight feet, I think. But Kevin was there, and he was alright, and that's all that mattered. As long as we were together, we'd get through this. I held him close, and he held me back, and everything was going to be okay...

But I didn't really believe it this time as the ground kept raining down around us. Kevin broke away from me and pulled a rope which I hadn't noticed before. The other end was connected to a plastic tarp sitting above the hole. I didn't understand what was going on until the tarp slid forward, dumping its huge payload of dirt directly on our heads. By then it was already too late. He'd buried us both alive.

The tarp must have been balanced on a slope or something, because after that first pull the dirt kept coming. The torrent was so dark and thick that I had to hold my breath. I got a last flash of Kevin gritting his teeth and hauling at the rope, then he was gone, lost in the avalanche which sealed us together. I managed to catch his hand before the dirt trapped my arms against my body. I felt the pressure of it building around my chest, then up my shoulders, packing around my neck, finally covering my head completely.

The weight was so intense that I couldn't budge. I squeezed Kevin's hand and felt the pressure returned. He was holding onto me for dear life—for something dearer than life, which he'd thrown away so casually. But as the weight of earth above us increased, the pressure from his hand was fading, growing limp. I was lucky that I held my breath so quickly—my expanded lungs occupied a little more space and gave me a small pocket of air. I tried to breathe as shallowly as I could, but even with the slightest intake of air I could feel the dirt sliding in a little tighter around me, making it that much harder to expel my next breath. A relentlessly constricting serpent, its coils drawing tighter and tighter around my chest.

I was going to die. Kevin was going to die, and I couldn't save him. But at least he wouldn't be alone. All I could do was squeeze his hand and wait for the time it didn't squeeze back. I started feeling dizzy as I labored harder and harder for air. The burning in my lungs mounted until my whole body felt like it was going to explode, and then slowly, slowly it subsided. Or maybe it was still there, but I didn't feel it so much because my consciousness was drifting off somewhere else...

...somewhere else where it was still pitch black, but I didn't need my eyes to see the tree. That was what Kevin called it anyway, although I would describe it more like a neural network, a billion tendrils connecting and separating to span across an infinite sky. Where two or more branches met, I'd see a face trapped beneath the tendril's skin. All ages, all races, all expressing a myriad of human emotions. Some had jutting brows bristling with hair like a Neanderthal, while others I could have passed on the street without thinking twice.

But I understand why Kevin said they were screaming. There was a sound coming from each, an infinitesimally small note in the grand symphony which encompassed me. Many were screeching, thrashing against their confines and howling in pain. Others babbled in an unknown language, laughing or crying like raving lunatics. Still others were tranquil, softly speaking a single word or phrase over and over again, though these too seemed mad and meaningless. I scanned face after face looking for Kevin, somehow feeling that if only I could find him, then even now I could bring him home.

I don't know how long I searched these infinite faces, but I knew I was growing too weary to continue forever. I might have already seen him and passed him by without noticing; there were so many faces that they all started to blend together and look the same. I was no longer able to even untangle their individual voices, each raucous note replaced by the mighty roar of their combined chorus, rising and crashing like the sea.

I screamed for Kevin until my scream was all I was, my contribution devoured by the song until the two were one. The combination of our outpouring joined the music, together creating something awesome from the ugliness. All the chaotic dissonance of our senseless pain was an integral part of that greater harmony, though I'd never know it from focusing on any one of the mad faces individually. And though I couldn't find Kevin in their midst, I knew I must be hearing his voice somewhere in the chorus too. And somewhere far away in another world, I felt the ghost of small fingers squeeze my hand.

My wife had found the note and followed us to the fort shortly after, keeping her wits about her enough to call the police. When I regained consciousness on the ground, the paramedics told me I was lucky to still be alive. I told them they were right.

Forgive the poverty of my words which seek to capture something too great to be confined. That hole was the tomb where I died and the womb where I was born. And now that I have seen the tree, I understand why Kevin knew he had to return, just as I will someday when I'm ready.

They never found Kevin's body, despite excavating an area four times the size of the original hole. I never found his face in the labyrinth either, but I don't suppose that matters. Whether it laughed or cried or whispered to itself is irrelevant, because he wasn't any of the unfathomable billions of interchangeable faces. He was the song itself: beautiful, eternal, and never alone.

## My Soul Is In A Paper Lantern

Do you know what it's like to live without a soul? Because I do.

It's like watching a romantic movie that's so perfect you find yourself falling in love with the character. Then the lights come on, and you suddenly remember that person doesn't exist. And even if they did, they would never care that you exist.

It's like running the wrong way on a racetrack. It doesn't matter whether you ever finish or not, because everyone else has already crossed the line and gone home. You've run farther than anyone else, your legs are agony and there's a fire in your lungs, but you're still running because you're afraid of the silence when you finally stop.

Living without a soul is sitting in the eye of the hurricane. Life is moving all around you, and sometimes it feels like you're part of it when it passes too close. But in the end nothing and no one can ever move you, and though the wind howls fierce in its savage glory and sweeps all the world from under your feet, you'll never know what it feels like join that wild dance. And that's okay. You tell yourself that at least you won't be hurt like all those other fragile humans burdened with their souls, but deep down you wish you could feel that hurt. Just for a moment. Just so once in your life you know there's something important enough to be hurt over.

I lost my soul when I was only six years old. My father didn't want me. My mother told me so. She said I was the reason that he left, and I believed her. I was in first grade at the time, and our class project was to make a paper lantern which was closed at the top. The hot air from the candle was supposed to lift the lantern, although mine wasn't sealed properly and couldn't leave the ground. I was getting really frustrated, and after the fourth or fifth attempt I got so mad that I actually ripped the whole thing to shreds.

My teacher—Mr. Hansbury, a gentle dumpling of a man with a bristly mustache, squatted down next to me and gave me the lantern he had been building. I was so mad that I was about to destroy that one too, but he sat me down and said:

"Do you know what I love most about paper lanterns? They might seem flimsy, but when they fly, they can carry away anything that you don't want anymore. You can put all your anger into one of these, and the moment you light the candle, it's going to float away and take that anger with it."

That sounded pretty amazing to me at the time. I settled down to watch him glue the candle into place, concentrating all my little heart on filling the lantern with my bad feelings. It started off with just the anger at the project, but one bitterness led to the next, and by the time Mr. Hansbury was finished I'd poured everything that I was into the paper. All the other class lanterns only hovered a few feet off the ground, but mine went up and up and on forever—all the way to the top of the sky. The other kids laughed and cheered to see it go, and my teacher put his hand on my shoulder and looked so proud, but I didn't feel much of anything. How could I, with my soul slowly disappearing from view?

I remember asking Mr. Hansbury if I could go home and live with him after that, but he said he didn't think my mother would like that. I told him that she would, but he still said no. I don't suppose it would have mattered one way or another though, because it was too late to take back what I did.

There's something else besides the numbness that comes when your soul is gone. I didn't see them the first night, but I could hear them breathing when I lay down to sleep. Soft as the wind, but regular and calm like a sleeping animal. I sat and listened in the darkness for a long while, covers clutched over my head; the breathing seemed so close I could feel its warmth billowing under the sheets. I cried for what seemed like hours, but mom didn't come, and I was too afraid to get out of bed. I don't think I fell asleep until it was light outside.

Mom was angry at me in the morning for keeping her awake. She'd heard me, but she thought I would give up eventually. I didn't get breakfast that day, and I didn't mention the breathing again. That was only the beginning.

I think a soul does more than help you appreciate the things around you. It also protects you from noticing the things you aren't supposed to see. And with it gone, they were everywhere. Beady eyes glinting from under the sofa, a dark flash at the corner of my eye, scuffling in the drawers, and late-night knockings on doors and windows. I never got a good look at them, but they were always watching me. I'd wake up in the middle of the night and feel their weight all over my body, pinning me down. Rough skin against me, dirty fingers digging into my nose and mouth. Worse still, their touch penetrated my mind, inserting thoughts so vile that I knew they couldn't be my own, although the longer they were in my head, the more difficult it was to be certain of that.

Did I want to insert a needle into my eye and see how far it would go? Probably not. Then why could I not stop thinking about it?

Were they making me think about beating my class-mates into bloody pulps? Or setting fires to people's homes to watch them weep on the sidewalk? Or was that all from me?

The first few nights I lay awake and cried to myself, but I soon learned to be more afraid of my mom than I was of the creatures. As much as I hated the shadows, they never hit me after-all. I wouldn't call it living, but I continued to exist for years like that. During the day I kept to myself: exhausted and numb. All colors seemed muted except for the glittering eyes which tracked me from unlikely crevices, all sounds muffled but for their scrapings and breathings. The only times I could really feel something was when I was lay awake in the darkness, but these were the times I wish I felt less. Neither screams nor silence brought any comfort from the intrusive probing, and my mind was flooded with persistent images of violence, self-destruction, and despair.

Over time I found a trick to help me get through the insufferable nights. I convinced myself that my body was not my own, and that nothing it felt could do me harm. The real me was flying safe somewhere, high up in the sky inside that paper lantern. And no matter what happened to my flesh—no matter what my flesh did to anyone else—that had nothing to do with me.

I kept everything below the surface as best I could until I was fourteen years old. By then I'd lost all ability to distinguish the origin of my thoughts. All I knew is that I wanted to hurt someone—hurt them as badly as I wanted to be hurt in return. I picked fights at school. I pushed my classmates around, and they stayed clear of me. I once drove a pencil into someone's hand when they weren't looking, grinding it back and forth to make sure to tip broke off inside the skin. I heard the creatures snickering at that, but it was a disdainful kind of laugh.

When I was called into the principal's office afterward, I was surprised to see Mr. Hansbury there too. The principal was all rage, lecturing me and stamping around like the Spanish Inquisition. Mr. Hansbury didn't say much. He just looked tired and sad. He didn't speak until the principal dismissed me, at which point he put his hand on my shoulder and leaned in real close to ask:

"Have you looked for it?"

I didn't have the faintest idea what he meant. I gave him a stare that a marble statue would find cold.

"Your lantern. Did you ever try to get it back?"

I told him to go fuck himself.

"I'm sorry for telling you to send it away," he added, gripping my shoulder to stop me from leaving. "I thought it would be easier than facing the feelings, but I was wrong. People can't hide from themselves like that."

The pencil was good, but it wasn't enough. My thoughts matched the sardonic tone of the laughter, mocking me for my pitiful attempt. As the creatures crawled over me at night and their intentions mingled with my own, I decided to bring a knife next time. I considered a gun too, but resolved that it wasn't personal enough. I'd rather look into one person's eyes when the blade slipped into them than shoot a dozen scurrying figures from a distance. And what happened to me afterward? It didn't matter, because the real me was safely floating in the breeze a thousand miles away.

It wasn't going to be at school this time. I wanted to take my time and not be interrupted. Instead I went out at midnight, the taste of those dirty fingers still fresh in my mouth. I didn't care who my victim was as long as they could feel what I was doing to them. My neighborhood was quiet at night and there weren't a lot of options, so I decided to head down to the 24 hour gas station on the corner.

Kitchen knife gripped between my fingers, cold air filling my lungs, goading laughter and applause from the creatures thick around me in the darkness, I almost felt alive there for a second. Just like I did with the pencil, but this would taste better. Holding the knife, I felt like a virgin on prom night with my crush slowly unzipping my pants. I wasn't in the eye of the storm anymore—I was the storm, and tonight would be the night—that I saw a paper lantern floating in the air, just a few feet off the ground. The shell was so filthy and stained that I could barely see the light inside. It was impossible for the fragile thing to have survived all these years, more impossible still for the single candle to have burned all this time, but I knew without doubt that it was my light by the way the creatures howled. They hated it with a passion, and would have torn it to shreds if I hadn't gotten there first. I plucked the lantern from the air and guided it softly to the ground, the shades screeching as they whirled around me, feral animals cowed by the miraculous flame.

Holding the lantern close, I found the note that was attached.

*"I found this in the woods. Took a couple days to find it."*
-Mr. H

I collapsed on the sidewalk, trembling for all the time I'd spent away from myself, blubbering and sobbing like an idiot until the flame guttered out from my tears. The howling creatures reached a feverish pitch, and then silence, all rising together into the sky with the last wisps of curling smoke from the lantern. It hurt like nothing I'd felt in years, but it was a cleansing kind of hurt. I didn't hide from it. I didn't send it away. I didn't drown it with distractions or fight its grip on me. I won't go so far as to say that pain is a good thing, but it is undeniably a real thing, and I'd rather hurt than send it away to live with the hole it leaves behind.

## The World's Oldest Tree

"Just because you can't see them doesn't mean they aren't real."

"How do you know?"

"Because you can feel them when they're close," I said. "The goosebumps on your skin, even though it's not cold. The way the air tastes, and the dry lump in your throat. That's how they let you know they're about to strike."

"How do you get away?"

"No one ever has. You get about ten minutes after you notice them before they force themselves inside you. Then it's all over. Wait—did you feel something? Clara look at your arms! You've already got the goosebumps!"

My sister squirmed, thrashing against the seatbelt which suddenly looked like it was squeezing the breath out of her frail body. Her skin was bone-white, although that was hardly surprising since she never went outside.

"Mark stop scaring your sister," mom clucked from the passenger seat. "We're almost there, just hold on."

"Moooooom, I can feel them!" Clara howled.

I was doing my best to softly blow air on her from the corner of my mouth without her noticing it was me.

"Ghosts aren't real, Clara. You're twelve-years old—you should know better by now," my dad said without turning. It had been a long drive for all of us, and he was gripping the wheel so tightly it looked like he was ready to swerve off the road and camp in the first ditch we found.

"See? I told you." Clara crossed her arms in an infuriating display of smugness.

"Then how come dad's mouth didn't move when he said that?"

I'm almost ashamed to admit how much pleasure I got from her double-take. Almost. Then came the rapid, aggressive burst of tapping on the window and Clara actually shrieked. I couldn't stop laughing as dad rolled down the window.

"Camping registration?" the park ranger asked, face shadowed by his wide-brimmed hat. He glanced disinterestedly into the back seats to catch Clara giggling and smacking at me. She wasn't strong enough for it to hurt, and I was laughing too so I didn't bother defending myself. Mom looked tired, but peaceful.

"Thank God. I thought we'd never get here." Dad handed the man an email printout.

"Long drive, huh? Where you folks from?" the ranger asked.

"California. I tried to tell them we have our own forests, but Clara was heart-set on seeing the great quaking aspen."

"Welcome to Utah then. You won't be disappointed. Did you kids know that the Pando is the oldest and biggest life form on the planet?"

"I did!" Clara raised her hand, flailing it around like an eager student. "Although each tree is only about 120 years old, they're all connected to the same root network which has been alive for over 80,000 years, stretching over 105 acres."

"Just 80,000?" The park ranger smirked. "I've heard it's more like a million. We're not sure exactly, but there's a good chance the Pando was alive before the first human being walked the earth. Pretty incredible, huh?"

"Yep! I wish I could live that long," Clara said. Mom and dad exchanged furtive glances.

"It's not about how long you live." Mom's voice cracked, and she had to take a long breath before she restarted. "It's about what you do with the time that you have. And I for one am grateful for every second we get to spend together as a family." Dad squeezed mom's hand. It must have been hard too, because their interlocked fingers were trembling. The uncomfortable silence which followed only lasted a moment before the park ranger handed us a pass and waved us on our way.

It's no secret that my sister is sick. Mom and dad don't like to talk about it, so I didn't know exactly what it was. She spent a lot of time in the hospital though, which seemed stupid to me because she was always weaker going out than she was going in. I've asked her about it before, but she just shrugged and said, 'they'll figure it out.' I didn't like the way her face looked when she said it, so I didn't ask again. Seeing her scared like that wasn't any fun.

It was almost dark when we got to the campsite. I helped dad setting up the tent while mom unpacked the car. Clara just sat on a log and stared at the sunset, which seemed really unfair to me, but it's not like she'd be much help anyway. The light was weird here—even after the sun went down, it didn't really get dark. The twilight felt like it went on for hours, and the air was so quiet that time must have frozen. I was half-hoping Clara would pick up on the weird atmosphere and start believing in my ghosts again, but I think she'd forgotten all about them. Maybe she was never even afraid in the first place, only putting on a show for my amusement.

"Can you hear them?" Clara asked when I went over to call her for dinner.

"Who?"

"The trees. They've been waiting for me for a long time."

I didn't buy it. She was just trying to creep me out as revenge. "What are they saying?" I asked anyway.

Clara's pale skin glowed in the enduring twilight, almost as white as her eerie smile. "It doesn't speak with words. It's more like feelings. Images. Ideas. The 'Trembling Giant' is angry. Slow, purposeful, smoldering, anger, like a glacier carving a hole in a mountain range. And it needs me to set it loose."

I wish she wouldn't smile like that. "Dinner's ready, come on." I turned back toward the fire in a hurry, not wanting to give her the satisfaction of seeing me shudder. Glancing back over my shoulder, I could still see the glow of her little teeth piercing the gathering dusk.

The next day was miserable and dull. I wanted to go out hiking and explore the forest, but Clara was too tired and mom insisted we didn't leave her behind. The whole point of this trip was to spend time together as a family, she said, so we were just going to do activities that we all could enjoy. So there we were, surrounded by spectacular natural beauty with adventure and discovery hidden behind every tree, while we sat in the dirt whittling sticks. Singing songs. Weaving baskets, watching the world drip by one excruciating second at a time.

"The baskets are fun! Look how nice your sister's is turning out."

"Can I make a really big one?" I asked.

"Of course! You can make whatever you want."

"Okay I'm going to weave a coffin then. You can just bury me wherever."

"Don't even joke about that," my father grunted.

"Or better yet, I'll make one for Clara. If she's too sick to do anything fun, then she might as well—"

"Mark!" Mom that time. I'd crossed a line, and I knew it, but I didn't care. I was bored out of my mind. I missed my computer and my friends. I hated all this lovey-dovey family time. They always took her side about everything and gave her whatever she asked for, but if I ever wanted something I was just being selfish.

"I'm going to be in the woods if anyone needs me. As if."

I heard Mom start to chase me for a second, but Dad stopped her to interject: "Stay close, okay? Don't get lost."

Getting lost didn't seem like such a bad option at the moment. White-barked giants stretching as far as I could see, with mazes of fallen trees and branches that I could use to build forts. Lush grass and ferns to run through, craggy rocks to climb, meandering streams to jump—I can't believe the rest of them sat 8 hours in the car just so they can keep sitting around here. I marveled at the natural grandeur as I walked, mesmerized by the idea that this huge forest was all a single living thing. I decided to dig with a stick to get a look at the connected roots, but the ground was hard and the going was slow.

This would have been a lot easier if I'd had some help. When Clara and I were little, we used to do everything together. She was like my side-kick, always enthusiastically following me around leaping to attention whenever I had a mission for her. What was the point of playing games with yourself when no one was there to cheer your victories or mourn your defeats?

My frustration at the futility of the dig was quickly mounting, but I used that feeling as fuel to ram the stick down even harder. Out of breath, sweating and aching, I thrust the stick so hard that it snapped in two. I don't know why that made me so angry, but it did. I dropped to my hands and knees and started digging with my fingers, hurling rocks and dirt clods around me in every direction. My fingers were accumulating cuts and scrapes, and I was about to give up when my hand suddenly broke through a thick clump of roots to reveal a hole in the ground.

Dirt and pebbles rained down the hole to disappear in the darkness below. It must have been deep too, because even with my ear to the ground I couldn't hear anything land. Unwilling to return and admit defeat, I spent the next few hours widening the hole and trying to find a way to climb down. By the afternoon I was so filthy that I was practically indistinguishable from the earth I churned through. My fingers were openly bleeding in places, and the beating sun frowned down with disdain at my efforts. None of that mattered though, because I'd opened the hole wide enough to slip inside the yawning darkness.

I climbed down the network of roots which were matted as densely as a net. My phone's flashlight prodded the darkness like a needle in an elephant, utterly underwhelming in the massive space I suddenly found myself within. The hidden cave was a converging point for the tendrils from innumerable trees which merged into larger roots, joining again in turn to weave great networked tapestries which dwarfed the thin trees above the ground. I continued climbing downward along the widening roots, tempted to hide down here all day and freak out my family.

Below the cave, my route terminated in a small circular space, not much larger than my own body. It felt like being inside an egg: completely encapsulated by the roots which were matted so densely now that they formed an impenetrable wall of wood. It was so quiet down here that I could hear my heart throbbing in my ears, my labored breathing a hurricane which fractured the stillness.

'Can you hear them?' my sister had asked last night, wide-eyed and serious.

Up above under the wide open sky with my family eating dinner? That question was child's play. But here in this hidden kingdom under the earth? I placed my hand on a massive wooden column and felt what she was talking about. This could have been growing before humans existed. It could have been touched by forgotten Gods or aliens who walked the Earth before history began. Or perhaps the Earth itself was living through these mighty pillars, lying dormant but for the quiet seething anger which slowly burned through the millennium.

The root was warm to the touch, and as I felt it, it was unmistakably feeling me in return. I had the unnerving feeling that a sound too deep for my ears to register was silently screaming around me. The feeling became more intense the longer I held on. I saw a fire in my mind's eye, running in infernal rivers from the depths of the world to drown the cities which infested the land like festering rot on clean skin. The root was getting hotter under my touch, and as much as I tried to clear my head, the thoughts returned—the decaying towers, the teaming crowds aimlessly running, the rivers of blood which flowed down crumbling streets.

I ripped my hand away and let go, panting for breath. This was better than ghosts. This was real. And all I could think about was showing it to Clara and watching her freak. I scrambled back up the roots, pulling myself hand-over-hand onto the surface to run the whole way back to the campsite.

"What in the world—" my mother started.

"Where's Clara? I want to show her something."

"She went to lie down for a little while. How did you get so filthy?"

But I didn't wait. I sprang into her tent, practically dragging her to her feet while my parents protested from behind.

"Just for a second, okay? You can sleep anytime, but this is what we're here for."

"Mark don't you dare bother her—"

"It's okay, mom," Clara said, dragging herself out to flinch beneath the sun. "I'm here to spend time with Mark too, right?"

There it was again. Mom and Dad holding hands, clenching so tightly they shook. That didn't matter though. All I could think about was Clara's face when I showed her my secret discovery. Our parents offered to come with us, but I figured that would destroy the whole fun of the secret. I was pleasantly surprised that Clara was so willing to go—it seems like she didn't want to do anything anymore.

"You heard it too," she said the moment we were alone.

"Not heard. Felt."

"This isn't a trick, right? You're not just making fun of me because I believe it?"

"When have I ever tried to trick you?" I put on my best facade of shocked-innocence. She snickered.

"How about when you wrote 'soap flavor' on the ice-cream box so you wouldn't have to share?"

"That's an isolated incident."

"Or when you told me the cactus had soft spines like a cat's fur?"

"I didn't think you'd just slap it."

She laughed again, and we walked on in silence for a bit. She was obviously struggling, but she was just as obviously making an effort to hide it, so I didn't say anything. It wasn't much farther anyway.

"Up there, right around that grove. Anyway if I trick you so much, then how come you still believe me?"

She shrugged, catching my eyes for a second before turning to look where I was pointing. "I guess I don't know how many more chances I'll have to be tricked. I want to make the most of it while I still can."

I didn't know how to respond to that, so I kept walking.

"That's why we're here. You know that, right?" she asked.

I kept staring straight ahead.

"This might be our last chance for the whole family to be together before I..."

"It's over here," I interrupted, squatting down beside the hole. I expected her to say something sarcastic or to complain.

"Give me a hand, okay?" She didn't even hesitate. Feet first, she began lowering herself down. I helped keep her steady while she climbed. I kept my eyes on our hands so I didn't have to look at her face. I fully understood what she was saying, and I didn't want her to say more. I didn't start climbing after her until her feet touched the cave floor.

"You're right. It's stronger down here," she said.

"You haven't seen anything yet. Come on."

I continued leading to the point where the roots terminated in the enclosed root-egg. There wasn't enough room for both of us to fit in the perfect nest, so I helped her climb in while I waited in the larger cave. Her fingers grazed the roots in silent reverence, hand jerking back from their warmth. That little smile glinted in the darkness, stretching into a euphoric grin as she touched the wood again.

"You feel it?" I asked. I knew she did, but I had to ask anyway because the silence was so heavy down here.

She simply smiled and closed her eyes. The sound of my rushing blood filled my ears again. I had to keep talking.

"What made you think it was calling for you?"

She wasn't the one who answered though. It was that scream again, too deep to hear, but I felt the echo in every vibrating root. It came from everywhere—all the mighty forest bellowing in silence, all the unknown depths of the roots, all resonating with a single, persistent, throb. Even outside of the egg I could start to feel the colossal intent seep into my mind. Incessant, irrepressible thoughts, so vivid I might as well be seeing them with my eyes. Imagery of burning rivers bubbling up from the Earth to exhaust themselves in the open air, leaving behind an abyss so deep that it must pierce through the core of the planet.

"Clara? What's going on? What do you see?" Even shining light in my face, I could barely see it. All was fire and the bellowing howl, mounting in pitch just enough for me to actually hear the low rumble like an earthquake.

"Clara, you have to get out of there. Something is going to happen."

"I know. I'm making it happen." The voice sounded so small and distant next to the enveloping presence. "We both need each other. "I need its enduring life, and it needs a body guide its will."

"Clara where are you? Quick grab my hand!" I fumbled to reach down to her, but the visions were too intense for me to see straight. My raw hands kept butting up against the roots.

"Tell mom and dad that I didn't die. That I'll never die."

Why couldn't I find the opening? I'd been standing right over it a moment ago.

"Tell them I'll be with them in the forest, even when they think themselves alone."

It took me going down on my belly to finally realize what had happened. It wasn't that I couldn't find the hole—it's that the hole didn't exist anymore. The roots had moved, fully sealing Clara inside the earth.

"Clara! Can you hear me? Clara get out!"

"I am out, Mark." The reply was so faint. "No more tricks between us. You're the one who should be running."

I'm not proud of the fact that I ran, scrambling back up the roots to pull myself onto the surface. Some might call it cowardice, but I know the certainty in her voice, and I trusted her more than I trusted myself in that moment. Even above the ground I could still feel the silent scream, so low and powerful that my entire body vibrated. Panting for breath on the surface, I started to scream with everything my ragged lungs would allow. I don't know how long this went on for, but by the time I stopped, the forest was silent again.

The earth wasn't shaking. The visions had cleared. All except for the hint of Clara's face outlined in the bark of an aspen tree.

## Am I Dreaming, Or Am I The Dream?

I've decided that it must be one or the other. How else could I explain seeing the same person everywhere I went?

He's impossible not to notice with his long gray mustache waxed to a pinpoint. Bushy eyebrows caught in a perpetual explosion, floppy white hair that looked like it was having an argument with the head. He doesn't always speak to me, or even look at me, but for the last two years he's always been there.

He first appeared as a substitute teacher when I was in my junior year of high-school. He introduced himself as Mr. Brice, although there was a long hesitation before he gave his name as though he couldn't decide what he wanted to be called. His voice wasn't right either—I remember him spending half the class switching accents, his speech collapsing occasionally into a variety of foreign languages before he caught himself and readjusted. The class found him "dapper" and charming in his fine tailored wool suit, and I didn't initially suspect him of anything more than being eccentrically addled.

The next day he was working in the cafeteria. Substitutes go where they're needed, I suppose, but oddly none of my classmates seemed to remember him. They remembered that we had a substitute teacher, but everyone was quite sure that it wasn't him. He gave me an extra scoop of chili and winked at me, muttering in an English accent: "I won't tell if you don't." I don't think he was talking about the chili.

Mr. Brice spent the next few weeks rotating throughout the school. One day he was the janitor, next he was a guest speaker, or even the principal himself. I quickly learned to stop bringing up the phenomenon when it became obvious that I was the only one who noticed. Mr. Brice was learning too—it didn't take long before his speech stopped fluctuating, and his clothing adapted to nondescript khakis and a polo shirt.

I tried questioning him more than once, but the man stubbornly adhered to the role he'd currently assumed, pretending he knew me only as well as the character he played. At the same time, there would always be little winks or enigmatic phrases thrown in which conveyed our peculiar intimacy. I caught him alone one day when I'd forgotten my calculator and had to double back for it. Mr. Brice was on the phone, casually reclining with his feet flung up on his desk. I distinctly remember the words:

"Of course he's caught on, but he isn't frightened yet."

He winked again when he met my eye. I stood in abject confusion while he politely disengaged from his phone call.

"Were you talking about me?" I asked.

The feet came down with a stomp.

"All the time," he said, leaning forward to fold his well-manicured hands demurely on his desk. He cocked his head to the side, studying me intensely. "You preoccupy most of my attention nowadays, but I mustn't get too attached to you."

"What the hell is that supposed to mean?"

"You don't belong here. I don't want it to hurt when I have to get rid of you."

"Um..."

He coughed. Then the infuriating wink. "What I mean to say is: the teachers can't go home until the last student leaves, so run along."

I snatched my calculator without another word. The whole situation was so unnerving, and I couldn't think of anything to respond. Mr. Brice blatantly picked up his phone again as I left.

"He's just leaving. No, I don't think he'll run yet. Where could he possibly go where I couldn't find him?"

I didn't see him at school much after that, but he was always somewhere, always watching me: on a bench reading the newspaper, or bussing tables, or working behind the counter at the gas station. I never confronted him, although I did try taking a picture of him a few times. The pictures would work, but only for a day. When I looked back at the photo after that, everything else would be the same except for Mr. Brice, who would invariably be replaced with the real person—the same person that everyone else remembered being there the whole time.

Like he said, I wasn't afraid yet though. The situation enthralled me for a few weeks, but after that it simply became part of life. And as long as Mr. Brice was there, my life was being steered in a particular direction.

Mr. Brice the school counselor took the liberty of submitting my application to a science program at Stanford University where he felt I would excel.

Mr. Brice the college administrator overlooked my mediocre grades in favor of my exceptional essay, which I never remember writing.

Mr. Brice the restaurant manager fired me when I mentioned wanting to wait a bit on college. He said he didn't want my life here interfering with my "future opportunities". I almost hit him when he winked that time. More than all his other meddling, that one really got to me. I was fired right on the spot in the middle of my shift with two co-workers watching. I just felt so angry and helpless and alone. I wanted to scream at him and tell him that I won't play his game anymore, but that would just make me look like the crazy one. I wanted to tell him that he didn't control my life, and that I wasn't afraid of him, but of course he already knew that to be a lie.

"Go quietly now, won't you?" he said. "You don't want an incident on your record."

"Why not?" I was conscious of all the eyes on me, but I had to say something. "Since when has anything I've done made a difference?"

"Oh but it can. Not to you maybe, but I'd hate to think of how other people might be affected by your stupidity."

"Are you threatening me?" I said it loud enough for the whole restaurant to hear. Five seconds of silence can feel like a very long time, and I gloated the whole while. He wasn't embarrassed or defensive like I thought he would be though. He glanced dispassionately at the surrounding patronage before taking two long strides toward me—close enough for me to feel his breath on my face.

"Yes. I'll threaten you, if that's what it takes."

I hadn't expected that. Neither had anyone else around us. One of the waitresses made a nervous giggle, but it was cut unnaturally short.

"I'm doing this for your own good," Mr. Brice added. "Don't test me."

We stared off for a moment before his phone started ringing.

"You're a piece of shit," I told him as I left.

He just smiled, speaking into his phone: "Please calm down. Nothing has changed. We own him, and he knows it."

I lingered by the door to listen in, but he'd already hung up.

Both of my parents were fired on the same day. Neither were given more than a superficial reason. I suppose I should be thankful that it wasn't Mr. Brice the serial killer that visited them instead. I'd gotten so used to his ubiquitous presence that I never really stopped to think how much power he had over me. Over everyone. I fantasized about trying to kill him for a while, but immediately thought of Mr. Brice the policeman and Mr. Brice the judge who would find me wherever I went.

The mood was really dark around my house for the next few days until I received a full academic scholarship in the mail. Considering their recent terminations, my parents made it clear that they wouldn't be able to help me with my tuition. They told me that I'd be an idiot not to accept it, and of course they were right.

It didn't seem like a bad life that he had planned for me. I was being handed opportunities that other people could only dream of, but it wasn't my life. If I just gave up without a fight, then who knows where it would end? Maybe he wanted to use me to build a new bomb, or design a weaponed virus. If I gave into him now, then I'd be surrendering my whole life to him. Trying to confront him again seemed too dangerous, but whoever he kept talking to on the phone must know what was going on. I just had to steal it and see who had called him while I was being fired.

This wasn't exactly a simple matter. I couldn't break into his house, because he could be anyone or anywhere. I had to lure him to me, and that meant doing something which threatened to destroy his plan for me. As long as he controlled the situation, it seemed like any criminal offense or outrageous act could be covered up by the people he posed as. It was overwhelming how powerless I felt, but with or without him, I could never control how other people acted. I just had to focus on myself—the one thing he couldn't take away.

I chose the top of a bank for this purpose. I was able to climb up pretty easily because of the adjoining buildings, and it had a nice flat roof that was high enough to do some real damage if I jumped. I stood up there for a long while, watching a street so familiar and mundane, yet so surreal and incomprehensible that I felt like a visiting alien. As the wind whipped around me I wondered whether I would still jump if he didn't show up to stop me. Would my death be a victory over him? Or was it the inevitable conclusion that he had always led me toward?

A hand on my shoulder meant I never had to find out.

"Took you long enough," I said without turning. I stiffened my shoulder under his grip. I wanted my tension to be obvious. I wanted him to really believe I would do it.

"It's a hard climb for someone my age. Couldn't you have found something a little lower to jump from?" I could almost hear the wink in his voice. His hand tightened slightly, but I pulled away—the toe of my shoe now over the edge.

"I'm not here to negotiate. I want you out of my life."

There was a long silence. I glanced behind me—Mr. Brice was dialing a call. "Hello hello—I have a bit of a pickle," he said into the phone.

I didn't waste my chance. Pinning his free hand against my body, I spun to snatch the phone from him. He lurched back, but I dove after him. A quick spin as he tried to shield the phone with his torso—hands buffeting each other out of the way—then another lunge and I had the phone. I wrapped my whole body against it, hurling myself to the ground to protect it. His arm was still tangled up in mine though, and with the turn he slipped straight out into the open air. Those few seconds watching him tumble were the longest of my life. I turned away before he hit the ground, but I still heard the sickening crack.

"Who is there? What's going on?" the voice in the phone. My voice, strained and weary, muffled and distorted, but unmistakably mine.

I didn't have time to decipher this. I couldn't decipher much of anything, except that the world was coming to an end. A man collapsed in the street, causing a small turbulence of panic around him. Then a second, and a third—everyone crumpling into discarded bags of meat. The buildings were dissolving into so much dust, and the light of the sky bled and ran like water color. A moment later and the building beneath my feet gave way, tumbling into blackness. I woke on a narrow cot, holding a phone in my hand. I tried to jerk upright, immediately regretting my decision as my tether of IV lines dragged inside my veins.

"A few more years and we would have had a cure." Mr. Brice's voice, but not Mr. Brice. The thing over my bed was more akin to the dissolving world I just witnessed than any human being I'd ever seen. Skin in constant dissolution, warping and reforming before my eyes.

"Am I dreaming?" I asked.

"Not anymore."

"You—you did this to me—"

"I spun the dream. A dream about the life you could have lived. And if you were to discover a cure in that dream, you'd wake up and still remember it. You'd be able to get better again, but now—"

I couldn't look at the creature. I turned away to look down the length of my body. My emaciated arms. The outline of knees as sharp as blades beneath my blanket. That was even worse.

I'm not writing this as a warning. There isn't a lesson here—although perhaps there is some merit in trusting one's dreams, no matter how outlandish. No threats or looming dread. I'm simply sharing my story because the dream spinner has left me. I'm alone, and angry at myself, and so very frightened. I'm going back to sleep in the chance I dream again, but if I do not wake, then I suppose what I'm really writing this for is simply to say goodbye.

## Our Ship Sailed Over The Edge Of The World

There wasn't a giant waterfall spilling endlessly into space, if that's what you're wondering. Only a damn fool would think the Earth is flat. Besides, I figure we'd run out of water pretty fast that way. The things we've seen though—the things that seen us back—well if they belonged in this world, then it must mean humans don't. I guess it's easier for me to tell myself I sailed right over the edge into some new place entirely than accept that those creatures are here with us.

Let's get our facts straight first. I know a lot of folks use fishing as an excuse to get wasted where nobody's around to judge them. They're the people who see four hundred pounds of flabby porpoise and swear they were visited by the fairest lady to ever trade her cooch for a tail. Not me. I'm stone-cold sober and proud of it. My buddy Jason—yeah he likes to knock back a few when we're out on the water, but he's not the one telling the story, so that doesn't mean shit.

Meet the Iron Cucumber—our pride and joy. 22 foot cuddy cabin that we bought together for our fishing trips. Last weekend was supposed to be like any other; we had our cabin stocked with our gear, an ice chest full of deli meats and beverages, and minds keen on pretending the city life was just a recurring bad dream. During the week we both worked as financial analysts at a bank, but by Friday we'd have trouble hearing all that blather over the rising call of the wild.

"We're basically werewolves," Jason had said on one of our trips. "Everyone we know sees us in our suits all day and assumes that's what we are. But that's just because they've never seen us under a full moon."

## Sleepless Nights

"So when the full moon comes you sit in a different chair and put a hat on?" I'd asked. "Hide yo' children. This one's feral."

"Say that to that thrashing 160 pounder I wrestled to the ground."

"160 pounds? Congratulations. To your wife for losing all that weight."

Jokes aside, Jason is a badass. He's got to be over 200 pounds himself, but he's 6'2", and with his bristling beard and those tribal tattoos running up his forearms, I've got to admit he looks a lot more dangerous than I do. He's a wizard at boating too—it was his idea to get the thing in the first place. He sniffs the wind and makes some crazy accurate guesses about the weather. Says he came from pirates on his father's side, with maternal gypsies to boot. I know for a fact his family were potato farmers from Ireland, but I never told him so. Point is that I know he's a lot of talk and bluster, but if we were going to war, then I'd want him as my captain. I guess that's why I never doubted him when he said, "Something unnatural about the air tonight."

Not as far as I could tell. There wasn't any breeze, and everything smelled like salt and fish and BBQ potato chips to me. I still nodded sagely, staring off into the vastness of the black waters.

"Tastes like oil," he said, spitting into the waves. "Like we're inside a giant machine that's turning all around us."

"If you didn't want to be a cog in a giant machine then you shouldn't have gone into banking," I said.

I expected a sarcastic quip back about how he 'ain't no tool'. It was unnerving to see him just staring off into the darkness, a slight shudder running down his massive frame.

"I suppose you're right," is all he said.

I don't know if it was just his mood, but within an hour I thought I began to feel it too. It was almost like hearing the screeching metal of vehicles colliding on the TV, then muting it and watching the silent picture. Just seeing it was enough to clearly imagine the sound, even though it was perfectly quiet. Our conversation was falling flat, so I brought out a book to read to distract myself from the unsettling sensation.

"There weren't any clouds when the sun set," Jason said, still staring vacantly into space.

"That's good, right? Clear sailing weather."

"So where are all the stars?"

He was right. Almost 9 PM and pitch black without a single bead of light. This far from the city they should be spectacular.

"Maybe the clouds moved in after the sunset?" I asked.

"With what wind?"

Quiet again. I shrugged and turned the page.

"If I had to die anywhere, I'd rather it be out here," he said after a long pause.

"What the fuck, Jason?"

"Think about it," he said. "Of all the ways you could go. Getting cancer and having your bedroom turned into a jail cell. Or Alzheimer's and forgetting your family and even yourself. Maybe a nuclear holocaust. I'd rather it happen out in nature when I'm still my own master."

"You're just saying that because I'm here with you. Look Jason, that's sweet and all but I don't think I'm interested in a relationship..." my words trailed off in the heavy silence. Even that couldn't lighten his mood. He sighed and dropped down to his sleeping bag on the floor. "You out already?"

"Yeah, I don't know what it is," he said, climbing into the bag. "I'm just going to sleep it off. Things will be better in the morning. And if they're not... well wake me before it happens."

"Before what happens?" But he didn't reply. I tried to put it out of my mind and keep reading, but I couldn't keep my focus. After about 30 minutes of re-reading the same page I got so frustrated I threw the book straight over the side of the boat. It felt good. Sitting there in the stillness listening to the gentle waves and riding the rhythmic sway I started to calm down. For a moment, anyway.

"There wasn't a splash."

"I thought you were asleep," I said.

"When you threw your book overboard. I didn't hear it hit the water."

Shit, neither did I. And I should have, right? It was really really quiet out there. I got up and peered out where I'd thrown it. Blackness. I turned on my flashlight and scanned to see if it was still floating there.

"Jason—you're going to want to see this."

I turned around, but he was already on his feet. He joined me at the side, and together we stared out at the emptiness beyond.

"Jason?"

"Yeah, I see it. I mean, I don't see it, but I see it."

"Yeah. Okay. Just making sure."

The water was gone. The whole ocean. We were sailing on inky darkness—like a black gas which twisted and bubbled in nebulous designs. Deep within the cloud there was thousands of tiny pricks of light, almost like stars. Jason leapt to the controls.

"What are you doing?"

"Turning the boat around."

"What's the matter? I thought you were okay dying out here?" He just glared at me. I know it was in bad taste, but I was freaking out and humor is like a defense mechanism for me. Jason brought the engine to life, but it began immediately making such a horrendous noise—like a car throwing up—that he immediately killed it again.

"No water," he grunted. "Can't run without water."

"At least we found our missing stars," I said. I would have done a more convincing job of playing it cool if my voice hadn't cracked in the middle.

"I don't think those are stars."

Back to the side of the boat—he was right. Of course he always had to be right. The lights were moving. Delicately but unmistakably moving, like fireflies drifting through a heavy mist. I watched transfixed as one began floating closer toward the boat.

"Catalina Harbor, this is the Iron Cucumber." Jason was speaking into the radio, but I couldn't turn away from the light.

Short static. "Catalina Harbor, this is a distress call. Repeat. This is a distress call. Over."

"Jason you need to see this." He gave me a distracted wave. The light was about the size of a baseball now. I couldn't tell how close it was, but it was clearly moving this way.

"Iron Cucumber, this is Catalina Harbor. Is your ship sinking? Over." Jason stared blankly at the receiver for a moment.

"Repeat—" the radio began.

"Yes, we're sinking. Please send help right away. We're approximately 14 miles west of—"

"Jason!" I shouted. "It's got a body!" I couldn't tell what exactly. It was nothing but a silhouette, mostly concealed by the bright light which had grown to the size of a basketball.

"Please repeat. 14 miles west of—" the radio began.

"Never mind. We're okay. Sorry about the confusion. Over and gone." Jason switched the radio off.

"We are definitely not okay. What the hell?"

Jason gave a mad grin. "I'm not sending another human being into this. We wanted an adventure, right?"

"This is not an adventure. This is a bad trip. This is the end of the world—this is—"

"This is the call of the wild," Jason said. He raised his head to the empty sky and let off a chilling wolf howl.

"Give me that radio—now!" I lunged for him, but he chucked it across the boat. I winced as it skidded along the floor, hoping to God it hadn't broken. I sprinted after it.

"Times like these are when you find out what you're made of," Jason said. "How do you feel about going for a little swim?"

I reached the radio. It was still intact. I turned it back on and spun to see Jason leaning way out over the boat, his whole torso over the side.

"Catalina Harbor—this is the Iron Cucumber—over." I shouted into the receiver. Then holding it against my chest: "Jason don't you dare—"

"Look buddy," the radio crackled, "I don't know what kind of game you're playing, but harassing an emergency line is a serious offense. Over."

"This is not a game. We are in immediate distress. Over."

"Iron Cucumber, is that right? Over."

"Yes sir. We're located—Jason where the hell are we? Jason!"

Jason leaned a little farther, and then he was gone. He slipped overboard without a sound, straight through the black mist.

"The Iron Cucumber is still in the harbor. Spot 427, right between The Goliath and Sister Beetle," the radio said.

"Excuse me?"

The radio went to static. I let it slide from my fingers and rattle to the ground. The place where Jason went over was so bright I could barely look at it. The light must have almost reached the boat, but I was too afraid to go to the edge and look.

"Jason?" I shouted. "Jason are you there?"

The light was beginning to recede. I couldn't stand it anymore. I went to the edge to look down, and—

Fingers gripped the railing. I'm not ashamed to say I shrieked and fell on my ass. A moment later, and Jason had climbed back on board. I didn't have time to say anything. The second he had his footing, he slugged me across the face and I blacked out.

I woke up screaming.

"Chill dude, we're almost back." I was in my sleeping bag, and Jason was sitting next to me. I recoiled immediately, pressing myself against the wall of the boat. "You okay? I thought you had a stroke or something."

"The water was gone. The lights—"

He laughed. "Man, what a relief. Just hold tight, okay? I'm going to get you to a hospital."

"So you didn't see anything weird out there?"

"Just you having a fit like a seizure or something in your sleep. You want a hand?"

"No, don't touch me."

"Okay man, you just rest. We'll call the hospital as soon as we're in cell range."

I didn't call the hospital when I got back though. I told him I was fine and made an excuse to get away. I called the Catalina Harbor instead. I asked them if they received a distressed radio call from the Iron Cucumber, and they said yes.

It wasn't a dream. It wasn't a fit. I'm not making this up.

So what the hell happened over the edge of the world? And what was it that came back in the boat with me?

## It Wasn't A Hit And Run. I Reversed Too.

I'm wearing the wrong suit. This one has a hole in the back. I forgot my phone charger at home, but it's too late now. I shouldn't have packed so much—I won't have time to check my bag. I never should have booked such an early flight in the first place. And I REALLY shouldn't have hit that pedestrian.

It all happened so fast. Accelerating through the blind corner in the pre-dawn twilight, I congratulated myself on beating the light. I didn't see him until I was a few feet away. I still didn't know what happened until I heard the crack and lurched from impact. He disappeared under the hood of my car and I slammed on the breaks, but it was too little and way too late. The car skidded to a stop about a dozen feet past where he went down.

The flight didn't exist anymore. My job didn't exist. Only my breathing did—great heaving gasps that I had to consciously force to keep myself from passing out. I could see his crumpled body in my rear-view mirror, but I was too scared to even get out of the car. I must have sat there for at least a minute, just staring at the smeared trail of blood. The unnatural angle of his right knee—the shoulder that flopped uselessly out of its socket—and finally the twitch of movement as he began to crawl.

I wish I could tell you I was too numb to know what I was doing, but I was thinking very clearly when I threw my car into reverse. It wasn't about missing the flight anymore. It wasn't just the insurance, or the medical bills, or the court cases that would come of this. My whole life was balanced on the edge of a knife, and a mistake like this was all it would take to ruin me.

I wish I didn't catch his eyes in the rear-view mirror when I hit him again. It wasn't surprise, or pleading, or even fear I saw there—just raw accusation. He knew he wasn't going to walk away from this. He knew exactly what I was thinking—exactly how selfish and cowardly I was. In that moment, I think he knew me more truly than my parents or my closest friends. The rest of my entire life didn't matter because the person who hit him a second time was who I really was.

And the third time. And a fourth. And the fifth. Back and forth over the body. It was almost light now, but it was still early enough for the street to be deserted. I pulled into an automated car wash at the end of the street. I ordered deluxe. That's where the numbness came—I didn't think a single thought as I sat in my car and watched the water jets and soap bubbles. Then I drove off, swearing to myself that nothing ever happened.

I still made my flight (miraculously). I had to run through the whole airport. My heart was beating so fast when the security looked at me, although of course it was absurd to think they knew what happened. The whole regimented travel routine coaxed me back into the illusion of normalcy though, and by the time I reached my boarding gate I'd half convinced myself that it never happened at all. I was just stressed and worrying about nothing. It was just a bad dream, but now I've woken up and it was time to go on with the rest of my life.

It still felt like I was dreaming though. I didn't walk. I drifted. Finding my window seat, I stared at the runway and marveled how surreal it looked. Airplanes defy all natural instincts for what is possible. All our technology does.

"Mind switching seats? You can have a window," I heard from the aisle. I was lost in thought though, oblivious to the outside world.

"Thanks a bunch. I just wanted to sit with my friend."

The shuffling of bodies, all moving in an orderly fashion. No one batted an eye at the absurdity of the whole show. Any kid can get behind the wheel of a five thousand pound unstoppable killing machine. If someone saw that hurtling toward them a few hundred years ago, they would have thought it was a demon straight from hell.

The sound of folding paper. "You keep up with the news?" the man next to me asked. I shrugged and kept staring out the window. Intrusive images of that unnaturally angled knee kept bursting into my mind, but I forced it out again. What if there was still blood on my car? I didn't have time to check that thoroughly.

"These politicians," my neighbor continued. "Absolute disgrace. Even the good ones—they don't care about who they're hurting. They're just afraid of being caught."

That made me look. Twice. And a third time. The man I'd hit this morning wasn't looking at me though. He was just calmly reading the paper. Now I know what you're thinking already—that it was my guilt making me see his face on this unrelated stranger. It wasn't just a passing similarity though. No wounds, no blood, no dislocated arm, but it was him alright. And when he looked up at me and smiled, it was the eyes I'd seen in my rear-view mirror.

The plane lurched, and I gave a little gasp. We were moving. Taking off. I unbuckled my seatbelt and started to stand, but the stewardess was quick to scold me back down. I couldn't think of an adequate reason for why I had to get out of there, so I just sat back down instead. That was stupid of me. I should have made up a medical condition or something, but I guess I was still in shock. It wasn't long before we were in the air and it was too late anyway.

"That's the worst thing about it for me," the person I killed this morning said. "Lack of conscious. If you're going to do someone in, at least show some respect. Say a prayer or something. But just doing it cold like that—" he gestured at his paper, but I didn't look. "It really boils the blood, you know?"

"Excuse me, I have to go to the bathroom." I started to stand again, but he grabbed my arm and dragged me back down to my seat.

"Seat belt sign is on. You're a grown man. Show some self-control."

I nodded, numbly buckling myself back in.

"I'm sorry," I mumbled.

"Sorry for what?" he asked.

I shrugged.

"Go on. Say it."

"I'm sorry," is all I could muster up.

"No you're not. You're just like the people in the news. You're only sorry you got caught. How long do you suppose this flight is?"

"Um, about 3 hours."

"That's plenty. You've got three hours to finish me off." He was looking me dead in the eye.

"Or...?"

"Or it'll be my turn. And one man to another, you have my word," he leaned in real close here, "I'll get it right the first time and won't need to back up."

"What the hell are you?"

He just grinned. The seatbelt sign went off, and he stood up to stretch. As he did so, something fell out of his sleeve and onto his vacated seat. I reached out and picked it up—a sharpened plastic shiv. He winked.

"I've got to use the bathroom. You take care now."

By the time he reached the end of the aisle I'd began to process everything. He wanted me to try to kill him again. Why? It didn't matter. Was he bluffing? I don't have much experience with immortal zombies, but my guess is they can do pretty much anything they set their mind to. It was one thing on a dark road without any witnesses, but on a secure and crowded flight without any escape?

But he'd given me the shiv, and he was alone in the bathroom right now. That couldn't be a coincidence. This was my one shot, and I was going to take it. Concealing the weapon, I moved to the bathroom at the end of the aisle. All those eyes on me—they're just passively tracking movement. They don't know. No one suspects anything. Then to the bathroom door—it was unlocked. I took a deep breath and opened it.

He was sitting on the toilet, his pants around his ankles, grinning up at me. When I was in the car, it took me a long time to work up the nerve to back up. This time I didn't even hesitate. I lunged at him, driving the plastic straight into his heart.

He barely flinched. I let go of the shiv, horrified to see it buried in his chest, even more horrified to see myself doing it. He calmly wiped his ass and pulled up his pants while I watched. Then he pushed past me, moving to exit the bathroom. I couldn't let him get away. I grabbed the shiv and stabbed him again, but he wrapped his arms around me and locked me against his body.

"Good luck turning your back on this one," he grunted as I struggled against the implacable grip. Together we tumbled out into the aisle—and this time all those eyes really were on me.

"Help!" the man screamed, appearing to notice his injury for the first time. "This man's trying to kill me!"

My hand on the shiv, the wound in his chest—there's no playing innocent there. I dropped my weapon and put my hands in the air. The man writhed on the ground, screaming and carrying on even though I knew he was fine.

"You're a liar!" I shouted as someone grabbed me from behind. "It's just an act! Can't you see he's faking?"

I swear I saw the man wink as they wrestled me to the ground, but I didn't fight back. But how the hell am I supposed to explain that in court?

Attempted murder. That's what I'm on trial for. As part of my guilty plea, my attorney advised me to tell a full account of what happened. That's what I'm doing, because I know it's still less than I deserve.

## The Missing Child Speaks

I don't have kids of my own, so I can only imagine how terrifying this must be for my neighbor Amy Galligan. I didn't know her well, but we've chatted a few times in the apartment mail room—her about the difficulties of being a single mother, me playing up my shipping job at Amazon to make it sound like I'm a big shot. It's a monster of a city though, and there are so many people with so many problems that I was hardly even phased when I saw the missing poster of her four-year-old daughter hanging around the building.

*Taken from a public playground at Fairbanks Park.*
*Any information, please call 818-***-****

"Maybe she tossed it," I remarked casually to my buddy Dave.

"Tossed what. The kid?"

"Yeah, or flushed it or something, I don't know. I know the woman, and she bitches all the time about how she has no life of her own anymore. Seemed to me like she would have been happier without it."

"It's not an IT, man, she's a baby girl. And you can't flush a four-year-old—what the fuck?" Dave and I knew each other since grade school, so it amazed me that I could still get a rise out of him with dark jokes like that. "Anyway, why would she put up missing posters if she didn't want the kid?"

"Duh, it's so she won't look suspicious." That was Sammy, Dave's girlfriend. Slim, beautiful dark hair, and snarky as a goth in church—I don't know how my goodie-goodie friend got so lucky. I pointed at her, then tapped my nose in what I hoped to be the universal signal for 'she knows'. Dave just looked bewildered and flustered.

"No one would do that to their own kid. The moment they're born, they take a part of your soul with them. It's not just like you're split in half either—they've taken all the best parts of you. All your innocence and hope and wonder at the world that eroded from you over the years—it's all right there in your arms,

# Sleepless Nights

promising a better life than you could ever live for yourself. And when you're looking at them, all those holes in your soul that you didn't even know where there are filled back in. For the first time in your life, you know that you truly matter."

"Dude, you don't even have a kid," I said.

"So what? I'm human, aren't I? I know what's what."

Meanwhile I swear Sammy was humming the tune to Family Guy's 'Prom night dumpster babies' song. I think my heart just did a back-flip.

"Screw you both." Dave bounced off the couch in agitation. "I'm going to go check on her and see if there's anything I can do to help."

"Seriously? You don't even know the lady," I protested, feeling a little flustered myself.

"Yeah, what gives?" Sammy chimed in. "I thought we were going to play paint-ball today."

I could handle Dave's anger. I even found it funny. If I'm being honest, maybe I was even a little jealous and wanted to torment him. That sad, pitying look he gave us though? That cut deeper than I'd care to admit. I guess Sammy felt the same way because a few moments later all three of us were standing outside of Amy's apartment.

Dave knocked first.

"Excuse me, Ms. Galligan? It's your neighbors."

Nothing.

"Are you sure she's home?" Sammy whispered.

"Yeah, I heard her toilet like five minutes ago. Thin walls." I matched her hushed tone.

"Oh, I didn't know she had twins," Sammy said. I almost burst a lung trying not to laugh.

Dave pressed his ear against the door. I expected another death glare from him, but he just turned around and grinned.

"It's okay. They must have found her. I hear the kid talking," he said.

We were about to go when the door opened behind us. Amy was standing in the doorway—bird's nest hair, loose bathrobe, face puffy with fresh tears and anxious stress—even Sammy didn't have anything to say about that. A little girl giggled from somewhere inside her apartment.

"Is your daughter...?" Dave began.

Amy shook her head and wiped her nose with the back of her hand. She turned around and walked inside her apartment, leaving the door open. Dave followed without question. I didn't move until a few seconds later when Sammy entered.

"There's lots of boxes, mommy." The slightly tinny voice was coming from an Amazon Echo Dot sitting on a coffee table. Beside it were scattered a halo of used tissues. "It's too dark though. Mommy, where are you?"

"It's okay Lilly," Amy said, her voice cracking. "I'm going to be there soon, just hold on."

Amy looked at us pleadingly, and we stared back in stunned silence.

"How long has she—" Dave began.

"About an hour," Amy cut him off. "She said someone took her from the park, and she doesn't know where she is."

"Was it an Amazon van?" I asked. Dave gave me another disapproving glare, but it melted as Amy nodded. "I think so. Lilly said it was black and orange."

Sammy was on her phone, typing furiously.

"Police?" Dave asked.

Sammy shook her head, showing us her screen a moment later: a picture of Lilly with a plain white background.

"This is her, right?"

"Where did you find that?" Amy asked urgently.

Sammy hit the back arrow, returning the screen to an Amazon product page. I would have laughed if I hadn't seen Amy's face.

Lilly Galligan.<br>
$1,495. Used. In stock.<br>
4.2 / 5 stars. 10 Reviews.

"4.2 stars though," I said, trying to lighten the mood. "At least she's got—"

Glares all around. I didn't finish that thought.

"Baby, can you hear me? What else do you see?" Amy demanded.

It wasn't Lilly who answered though. It was just Alexa's generic, robotic voice. "Would you like to place an order for Lilly Galligan now?"

"Come on, isn't anyone curious to read the reviews?" I asked. "Like, what are they going to say? 3 stars, can't color within the lines?"

"Shit, dude," Dave said.

"Yeah, seriously. Not the time." Even Sammy agreed.

"None of you are any fun," I said. "I put a lot of work into this. The least you could do is play along—"

I was ready when Dave took a swing at me, and I managed to back-peddle out of the way. There was a lot of yelling—some hysterical sobs from Amy—then Dave chasing me half way around the room before they gave me a chance to explain.

"She's at a warehouse, okay? God, what babies. Can't anyone take a joke?"

That time I did get punched. It's okay though—I took it like a man. They all insisted I drive them there right away, which is what I was intending to do all along, anyway. This will be the first time I've ever tried to sell adults, so I wonder how much I'll get for these three.

## Are You Happy Now?

Hair twined between fingers. Dirt bloodied into paste. Coiled muscle, panting breath, and a broken smile.

"What are you?" I'd shouted down at him.

"I'm me."

I hit him again—hard enough for the bones in my hand to rattle against each other. I don't know why it made me so angry that he was still smiling.

"I want to hear you say it! What are you?"

"Too much. I don't want it, I don't want, I don't—"

Again—the pain in my hand was triumph. The kid would have been flat on the ground if I wasn't still holding him up by his hair.

"Just say it. That's all you got to do. Admit what you are."

"I'm happy."

I dropped Chase to crumple in a heap. The boy was laughing, blood spraying from his mouth as he did. Exhausted, I sat down next to him. He rolled back and forth, body rigidly locked in the fetal position. He was taking great gasps of air and choking on his own blood, laughing all the while.

"God damn it. You're literally insane," I panted.

Chase chocked again. The coughing didn't stop this time. I helped him onto his knees and slapped his back to help clear the airway. He rewarded me with a giant bloody smile.

"I would have stopped if you just said it," I said, my voice calmer. "Why are you so stubborn?"

"You want me to say I'm autism," he slurred. He was hard enough to understand without a mouthful of blood.

"Autistic," I corrected. "I want you to tell the truth and stop pretending you're normal."

"I never pretended. I never normal—pretended normal." His breath was coming easier now. I couldn't look away from the long line of viscous blood which hung from his lip without quite falling. "Not many people are happy. I'm special like that."

We both laughed, although I don't think we were laughing at the same thing.

For the first few weeks I knew Chase, I hated his guts. All the special attention he got—everyone doing stuff for him and congratulating him for accomplishing absolutely nothing—for that big dopey grin he didn't deserve—I thought it was all just a big act. I hated that he wore clothes like a normal person and sat in class without doing any of the work. I thought I could beat the truth out of him, and I guess I did. The truth was that he really was happy—maybe the only truly happy person I'd never known.

"I know I'm autism," he told me later in his customary lurching speech. "I know what it means—I'm autism. I don't play around—play pretend."

"Then why don't you ever say it?"

"I do. I just say it last. If I say it first, people don't listen to the rest. They think they already know me."

I stayed quiet while we walked home. He was rolling his sleeves up and down his right forearm. Up and down. Then both down. Then both up. He never stuck with one tick very long. The next moment he was on his tip-toes, tottering along behind me. Then he was loudly humming some made-up tune, or flapping his arms like a bird, or spitting straight in the air and shrieking with laughter as he tried to dodge the falling drop. Whatever he was doing seemed to absorb him completely—so much that when I spoke again he jumped in surprise to find me still there.

"You're too busy busy," he said, even though he was the one doing everything while I just walked. "That's why it's—why you're not happy."

"I'm not even doing anything," I said.

"Too many things," he insisted, almost shouting it. I looked around to make sure no one else was around. I didn't want anyone to think we were friends. "Not nothing. You're looking at ten things. Thinking about twenty. Thirty forty fifty—not real things. Old things. New things. Could-be-things and shouldn't-be-things."

"So what? You're the one always spazzing out."

His whole face furrowed in confusion. Then he smiled.

"I just do one thing with my whole heart."

I was getting frustrated. "That's not true. In the five minutes we've been walking you've done like a hundred different things."

He shook his head, his grin widening. "Just one thing. All my heart—just one thing. Then when I'm finished, I do another."

"And that really makes you happy? It doesn't bother you that you're different?"

He didn't answer though. He'd stopped to pet a bushy plant as if it were a dog.

"I'm not waiting for you," I said. "I'm going home."

"The plants can't walk."

"I'm not talking about the plants—"

"Or drive cars. Or make friends," he rambled. Despite myself, I stopped and waited to hear where this was going. "They're different too. And some have flowers and some have spikes and some have flowers—"

"You already said flowers," I interrupted.

"Because some have lots," Chase declared, unperturbed. "It would be stupid if they didn't grow though—just because they were different. Everything grows—is different. Everything dies. Everything dies." He grasped the bushy plant he'd been petting with both hands and ripped it violently by the roots. A moment later and everything was in the air—stems and leaves and clods of soil all raining around us while he laughed and danced through it.

"You're retarded," I said.

Chase grinned. "So are you, but it's okay. We're still growing."

He wasn't so talkative the next day in school. He had a fresh bruise under one eye. I know that shouldn't have made me so angry after what I'd done to him, but it did. I asked what happened, but he didn't feel like talking.

"Tell me who did it," I demanded. "I'll make sure it doesn't happen again."

He shook his head, not looking at me. I tried to grab him by the shoulder and turn him my way to get a better look, but he yelped and darted into the corner of the room. He pulled out a notebook from his bag and began writing furiously, not looking up as I crept closer. If someone was hurting him, then I wanted to know. I liked the idea of getting into a fight with someone—like it was my penance for what I've already done.

I snuck a peak at what he was writing. Chase was halfway through the notebook, and I figured it was some kind of journal or something. I got too close again though, and Chase started shrieking. The teacher assumed I was picking on him and gave me detention on the spot. It was so stupid—when I was ACTUALLY trying to hurt him we got along, but now that I was trying to help I got in trouble. I shouted at Chase, telling him to explain that I was on his side. Chase didn't look up though. The only result was the teacher grabbing me by the arm to march me all the way to the principal's office.

"Boys will be boys—" I heard the principal say through the door. I waited outside on a hard plastic chair for him to finish his meeting.

"Chase is being tormented! You don't understand how hard it is to take care of a—" came a man's voice. I stopped kicking the wall to listen.

"Perhaps a public school is not the safest environment for—"

"It's your job to make it safe. If anything happens to him—"

"Mr. Hackent, please. The teachers will always do their best, but they can't be everywhere at once. What happens before or after school—"

I opened the door. Sudden silence. The principal in his sweater vest and the man I can only assume was Chase's father in a suit, both staring at me.

"I can keep an eye on him to and from school," I volunteered immediately.

The principal looked uncomfortable. He was well aware of my history of fighting. I guess he thought it was more important to placate the angry man sitting across from him though, so he nodded after a moment.

"That's settled then," he said. "The teachers will keep Chase safe during school, and now he'll be safe on the way too."

Mr. Hackent growled at me, his eyes narrowed in suspicion.

"What about at home?" I asked, staring straight back.

"What happens at home is none of your business," Mr. Hackent replied, standing up rigidly. "If anything happens now, at least I'll know who to blame."

The bruises didn't go away though. There was a fresh one at least once a week. Chase didn't want to talk about it, but at least he was talking about other stuff again—everything except what he wrote in his journal.

"One thing—your whole heart—one thing at a time," Chase said. "If you let that one thing be something bad, then that bad thing is all there is."

"Just ignoring something doesn't make it go away. If someone is still hurting you—"

I stopped because he wasn't listening anyway. He was just playing with his ears, not looking at me. Folding them back and forth. Back and forth.

"I don't ignore it," he said after a long moment.

"Huh?"

"I just don't take it with me," he insisted. "I write it down, then I leave it behind. Fists only hurt once. It's not too bad, and then it's over. Thinking about it hurts more—hurts longer. Most things are like that—it's the thinking about the thing that hurts more than the thing. So just stop thinking about it."

"Are you happy now?" I asked him.

"Always happy," he said, although he didn't smile that time. "I just got to focus on growing."

He didn't look at me very often, but he did this time. Right in my eyes, still staring while he hid his journal behind an electrical box. He put a finger to his lips, hissing a loud SHHHH before turning to walk away. He could have hidden it anywhere, but he was doing it right in front of me because he trusted me. I entertained the thought of just taking it to try to find out the truth, but now it seemed more important to prove I was his friend.

I hate how much sense he made at the time. I hate how easily I let it go.

I started seeing Mr. Hackent at the school more frequently. There'd always be shouting as soon as the principal's door closed, and I wasn't the only one who noticed. Pretty soon kids started talking, and someone must have spoken up about seeing me beat up Chase that one time. After that I was forbidden to walk with Chase, or even talk to him in the hallway.

The bruises didn't stop though. They weren't happening at school, and they weren't happening on the way to and fro either. I kept getting called into the principal's office. I tried to explain that it must be happening at home, but no one believed me. I started getting really angry at Chase. I wanted him to tell people the truth, but he couldn't handle the pressure. Detentions turned into suspension, with threats of permanent expulsion if Chase didn't stop getting abused.

It wasn't my fight. That's what I told myself. The little idiot was going to be happy no matter what happened, and the only thing I was doing by getting involved was making things worse for myself.

I let it go. I stayed the hell away from him—didn't speak to him—didn't even look at him. Even when he tried to talk to me, I just walked away. I thought no one could blame me if they saw that I wanted nothing to do with him.

It didn't stop me from blaming myself though. The lights and sirens were on my block a few days after I cut contact. I was taken down to the police station for questioning. There was so much going on that I couldn't even process it. I just remember rolling my sleeves up and down. Up and down. Trying not to think. Up and down, with all my heart. Because the moment I stopped, I know I'd hear everyone talking about the autistic boy—that's what they called him on the news, not even using his name—the autistic boy who took his own life with a razor blade. I'd hear about the incessant bullying which drove him to it, and hear his father blathering about doing all he could.

But I know Chase would never do that. He was happy. He was growing. And nothing could have stopped that except someone pulling him up by the roots.

The first thing I did was retrieve Chase's journal. There were a hundred things I could have done with it to prove what really happened, but I only picked one. One thing at a time. One thing with all your heart, and for me, that was revenge. Mr. Hackent is a dead man.

It took a few days snooping around his house to find a reliable way in: the broken grate which let me slip into his basement from the outside. I'd wait until I saw him leave for work in the morning, then I'd sneak upstairs to his bedroom. Over the next week, he'd find quotes from Chase's journal cut out and left around his house.

*He doesn't like hurting me. He just can't help it.* - on his bedside table.

*Dad wishes I was normal. I wish he wasn't.* - taped onto his bathroom mirror.

*He wants me to go, but I have nowhere else to go.* - on his leftover eggs in the refrigerator, ketchup soaking through the paper like blood.

It was working too. Every day Mr. Hachent left for work, he looked a little more tired. A little more on edge. On Thursday he skipped work entirely, and when he left Friday morning, it looked like he'd been wearing the same clothes since Wednesday. When he got home that night, this is what he found.

*Are you happy now?*

It wasn't a note though. It was spray paint this time. On every wall. Every counter. On the ceiling and across his bedsheets.

*Are you happy now?*

I heard him shouting the words when he came home. Screaming at the top of his lungs, the sound distorting as he ran from room to room, seeing it everywhere.

*Are you happy now?*

Neighbors reported a gunshot that same night. Rumor had it that he spent several hours ranting about ghosts to his family before it happened. The police concluded that he'd been driven to madness over the death of his son, which I guess isn't too far from the truth.

One thing at a time. And now that I've finished what I set out to do, I've got to keep myself busy. Really busy—incessantly jumping from one project to the next. I need to always be living, always growing. Because I know when it gets too quiet I'll have to stop and think, and I'm afraid of the moments when I have to ask myself:

Am I happy now?

## She Looks Like A Future Victim

How do killers and rapists choose their next victim? Does it have to do with some repressed childhood memory, fueling a blind hatred toward a particular type of person? Or is it just something they see in the moment: the shape of a body, or her pretty face stirring the blood into an undeniable throb? Whatever it is, I understand why he chose my co-worker Casey. It's hard even looking at her without letting your mind wander. It's not that she's overtly sexual or provocative or anything—it's more the way she moves, graceful and flowing to the point where even waiting tables looks like an intricately choreographed ballet.

It was at the end of our shift the other day when I noticed this customer staring at her. He'd been there for almost an hour, and he still hadn't ordered anything except a coffee. He didn't have a book or a phone or anything either—he was just fixated on her, tracking her every movement with his hungry eyes. Scruffy coarse beard, leather jacket, snake tattoo winding all the way down his hands—I wouldn't want him staring at me. I tried to warn Casey and offered to drive her home (she lives right around the block), but she didn't seem very concerned by him.

She should have been though. The second she walked out the door, the scruffy customer was on her heels, making zero effort to hide his single-minded fascination. I'm not one to be paranoid or anything, but there was a desperate urgency as he followed: a predator stalking the last few feet before the chase is on. Better safe than sorry—I hopped in my pickup and trailed them around the corner.

Casey glanced over her shoulder, and she must have seen him because she started walking faster. The man matched her stride for stride, almost breaking into a run the last few yards before she reached her apartment. I parked on the street until I made sure she got in safely. The building needed a key to enter the lobby, and watching the man rattle on the locked door it was obvious he didn't live there. I watched him pace restlessly for a minute before he began to circle the structure. My instincts hadn't lied to me yet; he was still trying to find a way into the building.

I got out of my car to watch what he was up to. I wasn't thinking about personal danger. All that mattered was that Casey was safe—that and her thinking of me as a hero for looking out for her. I lost sight of the guy for a few minutes after I turned the corner though, and I had to circle the whole building again before I realized what he was up to.

He was climbing the metal exterior stairs of the fire escape. He must have jumped from the top of a dumpster to reach the platform. A black ski mask was pulled over his face. This was getting serious. I should have called the police at this point, but I was still entertaining this fantasy about charging in to save her, and my nerves were on fire with the thrill of the hunt. I clambered onto the dumpster and made a wild leap, action-music playing in my head as I hauled myself onto the metal platform. I shouted at him to stop, but he was already four floors above me and disappearing into an open window.

How much could he do to her in the time it took me to climb four stories? I didn't want to think about it. My last fight had been in grade school. What the hell was I thinking? It was becoming way too real, way too fast, but I'd already committed this far and I couldn't turn back now. I raced up the rattling metal stairs with a sound like a herd of elephants. There was a scream—Casey's scream—but the air I inhaled had turned to daggers and I was already going as fast as I could. Reaching the window he entered by, I dove inside, utterly out of breath and ill prepared for whatever was waiting for me.

I was in a bedroom. Casey was stripped to her underwear, face down on the bed, hands roughly tied behind her back. The man was looming over her—that's all I needed to know. I grabbed steel reading lamp from her desk and smashed it two-handed into the back of his skull. I wish he wasn't wearing the mask just so I could see the look on his face as he crumpled on the ground.

"Hey baby? What was that sound?" she asked, muffled against the pillow.

I was still trying to catch my breath and couldn't respond. It gave me a moment to take in the whole scene: the Valentine's chocolates on the desk, the fuzzy pink ropes which tied Casey's hands, the fact that she wasn't struggling or trying to get away. How had he known this was her room from the outside anyway? Unless...

The truth hit me so hard that I wanted to crumple on the ground next to her boyfriend. Or even better, knock me out the window so she never saw me or figured out what happened. Absolute panic as she began turning her head in my direction. Mind-numbing, terrified, dry-mouthed panic as I dropped to the ground under the bed.

"Well? I'm waiting!" Casey said, wiggling her butt.

I could only think of one solution. I ripped the ski mask off her boyfriend's unconscious body and put it on, and I stood up.

"Please don't hurt me!" she wailed at an unexpected volume. Did she see through my disguise? "I'm all alone, Mr. Intruder Man! What are you going to do to me?"

I couldn't answer or she'd recognize my voice. I couldn't run because she'd already seen me. And seeing her tied up in her underwear like that, practically begging for it... well if my mind wasn't already numb from panic, then that would have been enough to purge the rest of my thoughts. I was in absolute despair and euphoria at the same time as I climbed on top of her, feeling the curve of her body squirm against mine in an erotic and fantastic nightmare.

Is it still rape if she wants it? If she loves it? If she's begging for more? The sex was phenomenal—the best of my life—and I can tell she felt the same by how she welcomed me into her and moaned. I was really starting to get into it when I heard another, deeper moan. She must have thought it was from me because it made her go even louder.

But I knew better. It was her boyfriend on the ground, starting to wake up. There I am, frozen mid-thrust, her desperate for more, now listening to her boyfriend waking up. Oh my god oh my god oh my god—I leap off and leap straight through the window, completely naked from the waist down. A second later there's the most ear-splitting scream, joined by a confused bellow. Casey appears at the window a moment later, still naked, watching me flying down the steps and leaping onto the dumpster below—sliding off in my panic to plaster flat on the ground.

Thank god I was still wearing the mask. I hope she leaves her window open again tomorrow night.

## The Exorcism Of An Angel

There is no greater curse than the possession of a Demon, nor greater honor than the visitation of an Angel. God has blessed our home with his presence, and I am nothing but grateful for the miracle which has occurred. And yet I tremble as I write this, because through this trial we have learned one lesson most truly of all:

*"His delight is not in the strength of the horse, nor his pleasure in the legs of a man, but the Lord takes pleasure in those who fear him."*
*Psalm 147:10-11*

To fear God does him as much honor as to love him, for both are equal expressions of belief.

God does not give us the choice of which laws to follow. The comforts of modern life have seduced men into a pitiful state of moral lassitude, but our family does not compromise on our beliefs. Righteousness can be feigned for the sake of impressing one's neighbors, but the truth of our souls cannot be hidden from God.

*"I do not permit a woman to teach or to have authority over a man; she must be silent."* -1 *Timothy 2:12*

But the insolent girl would not be silent before my husband. Not until I struck her. First she howled, then she whimpered, and then she was still. How beautiful the fear of God had made my child.

Elizabeth was only six years old when she turned from the path. She spoke when she was not addressed. Lies flowed from her mouth as naturally as truth,

## Sleepless Nights

she refused to pray, and she showed no shame in drawing blasphemous monsters and images which did nothing to glorify God. My husband, Luke, and I prayed for her every night, but the Lord knows that a child understands the weight of a cane more keenly than any word.

*"Foolishness is bound in the heart of a child; but the rod of correction shall drive it far from him." -Prov 22:15*

Her high-collared dresses hid the marks, and for a time Elizabeth showed enough respect for her parents not to speak against us. I should have listened to Luke and not sent her to that public school where her mind could be further polluted by the unfaithful. Her rearing was impeccable, so there's no other way I can explain the filth which began spewing from her mouth.

"I don't want to go!" she said last Sunday morning while I dressed her for church. "I hate him! I hate God!"

"God loves you," I tried to explain, but she wouldn't listen.

"No he doesn't. God hates me too."

"Why would you say such a thing?" I asked.

"Because he made you my mom."

We didn't go to church that day. After Luke heard what she said, she was in no condition to go anywhere. The Lord knows I wept as much as Elizabeth did. It couldn't go on like this, I told myself. Luke thought that she would learn in time, but I wasn't strong enough to endure her lessons. I cleaned my daughter's wounds and made her comfortable, but her blood was still on my hands when I prayed that night.

"Where did we go wrong?" I begged from the quiet. "Oh God, if you truly love us as we love you, send us an Angel to grant us the happiness we deserve."

I could see the light through my closed eyes, and I knew the Spirit was with me then. I felt his warmth on my hands and face. I dared not look, or speak, or even breath, afraid to disrupt the miracle in progress. For one divine moment I knew my prayers were answered and I was in heaven. The next moment, I heard Luke shout "Fire!"

Smoke was billowing under our bedroom door. The hallway was an inferno—flames gutting between the floorboards, climbing the walls, igniting the pictures and the wooden crucifixes pounded into the walls. I staggered towards Elizabeth's room—coughing and falling to my knees to crawl under the smoke. Luke grabbed me under my arms and heaved me toward the front door, but I kicked and fought him the whole way.

"Elizabeth! She's still in there!"

"The Lord preserve her," Luke said, uncompromising as always. I was dizzy from the smoke, and I wasn't strong enough to fight Luke off. Before I knew what was happening, I was panting and heaving on our front lawn while the house burned.

"Elizabeth!" I'd screamed through my strained throat. "Elizabeth where are you?"

Luke wouldn't let me go back in. I was screaming and crying hysterically, but he forced me to the ground and held me there until the fire department came. If Elizabeth was crying for us, I couldn't hear her over the roaring flames. Maybe she stayed quiet though, more afraid of us than the fire. Luke prayed while the firemen battled the blaze. I didn't, knowing my prayers had already been answered. This is the happiness we deserved.

Three strong men entered the house when the exterior had been doused. Veterans in full gear with masks and oxygen tanks. Elizabeth had nothing, and sore as she was from her punishments, I don't know if she could have escaped that house even without the fire. Three men exited the house, their arms empty.

Elizabeth was barefoot and walking unassisted between them. Her face was clear, unmarked from soot, her breathing slow and even. Her skin was pure white, unmarked by injury or burn.

"A miracle," Luke had said.

"A miracle," the firemen were quick to agree.

"A curse," I wasn't brave enough to reply.

We all stayed in a hotel that night. Luke was so exhausted from the ordeal that he slept soundly, but I couldn't help but lie awake and listen to Elizabeth whispering to herself. She was traumatized, my reasoning said. She was trying to process what happened, and she needed me to hold her and tell her it's going to be okay. I almost got up a dozen times in the night to comfort her, but each time my muscles locked from some nameless instinct as old as fear itself which begged me not to approach the mumbling girl.

"Elizabeth is a good girl. A good girl," I heard my daughter whisper. "Elizabeth will not punish them."

I pretended to be asleep, trying to match my husband's deep breathing. I couldn't get enough air though, and my involuntary gasps must have betrayed me because Elizabeth would sometimes sit rigidly upright to stare at me in the darkness. I watched her through slitted eyes, not daring to move.

"Elizabeth prayed too, you know," the girl was obviously speaking to me, but all I could do was lie there and keep breathing. "Do you know what she prayed for?"

I clenched my eyes tight. I felt so stiff that I might as well be dead. I didn't hear anything else, but I was too scared to look. A full minute before the silence became too loud, and when I opened my eyes again, the girl was standing right beside my bed.

I jerked upright, hopelessly tangling the covers in my surprise. Luke woke with a start and flailed around the nightstand until he turned on the lamp. "What is it? What's going on?"

Elizabeth was back in her bed, rigidly upright, just staring at me and smiling. I forced a smile in return.

"Nothing's the matter. We're all okay now. Get some sleep Elizabeth."

Luke grunted and turned the lights back off, rolling his back toward me.

"Goodnight Lady," Elizabeth said. I don't know how many hours it took me to fall asleep after that, but I never saw Elizabeth lie down the whole time.

Over the next few days, the insurance inspectors concluded that it was an electrical fire, although there was so little information in their report that it seemed more like speculation to me.

Elizabeth hasn't given us any trouble since. She's mild and dutiful in her behavior and her prayers. She still loves to draw, but the serene passionless faces she repeats over and over are far more disturbing than the monsters she used to decorate the pages with. Luke couldn't be happier of course—he's got the perfect little angel he's always wanted. He doesn't seem to realize that we've always had an angel, or that somehow she didn't make it out of that fire.

She's watching me as I write this, smiling and swinging her feet, but I don't care. She may even read it if she likes—it doesn't matter. God already knows there is more divinity in an imperfect child than all the angels in heaven. I worship him with my fear now, so if that truly pleases the Lord, let him hear me and send my daughter home.

But she's giggling now, so perhaps he has other plans in store for me.

## Now Hiring. Last Three Employees Killed Themselves.

Twelve weeks looking for a job and things were getting desperate. I'm talking water-and-electricity-off desperate, with the landlord playing my door like a drum.

I called my way through entire directories of offerings, often not sure what I was interviewing for until the morning of. I'd get three or four meetings on a good day, but nothing stuck until the excessively tan man from Mello Corp shook my hand.

"You've made a good decision," Cameron had said, pulling me in a bit too close. "Employees at Mello Corp are like a big family. They all stay for life."

I wish I'd gotten a chance to clarify what my actual responsibilities were. I just saw a salaried position and a plush dark-wood office, and that was good enough for me. It didn't help that Cameron only described the requirements in vague generalities about loyalty and teamwork. Even the liability forms didn't help—just a flash of an official letterhead and it was whisked away, leaving me nodding and smiling.

Truth is that I don't have much respect for office jobs. I figured a week lying low and Googling things would teach me everything I needed to know. So far so good—few days in, and I'd spent it all coasting around chatting with people. I was given some menial cleaning tasks, and a few organizing and carrier jobs, but mostly I was free to just watch and learn.

It seemed to be a delivery company, although they only shipped one product. No-one ever mentioned what the product was, and I didn't want to betray my ignorance by asking. Few dudes in their late thirties said they'd been here over 15 years each though. First and last job they'd ever take. The two women working the phones were both 10+ years, and another guy upstairs said he'd been here over 40.

Cameron wasn't joking about the commitment. The funny thing is though, no-one seemed the least happy or boastful in announcing their sentence. There wasn't any small talk in the break room, no affectionate nicknames or the inside jokes you'd expect with such long camaraderie.

All eyes were sullen, tracing patterns in the uniform carpet. Muffled voices, drudging steps, smiles that gave up before they started.

"I don't get it," I casually threw out to one of the guys. "Why does everyone stay so long if they don't like it here?"

"They don't all," he said, not quite meeting my eyes. "Last three with your job killed themselves to get out early."

I gave him a big grin, sucking up to show I appreciated his joke. His deadpan face betrayed nothing. My grin slowly faded as we sat together in silence, him shuffling one foot against the other. Then he left, and I was left standing wondering what the hell was going on.

I can't imagine myself in this gloomy place for 10, let alone 40 years. I resolved to keep applying to jobs and only work here until I found something better. Besides, I sort of enjoyed the thrill of the hunt, and this place was snooze-ville.

I wish it had stayed that way. Few days later and I was making my first outside delivery. Blank cardboard package, about the size of a cake. I was bored waiting to receive it, then bored waiting in traffic. I was bored when I rang the doorbell, and bored when she opened the package. And then something started buzzing. And it wasn't boring anymore.

Wasps were flooding into the air, and they resented their captivity with a vengeance. The sound magnified within seconds until it was all I could hear in every direction. I did what any sane person would do: scream like a little girl and run as fast as I could without looking back. Only I did look back—about a hundred feet down the driveway by my car. The buzzing had all stayed at the house around the woman.

She wasn't screaming anymore. Her throat had swollen shut, bulbous swellings covering her face and neck. She still flailed around with her arms and legs, but the movements were getting more sluggish with every vain stroke. The things were crawling through her hair, up her dress, even into her open mouth.

I've seen allergic reactions before. There was a kid in my middle school who ate a peanut and turned into a balloon animal, but it was nothing like this. I don't know if the wasps were purposefully stinging the same spots around her face and neck, or if that's all I could see, but the swellings seemed to stack on top of each other, one grotesque swelling budding off the last.

First things first, and I vomited. Then I wiped my mouth, got in the car, and made sure all the windows were rolled up. By then my phone was ringing:

"Now you really are family," Cameron's voice was a ray of unwelcome sunshine through a dreary morning.

"You knew? What was inside, you knew about the—"

"They're magnificent, aren't they? Put someone's scent in the box, starve them a little, and then that's the only one they'll hunt."

"You're absolutely insane. I know where you work. I'm calling the cops, and—"

"Smile for the camera, won't you?" he interrupted.

"Huh?" I looked up and down the street. A blinding flash. One of the guys from work was standing outside my window with a camera. He gave me a thumbs up and took another picture.

"That will go well with the live video," Cameron said. "Combine that with the signed confession you have plotting and executing her murder—"

"I didn't sign—"

"Are you really sure?"

It didn't matter what I tried to say. It was caught in my throat anyway.

"You have a break until 1, then two more deliveries in the afternoon."

The phone cut off.

Well I'd love to explain more, but my break is almost over and Cameron is very clear that he doesn't like lateness. Maybe I'll leave early instead, like the others.

## Sgt Dawson's Widow Deserves To Know How He Really Died

Dear Mrs. Dawson,

My name is Frank Tiller, and I was with your husband when he died. I don't know how to contact you proper, but the sergeant once told me the two of you used to read stories like this, so I figure you might find these words too. He used to read to you while you drew pictures from what's happening, isn't that right? He said you weren't scared of nothing though—didn't matter how dark it got, your laughter was a light to follow. I don't suppose you're laughing much these days. I know I'm not.

Two gunshots, one in the chest, one in the stomach. He didn't abandon his position, not as long as he could provide cover to give the rest of us a chance away from the ambush. That's what they told you, wasn't it? I was shocked when I read the report, but I suppose I understand why they lied. That's a hero's death they gave him. They knew you wouldn't question it, and really that's all they cared about.

Pardon if I'm overstepping my bounds ma'am, but if I were you I'd want to know the truth, even if it weren't so pretty.

The report said he died May 22nd, but you have to understand that this begun on the 13th when our squad encountered a land-mine. It detonated beneath the front left tire of our LTATV jeep with a sound so loud I only felt it. I was thrown clear when the jeep went into the air, but Sergeant Dawson got the worst of it in the driver's seat. What metal hadn't disintegrated had melted and run like candle-wax, leaving a crater in the car like a meteor just punched through.

Nobody could have told you how your husband walked away from that with hardly a limp, just like nobody could say he was the same afterward. Doctor said it was an acute case of PTSD, but I see what PTSD looks like every time I look in the mirror, and it didn't feel nothing like that to me.

I don't know how to right describe it ma'am, but when the sergeant talked, I felt like he was calling from the bottom of the deepest of deep wells, like he wasn't here at all but just a little echo that started a long time ago.

Sometimes he'd look right at me and say something like, "Frankie what you got waiting for you back home?" and we'd talk like a bunch of geezers on a park bench with all the time in the world. He was like that when the Captain came in —sober enough to be approved for his position again.

Captain wouldn't have been so quick if he saw Dawson at his dark times. He'd forget who I was, or who he was, wandering lost and scared until I found him and brought him back to his quarters. Other times he'll be screaming at a wall, really going at it, red faced with the veins bulging in his neck and spit flying like a drill sergeant.

Every day it seemed the dark side was a little more the only side. Even when he had it together, he'd forget my name or say something which betrayed how fragile his mind was. Once real loud in front of everyone in the barracks he ordered me to "Climb to the moon on the finest of ladders", his voice sing-songing like a lune.

The Captain didn't see it, but the rest of his men did. I'd hear them making fun of the sergeant behind his back, taunting him for his wild intellectual and personality fluctuations. Your husband only made it worse, ordering a man to grow a beard, or demanding to know why the King of England was so late in arriving. He was a laughingstock behind closed doors, and sometimes the doors weren't even closed.

Other men gave me shit for not joining in, but on my word I wouldn't do that. If the sergeant asked me to jump I'd ask how high, and if he said it was to the moon, then I'd give it my damn best. Count all the bricks in the barracks—it was 16,444, and I didn't leave until after midnight.

## Sleepless Nights

You see, I knew your husband was still in there, somewhere nobody could reach him anymore. He was the same man who had saved my life on more than one occasion, and I would follow him to whatever end. I thought that if he noticed I was listening—really listening, then he'd find his way back. If he knew he wasn't being judged or looked down on or forgotten, he'd have a reason to return.

God ma'am, those days scared the hell out of me. I wasn't just scared for the sergeant who seemed to keep getting worse, I was scared for myself. The only way I used to sleep at night is trusting the sergeant was going to keep me safe, and these days even pills couldn't settle me down.

I didn't give up on him. I want you to know that. Every damn impossible thing he'd say I'd look in the eye and say "Yes sir!" Everything except one—the night of May 22nd. The night he grabbed me by the shoulders and looked me in the eye, the night he really knew me, when he asked for me to take his life.

"I feel something bad coming, Frankie," he said. "Like my soul needs to take a really bad shit that's been brewing way too long."

I told him not to worry about it. We all feel like that all the time. He chuckled a bit, but he wouldn't lay off.

"I want you to put a bullet in me. Two to be sure. Something's coming Frankie, and I don't want to be around when it gets here."

The next question out of his mouth was how much would it cost to buy India. I told him I'd need some time to research it, and he let me go for the night.

He had no right to ask a question like that (not the India one). I didn't deserve to be put in this position where I had to just walk away in shame. Maybe the rest of the men were right, I thought. I ought to have called the medical officer and gotten him locked up a long time ago, for his own safety and everyone else. I just couldn't bring myself to admit he was already gone.

That's why I'm taking responsibility for what happened ma'am, and it's why I'm writing you this letter now. The sergeant wasn't wearing nothing but his skin when the midnight shift caught him sneaking around the base. I know for a fact that neither of the soldiers fired a shot before they were both dead, without even a chance to set the alarm.

There's a lot of different accounts after that ma'am. Some say he had fur growing down his sides and a mouth like the inside of a butcher's shop. Others think he was high on amphetamines or something, so much that he didn't feel no pain—not even remorse for the men he killed.

All I can tell you with certainty is what I saw with my own two eyes. That was the sergeant burying his head in a man's chest cavity like a starved dog. And when everything was all over, seven body bags were stacked against the far fence, his being one of them.

One in the head, one in the chest, two to make sure. I guess on that count the army told the truth. Just what the sergeant ordered. But I was a damn fool for not listening to him sooner, and there's six fine ladies who are going to have a man in uniform knock on their door holding a flag, just like how it happened to you.

What they didn't tell you though—what they didn't want to tell anyone, but I damn near forced it out of them—was that the sergeant was cold long before I shot him down. 8-10 days, that was their best guess, putting the actual death closer to the 13th. Nobody knows how your husband walked away from that, and it's my theory that he never did.

## Ugly Little Liars

Everyone I know is an ugly little liar. I can see it carved into their skin, open wounds gaping and sucking endlessly at the empty air. I can see it in their grotesquely swinging club foot, or the jutting disfigurement of their face. If they could see each other's ugliness, they would never leer and grin at each other the way they do. They'd never even leave the house, too ashamed of the truth of their soul that only I can see.

I used to be frightened of everyone when I was little. I thought I was the only boy in a world of monsters. Then came the day when I was in pre-school when my teacher (bulbous nose like an overripe pimple and sticky yellow pools for eyes) asked me if I'd taken Sally's pudding cup. I looked straight into that tremulous pimple and swore up and down that I didn't even like pudding. My hand itched all the while, the sensation mounting to an intense burning by the time I'd finished. I started to cry, so the teacher decided I was telling the truth and moved on.

I did lie though. The scar on my hand is proof of that. It looks like someone took a red-hot knife and twisted it in the flesh between my thumb and index finger. I tried to show the teacher, but even with a magnifying glass she couldn't see anything there. Neither could my mom. It didn't take me long to learn it was better not to talk about it at all. I don't know what makes me different, but I can tell you with certainty that I learned quickly not to lie.

Most children are pretty clean. Teenagers are generally the messiest, because their wounds are freshest. By the time they reach their 20s and 30s, most of that is just a latticework of old scars, dried and hardened to show their dishonesty is mostly left behind.

Of course there are the outliers too. The perfect skin of an angel drifting through a crowd. I like to watch them when they don't know I'm looking, as if their purity somehow redeems the rest of the filth they've submerged themselves in. On the other side there are the true monsters—the ones who don't even look human anymore. The bigger the lie, the bigger the mutation. I always keep my distance from those when I can help it, as much to avoid getting nauseous as for my own safety.

There's one particular instance I'd like to draw attention to though. I don't often see fully grown men with such profuse, dripping wounds. It wasn't the milky pus dripping from his eyes that bothered me most though, or even the blood which spilled from his suit pants to leave glistening pools wherever he walked. He was the first person I've ever seen with a second head, the second "neck" bridging off the first, composed of nothing more than a network of unconcealed veins and arteries. The second head looked much like the first, even wearing the same heavy horn-rimmed glasses, although the second face never smiled—stark contrast to the perfect teeth of the perpetual grin beside it.

I was just finishing a delivery to the hospital when I spotted him exiting the building. (Great job, delivery driver. Not much chance for people to lie when you're only asking their name). Ordinarily I'd just cross the street to avoid the ghastly figure, but his singular deformity made me stop and pause. The second head was staring right at me, almost as if it knew I could see it. The blank face betrayed nothing however, and I was about to get in my truck when the two heads spoke in unison.

"Come along, hurry now. Before anyone sees you leave!"

A half-dozen colorful children paraded from the hospital, close on his heels. They looked like they're dressed for a Mardi gras or something—decorative hats, scarves, rainbow beads and flamboyant masks. The misshapen man made a show of looking left and right as though playing a game, and all the children played right along, some even tip-toeing as he led them toward his black SUV.

"That's it, everyone inside. I'll keep you safe, don't worry about a thing."

A hole opened in the forehead of the original before my eyes. An inaudible gunshot which pulverized the skin and left a crack in the exposed skull beneath. I stood in shock for several seconds—several seconds too long. The SUV was already on the road by the time I got behind my wheel. It was none of my business, right? I'm glad I didn't say that out loud, because of course that was a lie. I might be the only one to know who that man was inside, so of course it was my obligation to follow.

I laughed at myself for the first few minutes in pursuit. I was being paranoid. There's a perfectly reasonable explanation for this. Then the SUV took a sharp turn onto a dirt road, and suddenly I wasn't so sure anymore.

The crumbling farmhouse they pulled up to was another red flag. High chain-link fences surrounded the property—the only new thing in the place. Two of the upstairs windows were boarded up, and the whole property stank like a corpse. I didn't want to raise suspicion, so I parked a ways back along the dirt road. I watched as the man parked inside the chain fence, locked it behind him, and then began to herd the children around the back of the house. I snuck forward through the dry reeds, keeping low and trying to get close enough to catch another lie.

"What's back there?" one of the older girls asked, 12 years at most. Old enough to be rightly suspicious.

"You have nothing to be afraid of. I won't let anything hurt you."

Something ruptured on his back underneath his shirt. A thick yellow and red liquid began to stain the inside.

"Come on, tell us!"

"What's your best guess?" both heads replied.

"A birthday party!" one of the younger boys squealed.

"Amazing! That's exactly right."

The stain was rapidly spreading, the wet shirt clinging to lumps like boils beneath.

I didn't waste any more time trying to be a hero. I called the police, and an officer promised to be directly on his way.

I couldn't just sit around and wait though. I had to get closer, but the chain fence had been padlocked behind them. The second head was watching me as the group rounded the corner of the building. I was already pacing along the perimeter to look for a way in.

I heard the first scream. A few seconds later, more shrieks swiftly joined in. I leaped onto the fence, desperately trying to haul myself up. The links were too small to get my foot into though, and I wasn't strong enough to climb with just my fingers. I heard the man's roaring laughter and I redoubled my efforts, this time trying to dig underneath. I managed to bend part of the unsecured links at the bottom, churning through the loose soil to make some room.

I strained my ears, but all the children were drowned out by the loud carnival music which began to play. I vaguely heard another shriek climb its way through the noise. A few moments later and I'd widened the hole enough to wriggle through on my stomach. After that it was just a mad dash around the building, dreading what I might find, and even more terrified of lingering long enough to hear one more child scream.

I almost ran head-first into a donkey who didn't look the least apologetic for being in my way.

"Hey mister can you help me up?"

I stared down at the little boy trying to clamber up the stoic donkey's leg. I hadn't noticed he was bald while his hat had been on.

"This isn't any ordinary petting zoo," the disfigured man was saying, his bloody back to me. "These are magical animals. All you have to do is play with them, and you're going to feel all better."

The second head was looking right at me. It coughed a great mouthful of blood onto the ground. Another shriek—coming from two girls chasing after a pair of chickens. One of their headscarves unraveled as they ran, revealing a second bald head. The stench was even stronger here, although that wasn't too surprising considering all the animals.

"And the plants that grow here—they're magic too," he was saying. "Everyone gets a carrot. They'll make you grow up big and strong."

The second head was coughing so much blood that the skin was visibly dehydrating, shrinking down like a prune.

"I don't want to grow big! I want to stay little!" one of the girls wailed.

"That's okay too. Go ahead and take a bite. You'll never grow up at all."

I waited for the next wound, but it didn't come.

I left the way I came, crawling under the fence. The police car was already parked outside.

"What's the situation? Where's the kidnapper?" the officer asked me.

"I was wrong, I'm sorry. He isn't a monster."

"And the kids?"

"The kids are all going to be fine," I said, already feeling the red-hot burn radiating up my leg.

I used to think lies were the worst thing in the world. That they turned people into monsters. The real monsters—they're just as fine hurting people with the truth as they are with lies. Truth and lies—those are facts. Those we can see and know. Ugliness isn't created by the subject though, it's created by the perceiver in passing that judgment, and I'm the only ugly one here today.

## Message In A Bottle

Last year my wife Janis and I were walking on the beach near our house. We've been married almost twenty years and still hold hands wherever we go, so my first awareness of the bottle was when she started racing ahead and dragging me across the sand.

"Hey Matt! Look at the size of that shell!" she said, simultaneously blocking my view of it as she ran. "Oooh wait. Is that what I think it is?"

"Probably. Assuming you think it's a piece of trash."

Janis let go of my hand to drop to her knees, allowing her skirt to pool around her on the sand. "It's not! It's a treasure!"

"It's probably some homeless man's piss pot."

Anyone who has been married knows exactly what look she gave me. Sort of a 'I've known you long enough that I don't have to pretend you're funny anymore' look.

It really was a beautiful bottle though, despite the erosion and clinging barnacles countless years had stained its surface with. It seemed to be made of some type of ceramic, and the fat base was surrounded in intricate geometrical designs. A leering face was carved into the neck, and a moldy cork with a pungent smell was wedged in the top. Janis wasted no time trying to pry it open with her nails.

"It looks like something that might have been on an old ship," she said, grunting with the effort like an offended farm animal. "How can you not be excited by this?"

I shrugged, looking out to sea. "I like to save all my excitement for the big things. Like weekends and pizza night. Speaking of..."

But she had it opened now. She'd turned it over to shake the contents into her outstretched palm. I expected a rush of water and nothing else, but the thin rolled parchment which slipped out was immaculately preserved. Janis unrolled it and studied the page. The wonder in her face gave way to amusement, then incredulity, her brow continuing to furrow into a bitter anger.

"Well don't leave me hanging! What's it about?" I asked.

"I don't know. Ask your girlfriend." She shoved it against my chest and turned to stomp back toward our house without another word. Bewildered, I opened the letter and read:

*Dear Matthew Davis,*
*I miss you. I need you. How much longer will you make me wait? If your love endures as mine has done, what keeps you away from me?*

"Janis? Honey?" I called, unable to tear my eyes away from the note. The paper—the bottle—even the smooth archaic penmanship, all seeming ancient and untampered with. So what were the chances that it would be addressed to someone else with my name?

My wife was already gone though. She didn't talk to me until late that night when I finally got frustrated enough to snap at her. It was either a coincidence or a practical joke played on me, neither of which were my fault. She wasn't convinced, but at least she opened up about her fear that I was cheating on her. She thought that someone hid the note near my house where I would find it as a romantic gesture. Eventually she came around, but it was an uneasy peace at best.

And it only got harder from there. There was another bottle almost every morning, wedged in the sand at the high tide line as though it had washed up overnight. Sometimes my wife would find them, other times I would. I posted pictures online of a few of the bottles, and the closest match I was able to find were potions used by 17th century alchemists. That seemed like an important clue to me, but all my wife ever focused on were the notes.

*The ocean ends, though we do not see it. The summer fades, though the sun seems unassailable in the sky. Only our love will never grow old. I will not give up on you Matt.*

Or

*How long has it been since we've made love? Do you still remember what it felt like to be with me?*

Janis did her best to play it off as a joke, but I could tell that it was getting to her. She kept making excuses to spend more time alone, and when I pressed her to talk about her jealousy, she'd only treat it like an accusation and get defensive. We'd start fights over nothing, until by the end of the night we were screaming at each other and the next morning not remember why.

One night all it took was me coming home late from work and she was yelling before I even opened the car door. I couldn't take it anymore. I just slammed the car into reverse and left without a word, driving down to the beach to be alone. All the bottles were arriving within about a hundred yard stretch, so I resolved to spend the whole night there until I caught whoever was really leaving them.

Despite living within walking distance of the ocean, I'd never spent any time there after the sun went down. It's amazing how alien a familiar place can feel when the night closes in. The gentle rhythm of the waves seemed less innocent somehow, like I was listening to some colossal creature slowly breathing beside me. The reflection of the moon cast strange shapes into the water, and the cresting of each black wave seemed like it was being distorted by unseen creatures just below the surface.

I maintained my silent vigil until just after midnight when the moon was masked by a thick layer of clouds. My phone had run out of batteries, and it was so dark that I don't think I would have seen someone drop the bottle ten feet away. It would have been completely black if it weren't for the reflection in the ocean. I was getting ready to give up, or at least go back to the car and look for a flashlight, when a thought occurred to me.

If the moon was completely obscured, how was its light still reflecting from the water? The longer I stared, the more sure I was that the light wasn't a reflection at all: the soft luminescence was coming from below the waves. I raced back to my car to check for the light, but I didn't find one. There was a snorkeling mask in the trunk though, so I took that instead and returned to the beach.

I stripped to my underwear and took a step in. The water was ice around my ankles and I almost turned around, but the light was even stronger now and I was drawn like a moth to the flame. By the time the water reached my knees, my feet were so numb that I couldn't even feel them. The light was moving too, twisting and dancing like a living thing, one second drawing close, the next leading me out a little deeper.

Deep breath before the plunge, and I flung myself into the oncoming waves. The cold water closed over my head, but the thrill of my discovery made it feel like liquid energy washing over my body. The light was coming from a woman, shining out through her translucent skin. She was gracefully twirling through the water, her slightest movements propelling her more easily than a practiced stroke. At first she looked like she was swimming, but as I drew closer it quickly became apparent that all the movements were wrong.

Her elbows and knees moved in unnatural, double-jointed arcs. Her neck appeared to have no bones at all, and it turned fluidly to track me independently of her turning body. In her right hand she carried a bottle, just like the kind that had washed up on shore. If my mouth hadn't been full of water, I might have screamed. I also might have said, "Hello Janis," and she might have said, "I've been waiting for you."

I don't know how long I followed her for. She'd let me get almost close enough to touch her before drifting back just out of reach. I was mesmerized by the light and couldn't resist trying to get a better look. If it weren't for the eldritch radiance and the strange movements, I would have sworn it was Janis, and I thought if I could only get close enough to catch her then I'd know for sure.

I was getting tired though, and stretching for the ground and feeling nothing I suddenly realized how deep I had actually swum. I surged to the surface in a panic. The lights of houses on the shore were so far away that they looked like stars. I spun helplessly in place, trying to get a bearing of where I was, when a hand grabbed my ankle. She didn't try to yank me down. The caress was gentle, but as soon as I tried to pull away, her grip tightened. I felt her fingers climbing up my leg, the incessant pressure building like a constricting snake slowly strangling its prey.

I tried to start swimming back toward shore, but the more I fought against her, the harder she pulled. A moment later and I was underwater again, bending double to vainly pry her hands off with my fingers. Water was flowing into my nose and mouth at this point, the bitter salt igniting my throat and flooding me with fresh waves of panic. The more I panicked, the harder I fought, and the harder I fought, the deeper down I was dragged. The last thing I remember was Janis wrapping her whole body around me, her limbs and spine completely encompassing me as though she had no bones at all. I remember the icy waters giving way to numbness, then the suffocating pressure giving way to oblivion.

It was early morning when I woke on my back on the beach. There was a bottle still clutched in my hands.

*Can you forgive me?* it read. *I forgive you. As long as you visit me every year, I can wait a little longer for you to be mine again.*

Even when I went home, it didn't feel like home anymore. I found Janis' body lying in bed with nothing but an empty bottle of Jack Daniels and two empty containers of sleeping pills. I was sick of notes, but there was one left for me to read on the night-table.

## Sleepless Nights

I saw you with her in the water, and I'll never forgive you.

It's been a year since my wife died. Maybe when I go back down to the water to visit her again, she'll finally understand.

It's only her that I've ever loved.

## Illuminating The Dark Web

### July 1st, 2018

A face is staring into the camera. Sandy hair, mid-twenties, male, somewhat reminiscent of a squirrel in his rabid mannerisms.

"The big day is finally here. This is our first time testing out our new SPYDER bot on the dark web, and we're both pretty excited. We've only got a week left to iron out the bugs before Kevin has to defend his thesis, but I don't anticipate any problems. Kevin is nervous as hell, but the kid is an absolute genius. He's still configuring his TOR network and VPN, so I'm going to catch everyone up who are just joining the stream now.

"Typical web crawlers haven't been able to explore the dark web because they can't index specific inputs like forms or authentication pass-phrases. I'm mostly here for moral support and don't understand it completely, but Kevin's SPYDER bot has machine learning algorithms which have been training the last few weeks to learn a new adaptive method of keyword selection.

"You hear that derisive snort at my oversimplification? Yeah that's Kevin. Say hello Kevin!" The streamer looks off camera.

Off camera voice: "Shut up Brian."

"Whatever, fuck you too, man. Based on the training results, we should be able to index a couple thousand pages a day. Google only reaches 16 percent of all available websites, so that means it's going to take us approximately... forever to get through it all with our current computing power. This is just a proof of concept though. All we're using at the moment is Kevin's old laptop that his dog Crinkles practically smashed. The power chord was stretched across the room and this little bulldog comes barreling right through—"

Indistinct grunt off camera.

"Hold on, it looks like we're good to go. If all goes well, then in a couple of months you're going to start reading about how the dark web ceased to exist because of our little SPYDER. I'm going to end the stream now to let it get started, but join us again tomorrow to explore all the cool stuff we found!"

### July 3rd, 2018

The sandy haired man is back. There are bags under his eyes, but he's as enthusiastic as ever.

"Hey guys, it's me again. Sorry for the delay, but we hit an unexpected bump. SPYDER was doing great and had already logged a few hundred sites when it abruptly stopped with this weird error. It keeps telling us that it has already indexed everything. Kevin is able to manually direct it to keep finding new sites, but as soon as its automated it just says it's finished again.

"Kevin is practically ripping his hair out, but it's not like this has been a complete waste of time. We did discover a brand new, never-before-seen color that I'm pretty sure didn't used to exist. All Kevin had to do was put on a white t-shirt a week ago, then eat nothing but BBQ chicken wings and sweat out the sauce."

The camera starts to pan to the left. An unseen hand shoves it back into place.

"Anyway," Brian rambles, "it looks like we might still be awhile, so—"

Off Camera Voice: "Got it. I don't understand it, but I've got it."

"Well whip me red and call me apple sauce, because it looks like we're back in business."

Off Camera Voice: "What? That's not a saying. Nobody says that."

"Kevin Kevin Kevin, you have GOT to get out more. People are saying that like ALL the time. So what was the holdup?"

Off Camera Voice: "It's all linked. Look at this—a drug marketplace, an anime-forum, a counterfeit producer, some dungeon-porn—"

"You have my attention."

Off Camera Voice: "It's all referencing the same destination. SPYDER stops indexing because it thinks the whole dark web is this one site. I'm going to try to get in..."

"That relates to a joke I know. So a drug lord, a weebu, a conman, and a pornstar all walk into a bar..."

Off Camera Voice: "This isn't a real joke. Just shut up, I'm trying to concentrate—"

"—and the barman says, 'what are you guys doing together?' So the drug lord says—"

Off Camera Voice: "They've all got something to hide."

"Even the pornstar?"

Off Camera Voice: "It's gotta be a blackmail thing. These guys must be tunneling into other websites to get info or hold them ransom. But there's no way they can be everywhere. Every single site SPYDER finds... shit. Shit-mother-fucking-bitch-sticks."

"Oh like that's a real saying."

Off Camera Voice: "They're on my computer. I have no idea how they traced SPYDER back, but the mouse is moving on its own. It's typing an address into TOR..."

"What are you doing?"

## Sleepless Nights

Off Camera Voice: "Popping out the battery. The power button isn't working."

"No don't!" The streamer dives off camera. Bumping noises.

Off Camera Voice: "Dude give that back!"

The streamer returns in front of the camera holding a battered old laptop. "Nah man, this is what the people are here to see! Let's find out where these hackers are trying to take us."

"I swear to God, Brian." An overweight torpedo wearing a blotchy shirt of unclassifiable color hurtles across the screen. The streamer's chair tips over, and both men go down. The laptop is left in front of the camera where a long line of seemingly random letters and symbols are typing themselves into the address bar of a TOR browser.

Indistinct muffled swearing.

The website loads. A countdown timer starting at fifteen minutes begins to tick down. Kevin and Brian stick their heads up over the desk in unison to stare at it.

"At least shut that damn camera off," Kevin says.

"Only if you'll let it countdown so we can see what happens," Brian replies, swatting away Kevin's hand which stretches for the laptop.

"God, you're such an asshole. Whatever, fine, just shut it off."

The sandy man begins to wave, but the screen cuts off halfway through.

When the stream returns, the timer reads 15 seconds. The angle is weird, as if the camera is in his lap hidden beneath the desk. The looming Kevin is pacing and muttering to himself in the corner of the screen. Brian surreptitiously leans over the camera and gives a thumbs up, mouthing the letters OMG. The timer hits 0 and stays there.

A dog starts barking somewhere in the distance.

"Are you happy now?" Kevin grunts. "Give it back, okay?"

There's a knock on the door. A single knock—loud and deliberate. The barking intensifies, snarling, growling, all hell breaking loose in its little world.

"Not really," Kevin whispers.

A second knock. Then a third, each about three seconds apart.

"You get it." Both men say at nearly the same instant. They stare at each other until the next knock.

"This is your fault!" Kevin wheezes in a voice halfway between a whisper and a shout.

"Yeah, yeah," he replies. He approaches the door, the camera angle still at waist height. Then in a louder voice: "Who is it?"

"Are you still recording?" Kevin hisses. "Unbelievable."

The screen is filled by the door as Kevin gets closer. He's right up against it, so he's probably looking through the peek-hole. CRASH—a sound loud enough to max out the speaker volume. The door explodes inward in a wave of splinters.

The screen shakes erratically, and there's nothing but splinters and lances of light and screaming.

A gray-skinned hand streaks across the camera. If you freeze the frame, you'll notice that the skin looks more like coarse cloth, and that there is stitching running up and down the fingers.

The stream cuts off.

## *July 10th, 2018*

Brian has turned the stream back on. His face seems paler. His skin is breaking out, and his hair hangs in greasy strings around his face. He's sitting at a bare table in a concrete room. The lights are dim, but there's a large man standing in the back of his room. His hands are folded motionlessly in front of him.

"Um, yeah, hi guys. This might be... my last broadcast for a while." He glances back at the figure in the corner, but there's no movement. Back to the camera: "Kevin's okay. I mean, he's different, but he's okay." He glances back to the corner of the room, but the figure still hasn't budged. Brian's shadow shifts with his movement, and for a moment the stitched cloth/skin of the person in the corner is visible running all the way up his arm.

"I guess they had something like **SPYDER**. They were only tunneling into websites on the dark web, anyway. I guess those kinds of people could disappear without as many questions being asked. They wanted my followers to know though..."

Brian swallows. He looks behind again. Then a sudden burst of movement—grabbing the camera and dragging it up to his face. "Close your browser now. Shut off your computer."

The figure in the back has started to move. Great, lumbering steps, charging forward.

Brian's words are a breathy rush. "It only takes fifteen minutes for them to find you once they've established a connection."

The cloth hands seize Brian from behind and drag him off camera.

"Don't do this Kevin!" He shouts. "How long has your browser been open already? Just shut the damn thing off!"

There's a heavy THUD. A heavyset face appears in front of the camera for a moment. The human eyes look strange embedded within the cloth. Stitches run down either side of the face along the jawline. The cloth might just be sewn to the skin, but it fits so closely to the anatomy of Kevin's face that it looks more like the cloth has replaced it.

The stream cuts to black, replaced by the last few seconds of a depleting timer.

## Me, Myself, And I Play Games Together

We all have the same God, and his name is chance. And we're all praying every second of our lives.

If only I had jumped a little higher when skateboarding, then I wouldn't have clipped the barrier and hurt my ankle. If only I hadn't hurt my ankle, then I would have been on the soccer team with my brother and sister. If only I hadn't stayed home instead of going to watch them practice. Then all three of us would have died driving home one Tuesday evening, and I wouldn't have to sit wondering why I'm still here.

Were we close? Triplets have that tendency, yes. We were practically identical, enough so that dad couldn't even tell which of us was the girl when our hair was covered. We were each other's shadows for twelve years, sharing clothes and toys and doing almost everything together until the day I learned to do everything alone.

Nelson, aka Nelly, was the smart one. My sister and I would take credit for his grades as if they were proof of our identical genius, even though we never did as well. Teresa was a gentle soul who was most easily identified as the one with the cat on her lap. Now the cat sits with me, always mewing softly to echo the empty longing we both feel.

My mother survived the collision with the drunk driver, but she hasn't been the same since. Sometimes she'll call me by the wrong name, not realizing her mistake until halfway through the conversation when she'll suddenly freeze and fall quiet. Then she'll close off and become guarded, looking at me as if I was a stranger.

One such occasion happened a little over a week after the accident. I was passing through the living room to the kitchen when Mom called out to Nelly, asking for a glass of water on his way back. I didn't correct her, but Nelly did.

"I'm busy, ask Teresa," he said. He said it with my mouth, not having one of his own anymore.

That snapped mom back into awareness. She realized her mistake at once and the hoarse strain in her voice returned.

"I'm so sorry," she said. "I know you aren't Nelly. It's just —"

"I am too Nelly. I'm just busy." I didn't mean to say the words. I certainly didn't think them before they left my mouth. But neither did I choose to turn around and head back upstairs even though that's exactly what I did.

It was surreal to watch my legs move on their own, almost as if I was sleepwalking through a familiar dream. The cat rubbed against my legs at the base of the stairs, and I automatically reached down to pet it, marveling at her unusual affection.

"Whose a kitty kitty kitty? You're a kitty kitty kitty!"

It's not the type of thing I'd normally say, but then again, I wasn't the one saying it. That was Teresa, and by the way the cat sat down on my feet and rolled onto her back to be scratched, I knew the cat understood that too.

I raced up the rest of the stairs and slammed the door behind me. I couldn't understand what just happened, and I needed to be alone to clear my head. But I wasn't alone at all, because Nelly and Teresa were still with me.

Nelly thought it was tremendously funny how furiously I gasped for air. I know because I could hear him laughing as clear as if I was wearing headphones. The cat began to meow outside the closed door, and Teresa wanted me to open it and let her in. I'd already begun to turn the doorknob before I realized what was happening and forced myself to stop.

"It's no fair if you don't let us have a turn too," Teresa scolded. "I would have let you if it had been the other way around."

"We'll take turns," Nelly offered. "We can each do every third day, or if you'd rather, we can break it up hour by hour."

"As long as you don't try to make me waste my turn on sleeping," Teresa said. "Eww, does that mean you two are going to make us kiss girls and stuff? 'Cause I wouldn't make you kiss a boy."

The knock on the door made me jump. I still hadn't caught my breath—if anything I was breathing harder than when I'd been running up the stairs.

"Do you want to talk, or…?" My dad's voice trailed off from the other side.

But Nelly and Teresa hadn't stopped their chatter inside my head. They were having a heated debate about what to do about sharing boyfriends and girlfriends, and with dad talking through the door, I couldn't make sense of them. I could tell that dad was worried though, because he kept trying to push the door open. Nelly and Teresa kept getting louder and louder, talking over each other until they were almost shouting and—

"We're busy!" I screamed to be heard over the din.

The pressure on the other side of the door vanished. Nelly and Teresa went quiet. There was a long pause before Dad said, "Okay, yeah. Sure. Just know that we love you very much and…" Pause. "… and things are going to get easier as time goes on."

But he was wrong. Things got much, much harder soon after.

Laying awake that night, we all came to the conclusion that it would be best not tell anyone there were three of us. We agreed to take turns by the day, on the condition that we could overrule big decisions by a two-to-one vote. Of course Teresa protested saying the boys would team up against her, but she was quickly overruled by Nelly and I and so the rule stood.

Besides, we quickly realized that any two of us could quickly overpower the third, rule or no rule. If Nelly wanted to sneak downstairs and eat a bowl of ice-cream, I could stop him as soon as I realized what was happening. But if Teresa decided she would like some ice-cream too, then there was nothing I could do to prevent the two of them from lurching my body out of bed and crawling downstairs through the darkness.

The other unsettling realization was that while I could stop one of them from taking control, I could only do so with a conscious effort. In such cases my muscles would lock up as if performing a static exercise until gradually one conceded, or the third broke the tie. If one of them moved suddenly without announcing their intentions however, then I wouldn't realize what was happening until I had already watched myself move.

This arrangement came with a number of advantages. We unanimously agreed to let Nelly take our tests for us, and we gave him a little extra time so he could study and do our homework too. I was also able to join the soccer team as soon as my ankle was strong again, and my new teammates were amazed to see that I already knew all the drills and shots without having practiced a day in my life.

It all ran quite smoothly until the day at soccer practice when one of my teammates pulled us aside and pointed to the bleachers. They were mostly empty except for a scattering of parents huddled together on the front row.

"Isn't that Mr. Thrope? Morgan's dad?" my teammate asked, gesturing to a rather fat man with a baseball cap pulled low over his face.

"Who is Morgan?" I asked. I would usually hear Nelly and Teresa whispering to each other even when it wasn't their turn, but they were both completely silent now.

"Donno, he's in an earlier grade," my teammate said. "But his mom is the one who hit your mom's car, right? I think she's in jail now."

"What's he doing here if his kid doesn't play?" I asked.

The coach blew the whistle though, and we all had to jog back to our positions. I spent the next half-hour making a mess out of every shot because Nelly and Teresa weren't helping out. It's the quietest they'd been since they first spoke.

I covered by pretending that my ankle was hurting again and sat down to rest. Mr. Thrope immediately got up and started walking toward me. I tried to leave, but found my muscles stiffen and lock me in place. My brother and sister still weren't saying a word. I waited frozen as the man stepped into the second row and sat directly behind me.

"Hey kid. You were looking good out there," the man said.

"No I wasn't," I replied.

"Maybe, doesn't mater. We all have those days where things don't go as planned, eh?"

I swung my feet beneath me and kept my eyes on the field.

"We all got some days we wish we could take back," the man continued, his voice unsteady.

"It wasn't your fault," Teresa spoke through me, turning us to face him.

"I know I know…" He'd removed his hat and was crumpling it with his hands. His face was twisted and quivering. "It's not about whose fault it is. I'm just sorry it happened, that's all."

"How old is Morgan?" Nelly asked.

"He's ten. Going to be eleven next month."

"Do you love him?" Teresa followed seamlessly.

"'Course I do. And I love his mom too, even though—"

"And you'll miss him when he's gone?" Nelly prompted.

The man furrowed his brow and said nothing. I tried to turn back to watch the field, but Nelly and Teresa were both pulling the other way. I must have looked quite odd inching closer to the man in short, jerking motions.

"What's sorry supposed to do?" Teresa asked. "If you didn't do it, then you can't apologize. If it didn't happen to you, then you can't sympathize."

"You're not really sorry," Nelly added. "Not yet."

The man gave us a queer look and put his hat back on. "I didn't have to come here, but I did. I'm trying to be good to you."

"I'm not the one you should be worried about," I said. I felt cool and dangerous watching the color drain from his face. Then his scowl returned, and he walked away, muttering something that sounded like 'psycho' under his breath.

I didn't feel nearly so impressive after he'd gone. I was scared.

"Morgan really has nothing to do with it," I told my siblings.

"Neither did we," Teresa said. "Neither do you." I'd never heard her voice so low and angry.

"I veto it. I won't let you hurt him—" I said.

"Two against one," Nelly cut in. Teresa said nothing to disagree.

---

WHEN THE LUNCH bell rang the next day, I didn't run for the door like I usually do. I stayed seated in my class until all the other kids had gone. I felt my mouth open and heard the words come out as though in a dream.

"Is Morgan in your next class?"

Mrs. Wilmore nodded, not looking up from the papers on her desk.

"He told me to tell you that he won't be making it today. He's got a doctor's appointment."

My teacher looked at me from over her glasses. "Tell him to bring a note."

"Yes ma'am," Teresa said. "I think it's pretty serious though. He might not be back for a while."

Mrs. Wilmore thanked me and went back to her work. I was slow to leave the room, trembling with each step as I fought against the irresistible betrayal of my limbs.

"I'll warn her. I'll warn him—I'll tell on you, and someone will stop you," I said internally.

"Go ahead and try," Nelly replied cooly.

"Mrs—"

My throat might as well have turned to stone. I couldn't even swallow. I tried to turn around, but my progress from of the room was relentless.

"It won't do any good to tell," Teresa told me soothingly. "They'll think you did it. And they'll punish you."

We'd already spotted Morgan in the lunch room. He was waiting in line for pizza at the counter.

"I don't care. This isn't right. Teresa, I know you wouldn't—"

"Shut up. Seriously, just shut up," Nelly interrupted.

My hand was reaching out to Morgan. He was a small boy, even considering that he was younger. I could clearly feel the bones in his shoulder where I lay my hand.

"Your dad is waiting for you outside," Nelly said out loud. "He said it's about your mom, and that you should hurry."

Morgan turned around and looked at me with eyes that looked too large on his small angular face. I don't know which bothered me more: that he was scared, or that I could feel Nelly and Teresa loving it.

Morgan willingly left his place in line and followed me through the empty hall. "Not that way," Nelly said. "He's waiting behind the school."

One of my hands was still on Morgan's shoulder, steering him out of the building. The other was clenched in my pocket. It was holding something smooth and cold and hard. I don't know what it was, but I'm sure I wasn't the one to put it there.

I couldn't force words through my lips, but I could still plead with the others inside. "Don't you think he's been through enough? With his mom in jail—"

"Shut up!" Nelly screamed internally. "You don't know anything. You don't know what it feels like to die. You don't know where we went, or how hard it was for us to come back. You don't even know how much it hurts watching everyone move on like we never even existed."

Morgan glanced at me and my face smiled back, showing no sign of the internal conflict. He tried to shrug my hand off, but my grip tightened as we neared the exit.

"We need this," Teresa agreed solemnly. "You wouldn't understand."

"This isn't you," I begged as we stealthily crossed the carpet. "I know you'd never hurt a fly—"

"The one you know died," Teresa replied sternly. "You don't know us anymore."

"Where is he?" Morgan asked as we stepped outside.

"Funny, I bet that's what he'll say too. When he comes to pick you up after school," Nelly said.

My hand withdrew from my pocket, the hard object still clutched inside. I don't know how they got a butterfly knife. Morgan was even more surprised.

I wish I could tell you that we were able to talk through it. That I made them understand that one death does not pay for another. I wish I could have gone all the way back to that day I was skateboarding and never hurt my ankle in the first place. Then all three of us would have died, and Morgan would have still been alive.

When my brother and sister died, I thought that loneliness was the worst feeling in the world. I'd give anything to feel the peace of loneliness again, but I don't think I ever will. Nelly and Teresa are still giving me turns though, and I'm using mine to write this.

I'm sorry Morgan.

I'm sorry Mr. Thrope.

I forgive you Mrs. Thrope.

Nelly and Teresa are getting loud again, and my fingers are having trouble typing. I guess I'll be spending my next turn writing another apology to the next ones we hurt.

## Putin Doesn't Like My Father

None of my friends will listen to me anymore, and I don't know who else to tell. I don't have any ghost sightings to report, and there aren't any monsters under my bed, but I'm not afraid of that sort of thing. I'm afraid of what's happening to my family, and even worse, that everyone sees it happening but does nothing. It feels like drowning at a pool party, struggling and shouting and begging while all my friends silently watch.

It started a year ago with Dad's YouTube channel. He used to work as an aide for a political leader (A.N.), but then the campaign started traveling and Dad decided not to move. My mom is a teacher, and she tried to get him a job at her school, but he wouldn't have it.

"Мертвые не сражаются. Я мертв?" he used to say. Dead men don't fight. Am I already dead?

Papa is not the kind of man you can argue with. His voice is low and measured, rumbling out of his barrel chest like he's patiently explaining some irrefutable law of the universe to a child who isn't expected to understand. He always seems exhausted, grunting and groaning when he has to stand up or do anything, but you only have to see his eyes to know there's a bottomless reserve of spirit that could march him through an endless winter night.

He kept contact with all his political friends, and whenever they'd uncovered corruption or scandal, they'd tell my father. They were too afraid to mention it

## Sleepless Nights

over the phone, not daring to speak above a whisper even in person. I'd sit at the top of the stairs out of sight while they talked though, and all those things they were too afraid to even think out loud would be spoken clearly on papa's show.

First came the letter. Polite, formal, from the Ministry of Communications. I'd picked up the mail and opened it because I was impressed by the official government stamp. I thought Dad had won some kind of award for his show. He didn't smile often, and I wanted to be the one who made it happen.

Instead, I found a generic letter informing papa that his channel was in violation of slander laws and needed to be closed. It thanked him for his "attempt at public service", even listing a variety of other "safe" topics that he could talk about instead. That same night, after everyone but papa had gone to sleep, we were woken by a splintering-crashing sound. We found papa standing in the living room holding a brick, staring out our broken window, his bathrobe fluttering in the freezing wind like some kind of battle flag. Mom was horrified, but papa was grinning from ear-to-ear.

"Они только пытаются заткнуть вас, если вам что-то стоит сказать." They only try to shut you up if you have something worth saying.

It was another four months before the next incident. My older brother was expelled from the University. They told him that they'd received multiple anonymous reports about his disorderly and rebellious behavior, but he swore up and down that he never did anything. We all thought that he was covering up something until that night when a second brick came through our window. The message couldn't have been clearer, but neither could papa's response.

His influence was expanding. He had several investigators reporting to him at all hours of the day and night. Over 10,000 subscribers. Every day a new video, a voice of reason cutting through the miles of red tape and political side-talk. Turning on the TV or reading the newspaper, it was impossible to tell what was real. Papa says uncertainty is a seed which grows into fear. That must be true, because I didn't know what was going to happen next, and I was afraid all the time.

Mom lost her teaching job shortly after. The school said that parents were concerned she wasn't sticking to the syllabus, instead feeding her own propaganda into the class. No one had ever complained to mom about it, and she said she'd never so much as mentioned politics (she taught math). She tried to get an appeal with the board, but after the meeting there were tears in her eyes and she wouldn't say a word about what happened. She'd taught at that school for the last 21 years. There wasn't another brick that night, but there didn't need to be. In the morning I found her teaching award from the governor in the trash, along with a carefully folded Russian flag.

Papa didn't stop, and no one asked him to. Not even when he started receiving death threats in the mail. He was arrested twice, first taking him at the grocery store for spreading libel. He was only gone a few days that time, but when he came back, he was more insistent than ever. He was working on something big. Something that would change Russia—change the world, even. Wherever someone in power feared what the truth could do to him, things would change.

They didn't give him the chance though. The second arrest happened at our house with someone knocking on the door. They didn't even bother to tell him why he was being arrested that time, but he didn't resist. That made me angry. Someone coming into our house and dragging him away from his family—he always told me he was a fighter. The silent, willing man who they marched into the night didn't look like a fighter to me.

The harassment only got worse while he was gone. Friends and neighbors who had known us for years stopped talking to us, turning the other way when we said hello. People at school treated me like I had an infectious disease. There was a rumor going around that my father was an anarchist. I heard everything—about his treason, his hatred for Russia, even accounts of how he raped and killed someone.

Defending him only made it worse for me, but I couldn't help it. I hit a boy in the mouth when he kept telling me I had to go to the station and suck someone's cock to get papa out. I wasn't even sure I wanted papa to be released. That's what I was thinking sitting outside the principal's office, waiting to be expelled like my brother was. I wanted papa to disappear—to have never existed at all. I was so angry that I almost stormed off right then, but I'm glad I didn't because I was able to hear what the principal was saying behind his door.

He was talking about my father. The person he spoke with sounded like he was giving the principal orders.

"Уничтожьте его семью," he said. Destroy his family.

Then the man starting listing things off, as calm and clear as though he was ordering food at a drive-through.

"Скажите ученикам, что его сыновья тоже предатели." Tell the students his sons are traitors too.

"Его дом должен быть сожжен." His house must be burned.

"Его жена должна быть изнасилована." His wife must be raped.

All done before next week when papa was to be released. The principal didn't even hesitate.

"Будет сделано," he replied. It will be done.

I didn't wait for the door to open. I ran home—7 miles, but I didn't stop once. I wasn't even angry anymore. I understand how pointless it is being angry at something that big and powerful. It would be like cursing the ocean for its waves. I also understand why papa was so compliant with being arrested. You can't fight something like that. It was fear, not anger, which kept me moving—desperately trying to think how I could explain this to Mom, and where we could sleep tonight where they wouldn't find us.

That fear—that numbing, helpless, lonely fear—was all I had to keep me company while I ran. And when the pain in my side came like a knife between my ribs and my legs trembled as I lifted them from the concrete—that fear was stronger. I just kept marveling at how powerful a thing fear can be—stronger than pain, or loyalty, or even human empathy. I thought it must be the strongest force there is in the world, and that must be why the government uses it to control us.

The fear that right and wrong don't matter when you are one and they are many. But it's a ridiculous fear, because the cowering people are the ones who are many. And it seems to me the government must know that too; they only try to frighten us because they are frightened of us. They're scared of us not being scared anymore. And how do we stop from being scared?

Papa said uncertainty grows into fear, so we must leave no doubt. I warned my mom and brother, but neither of them have left yet. They're helping me sort through papa's notes and recordings. We're going to find what he was working on when they took him. We're going to find what they were so afraid of, and we're going to release it to the world.

There's no uncertainty about it anymore. I'm not afraid, even though I know I will be arrested or killed for this. And when the word gets out that uncertainty will be gone from the people too. We are many and they are one. And it is their turn to be afraid.

## The Taking Tree

My earliest memory of Grandma Elias was a Sunday morning at her house. The eggs were firm and golden and the hash-browns were burned, just like they were supposed to be. Everything at Grandma's house was exactly right, all the way from the Christmas lights which never came down to her little corgi Muffins who followed her like a shadow. It was time for church, but I didn't want to leave.

"How come Grandma doesn't have to go to church?" I asked.

"She already knows all that stuff," my mother said, forcing me into a jacket like meat through a grinder. "You still have to learn though."

Grandma stuck out her tongue and waggled it about behind mom's back. I wasn't amused. It wasn't fair.

"Don't you want to visit God?" I asked Grandma.

"God doesn't live in a church, silly," Grandma Elias said. "He lives in that crab-apple tree in my backyard. Would you like to meet him?"

"Yes! Can we mom? Instead of church?"

I recognized mom's expression from the time she accidentally drank sour milk. "Absolutely not. Please don't joke about that kind of stuff, Elias. You know how impressionable they can be."

Grandma shrugged and winked. "I was counting on it. Another time then."

She didn't mention it again though, and I forgot all about the God in her apple tree. The subject didn't come up again until years later when I was in the 10th grade. Mom was in the hospital to remove some ovarian cyst, and I'd been left at Grandma's for a few days while she recovered. Every morning I'd wake up to find Grandma kneeling beside her apple tree, digging around its roots. I assumed she was just pulling weeds or something until I caught her burying a row of sealed Tupperware filled with leftovers.

"Is that for God?" I asked, suddenly remembering what she'd said when I was young.

"Yes. I wanted to thank him for looking after your mother."

"So it's like a prayer?"

She shook her head. "Is that what they teach you in that dusty old Sunday school? No, you must never ask God and for anything. You must only thank him for what he has already done."

I watched as she carefully patted the soil into place.

"Is he going to eat it?" I asked.

"What are you asking me for?" She moved to put her hand on the tree and invited me to do the same. I did so without thinking, but jerked away immediately. The bark was warm and pliable like rough skin. My fingers were still tingling, almost vibrating as though a whisper, too deep to decipher, still echoed through my body.

Grandma Elias just laughed and turned to go inside. Somehow I didn't feel like staying there alone.

Mom was released from the hospital shortly after, but a few days later she started getting sharp pains and had to go back in. No-one told me what was going on, but that alone made me know it wasn't good. I made a point of setting my alarm for the crack of dawn so I could watch Grandma digging around the roots of her tree. I waited until she left to investigate and see if there were any treats I could steal.

The first thing I uncovered were the Tupperware. They were all empty. Absolutely clean, like they'd gone through the dishwasher. I figure she must have traded them out for her latest donation, so I kept digging into the newly disturbed earth. The soil was damp here, but I kept going until I uncovered a patch of golden fur. Muffin was buried under the tree.

I was trembling from head to foot while I slowly covered up the little body again. It wasn't just the horror of what I found either; I could feel the vibrations emanating from the tree. The bark was so hot to the touch that it almost scalded me, but I forced my hand to remain to feel the hum of the presence. Not quite a sound, not quite a thought, but something suspended between flooded my senses.

I wasn't myself in that instant. I was looking through Grandma's eyes as she sat on her bed, hands clasped and shaking. I was in a hospital room watching a daytime soap opera on the television in the corner of the room. I was a hundred people doing a hundred things, thinking a hundred thoughts, dreading a hundred futures, and then it was gone. It was just me standing before the tree, panting for breath, staring at my swollen red fingertips that still stung from where they'd touched the rough skin.

I was scared and confused, but I didn't speak of it to anyone. Grandma didn't say a word about why Muffin wasn't in the yard anymore, and I didn't ask. She seemed to be in a better mood afterward though, singing or whistling to herself wherever she went. Then a few hours later we got a call from the hospital—that it had been a false alarm and that mom was already on her way to pick me up. For the first time, I was only too happy to leave Grandma's house.

A couple years later and I'd left my hometown to go to college. I got swept up in the daily dramas of life and didn't look back. Not until I visited again Junior year to help Grandma Elias start to pack up her home. She'd grown too old to look after the place herself, and she'd decided to move into a facility. All the conversations had been light and optimistic as though this would make her life so much easier, so I wasn't prepared for the shock of seeing her again.

The electric wheelchair was the first surprise. My family isn't exactly open about their problems, and nobody had told me that her arthritis was so bad that she couldn't even walk or open doors anymore. Her face was dried and loose, and her eyes were deep and sunken. I looked up the place she was moving into, only to discover it wasn't a retirement home at all: it was a hospice. My mom still kept talking about all the friends Grandma would make there, and Grandma said she was looking forward to the activities and the company. They were living in stubborn denial, and I couldn't take it.

"The only thing I'll miss is my garden and my tree," Grandma said, looking around her old home. "It's not like I can get down on my knees and dig anyway though, so I suppose it's for the best."

Luckily I knew where God lived, and I was sure he'd intervene. A small bribe or offering wasn't going to cut it though. It had been a life for a life when my mother was sick, and I was ready to pay that price again. The more I thought about it, the more sure I was that I could follow through. This wouldn't be a thank you gift though, and I had no intention of being subtle and simply hoping for the best. In other words, I felt that it had to be human, the most valuable thing I could think to offer.

The digging took a lot longer than expected. I came back with a shovel that night. Grandma Elias hadn't moved out yet, but I was comfortable in the familiar darkness and didn't make too much noise. When I finished the hole, I'd go find some drunk coming home from the bar and knock him out. Push him into the hole and cover him up. No one would ever know—not even Grandma.

If Muffin was still here, then he would have set off the alarm by now, but I couldn't even find the little body anymore. I kept at it for a few hours until the hole was a little longer than I was tall. I hopped inside to test its depth and found the earthen walls rose almost to my chest. That should be plenty. I started to climb out again, grabbing one of the roots for support while I pulled myself up. The root was fire, and I let go immediately, reeling backward to nurse my injured hand. I overbalanced and was about to fall, but something lashed out of the darkness to snatch me around a flailing arm.

I stared in dumb shock at the root twined around my arm for several seconds before the burning began to penetrate my long-sleeved shirt. The intensity of the heat was increasing by the second. I scrambled in the opposite direction, trying to hoist myself out of the hole without touching the tree. I barely got two steps before another blast of heat penetrating my ankle and dragged me to the ground. Back up to my knees, but an irresistible weight flattened me back to the ground. The heat of the roots withdrew, but the weight was increasing by the second.

Dirt and rocks were raining around me so hard it felt like a hail storm. The roots were sweeping all the piled earth directly on top of me. I managed to raise myself onto my elbows and knees to create a small air pocket, but I could go no farther. The last of the meager starlight quenched above me, and I was buried alive. I could still hear the muffled sound of the dirt packing in tighter above me for a little while, but it was becoming fainter and more distant by the second. Another sound was replacing it, the same vibrating whispers I'd heard all those years ago.

Part of me was still braced on my hands and knees in the darkness, but I hardly noticed anymore because I was also sitting on a hilltop and staring at the stars with a beautiful girl warm against me. I was sleeping in a bed—a hundred bodies in a hundred beds, all breathing slow and regular. And every passing second made me aware of a hundred new people, experiencing their bodies and hearing their maddening cacophony of thoughts. I was grieving, and celebrating, in ecstasy and agony, all so real that it might as well have been my own body experiencing these things.

It kept going. Faster and faster until the part of me that was buried under the tree was so insignificant that I hardly remembered it. Within moments I must have been every man, woman, and child on the planet, all their experiences mingling into a single omnipresent hum of consciousness. I felt myself being born in ceaseless explosions of sensation, and just as often did I feel myself die, snuffing out entirely. But each coming and going didn't matter, because I could feel the hum everywhere and in everything, eternal and immune from the fluctuations of its composition.

The feeling didn't last. One by one, then in hundreds and thousands at a time, those minds closed to me. My awareness was shrinking again, and my shaking body buried underground and my shallow breaths were becoming more real. Soon I had but one mind, one body, one life, and one desperate urge to not let this slip away like the others. I began to wiggle back and forth, using my small opening to continue displacing dirt above my back. I managed to make enough space to get my feet underneath me, and then the additional power of my legs helped to push upward through the earth. The air was thick and heavy with my own stale breath, but the higher I got, the less densely packed the soil was. My head was growing light, and I was afraid I'd pass out, but my hand broke through the surface and a clean cold gust of air filled my greedy lungs.

Inch by laborious inch, I widened the hole and crawled back onto the surface to lay panting on the ground. I thought I was alone until I heard Grandma Elias' voice only a few feet away.

"Well? Did you get what you asked for?"

I was too weak to do anything but lift my head. She was wearing a bathrobe, sitting in her wheelchair with her wrinkled hands folded demurely in her lap. She seemed as frail and ancient as ever.

"Asking doesn't work, does it?"

I managed to shake my head. I thought she'd be angry or disappointed, but she only smiled.

"When your mother was sick, I did something terrible. I asked God to make her better. She was going to get better anyway, but I didn't know that. I thought that if I gave up a life, then I could protect a life. The tree doesn't stop death though—it gives us something much more valuable than that."

"You're still going to die, aren't you?" I asked, unable to help myself.

"Does that frighten you?" she asked.

I said nothing. I'd felt what it was like to die. A drop of rain in the ocean, gone in an instant but still part of the whole.

"Me neither," she said, "and that is the true gift of the tree."

## Have You Seen This Child?

I don't have any kids, so I can't really imagine what it would be like to have one missing. I do have a half-coyote dog who used to sneak out of the yard all the time though (Colonel Wallace), so I at least have a general idea how desperate and helpless it feels to have part of your life suddenly go missing.

Like grief, it comes in stages.

The denial: I just saw him a moment ago, I'm sure he's around here somewhere.

Anger: it's his own fault, bloody idiot. If he gets run over by a car, then I'm getting a turtle next time.

Bargaining: missing posters. Flyers in local groups. Calling every shelter in a ten-mile radius...

And so on, although I'm not sure any mother will ever fully reach the "acceptance" stage. Once they hit depression, it just loops back to denial and starts all over again. That's the feeling I got from reading the advertisement, anyway.

"Timmy Preston, age 7. Missing two weeks. Last seen in the Jefferson Heights playground. If you have any information on his whereabouts, please contact (818)-***-****. I never turn the lights off anymore in case it helps him find his way home, but the house has never been so dark. I'm not old enough to shake like this. Please have mercy on a grieving mother."

It was the first time I've ever seen a Facebook ad for a missing person, but I guess it makes sense. They allow you to target specific locations, and Jefferson Heights is only a few blocks away from my apartment. Next time Colonel Wallace finds a new angle to dig through my bushes, I might have to try that too.

Was I going to gather a mob and start combing through the city? No. There's too much tragedy in the world to chase down every wrongdoing. But that message really stuck with me, and so did the kid's photo: bright blue eyes, a sweep of blond hair, and a light drizzle of freckles. I took a screenshot on my phone just in case, then forgot all about it.

Until the next day. And the day after. And the one after that. I don't know how much money that lady was dumping into advertising, but that post never seemed to go away. Shit, now there's a sobering thought. The only thing worse than losing a kid would be draining the rest of your resources trying to find someone who couldn't be found. I once read an article about a woman who mortgaged her house to pay a private investigator to track down her daughter. The kid was never found, and the woman was driven to homelessness when she couldn't make the payments. I don't remember exactly what the quote was, but it was something like: "Do I regret it? Of course not. Getting me onto the streets will only make it easier for me to keep looking."

Well I still didn't search for Timmy. Not consciously anyway. I began walking my dog on a different route though—one that circled around Jefferson Heights and the surrounding neighborhoods. I didn't expect to see him, but that image was burned into my mind enough that I'd notice if I did.

I'd notice a blond kid with freckles peeking out over a fence. I'd notice how quickly he disappeared and ran back into the house, like he was afraid of being caught. I stood staring, not quite believing what I saw. An exact match of the screenshot on my phone—I called the number immediately, reporting what I found.

The woman on the other line was hysterical. She thanked me a dozen times. She said that was her ex-husband's house, although he denied ever seeing the boy. She told me she was going to call the police right away, and that I might want to get out of there if I didn't want to get involved.

I'm not ashamed to say I felt like the world's biggest hero for the rest of the day. At least until the evening news when I saw that familiar picture flash once more.

"Timmy Preston, abducted from his legal guardian," the local news reported.

I turned up the volume, half-expecting to hear the woman thank me by name. "Taken from his backyard this afternoon."

I turned off the TV and just stared at the blank screen. I guess I'm still in the denial phase.

## When You Die In A Dream

The wind pummeled me as I dove through the lower atmosphere. My eyes were watering so bad that I couldn't see straight, although I don't know if it would have mattered considering how the landscape blurred from my speed. All I could distinguish was the looming wall of earth growing exponentially as I hurtle closer and closer, needle sized trees growing into a behemoth's grasping claws, until...

Right before impact, I wake up gasping. I've had that dream at least once every few months since I was four.

There are others too. I remember fighting in one of them. Some kind of a street brawl with dozens of swirling bodies dancing to choreographed violence. First I'll be pushing the other combatant back, then he'll push me, back and forth, back and forth. Until I'm about to land the finishing blow and he whips out a gun. I hear the sound, and see the flare of the muzzle, and my whole body tenses for a force it can't resist, but...

Right before impact, I wake up gasping.

So what would happen if I didn't wake up? Would I feel the bullet, like I felt the wind and the swinging blows? Would the dream dissolve into some unspeakable hellscape where I continue to experience the beyond? Or would I never wake up at all?

I finally got my answer thanks to a teenage girl who couldn't wait five minutes to text her friend back. Her left wheel slipped over the double yellow line, and her bumper clipped my car going 45 in the opposite direction. Before I knew what was happening, I suddenly felt the impact absent from my dreams all those years.

It didn't last more than a second. A wave of pressure too intense to be pain washed over my body. My face slammed into the airbag which felt like it was full of sand. All the light in the world constricted into a pinprick, the screeching roar devouring me until only a ringing tingle remained, and then silence.

I was out cold and didn't dream that time. I was pretty disoriented when I woke up in the hospital, but I remember grabbing the arm of a nurse and begging her not to let me fall back asleep.

"I know how it feels to die now!" I told her. Or at least I tried. My words were slurring, and I couldn't be making much sense. A moment later I felt a sting in my arm, and my vision swam.

The next thing I felt was the wind stinging my face and whipping the tears from my eyes. I was far enough up to see the curvature of the earth, but I couldn't appreciate the magnificent sight knowing what was to come. I could picture the impact so clearly now. Part of me knew I was still in the hospital bed, but I was so fixated on the rush that I couldn't convince myself it wasn't real.

This was a hundred times worse than the accident. Everything happened too fast in the car for me to be afraid, but this time I had a few minutes of excruciating anticipation. My stomach was a knot of snakes trying to strangle each other. The air flooding into my lungs was thin this high up, but it came so fast that I felt like I was perpetually caught between breaths.

I wanted to wake up so bad. I screamed the best I could, thrashing around and hoping that the nurse would notice my disturbance. I tried to convince myself that I could fly, but the rush wouldn't stop. I tried to spit, disgusted to feel the saliva dribble down my chin, unaffected by the surrounding torrent. I'm still in bed! This isn't real! But it felt real. And when my body was obliterated on the ground, I just knew that was going to feel real too.

Watching the ground speed toward me was torture. Closing my eyes and bracing for an unpredictable collision was even worse. I had a glimmer of hope when I heard the nurse speaking, her voice distant and muffled from the wind. A last desperate call for help, but I couldn't reach her. The muffled voice grew even fainter as it mingled with the city noises below.

No trees or branches to slow my fall. No water or soft earth to dampen the blow. Just concrete and asphalt for as far as I could see.

The landing was everything I knew it would be. I smashed through the roof of an apartment building, legs first. I felt my bones in my feet pulverizing to dust, but the shock wave was so brutal that I could feel my skeleton rearranging throughout my body. The roof caved in beneath me, and I tumbled through in a hail of broken tiles and splintered debris. There was a brief, horrible moment where my body knew it was dead but my brain hadn't caught up yet, and then...

Right after impact, I wake up gasping.

The clattering of the falling debris was still ringing in my ears, but it was over. Disoriented, I got up and staggered toward the bathroom. Even though I knew it was a dream, it was a relief to feel my intact body responding to my commands. At least it means I walked away from the car accident without too severe injuries...

The car accident. The hospital. But I wasn't in the hospital, where was I? I rubbed my eyes, finally noticing the giant hole in the ceiling of my apartment. And the twisted remains of a corpse on my floor. I almost threw up. Taking a step closer to inspect, I could no longer deny the bile rising in my throat. My dead body was lying in the middle of the room. In the distance, the blare of sirens cemented the absurd scene into reality.

I rushed to the bathroom and hurled in the sink. It took a few moments of heaving and spluttering before I was able to pull away and look into the mirror. I didn't recognize the face staring back.

THUMP THUMP THUMP—pounding on the door. I nearly jumped out of my unfamiliar skin.

"We heard an explosion. Are you okay in there?"

THUMP THUMP THUMP—my heart playing along. This was a dream. I was still in the hospital. I had to wake up. The pounding on the door was getting louder, and I couldn't think straight. I ran to the balcony to get some fresh air, noticing that I was still over a dozen stories in the air. Someone was trying to force the door now, and I didn't have the stomach to stand over my dead body and attempt to explain the macabre situation. I swung my legs over the metal railing, and hesitating only a second, let myself fall again.

This time I'll wake up for sure...

The wind. The snakes in my belly. The scream of onlookers, and the full body immersion of pain. Next I knew, I was gasping for air. People were screaming all around me, so I started screaming too.

I heard a shrill, piercing shriek tear from my lungs. I clapped a hand over my mouth—a shriveled old hand, frail with a road map of bulging veins. I staggered away from the scene on the sidewalk against a stream of people. They're crowding to see the broken body of the poor fool who nose-dived from an apartment balcony a dozen stories up.

THUMP THUMP—my weary heart fluttering as I stared at my reflection in a car window. An old woman was staring back at me, her face distraught and confused. I watched one of her hands raise to her face and felt the leathery skin beneath trembling fingertips. THUMP THUMP THUMP—my heart going faster and faster, the strain of half-filled arteries vainly trying to keep up, then a sharp pain radiating through my chest. A heart attack this time, and I was dying again.

I had no disillusion about it this time. I continued watching my reflection for as long as I could stand until all color faded from my face and the pain in my chest had echoed into an all-encompassing throb. My vision swam, and everything started to slip away...

I've died twice more since writing that. If I'm careful, it seems like I can last a few hours before something gets me. Almost as if it's the will of the universe to track me down and snuff me out. I'm writing this to keep some record of what is happening while I still have a chance.

I think I always used to wake up because my brain had no experience of death to relate to. It's not really the impact waking you up at all, merely the shock of your scrambling brain saying "oh shit, what comes next?"

If you've led an easy life, I don't suppose you have anything to fear. If you've never broken a bone, or suffered a trauma, then the near-death experience is a safety valve that will shield from this revolving nightmare. But if you've suffered exquisitely in life and your mind knows how to retrace that dark path?

Even death won't be an escape.

## Dead Dogs Don't Do Tricks

The best thing about dead dogs is that you don't have to feed them.

The worst? Probably the smell...

That's what mom complains about, anyway. She thinks there's a gas leak under the house; she'd never let me keep Misty if she knew where the smell was really coming from. It was hard for me to keep a straight face when she called the company to complain, but I don't think she noticed my guilt. When mom is angry, she isn't very good with minor details like me.

This all started about two months ago. I wanted a dog. Dad wanted a dog. Mom didn't want dad. So we got a dog and called ourselves a happy family. Misty was a lean greyhound with a white patch on her chest like a plume of lace. I thought she looked like an alien because she was so skinny, but that was part of her charm. She was pretty skittish and didn't like being held, but she could always sense when I was feeling down and would run to plop her head in my lap.

Misty was the magic pill that was supposed to fix my family, and it worked for a while. Whenever anyone raised their voice, Misty would start scampering around or whimpering and the argument fizzled out. It didn't matter which side was right: if you scared Misty while trying to prove your point, then you've already lost the moral high ground.

My parents adapted. They learned to fight in a chilly monotone that was even worse than yelling. Misty could sense the tension in the air too, and I know it made her nervous. I tried telling my parents, but they insisted that they were speaking in ordinary voices and that I was imagining things. What could a twelve-year-old boy possibly understand about grownup matters or animal psychology?

Well here's something I learned: nervous dogs have accidents inside the house. A little damp spot on the carpet, sometimes a poop on the kitchen tile— no big deal, right? Wrong. It was the little extra stress that pushed my parents over the edge. Suddenly Misty took on a new therapeutic role as the household scapegoat.

Monthly bills higher than expected? Yell at the dog for being too expensive.

Dad sleeps in and doesn't have time for his morning walk? Yell at the dog for making a mess.

Family drifting apart? Yell at the dog for preventing a weekend getaway.

"Don't listen to them," I tried to tell Misty. She slept on the foot of my bed, and I could feel her trembling as my parent's voices filtered through the wall. "They're all bark and no bite. You'd understand if you were human like me."

The louder they got, the more she whined. Then doors started slamming, and the whine turned into a long howl. Mom ripped open my bedroom door and started screaming at us—Dad was in the living room dragging a suitcase toward the front door.

"Shut that thing up!" she yelled. "No wonder we're stressed, listening to that damn howling all the time."

He was leaving—fine, what do I care? But they had no right to treat Misty that way. Misty must have agreed too: the moment Dad opened the front door, Misty bolted. I'd never seen her move so fast, leaping straight over the couch like a flying deer. Dad dropped his suitcase and chased after her, and I was close behind.

The shouting was bad. The swearing was bad. The screech of tires on asphalt and the wet thud to follow were much, much worse. The little gray body was hauled out of the street, hanging limp in my dad's arms.

"Dead on impact," he grunted, dropping the body on the sidewalk. "She didn't suffer."

That was the first time Misty stayed still enough for me to hold her.

My dad was screaming at the man climbing out of his car. Mom was screaming at dad for leaving the door open. The driver was screaming at both of them. No one seemed to notice me burying my face in Misty's wet fur. I couldn't help but wonder whether they'd be acting the same if I was the one who wasn't moving. It was too much to handle—I dropped the stiffening body and ran blindly down the street in my pajamas.

My heart had never beaten so fast as when I sprinted away from that horror. And it never stopped so suddenly as when I heard the pattering feet behind me.

Misty was following me, gaining swiftly. I looked back at the arena illuminated by street lamps in front of my house. My parents were still yelling at the driver. Eyes back to the dog—the crushed face clearly stiff and dead. I could even see patches of exposed brain where the skull had caved in.

Misty didn't seem to notice. She just sat at my feet, white eyes staring at me, tongue lolling a little too far from the mouth to be fully attached at the base.

"We got to hide you," I said. In retrospect, I guess I should have been afraid, but at the time I was just relieved. I needed her, and she needed me, and everything else was someone else's problem as long as we didn't lose each other.

I looped around and let myself in the back door, my parents still arguing out front. I slipped Misty into my room and hid her under the bed. Then I lay on the floor to reassure her.

"Don't let mom or dad see you, okay? They wouldn't understand."

Misty seemed to nod, part of her jaw slipping loose for a moment as she did.

"You aren't hurting, are you?"

Misty shakes her head. I pat her, trying not to wince at the damp, cool skin.

"You understand me though. Hey, you know how to shake hands?"

She didn't, but it didn't take more than a minute for her to learn. By then my parents were coming back inside, so I jumped in bed and pulled the covers up. The door cracked open. I rolled away from the lance of light. The tension of hesitation, and then the door closed again.

I didn't speak a word about Misty the next day. Neither did Mom. Dad wasn't there, and neither of us mentioned that either. It's okay though, because I had a secret that I couldn't wait to get back to.

I spent a lot of time in my room after that. Or out after dark—any excuse to be with Misty. She never made a sound, and she never left my side. She'd always stare at me, prompt and ready for anything. Watching shows? She let me use her as a pillow. Late night bike ride? She was my shadow, a phantom just beyond the street lamps.

It wasn't just tricks she was learning anymore either. She mimicked everything I did. If I started brushing my teeth, Misty would lean up on the counter and lift her paw. She tried to wiggle into my pajamas when I got ready for bed, and when I whisper for her to hide, she whispers back.

"I hide," she'd say, each syllable laborious and strange from her mouth. "Hide and quiet."

It gave me the shudders the first time I heard it. Of course it was amazing, but listening to her struggling with the words made me think of a deaf person slurring things he can't hear.

"You don't have to speak," I told her.

The dog smiled, an unnatural expression which barred her fangs. "I will be... just like you."

I still loved Misty, but something changed after that. I felt like the more she understood me, the less I understood her. I also started catching her doing more things without me. I woke up in the middle of the night once to find her missing, although she was there again when I woke in the morning. Then once in the bathroom alone—she was just leaning on the counter and staring into the mirror.

"Happy face," she said, trying to smile.

"Angry face," she said, the expression only changing subtly.

"I love you... mommy... thank you... for breakfast," she said, working her way slowly through each word.

She wasn't just learning how to be like me. She was learning how to be me. I think that's the first time I was actually scared of her.

I couldn't exactly confide in Mom. She's been worse than ever since Dad left. She doesn't come home until late at night, and she's always ready to snap at the first thing she sees. So I just kept the secret to myself. And every day, I got a little more scared.

"Happy face," Misty said, and she really did smile. Her teeth even looked a little more human.

"Angry face," she said. I never noticed her having eyebrows before, but they were clearly furrowed.

This is about the time she started walking on her hind legs too. She fell over a lot at first, but within a couple of days she almost moved naturally. She wore a pair of my underwear because the elastic was the only thing that she could keep on. It bothered me, but I didn't tell her so. I didn't like it when she looked at me anymore. It felt too much like I was being studied.

This goes on for about two weeks before Dad comes home again. I lock my door as soon as I hear my parents talking in the living room. The tension in the air is like suspended electricity before a storm. That voice they're using—the strained, fake normal they used not to scare the dog—it's an explosion waiting to happen. It takes less than 30 seconds before the voices start to rise, and they begin talking over each other.

A silent lull—I press my ear to the door. Then I flinch as something glass smashes—a picture frame, maybe?

"Run," the voice under my bed whispers. Misty starts to drag herself out. I knew she was under there from the smell, but I didn't even recognize her. The joints were a little wrong, the face a bit elongated, but otherwise I might as well have been looking into a mirror.

"You're drunk," my mom shouts. "Get out and stay out!"

"Out of my own house? Goddamn idiot."

"Let go! You're hurting me!"

"The window," Misty urges. There's another smash from the living room. I can't make out the words anymore—the screaming is incoherent. I slide through the window and drop onto the grass below. Turning around, I see my bedroom door closing. Misty is nowhere to be seen.

"Mom, Dad. Please stop fighting." The voice distant, muffled, but unmistakably mine.

Three full seconds of silence. Then the screaming. Somewhere in that awful din, I heard my own voice say: "Can't you see what it's doing to me?"

I waited a full hour before going back in the house. My parents were in their room, speaking softly. Misty was waiting on the couch, grinning with human teeth.

I don't know if things are going to get better from here, but if they get worse... well Misty is looking out for me, and she's figured out some tricks of her own.

## Blood Games

I was almost friends with a monster when I was eleven years old. I would have preferred a human friend, but my family had just moved to a new city where everyone was cold and distant. My father promised that I would meet new people at school, but there were still a few weeks of summer and I had nothing to do.

Elisa Williams was the one I really wanted to be friends with. She lived next door in a beautiful gray house with a high-fenced yard. I used to sit with my back to the fence and listen to her playing and giggling; the sound bubbling up like music made for everyone but me.

I wasn't brave enough to introduce myself, but after a few days of moping around the house, my mother volunteered to do it for me. I stood behind her, carrying a basket of cookies while she knocked on the neighbor's door.

"Elisa!" The man who opened it looked like a poorly shaved bear. "Get over here and meet your new friend."

"We're busy!" came the shrill response from somewhere deeper in the house.

My mother marveled about the woodworking and craftsmanship and asked the age of the venerable structure.

"Now, Elisa!" the bear bellowed. "I know you're alone up there."

A short, angry sigh, like what circus lions must do before they're forced onto the stage. Then footsteps creaking down the stairs.

"I've got cookies!" I supplied hopefully.

"Elisa spends all day playing by herself," the bear said. "She's been so lonely since her mother passed. Some company will be good for her."

I thought about the giggling I heard through the fence, and I didn't understand how someone could have such a good time on their own.

Elisa appeared a moment later, her head hanging low in surly obedience. She wore shorts and long socks pulled halfway up her thighs: one bright green and the other purple. That's all I really saw, because I was so embarrassed that I couldn't look up from the basket of cookies I held out.

Elisa snatched the whole basket and briskly turned around again. I glimpsed a wave of black hair, curly like her father's, but not so wild. After a few steps she turned to glare over her shoulder with the resentful expression a vegan might give a BBQ.

"Well? Are you coming or not?"

I hadn't taken my second step before she cut in.

"Shoes off." I hasted to obey. "No, the socks stay on. What are you, some kind of barbarian?"

"No ma'am." I don't know why I said that, but I was scared of her and I didn't want to give her any reason to send me away.

Elisa seemed satisfied with the answer though, and she permitted me to follow her up the stairs toward her room. I felt like I was on solid ground until she said:

"We don't need any more friends. None of our games have room for a third person."

"Your dad said—"

"He isn't my dad. He killed my father and took me prisoner."

"Um—"

"Oh yes," Elisa said, pivoting her socked-heel on the wooden floor so smoothly that she seemed to almost float. "But that's okay, because sometimes he brings me little boys to eat."

I could only hope that my stunned silence was mistaken for composure. Elisa rolled her eyes and opened the door to her room.

"Just kidding. You're not stupid, are you?"

I was holding my breath, too afraid to even reply.

"I'm sorry. That wasn't a fair question. Most stupid people don't know they're stupid, and I suppose it's perfectly fine if you are as long as you don't try to perform surgery, or vote, or do anything a normal person would do," Elisa rambled.

The stairway and hall we passed were heavily decorated with framed portraits, hanging tapestries, and ornate tables littered with precious and intricate things.

It was a stark contrast to Elisa's room which had a simple metal-frame bed in the corner and a dark-wood cabinet on the other side. The walls were painted black, and the window was concealed beneath a thick curtain. There was nothing on the hard-wood floor to disrupt the monastic austerity.

"How do you play games without any toys?" I asked.

"We play blood games," she said sternly, stressing the plural again. "The kind that need magic to work. You do know about magic, don't you?"

"Yeah sure. Of course." I didn't want to say anything more to betray my ignorance. I reached for a cookie from the basket, but she slapped my hand away. I stood in disbelief as she ate one of the cookies herself.

"My mother taught me after she passed," Elisa said casually, moving to set the cookies on the cabinet. She retrieved something and turned to face me again. "If you want to play, then you'll need to give me your hand."

"What do you mean after she passed?" I tentatively stretched out to her.

"Now close your eyes."

She could have told me to jump out the window and I probably would have done it. She had the sweetest smile on her face, and the soft brush of her fingers tracing my palm made me blush. I closed my eyes and took a deep breath.

"Don't scream. Mother hates screamers."

I opened my eyes a sliver, just in time to see a metallic flash in the air. Elisa's grip tightened around my wrist while her free hand gouged a needle into the center of my palm.

I didn't scream exactly. It was more of a shrieking yelping sound, like a rabbit trying skydiving for the first time. I tore my hand away with the needle still in it, blood freely running between my fingers.

"Come back here!" Elisa shouted. "You're going to make a mess!"

We both dashed for the door. I hesitated to avoid running into her, but she pushed me aside and didn't slow until she'd slammed the door shut and locked it from the inside.

"You're wasting the blood. Give me your hand."

"No! You'll stab me again!" I gingerly pulled the needle out of the skin, prompting a fresh swell of blood. I felt dizzy.

"Baby." She snorted. That hurt slightly more than the needle. "You're already bleeding, so I don't need to stab you again as long as you play along. Here, wipe some on me."

She offered me the back of her hand. Bewildered, I rubbed a long smear of blood on her pale skin. Her dark eyes sparkled as she watched with eager fascination.

I almost took the opportunity to flee, but I couldn't resist asking: "How does blood magic work?"

"Mother said that when the world was young, all living things were connected and the same blood flowed from one to the next." Elisa plucked the needle from my fingers and pricked her clean hand daintily to draw forth a single drop of blood. "We started to fight one another though, and it got worse and worse until we had to pull apart into separate entities. We became so distant that we started taking different shapes, and some animals even preyed upon others until we forgot that we were ever the same. The blood is the only part of us that never forgot."

Using the nail of one index finger, she deftly traced a pattern in my blood. A circle, with a triangle inside, and a square inside that, and perhaps even a tiny pentagon within.

With deep concentration she pressed the single drop of her blood into the center of the design.

"Now what are you doing?" I asked.

She smiled, but the gesture seemed strained and unnatural, like a dog baring its teeth for a dog food commercial.

"Duh," she said. "I'm making magic."

And she was. The pattern of blood on her hand was glowing. Soft at first, but growing brighter in even pulses. My heart began to race with excitement, and the pulsing light increased to match its rhythm.

"What's it do?" I asked.

"I'm going to grow you a friend," she said. "That's what you want, isn't it?"

I wanted to tell her that I didn't need a friend anymore because I had her. But we don't always get what we want, even from ourselves. Especially from ourselves.

"Yeah sure. That's what I came here for," I said.

"Okay watch."

The light grew stronger, but I couldn't look away. The pattern was moving now. The triangle was turning within the circle, and the square within that, which moved in the opposite direction. And from the center grew a red stalk, like a time-lapse growth struggling through her skin to sprout and curl into the air.

Within a breathless moment the stalk had grown over a foot. The veins of Elisa's hand glowed beneath the skin like a network of roots. And from that strange plant, an even stranger fruit began to swell.

"What is his name?" Elisa asked.

"Um, how about Sid."

The fruit looked like an organ with a face. I didn't know what a fetus looked like at the time, but when I saw pictures when I was older I knew that's what it was.

"How big should he be?"

"I want to be taller than he is," I said.

Elisa smiled.

"What?" I said. "We'll be playing sports and stuff. I want to win."

"What does Sid like to eat?" she asked.

"Uh…" I glanced around the empty room, spotting the basket. "Cookies, I guess."

It was larger now. I could make out tiny blue hands and feet pressing against its transparent cocoon.

"And what does he love?" Her voice was fainter now, straining with exertion. Her glowing veins extended all the way down her arm now, and for the first time I realized the concentration on her face was mixed with pain.

"I don't know. I don't think I like this game. I don't want to play anymore."

"You can't stop now. What does Sid love?"

Elisa took a sharp intake of breath and grimaced. The plant had stopped growing, and the swiftly gorging fruit was about the size of a watermelon. How was it getting so big? Was it filling up with her blood?

"Stop it," I said. My voice cracked, but I didn't care. "Make it go back. Cut it off."

"It's not an it," she grunted. "His name is Sid, and he is already alive. You have to tell me what he loves, or he will be nothing but—"

"I hate it. I hate him. Make him go away, please."

"Hurry! You're part of the spell too. I can't do this alone," she said.

It wasn't a watermelon anymore. It was the size of dog and beginning to grow coarse fur. Now it was heavy enough that Elisa had to kneel and rest it on the ground. The hands and feet were becoming more defined and solid by the second. Its eyes fluttered once, and then opened to pierce me with pale sightless orbs.

"Mr. Williams!" I screamed. "Mr. Williams help! It's hurting her!"

Thunder on the stairs, but the wretched thing reacted to the noise and flailed its arms. One wild claw pierced straight through its encompassing sac and clawed the open air an inch from my face. Bright red fingers clutched the tattered opening and ripped it wide in a rush of blood. All at once Sid was free and on the ground, standing almost as tall as me.

Pounding on the door. It was still locked. "What's going on in there. Elisa? Are you okay?"

She lay panting on the ground. The blood was beginning to evaporate into a thick red mist. I choked and fell to the ground to avoid breathing in the heavy wet air. The tattered sac, the discarded dying stem, both withering before my eyes. Sid was crouched in terror, its matted blue fur showing through the evaporating blood.

"Open the door! Boy are you in there?"

I crawled across the ground to unlock the door. More pounding, louder and more desperate than ever. Out of the corner of my eye I saw Sid flinching at each resounding crash.

The instant I fully turned away from it to unlock the door, I heard Elisa scream. I pounded back the lock and the enormous pressure on the other side made the door spring like a trap.

The man was roaring, but it was too late. Elisa's stomach had been savagely opened. Sid loomed over her, digging through her stomach as though searching for something. When it turned to face Mr. William's onslaught, it was shoveling a bloody clump into its mouth.

Mr. Williams almost caught it, but it bounded away just in time. The bear man moved to the window to block its retreat, but he missed again when Sid lunged for the basket on the cabinet instead. By the time the man caught up with it, Sid had already fled through the door.

"It's my fault." I heaved for air.

Mr. Williams knelt above his daughter, clutching her soaked body to his chest.

"I could have shaped it," I said. "I could have told it not to hurt anyone. I'm so sorry."

"We need to get out of the house," he said.

I followed him downstairs though I knew it wouldn't return. The monster had been born with but one desire, and it would stop at nothing to get it. There was nothing left to satisfy it here.

A cookie monster was born that day.

## The Stillbirth Lie

"Time of death: 10:27 AM."

Doctor Francis turned his back on the exhausted mother, the tiny body shielded in his arms.

The sound which escaped the mother's body was more like a wounded animal than a human: raw emotion without words. She reached toward the small bundle, but the doctor turns sharply and walks from the room.

"Let me see him at least! Just for a moment!" she cries.

"It would be too hard on you," the doctor says, pausing at the doorway. "Try to get some rest. You've had a long day." And he was gone, carrying the child with him.

I've been a nurse at Mercy Hospital for two years. I've seen more than my fair share of tragedy and heartbreak. I've seen grown men blubbering like babies, amputated limbs, inconsolable children with an incurable disease, but this was a first for me. I've never seen a doctor pronounce a child stillborn with a hand over its mouth to suppress its cries. The baby was still squirming in his arms as he carried the little boy from the room.

The doctor must have had a reason though, right? He noticed something was wrong, something fatal, and he thought it would be easier for the mother to bear this way. It just seemed so cruel. I had to confront him in the hallway outside.

"Where are you taking him?" I asked.

"B-1."

"The morgue?"

A feeble cry escaped the child's lips, but it was drowned out by the swelling wail from inside the maternity room. The doctor wrapped the tiny form in his lab coat and hustled off at a quickened pace.

"You can't seriously..."

"I could have you fired, you know." Doctor Francis said it as casually as though commenting on the weather. "All I'd have to do is tell the administration about that time you molested an unconscious person."

"That never happened. What you're doing now though—"

"Just your word against mine then, isn't it?" He stopped at the service elevator. The down arrow lights up. "And who do you think they'd believe? A lifetime veteran and beloved family doctor, or some sketchy nurse trying to save his own skin?" The elevator opened, and he stepped inside. He readjusted to tuck the bundled child under one arm.

I tried to enter with him, but he blocked my path.

"Don't be an idiot, okay?" he said. "You can trust me. I know what I'm doing."

"Yeah, because stealing a child and threatening an innocent witness is totally trustworthy behavior."

"This is for their own good. Them and their parents."

"Them? How many are there?"

Dr. Francis grinned as the door closed. The shifting light seemed to highlight his teeth into something like a snarl. The elevator whirred down. I helplessly mashed the down arrow, but there was only one shaft and I'd have to wait.

I sprinted to the stairs instead, racing against my own morbid thoughts. The door exiting the stairwell to the basement was locked. I fumbled through my keys. I'd never needed to go down here before, and I couldn't remember which one opened the morgue.

I heard a child cry on the other side. Was I too late? Was he already killing it? My fingers were shaking enough that even the right key wouldn't fit. Deep breath. Deep breath. Concentrate. Another cry, muffled and distant this time.

Then the key slid in and I flung open the door. The morgue was still and quiet. There was no sign of the doctor. I searched the room for several minutes, but the cold dead air seemed to mock the very possibility of what I'd seen. I probably would have given up and left soon, but a rattling sound froze me in place.

It was coming from inside one of the body drawers. It was beginning to open from the inside. I leapt across the room to hide behind an upright supply cabinet just in time before the drawer opened.

Doctor Francis crawled out and closed the drawer behind him. He straightened his lab coat, looked from side to side, and then proceeded to the elevator. The child was gone.

I waited until the elevator door closed behind him before rushing to the wall of drawers. Opening the one he crawled from, I immediately realized that it wasn't a drawer at all. It was a passage way.

Fresh wails from the other side prompted me to lie flat on my stomach and crawl through the tight metal space. The crying got louder as I went, until after about 10 feet I emerged into a room I'd never seen before.

Candles lined the walls with long lines of melted wax to mark their enduring vigil. Occult symbols were splashed on the floor in a dark liquid I preferred not to speculate about. And the cribs—a dozen of them arranged in a circle, each containing a frightened infant.

Thank God the cribs were still labeled with their medical charts. These children were all dead—if you believed the official statements, anyway. Their parents were all told that they were stillbirths.

How many heartbreaks and broken lives were there because of this profane room? It was enough to make me sick. I spent the rest of the day removing the children one by one, belly-crawling through the tight passage to bring them back up to the hospital and the world of the living.

The phone calls to the parents were bittersweet. I couldn't even begin to explain what happened. Some children had been down there for as long as a month, and the parents' shock at hearing they were still alive was absolute.

One tearful reunion after another depleted me to my very core. After the initial relief, the parents would start to ask questions that I couldn't possibly answer.

In the first meeting I tried to spin a complicated story about mixed medical records, but it sounded impossible even as I said it. After that I simply told them it was a miracle, and honestly that's what it felt like. By the time all but one child was sent home, I felt like an angel bringing the children back from the dead.

## Sleepless Nights

The parents of the last child were out of town, so I'd have to wait until they could get back. It was a little girl named Emma with a single soft blonde curl. She'd have to stay in the hospital one more night, and I volunteered to stay with her to make sure I was there when the parents arrived.

I'd alerted the security about doctor Francis, but all the commotion of the reunions afterward had driven him from my mind until that evening. I'd spun so many false tales to explain what had happened to the children that I hadn't even considered what the actual justification was.

I sat with Emma in the extra patient room where I'd be spending the night. She slept peacefully, soft little hands curled and still. Even if doctor Francis was insane, he must have chosen these children for a reason. He'd delivered hundreds of children over the last month, but he'd only hidden a few of them.

The hospital was growing quiet around us. The day staff were going home, and the lights in the hallway were dimmed. The peace was disturbed by a sound outside my room:

"Where is she? Where's Emma?"

"You're not allowed to be here, sir. I was told—"

"Nonsense, I work here. Where is she?"

"314, but doctor Francis—"

I tensed as the door swung open. I caught a glimpse of a security guard hurrying toward us, but doctor Francis slipped inside and slammed the door behind him. I was on my feet, but too late to stop him from snatching a metal IV pole and barring the door.

Emma was awake and starting to cry.

"Give her to me!" he demanded, striding toward the girl. "Where are the others?"

"What the hell do you think you're doing?" I asked.

I tried to maneuver around him to unblock the door, but he shoved me roughly back onto the bed.

"I won't let you hurt her!" I said, jumping upright once more.

"Hurt her? God damn idiot. Emma was stillborn. There's nothing that can hurt her now."

Emma was wailing now, frightened high-pitched sobs.

"She's obviously not—"

The doctor shoved a folder into my chest. Security was pounding on the door. Francis wasn't moving toward Emma anymore though, so I allowed myself the time to look inside the folder.

"Where are the others? Don't tell me you..."

"I sent them home," I said. "They were obviously happy, healthy, living..."

I was staring at a set of x-rays, but I didn't understand what I was seeing. The outline looked like a child, but there was something like an eel or a snake coiled tightly within, filling the entirety of the body.

Emma wailed louder as the door rattled harder.
"Can't you hear how scared she is?" I demanded. "You've got to stop this."
"Her mouth is closed," the doctor replied.
"What?"
The wail intensified into a shrill shriek, although it still sounded muffled. But he was right. Emma's mouth was still closed.
"She isn't crying," he said, his voice softer now but still audible because of the terrifying intensity. "Dead children can't cry. But the thing inside them can."
Emma was starting to squirm. Not just her arms and legs either—it was more like the skin was being pushed from something within.
"Do you want to call the parents, or should I?" he asked.

## The Mercy Killing Appointment

"I live in hope I can jump before I am pushed."
-Sir Terry Pratchett on the right to die.

IS any life better than any death? Even a life of profound grief and suffering, carrying the guilt of knowing how much of a burden you've become to those you love? Should our spirits be kept locked in a feeble corpse until the last drop of blood has dragged to a stop through withered veins? Or should we alone be the judge of what burden we can bear; should our pleading be heard when we reach out in our final hour?

Assisted suicides are illegal where I live. A caring doctor should not go to prison for administering the final cure to his grateful patient. When I asked openly about the option, the hospital staff couldn't even meet my eyes. They mumbled excuses and aversions as though they were embarrassed. If anyone should be embarrassed, it was me for admitting that all life had value except this one. I was given a long list of exercises and diets and painkillers intended to add a few more months, but no-one pretended it was a cure.

"A full life deserves a full death. I don't want it to linger on the doorstep. I want it done now. Actually Monday would be better. It's supposed to rain that day, anyway."

The doctor said it was quite impossible. He left in a huff, promising to return with either a psychologist, or a policeman if I couldn't be dissuaded. He of all people should understand that the tumor wasn't in the brain. This decision wasn't an idle fancy. I wasn't some teenager declaring that life was pointless after I got dumped. I was at the end of a very long rope, ready for release.

I would have done the deed myself with a gun or a bottle of pills, but I knew my wife would never forgive me in this life or the next. Better it was clean and professional and out of my hands. I sighed and made my way to the door, but

Susan, one of the nurses, stopped me. She had a bright and perky energy about her that always lit up the room, but I could tell by her hushed tone that she understood the gravity of my request.

"Monday." Just one word. It was enough.

I nodded. I slipped her my business card with my address and mouthed the word 'thank you'. She returned a tight-lipped smile, and we stood staring at each other for a moment. Then she hugged me out of nowhere. I was uncomfortable at first, but I held on anyway. Just so she wouldn't see the tears in my eyes.

At last I pulled away and cleared my throat. "Now if you'll excuse me, I'd like to spend the weekend with my wife."

Of course I didn't tell my wife about the appointment. This weekend was a celebration of life, and I didn't want it to be tainted by the unpleasantness to come. We went to the beach on Saturday and dined at a waterside cafe with our feet in the sand. On Sunday we drove up into the mountains to spend time with her family. The word 'goodbye' stuck in my throat when we hugged and parted.

The sand doesn't stick in the hourglass though, and the clouds are already gathering overhead. My wife is sleeping in the bed next to me, but I still haven't told her. Tomorrow will be Monday, and I trust Susan to meet me soon.

Won't my wife be surprised when she finds out about the appointment I made for her. With her out of the way, I can really start living again.

## Don't Follow Tail Lights Through A Fog

I might as well have been smothered in a blanket for how well I could see. Sliding, oozing, pouring through the air to swirl around me. The thick fog that rolled in from the ocean behaved more like a wave of viscous liquid than it did a cloud. The road I was driving on ran parallel to the water, and it only took a couple of minutes after the fog hit the beach before it had fully encompassed my car.

I've never seen anything like it in my life. Leaning out the window, I couldn't even see the ground a few feet below. I would have been smart to pull off the road and wait it out, but I was suffering from an acute case of love at the time and my rational voice was a ghost beside the thundering of my blood. My son was going to be born today, and I was going to be there to see it happen.

Despite my best intentions, it would have been impossible for me to continue without the taillights in front of me. I'd been following this beat up old pickup with a "Crazy8" license plate for the last few miles, and if it wasn't going to stop, then neither was I. The lights in front of me slowed to a crawl, and I kept pace going as close as I dared for fear of losing him.

The two of us were the only ones stupid enough to still be driving. We passed a half-dozen other cars all pulled off the road with their emergency lights glowing through the heavy air. The lights in front of me never stopped though, deep red beacons promising me a safe road ahead. I figured that even if he hit something, then I'd be going slow enough that I could still stop in time. I was more worried about him running off the road, but he continued to navigate the winding way flawlessly and I never even brushed up against the rumble strips that warn when you're getting too close to the edge.

It was slow going, but it gave me a chance to check in with my wife. The contractions were becoming more severe, and I told her not to wait, but she just pretended it was no big deal.

"I'm going to be telling this story for the rest of my life," she said through heavy breath. "Do you want to know how it ends?"

"With me holding the baby so you can get some God damned rest?"

She laughed. "Damn straight. You remember our deal, right?"

"Of course. It's not going to be like with your dad. I'm always going to be there for both of you."

"Well you can start any time now. I swear to God that if you don't show up I'm going home with the first doctor who smiles at me."

I think she was saying something else too, but my focus was diverted by the latest car I passed on the side of the road. A beat-up pickup—the Crazy8 plate whose tail lights were still glowing through the fog ahead of me.

"Okay honey I'm going to focus on driving, but I'll see you in just a few minutes."

I hung up and gripped the wheel with both hands. Is it possible that the car in front pulled off the road and another car had taken his place without me noticing? Absolutely not. I'd been directly behind him with my eyes glued on the lights the whole time. They hadn't changed either—it was the same red glow. I checked my mirror, but the old pickup had already disappeared into the fog behind me.

I put a bit more weight on the gas and surged closer to the car in front of me to check for the "Crazy8" license plate. The lights ahead of me sped up in perfect unison as though we were magnets repelling each other. I dared going as fast as 30 mph, but I couldn't close the distance and quickly dropped back down to 15. The lights maintained their distance exactly—just close enough for me to see the light, but not close enough to see the car.

Fast, slow. Fast, slow. I played this game for the next minute. The distance between me and the lights never changed, and the obscured landscape made me feel as though I was standing still. No one could have the reflexes to keep matching my speed like that. Or even if they could—then why? Unless of course, they wanted me to follow.

I slowed to a stop to check my GPS and make sure I hadn't accidentally missed my turnoff. Right on cue, the lights ahead stopped as well. I fiddled with my phone to bring up the maps, breathing a sigh of relief to see my next turn a few hundred feet away. Looking up, the breath caught in my throat. The lights were coming closer now, burning through the fog with a nameless menace that raised the hairs on the back of my neck.

The lights flashed once. As they drew closer, a shape began to resolve itself from the fog. The lights flashed again—no, not flashed. They didn't go on and off. Something slid over them and then slid back. It would be more accurate to say that they blinked. It took about ten seconds for my brain to process that I was staring into a set of red eyes, much larger than could fit in a human head.

My first instinct was to slam the horn for all I was worth. The eyes immediately retreated, but only a few feet. A torrent of sound replied, like a whole herd of braying animals, berserk with fear and pain as they trample one another to death in their mad dash to escape their own slaughter. Only a herd of animals wouldn't all start and stop at the same time. The whole chorus fell eerily silent together. The eyes turned away from me, the light vanishing into the mist to leave me suspended in the opaque white walls which felt closer than ever.

My suspended breath exploded out of me in a gasp. The creature was leaving, and I was safe inside the car. I started to inch forward again, now using the rumble strip to guide me toward my turn. I white-knuckled the steering wheel, trembling with the car as it eased along the invisible bend.

The turn the creature had taken a few moments before. The turn which led to the hospital where my wife was giving birth. But it couldn't be...

I had no warning before the massive impact broadsided my car. The wild braying mingled with the screech of twisted metal. The car spun almost ninety degrees from the force of the blow, leaving me even more lost and disoriented than I already was. I stomped the gas and shot straight off the road, bumping and lurching and spinning my tires to a standstill in the sandy ground.

Another impact—this time from behind, propelling me back onto the intersecting road where I'd been trying to turn. 30—40—50 mph, I accelerated blindly through the fog. The red eyes filled my mirror, easily keeping pace with me. I was pushing 70 before they started falling behind. My front right wheel kept slipping off the road, but I kept readjusting and didn't dare slow down. If there was a sudden curve, then I was dead. If there was a tree, or a sign, or an invisible barrier hidden in the fog—dead. My whole body was rigid with tension, braced every second for a collision that could happen any time.

I didn't see the eyes anymore though, and gradually I slowed once more. I started to pull up my GPS again, but the second I took my eyes off the mirror I heard the sound again. Red eyes filled the mirror, rushing toward me in a reckless charge as though planning to barrel straight through my car. I swerved to get out of the way, sliding off the road once more. The wall of sound crashed around me, then just as quickly it was gone.

The fog was lifting with it. I sat stunned for several seconds as the air miraculously cleared around me. Directly ahead was the hospital. The relief only lasted a moment. I hadn't gotten away from the creature. It had gotten away from me. I hadn't escaped its pursuit. I'd lost the race.

I was inside the hospital by the time I heard the sound again. Rabid, feral, and yet with such focused intensity that there was surely a malevolent intelligence behind its bestial roar. I sprinted to my wife's room, terrified of what I'd find yet dreading not knowing even more.

My wife sitting up in bed, holding her son—our son, in her arms. The sweat on her brow, the sweet smile on her lips, and the proud victory in her lifted face.

"He's beautiful," I whispered, hardly daring to breathe and disturb the perfect moment.

"Shh—you'll wake him."

But I was too late. He was already stretching his tiny fists and opening his little red eyes.

## Alektorophobia: A Fear Of Chickens

Her freckles make my knees weak. I can feel heavy drops of sweat squeezing through my pores. It's going to be my turn next, and I've spent the last few minutes carefully rehearsing my words and their casual inflection in my mind. Missy's left knee is almost touching my right one as we sit on the same log, and the faintest sensation of her body heat is burning a hundred times hotter than the campfire.

"Your turn, Wobbles," Jeff says. I don't bother correcting him because my real name of Webster is just as bad. "Truth or dare?"

"Dare," I say without hesitation.

My face is a carefully maintained a mask of boredom. Jeff is smirking at me because of our deal. I've been giving him my dessert for the last week, even though the camp always has the best food at the end. I've been doing his craft projects to cover for him while he sneaks behind the toolshed and drinks with a few of the older boys. I even let him beat me at ping pong while a dozen people watched, even though I could have kicked his ass, and he knows it. It's all going to be worth it though, because he's about to dare me to kiss Missy.

"You sure you're brave enough for a dare?" Jeff asks, languidly drawing out each word. He's trying to make me squirm, but I'm not taking the bait.

"I'm ready. Shoot," I say. My breathing is almost steady.

"'Cause I'm sure everybody is just dying to know more about that time you took a piss in the creak, and—"

"Come on Jeff, just dare him already," Missy says.

Every muscle in my body is a painful knot. Somehow all the moisture in my mouth has teleported into my armpits. Missy shouldn't be able to smell it over the burning logs though. I hope.

## Sleepless Nights

"Okay Wobbles. By the power invested in me by the sacred games of Camp Tillwaki, I dare you to..."

I was already standing. I wasn't going to over-think it. I wasn't going to give anyone else the chance to over-think it. I was just going to duck in there, and...

"... try to catch Scar Face, the one-eyed chicken!"

I'd already turned toward Missy in anticipation. She got a full view of my gaping mouth and the startled fear stamped across my face. She covered her mouth and tried not to laugh, failing in the most delightful way. I spun to face Jeff and his giant sloppy grin. He'd stepped aside to reveal a cage containing the most hideous monster I've ever seen. A few other boys had already taken up chanting "Scar Face... Scar Face...".

Jeff's hand is poised on the latch to open the cage. "Unless of course... you're scared of him."

Scar Face cocked its mangled head to the side and glared at me. It was all black except for its disgusting fleshy red crown and malicious beady eyes. The counselors said that a fox almost got Scar Face once, but it fought back and pecked out both the fox's eyes. Legend has it that it didn't stop there either, but continued to attack the blinded fox until it had pecked its way straight to the brain through the eye sockets.

"Afraid of a chicken? Don't be stupid," I said. Even with my back to Missy, she's still the only thing that I can see.

The cage flies open and Jeff scrambles backward to get out of the way. Scar Face takes his time strutting out, eyeing us all one at a time like a lord surveying his subjects. I crouch, ready to spring, but that only makes the trembling in my legs more evident.

I don't give myself a chance to over-think. Before the chicken has taken two steps, I dive on it with outstretched arms. It gets a vicious peck into my shoulder, but my adrenalin is raging through me and I barely feel it.

I'm about to stuff the creature back into its cage when my legs give out beneath me. I'd been so busy trying to keep its beak away that I hadn't noticed Jeff sneaking around the side. He'd swept my legs with a sharp kick, and Scar Face and I tumbled to the ground. By this point the creature was berserk with rage. Catching it again wasn't nearly as important as making sure it didn't catch me.

"Come on, that's cheating!" Missy wails. Her sympathy was a small condolence beside the throaty squawks.

I was still laying stunned on the ground when Scar Face began his attack. The razor beak sank into my chest again and again, and the more I tried to fight it off with my hands, the farther it worked its way up my neck and face. Jeff was howling with laughter, egging the chicken on by nudging it in the butt with his foot. I managed to drag myself to my feet, but the enraged bird launched itself into the air to continue its relentless assault.

I'd been using my hands to push myself up and wasn't shielding my face for just a moment, but that's all it took. The talons planted themselves around my shoulder and the beak dove straight into my face. I could see it growing exponentially larger by the second as it hurtled towards my eye, and the next I knew an explosion of pain cascaded through my body. The surrounding laughter turned to screams and mad panic as the blood ran freely down my face. I flailed madly until the bird dropped back to the ground. I stumbled blindly trying to get away until I tripped over a log and fell too.

I still had one good eye, but it was so filled with sweat and blood that I couldn't see a thing. I curled into a fetal position, listening to the awful squawking and screaming, just waiting for the unpredictable beak to gouge into my prone body.

I vaguely heard the gruff voice of one of the counselors, but I was loosing a lot of blood and nothing seemed quite real. I passed out shortly afterward. The last thought in my head was back to the fantasy of being dared to kiss Missy, and the softness of her lips against mine.

Camp ended one week after that. I spent most of the time in a medical building with a giant swathe of bandages compressing where one of my eyes used to be. Missy visited once, but only briefly to check in. She stayed near the back of the room and showed about as much interest in resuming my fantasy as I had in kissing Scar Face.

Yeah it was a tough week, but there was one silver lining. The counselor (who was probably just desperate not to get sued), told me that the chicken had been put down. He practically begged me to tell him if there was anything else he could do to make this right, and I told him that there was: I wanted to cook the chicken myself for the farewell banquet, and I wanted him to assign Jeff as my assistant. The counselor blurted out immediate consent, talking over himself in his hurry to promise us the whole kitchen for as long as we needed it.

Some might think this is petty revenge, but I don't. I'd need a glass eye to replace the one that was gouged out, not to mention a lifetime of alektorophobia. And when I stood at the head of the long table and watched everyone eat the final meal I'd prepared, well that felt almost as good as a kiss.

I don't know if they were just being nice because of the incident, but people raved about that meal. I tried to stay humble, but I had two plates myself and know it wasn't just empty words. Jeff really did taste better than any chicken would have.

## My Stalker Wishes Me Happy Birthday Every Year

"Happy Birthday Mahjouba. I hope someone gets you the new phone I saw you looking at last week."

-Love X

## Sleepless Nights

"Another year already. It seems like only yesterday your mom dropped you off for high school. It's been such a pleasure watching you grow up."
-Love X

"You should be more careful about closing your windows at night. You never know when someone might climb up from the balcony below. Happy birthday, stay safe."
-Love X

They might sound creepy to you, but you have to understand that I've been getting these cards every year for as long as I can remember. My mom made a big fuss about them for a while, but we never got the slightest clue where they were coming from and nothing bad ever came from it. Over the years it just became a fact of life; I even looked forward to the mysterious messages.

We all had our theories, of course. Mom thought it was some socially handicapped secret admirer with a lifelong obsession. My half-sister Amina couldn't stand the idea of anyone being in love with me. She insisted it was a psychopath who was just biding his time to strike. I even caught her slipping her own menacing anonymous letter into the pile one year just to scare me.

Personally I always thought (or at least hoped) they were coming from dad. He left my mother while she was still pregnant with me. Mom thinks that's proof that he doesn't care and wouldn't bother. I think it's proof that he knows I exist. The fact that Amina never gets a card seems to support the idea.

This never caused a problem until I was in my twenties and living on my own. I'd started dating a guy named Ranja who was almost charming to a fault. He wouldn't say that I looked beautiful. He'd tell me that the rain came from angels weeping over losing me from heaven. Or that the puddles loved me so much that they'd hold on to my reflection even after I'd left. A little over the top maybe, but I'd be lying if I didn't admit to feeling myself all mixed up at his words.

Ranja and I had been together for almost eight months before we celebrated my first birthday together. That's the first time I saw the other side of him. I guess I never realized how closely linked passion and jealousy are before he opened my mysterious card. His brows knotted together while he read, his pressed lips began to tremble, and all the color drained from his face.

"It's no big deal, really," I told him. "What's it say?"

Ranja didn't answer. He threw the card down on the table and walked to the other side of the room, breathing heavily. I picked it up and read:

"He's going to hurt you, Mahjouba. You wouldn't be the first either. Get out, or this may be the last card you ever receive."
-Love X

When I looked up, Ranja was standing on the opposite side of his living room, just glaring at me. "Well?" he asked. "Explain yourself."

"Me? What did I do?"

The space between us closed more rapidly than I was comfortable with. I took a step back, but that only brought him closer—trapping me against a wall.

"What's his name? How long have you been seeing him?" Ranja pressed.

What followed was the worst argument we've ever had. He refused to believe me when I told him it might be my father, and I got a glimpse of the person the message warned me about. I told him he could check with my family, but he seemed to think they would lie to protect me. We managed to avoid talking about it for a few days until one morning when Ranja triumphantly slammed a piece of paper on the table.

"He's dead. Twelve years he's been dead."

I don't know how Ranja did it, but I was staring at my father's death certificate. Have you ever felt a lifetime of hope shatter in a few seconds? It's like being conscious of your own death. Your body keeps moving and you can feel it go, but there's no one inside anymore.

"Stop pretending you care just to get out of trouble. I know you never met him."

And then the argument started again, but my heart wasn't in it anymore. I couldn't explain who was sending the letters. I could barely even talk, and he took my silence as an admission of guilt. He didn't understand that I wasn't hurt because I lost my father. You can't lose something you've never had. I was hurt because I lost every possible future with my father in it. I lost him dancing with me at my wedding and carrying my future kids on his back. I lost him telling me that he never stopped thinking of me, or loving me, even if it was only from afar.

And all I gained in return were threats, insults, and the unsettling realization that a stranger really had been following me my whole life long. Now Ranja was laying it on the line—I could either trust him, or the letter writer. He demanded to know why I would throw away the life I was building for some creep I'd never met. How could I possibly take care of myself without him? How could I find another man as good as him when even my own father didn't want me?

If my life was a movie, then things would have gotten better after that. I would have stood up for myself and learned to live on my own terms. But I was scared, and I was alone, and I thought that someone who said the angels wept for me would never dare blasphemy the object of their love.

I thought I deserved it when he started to lock me in my own room. What else could he do if he didn't trust me?

I thought I could be strong when he hit me or pulled my hair. At least he didn't leave. My mother would have been lucky to have found a man like Ranja.

And for the next year, I hated myself for spending my whole life waiting for a fairy tale that would never come true.

Until my birthday came again, and I finally found the will to leave. It wasn't what the card said that convinced me—just a benign, generic well-wishing straight off the shelf. It was where the card came from, because this was the first time there had ever been a return address.

In the cool and safety of the dark I stole out of Ranja's house with only what I could fit in a suitcase. It was hard going dragging my things, but I knew that if my life was going to start over, then it was going to start with the only person I've ever trusted—the one sending the letters. And when I found myself entering the cemetery, I knew I had found what I was looking for.

My father's headstone, which read: "Are you there, Mahjouba? I will always be with you."

### My Diary That I Didn't Write

I'm that guy who will swerve across three lanes of traffic without hesitation because I spotted a sign for a garage sale. Doesn't matter that I don't need anything, doesn't matter if there are three other people in my car with busy lives and no interest in digging through someone else's trash. Garage sales are like magical dimensions where anything is possible and reality is only a suggestion.

Entire sofa for $50? No problem, they're just happy for someone to get rid of it.

Grandpa's medals from the war? Well, who is he trying to impress now?

The literal holy grail? Why not? It's got to be somewhere. Some dude's kids were probably eating cereal out of it.

But by far the strangest thing I've ever discovered in years of hunting was a little black notebook bound with leather straps. When I noticed there was writing inside, I snuck behind a big stack of old garden chairs to snoop mercilessly through someone's personal life. The erotic short story of a bored housewife? Maybe the daughter's scandalous journal full of young love and heartbreak? It's a garage sale, baby. It's all fair game.

I was immediately disappointed upon closer inspection. The first few entries were composed of big blocky letters like a child might write. A day at the pool, the stuff he learned in class, the new friend he met at the park... I was quickly losing interest and was about to return the notebook when I realized I recognized the person he was talking about. Devin was my best friend in third grade. We used to build pillow forts in his parent's house—And there it was. The next entry talking about the fort. About the secret passage we made in the back so his cat could still visit when the door was closed. It's been years and years since I last thought about that. But how did these people get my diary? I wasn't even in the same state that I grew up in anymore. I watched the homeowner suspiciously while he bartered over an old TV. Clean face, slightly balding, a broad smile—nothing out of the ordinary. I considered asking him about it, but decided it was too personal to explain.

I slipped the notebook into my pocket and stood to leave. It couldn't have been stealing if it belonged to me, right? As I headed for my car parked on the street, I heard him call after me:

"Couldn't find anything you liked?"

I gave my best straight face and shook my head. "Plenty I liked. Nothing I need."

"It's hard to tell what we're going to need... until we need it. Take care now."

I was gone without looking back. Too impatient to drive all the way home, I stopped in a coffee shop around the corner to continue pursuing this bizarre discovery.

Flipping through the book, I noticed the handwriting slowly refine as it progressed until it identically matched my own. This wasn't just a childhood relic: the entries spanned over the course of years. It seemed impossible that I could have kept this for so long without any memory of it. There was no denying it was mine though, complete with my fleeting obsession over a girl in one of my college classes. I was too shy to talk to her, so I'd just sit in the row behind and daydream the hour away. She dropped out a few weeks later, and I missed my chance of ever saying hello. I was so embarrassed by my ineptitude that I never breathed a word about her to anyone. And yet here she was, immortalized on paper in my own hand.

So why didn't I remember writing it?

The farther I got through the book, the more unsettling that question became. The writing became sloppier as though rushed. Entries became short and far between, just a few lines per month. I could still recognize the events of my past, but the language became darker than I was expecting.

*I should just kill her. Necks break as easily as hearts, maybe easier. She didn't love me, she can't love anyone but herself. I'd spare the next sucker she decides to fuck a lot of pain if I just killed her now.*

That was written about my ex fiance, only a few months ago. The breakup was stressful for both of us, but we'd parted on good terms. Sure there was some lingering resentment and disappointment, and I'd had some pretty nasty thoughts about her, but I never once considered something like that. My diary said otherwise.

*She gets home late on Tuesdays and Thursdays, it read. 10:30 PM at the bus stop. She has two blocks to walk, and there won't be any people around. All I've got to do is take her purse and it will look like a mugging gone bad. No one will ever know.*

The next few pages were hard to read. I kept glancing over my shoulder in paranoia as though someone in the coffee shop would read over my shoulder and call the police. I moved to a corner table which had opened up and continued reading.

*It was even easier than expected. She didn't look up from her phone, even when I was right behind her. One hand under the jaw, the other on the top of her head. One quick motion—I can still hear the splintering crack, like stomping on dry wood except for the wet, sucking sound of separated vertebrae.*

I stopped reading and looked away. For a second I thought I remembered what that sounded like, but it might have just been the power of suggestion. I pulled out my phone to text her and make sure she was okay, but changed my mind at the absurdity of it. I flipped ahead to the last page containing writing. It was dated yesterday.

*It was supposed to be easier this way. I thought killing her would be the end, but I'm thinking about her more than ever. Every face is her reflection, every smile a sneer, every voice heavy with accusation. I think I'm going to go insane if I can't get her out of my head. I want to forget. I need to forget. And yet if I do, how much of me will disappear with her?*

Need to forget. The words rang a bell in my mind. As I was leaving the garage sale, the man had said it's hard to tell what we're going to need until we need it. It had to be a coincidence. Or maybe I just needed it to be. I scanned every page until the end of the notebook, but they were all blank.

I picked up my phone and called my ex. The ringing seemed to go on for an eternity, but it was only three repetitions before it connected. I asked if she was there, my voice catching in my throat.

There was crying on the other line, then a sniffled apology. I recognized the voice as her mother.

"She's gone. Last week—please don't call this number again."

The call ended abruptly. The coffee shop suddenly felt much louder than it had a moment before. The sound of the cash register opening made me jump. People seemed to shout at one another across the room. I stumbled outside, and the traffic was a hurricane whirling around me. Then to my car, lurching onto the street with a chorus of horns shaking me to the bone. I didn't slow down until I slammed to stop at the garage sale once more.

All the other perspective buyers had gone home. It was just the homeowner sitting in an old garden chair facing the street. He wasn't reading or doing anything, just sitting there and waiting. He smiled as though expecting me when I got out of the car.

"Forget something?" he asked, his voice coy.

"I didn't kill her," I blurted out. I hadn't intended to say that. I don't know what I'd intended to say, but it wasn't that.

He only laughed. "Why not?"

"Because I'm a good person. We both are—were, whatever. It didn't go like that."

"How did it go then?" he asked, casually reaching under his chair. "Like this, maybe?"

He produced a small stack of notebooks, each a different color. He opened the red one seemingly at random and began to read: "Love survives, love endures. There was once a time when we fought a lot, but in fighting we learned more about each other than we ever did from the easy times. We showed each other our deepest insecurities and vulnerabilities—we gave the other the power to destroy us, and we loved each other for our mercy. I liked her because of her virtues, but I loved her because of her faults, because I knew she trusted me enough not to hide herself from me."

"What's that supposed to be?" I asked. I'd been moving closer while he read until I was only a few feet away.

"You were working on your wedding vows. Don't worry—it was just a first draft. Here, take it." He handed me the red notebook.

I snatched it suspiciously as though the man taking me hostage had just offered his gun. I immediately flipped to the end and saw my handwriting with yesterday's date once more.

*1 dozen eggs.*
*Diapers—not that plastic crap.*
*Garden hose...*

"What the hell is this?"

"Things your wife wanted you to pick up on your way home. You'll find her waiting for you if you go now. Or maybe you'd prefer the blue notebook. You never met her at all because you went back to finish your PhD. Is that what you want?"

My face must have betrayed my confusion because he laughed again. "A lot of folks think they can only affect their present because that's all they see, but every second you're alive you're only making more past. Keep that in mind next time you make a decision—is this the past I want to live with someday?"

He offered his open hand to take the red notebook back, but I clutched it to my chest. I turned away without another word, gripping the notebook so tightly that the cover cut into my fingers. I was scared to think what might happen if I spent anymore time here.

Besides, my wife was at home, and I wasn't going to keep her waiting forever.

## Relive Your Childhood

The only reason to go to a high school reunion is to rub your success in everyone's faces. For me, that meant letting them know I married the prettiest girl in our grade. There's nothing more satisfying than watching them glance at me, then at Kimberly holding my hand, then quickly back to me with the wide-eyed shock of realization.

I'll just smile and nod. Yep, you caught us. Me, a little fatter with rough stubble on my face. Her as beautiful as ever, the short tangle of ginger hair she wore in high school replaced with a luxurious wave flowing halfway down her back.

"I want everyone to remember that as long as you're here, it's still 2008."

That was Brandon with the microphone standing at the head of the gymnasium. He was always a weird loner that I never knew very well, but I'd gotten the Facebook invitation from him because he did all the organizing for the reunion.

I have no idea how he got permission to use our old school which had been out of operational for years. An overly ambitious remodeling project had been terminated halfway through for whatever reason, and there were still discarded building supplies and stacks of lumber everywhere.

"I'm serious," Brandon growled, hands plastering his greasy gelled hair back against his head. "Smart phones in the plastic bin. Those things didn't exist when we were in school."

Nobody wanted to make a defiant scene in front of their old classmates, so we all reluctantly dumped our gadgets into the bin as we entered.

Brandon had gone to great lengths to make the place feel like it used to. Old science fair posters were hung on the walls. Stacks of molding brochures advertised Grease with the 2008 school cast. There was even a collection of trophies that our track and field team had won that year, God knows where he got them.

"Kimberly, huh? Congratulations man." My old friend Chase clapped me on the back. "I'd always hoped you two would end up together."

"As if." I grinned. "You told me my only shot would be to wear a wig and ask out the only lesbian."

Kimberly snorted as she laughed in the most delightful way.

"Shit, is Casey here? Don't tell her I said that." Chase laughed too, but the sound cut suddenly short as he became aware of Brandon standing behind him.

"Strike one," Brandon said, his voice barely above a whisper.

"Huh?"

"They weren't married in high school. They weren't even dating," Brandon grunted. "That means they aren't together here."

"Chill out Brandon," Kimberly said. "We can be nostalgic without literally repeating high school."

"Seriously," Chase added. "I didn't have a tattoo in high school. You want me to scrape it off?"

Brandon seemed to seriously consider this for a moment. "No, that's not necessary." Chase had already half-turned away from him before Brandon grabbed his shoulder and turned him back. "You can just cover it up with some foundation."

"You're being ridiculous. Nobody cares."

"I care," Brandon said softly. "The spell doesn't work unless everything is perfect. Strike two."

"Screw you, man." Chase turned away and started walking toward the door.

"You can't leave before the bell rings!" Brandon shouted. Kimberly gave me a tight-lipped smile and rolled her eyes.

"No wonder you never had any friends," Chase shot back. "Guess some things never change after-all."

Snickers from all around. Brandon looked like he was holding his breath. His face was going bright red. Chase reached the door and heaved, but it didn't budge. Again, this time with both hands, grunting in exertion.

"You seriously locked us in here?"

"Strike three."

The gunshot shattered the air into so many ringing shards. We were all too stunned to make a sound as Chase's body slumped against the door and slid to the ground, leaving a great red smear on the door to show where the bullet exited his body on the other side.

Then the screaming started all at once. Still clutching his handgun, Brandon sprinted back to the microphone and howled at us until it was quiet enough for him to be heard.

"That's enough!" he shouted, still brandishing the hand gun in his free hand. "If you're not going to play by the rules, then you shouldn't have come. We didn't all get out of here in one piece. We didn't all get the job of our dreams, or find someone who loved us, but that doesn't matter anymore. Tonight we're back in 2008 with our whole lives ahead of us, and anything is possible."

He strutted to the stereo and turned up the music—Viva La Vida by Coldplay. The screams gave way to an electric silence as the assembly stared at Brandon in disbelief. He was getting red in the face again.

"Well?" he shouted. "What are you waiting for? Start dancing!"

The only movement was a few people cowering a little closer together. Kimberly hung onto my arm, her nails digging through my shirt.

Brandon was getting visibly more irritated the longer we waited. "You with the green dress," he shouted at a woman who was kneeling over Chase's crumpled body. "You used to date him, right?"

That was Emma. She and Chase had been together for a few months, but they split upon graduation. She held a hand over her mouth, stifling back sobs.

"Yeah, I remember seeing you together," Brandon continued, his words slurring together in their haste. "Act like it."

Emma stared in confusion, her face a mess of running tears and snot.

"Grab him by the hand. Dance with him," Brandon ordered.

"He's dead!" she shrieked. "You killed him!"

"He wasn't dead in 2008!" Brandon screamed back, limp hair whipping across the ghastly shade of purple his face as turning. He might have been intoxicated, but I'd never seen alcohol affect someone like that, the strange light almost glowing from his face. "Strike one! Don't let me get to three."

Still sniffling, Emma hoisted Chase's body up to its knees with visible effort. She kept looking back at Brandon and his leveled gun. Emma let the body's weight lean against her, his blood soaking through her dress. They began to sway to the music as she broke into fresh sobs.

Another gunshot. Emma gasped and let the body fall. It wasn't her though—it was Brody who used to play football. He'd tried to sneak into the cell phone bin while everyone was distracted. The shot hadn't hit him, but it was enough to make him freeze—standing stiff as though he were a scarecrow with a wooden pole up his ass.

"Brandon, please stop!" Kimberly shouted. She broke away from my arm. I tried to stop her, but she gave me that look that said 'trust me' and I let her go. The funny thing was that I really did trust her. More than the gun, or the dead body, or my own terror—she was more real than any of it, and she would know what to do.

"Why? Did you fuck him too?" Brandon asked, his face twisted into a cruel sneer.

"If we're all getting another chance," she said in a forced calm, walking toward Brandon with small, tense steps, "then I want to use mine to get to know you. We never talked much in high school."

I don't know what game she was playing, but I didn't like it. She was back in 2008 and wasn't my wife anymore though. She was her own person making her own choices, and anything I did to interfere would probably just get us both killed.

Brandon looked as uncertain as I felt. He shifted from one foot to the other, still loosely pointing the gun in her direction.

"No, we didn't talk much," he conceded at last. "I wanted to, but I didn't know how."

"I know," Kimberly said gently, still edging closer. "I felt the same way. Did you know I used to watch you when you weren't looking?"

Brandon opened and closed his mouth, but no sound came out.

"I used to see you eating lunch all alone and wonder what secrets that boy was hiding," Kimberly said, her voice trembling ever so slightly as she continued her approach. "But you never told me."

Brandon glanced nervously around the room. All eyes were on him. "No. I guess I never did."

Kimberly looked around as though noticing everyone for the first time. "It's not too late. You and I, we could go somewhere private. Everyone else can go, and you and I can have a chance to be alone together."

So that was her plan. To sacrifice herself so the others could escape. I had to do something, but what? I couldn't think of any way to interfere that wouldn't put everyone else in danger.

"Would you like that, Brandon?" Kimberly was close enough to his microphone that her seductive whisper was carried across the whole room. "Would you like to be alone with me?"

Brandon swallowed hard. Then nodded. He fumbled around the stereo controls until he found a button that made the bell ring. A heavy click resounded as the doors unlocked.

"Everyone out," Brandon ordered, not taking his eyes off my wife.

The doors burst open and everyone flooded through them. Everyone except me, still frozen in place.

They hadn't had a chance to get their cell phones. How long would it be before one of them was able to call for help? I had to stall.

"Strike two." The words as sharp as a slap across the face. Brandon was looking at me though—the barrel of his gun was looking too.

"I didn't do anything—" I protested.

"Strike one was pretending you were married to Kimberly when you came in," Brandon said. "Strike two was not leaving when the bell rang."

I took a hesitant step toward them, but before my foot had even touched the ground a bullet planted in the floor with a cascade of splintering wood.

"Please go." Kimberly's whisper still traveled across the room, so intimate yet so cold. Her eyes were pleading. "Brandon and I want to talk in private."

"I'll find you," I promised.

What else could I do? I turned and ran. I'd get to the closest store that was still open and call the police from there. Or knock on houses if I had to—one of them would see the desperation on my face and let me in.

It took less than five minutes of sprinting before I found a gas station, but it felt like hours. Every step was taking me farther away from my wife, and every second was bringing her closer to disaster.

The police didn't find them at the school. They didn't find them in their sweep of the neighborhood, and even more peculiar, didn't even find a trace of the bullets that had been fired.

They did find Brandon eventually though. He was sleeping in bed in his home a little over ten miles away. Kimberly was there too, confused as to what all the fuss was about. She'd spent a quiet evening with her husband, a high school sweetheart whom she'd gotten to know after an unlikely intimate conversation the two had shared 10 years ago.

Chase was at his home too. He'd never heard about a reunion, but he was happy to hear from me and didn't understand why I was so upset. No one understood why I was still so hung up over a girl from high school. Or why it hurt so much when she smiled her secret smile at someone other than me.

## Heart Eater

I'd already found the engagement ring my boyfriend Niles hid in his sock drawer. Now he was taking me on a romantic weekend getaway with a private dinner at the base of a waterfall. It was supposed to be the best day of my life, but now he's dead and it's all my fault.

I was ready to say yes. It's all I could think about on the drive through the state park. My family never thought it would last, but I was going to prove them wrong. Dad called Niles a "pretty boy", and every time he saw a Disney Princess he'd point and ask "Hey, isn't that your boyfriend?"

I'd just smile and roll my eyes. They thought that just because Niles was handsome that I was superficial for being with him, but he was so much more than that. He was kind, and smart, and funny, and even more important, he made me feel like that's exactly what I deserved.

Everything was perfect that night except me. 'Something' by the Beatles was playing on a handheld stereo, and a dozen candles were scattered on the surrounding ground. There was chilled champagne in the ice chest, and stars in the sky, and the love of my life getting out of his chair to drop to one knee.

"Umm," probably wasn't the answer he was expecting. It wasn't what I was expecting to say either, but it was the best I could do.

"Umm?" Niles asked in disbelief. "I didn't drive all the way out here for an 'umm.'"

I was frozen. I'd rehearsed this moment a thousand times in my head, but my rehearsals hadn't prepared me for the breathless terror of the actual moment. All I could think about was my dad's words, wondering if it really was just his looks that I was attracted to.

In ten years, when he's started to bald and put on weight, am I still going to think his jokes are funny? When we settle down and have kids and romantic moments like this are replaced by daily chores and routines, will I still look at him the same way? Or even more likely, what if he's the one who gets bored of me?

"Umm," I said again.

"Unbelievable," Niles said. "Un-fucking believable."

"What? I didn't say no!"

"You didn't have to." Niles wasn't kneeling anymore. He wasn't even facing me—just staring off into the emptiness of night.

"It's a serious question!" I could have said yes then, but I felt obliged to defend myself. "There's nothing wrong with taking a moment to think."

"Take all the time you need. I'm going for a walk."

Again I had a chance. I could rush up to him and hug him and say of course I want to spend my life with you. But it only took him a few steps to exit the meagre light of the candles, and Niles was gone before I could gather my wits.

The song finished playing, and I was able to distinguish a strange plopping sound separate from the crash of the waterfall. My rapid breathing became louder, but it didn't drown out the mumbling whisper from the dark water.

"Niles? Are you still there?"

The whispering grew louder—a low rasping voice that sounded nothing like Niles, coming just beyond the ring of light. I couldn't make out every word, but a few were unmistakable.

"… your doubt… your fear… delicious."

That last word sounded with particular clarity, drawn out and savored as though each syllable was tasted.

Niles was playing a trick to get back at me. That meant he couldn't have taken my hesitation too seriously. I breathed a deep sigh of relief, but didn't even have a chance to fully exhale before I heard the crack of twigs. Then a muffled swear—all the way up the hill we'd hiked in on.

"Niles, was that you?" I called, my own voice so feeble and insignificant in the looming wilds. "Come back! Let's talk."

"Alright. I'm coming." That was from the hill again. So he hadn't been the one whispering.

"I can tell you," hissed the whisper. A stir of movement behind me. I spun just in time to catch something like a long slug disappearing beyond the light. "How he feels," the whisper came from the same place. "What he's really after, and whether you can give it to him."

I heard Niles stumble—still a fair distance away.

"Okay yeah," I said. "I need to know."

If a sound could curl like a smile, then that's exactly what the hiss did. Then it was gone, its barely perceptible shadow slipping into the deeper darkness beyond.

"Hold on, I'm almost there," Niles shouted from the same direction.

"Niles watch out!" It had only just occurred to me what I'd done. "There's something out there—"

His scream overwhelmed the splashing water and filled the sky from horizon to horizon. Tortuous, guttural, and long enough that he had to pause to draw breath to begin screaming again.

I was rushing toward him as fast as I could, but I made slow progress as soon as I pitched into the blackness. I kept stumbling over hidden rocks or blindly charging through thick underbrush, led by nothing but his screams which seemed to go on forever.

But forever is a dream from which all are forced to wake, and he was silent by the time I found him. The slug I'd glimpsed rested on his chest, pulsing as it burrowed its way into his flayed chest cavity. It was as wide as a tree trunk, maybe four feet long, perhaps more depending how deeply it sank within Niles' body.

"Do you still want to know?" The whisper came from the free end of the slug. "Everything he knew, everything he felt, his heart is not hidden from me."

Would it be wrong to listen to this monster which feasted upon him? Or would it be disrespectful to turn away and forever lose his final thoughts? For the second time that night, I was frozen and said nothing.

"I can taste his admiration," mused the creature. "From the first time he saw you, sitting alone reading a book. The intelligent focus on your face—the way the light played through your hair—he watched you for almost an hour before he worked up the courage to say hello."

"He never told me he was watching…"

"I can taste his love," it hissed. "Fresh from his heart, it fills me up. Enough to endure a hundred years of adversity. Until the night at the end of all days when age has stolen everything but the grace of your spirit, he would have loved you."

I had to hear this. Even though I was crying, I wouldn't leave. This was my solace and my punishment in one. The monster was silent for a long moment before it said:

"I love you too."

It was enough of a shock to suspend my heaving sobs.

"With everything he was, I am," it hissed. "I love you with all his heart."

The creature pulsed. Then again, the ripple cascading up and down its fleshy mass as it wriggled free. Niles heart was in full view, raw and wet and still beating where it was clutched in the creature's mouth. Then swallowing, the heart vanished still beating all the way down.

"I'm back," the second mouth said, speaking with Nile's voice as clear as the mountain air. "Let's just start over, okay? Don't over-think. Don't make assumptions. Don't be afraid. Will you marry me?"

I started to cry again. "Yes Niles. It was always yes."

I wasn't about to lose true love twice in one night. Besides, maybe now dad will finally shut up about me only loving him for his looks.

## Xenophobia

*Patient Name: Jordan Malone*
*Age: 42*
*Sex: Male*
*Diagnosis: Xenophobia*
*Time of death: To be determined*

This report documents the performance of MJ220717 in the Skinner Prison Experiments. Due to the overcrowding of [REDACTED] State Penitentiary, we have been provided with an operational license to transfer qualified subjects to our rehabilitation facility.

MJ220717 was selected based on the following interview that our agent recorded in his blue notebook.

Agent: Please state the reason for your incarceration.

MJ220717: A beaner was threatening me, so I set his house on fire. You guys going to get me out, or what?

Agent: The police statement says that you were armed and accompanied by three accomplices. The victim was unarmed and living with his wife and five children. How was he threatening you?

MJ220717: Five children? Damn.

Agent: You were unaware?

MJ220717: I knew there were too many of them, but I didn't know they bred like roaches. They're threatening our way of life and will flood the country if somebody don't burn 'em out.

Agent: Do you plan to 'burn out' all 11 million illegal immigrants estimated living within the country?

MJ220717: We killed 6 million Jews last time. Yeah, I reckon we can do 11 if we work together.

Agent: So you and your hate group—

MJ220717: Hate group? Shit, we don't hate anybody. My momma don't raise me like that. Let me ask you something though—you go to church?

Agent: That's not relevant—

MJ220717: 'Cause I do. Me and [REDACTED] were doing God's work. Doing the Law's work that the police are too chicken-shit to do. Now I'm in jail while those fuckers walk around free in my country. So yeah, maybe I do hate that. That's injustice, pure and simple.

Agent: I understand. Thank you, Mr. Malone. I think we can help each other here.

MJ220717 was transferred to our facility two days later. He was happy to be released and provided no resistance as he was introduced to his new living quarters. He was provided with a standard suite, approximately 500 square feet with a private bathroom and mini kitchen.

There were no altercations when he was briefed on the details of his rehabilitation.

Agent: Our team has diagnosed you with xenophobia. Are you familiar with the term?

MJ220717: I'm not sick with nothing.

Agent: It means a fear of the unknown, based on your fear reaction with unfamiliar races and cultures—

MJ220717: I'm not afraid of them! I'm standing up to them. If a snake got in my house and I strangled it before it bit somebody, that's bravery right there. I'm protecting my country.

Agent: …are we finished?

MJ220717: You said we could help each other.

Agent: I got you out of prison, didn't I? Now it's your turn to help me with my study. Unless you'd prefer to go back, of course.

MJ220717: Let's get this over with. What do I have to do? Talk to a counselor?

Agent: Something like that. We're pursuing a form of exposure therapy. It's only going to take two hours a day. The rest of the time will be yours, with access to television and recreational facilities.

MJ220717: I've heard of the exposure thing. So what, you're going to lock me in with a spic? We gonna play checkers or some shit?

Agent: This isn't about your relationship with foreigners. We're more interested in the deeper underlying issue—your fear of the unknown.

MJ220717 did not protest as he was locked inside his living quarters. Security footage continued to monitor him as he paced the room in agitation. This continued for several minutes before he returns to his bed and points the remote at the TV.

The screen remains black. He points again, mashing the buttons in visible frustration. He gets off the bed and approaches the TV, reaching to turn it on manually.

He isn't expecting the hand which reaches out of the screen to intertwine its fingers with his own. He stumbles backward and falls onto his bed. The hand is gone by the time he returns to the screen to smash it with his fist.

MJ220717 hyperventilates as he removes the shards of glass from his knuckles, but he otherwise seems unaware of the [REDACTED] entity now sharing his living space. All agents have vacated the area to give it space to work.

MJ220717 goes to the bathroom, presumably to look for medical supplies. He isn't expecting the swarm of spiders that flood from the medicine cabinet. The capacity is only a few cubic feet, but the contents are sufficient to cover the entire surface area of the bathroom within seconds.

MJ220717 flees the bathroom and closes the door behind him. He presses his back against it for several seconds, his hyperventilation exasperated. When he notices the spiders crawling under the door, he retreats to the bed and pulls the sheets to seal the gap.

He's hammering on the apartment door, calling for help. There is still an hour and forty minutes left of his session, and the door remains locked.

The [REDACTED] entity doesn't remain idle during this time. The hand has reappeared out of the garbage disposal, feeling its way around the kitchen sink.

MJ220717 notices it now. He approaches and stares at the thing, apparently realizing that it is growing into the room rather than reaching. Similar to the development of a time-lapsed plant or mushroom, the hand and arm are swelling. The joints grow more gnarled and misshapen, and additional fingers begin to bud.

MJ220717 tries to turn on the garbage disposal, but the hand intercepts him and interlocks its fingers once more. They struggle briefly before the subject is able to maneuver his free hand to reach the switch. He turns it on, but the intertwined hands drag him into the blades.

He manages to turn off the garbage disposal before his hand enters. He flees once more to the front door, pounding and screaming.

The bathroom door opens. The spiders have been growing in the same manner as the hand, and each are now the size of a rat. They're now large enough for him to realize that they are scuttling on tiny fingers instead of legs.

MJ220717 spends the remainder of his two-hour session pressed against the door while the growing [REDACTED] entities crawl over him. He's still crying when the agent retrieves him and permits him to move to a fresh living space.

Agent: Ever see anything like that before?

MJ220717 is quietly crying.

Agent: We're not so different, you and me. Or you and those people whose house you tried to burn down. Or you and your ancestors ten thousand years ago. We're all pretty much the same, compared with something like that. Don't you think?

MJ220717: I want to go back to jail. Please.

Agent: You have 22 hours before your next session. Feel free to take comfort with your fellow humans in the recreational area until then. You have more in common than you think.

## A Global Religion

It began with alcohol, as more than one religion must have done before. I wanted to be drunk by the time I got home. It's a habit I picked up after my divorce when I realized how cold an empty house can be without a little fire in the blood.

There's a pub around the block that lets me park my car overnight. I'd stop after work and walk home when I couldn't feel my face anymore. The chill morning air on my walk back helped wake me up enough to drive to work, and then I'd do it all again.

I'd thought about going to Alcoholics Anonymous, but I figured I could do the same stuff they did on my own. All I had to do is surrender myself to God, right? To admit that I'm helpless and he's all powerful, and to accept that he doesn't want anyone to have any fun.

It's getting to be winter here though, and one night it was so damn cold that I felt like my skin was peeling off just standing outside. I'd drive home—just this once. No one else was on the road, and I thought I could inch along without any trouble.

I don't know how I turned down an unfamiliar road this close to my home, but whether it was a trick of the darkness or the alcohol, I presently found myself before a row of strange houses. Piles of trash, boarded windows, and even the gutted skeletons of burned houses loomed above me on either side. I was about to turn back when something dark dashed in front of my car.

I slammed my foot down, but somehow the shock crossed my wires and I hit the gas instead. The car lurched forward, and I heard a loud, wet noise, like someone belly flopping into a pool from ten stories up. I heard the second bump as my back tires rolled over it before I could stop.

I threw open my door and stumbled out. There was a long glistening streak behind my tires. A crumpled shape in the road, and one naked white bone jutting out to reflect my taillights.

I threw up. It was a long one where I kept heaving and spitting up bile and drool long after my stomach was empty. I could hear this pitiful moaning the whole time, but I was helpless to my trembling contractions and couldn't help him.

I thought I was too late by the time I walked back to the mess on the road. There wasn't an inch of unmarked skin or a limb that wasn't folded back on itself. The broken form looked more like it had gone through a blender than been hit by a car.

"Please..." the voice said, gurgling and spluttering as it did. "Please forgive me."

"Forgive you? Shit, I was the one—hold on, I'm going to call for help."

"I'm sorry. I'm sorry. I know I deserve this, but have mercy."

It took supreme concentration to force my clumsy fingers to dial 911, but I froze before I hit call. The broken form was rising, and dozens of fingers were intertwining in front of it in a gesture of prayer.

Dozens. I kept blinking, sure that the alcohol was playing tricks on me. As it continued to stand, it became undeniable though: whatever I was looking at wasn't human.

I couldn't understand how my car could have done that much damage, but now I saw that it hadn't. The creature's body was covered in boils and welts, many of which were long since ruptured to weep rivers of dried blood and pus. Its third leg was shriveled as though devoid of muscle or bone, dragging limp on the ground behind it. Veins across its body stood out like knotted rope beneath the skin, except in the many places where they exited the skin entirely to tangle with one another before sinking back into the flesh.

I felt the nausea swelling up within me again, but I was too empty to vomit again. We stared at one another for a long moment before it said:

"You're not one of us."

I shook my head.

Something like a snarl crossed its face, destroying its last visage of humanity and replacing it with a mask of bestial terror.

"You don't know how long we've waited for you," it hissed.

I turned and began walking toward my car, swaying but remaining upright.

"Please don't leave us!" The terrible wail behind me only made me hasten my pace. "The others are coming."

I dropped heavily back into the driver seat and slammed the door. I spent a few moments fumbling with the buttons before I heard the doors lock. I re-locked them a dozen times just to be sure. When I looked up, I could see the face of the creature filling my rearview mirror.

It bore traces of being human, but only so much as butchered meat hints at the finally prepared meal which might be made from it. The car's side panels on either side shook, and there were more of the creatures peering through the windows. Then a loud thump on the roof, and the pitter-patter of those dozens of fingers probing along the surface, feeling each ridge for a way in.

Though mired in the dead of night, the surrounding street had come alive. The light of flames flickered into existence in the surrounding houses, and where there was no flame a sea of eyes reflected the light from the shadows. Long fingers pried away the boards on the windows, and much of what I'd mistaken for trash now shifted with the teeming beings which had huddled underneath.

"Don't leave us, my pure-skin, my love." A living echo which multiplied with every utterance. "Love, love—never leave."

I maneuvered the car forward, trying my best not to hit anyone. My hesitation only made it more difficult as the creatures continued pressing in around the car. I had no choice but to floor the pedal and press through them, hoping they'd get out of the way.

They didn't. If anything, they made an active effort to hurl themselves before the car as though their bodies could slow my departure. The wails rose in pitch around me, the agony of the fallen growing more frenzied and desperate by the second.

Each that was crushed or wounded by the relentless passage of my car would be swiftly seized by their massing brethren. Such victims could not defend themselves and were swiftly torn to shreds, devoured alive before my eyes. The empty space was filled at once with more creatures who hurled themselves before me only to be met with a similarly gruesome fate.

Crawling headfirst down from windows, or digging up from the ground, or manifesting from the darkness, this swarming legion flooded toward me from all directions. I increased my speed and gave no regard to the constant buckling of the car as it rolled over the incessant mob.

But I could not block out the wailing grief, nor the chanting which arose from every corner of this blasphemous street. Dark hymns whistled and shrieked with feverish pitch, and again the echoes which spread through the chaos like an infectious disease.

"We need you—we love you—our pure-skin God. Take us with you—don't leave us—our pure-skin God."

Until I'd finally gained enough acceleration to tear through the last of them and break free onto the open street. Many tried to race alongside me for as long as they could, their deformed bodies moving with desperate urgency until they collapsed in exhaustion and were beset by those behind.

I didn't dare slow until I'd left that madness far behind and found myself on a solitary hill. I paused to look at the view and get my bearings, but I recognized nothing that I saw.

Unfamiliar towers gouged the sky, mountains lit by firelight. The neighborhood I passed was no anomaly, for as far as I could see the ruined buildings were writhing to life with the swarming creatures. I couldn't stay long though, for already bright eyes were reflecting from the darkness around.

I drove again until I found a larger road, and then taking that I kept going until I found a highway. The echo had spread far past the street of its origin, and I heard the phrase "pure-skin" follow me where I went like rolling thunder across the land.

I was the only car on the highway and remained so for many miles while fleeing that awful den. My head ached, and I was exhausted, but I forced my eyes to remained locked on the road ahead of me and didn't deviate from my path.

It wasn't until the early hours of the morning when I heard a siren and suddenly realized I was no longer alone on the road. The daily traffic had gradually resumed around me, each car occupied by a human driver—bored, sleepy, and ignorant to the denizens of that dreadful night.

"Do you know why I pulled you over?" the policeman asked when he got out of his car.

"Because I'm wretched and I deserved it," I managed to reply.

"I'm more concerned about the blood on your car," he said.

Good thing it wasn't human blood, or I could have been in real trouble.

I don't know how I stumbled into that world, but I think I accidentally started some sort of religion there. So must all things seem glorious to the wretched. If only they understood how small and powerless their pure-skinned God really was.

## First Rule of Fright Club

The first rule of fright club is that you can't join if you have a heart condition or high blood pressure. That's just common sense though, right?

The second rule is that you can't leave the room until the bell rings. Whatever you see or feel in there—whatever sees or feels you—that's your reality until the round is over.

The third rule is that you cannot take anything with you or let anything follow you out. The poster said that breaking any of these rules makes the participant ineligible to win the $10,000 grand prize, which comes with a unique internship opportunity.

The cartoon pumpkin and witch stickers didn't make it sound very threatening. Besides, the poster had my University logo on it, and everyone knows that school-sponsored events are lame and politically correct by necessity.

"You can't not do it," my friend Jesse told me. "It's free money." This coming from the guy whose retirement plan is buying a lottery ticket every month.

"There has to be a catch," I told him. "They charged me to print out my resume so I could apply to their own job offers. You aren't going to get it."

"Let's make it more interesting then," Jesse said. "Bet you $100 bucks that I last longer than you, whatever it is."

$10,000 is $10,000, but showing up my friend and taking his money? Now that's priceless. I agreed to check it out, and we both went to the specified room in the psychology building after our classes finished for the day.

The stickers made it easy to find the right place. Big black cauldrons with frothing brew, zombies and skeletons, ghosts with their billowing sheets and demons with pitchforks. The scrawny teenager in the long black cloak who checked us in was even less intimidating.

"You know the three rules?" the guy in the cloak asked when we said we'd like to join.

"Yeah. But what's up with something following you out?" I asked.

The teenager shrugged. "Donno. I figure they just don't want to make a mess in the rest of the building."

"Has anyone won yet?" Jesse asked.

"Maybe?" The teenager scratched the back of his head with the intensity of a dog chasing fleas. "Man, just let me read from the script, okay?" He coughed and held up a clipboard, beginning again in what he must have thought was a dark and spooky voice. It sounded more like Dracula's gay lover to me.

"Once upon a time in a far away land, an aging King had to decide which of his three sons would next sit upon the throne. Believing bravery to be most important, the King devised Fright Club to test which of his sons were worthy."

"Seriously? What self-respecting King would call his test Fright Club?" Jesse asked.

The teenager gave us a long suffering look, like a waiter when you ask him to taste your gluten-free food to see if he thought could still taste the gluten.

"Ever since, Fright Club has been passed down through the generations," the cloaked guy continued. "Dare ye enter to see if you too are brave enough to be King?"

"Is that what we're interning for? Being King?" Jesse quipped.

"Just sign the damn form," the teenager snapped. "I don't know anything more than you do."

I picked at one of the pumpkin stickers on the wall while Jesse was signing. It peeled cleanly back to reveal a little hole in the wall. It was time for me to sign though, so I pressed the sticker back into place and pretended I didn't see anything. I thought that I might be able to get an advantage from this insight later.

The teenager meanwhile produced a large uncarved pumpkin from beneath a table and left it in the middle of the room. He set a timer on the table for ten minutes and said he'd check back after the first round was over. Then he was gone, and it was just me, Jesse, and the pumpkin.

"I don't get it," Jesse said, pacing the perimeter of the room. "What are we supposed to—"

The lights went out, suspending the room in nearly complete darkness. The only glimmer came from the stickers which apparently glowed.

"Oooh I'm a four-year-old. I need a nightlight because I'm scared of the dark," Jesse whined.

"Shut up. Do you hear something?" I asked.

"Yeah, I think so. It sounds a bit like the easiest $100 I ever made."

I didn't reply. I was intent on the scraping, scratching sound. Like a knife peeling a potato, or—

"Something is carving the pumpkin. Listen."

I felt my way toward the center of the room and the sound grew stronger. It was a wet, juicy sound, and I could clearly smell the freshly cut pumpkin.

"My phone isn't turning on," Jesse grumbled. "Can you see what's happening?"

I fumbled in my pocket. My phone was dead too, although it had been at half battery the last time I checked. I gingerly probed the darkness with my foot until I found the pumpkin. I reached down to feel it with my fingers, but immediately recoiled at the soft, warm touch.

"It doesn't feel like a pumpkin…" I said.

Jesse traced my voice and quickly located it as well. I felt him kneeling beside me.

"That's a head, dude. Check it, I've got the nose right here."

I felt along his arm until I reached his hand. Then back to the invisible 'pumpkin'. It was undeniable. The shape, the flexible cartilage, even the lips and teeth below it. There was a human head where the pumpkin had been.

"This is kid stuff, dude," Jesse said with the slightest tremor in his throat. "I wonder how much time we've got left."

"So what's the sound coming from if it's not a pumpkin?" I asked. My hand was still tracing the face when I felt the jaw suddenly open. The scraping sound grew louder. Something brushed against my fingers, evidently exiting the mouth.

I stumbled back a few paces. "Jesse? Did you feel that? Where are you?"

"Over here man. I'm getting some glow stickers to try to see what's going on."

I spotted him against the wall, his hands vaguely illuminated by the small stack of stickers he'd already peeled off. The scraping sound was coming from the walls now too. Something was coming through the holes behind the stickers.

"Stop it. Put them back," I said.

"Chill, dude. You're just jealous you didn't think of it first."

"Hurry then. Come on, that's enough."

His pale illuminated hands were carrying about a dozen glowing stickers. I watched him grab two more before carrying the pile toward the middle of the room. Then his hands hesitated, and he changed direction.

"Hold on a second. I'm just going to check the timer."

The scraping was getting louder by the second. Like sandpaper along a rough surface, or hundreds of tiny legs skittering—

"Three minutes left. No big deal."

Something flying brushed my face. Then another one. The whirr of unseen wings beat against the blackness all around me.

"I want out of here," I said.

"Come on, we're almost there. I bet it's just like stuff on strings swinging around." His glowing hands were moving toward the center of the room.

"Are you encouraging me to stay now? Don't you care about winning anymore?"

"Whatever, I can win next round instead. I just don't want to be alone in here."

"Aha! I knew it! You are afraid!" The triumph of that realization gave me courage. It was easy to forget that we were still at school with the dark buzzing all around us.

"Do you remember when we were freshman and those three guys started following us one night?"

Jesse was standing directly over where the head was, but the light didn't reach far enough down.

"Yeah, so what?" I asked.

"You remember how we kept taking random routes to lose them, but they kept making all the same turns?" He still wasn't moving.

"What are you waiting for?" I asked. "Light that sucker up."

"Then how we started running, and they ran too? But they were just playing a prank on us to scare us."

More flying things were brushing against me. They kept landing on my face or the back of my neck. My hands were nonstop windshield wipers now, but it still wasn't enough to keep them off.

"What does that have to do with anything?" I asked. "Is this a pep talk or something?"

"No," Jesse said. "I just wanted you to remember." He finally knelt down with the glowing stickers. If that was a fake head on the ground, then it was the realest fake head I'd ever seen. From the congealed blood at the base of the severed neck to the flies and maggots swarming out of its mouth, everything looked exactly how I'd imagine it should.

"I just want you to know how well I tricked you. I know everything Jesse knew, because I already got him the second the lights turned off."

The glowing handful of stickers illuminated Jesse's head on the ground. But it couldn't really be him because I've been hearing his voice the whole time. Hadn't I?

I studied the hands that were holding the glowing stickers. For the first time I noticed how large and rough the fingers were. How much hair was on the knuckles. The light wasn't strong enough to see the rest of him, but in that moment I was 100% certain that those were not Jesse's hands.

"Run," Jesse's voice said from the darkness.

"I'm not leaving before you do, Jesse," I said, addressing the head on the ground. "$100, that's the deal. But I'm not leaving without you either."

"That's good," said Jesse's voice. The pitch of the voice grew deeper with each word. "I'll see you again in round 2 then."

The hands cupped to cover the glowing stickers and disappeared along with the head. There was no sound but the mad buzzing of insects, although this too grew fainter and more distant by the moment.

I crossed my arms and stood stubbornly still until the bell rang. The lights came on an instant later, just in time for me to see the last few insects crawling back into the holes in the wall. They looked like wasps, but were at least three inches long with monstrous spiral stingers. They reminded me of those army knives that were supposed to leave wounds that couldn't be closed.

"Round 1 clear!" the teenager said with forced enthusiasm. "Congratulations."

I blinked rapidly to readjust to the light. There was a pumpkin in the middle of the floor again. Jesse's head and the other figure were nowhere to be seen.

"What about Jesse?" I asked. "Did he leave early?"

"Who?"

"Jesse. The other guy who took the test with me."

The teenager scratched his head vigorously. Hard enough for there to be blood under his fingernails when he withdrew his hand.

"I don't know what you're talking about. Only one person at a time is allowed to take the tests. You came in here alone."

Jesse hasn't answered my calls since I got out. No one has seen him anywhere. I can only hope there will be more answers in the second round.

## Second Rule of Fright Club

The second rule is that you can't leave the room until the bell rings. Whatever you see or feel in there—whatever sees or feels you—that's your reality until the round is over.

I guess I shouldn't have been surprised to find Jesse waiting for me inside the Fright Club room. The severed head had been pretty convincing though, and I was cautious not to close the door completely behind me. We were the only ones in the room, and it was empty except for a table covered by a white sheet.

"Nice robe," I told Jesse. "What happened to the other guy?"

Jesse was scratching his right forearm. Hard. It sounded like the nails were splintering. I studied his face hard, trying to discern whether it was really him or only the thing pretending.

"Huh? Hey man, haven't seen you in…" his voice trailed off. He turned his attention back toward scratching his red arm.

"So you work here now?" I asked, trying to keep my voice casual.

"Yeah since…" Scratch. Scratch. Scratch. Then he stole a glance at me, shying away from meeting my eyes. "Your hair is different," Jesse said. "Longer. A lot longer—is that a wig?"

The shock of finding him occupied my initial attention. Now that he mentioned it though, he looked different too. He was paler and skinnier than he was yesterday, with rough stubble that couldn't have grown overnight.

"No. Just combed weird," I replied cautiously. I could only hope that this was the real Jesse, but I couldn't let my guard down.

"You know how it is, man," Jesse said. "It's not like the King asks whether someone wants the job or not. Someone's got to do it though, right?"

"Sure," I lead him on. "Otherwise how would the King know who was going to rule after him?"

"You know what's up," Jesse bobbed and nodded. He moved towards me, but I got out of the way to give him space.

My mistake—Jesse was headed for the door, not for me. Now I'd let that thing get between me and my only exit. He roughly closed the door and turned to face me.

"Are we ready to begin?" Jesse asked.

A muffled ticking began before I could answer. I couldn't make out where it was coming from though.

"How long have we had a King?" I asked.

He grinned like he was in on the joke. I didn't follow up with anything though, and gradually the smile cracked at the edges to draw the lips tight and thin.

"Always. But you've just got ten minutes." I felt an anxious rush as though it was my time running out instead of the game's.

"I saw you dead," I said accusingly, unable to maintain my forced nonchalance any longer.

"Yeah…" Jesse replied hoarsely. "I felt it too. Like lightning through my throat, and then everything went numb, and I saw my body tumbling away…" He turned away, his hands on the back of his neck. Scratching. Blood between the nails. "That was only my other, though. I guess your other is still alive?"

I hadn't considered that. I didn't want to consider what he meant.

"The King said we'll know when our double dies, even if he's in the parallel universe," the other Jesse continued. "I thought it would be more like a notification though. I didn't expect to actually feel him die."

"I don't understand this round," I interrupted. I was getting impatient and frustrated. "What's supposed to be scary about this?"

"This one isn't supposed to be scary," the other Jesse said. He went to the table and began rolling back the sheet. "There's more to bravery than not being scared. Like enduring pain, for example."

A thin naked body was revealed beneath the sheet. I winced as it turned toward me, recognizing my own face staring back.

"Yeah, that's the short hair I remember," Jesse said, staring at the thin body. Then to me: "I guess that makes you the other."

The ticking was louder now. It was coming from the body on the table. Jesse continued rolling back the sheet until he reached the stomach, revealing the alarm clock embedded deep within the flesh. It looked like an old wound because the skin had grown around it to hold it in place with hardened scar tissue.

"What's it like? The other side?" Jesse turned away from the body. I wish I could too, but my eyes were fixed. "What's the King like?"

The ticking stopped. My other groaned and shifted on the table.

"We don't have a King," I told the other Jesse.

"No King…" the other Jesse sighed. "I wish I could go back with you."

I may have been slow to realize it, but that's when it really hit me. This room—maybe the whole building, but definitely this room—wasn't in my reality. I was already on the other side.

"What's going on?" I asked. "Why did the clock stop?"

"You've got to take it out to resume it," Jesse said. "Otherwise the round will never end."

The face of the clock barely protruded from my other's skin. I didn't know how far back it extended, but removing the clock would leave a gaping hole that would doubtlessly be a mortal wound.

My other whimpered and closed his eyes. My eyes—his eyes—it didn't matter. I shook my head and went for the door.

"I'm not going to kill him," I said. Jesse didn't move to stop me, so I accelerated until I reached the exit. "I only came back because I thought I could save you. You can come with me—"

"Third rule," Jesse replied.

"Fine, suit yourself. I'm going."

Only I wasn't. Opening the door, there was no school hallway or decorated walls. There was a long corridor of rough stone with red flickering electric lights. And a rising echo—a distant scream reverberating through the stone. I swiftly closed the door again.

"The second rule—"

"Shut up. Shut the hell up," I said, angrily pacing back. "I'm not going to do it."

Jesse shrugged and resumed scratching.

"What the hell is wrong with you, anyway?" I asked.

He shrugged again, focusing on his task.

I was getting really agitated, but I couldn't control it. I paced restlessly, trying not to look at my other's frail body. The only other place to look was the other Jesse and his incessant scratching.

Scratch scratch scratch—he was beginning to draw blood again. It beaded out of his forearm to dribble down toward his wrist. I stared as he picked at the tattered skin, peeling it back like a child playing with dried glue.

There was something moving underneath. Small black fingers, quick as anything, darted out of the wound to draw the skin back together. I only saw it for a moment, but it was enough.

I worked up the courage to stand over my other on the table. He wasn't me, no matter how much he looked like it. He wasn't human, although that thought was an even harder sell because his face held so much suffering and resignation.

"Okay. Okay okay." Deep breath. "I'm sorry," I said to the thing wearing my face. It didn't hear, or didn't react if it did.

I grabbed the clock with my fingertips and began to pull. My other started to scream, and I reflexively released, feeling the building pressure in my own stomach release as well. Then gritting my teeth I grabbed again, dragging it out one excruciating centimeter at a time.

Blood was swelling from beneath the clock, soaking my fingers and making it slippery and hard to hold. At the same time I could feel the gouging pressure in my own stomach explode into a white-hot knot of pain.

My other began to thrash on the table, but I pulled even harder. This wasn't happening. He's not human. I'm not really killing him. I'm not really dying. The words made no impact on the agony of the moment. It doesn't matter whether this was reality or not. It was real to me.

The small black fingers emerged from my other's open wound and danced around the clock, dragging it back inside. I wrestled with them, but they were incessant and I was growing weak from pain. I needed something sharp—something to cut it out with, but I had nothing but my own hands.

I managed to get the clock completely out of the skin, but I couldn't break the grip of the dark fingers. My only choice was to hold the clock with one hand while using the other to reach inside the wound, feeling around the back of the clock to try to turn it back on. This blind maneuver was subtle, and it as almost impossible to concentrate because I could feel a hand rummaging around in my own stomach the whole while.

Click—then ticking—at last the clock was going again. I released the clock and dragged my hand out of my other's stomach cavity. The pressure immediately vanished in my own stomach, but the shock was enough to leave me panting and heaving on all fours.

I heard my own scream, but I couldn't be sure whether it was coming from me or my other. I stayed there on my hands and knees, waiting for the pain to slowly subside until it was nothing more than a dull ache.

The bell finally rang.

"If I finish all three trials, do I become King?" I asked at last.

"That's how it's usually done," Jesse said.

"And I could do whatever I want then, right? I could break my own rules and let people out, or stop playing games with them, or anything I wanted?"

"I don't see who would stop you."

"So when does the final round start?"

## Third Rule of Fright Club

The third and final rule is that you cannot take anything with you, or let anything follow you out. It's the only rule I broke during my trials.

I wanted to bring my double with me when I left the second round. The black fingers did wonders to mend his wound from the inside, and though broken in spirit, there was still breath dragging from his lungs when I left.

But for an accident of birth, I could have been that tormented pawn in this unholy game. Or maybe I was no less of a pawn than him—maybe I was him, and there was no difference at all—it's still very confusing for me. Ultimately, I decided that I would do no good for anyone unless I could pass the third round though, and I left him so as not to jeopardize my chances.

The King was waiting in the open door of the Fright Club room for the third round. On his head rested a thin crown of twisted black wire, but I didn't need that to recognize him. The thick hair on his hands—the deep voice when he welcomed me—he was the man who had killed the real Jesse in the first round. More than that though, it was the familiarity in his ancient face that made me so certain.

"Is that really what I'm going to look like when I get old?" I asked him. From the set of his jaw to the sharp angles of his nose and high arching brows, I knew I was looking at another version of myself despite the toll of years.

"If you get old," the King replied somberly.

He smiled and stepped aside graciously, gesturing for me to enter. The room didn't have the facade of a classroom anymore—cold stone and red electric lights trailed off into a sea of shadows in the massive space.

The air was musty and cold when I stepped inside, and sound echoed and lingered beneath the massive dome overhead. It reminded me of a gothic cathedral, except that in place of religious iconography there were only statues and carved designs of strange and monstrous creatures that had never been seen on Earth.

"Stand with your others," the King said in a voice accustomed to being obeyed. "We'll begin when the last contestants have arrived."

I shivered as I moved toward the dozen other shapes. They were sitting on a row of benches which were arranged around the perimeter of the round room. I can't say I was surprised to see each wearing my face as they tracked my progress toward them.

That's not to say that there weren't still variations between us though. One was young—looking just as I had ten years ago, wearing the bright red sweatshirt that I remember wearing to school every day. Another was hardly recognizable because of his dozens of piercings, and a third was even female, sharing my features in the way twins might. Their clothes ranged from coarse hand-sewn linens to sleek suits and everything in-between, including two wearing a seamless metallic substance which fit them as close as a second skin.

"Um, hi," I said to the assembly of my others. "My name is—"

They knew my name because it choroused back to me at once.

"That's what we're all called," the youngest one chimed in.

"Sure, okay," I said. "That's going to get confusing though, don't you think?"

The female version of myself said: "It shouldn't be a problem. Only one of us will leave this place."

"Did the King tell you that?" I asked.

They all glanced back and forth, reading each other's faces with unspoken acknowledgement. No, they didn't have to be told. Deep down they just knew—and so did I.

"How are we the only ones to make it to the end?" I asked. Again I knew the answer before I'd even finished asking, but the cold silence of this place begged to be filled.

"The rest of us didn't survive the first two rounds," the woman said. "We're the only ones he wants."

"But why?"

The King's deep voice echoed indistinctly. All froze and turned their attention toward two more of us—me twenty years from now, with a large belly and receding hair, and another me whose gaunt and haunted expression looked like the mugshot of a heroin addict.

"It would be best if I answered that," the King said, following the two latest arrivals toward us. "It all begins with a King and his three sons. Stop me if you've heard this one."

"None of the three sons passed," my other in a suit said. "They all died in this round."

The King beamed. I half-expected him to take a treat from his pocket and throw it at my other. Instead, he said: "Correct. And it is a blessing that they did, for it would be a greater tragedy by far to have a weak King sit upon the throne. Imagine now that poor old King whose sand ran swift through the hourglass. He had watched all three of his dear sons die, and now his Kingdom would be lost without a strong hand upon the reigns. Follow."

The King continued walking toward the center of the great chamber as he drew level with us. We stood and followed him across the uneven stone.

"None were worthy to sit upon the throne," the King continued, "save for the King himself. If he could conjure a magic draught to live forever, doubtless he would be ruling still. Instead he did the next best thing—he found a way to create his other and crown a younger self, and so he began his rule again."

The King stopped at the center of the room where a large pit was carved into the floor. Inside the three-foot drop, the pit was filled with fine-powdered sand. Embedded in the sand were swords, spears, axes, and other strange bladed devices that I could not recognize. In the very center of the sand was a large-faced clock.

"Each King has refined this subtle art and passed on his knowledge, until now we are no longer limited to a single other. We create all the variations of ourselves and spread them so each may have different experiences and lives. Each comes from different epochs with different talents. Only this King among Kings is fit to rule hereafter, and only one of you is worthy to replace me."

I closed my eyes but could not block the image of what must surely come next. He would have us fight and kill one another here until only one was left. And worse still, each wound and death that we inflict upon one another must also be felt upon ourselves, such was the agony of the clock in the second round.

"And if we don't?" I was first to break the heavy silence. "If we all refuse to rule and you are left to wait for age to take you?"

"You aren't the first to ask that." The King sneered. "It only takes one of you to want it though, and knowing myself, at least one of us is ready to kill."

My others sensed it too, as they must thinking with my mind. We looked to one another for comfort, but saw only the eyes of our victims or our murderer looking back at us. The same ambition which drove me to return for the final round must also burn in their hearts. I could trust none of them any more than I could trust myself, and in such desperate circumstances I did not value my nobility high.

"I won't kill you," whispered the girl out of the corner of her mouth.

"Thanks," I whispered back. "That's the nicest thing anyone has said to me all day."

She coughed discreetly. The King glanced at us, then turned away.

"And?" she prompted urgently. "You're supposed to say you won't kill me either."

"Oh right, yeah. Definitely not. I mean, there isn't really another option, but hopefully not."

The King was starting to pull the weapons from the sand. He was still talking—something about the glory of victory and the honor of besting yourself. I wasn't really listening anymore.

"We could run." She barely mouthed the words, but our minds were already running down the same road.

"We'd have to break the third rule," I said. "The King—"

"The King is our other too," she interrupted. "When one of us is killed—he'll feel it too. That will be our chance. I don't want to go alone."

The King was looking at us again. I didn't reply, but I gave the slightest nod. That would be enough for her to understand. It was enough for the King too.

"You, boy. From the University. You're first." The King hurled a sword at me, handle first. I snatched it and almost dropped it immediately, surprised by its weight. "Suit—you too. Let's make this quick."

I felt several hands on my back pushing me toward the pit. I glanced back at the girl—the subtlest nod. But before we could break for it, someone had to die. And if I was in the first round, that meant that I had to kill.

The suit was fumbling a set of javelins when I dropped onto the sand. If I were him, I wouldn't hesitate. That's why I rolled the instant I hit the ground—just in time before the first spear quivered in the sand beside me.

The ticking of the clock began, but I wasn't playing anymore.

There wasn't anywhere left to hide. He'd expect me to charge straight at him, trying to close the distance to use my sword. I took a sharp right instead, feeling the air of a second javelin digging into the ground. He'd be ready for that trick next time, but I wouldn't give him the chance.

I dashed across the sand directly toward him. My feet were sinking with every step though, and it was taking longer to reach him than I expected. I tried to dodge again as he raised his arm, but he held the javelin this time and waited until the last possible moment. I tried to switch directions again, but I lost my footing in the loose sand and tumbled to the ground. A few feet away from him and helplessly mired, he wouldn't miss again.

The pain came with an explosion of light and heat. In one side and out the other, straight through the heart. I was dead, and the only mystery left was wondering how I knew I was dead.

"Run! Everyone now is your chance!" the girl screamed.

I was back on my feet before I realized what happened. My combatant fell to his knees, the tip of a knife protruding from his chest. The girl was standing behind. He never threw the last javelin—it was his death that I'd felt.

I scrambled out of the pit and helped her out behind me. The old King was clutching his chest and gasping for breath—everyone was in an equal state of shock and pain, but the older ones were slower to recover.

Some of us broke away and started running for the door—the youngest boy, the girl, and the middle aged man.

"Kill them!" the King roared. "Shoot them in the back. It'll save you trouble in the arena."

Swords bouncing off the stone, the whir of projectiles in the air, neither as terrifying as seeing my faces contorted in rage and bloodlust as they charged after me.

"He recovered too fast," I yelled. "He won't let us escape."

"Keep going, trust me," the girl said. I wanted to explain that I couldn't trust her because I couldn't trust myself, but I decided not to waste the air.

We leapt over the benches. Behind me I heard one of them turn over as someone stumbled and fell. It was the youngest boy, sprawled out on the stone on the other side of an upturned bench. The boy was on his knees again in a second, but not fast enough—

The whir of a crossbow and the fatal pain returned. Like a drill bursting through the back of my skull. I kept running—there's no way someone could have survived a blow like that.

It bought us enough time to get to the door. I flung it open and stood staring at the empty stone corridor beyond. I slammed the door shut again and re-opened it to the same sight.

"No one is going anywhere," the King's booming voice reverberated through the chamber. "Not until they finish my game."

The girl arrived beside me a second later. She ripped open the door a third time to see the same hall.

"His game, his rules," she sighed in exasperation. The others would be on us in a matter of seconds. "On my signal, you open it again."

"It's no good. We're still stuck in—"

"You have to trust me," she said.

"What signal?"

But the signal was impossible to miss. A blade in my heart, staggering me to my knees. I forced myself upright and opened the door at once, seeing my school corridor with the Halloween stickers beyond.

I leapt through and turned to see the girl still on her knees, hands pressing the knife into her own heart. The King was bellowing somewhere beyond—the shock must have been enough to break the spell separating the two dimensions for just a moment.

With the last of her strength, the girl lunged forward and slammed the door in my face. I instinctively tried to open it once more, but the pain which overtook me was unbearable.

I died a dozen times in the next few moments. My head was caved in, or lopped off entirely. The piercing of blades sliding between each rib, and other wounds which were harder to classify. There was a slaughter in progress on the other side of the door, and I was helpless to stop it.

By the time the worst of it passed I stood and flung the door open, ready to rush back and save who could be saved. I nearly tripped over myself entering the empty classroom. Lights off, desks pushed against the wall, there was no sign of the other world which I'd been cut off from.

I don't know who survived in the end, if anyone. I can only hope that whatever black magic preserved us with the mending fingers saved her somehow. I hope that there is a Queen who sits next upon the throne, and that she will break the tradition and go in peace.

I tell myself that I'm the lucky one, but I don't know. How can I go back to living my life when so many parts of me will never leave the Fright Club room?

## Antennas on Every House

The antennas weren't installed during the day. Someone would have noticed the electrician's van in the street. I don't see how they could have been put in at night either though. I can clearly hear when squirrels chase each other on my roof—there's no way I wouldn't notice someone walking around up there.

Mrs. Jackson on my left noticed first. She had already called the power department, our internet and cable provider, and the homeowner's association—none of which had a clue.

She insisted that I step outside and look at them, despite my face clearly expressing zero interest. Her voice was getting more shrill with every word though, so I eventually allowed her to drag me outside to avoid waking my six-year-old daughter Emma.

Bleary-eyed and still in my bathrobe, I followed Mrs. Jackson to the street to get a proper view of the thing. The antennas had three metal prongs a bit like a pitchfork, pure black unlike the typical metallic ones. I spent several minutes nodding seriously as she rambled, wondering how long I was expected to stand there before I could politely resume my apathy.

"You can probably climb there from your balcony," Mrs. Jackson told me. "All you'd have to do is jump up and grab—"

"Wouldn't it be just as easy from your balcony?" I asked.

Mrs. Jackson gave me a critical look as though trying to decide whether to be offended. It was only a subtle change from her usual expression.

"My husband won't be home until tonight," she said, as though that was my fault somehow. "It'll only take a minute."

It was just cold enough for politeness to suddenly become optional.

"Oh, wait, I remember what that is," I said, turning back. I drawled out my words so I could make it all the way to my door before I finished. "That's just the government secret surveillance program. Don't blow up anything and you should be fine."

I swiftly shut the door before she could reply and congratulated myself on a successful escape. I let my wife answer the door next time and heard her apologizing on my behalf. My wife managed to get me out of climbing on the roof, but somehow we lost Emma to our neighbor's daughter's sleepover during the negotiation.

I didn't think anything more of the antennas until I left for work and they caught my eye. There were two dead squirrels on my roof beside them, lying in a small pool of blood which dribbled into the gutter.

When I got home that night I found Mr. Jackson kneeling on his roof beside his antenna. He was motionless and intent upon the thing, staring with such ferocity that I expected him to lunge and snap it off at any moment.

"Hiding from the Misses, huh?" I called up to him. "Good spot."

He started to move his head toward me but stopped part way, his eyes never leaving the antenna. Slowly his head returned to its fixed position. I thought he might not have heard me and was about to try again when he said quite softly, "Can you hear it? Like static in your brain."

"Hear what? Hey look, while you're up there would you mind tossing those two dead—those four dead squirrels from my roof?"

Four now. I shuddered, trying not to look at them. There must be a hawk or something that lived up there.

Mr. Jackson slowly turned his head toward me again, his eyes finally breaking away from the antenna at the last moment. His mouth seemed to be moving, but I couldn't hear anything.

I stepped closer until I could hear a faint buzzing sound. He was blowing air through his lips like Emma did when she was trying to make a fart noise. The vibrating of his lips sounded more like static though. We locked eyes for about ten seconds, him softly blubbering the whole while. Without another word I turned and went inside my house, glad to be rid of him.

I didn't feel comfortable about Emma sleeping there that night, but I couldn't think of a good reason not to let her go either. I packed her school bag with her dolls, a board game, and a whistle—just in case. I told her all she needed to do was blow the whistle if anything was wrong, and I'd hear and come get her.

After ten minutes of continuous whistle blowing—including once when she tried to make it sound different by sneezing into it—I'd changed my mind and was happy when Mrs. Jackson knocked to pick her up.

"Did you ever figure out what the antennas are for?" I asked her.

She gave me the stink eye. "Government surveillance, no doubt."

"Oh that's nice. You hear that Emma? You've got to be good or the government will take you away."

"Sounds good!" Emma said cheerfully.

"What a horrible thing to say to your child," Mrs. Jackson sniffed.

"How do you get your daughter to behave?" I asked.

"Shirley doesn't need to be threatened. She knows good girls go to heaven and bad girls go to hell, and that's all there is to it," Mrs. Jackson huffed without the slightest sense of irony.

We were interrupted by the blast of a whistle.

"I want to go!" Emma demanded. "What are we still doing here?"

I felt slightly sick watching Mrs. Jackson take Emma by the hand and walk away. I watched them all the way until they got to their house. Mr. Jackson was still on the roof, but he turned away from the antenna to watch them go inside. It was hard to tell from here, but it seemed like his lips were still moving.

I closed the door and took a deep breath. My wife and I had the house to ourselves though, and that was enough reason to celebrate.

It was freezing outside, but I left the window open that night so I could hear the whistle. My wife thought I was being paranoid, but apparently paranoia is cute when it comes to our daughter, so she let me keep it open. That should have made me feel better, but it didn't. In fact I felt even worse because every moment that I didn't hear the whistle made me wonder whether something had already happened to her.

I'd bothered my wife enough already though, and I kept my fears to myself. I lay awake listening for the static in my brain—for the whistle—for something on the roof—for anything. But the night was dark and still, and little by little I allowed myself to lower my defenses and drift off to sleep.

That night I dreamt of falling from a dizzying height as though I was dropped from space. I kept going faster and faster, the wind whipping around me. But no matter how fast I went or how far I fell, I never seemed to get any closer to the ground.

I could still hear the wind when I woke up the next morning. It sounded a lot like a whistle. The next I remember, I was in my kitchen with three police officers standing around the table.

They believe that Mr. Jackson had killed his wife during the night. The hushed tones and ashen faces of the police told me not to ask exactly how. Most of their daughter Shirely was found in the living room beside her mother, although they're having trouble finding the rest. Mr. Jackson was nowhere to be found.

Thank God that Emma escaped in time. The police found her hiding on the roof, clinging to the antenna all night long to keep from sliding off. She must be suffering from shock and cold, they said, because when they found her she barely responded. She couldn't tear her eyes away from the antenna, or reply with anything besides the soft static nosies she made with her mouth.

## I Lost My Innocence at Serenity Falls

My father was a diplomat who shook hands with the most powerful people in the world. A business man with foreign affairs, managing an empire so vast that the sun never sets upon it. He was an army veteran in Afghanistan and a doctor in Ethiopia. In fact, he was so important that he went everywhere and did everything—except for coming home, that is.

When I was little, I used to love hearing stories about him. I liked to imagine that I'd get to meet him someday, and the two of us would go everywhere I heard about in mom's stories. It wasn't until I was eight years old when I realized how strained her voice was when she talked about him, or how selfish I was for always bringing him up. I didn't ask for any more stories after that, and mom never brought him up on her own.

She must have loved him terribly for it to still hurt after all these years. My mother once said the longer you wait for something you want, the better it is to have, like interest building up in the bank. So every day he didn't come home wasn't a punishment; it would only make their reunion that much happier when it finally did happen.

It would have been so much easier if he did come back though. I wouldn't have to walk home from school because mom would be there to pick me up. And I wouldn't have to make my own dinner, because mom wouldn't need a second job in the evening. Some nights I'd try to stay up until she got back, but I'd usually fall asleep on the couch watching TV and wouldn't see her until the morning when she woke me in my bed.

The older I got, the more mother's stories didn't make sense. Even if only one of them was true, my father must have had an opportunity to visit by now. Army contracts are only 4 years, and if he was as rich and important as she said, then he must have been able to send a little money so mom wouldn't have to work so hard.

The only explanations I could think of was that he was either dead or lost. If he was dead, I intended to find out where he was buried so mom wouldn't have to keep waiting. If he was lost, I'd help him find his way home again. A friend suggested that my parents might have gotten divorced and just didn't love each other anymore, but I didn't think that was true. Mom wouldn't still be hurt if she didn't love him, and I didn't think it was possible for anyone not to love my mom.

So I started my search. I asked my grandparents on my mother's side, but they were tight-lipped and quick to change the subject. I spent my lunches looking for him online on the school computers, but there were hundreds of people with the same name, and I only had a single grainy photo to compare with. He might have gained weight, or grown a mustache, or even lost an arm in battle for all I knew.

The one thing I was sure about was that he never changed his name, because if he was lost then he'd want to be found again. So I started going down the list of the hundreds of people with the right name and sending each a message asking if they were my dad.

Most didn't reply. Some seemed concerned, others creepy, but I didn't let that bother me. I started out with my city, Serenity Falls, but quickly expanded my search to the whole state of Wisconsin. We'd moved around quite a bit when I was younger, but we'd never left the state so I thought that's where he must be looking for us.

Then one day I messaged someone and asked if they were my father, and he replied with my mother's name and I knew I'd found him. He was older than I expected and most of his hair was gone, but he still looked a lot like the photograph. A lot like me. And no one using the other school computers could understand why I started to cry.

He asked a lot of questions about my mother. He asked for pictures of her and wanted me to tell him everything. I told him what city we lived in, and he promised to drive there right away even though it was over a hundred miles. He didn't seem to mind that mom would still be at work, because he was excited to meet me too.

For the first time in my life my dad was going to pick me up from school. I couldn't focus or sit still through any of my remaining classes. When the final bell rang I exploded out of my chair so fast I knocked my whole desk over, but I didn't stay to pick it up. I was the first out of the building and was waiting on the sidewalk within a minute. He was already waiting for me.

My dad had even less hair than his picture, but I didn't mind because he drove a red sports car. I asked if he really was an international businessman, and he laughed and said he did that in his spare time.

He didn't want to meet mom at home or at work because that wasn't romantic. Instead he wanted to take me to the real Serenity Falls the town is named after. That's where they had their first date, and mom could meet us there. I texted mom and let her know a surprise was waiting for her there, and she promised to get off work early.

It was only about a twenty minute drive, but I feel like we really bonded in that time. Dad didn't like talking about himself and asked me a thousand questions instead. What games did I like to play? How was I doing in my classes? Who were my friends, and on and on. His eyes would light up with even the most boring answer as though it was a miraculous revelation from on high.

I teased him for that, but then he got all serious and said, "You don't understand. I didn't even know you existed until today. You aren't just telling me about yourself—you're being created from nothing right here in front of my eyes. It really is a bit like a miracle."

Serenity Falls was quiet around the Christmas season. We were the only ones in the parking lot, so we got to drive all the way to the head of the trail which led to the viewpoint. The water was all frozen in snow and ice, and it wouldn't be a waterfall again until the thaw of the spring. It was still beautiful because of the long icicles lancing off the jagged rock. The light seemed trapped within the crystals which shimmered as the light faded.

We stood together in silence overlooking the falls for several minutes. I started to shiver, but he put his arm around me and drew me close, and I almost started to cry again without knowing why.

"When is your mom going to be here?" he asked at last.

"Not for at least an hour."

"Do you want to wait in the car where it's warm?" he asked.

"Why did you really leave?" I blurted out.

He withdrew his arm from around my shoulders and we stood together in silence again.

"I lied earlier," he said, still staring at the hanging ice. "I did know you existed before today."

"Then why did you—" I cut myself short.

"I wasn't ready. I loved your mother, but I didn't want to have a family yet. I'm sorry."

I shrugged as if it had nothing to do with me, but I couldn't look at him.

"Were you really in the army?"

"I was."

"And a diplomat? And a doctor?"

He laughed in response. It was a warm sound, and I wasn't shivering anymore.

"But you really did love my mom?" I asked.

"I still do. More than anything," he said. "That's why I'm here. But I'm still not ready to have a kid. I don't think I'll ever be."

It hadn't gotten any colder, but I started shivering anyway. He put his arm around me again, but it didn't feel as comforting as it had before. His fingers were gripping my shoulder a little too tight.

"It's only going to be cold for a minute," he said. "After that you won't even feel it. It'll just be like drifting off to sleep."

"I want to go back to the car." I tried to pull away, but he wouldn't let go.

"Everybody wants something," he said, "but not everybody is willing to do what it takes to get it."

He slid behind me, and suddenly both his arms were around me. I struggled and kicked, landing a solid one into his thigh before he got me off the ground. He grunted but didn't let go as he lifted me over the railing. I braced my feet against it and tried to push back, but he lifted me even higher until I couldn't reach it anymore.

My dad flung me over the ledge to tumble down the twenty foot drop to the frozen water. I smashed straight through the ice and plunged into the numbing depths. I spun over once or twice trying to orient myself, and by the time I was able to surge upward again I couldn't find the hole I'd broken through.

All I could feel was the underside of the ice. It was thicker than it seemed when I fell through. My numb fists moved sluggishly through the water, pounding feebly. I went back to searching for the hole instead, but the freezing water stung my eyes so badly I could barely see.

I saw the vague outline of his shape through the ice though. He was standing directly over me, looking down. He watched me flail against the underside. The weight of my wet clothes was beginning to drag me down, and my chest felt like it was about to explode. Each time I surged upward it became a little harder to reach the ice, until the time I couldn't reach it at all and began drifting down.

I watched him turn and begin climbing up the slope, and everything went black. I came to a moment later when I heard the sports car rev to life and pull away. I lurched upward again, and by blind chance one hand slipped through the hole in the ice. I couldn't feel my fingers as they latched onto the edge. Somehow the air was even colder than the water, but inch by excruciating inch I dragged myself upward until I'd pulled myself from the water.

I was barely alive when my mom found me. I didn't want to tell her what happened, but even lies meant to protect someone can do more harm than good. I told her everything, and she promised never to let that man back into our life again.

If my future children ever ask me about my father, I'm going to tell them the truth. That he tried to kill me, that he was never caught, and that no family is incomplete that has love.

## Bury The Pain

My grandfather Jerry has a mean temper, but you'd never guess it from looking at him. He's got these little spectacles which slide all the way to the end of his nose that do nothing to hide his twinkling eyes. The poof of white hair around his head looks almost like a halo, and the lines of his face are so deep that he seems to be smiling even when he's not.

I've never seen him yell, or swear, or break anything, but I'd hear him whenever I spent the weekend. The first time was one night after I'd already gone to bed and the lights had been off for a little while.

I was laying real still, getting ready to fall asleep, when the porch-light starts sneaking past my curtains. I peaked out to see Jerry softly closing the backdoor behind him and creeping down into Grandmother's vegetable garden. He went about twenty feet from the house at the very edge of light and began to dig, even though the ground was hard and frozen and the wind must have been bitter cold.

He dug for a few minutes before dropping to his knees to bring his face against the hole. Then he started to scream.

For a good few seconds there weren't any words to it—just a rush of anguish I didn't know one man could bear. I thought he was having a heart attack or something, so I rushed out of bed and opened the backdoor.

"Whiny, ungrateful little bitch. Somebody ought to bleed him dry and make him drink it back up."

The earth muffled a lot of it, but I heard enough to stop me from running to his aid. He couldn't see me while his face was pressed to the ground like that, so I just stood and watched from the porch.

"The girl's no better," he shouted. "Should have raped her when I had the chance. She would have liked that. Deserved it even if she didn't."

The words morphed into another wordless, guttural scream. I turned around and raced back inside, heart pounding 100 for every breath I took. I jumped back in bed and pulled the blankets over my head, just laying there shaking and listening until he fell silent.

The porch-light went off, and I heard the backdoor close real soft again. Then not another sound for the rest of the night, which I know because I didn't fall asleep until morning.

I got a few hours sleep before I woke to a knocking on my bedroom door. It was Grandmother promising fresh pancakes in the kitchen. Grandfather Jerry was there too, all smiles and cheerful jokes about the newspaper he was reading. And life went on like it was supposed to.

Until the next night when the porch-light flicked on again. I didn't get out of bed that time. I just lay there and listened to the distant muffled screaming. I caught the phrase, "Nail him to a cross if he wants to act so damn holy." I wouldn't have gotten out of bed again for anything.

Jerry continued to be as pleasant as always, graciously thanking anyone for the smallest service and going out of his way to help whoever needed it. But every time I stayed the night I'd watch for that porch-light, and every time I was falling asleep I'd hear him going on.

When I got old enough to stay home alone, I stopped sleeping at my grandparents. I moved to another city when I went to college and never told anyone. I didn't even like to think about it. Then my parents moved for my dad's new job, and I didn't see my grandparents so much after that.

Fast forward to a week ago when we got the news that Grandmother died. My parents had long since sold the house I grew up in, so we were all going to stay at my grandparent's house for the funeral. As chance would have it my parent's flight was delayed though, so the first night I arrived it would be just me and Grandfather Jerry in the house.

I could have handled it if Jerry had been in mourning. It would have been tough to see him like that, but at least it would have been natural. Instead he was just as cheerful as he'd always been. He whistled to himself while he cooked me dinner, making a show of juggling cans of green beans with a great wide grin on his face.

By the evening I'd half-convinced myself the whole thing was in my head. I still felt like a little boy when I got into bed in that old room though, and I still dreaded seeing the porch-light through the window as I waited for sleep.

And there it was. Half-past 11 when I'd just plugged in my phone and was starting to undress. The soft click from the backdoor sent a shiver down my spine. It was absurd for a grown man to be afraid of that decrepit tottering fool. I reasoned that I couldn't be afraid of him, that it was only the memory of being afraid as a child that I was holding onto.

To prove the point, I forced myself to go to the backdoor and open it. It took a moment for my eyes to adjust to the dark before I spotted him. He was kneeling down into the earth again, but he wasn't screaming this time. I watched his old shoulders tremble as he wept into the hole for a long time before I quietly closed the door and went back to my room.

Soon after I saw the light go off. I waited until I was sure he was in his own room before stealing out of the house. It wasn't hard to find the place where he'd been digging because the garden had been neglected for a long time, and there was only a single spot where the ground had been disturbed.

So I began to dig. I didn't know how deep I was supposed to go, but it only took him a few minutes so I was careful not to push the blade too far. I didn't know what I was looking for, but I knew I'd found it when I saw the earth start to move on its own.

Slow, even pulses, like breathing which raised and lowered the last layer of dirt. I produced the flashlight on my phone and turned it on, staring at the beating heart embedded within the earth. With every beat the heart pushed a small gush of blood out of its aorta to dribble down the sides and soak into the ground, despite there being no obvious source for the blood.

The house was dark and quiet except for the porch-light. I briefly considered screaming at it like Jerry did, but I didn't see the point and didn't want to risk waking him.

I wanted to get a better look though, so I reached down with my hands to clear more of the dirt away. One of my fingers accidentally brushed against the thing's side while doing so, and that's all it took. A flood of feelings swept over

## Sleepless Nights

me all tumbling over one another, senseless and maddening in their conflicting natures. I'd never had a panic attack before, but that's the closest parallel I can draw.

Grandfather took two bullets in the Vietnam war. I'd forgotten, but I remembered it now because I suddenly felt them in my left shoulder and thigh. He'd once been swindled by a building contractor—his name was Jeffery Wallace, and I'd never hated anyone so much in my life. He'd been cheated on by a girl he loved, fired from a job he put his soul into, and once falsely accused of rape.

All the rage and injustice and misery he'd felt in his life was all coming to me at once. Voices in my head were shouting over one another to be heard, and more voices were joining by the second. I couldn't tell one from the other, or even understand where the hurt was coming from, just that it was all there at once in one great red wave of anger and remorse. It flooded through my veins, poured through my body, then up through my throat and out my mouth in one long wordless scream.

The one wound that rose above the rest was the absence of my Grandmother. She wasn't the old lady who let me watch cartoons and made pancakes though—in that moment she was the center of my life that everything else revolved around. But she was gone, and everything else had stopped revolving, and I didn't see how anything in this world was going to make it start again.

I don't know how long that lasted, but it didn't stop until I felt a hand on my shoulder. The scream cut short, and I collapsed on my hands and knees, gasping for breath.

My grandfather didn't say anything. He just stood behind me and squeezed my shoulder. Once I'd steadied myself I turned to look at him, standing there in the cold with just his pajama bottoms on. My eyes fixed on the long scar on his chest, right over where his heart should have been.

"I can take yours out too, if you want," he said. "If it gets too much."

I didn't realize how much I wanted that until he said it. How much easier it would be to leave all this behind.

"Please," I begged.

"But I'll tell you something I wish my father told me before he showed me how," he said. "You can bury it and keep walking, but it never goes away. And you'll have to come back to it every time you bury a new hurt, and it'll be worse than ever because all that stuff you tried to bury will be right there waiting for you."

"I don't want to feel like this," I told him.

He squeezed my shoulder again. "You're going to feel it," he said, uncompromising but not without sympathy. "Either when it happens, or years down the road. And it's a lot easier to feel one thing fully at a time than bury it for when you're ready. Even if you live to be as old as I am, you're never going to be readier than you are now."

My parents arrived the next morning, and we all attended the funeral together. I don't think there was a dry eye in the house except for Grandfather. I overheard a few whispers looking down on the man for his lingering smile, but I knew better. She had a special place in his heart that none of them would understand, and she'll still be there long after he's gone.

## The Scariest Story In The World

Though the wind bellows fierce across my face like the howl of a nameless beast, though the moon twists shadows into abyssal creatures and the gates of Hell within my companion's eyes, I am not afraid. I will be, he promises, but not yet.

You see this is not the scariest story in the world. This is just a tribute.

My brother Jake read the fabled story on an ancient scroll, or so the old man swore to me. I believe the psychiatrist preferred the explanation of "sudden onset psychosis".

All I know for sure is that last week I met Jake for a drink after work and listened to him complain about his wife for an hour. The way she bossed him around, the way she never considered his feelings, then on to ramble about his job and a camping trip he and his coworkers had planned to get away from it all.

Three days later, I received a phone call from the police station. Did I know Jake? Of course, he's my brother. Did I know why his naked body was covered in blue paint, or why he was running down main street screaming at pigeons?

No, officer. I'm not sure why he was doing that.

Speaking to Jake in the hospital was the most difficult thing I've ever had to do. His eyes were milky pools which bulged so disgustingly from their sockets that I was afraid they'd fall out. His breathing came in short bursts of ragged gasps as though he was constantly forgetting and then being reminded that he was being chased. Even his skin seemed to have aged, fresh wrinkles threatening to melt off his face entirely.

"I never knew a nobody. Nobody never knew me." He repeated that line frequently, sometimes looking in my direction though never quite seeing me.

It was punctuated with other nonsense, such as:

"You see 'em born, but you never see 'em unborn."

Or

"I felt it drinking me. Like I was a bottle and it couldn't be quenched."

I couldn't make heads or tails of it. Neither could our parents, or our relatives, or any of the long line of doctors who paraded through the room. By the third visit I was seriously considering leaving and never returning. What was the point? Whatever had happened to him, my brother wasn't in there anymore.

I wrestled with that thought all day, making excuses to delay until finally near midnight the guilt overpowered my hesitation. I decided to drop by for just a moment to see if his condition changed.

It hadn't. But something had. There was an old man sitting beside his bed, endlessly wringing his hands and muttering to himself. His stained trench-coat and wild matted hair suggested a homeless person, and I wouldn't have been surprised if he had his own room in the psyche ward.

"Do you know Jake?" I asked cautiously.

"Does anyone, anymore?" the old man replied with the articulate, measured words of a stage actor.

"Do you know what happened to him?" I asked, still standing by the door.

"Mr. Sandman," Jake's voice gurgled like wet mud. "Mr. Sandman, dream me a dream..."

"I do," the old man answered. It was almost surreal to hear such an even, intelligent voice from such a disorderly man. "He read something he oughtn't to, and it's driven him quite mad."

Convinced by my companion's certainty, I sat in the chair beside him and searched his face for answers. The eyes which met my gaze, as I have already mentioned, were akin to the gates of Hell. I suppose such a fanciful description requires elaboration. It's not that his eyes were abnormal, just as an arch of stone may seem quite natural almost anywhere. I simply had the feeling that the world on the other side of those eyes had very little in common with our own.

"What did you read?" I asked my brother, needing an excuse to look away.

Jake's breath was coming fast again. His fingers gripped his bedsheets on either side of him as though he was hanging from a precipice and clinging for his life.

"The scariest story in the world, that's all," the old man said. "Would you like to read it too?"

Jake was practically convulsing at the words. I was about to call a nurse, but the old man ran his long fingers down my brother's face and his breathing immediately eased.

"You can't get through to him if you don't know where his mind has been," the old man's voice had grown as melodic as a lullaby. "Read the story, and if you keep your wits about you, then you will find the words to call your brother home."

"Okay. Sure, yeah," I said. Part concern for my brother, part sibling rivalry in wanting to test myself, but mostly it was just morbid curiosity. "Is there a chance I'll end up like that?"

The old man smiled and stood. Saying nothing, he turned to exit the room.

"You can't expect me to follow you if you don't answer," I called after him.

"I absolutely can," he replied, and he was gone. And of course he was right. How could I not follow that begging question mark?

And so the wind howled as I walked into the night with my companion. I asked his name, and his voice betrayed nothing when he answered "Mr. Sandman." I assume it was in jest, but I can't be certain. While we walked, he told me the tale of the demon scroll.

"The story was written over the course of four generations, beginning in the 6th century. After the man had fathered a son, he would take up the story and pour all he knew of fear into the manuscript. Once he had contributed what he was able, the man would collapse into insanity, passing the manuscript onto his heir when he came of age."

"If they knew the thing was evil, why wouldn't they just destroy it?"

"Will you destroy it?"

"Not until I've read it..."

"Ah," Mr. Sandman said, tapping the side of his nose. "And so it passes. Each son thought they could save their father through their own sacrifice, yet each fell as their fathers had into madness."

The old man had taken a turn on a street I didn't recognize, but I was too absorbed in his tale to pay it much mind.

"Well maybe I will destroy it then. If everyone who has ever read it—"

"Not everyone," my companion interrupted. "Four generations passed the scroll, until one son endured the trial. He maintained his sanity, helped his father to recover, and even prospered for his greater sight into the heart of terror. Such was his love for the fear he found that he kept the scroll hidden and safe. Until your brother discovered it by accident, of course."

"What happened to the boy? And how do you know this?"

The old man smiled over his shoulder, saying nothing.

"Well what made him different that allowed him to prevail?" I pressed.

"The boy wasn't brave like the others." Mr. Sandman had left the road entirely and was now walking along a dirt path through a dark copse of trees. I was helpless but to follow. "When you are brave, you fight against fear as though to conquer it. Only the cowardly know how to make fear their friend as that boy once did. Here we are though, just where your brother left it."

Mr. Sandman reached inside a rotted stump to produce a scroll. It was a stretch of animal hide, about three feet tall, its surface yellowed and edges burned or tattered by age. He offered it to me freely, and I accepted.

"Can't you give me any idea what to expect?" I asked. The thing was clenched in my hand, still rolled.

"I already have." Mr. Sandman's eyes didn't waver, fixed on my own. The wind held its breath as I held mine. I nodded, my mind made at last. Still meeting Mr. Sandman's eyes, I took a lighter from my pocket and set the flame to the scroll.

If his eyes were the gates of Hell, then now they were opened. An animal snarl escaped his throat as he launched himself at me. Decrepit fingers clawed at my face, feeling like shards of bone digging into my skin. I tried to fend him off, prompting him to sink his yellowed teeth into my defensive forearm.

There was no chance to reason with him. I couldn't flee with him latched onto me. All I could do was pummel his scruffy head with my free hand, over and over, each blow harder than the last as his teeth plunged deeper into my skin. By the time he let go his mouth was a fountain of blood which spurted between his rotten teeth.

"You've read it, haven't you??" I demanded, looming over the crumpled body. "Tell me what's inside!"

The wet laughter was nauseating. Then it stopped, and that was even worse. The wind started to whistle again, finally daring to breathe.

The thick animal hide was slow to light, but I got it going with a little kindling. The stump, the scroll, and Mr. Sandman's body all joined in the pillar of flame. Fear is an evil thing. That's what I told myself in the heat of the moment, my bloody arm in agony. That it was a cursed knowledge the world would do better without.

But each night as I lie awake my thoughts are bound to what was inside that scroll. And when my brother took his own life in the hospital, I had to wonder how things would have been different if I had striven to understand fear rather than flee from it.

Maybe fear is an evil thing, but the fear of fear is even worse.

## 54 Sleepless Nights

### My Wives Don't Get Along

Have you ever wanted to love someone, but couldn't?

That's how I felt about Tammy. We never should have gotten together in the first place, but it was her birthday and I didn't know what I was getting myself in for. She invited all five of us from the office and I was expecting to just have a drink and go home. Fast forward to the bar, half an hour past when we were all supposed to meet, and every time her phone buzzed I knew it was another person canceling at the last minute. But she was glowing with warmth that wasn't dampened by her disappointment, and I had nowhere else to be, and hours can melt together so fast when you've found someone to be lonely with.

Tammy blamed herself for how the party turned out in a vicious, self-deprecating way that left me scampering to reassure her. And the harder she was on herself the kinder I had to be, until somehow without meaning to I called her beautiful because I couldn't bear her thinking otherwise for another minute. The way her face lit up in response was proof that I wasn't lying, and the way she smiled back made me feel like it was the first time she'd ever really believed those words.

Tammy stayed close to me as we were leaving together. Close enough to feel her breath on my neck. Then her arms were wrapped around my arm and her warmth wasn't just something to be imagined anymore. Just to keep her balance, she said, but no amount of steadying herself was enough for her to let go. She'd been drinking after all, and needed someone to drive her home…

Well I think she really was beautiful that night, and the more of her she trusted me to see, the more beautiful she became. But love? It wasn't her fault that she came to love me, and it wasn't my fault that I couldn't feel the same.

A starving man doesn't care what he eats, and the lonely will cling to anyone who makes them forget what it's like to be alone. Tammy and I stayed together, and the phrase "maybe this is what love is supposed to feel like" kept popping up in my head. Tammy treated me with devotion and smothered me in kindness, and the longer we stayed together, the harder it became to imagine my life being any other way.

Tammy would do anything to keep me, and she reminded me every day. I could think of no better way to thank her than with everything I had to give. She was nothing but joy on the day I asked her to marry me, and basking in that light I told myself that her happiness would be enough for the both of us for all my years ahead.

Then there was my other wife. The one with the shaved head. The one with the nose rings, and the leather jacket, and the tattoo of snake twisting from one thigh to the next. I don't know if you could call Zara beautiful—certainly not in the same way you could Tammy—but you could call her other names and they'd all turn her on.

I met Zara in another town where my company headquarter's was. I had to go once a month, every month, but it didn't take long before I found an excuse to go every weekend instead. Tammy was pregnant, and I wasn't proud about what I was doing. But neither was I ashamed, because any guilt I should have felt was a drop in the ocean that was love.

Zara was everything I'd never known I'd wanted. She was wild, unrestrained, insatiable. She was a witch who put me under her spell, a demon who had claimed my soul. These are the types of excuses I'd tell myself whenever the guilt began to crawl up my spine. When I'd hold Tammy at night I'd tell myself stories of all the mad things men have ever done for love, and I'd put myself in their noble company. And when I fell asleep, I'd dream of being back with the girl whose touch was fire.

A weekend was never enough to spend with Zara, and every time was harder to leave than the last. I couldn't leave Tammy with the child though, and the anxious worry that this had to end began eating away at me night and day. I kept them both a secret from each other, swinging back and forth, barely trusting myself to call one by name without my tongue betraying me with the other's. The more the pressure grew, the more insecure and defensive I became, until one day by surprise Zara told me she was jealous of my time. She didn't want me to leave again. She wanted to be my wife, and fool that I was, I told her that I wanted the same.

It wasn't a very official wedding—Zara wasn't into that sort of thing. Our hands were clasped in the forest and our feet were in the stream when I placed a ring upon her finger. My life as I knew it had ended forever, and I couldn't imagine anything but happiness to come.

I told myself then that I would make one last trip to end things with Tammy. She'd be better off alone—I wanted to believe—than with someone who didn't need her anymore. I would do my part and help pay for the child, and I wouldn't need much money because nothing I could buy would fill my heart the way holding Zara did. Tammy would cry, but I wouldn't break, and in five years time—in ten years time—when I'm old and grey with shaking hands—I'll hold Zara all the tighter knowing that I was almost too weak to follow my heart.

And maybe that's how it would have gone if Zara hadn't followed me back. She thought she would surprise me by making the trip to help me move. She thought she was being clever by calling my work and pretending to be a client setting up a meeting at my home. How could she have known that Tammy was home while I'd gone to the store to pick up some things for our new born child?

The police were home before I was. The weeping young mother and the screaming punk—it wasn't hard for them to figure out what happened. The knife-slashed curtains and the shattered plates—there must have been quite a fight to be loud enough for the neighbors to call the cops. The blood-stained carpet and the dirty tracks into the nursery—there was no way to hide the evidence, or mistake what happened to my daughter who was slashed into ribbons before she'd ever learned her name.

Zara and I never spoke again. Not even at her trial where I was called as a witness. I couldn't even meet her eyes when I told the jury about the affair, that I'd loved her, and that I knew it was wrong. I told them that Zara had been jealous, that she'd killed the child, and that I never wanted to see her again.

The only thing that could have been harder to bear was when Tammy forgave me. She said it wasn't my fault. That I'd made a mistake. That we could learn to be happy together again. And I believed her, because as heavy as this weight was for me to bear, I knew that I couldn't bear it alone.

That was almost twenty years ago, and Tammy and I have moved past it the best we could. We had two more children, both boys. I'm glad of that, because if we'd had a girl I don't think I could have looked at her without thinking about the child who had been cut from us. If Tammy can still love me after all that, then who am I to say that I can't love her in return? Despite everything I'd done to avoid being alone though, I know that it's only a matter of time.

Tammy is sick, and she isn't going to get better. I've been spending every day at my wife's side, and our youngest will be leaving to college in a few weeks. Then it's just going to be me and my regrets, thinking about the words Tammy said to me last night.

"I told you I'd do anything to keep you, and I did," she told me. "If you didn't think Zara killed our daughter, you never would have stayed with me. I had to do it, don't you see? We've made each other so happy through the years."

I always knew I never loved her, but it's taken me my entire life to find out why.

## The Taxidermied Child

Before this week, I would have told you that running the acquisitions department at the American History Museum was the best job in the world. Never a day goes by where I'm not learning something new, discovering lost artifacts which force me to continually reassess my understanding of our rich culture.

Most people don't understand how glamorous the work really is. You have to understand that our donations generally come from extremely wealthy families, each with long histories of their own and treasures which are passed through the generations. These donors are typically motivated by the large tax breaks they receive for their charitable contributions, so I am often flown across the country and treated to the highest comfort that money can buy, no doubt buttering me up in hopes of a favorable appraisal and acceptance of their donation.

When I accepted the invitation to Mr. Calomney's estate, I had every expectation of the luxury and finery befitting the Tudor-style mansion depicted in the enclosed photograph. From the steep gable roof to the elaborate masonry and embellished doorways, the residence itself was a relic of the unimaginable wealth with which the plantation owners once ruled the southern countryside.

Mr. Calomney was there to greet me at the end of his cobblestone driveway. Hands in the pockets of his pristine white suit, a golden chain dangling from his breast pocket, silk around his neck and a beige fedora with a roguish tilt, he might have stepped straight out of an oil painting from the era. He was gracious to help me with my bags and show me inside, incessant welcome and gratitude spilling from his mouth with a heavily-accented drawl.

I followed him from room to room, keeping careful tally of everything he was willing to part with. Dark wooden furniture from the West Indies, ornate baroque chests of drawers, exquisite colonial paintings—he breezed by each of them as though they were hardly worth the effort of describing. All the while he continued gesturing me onward with an almost conspiratorial hush to his voice, promising a prize that he guaranteed was unique to his collection.

Everything I saw was of impeccable condition, seemingly untouched by age or refurbishment. At least, until we reached the worn wooden doorway where his intention was most fixed upon. Opening this with a flourish, he led me inside to a bare and dilapidated room. Once painted red, the humidity in the air had long since stripped all life and color from the walls to leave the most dreadful pale streaks and blotches around us. The sole furniture was a splintered three-legged stool; the sole occupant a small brown-skinned boy sitting atop it.

"He's held up well, hasn't he?" Mr. Calomney said, puffing out his chest with pride. "They don't usually last more than a year, you know. The skin discolors something awful and starts to stretch and peel away. It's been over a hundred years since he died, but he still looks like he could jump up and skip around, doesn't he?"

I'd never seen a taxidermied human before, and I didn't feel qualified to comment on the condition. He was right about how real it looked though—I had the most unnerving feeling that the boy was looking right at me, and that if I were to turn away for a moment I might find him in an altogether different position.

A clear stitching was visible in the dark skin which ran up one side of his body, disappeared into his curly black hair, and emerged again on the other side. His eyes were made of glass, but a stern judgement still lingered in his furrowed brow as though he knew exactly what had happened to him and blamed me for his fate.

"Would you like to know the secret?" Mr. Calomney pressed with a hot whisper down the back of my neck. "Why the skin stayed so fresh?" He waited for a moment, then continued without the least bit of encouragement. "Even modern taxidermists couldn't preserve someone this well, because they all make the same mistake. They all wait until the subject is dead to begin the tanning process."

Mr. Calomney rolled back on his heels, puffing out the gold on his chest and looking immensely pleased with himself. Then to address the shock and disgust on my face, he added, "Don't worry, it was all perfectly legal. The boy was my family's property, after-all. It's better than what could have happened to him. Now wouldn't that be an interesting exhibit in your museum?"

Still too shocked to address the macabre sight, I professed interest in returning to inspect the rest of the house. Mr. Calomney became indignant though, insisting that this was his rarest and most valuable possession. I told him directly that our museum would not feature such a disturbing display, visibly angering the man whose voice quivered when he next spoke. He told me that he would give nothing to any museum with such a 'selective view of history', and that I was no longer welcome in his house. I was only too happy to oblige, grateful for the cleaner air outside that vile room.

I left Mr. Calomney on no uncertain terms and returned to my museum empty handed, telling nothing of the incident and doing my best to put it out of my mind entirely. That should have been the end of it, but not a week later I was in my office preparing for a meeting with Professor Horvat of New York's natural history museum when someone began to hammer on my door. Before I could welcome my unexpected guest, the door opened and I was confronted with Mr. Calomney once more.

I don't believe he had changed his clothes since the day I had seen him last. His white suit was dull and stained with yellowed sweat, his hair unkempt and greasy. Too surprised to protest, I backed away and made room for him as he entered my office dragging a luggage cart behind him. The object on the cart was concealed beneath a white sheet, but by its size and shape I could easily guess that the boy was seated underneath. Mr. Calomney ducked back into the hall for a moment to ensure his discretion, then returned closing the door behind.

"What are you doing here? Get out, get out!" I insisted, but he only shooed me away with his hands before sitting heavily before my desk. His face was flushed as though he'd been running, and he seemed to need a moment to catch his breath before he could speak a word.

"Look, maybe if you scheduled an appointment I could work something in this afternoon," I said, trying my best to sound reasonable, although I was trying to think of excuses to cancel even as I said it. "As it is I'm already expecting—"

"You've got to take him," Mr. Calomney interrupted with passion. "I can't have him in the house anymore. Not for another night. I won't."

Already I could hear voices and footsteps in the hallway outside. The thought of being caught by professor Horvat with this wretched thing in my office was too much to bear.

"There's a storeroom on the right," I replied automatically. "Hurry now, you can leave it there for the time being. But you must retrieve it this afternoon, do you understand? And don't think about skirting off either —I know where you live and will have it shipped back at once if you do not return."

He thanked me profusely and together we wheeled the cart into the adjoining room. There were more questions that I wanted to ask, but there was already knocking on the door and there was nothing that could be done. Professor Horvat entered, regarding Mr. Calomney with surprise and perhaps even revulsion as my disheveled visitor pushed rudely out of the room. The sudden thunder of footsteps outside indicated that he was running as soon as he got the chance.

Fortunately the meeting was otherwise undisturbed, and none of my colleagues were wise to the fact that the taxidermied boy sat concealed in my storeroom. It was no great shock that Mr. Calomney failed to return that afternoon, but I was caught up with other appointments and didn't have a chance to dispose of the boy that day.

In fact the whole situation was so out of the ordinary and surreal to me that I hardly thought about it when I returned to work the next morning. When I did arrive, the whole museum was in an uproar over an ongoing school field trip that had misplaced one of its students. The whole building was searched from top to bottom, and I was so distracted by the ongoing efforts that I didn't spare a thought about the strange events of the previous day.

It didn't return to my attention until I had joined the search only to find a second taxidermied child in the store room beside my office. A little girl beside the boy, with freshly stitched skin running up one side and down the other. With little glass eyes and a little furrowed brow, silently judging me for all the sins I've never done.

"It wasn't my fault," I told the glass eyed children. "I didn't do anything to either of you. And I would have stopped it if I could, but—"

But of course that didn't help them in the least. And they couldn't stay here, or it would only be a matter of time before the missing student was identified. I keep them both in my house now, waiting to hear back from Mr. Calomney. The house I visited has been sold already, and I can't exactly ship them back to the innocent people who live there now.

I know I should burn them or bury them or chop them up and throw them in a lake. I know I shouldn't feel guilty for what happened to them, but I can't even hide them in the closet without feeling ashamed. Instead the boy is sitting at my kitchen table, the girl propped up beside the dresser in my room. I didn't do this to either of them, but I know that if I treat them poorly or ignore how they suffered, and I find a third has joined them one day, then that one really will be my fault. And that would be as bad as stitching them up myself.

So I wish them good morning and good night. I read to them from the paper, and I keep the light on when they're alone in the room. And I wait. For the day their brows are smooth and I catch them smiling again.

## Redemption for Murder

You can blame it on the alcohol, but that wouldn't make me feel any better. People drink everyday without killing someone. Besides, if I'm being really honest here, I probably would have still killed him if I'd been sober.

You can blame it on my childhood too. Something to do with my father not being around, or not sticking with school, or falling in with a troubled crowd. That's not quite true either though, because I would have ended up even worse if I admired someone as selfish and unstable as my father. And if the kids I knew were trouble, then it's probably my fault for making them that way so I wouldn't feel so alone.

I guess that leaves the blame on me where it belongs. I knew exactly what I was doing when I borrowed the money in the first place. Markie made it clear he'd taken the money from his father. He said the old man was too senile to notice though, which was fine with me since I never had any intention of paying it back. I couldn't plan six months in the future, but even if I could, I didn't expect to still be alive when the bill came due. But the money burned fast, and I always woke up again no matter how much I drank, until one day Markie comes banging on my door demanding something I didn't have to give.

I could have opened the door that night and begged his forgiveness. I could have sworn to get clean and told him about the jobs I'd considered and made an incremental payment plan to get him his money. Sucker that he was, Markie probably would have believed me. He might have even loaned me more if I'd been sincere about it.

Twenty seconds, maybe longer. That's how long I held the hammer in my hand and thought about what I was going to do. More than enough time to change my mind before I opened my door. I wasn't even angry at him when I struck the first blow. I was only angry at myself, and somehow it seemed like I could pour all my anger out of me and into him until he was dead and I was whole again.

Would it change your opinion of me if you knew I cried afterward? Doesn't matter, I'm not writing this for you to feel sorry for me. I would have turned myself over to the police, or to God, but the police would act on me without understanding, and God would understand too much while doing nothing. The only person I felt like I needed to confess to was Markie's father. He deserved to know where his money had gone and why he wouldn't see his son again. If anyone had the right to judge me, it was him.

I hardly recognized Mr. Methusa when I tracked him down. He was a lot older than I'd remembered him. Back in the day he caught Markie and I trying to break into a car together and he let us both have it with a belt. He hardly looked strong enough to lift his cane now, but I was still more afraid of him than ever. I was shaking from head to foot when he looked me up and down, slowly, agonizingly, as if he was deciding my punishment before I'd even told him what I'd done. Before I knew it I was on my knees, although I didn't know whether it was to beg or because my legs weren't strong enough to stand anymore.

"You're late," he told me. "Where have you been? I've been up waiting for you. Stop playing around and come in, Markie. I'll get your dinner back in the oven."

His mind really must be slipping to mistake me for Markie. With those words he passed judgement over me though. Now it was my turn to make a choice. I could break the old man's heart and tell him that his son wasn't coming home, or I could play the part and bring Markie back to life. I let Mr. Methusa feed me and I stayed the evening with him, and the more he talked, the more convinced I was that I was doing the right thing in letting him believe.

His mind hadn't completely gone. He really had noticed the money Markie took from him. And while I couldn't apologize for what I had really done, I found solace in apologizing for all the things he blamed his son for. Over the course of the evening I promised to make it up to him, to visit more often, to take him to the park to watch the ducks, and a hundred other things besides.

He marveled at Markie's sudden transformation and insisted I stayed the night in the spare room. After I'd gone to bed he brought me a glass of water and kissed me on the forehead and told me I was home. Lying in bed in the dark I cried for a second time that night.

I couldn't forget what I had done, but that knowledge made me try all the harder to be everything Markie should have been. Mr. Methusa had lived alone since his wife died four years ago, and he was overjoyed to have the company again. He showed me all his old baseball trophies, and his eyes lit up with delight when I told him I forgot the stories and asked him to tell me again. He had a big cupboard full of early musicals, and we'd watch one together every night. For the first few nights all I could think about was slipping out to get a drink, but every time I mentioned leaving I'd see this empty look on his face and knew my duty was to stay. Before I knew it I was going days at a time without even thinking about alcohol.

Not long after I found work at a pharmacy around the block and started making the old man's money back for him. It wasn't hard to save up now that I wasn't drinking and he was letting me stay rent-free. I honestly can't remember a time when I was so happy. I thought that this was how my life was going to be forever until the night we received an unexpected visitor.

It was around midnight when I heard the rustle of a key in the lock downstairs. I got a flashback to when I lived alone in an area that got break-ins all the time. I crept out of bed and spotted a flashlight beam lancing around the living room. Part of me was afraid, but I knew I didn't deserve to be here if I couldn't protect what I'd come to care about.

I waited until the flashlight turned toward the kitchen before I crept downstairs. The intruder was facing away from me, and I'd lose my chance if I waited any longer. He might have had a gun, or a knife, but I had a bronze baseball trophy and an arm that had done this before. I used the sharp corner of the base and got a clean blow in before the intruder could fully turn around.

The man crumpled to the floor, dazed but not out cold. He started to crawl away, but I pinned him to the ground, ready for another blow. It would have landed too if shock hadn't stayed my hand. Markie was lying on the floor below me, looking just as surprised and angry to see me as I was to see him. His skull still looked slightly misshapen where I'd pummeled him with the hammer what felt like a lifetime ago.

I told him he was dead if he made a sound, and he believed me. He wanted to know what I was doing there, but I still had him pinned and he was the one who had to talk. Markie confessed that he'd recovered, but had been too afraid to return to his father without his money. He figured he could come back and steal again, then later blame the second robbery if his father ever noticed what was missing.

I then confessed what I had done, and that he wasn't welcome back anymore. I told him he was rotten through and through and didn't deserve his father's love. He was angry, I was angry, and it was only a matter of time before one of us got loud enough to wake the old man. If he saw us together he'd know I was an imposter for sure, and I wasn't willing to give up the life I'd found.

It wasn't the alcohol after-all. I proved that when I brought the metal statue down on Markie's head again and again, not stopping until he did. I was more careful this time and made sure to finish the job, cleaning and disposing of everything properly. It didn't hurt me the same as it had the first time.

Mr. Methusa hadn't lost a son after-all, but I had gained a father.

## She Only Wants Me For My Body

There's nothing wrong with physical attraction opening the door to a relationship. I wouldn't even mind if she only wanted me for sex, because I understand that physical intimacy breaks down social barriers and makes it possible for us to get to know each other on a deeper level. I'm worried that my girlfriend wants to use my body for something else though, and its been keeping me up at night.

When we first started dating I used to think it was cute how she liked to watch me fall asleep. She was subtle about it before I called her out—just peeking out of the corner of her eye with this little smile on her face. She was really embarrassed when I first asked her about it. She pretended not to know what I was talking about, getting all flushed and flustered trying to come up with an excuse for what she was really looking at. Eventually she admitted that she always had trouble falling asleep though, and that watching me breathe was relaxing and soporific for her. I promised her that I would never judge her for her secrets, and she promised to love me for it.

After her secret was out she dropped all pretenses and turned it into a joke. She'd use two pillows under her chin to prop up her head, turn practically horizontal in bed with her legs dangling over the edge, and just stare at me with her wide hazel eyes. It was the first of many quirks that would transform her from a stranger into my best friend, and I cherished all the little building blocks that made her the only one for me.

Then came the day I lost my job. It was honestly my own fault for a string of stupid mistakes: an order sent to the wrong person, losing a check I was supposed to cash, mixing up my schedule and showing up late… I tried to tell my boss that I'd just been fatigued and not thinking clearly, but I was ashamed about my blatant screwups and couldn't muster much of a defense. Part of me was even relieved, because it meant I'd finally have a chance to rest and recover from whatever was making me so tired. Adding insult to injury though, I had even more trouble settling down at night because I kept worrying about money whenever I closed my eyes.

I didn't want my my girlfriend to worry too, so I told her everything was fine. I couldn't fall asleep the first night after I was fired, but I closed my eyes and pretended, making sure to breathe slow and even to help her fall asleep beside me. After a while of faking it I heard her rustle around and get out of bed. I peaked out of the corner of my eye to see her open the bottom drawer of her nightstand. I closed my eyes again and focused on breathing before she caught me awake. The last thing I wanted after a hard day was a midnight conversation about the future.

A few moments later and I felt her climb back into bed. Pretty soon I started feeling this brushing tickling feeling on my ear. My first instinct was that she suspected I was awake and was trying to test me, so I concentrated really hard on laying still and breathing slow. The tickling intensified to a persistent itch though, growing more powerful and intrusive as it moved deeper into my ear. I jerked upright when I couldn't take it anymore and swatted at the itch, expecting my fingers to close around a feather or whatever she was harassing me with.

I didn't predict the hard mass of squirming legs like a centipede. I let go out of dumbfounded shock. That was a mistake—it reacted to my touch by burrowing deeper into my ear. The sensation was now coming from inside my head more than it was on the exterior. I tried to snatch at it again to pull it out, but something sharp stung my finger and I yanked away—another mistake. By the time I realized what was going on it was almost entirely inside me.

My girlfriend started shouting, but I was so distraught that couldn't process what she meant by "Don't hurt it!" I ran to the bathroom and turned on the light just in time to see the the last inch of the creature kick and squirm and wriggle inside my ear. My girlfriend appeared behind me in the mirror, wringing her hands and averting her eyes.

"What do you mean, 'don't hurt it'?" I asked, her words finally getting through. The interior itching feeling was already subsiding, but I felt heavier and more tired than ever.

"You had a bad dream," she told me. "Come back to bed."

I wanted to believe her so badly. I stared into the mirror, at the reflection of her wide eyes, and all I could think about was all the nights she'd watched and waited for me to fall asleep. I turned without saying a word and pushed past her. She didn't try to stop me until I had reached her nightstand, and by then it was too late.

I pulled open the bottom drawer and saw a glass jar half-buried amongst her socks and underwear. She tried to pull me away, but I managed to lift it out and look inside—at all the squirmy, crawling, bug-like creatures crawling around inside. At the two empty glass jars beside it. I sat and stared while my girlfriend's words washed over me, the lapping of cold water I was too numb to feel.

"They aren't so bad. I've got them in me too."

"They need to be somewhere warm and safe."

"You promised not to judge me. Why won't you look at me?"

"They won't forgive you if you try to leave."

## Sleepless Nights

### Yesterday Was Better

I want to tell you about a curse I have. It's not a loud curse. There are no magic sparks or green smoke. It's a very quiet curse, so quiet that I didn't even notice right away. The spell is cumbersome and rare because it has to be cast on yourself at least nine times before it works. I've had it for a few years though, and I've done my research: it's called Happa Ma Palu, which can be translated simply as "Yesterday was better."

It's quiet because we all have a lot of yesterdays, and most of us have a good deal of tomorrows. Who is to say how one day measures against another? Happa Ma Palu knows, that's who. One day the happiest day of your life will be behind you, and you'll never feel it go, floating softer than the wind.

One day the sun won't be quite as bright as the day before, and the flowers will seem a little more gray. Did the sound of laughter always have that cynical ring to it? Did she always hesitate so long before saying "I love you too"? I thought it was my imagination at first, but since then I've seen it so many times, there can be no doubt.

I know the look on their faces. If you don't know what I'm talking about, then try to imagine a dog that runs back and forth through the yard all day, chasing butterflies and its shadow and every passing scent along the breeze. Yet every night someone pulls out one of the fence posts and moves the wall in a little closer, just a couple inches at a time. Until the day the dog runs out of the house and into the fence which has crept so close. The dog can't run; it can hardly turn around. But why did it ever think it had space to run? And why does it miss something it couldn't have done? That's the way it has always been, and that's the way it will always be.

Sound familiar yet? Happa Ma Palu knows. And tomorrow won't be any better, but people can learn to live just fine like that. As long as it's only a little bit every day, they can get used to it before it gets even worse. And before you know it, your body hurts all the time, all your food tastes rotten, and life is as bad as it can possibly be. But that's not quite true, because Happa Ma Palu means yesterday was better, and tomorrow is yet to come.

The cripple may look back on his limping days with nostalgia. You hardly notice how easily you draw breath until it begins to rasp through a throat worn dry and raw. You don't feel your skin until it breaks out in marks and sores, or pay mind to your sight until the shadows start playing tricks on you. I know I didn't pay her the attention she deserved until her heart was forever closed to me, but that was yesterday and who knows what tomorrow will bring?

Happa Ma Palu knows. If you could roll back the time, you'd hardly recognize the two of you standing together, you and who you used to be. And by the very end, it would be hard to recognize you were once human at all. A mind is nothing but a reflection of the world that peers into it, and enough pain and bitterness and hate pouring in will poison any heart. And whether mind follows body or body follows mind matters not when both are driving each other inexorably into the monstrous, the abominable, the profane.

You will feel so empty, ravenous, angry—aimed at those who never had this curse to bear. And you will hate, hate, hate, hate, hate, everyone who couldn't recognize you for who you used to be. They will treat you like an animal, and you will treat them the same, until one day your hunger gets too great and they will matter too little. You will lash out with all that suffering that has festered inside until you are empty again, and then you will need to feed. And you will chew, chew, chew, chew, chew, and never taste a thing.

It seems each of us is unique in how we suffer until a certain point, and then we suddenly find that we are the same. No matter what tortured form the body takes, nor which loathsome obsession fills our thoughts, one day will be the end of our tomorrows and we'll have all reached the same point. That's the day when I didn't just have the curse; It's the day I was Happa Ma Palu too.

And that's it. That's the end. I've reached the worst day and now I'm through. I'm on the other side, and the curse is lifted. And suddenly all my tomorrows are better than my yesterdays, and the rest of my life is just a game to see how much happier I can be. Then I can't wait for every day to show me what treasures it held secret from all my days behind. If you don't show up, who will ever know what those treasures could have been?

Happa Ma Palu knows.

Say it bright and clear in your head, loud enough for me to hear you. Happa Ma Palu. Nice, clean, crisp words. Happa ma palu, it's fun to say and feel your lips bubble together like a newborn infant. Because that's what you are, you know. You're a new beginning.

And now that you've said the name nine times, it's my new beginning too.

Tonight is the night I lost my mind and found something better. It's the night I found you to take my place.

## Inside A Human Zoo

It was one of those nights where nothing went according to plan.

An evening out with friends, but I couldn't find a parking spot anywhere around the place. Two blocks down the street, then hustling through the chill, puffing breath like smoke. All that only to discover I'd shown up at the wrong place. Then back toward my car, the skin around may ears prickled and numb, feeling like an idiot, just in time to see the parking enforcer glide past me without a word like a specter of death.

Too far from the curb. I didn't even know they gave tickets for that. But I was already so late. I couldn't let that bother me as I raced through the dark neighborhoods for a shortcut—not until I slammed to a stop in front of construction

## Sleepless Nights

work closing off the road. I remember thinking how this night couldn't get any worse as I pulled a sharp U-turn, but that was before a loud pop and a lurch nearly spun me off the road.

I was out on the street, ready to fight whatever hit me, whether it was a tree or a sign or a mailbox or a man. Then I found it—a power drill that one of the workers had left by the side of the road. The drill-bit was lodged securely in my tire, which like my hopes of meeting with my friends, deflated before my eyes.

It was one of those nights where everyone was the worst and everything was everyone's fault but mine. The kind of night where the lights seemed half as bright as they ought to, and the wind carried whispers of forgotten names. The kind of night not to talk to strangers.

"Flat tire, huh?" asked the fattest man I had ever seen in my life. I don't know where he could have come from for me not to have seen him, but now I could hardly see anything else. The segments of his legs overlapped each other in great wads, his bulk swinging sluggishly to catch up beneath his baggy shirt.

I bit my tongue to avoid lashing my frustration on this hapless bystander. Fumbling with the trunk, checking for my spare tire that I knew wasn't there.

"Want some help with that?" I could hear his weight even when I wasn't looking at him. Every word seemed swollen somehow, as though they could barely crawl over his blubbery lips. I looked him up and down, my expression intending to convey that he was doing enough just getting one foot in front of the other. He must have gotten the idea, because he dismissively waved a hand like a passing manatee.

"Bah, you don't know. At least pull it off the road. We don't want to draw too much attention to ourselves tonight, eh?"

"Who is this? A friend of yours, Sebastian?" A second voice, speaking in clipped tones. This man might as well have been a parody of the other, for he was so terribly thin that I could clearly make out his knuckle bones beneath his skin. Sharply inward drawn cheeks, eyes sunken into their sockets, and a curly knot of brown hair on his head.

"Never mind about his car, we're going to be late," the thin man continued. "It won't be in anyone's way while the road is closed."

A long, thin hand caught me by the back of my shirt as I tried to get back in my car. I wrestled away from him and he snorted in amusement. "No skin off my back. Here, hold onto your own ticket." Then turning sharply from me—"Sebastian! Wait for us, Sebastian. Oh I do wish I'd brought a camera."

I stared down at the ticket in my hand, with its elegant handwritten note glittering in gold ink.

*The Human Zoo. Admits one. Every flavor of human.*

The night wasn't going according to plan, but why let it be a complete waste? Curiosity can race twice way round a head before better judgement has a chance to put on its shoes. I never exactly made the decision to follow him, but neither did I stop once I realized what I was doing.

It wasn't difficult to catch up with the fat man who was plodding his way down the sidewalk. By that point they both seemed to think that I was here with the other one. Neither of them paid me much attention as they approached an iron gate which protected a strange and crooked house. The planks of wood bent and splintered as they struggled to support the slouching building, and in place of electric lights spluttered burning oil lanterns enclosed in twisted iron. The thin man produced a key to the gate. Moments later, he was knocking upon what once might have been a bright green door, though it was now peeling and faded into a ghastly shade.

The Human Zoo, in small golden letters above the door. A thousand questions on my lips, but I kept them unvoiced so as not to betray that I didn't belong. Maybe it was something like a freak show. Whatever someone looked like, I didn't like the implications that they were less than human though. Maybe there was human trafficking going on, and people were being bought and sold like animals. Or were the series of unfortunate events of the night making me paranoid, and there was a much more innocent explanation? All I knew is that I had to take a peek, or be left wondering forever what I might have seen.

The door opened to reveal a rather stiff, unpleasant man in a dark suit. He had the face of a man who might order a drink, discover he didn't like it, and pour it on the floor rather than return the offending beverage. It was certainly the type of expression he gave the three of us as he collected our tickets and ushered us into the dark hallway.

Low burning lanterns were mounted on the wall, the guttering light shifting the thick shadows across the dozen or more people already here. There wasn't enough light to see them clearly, but several bodies were strangely proportioned, possessing a clubbed foot, or dreadful swelling, or tumorous bulges. A few inquisitive faces caught the light for a moment, but swiftly they returned to the main attraction: the long line of ornate picture frames which occupied both sides of the hallway.

Well that was a relief. Here I was imagining the worst when there was nothing but a gallery inside. Stepping away from the people I arrived with, I hoped the pair wouldn't have a chance to figure out I hadn't been invited. I pressed myself toward the thickest part of the crowd where I hoped to blend in. I still felt conspicuously out of place though, and I had gone a good way before I found the courage to look up and see the paintings at all.

There was a painting of a girl: a teenager, or maybe her early twenties. She had long brown hair twisted into a braid. The painting style focused more on shades of light than any specific detail. It was clearly a painting though, which is why I was so surprised to see the girl step away from the frame to kneel beside a backpack. She proceeded to withdraw a small stack of books and set them upon her bed.

I turned to look at the painting on my other side, and found myself face-to-face with a middle-aged woman. The viewpoint was fixed, and I could only see her from the back. That was enough to tell she was in the kitchen, silently chopping something with a knife. I waited a minute to see if she would turn and face me, but she showed no realization that she was being watched.

"Oh oh oh, that's more like it," croaked an elderly man. Several other people and crowded around the painting he stood before. "Sarah Berkley, 242 S. Colver Street. I didn't know she was expecting company."

My eyes caught on the bronze plaque below the painting of the cooking woman. A name and an address—all of them had one. I followed the shift of people and tried to get a glance at what everyone was looking at.

"Let's get some sound from her. What do we pay you beastly people for?" another voice like a shrieking bird rose form the group.

I had almost made room to get a proper look when a distorted pop crackled in the air. It sounded like an old-fashioned record player spinning to life. Filtering through the gentle static came a sudden heaving breath, intermingled with a soft moaning sigh.

"A thousand bucks says she regrets it," the elderly man said, leering.

"Are you mad? She's fancied him for weeks. Thousand bucks, you're on," said another.

"Oh no, not with you. I'm still waiting on that five large for the man who hit his wife."

"He only pushed her out of the way, and you know it. That doesn't count!"

"Thousand bucks says she likes it, and she does him again before the week is out," rolled the fat-man's distinctive blubbery words.

"Done and done, shake on it Sebastian and we've got a deal."

The moaning was getting louder—the breath more ragged. I still couldn't get a clear look, but I was starting to feel really uneasy. I kept my distance from the painting and pretended to be interested another adjacent one. It was a man at his desk before a computer. I couldn't focus—there were more and more people arriving, and it kept getting louder."

"Look over here—we've got one crying."

"Pretty little thing. Want to pay her a visit and see if we can't give her a better night?"

"You go. I'll watch. Whatever you do, don't make it boring, eh?"

Then from farther down the hall— "Oh Wesley, you're such a fool. I can't believe you thought she loved you. That's right, runaway. Runaway you fat ugly fool."

"Hold on a second. Everyone quiet!"

*Hold on a second. Everyone quiet.* The distorted echo of those words were repeated from the darkness.

"I thought so. One of the animals has found its way into the gallery. Look, you can see the windows behind him!" Then the voice said my name, and then my address. I slipped back toward the door as unobtrusively as I could, but I was the only one moving. One pair at a time, the eyes of the patrons shimmering in the flickering light as they turned toward me. Then I was running out the door, the gasp of cold air flooding my lungs as though I'd been drowning.

"Pick him up after he falls asleep." Those were the last words before I heard the door close behind me.

I know you aren't supposed to drive on a flat tire, but the rumbling protest of my car was nothing beside the silent screaming between my ears. How can I go home knowing they're watching me? How can I ever know that I'm alone when they know where I am? And how can they even call that a human zoo, when they are nothing but animals themselves?

## I Don't Trust The Little God

We were happy once.

I'd just gotten my first real salaried job, and my wife was pregnant with a little one on the way. For once in our life we weren't worried about money, and I even had some set aside to make all the preparations ahead of time. We converted my study into a nursery and painted the walls sky-blue for our little boy. She added trains of yellow ducklings following their mother, and I was in charge of the white puffy clouds, the only thing I knew how to paint. We had a closet that we couldn't close because it was so full of diapers, stuffed animals, children's books, and toys. We weren't intentionally hoarding, but every time we went out my wife would see something that made her heart melt, and I was so happy to see her so happy that I never thought twice.

It felt like we had waited our whole lives for a day which never came. At first the doctor thought the pockets in his brain were temporary abnormalities that would disappear before birth, but less than a week later we received the diagnosis of Trisomy 18, a fatal chromosomal defect. We were given the choice whether to terminate the pregnancy or let the baby be born only to hold him once. To memorize every detail of his face, the feel of his skin, the look in his eyes before we had to say goodbye. My wife wanted to go through with it, but a few late nights later I convinced her it would be easier to never see his face at all.

I was always the more pragmatic of the two of us. I thought we could just try again, and that in a few years this would be nothing but a speed bump on the road to our happy family. Fool that I am, I made the mistake of trying to cheer her up by saying we already did most of the work by preparing the nursery and all the things. I guess I didn't understand how much harder this was on her than it was on me, but I found out soon enough.

The next day when I came home from work I got the message loud and clear. Everything we'd bought for the baby was piled in the yard and burned, with only a few charred book spines and loose buttons amidst the ash to reveal what they once had been. I didn't care about that though. I found my wife sitting in the nursery with a kitchen knife at her feet, her head buried in her knees. There were long gouges in the wall through all the little ducks, each puffy cloud shredded into loose hanging tatters. She was clutching a doll of the Little Prince, blond and blue eyed and charred at the corners. There were burns on her hands, and I can only assume that she impulsively saved it from the fire at the last second.

She was mumbling and incoherent for a while, but I got the impression that she hadn't forgiven herself for not holding her baby even once. I helped her into bed, but she wouldn't let go of the doll for a second. We talked a long time. We cried a long time. We talked again, and by the early hours of the next morning we both had a sense that the worst was behind us. My wife promised that she would be alright, and fool that I am, I believed her.

I resolved not to bring up having another kid, not until she did. I was going to let her deal with this in her own way, on her own time. That meant letting her sleep in every morning when I went to work, and finding her still in bed every night when I got home. That meant watching her once luxurious brown hair grow greasy and tangled without showering; watching her gain weight as she took out her pain on cartons of Ben and Jerry's and family sized bags of snicker bars. Apart from that, she didn't act too depressed though; she always made an effort to engage me with cheerful conversation, and I still believed we would get through this and be alright.

The only new habit that I had trouble moving past was the way her prayers changed at night. She didn't pray for her to get better, or anything about the future. Her prayers were always about the boy who never came. She had this notion that he was happy somewhere and growing up in his own way in his own place, and she prayed for him in that other life. And every time she prayed, she prayed to what she called her "little god", the charred doll which she'd never let out of her sight.

Sometimes I'd wake up in the night and hear her whispering to it, muttering thanks for keeping her safe and watching over her little boy wherever he was. That was uncomfortable for me, but it was her process and I let her work through it. Over time the nature of the prayers began to change though, and before long she was saying things like "next time around" and "my future boy". Those comments made me feel hopeful that she might finally be ready to give our family another try.

There were other things she said that made me less certain though. She kept asking the doll "if it promised". Other times she'd get angry at it, and when I asked her to explain, she'd get defensive and close up, only hinting that the doll was lying to her. Even worse were the times when she affirmed a promise she made to her little god, these usually in furtive whispers when she thought I was asleep. She'd swear over and over again that she was going to follow through, only to ask over and over if it would do the same. I didn't want to intrude or make her defensive, and I never found out what that promise was.

Through it all she was putting the nursery back together and repainting the walls though. She began taking better care of herself, although she'd still put on a lot of weight. Not long after the doll was gone, and that was the best sign yet that things were going back to normal. We were being intimate again for the first time since the incident, and I thought life had found a way to endure.

The day after she'd gotten rid of the doll I got a call while at work. It was the hospital—it was my wife—how fast could I get there? I couldn't make sense of what they were saying—something about a fire—but I hauled ass to get there and found out soon enough. I hardly even recognized her for the burns, every inch of skin either red and blistered or charred so black that I could see it crumbling off before my eyes.

The doctors told me a neighbor had called to report smoke coming from the house, but my wife's condition was the only trace of the fire except for the blackened ceiling directly above her. I heard the phrase spontaneous human combustion more than once. They told me that they didn't think they could save her, but chances were good of saving the child.

I told them there had been a mistake. That it had only been two months since we'd lost the last child, and that there was no way for her to be pregnant. My words seemed to get lost in all the rush and bustle though, and I was swept through one waiting room to the next, one medical form to the next, until before I had even had time to process what was happening, I was told that the boy would live. And every time I asked about my wife, the doctor just repeated that my son was going to be okay.

My "son". The blond haired boy with blue eyes, the boy who looked nothing like me and nothing like my wife, but who looked a whole lot like the little god who had made a promise to her. There were two of us yesterday, and there will be two of us tomorrow, but today it feels like there are less than one.

I hate myself for feeling so helpless. I miss my wife who would have known what this meant. And I don't trust the little god who sleeps alone in the nursery downstairs.

## A Ticket Out Of Hell

There are only two things worth knowing about hell: you wouldn't be there if you didn't deserve it, and you can't get out unless someone offers you a ticket.

You're probably imagining all sorts of other things worth knowing, such as what the demons look like, and how you'll be punished, and what exactly the thermostat is set to. There's no point speculating though, because all the unpleasant sights and feelings you're imagining are the sensations of a living body that you've left far behind. There's no torture worse than the knowledge you're right where you belong, and if you don't believe me, I politely suggest you go to hell and see for yourself.

When I was alive, I would have done anything in the name of love. The lengths I would go through just to see her, to hold her, to lose myself in her until I didn't know myself when I was alone. Until inevitably came the day when I became a stranger to myself, and she became a stranger to me, the two of us turned to poison in the other's veins. Then I would leave her to pursue a fresh intoxication to make me feel whole again, happy so long as I didn't remember those I left behind.

I had a child. More than one, perhaps many more. I know there was a little girl who suffered for me, shuffled from home to home until she was swallowed by the streets. I know there was a boy who wished his father would come back again, although perhaps he wouldn't have if he knew his father was someone like me. I would tell you their names if I could. I would have recited them to myself every moment I was in hell, wishing the best for them though I know they didn't get the best from me.

But I was dead, and they were lost, and that's how it would always be if I hadn't received a ticket out. It wasn't something I earned, or found, or stole, though the devil knows what I would have done to get it. I don't know how long I was mired in misery, but I do know there was no shortage of others who have languished far longer. All that matters is that it was into my hands she pressed the folded paper, and my ears that were blessed with her sweet words.

"You're free to leave. No one will try to stop you anymore. And don't worry if you ever change your mind. It's a two-way ticket, and you can come back whenever you want."

I wish I could describe her, my savior, but what word does justice to those who dwell beyond living senses? I could call her grace, but you would only see slender feet dancing through the grass without capturing the light of her soul. I could call her hope, but you would only feel the flush of excitement beneath your skin and miss the infinite in her cloudless eyes. No, I shall not sully her with any of our impoverished words. It is enough that you know she had a ticket, and that she was giving it to me.

"Why would anyone ever come back?" I asked.

"You might as well ask why anyone would ever come at all," is all she would reply.

And so I passed beneath the shadows that were cast without light. And each time the horrors of the shade loomed over me, I would close my eyes and present the paper in my hand only to feel the pressure of their presence melt back into the dark. I did not slow to listen to the anguish of those left behind, nor was I hindered as I rose into the endless light. All I could think of was getting out—starting over—not sparing a thought for what lay waiting on the other side.

The light I entered was more than something to be seen. It was something to be felt, to be heard, to be smelled, all rushing back to me in a crushing wave. I'd persisted in the emptiness beyond life for so long that I'd forgotten what it was like to *be* again. It was all too loud, too hot, too bright, all intermingled so I couldn't tell which was which, nor up from down, nor good from bad. Too much, too fast, too hard—I did the only thing I could. I began to cry, and then sob, and then wail, and that was exactly what I was supposed to do.

I had been born again, but it was different this time. Staring up at my mother's face as she cradled me in her arms, I remembered everything that I had endured thus far. I even remembered that this woman was my mother, and that the man with his arm around her was my father, and that they were going to take me home to the same blue-carpeted room I always remembered growing up in.

I hadn't just been born. I had been born into my own body, but if that were true, then why couldn't I stop crying once I realized what was going on? Why would my arm move without command—why would I grab hold of the end of the fork even though I knew it would be sharp? Why did I think these thoughts, yet be locked inside a child that couldn't speak aloud?

I hadn't just been born into my body. I had been born into my old life, and I was trapped inside without being able to change a thing. A prisoner to my every mistake, a helpless victim to rise and fall with the iron whims of fate. I could see and hear and feel everything that the body experienced, but my thoughts were cut off from those of the boy that would grow up to be me. I couldn't warn him of what was to come, or change my inevitable actions, or so much as whisper to let him know that I was there.

The newborn body spent most of its time sleeping, and that gave me lots of time to really think about what was to come. I was going to relive every embarrassing moment, every sickness, every defeat, all the way until my own death. Every long night, every heartbreak, every regret, even worse this time around for knowing they were coming despite my body fooling itself into fleeting happiness.

Somewhere in the back of the child's mind sat I, with a piece of folded paper still resting in my hand. It was a two-way ticket, and I could go back. But right now the child was only sleeping, and how could I say that I would prefer hell to this? I would wait, I told myself, until I couldn't take it anymore. One day I'd know my life had been ruined and I'd use the ticket, but not today.

Or tomorrow, or tomorrow, or tomorrow. Because I had spent a long, long time in the darkness, and I had forgotten how beautiful the world could be. Even if I couldn't control this new body, I still experienced its thrill of pleasure as it made each new discovery. The first strawberry—the first dog—the first time seeing the ocean from the window of a car. I had seen infinity after I had died, and I saw it again now through a child's eyes.

And before I knew it the years were starting to pass me by. I knew I was reliving my exact life, but it was amazing how many things I had forgotten over time. Even the childhood memories that I did possess, vague and faded as they may be, did nothing to ruin these visceral experiences. It was almost as good as living for the first time.

By now I had spent so long as a silent passenger that it didn't even feel strange not to choose how the story would play out. I'd wince when I knew I was about to slide down that splintery post, but I'd also remember that it barely even hurt when I woke up the next day. I felt the hot rage of not getting a toy I wanted at the store, and then remember that I'd gotten that toy on Christmas that same year, and that it had broken within the first twenty minutes. Every hurt and injustice that I had been dreading so much had seemed like the end of the world at the time, but now that I was living through them again I knew that none of it would matter forever.

So I let the years slip on, and watched as I grew into the same man I ever was. And then I met her again, my first love, and I felt the heart in my body stop as if it were my own. Looking at her as I did in the moment we first met, I couldn't understand how I had ever stopped loving her. But I would understand, because I had no choice but to live through it all again. I'd relive every little stress, and insecurity, and petty jealous which would grow until it swallowed me up. I'd yell at her, and lie to her, and hurt her in ways deeper than flesh can heal.

Yet here I was, trapped and helpless as I watched how she couldn't stop smiling, how her eyes would dart away but always find their way back to mine. I knew what it would feel like when all the love drained away from those eyes, only to be replaced by revulsion and remorse. My body didn't understand any of that though. It only felt the flush of youth and the bubbling of love, so blind and lost that it would chase her again no matter the end.

But I knew better, sitting alone at the back of the mind with a folded piece of paper in my hand. There was no point in going back to hell, if I was only trying to avoid grief and pain. Hell would be no kinder to me. Here there would still be moments of happiness to come, but going back to hell would banish even these.

If I was only living for myself, then staying must be the right choice to make. And yet if I stayed, I knew I would not be the only one who suffered. Whatever I endured in hell, at least I would be sparing my love and her future children a life with me in it. Better that I should go back where I belonged than force fate to play this hand again.

"I'm ready to go back now," I said to no one in particular. "I've still got my ticket, and I want to go back."

I closed myself away from the light and the noise and the smells of the world, and I was in the darkness once more. And out from that darkness I felt a touch upon my wrist, and I thought it was my savior, my grace, come to take me back to the other side. Yet when I opened my eyes I saw myself still in the living world with my future love smiling back at me, and I knew that I was the one opening my own eyes this time. And when I folded my hand over hers, I knew that was a choice I was making now, one that had never happened the first time round.

"Whether you're ready remains to be seen," said no one in particular in reply.

"Are you feeling okay? Do you want to get out of here?" my love asked me, just the way she had on the day we'd first met.

"No. I don't want to leave. I'm right where I'm supposed to be," I told her. From the way she smiled, she must have known I was talking about her.

My ticket has gotten me out of hell, but will it bring me back again? I suppose that's up to me to decide.

## Sharing A Dream

I read once that dreams shouldn't be taken seriously. That they're nothing but our unconscious mind interpreting random brain activity which happens naturally during sleep. But if all that noise and color and life is just coming from my brain, then how can two people share the same dream?

I didn't recognize the other person in my dream, but I saw him in such vivid detail that it was hard to imagine him not being real. I'd guess he was about my age, in his late 20s, thick curly brown hair, with broad blue-tinged glasses perched upon a wide nose. His face was covered in rough black stubble which progressed part way down his neck. I could see every individual hair, the pores of his skin, and the slight chip on one of his front teeth.

I could see him in such detail because, in my dream, I stood directly over him while he lay in a shallow pool of water. It was just deep enough to cover his face, and his eyes were open. I remember that he tried to speak to me, but the water filled his mouth and I couldn't understand what he was trying to say. Logically he should have stood up if he wanted to talk, and logically I should have helped him up if I wanted to listen. But it was just a dream, so I just kept asking him to repeat himself and he just kept on trying to talk, growing more and more frustrated the longer this went on. It wasn't until I was about to wake up that I realized my foot was on his chest and that I'd been holding him down the whole time.

The dream dissipated within moments of waking as usually happens with me, and I didn't think anything more of it until noon the next day. That's when I saw the same man, looking exactly as I'd dreamt him except that his face was cleanly shaven this time. I was walking with my boss down the hallway of my office building when he comes round the corner and passes us from the other direction. I guess I must have been staring a bit because he slows down as we pass, and for a moment we both stop in the middle of the hallway and stare at each other.

I couldn't think of any pretense to talk to him though. It's a big company, and most of us don't know the people who work in the other departments. Besides, my boss was with me I didn't want to say anything weird, so I just kept walking. I did look back for a second before I turned the corner though—just to see that he was still standing in the middle of the hallway, still staring at me over his shoulder.

By the end of the day I'd decided that I was overthinking things. We worked at the same place, so I must have seen him once and then forgotten until he showed up in my dream. And it didn't have to be weird—I'd probably look back too if someone was staring at me like I'd done to him.

Fast forward to the next night when I had the same dream. Only this time he was cleanly shaven—just like I'd seen him last. He wasn't as calm this time either. He must have remembered that I was holding him down because he started thrashing in the water almost immediately. The water boiled and churned with the energy of his gargled shouting. I was afraid that if he got up he'd attack me, so I did the only thing I could think of and held him down. I held him down and I waited for what seemed like hours until his violent motions finally subsided. By the end of the dream he wasn't trying to talk or move anymore, and when I woke up I could still remember his sullen, angry glare.

I was almost afraid to go to work the next day. It took an extra long shower for me to convince myself that I was being stupid. I usually have a pretty precisely timed morning routine, so that was enough to ensure I was late. My boss is pretty chill and that wouldn't have bee a big deal if it weren't for the guy waiting for me. I didn't see him until he rapped on my driver's side window with his knuckle shortly after I'd parked.

We stared at each other through the window which felt chillingly reminiscent of the thin layer of water which divided us in my dream. The same sullen glare —the same instinct that he was going to attack me the moment we stood on equal footing. But of course this was the real world, and I'd already spent the whole morning convincing myself how stupid I was for giving credence to a dream. I took a deep breath and rolled the window down.

"Yeah?" I asked him, trying to play it cool. "Do I know you?"

"Why didn't you let me up?" he asked at once without the slightest pretense. "I was drowning, and you knew I wanted to get out of there. So why were you holding me down?"

I couldn't decide whether to acknowledge that I knew what he was talking about. I wanted to tell him that it was just a dream—that I was scared—that it was somehow his fault for being underwater in the first place. I must have panicked though, because the only thing I said was, "I don't know what the hell you're talking about."

I tried to open my car door to get out, but the second it started to open he slammed it shut again. His face was getting bright and flushed and he looked equally capable of screaming at me or bursting into tears.

"How's it feel being trapped, huh?" he said. I tried opening the door again, but it was my arm against his whole body weight leaning against my car and I couldn't budge him. "I was drowning. I don't care why you were doing it, I just want to hear you say it. I want you to admit that you were doing it to me."

"You're crazy, man. Get away from my car."

I started to roll up my window. I wouldn't have to admit it if I could just wait him out. Sooner or later someone else would come through the parking lot and they'd help me. They'd call security—he'd be dragged away—or fired. I didn't care what happened to him, as long as I didn't have to admit that I knew what he was talking about.

His arm lashed out to block the closing window and he snatched at me. I just kept closing the window until it caught his arm to prevent him from getting me. I figured he'd retreat at the last second, but he didn't. His arm was caught by the rising glass, and his face kept getting redder. He starting yelling and cursing, and then I was yelling—demanding he pull his arm out of there even though it must have been pinned. He wanted me to reverse the window, but I didn't because I knew he'd grab me the second he had the space to move. I was freaking out, and the only thing I could think to do was keep holding the button, putting more and more pressure on his arm until—

All at once the window shattered, a thousand cracks and fractures appearing from nowhere. He screamed and ripped his arm away, and the whole window bent and wrenched free with him. A second later we were staring at each other through the open window, him red-faced and snarling, and me terrified out of my mind. I hit the car into reverse and lurched out of the parking spot, not looking back until I was out onto the street.

He wasn't chasing after me or anything—thank god—but I could still see him in the rear view mirror. I left him and my broken window in the parking lot and drove straight home, calling my boss to tell him I wouldn't be in that day. I've been pacing my room ever since I got home, unsure how I can ever go back to work and face him again. I'm seriously considering quitting my job, but I don't think that will even help. Because whatever I do, I can't erase the last thing he shouted after me as I pulled out of the parking lot.

"See you tonight, motherfucker!"

## The Suspicious Butcher

Let me begin with a disclaimer: I'm a vegetarian, and the idea of any human eating the carcass of another sentient animal is absolutely disgusting to me. It would be one thing if we had to kill to survive, but that isn't the case for the vast majority living in a modern society. The only reason we still kill is because we're bored.

We're bored of how our food tastes, and that boredom is a death sentence. We're bored of shooting animals in games, so we go and shoot one in real life. We even kill each other because we've gotten bored of trying to achieve our goals peacefully.

I try not to be preachy with my convictions though, so when my wife asked me to pick up some beef for her dinner party, I played the dutiful soldier. I shot down to a local butcher and tried my best not to breathe for the duration. This was the first time I'd ever actually gone to a dedicated butcher, and walking inside felt like I'd just stepped down the the throat of a living animal.

Ribeye steaks, brisket pastrami, beef tongue salami, corned brisket, all heaped in piles behind the glass. Canadian back bacon, kassler pork, peppered cutlets, all blending together in a great red wall. Dangling chains of sausages, salamis, bologna, hung up like Christmas lights all around me. The butcher must have noticed how overwhelmed I was because he came around the counter to help me. He was a kindly old man wearing a clean white apron, and he gave me a short tour of his shop.

He pointed out a hundred different cuts of meat, but I'd never tried any of them and had no idea which I was supposed to get. He laughed with good nature at my confusion and offered to pick his favorite one for me, and I was quick to accept and get out of there.

I don't know what kind of meat I actually bought. It looked bright and bloody, and the paper package only said "Grade A Meat". My wife wasn't impressed though—she lifted the corner of the paper and took one sniff before blanching. She was mad that I didn't notice how awful it reeked, but in my defense I thought that's how meat was supposed to smell. We didn't have time before our party to pickup anything else though, so we just left it in the fridge and scrapped together the best impromptu dinner we could.

The 'Grade A Meat' sat in the fridge for about a week because we didn't want to waste it, but by then neither of us could take the smell anymore. We compromised by tossing it into the alley behind our house for the stray dogs that nosed through our trash. It was gone the next morning, and a big scruffy black lab was hanging around so I'm sure he enjoyed it.

I went back to the butcher store to try and get a refund, but there was a different man working there and all he'd give me was store credit. Whatever, better than nothing, I picked up some other random pieces to give to the stray dogs. This butcher, a round mustached man, told me he throws out a lot of scraps every Friday and that I can pick them up for the dogs every week if I wanted. It seemed better than letting them go to waste, so I began this weekly tradition.

The odd thing was that I'd never actually see the dogs get the scraps. I'd put them in a bowl in the alley, but no matter how long I watched I never saw one of the dogs come by. The meat would always be gone by the next morning though, so I just assumed it was going to the right place.

My wife observed that he black lab hadn't been back though. Neither had the little terrier we saw sniffing around one day. It was weird, because once a stray dog finds a reliable source of free food they're unlikely to ever forget. We kept seeing dogs in the alley behind our house, but we never seemed to see the same dog twice.

A few weeks into this routine and the mustached butcher asked to see pictures of the strays eating his scraps. I told him that I'd never actually seen them eating it, and he got all huffy saying a wild animal was probably stealing it. He didn't want to give me any more after that, and we had a bit of an argument about it. He thought I was trying to scam him, and even went so far as to deny that I'd ever bought meat from him before, telling me there was no old man who worked at his shop.

More to prove him wrong than anything else, I made it my mission to prove where the meat was going. I went as far as to buy a big fatty New York steak with the bone still in as bait, then set it out beside a battery powered lamp so I could watch. I found a spot that I could see from my bedroom window, and I glued myself there waiting for something to happen.

About an hour into my vigil, my wife tells me I'm watching the wrong spot. I tell her that's impossible because I'm staring right at the bowl I put out under the lamp, and she tells me there are some dogs going at meat on the other end of the house.

It was black outside, but I had my phone for light and could hear the dogs growling and yipping ahead. Glad to have my proof, I had my camera and its flash ready as I rounded the corner.

My first surprise was seeing the bright, bloody red slab of meat we'd tossed out the first day. The color was the only recognizable thing about it though, because it was now several feet across and at least two feet high. There had been two dogs fighting over it—one ugly old bulldog, and hyper aggressive chihuahua that barely touched the ground. The chihuahua was getting the upper hand and had just managed to get the older dog to back off as I arrived.

The chihuahua had its back turned toward the meat so it could focus on the other dog. It didn't see the meat moving. Not like a natural creature, but swelling and oozing, contracting and expanding to drag itself across the ground. I started shouting to scare off the dog and get my wife to come see, but the chihuahua only turned to snarl at me instead. The slab of meat reared into the air and slammed down on the small dog with a wet thud and a high pitched squeal. The dog was utterly engulfed, and all I could hear from it were the sound of snapping bones and the wet tearing of meat.

I tried to save the dog by grabbing the meat and dragging it away. My fingers slipped along its slimy surface, and I had to drop my phone to try and get a better grip. The tighter I held, the more my fingers burned, until the corrosive pain was too much and I had to let go.

The bulldog was barking like mad now, and my wife was shouting back from the house. The meat reacted by swiftly dispersing, ripping itself to shreds like ground beef while each piece wormed its way into the ground. I grabbed my phone again to try and take the picture, but my fingers were slippery with blood and I couldn't operate the camera before the thing had vanished. All that was left of the chihuahua was a red smear on the ground.

I told my wife that I'd just slipped and cut my hands, and I hurried inside to wash off. I couldn't bring myself to tell her what I'd seen, but I'm writing this now to explain what my thoughts and words have failed to do so far. I don't know if she'll believe it, but I have to try. If this doesn't convince her that meat is murder, I don't know what will.

## My Neighbor's Infestation

I have two immediate neighbors in my apartment building. Ms. Bangles is a sixty year old woman who somehow has a different man over every other week. Based on the noise I hear filtering through my wall, I'm inclined to believe she really likes the discovery channel and has the hippo mating season on DVD.

It's the quieter neighbor, Mr. Receesh, that I'm worried about. There's this skittering, shuffling sound that makes my skin crawl. I never notice it during the day, but without fail once the hippos have settled down I can hear something scuttling around. I still don't like to cause problems though, and I've gotten into the habit of just playing soft music at night so I don't have to listen to it.

This worked pretty well until I started dating someone and she spent her first night at my place. It turns out she can't sleep with the music on, or with it off, given the symphony of the thin-walled building that plays every night. I told her I felt uncomfortable bringing up the heaving, grunting sounds from Ms. Bangles, so we agreed that she would speak to her about it in the morning if I talked to Mr. Receesh.

I got the bad end of that deal. Mr. Receesh is a short, dark haired, man with a mustache and glasses. In other words, somewhere between an IT guy and the man at the playground with no kids. He was wearing a bathrobe when he opened the door, and there was more hair spurting out of his chest than I have on my entire body.

"Police?" he asked, standing in the crack of the doorway like he didn't want me to see inside.

I was in sweats and a baggy T-shirt. Nothing about me looked like police. I told him no, I was his neighbor, and I just wanted to say—

*Click.* Door snaps shut, right in my face. I knocked again, feeling more than a little insulted. Again the door opens, and he looks me up and down. Then I heard the *scuttling* sound, and right there on his foot was this cockroach looking critter at least three or four inches long. It was crawling between his toes on his bare foot, but he didn't seem to mind.

"That. That's why I'm here," I said, pointing at the giant insect. "What the hell is that?"

His mustache wiggled when he grinned. "Her name is Percy. Do you like them?"

He opened his door a little wider as if to invite me in. I threw up a little bit in my mouth. The floor was covered in them, so thick I could barely see the tiles. More on the counters, scampering over the spoiled and uncovered fruit and open cereal boxes. Scaling the walls, wiggling through the carpet, and burrowing into the couch that had so many antenna sticking out through the rips in the fabric that it almost looked furry.

Sitting in the corner was a thin, unhappy looking woman who stared down at her magazine without looking up. Her baggy skin hung loosely from her bones as if she'd recently lost a lot of weight, which I'm sure I would have done too if my kitchen looked like hers. She made no move to shoo away the creatures, and it would have been a futile effort as she already had a good number visibly crawling through her frayed hair.

"This is Ulean, my wife, and all our wonderful children." Mr. Receesh beamed. "We would do anything for them, wouldn't we Ulean?"

"Mmm," Ulean grunted, flipping a page. She glanced up at me briefly with heavy eye-lids—a weary, long-suffering face—before letting gravity droop her head back down to the magazine.

A few of the insects made a mad bounding rush for the door, but Mr. Receesh closed it most of the way again and wedged his bare foot to block the exit. I tried not to look at the especially large insect trying to squirm free of his toes to get away.

"Well don't just stand there," he told me. "You can come in and meet them or go, but we can't just chat here or they'll escape."

I honestly don't know what I told him. I was feeling a little dizzy and my brain couldn't quite register what I'd seen. All I know is a moment later the door had closed, and I was standing there like an idiot, not wanting to knock again.

"I'm going to tell the managers at the front desk!" I shouted through the door. "You aren't allowed to keep those things. They need to send an exterminator!"

"How dare you threaten us!" the voice came back through the door. "Ulean and I would die for our children! Wouldn't we, Ulean? Don't you dare come back!"

I didn't stick around long enough for him to open it again. I ran straight to the administration office on the first floor, but it was closed. Sunday—they didn't open until 11. I didn't want to go back to my room and explain to my new girlfriend what was there, because that would be the last time she ever visited me. I just waited at the office for someone to come.

About ten minutes later, I see Mr. Receesh, fully dressed, hustling for the door with a suitcase. It squelched as he dragged it, and a little red liquid drizzled out through the zipper. I called after him, but he just flipped me off and rushed out. My girlfriend started texting me asking where I was, so I made up the excuse of going out to get us breakfast while I killed time until the office opened.

The only thing more disgusting than seeing those teaming masses of insects was imagining them while I was getting food. I felt like I didn't want to eat anything ever again, but I picked up some stuff for her and hurried back. The office was open by then, and I explained everything I saw to a bewildered lady who looked at me like this was all my fault somehow. She said she'd call someone about it, but I wouldn't back down until she agreed to come upstairs with me and see for herself.

Mr. Receesh was home again by the time we knocked. He fully opened the door and grinned, his stupid little mustache wiggling as he did. The office lady seemed embarrassed, but he laughed at her stumbling questions and invited us both inside. The moment the lady had passed, his expression changed to one of brooding anger in my direction.

The place was spotless, and I felt like the biggest asshole in the world. Clean counters, clean floor—I know I wasn't imagining it though, because the couch was still perforated in a hundred places where the insects had been burrowing a moment before.

"… no, no pets. Just me and the misses, sleeping in the other room," Mr. Receesh was saying. The office lady apologized again, and glaring daggers at me, moved to exit his apartment.

"Let's see the bedroom," I demanded.

"This is getting absurd," Mr. Receesh protested. "These baseless accusations are no excuse to harass my wife—"

I didn't wait for an invitation. I barged through the place and flung open the door, half-expecting a torrent of insects to come tumbling over me in an avalanche. The room was dark with no sign of the creatures. There was only the fat lump of Mrs. Receesh, peacefully lying in bed.

"That's enough out of you," the office lady said. She grabbed me by the back of my shirt and began to drag me from the room. "I'm so sorry for disturbing you, sir, I promise you won't be hearing from us again."

How could I explain what had happened without sounding insane? It doesn't matter how many layers Ulean wears when she goes out, it doesn't hide how much larger and lumpier she is now. It doesn't hide the limping shuffle she makes as she staggers along, always leaning on Mr. Receesh for support. What kind of monster would I be to criticize a woman for her handicap? Not to mention the ripple under her skin, like a thousand marching feet going about their business…

More importantly, how am I ever going to sleep at night with that damned scuttling sound?

## Should I Stop Selling Bodies?

Either you have a soul or you don't. It's the same to me either way.

If there is no soul, then a human corpse is no more sacred than ground beef in the grocery store or the roadkill smashed into the asphalt. If you do have a soul, then it is already gone by the time you close your eyes for the last time. Either way, the body you left behind no longer belongs to you.

Now some might protest and say that a person is the owner of their own body, so once they die their body is inherited by their family along with the rest of their possessions. If this were true then anyone would be free to take that body home with them. Maybe they'd prop it up in an armchair or keep it in the freezer until the weather is nice enough to bring along on the next family fishing trip. If anyone tried to do this, however, their family gathering would doubtlessly be interrupted by the police who would be quick to convince you that the body is not your property to do what you like with. That in reality your body belongs to the state, and that it's up to them to decide your ultimate fate. In other words no, I don't feel bad about stealing bodies from the state who has no right to them in the first place.

I work in a mortuary, but I'm not going to tell you which because that would be bad for business. The first body I took was destined for a closed casket funeral. She hadn't been wearing a seatbelt during a car accident, and the force of impact from her face hitting the windshield caused her skull to completely flatten like someone had taken a hammer to play-dough. I commented on the incident at the time to a friend, a male nurse who worked at a nearby teaching hospital. He offered me $500 on the spot so he and his friends could have some extra autopsy practice, and I couldn't think of any justification to say no.

The reasoning was straightforward enough. He and his friends would benefit from the extra experience. That experience would then benefit other people during their medical careers. And of course I would benefit from the extra cash. Meanwhile the corpse certainly wasn't going to mind, and the family was never going to find out, so a strictly utilitarian philosophy dictated that this was the right thing to do.

The woman weighed 126 pounds at the time of her death, exactly the same as the 28 bricks which I lined the bottom of her casket with. The funeral went as all funerals do, with tears and speeches and many furtive glances at the clock hanging at the back of the church. It wouldn't have even been worth mentioning

## Sleepless Nights

if the woman's father hadn't made the selfish request to see his daughter one last time.

I possess a good deal of confidence in my ability to be persuasive, added by the air of authority I've cultivated in being a medical professional. Somehow I doubted that I could conjure any medical terminology of sufficient verbosity to convince the man that the accident had condensed his daughter into a pile of bricks though. Instead I was forced to rush from one member of the family to the next, convincing each in turn that seeing the mangled corpse would instill a traumatic memory in them that would forever taint their recollection of the deceased. Once I had sufficient support for this idea we all descended upon the father in a flurry of pleading for him to forgo the request. It was a weight off my heart when he finally acceded and withdrew his intention.

As you can imagine I learned my lesson after that. I would never again let myself be put in that untenable position. From then on I would only sell the corpses of those destined for cremation instead.

It's not like I had much choice in the matter anyway. It turns out that 'Wagner', one of my friend's colleagues who participated in the unsanctioned autopsy, wasn't satisfied with a single body. Not only would Wagner require a steady stream of them, but he even threatened to report me to the authorities if I did not provide. If I were the only one who paid the price I might have fought back, but then Wagner went on to say he would tell the family of the deceased. I couldn't bear the thought of how they would react, particularly the father who had only wanted to see his daughter again.

One body a month, that's what he wanted to purchase, an insignificant number compared with the volume of business my mortuary processed. It wasn't difficult at all to move the covered bodies into the back of his van, nor was it hard to disguise the incinerated remains. Everything looks pretty much the same after its been blasted with 1800 degrees in the cremation oven for a few hours. Perhaps simply working with corpses all day has desensitized me somewhat, but it didn't take long before these monthly transactions had become a regular part of my business. It's not like I was only in it for the money either—I've actually been donating all the money I get to help the families with their funeral costs.

One time I was already waiting for Wagner by the back door with the body ready to go. He took one peek under the cloth, turned up his nose and said, "I don't like that one. What else do you got?"

"What's not to like?" I asked. I grasped hold of the deceased man's fat belly and shook it with both hands. "He's jammed full of lovely organs to play with."

"We're studying the removal of ovary cysts," Wagner told me. "I only want females from now on. The younger the better."

It just so happened that I had a girl in her mid twenties scheduled to be cremated, and I saw no difference in making the switch. This continued for another four months before I had the chance to catch up with my friend again over coffee, and he was shocked to hear that Wagner still wanted bodies at all.

"Didn't Wagner tell you that he dropped out of medical school last semester?" my friend asked me.

"No. He didn't mentioned that."

"What's he using the bodies for then?" my friend asked. And as we stared at each other over our coffees, the unsettling possibilities began to float up from those dark places in the mind that we try to forget are there at all.

"Well it could be worse," my friend said after a long pause. Then another as he took a sip of coffee. "At least he isn't hurting anyone."

"You don't think he's…"

"Wagner's always been a weird dude. What's wrong with it though?" my friend asked, nonplussed. "It's not like doing it with a kid or an animal or anything. It's not like anyone is suffering."

"We have to tell someone, don't we?" I asked, not sure what I was hoping to hear.

My friend shrugged. "Telling someone would hurt people. Not telling would not. Besides, I heard Wagner used to have a girlfriend but it ended badly. She got roughed up and the police had to get involved. To this day he swears she's the one who started it and he was only defending himself, but she was like a foot shorter than him and half his weight so none of us really believed it. So you're really doing the community a service by keeping him away from living girls."

"But why would he need a new one every month?" I asked.

"What do you care? It's not like the other girls are going to get jealous. Anyway he's had enough medical training to know how to preserve them properly, so it's not like it's going to be a health issue."

Shortly later my friend got a call and had to go back to work. I kept sitting there for about an hour, not drinking my coffee, just thinking while trying not to visualize anything too clearly. I know it's wrong, but for the life of me I can't figure out why.

Of course my instincts revolt at the idea, but does being offended make it wrong? After all, humans have a long history of being offended by everything from scientific knowledge, to using birth control, or even eating the wrong kind of meat on the wrong kind of day, and none of those hurt anyone either. And even if the offensive thought itself is the sin, then the only way the families would suffer is if I stopped providing the bodies and Wagner followed through on his threat to tell them. Not to mention that I wouldn't be able to donate to the funeral expenses anymore.

That's why I'm writing—to ask for your opinion. Should I cut Wagner off, or let him have his fun?

## The House No One Built

Old houses have a spirit of their own.

We don't usually notice during the day when the sun is warm and the windows are open. Fresh breeze carries familiar scents from the garden and the flowering jasmine vines snaking their way through the crumbling stonework. There is always too much going on in my house during the evenings to notice then either, with mom bustling around the kitchen and my two brothers jostling over their games in the living room. From somewhere upstairs echoes my uncle's warbling chuckles along with the canned laughter of his shows. And underlying it all comes the scratching, popping jazz playing from the ancient record player in my father's den, muffled and distant around the many twists and turns of the narrow hallways.

The house is comforting and warm and safe until everyone has gone to bed and the house begins to breathe. When the shadows never stay put where they're supposed to, and the stagnant air drags heavy with unfamiliar taste. The lights are never enough to fill the room, no matter how many switches are turned on. And the silence is never fully silent: a conspicuous sensation of emptiness even softer than the creaking floor boards or the rustle of wooden shutters against the wind. There's something else, something deeper, almost like someone figured out how to play the sound of silence to cover up something we weren't supposed to hear.

There's an unspoken rule in our house that keeps us quiet at night. Sometimes we'll catch one another in the hallways on our way to the bathroom, or when we're poking around the fridge looking for snacks. We'll greet each other with a nod or a gesture, or sometimes a whisper if we have to, but we'll never speak out loud. Even as children, my brothers and I never broke the silence at night. It always felt disrespectful, like shouting during church, as though we were interrupting something sacred that was there before we were born and would linger in those walls long after we were gone.

"Old electrical wiring can have that effect," my father had said once. He never elaborated on exactly what 'that effect' was, or gave us an explanation for how a faulty fuse box could feel like something in the dark was listening to you breathe. "I sort of like it though, you know? Makes me feel all snug, like the house is tucking me in at night."

"It has to do with the ventilation system," my mother said. "I felt it too when we first moved in, but honestly I hardly even notice any more. Just leave a window open if it's bothering you."

I didn't know how to explain to her that the house didn't want the windows open at night. It was as if I had pushed one of my brothers off the sofa, and then immediately turned my back on him. I wouldn't have to see his face to know that he was angry. He wouldn't need to shout or hit me back. I would just feel the anger stirring behind me in the air, an insubstantial thing which glowered down at me until I apologized and gave him his seat back. That's how it was with the house, suffocating me with its anger until I closed the window and let it settle down.

"No one builds a house to feel like this. If you're asking me why, then that's your answer. No one ever built this house, it just grew this way."

I liked my uncle's explanation best, even though I never fully understood it. My parents were always busy with something, and my brothers would never let me live it down if I told them I was afraid. My uncle liked having me visit though, because no one else ever did. His legs didn't work anymore, and he never got up except to drag himself to the bathroom. I'd sit on the end of his bed after bringing him food, and listen to him while he told me about the feelings I couldn't describe.

"Don't give me that face. People act like I'm broken just because I don't get around any more, but being inside all the time has given me and the house a chance to get to know one another. It told me about how people come along sometimes and cut down trees and build up houses, and how the land is hurt by it. How do I know? Because as soon as those people get up and leave, the land is going to try and heal itself. The gardens will start taking over the house, and the weeds will grow up high, and the animals will start jumping fences, and given enough time, you'll never know that people were there at all.

"Well it's the same way with this house, only the other way around. The land here was hurt by something a long time ago, hurt by something that was here even before the settlers came. And so the land did what it always does, it grows and it heals. Only some hurts run so deep they never heal right, and so the land has to grow up a house to trap the hurt inside and not ever let go."

"You're only saying that because you're thinking about your legs," I told him. "How is a house supposed to grow out of the ground, with all the wires and pipes and things?"

My uncle laughed, the familiar deep chuckle that was so much apart of this place that it might as well be coming from the house itself. "The house didn't grow from scratch, carpets and wallpaper and all. The shape of it grew up, swelling like a blister on the land. And then the people came along, and they must have thought it was an abandoned house that someone before them built. So they fixed it up and made it comfortable for people to live in—as comfortable as they could considering where it came from—and now its our turn to watch over the place."

"What about the hurt that caused it to grow? Where did that go?"

"You wouldn't be up here asking that if you didn't already know. You might not hear this in many songs, but there are some hurts that don't ever go. So you might as well make them your friend, because they're going to be there until the end of you. If the house ever decided that it doesn't want us to be here, then you won't need me to tell you that."

I wouldn't have remembered those words if they'd been wrong. I think my house really did care for my uncle. And my uncle must have cared back, because even when he got worse he wouldn't let my parents bring him to the hospital. He never raised his voice, but he was adamant that there would be anger if they made him leave. I remember thinking at the time how odd he said it, that 'there would be anger', and not that he would be angry. But the only thing that seemed to matter was that he was staying put and my parents were very worried. And like the house, they never told me exactly what was wrong.

I didn't sleep much that night, and I was awake when I heard my uncle gasping for air. It surprised me that my first thought was to be angry at him for making so much noise when the house wanted it to be quiet. The sound from my uncle was getting more desperate though, and it didn't take long for me wake my parents. Everything was loud after that: my brothers shouting, my parents arguing, and even the wail of an ambulance screeching up our street. I think my uncle would have tried to fight them off if he'd still been awake when they carried him out. I know he would have done more to convince us if he could, to make us believe there would be anger when he was gone.

My parents both rode with the ambulance, and it was just me and my brothers that knew what happened. We were already scared and anxious about our uncle. It wouldn't have taken much to set us off or make us imagine devils out of the darkness. My brothers were so worked up about what happened that they wouldn't stop talking though—about all the neighbors standing on their porch, about the beeping machines the medical responders carried, about what was going to happen to my uncle. Back and forth, louder and louder, then shouting again when one of them said my uncle was going to die.

The shouting didn't stop, not even when both of them had finally shut their mouths. It sounded just like my brothers, the sound reverberating through the halls upstairs, only the voices weren't shouting about my uncle anymore. The voices were threatening each other with such cruel and violent acts as to make me flinch in phantom agony. My brothers didn't seem to understand what was happening, and they kept getting angrier at one another, threatening each other for real as they accused the other of trying to frighten them. Then one of them got his hands around the others throat, and the other did in kind, and both were flaming red in the face as each precious breath was squandered on a snarl of hatred for the other.

I involuntarily held my own breath from the tension as I tried to drag them apart, and it was then I noticed that something beside us was still drawing air. Hot and heavy and angry, the force growing with every disembodied breath. A wind inside the house dragged over us so powerfully as to draw us up the stairs, the blast of each rhythmic pull whipping the curtains, twisting the rugs, and ripping pictures from the wall. Hot and wet and insatiable panting, and all the while my brothers doing nothing but fight each other as they tumbled end over end.

The cruel shouts and threats filled the air more powerfully up here, joined in by the voices of others I did not recognize. Men and women of all ages, their voices filled with such despising loathing hatred as though we alone were the cause of every harm and misery in their lives. Spitting, roaring hatred, wishing our deaths and shouting at us between each infernal breath. Hardest to bear were the voices of children, wailing and screaming at us with such revulsion and betrayal. Their suffering made me feel so guilty in that moment that I was absolutely convinced I deserved whatever punishment I was about to receive.

One of my brothers had stopped fighting back by now. He lay limply on the ground with the others hands still clamped around his throat, both faces nearly unrecognizable for the savageness of their exertion. The heat and the pressure was subsiding around us, however, and the wind was retreating through the cracks in the floorboards and walls. Now suddenly the air came sharp and cold as each window and door was hurled back against its hinges, snapping brittle into place like the fracture of bone. I knew at once the house was giving me this chance to leave it to languish in its hurt and its hatred. I can't explain how, but I knew that I would be safe if I ran for it now, leaving my brothers to whatever fate was bestowed them by the others hand. But just as clearly I knew that I would carry the hurt of what I let happen with me from that day until the end of me, and no redeeming glimmer of solace would ever turn that hurt into my friend.

I went through one of the open doors that was offered me, but not to go outside. Instead I went to my uncle's room, climbing into his bed and pulling up his blanket that was still damp with his sweat. I covered myself in that blanket and I cried until the last haunting echo of anger had settled into quiet, and then into something deeper, that sound of soft chuckling that had always come as though from the house itself.

There is a spirit in the house that no one built. And with it carries a hurt so old that I don't think will ever heal. But I know that spirit by name, and I call him my uncle. I told him that it's okay if he never leaves, because I'm never going to leave him either. At night I keep the windows closed and I stay very quiet, and together we have found peace. And someday another will name their hurt, and they will know that it is me, and I will never be alone.

## The Other Me

There are walls in this world that cannot be crossed. There is no force so great, nor light so harsh, nor sound so loud as to penetrate them. These walls are hidden from us, and we may go our entire life not realizing what secret places we are forbidden to enter.

## Sleepless Nights

How can one know about such walls that cannot be seen or felt? There are secret places where the walls are stretched thin, where it's no longer clear which side is which. Places where things that do not belong to our world slip in without notice, places where one of us can disappear and never find our way back again. I know because I found such a place two nights ago.

Like most things, it began with a girl. I would have killed for her, and I wish that she knew it. She was my classmate during my senior year at university. I didn't know what love was supposed to feel like, but she burned a hole in my awareness that left little room for anything beside. Her slightest murmur drowned out the surrounding noise, the barest turning of her head in my direction causing all other motion to cease. I remember how the half-dozen words we shared played on repeat for the rest of the day, and by the time I lay down to sleep that night, burning from the flush of my own thoughts, I knew that I was lost.

As the semester progressed we grew closer than I dared hope possible, but I was a fool to think I was the only one to notice her grace. Of course she was already engaged to marry, and I accepted that it was my roll to only admire her from a distance. The wedding was fast approaching though, and I couldn't bear the thought of us going our separate ways in life without her ever knowing how much better my world was with her in it.

I began to fantasize about situations where her fiancé humiliated himself in some impossible competition between us. I dreamt about making some grand romantic gesture that I lacked the courage to even whisper aloud. Each dream grew more vivid and elaborate, distracting me from the ache of jealous desperation that I could never bury deep enough to forget.

Then came the night before her wedding. The night she kissed me on the cheek and thanked me for being her friend. I couldn't sleep after that, couldn't sit still, couldn't hear myself think over the pulse of my own frustrated desire. Sweating, miserable, anxious without relief, I forced myself to go for a walk to clear my head of her. Past unfamiliar streets, down unknown roads, I walked so far that I left the city lights behind and found myself amidst the slouching ruin of long abandoned houses.

I'd been walking for hours, but I hadn't succeeded in leaving her behind. I sat down beside an old boarded-up well to rest. I noticed a small hole between the planks large enough to fit a coin through. Fishing around in my pocket, I found some loose change to drop through the opening, wishing myself happiness in a life without her, and wishing her the best even if that meant a life without me. I didn't expect there to still be water in the well, but it wasn't the plopping of my coins that surprised me. It was the rattle of something underneath the boards, and the quarter which slipped out from the hole to roll at my side.

I thought it must have hit a rock and bounced back up at me somehow for a moment, but that moment ended when I heard a voice echoing from below.

"Hello? Is there someone down there?"

"Do you mean up here?" I called back. "Are you stuck in the well?"

"What are you talking about? You're the one in the well."

The only thing that made sense to me was that someone was trapped in there all the same. I worked at one of the planks until I could get it loose, flinging it aside to get a proper look below. There wasn't anyone there though, nothing but the dark water and my reflection peering into it. Then I watched as my reflection dropped another coin. The spinning metal hit the water on his side, then continued falling upward until it rattled on the bottom of one of the remaining boards.

The two of us were identical, right down to the clothes we were wearing and the smudge of lipstick on our cheeks. That stood out to me the most, and on impulse I asked him if he was here because of her. He said yes, and I knew the two of us were living exactly the same life. Only we were living it in different worlds, not knowing the other existed until that very moment.

There are a million things we might have said to the other in such a circumstance, but the two of us knew without words that she was the only thing on our mind. It felt so good to finally admit my feelings openly to the only person who could completely understand. We both shared the same hopes, and fears, and sullen depression as we accepted our fate, but I was the one who figured out what had to be done.

"If we don't tell her, we'll always wonder what could have been," I said. "But if we do, we might ruin her own shot at being happy, or lose her forever as a friend. The only way we won't always wonder is for the two of us to each do something different."

"We'll fip a coin," he said, because of course he must have liked the idea for me to think it.

"Heads you tell her, and I don't."

"Tails you tell her, and we'll meet back here tomorrow night to tell the other how it went."

He flipped the coin down to the water, and it kept flipping all the way until it got to me. I snatched it out of the air and slapped it against my wrist, and the other me and I locked eyes.

"I'm scared," he said, but he was smiling.

"Heads. I'm going to tell her," I said, showing him the coin. His smile broadened, and I could easily imagine how relieved he must have felt. I was terrified, and he knew it, and somehow that made it all okay.

"Do it in person," he told me. "Don't hold anything back. Make it count. I really hope it works out for you. I hope it works out for us."

So I told her that I loved her.

It was after two in the morning by the time I got back home, almost three by the time I got to her place. I didn't text or call, I just knocked on the door. I was so occupied rehearsing everything I might say that I didn't even realize how freaked out she must be to hear someone knocking at that time. I almost ran away right then, but I held my ground until she opened the door. She leaned against the frame with a smug curiosity, wearing nothing but her underwear and a baggy t-shirt. All the words I had prepared dissolved like mist. So before she asked me a question I couldn't answer, I just blurted it out. I told her I loved her, and that it was the will of the universe that she should hear it from me tonight.

For the second time that night she kissed me, and the universe rejoiced with me.

We stayed up all night talking, and she didn't get married the next day. She said she'd suspected the truth, but hadn't trusted the feeling enough until I'd had the courage to come to her door. She told me she was so happy that I told her in time. I asked her what she would have done if I'd waited until after she was married to tell her. She shook her head and wouldn't say, and I knew the answer hurt her too much to try and pry. She was going to have a hard enough time explaining her change of heart, and I promised to be respectful and not rush her in any way.

We spent all the next day together, and I was so deliriously happy that discovering a parallel dimension only seemed like the second most magical thing to happen.

That night I drove out past where the city lights dried up to the boarded up well. I couldn't wait to tell the other me the good news. He started laughing when I told him, and then both of us were laughing without quite knowing why. He made me tell him every detail of what I said and did and how she reacted, and I told him everything—everything except when I asked her what would have happened if I'd waited one more day. I wanted the other me to be as happy as I was, and I couldn't bear to steal the joy from our eyes.

We made a promise to return the next night, and I did. The next time I looked into the dark water he wasn't there yet though, and I saw nothing where my reflection should have been peering over the lip of the well. I sat with my back against the stone and waited for him a long time before I finally heard his voice.

"I kissed her," he said.

I jumped up and peered over the rim of the well. I was sure I heard him, but I still couldn't see any reflection on the other side.

"She didn't kiss me back," he said. "I didn't catch up with her until she was in the train station. They were going on their honeymoon up state, and I managed to get her alone and I kissed her. She said we would have to talk about this when she got back. I told her I loved her, and she pushed me away."

The voice sounded different than I remembered it. There wasn't as much of an echo to it, and it took me longer than it should have to figure out why. I didn't realize what had happened until a heavy blow beat against the underside of the old boards. He'd gone through the water and climbed up my side of the well.

"Why should you get her and I don't? It isn't right," he said.

"We flipped a coin. We had a deal."

"You cheated!"

Part of the old wood ripped away in his hand. He was bracing with his back and legs against the sides of the well to stay in place while his hands were free to widen the opening.

"How did I cheat? I didn't stop you from telling her."

"You did. I might have told her myself if you hadn't stopped me. This is your fault!"

Beating, beating on the decaying barrier. The pounding sound frightened a flock of settled birds nearby, and they all went up in a frightened rush. My heart was running wild with panic. I couldn't fully process what was going on. All I knew is that I couldn't let him get above the rim of the well. That if we were both here on one side, then I wouldn't need to be physically attacked to suffer for it. I wouldn't be myself—my life wouldn't be my own, and she wouldn't be mine so long as he and I stood on equal ground.

That's why I grabbed a piece of the broken wood and brought it down on his head. I didn't know I was going to do it before it happened, and he looked just as surprised as I was. The blow was enough to make him slip and tumble back toward the water. He fell straight through, but he caught himself on the other side. Through the water he stared up at me, blood from the gash across his hairline dribbling down his face.

What could I do? I couldn't stand there forever and wait for him to try and crawl back up again. I couldn't go down into his world and let him live in mine, not without losing her.

All I know is that I shouldn't have done what I did. I shouldn't have turned and ran to my car. I shouldn't have given him the chance to escape into my world, because I know that's what I would have done. I would have killed for her, and so can he.

He knows where I work. He knows where I sleep. He knows everything about me. And if I were to disappear, he could take my place and no one would ever know.

Lauren Daniels, you need to know. That's why I'm writing this down.

If you read this, you'll know to ask me about the well. I'll tell you the truth if you do. But if you ask him, and he pretends that he doesn't know…

Then love him all the same. This is proof that neither of us could live in a world without you.

## The Invisible Door

Back when I was in fourth grade, I was friends with this super clean-cut kid who always tucked in his collared shirt into his khakis. He was brought up religious while my family wasn't, and we had this running game where we both tried to come up with questions to trip the other up. I remember one time sitting on my couch playing video games when I told him everything could be measured, and his counter was to ask how I could measure the distance between Heaven and Hell.

I was completely stumped, but I knew my dad would know because he knew everything. We ran to ask him in our dreadfully white kitchen where he spent most of his time because it was the room with the best light. He put down the book he was reading real slow, looked at me over his glasses, then at my friend, then back at me before finally saying:

"A second is more than enough time to get there, if that second is bad enough."

That answer always stuck with me. It came back years later when I was a sophomore in high school and the vice principle peeked into my English class to call my name in a low, hushed voice. I thought I was getting in trouble for something until I got into the hall and she handed me a cell phone, from which an excessively calm voice told me that my father had suffered a massive heart attack and had passed before he even got to the hospital. I remember thanking the faceless voice for telling me and hanging up. After the call, I looked down at the phone screen and noticed that the call lasted 10 minutes and 23 seconds from the time the vice principle first picked up, and I wondered which of those was the one where I made the journey.

The best man I've ever known died when he was only 42 years old. And anyone who has lost the one they admire most knows how it feels for part of themselves to die with them.

It didn't occur to me then that my second between heaven and hell hadn't happened yet though, and that it wouldn't happen until a night in college when I discovered the secret door in my house. It was an old victorian style house that looked more like a bunch of smaller houses had randomly smashed together than any deliberate construction. There was a group of 8 of us who pooled together to rent the place, which ended up being way cheaper than individual dorm rooms. Even after we'd been there for a few months we kept discovering new things about the place, like a fireplace that had been boarded up or the dumbwaiter shoot hidden in what we thought was an electrical box.

Well one night five of us were hanging out in the living room when Derek, engineering major with a mouth that never seemed to fully close, showed us this trick he learned. He put a layer of clear tape over the phone's flashlight and colored it blue with a marker, then another layer colored purple, and a few more going back and forth like that. When he was done he turned on the light, which was now filtered into UV-A and worked like a blacklight.

We had all been drinking a bit by this point and laughed enormously at all the gross glowing splotches on the couch. We turned out the rest of the lights to make the colors pop and took turns shining the light on our teeth to make them glow. Then we chased around Chrissie, the only girl in our group, whose makeup reacted to make her look like some sort of demonic clown. She was less amused (and probably less drunk) than the rest of us, so she took off up the stairs while we all followed. Gregory had a perfect Australian accent, and he made the Steve Irwin voice like we were stalking some exotic beast that we didn't want to frighten off.

It was all in good fun, but Chrissie was in no mood and she locked herself in her room. The slamming of her door cut through our buzz a bit, and we all felt like assholes and the game didn't seem so fun anymore. It was during this moment of sudden quiet that the light fell on a blank patch of wall and the outline of a door suddenly glowed from nowhere. Derek, Gregory, a third guy named Preston and me, all staring at it in silence like we'd just been visited by a UFO.

"Dude," Preston said.

"Dude," the rest of us replied in a solem chorus, the only appropriate response in such circumstances.

Derek ran his hands over the outline. It quickly became apparent that the light was shining through the wallpaper. As you can imagine with four buzzed college boys, we respected the property and wouldn't dream of tearing off the wallpaper on a rental just to satisfy an idle curiosity. At least for a few seconds anyway.

Derek had a pocket knife on his keychain and he slid it into the wall to trace the outline of the door, which was positioned almost exactly between his room and Chrissie's on the other side. It didn't seem like there was enough space for a third hidden room between them, and consensus said it couldn't have been larger than a closet that had been sealed up. We peeled back the wallpaper to reveal a solid wooden door that matched the design of the rest of the house, but it wasn't the door that was glowing. There was a thin gap around the edges, and whatever the UV light was reacting with was coming from behind.

"What if it opens into Chrissie's room?" Gregory asked. "She would literally kill us if we all just tumbled through."

"Don't worry about it," Preston said. "We'll just tell her it was your idea and that we were trying to stop you." He pushed against the door and it gave a little, seeming more stuck than locked.

"Chrissie you'll want to come see this!" Gregory called through the wall. "We promise not to shine the light on you!"

The language in her reply would have been sufficient to embarrass a career criminal and doesn't need to be replicated here. It was too late anyway because Derek had put his shoulder to the door and had already forced it open.

"Woah it's bigger in here than I thought," he said. "Damn, brighter too."

The harsh light was reflecting from a room painted entirely in white. From the cabinets to the white counter to the white tiles on the floor. Even the furniture—a familiar set of white wooden table and chairs.

"Why would they need an extra kitchen upstairs?" Preston asked, wandering inside.

"Duh, for the servants," Gregory said, moving down the line of cabinets to open and close each one. "Hey there's food in here! Cereal and rice and shit."

Cheerios and Frosted Flakes. I already knew that without looking.

"Servants don't need their own kitchen, idiot," Derek replied. "Rich people with servants don't even go in the kitchen. You're going to suck at being rich as much as you suck at being poor now."

"Damn dude, that cuts deep," Gregory said. "The fridge is working too. And this food looks really fresh."

I reached through the darkness on my right and flipped on the light switch, exactly where I knew it would be. How could I fail to recognize the exact kitchen in the house I grew up in? Everything from the design of the room to the same brand of microwave and same blue curtains with white clouds hanging on the opposite end of the room. The only difference was that the windows were all walled up now. Every detail was the same—family pictures hanging on the wall, fresh tomatoes on the counter from my mother's garden, and yes, as hesitant as I am to say aloud for the pure absurdity it sounds even to me, there was my father sitting at the kitchen table with a closed book in his hands.

My friends all flinched from the light of my flipped switch, their sudden unease apparent.

"How could the food be fresh?" Derek asked quietly. "We've been here for months and it must have been sealed up for longer than that."

"You don't think someone has been living here, do you?" Preston asked, taking a hesitant shuffle back toward the door.

"No way," Derek said. "I don't even know how there's space for a room here. There definitely couldn't be anywhere else for them to hide."

I don't know what bothered me more, that I was seeing my father again for the first time since his death, or that my friends obviously couldn't see what I sensed directly before me. My dad was staring right at me, looking at me the way I remember him in my most nostalgic childhood memories, strong and healthy with straight brown hair without a hint of grey. Keen stern eyes over the rim of his glasses were locked on my own.

"There had to have been someone," Gregory said, agreeing with Preston and backing toward the door. "There's still dishes in the fucking sink, and they aren't even moldy or anything. Let's get out of here."

"Yeah, I bet the landlord lives here. Fuck, I bet he's still been living in the house to keep an eye on us and we hadn't noticed. This place is big enough, and he could have just been using the back door and not leaving his room."

"I knew he seemed suspicious, even after we paid the security deposit," Derek said. "We're probably in his kitchen right now."

By this point all three of them had crowded back out the door. I still hadn't broken eye-contact with my father, who was now smirking softly. I felt helpless to blink, let alone follow my friends.

"Hurry up, man," Gregory called to me. "If he catches us here he's going to be pissed. We can just use Derek's clear tape to put the wallpaper back up and he will never know."

"You should go with them," my father said, his voice as thoughtful and measured as it had always been. "You wouldn't want to be caught somewhere you don't belong."

"I'm going to stay," I said to my friends, my back still to them. "You guys go ahead. I'll catch up."

"Seriously man, the landlord is going to kick us out if he catches us," Derek said. "Please hurry up."

"The second that you've been thinking about your whole life…" my father was saying. He pushed his chair back roughly across the floor and stood to face me.

"Did you hear that?" Preston asked, clearly reacting to the sound of the chair. "He's coming. Screw it, let's leave him. If he gets caught it's his own fault. I'm not going down with him."

"… is almost here," my father finished.

I didn't move. I think I'd forgotten how to. I was in such a state of shock that I didn't know what to do, and all I could think was that if I left now then I was sure I would never see him again. A few frozen seconds passed together in one big clump of time, and before I could react I heard the sound of the door closing behind me. The slam snapped me to my senses enough for me to turn and look at the place my friends had stood a moment before.

I jerked back to face my father once more. He had taken a step closer. A brain makes sense of scaling and distance so naturally that we hardly ever notice the process until it stops working. That's the effect I felt when my father had grown several inches in apparent height from the single forward step he'd taken. The effect was replicated with his second step, which brought him towering over me in a way that I hadn't seen since early childhood memories. And as he moved he seemed to be aging, putting on weight as his skin creased and wrinkled before my eyes, his stature shrinking back toward a more moderate perspective, so much less powerful and sure than he had a moment before.

This process didn't slow as he reached and then passed the age he appeared when I saw him last. Second by excruciating second I watched him growing old as he never did in life. He appeared more wise than ever as the grey blossomed into thick white hair, his eyes sparkling all the more for their piercing insight. All too quickly this too had passed, making way for the shriveling and decrepit decay of old age. He was still moving towards me—only a few paces away—but he trembled every time he lifted his leg to move.

One step away, but he never made it any closer. His tremulous leg collapsed suddenly under his own weight and he pitched toward the floor at my feet. I dove to catch him and together we both tumbled, although I at least managed to cushion his fall. I held him against my chest for several seconds, afraid to pull back and look at his face for fear of what withered shell of a human being which would remain at the very end of these prophetic years.

I felt his fingers clutching feebly against my shirt. Then they stopped. His last breath rattled free, and all the heat fled from his corpse against me. And in that breathless second I think my own heart must have stopped as well, because never in my life have I felt such a profound stillness, broken only by the probing fingers which began to stir once more.

The fingers weren't soft and warm anymore. Rigid and bony, pushing into my chest like I had fallen against sharp rocks. Harder and faster with every moment, pawing at me like an animal desperate to dig into the ground. I tried to wrestle free from the cold form wrapping itself around me. It heaved upward and pushed me into the floor, its rigid legs pinning me painfully while its hands tore into my chest.

I managed to get my arms out from under me and tried to cross them over my body to shield myself. I might as well have been trying to stop a crowbar with my hands. The force of the flashing bone pummeled through my defenses and tore my chest open, but I didn't feel any pain. The skin parted as cleanly as the knife through wallpaper had. The skeletal hand inserted a finger into the crack and slid it down toward my stomach, and my whole torso began to open in the same clean fashion. I couldn't breathe or call for help, and I was helpless but to lie and watch as the skeleton inserted its second hand to widen the cavity in my body. I willed myself to watch and not look away; I couldn't not see the leering skull above me grinning in blasphemy against my father's gentle smirk.

The skeleton kept at its work until it had split me from head to groin, cleanly separating me into two equal halves. I distinctly wondered which half of me was doing the wondering, but that thought quickly gave way to a fixated awareness on the empty darkness which existed in place of blood and bone and internal systems. No—not darkness at all—there was a single light in there too, perhaps a single soul for us both to share, and like a single star in the night sky it was made all the brighter for the vast emptiness around it.

Gently, slowly, with reverence as though stooping at an altar, the skeleton lay down inside of me. It's arms were my arms, its legs were my legs, its skull sliding into the black emptiness of my head to fit snugly into place. Then those arms which were not my arms curved around my body, hugging myself and pulling the two halves together to form a single whole.

I didn't go in that room again after the wallpaper was put back up. That must have been the first night since he died that I didn't miss him anymore. I don't know how long this process took—maybe ten minutes or more—but whenever I remember it, I like to think of it all happening in a single second. After all, if that's all it takes to get from heaven to hell, then why shouldn't someone who is made whole again make it back just as fast?

## Where the Devil Keeps His Pets

The fire at my campsite was burning low when the stranger separated from the shadows to join me. The collar of his long coat was turned up against the chill, and his bony fingers clutched a rough rope leash which extended behind him into the gathering night.

"Howdy camper," I grunted, barely taking my eyes off the comforting flames. There was a row of fires burning all along this side of the hill, a testament to how many people had fled the city this weekend in search of peaceful isolation. My old husky lifted her head to sniff the smoky air in the opposite direction of the man, apparently oblivious to his presence.

"You lost or something?" I assumed he had just stumbled into the wrong campsite and would soon continue to his own plot, but he maintained his rigid posture at the edge of light. I watched his hands tighten as the rope pulled taunt, long fingers remaining clenched as it fell slack again.

"You got a dog too?" I broke the silence again, shifting uncomfortably on my uneven stump. "Don't mind Ambus here, her guard days are over. She's almost blind, and won't hear a thing you say unless it's about food."

Ambus perked up again, leaning into me as I scratched the thinning fur behind her ear. The man in the coat took a step forward and perched upon a rock, about twice the distance from the fire that I was. His face was sour with pursed lips, the dark stubble on his face doing little to fill his sunken features. He gave a sharp tug on the rope, but it went taunt as his animal resisted the effort. I could only distinguish his dog's silhouette in the shadows, but it seemed oddly lumpy and misshapen from here. The man pulled again, viciously this time like the animal was out of control, even though it was just sitting there on the ground. The animal didn't relent however, and the man just shook his head and let the rope fall slack again.

"Ambus used to be like that too, but there isn't much fight left in her now." I chuckled. Ambus was giving into the scratch and had been slowly rolling onto her back to grant me access to her shaggy belly. "We used to hike out here all the time when she was younger. There were less people back then, and she could just run without a leash as far as she wanted in any direction. Sometimes I wouldn't see her for an hour and I'd get so worried, shouting for her until my voice was hoarse. But she always came back, trotting and frolicking, so happy and carefree that I didn't have the heart to stay mad at her."

"Wargol," the man spoke at last, a dark and guttural articulation.

"What's that now?"

"My dog. Wargol. Come, Wargol. The fire won't hurt you." The man pulled again, this time with both hands. A deep reluctant growl answered him, as though bargaining to be repaid for his troubles. The creature finally consented and plodded up to sit beside him. I laughed when the firelight illuminated the animal wearing a puffy green dragon costume, with soft cloth ridges and wings sewn on the back and sides. The black lab had narrow yellow eyes which indicated it knew exactly how ridiculous it looked.

"Well no wonder he's not happy," I said. "I'd be embarrassed to be seen in that getup too."

"So he doesn't scare the children," the man said. He tried to pat the animal, but the dog growled and barred his teeth until the hand was removed.

My husky rolled onto her haunches, crouched and alert. The hair was rising on her back, but I stroked her comfortingly until she settled to the ground.

"Well that's something new for you, isn't it Ambus? Never seen a dragon before. She did catch a rabbit once though. I saw her chasing it, but never thought she'd actually catch it. I think she was surprised too, because the moment she had it in her jaws it kicked her in the chest and she dropped it right away." I laughed and leaned back against my hands to stare up at the stars. "This is probably the last trip out here for us though. I don't think my heart could bear seeing these hills without her at my side."

I tried to laugh again, but the sound came out all wrong.

"I keep Wargol close too," the man said. "He loves me deeply, because he doesn't know any better."

"Yeah?" I didn't know what to say to that. "Dogs sure are great like that."

The man reached for the dog again, and it snapped at him this time. The man didn't flinch so I thought the dog was just playing, but when he pulled his hand away I saw blood flowing freely from a deep gouge in the fleshy base of his thumb. The man stared dispassionately at the red trickle running down his forearm.

"Um, are you okay?" I asked.

The man smiled, and the firelight glistened off long sharp canine teeth filling his mouth. A low growl began rising in his throat. The dog in the dragon costume pulled sharply back on the leash though, just as the man had done to the dog. The jolt was enough to silence the growl from the man, who now stared sullenly at me.

Ambus began to howl. She was always a quiet dog, and it had been so long since I heard her make a sound like that I thought I'd heard a wolf. She looked like she was getting ready to lunge again, but I grabbed her by the collar and snapped her leash back on. The old dog sprang anyway, launching herself a few feet before the leash snapped her back to the ground.

"Ambus, no! Leave it!"

The man began to growl again in response, but the black lab gave another sharp tug on the leash to calm the man. Ambus dropped to my feet and whined, looking at my helpless confusion for guidance.

"I do so love having an animal companion. Wargol and I, we are going to be together forever."

It was the black lab speaking now though, while the man continued to growl. I even caught a glimpse of evenly spaced, human teeth in the dog's mouth.

"Together forever. Would you like that? For her to be like Wargol?" the black lab inquired innocently. The voice matched the man perfectly, and my eyes kept flashing between the two to catch how the ventriloquism act was performed. The man's lips were tightly pursed again though, the subliminal growl never quite vanishing…

"I don't want forever." The words caught in my throat.

"Then you don't love Ambrus like I love Wargol," the black lab said. It twisted and pulled, and suddenly the rope slipped free from around its neck. It was advancing, but Ambus was ready.

I wasn't expecting how powerfully my old dog launched herself. The leash tore free from my numb fingers. I flailed after it—too slow.

The two dogs collided beside the fire. Interlocking jaws, a howl from Ambus, a human scream from the black lab. They were rolling on the ground now, through the burning embers, two writhing bodies intermingled in their violent dance.

I tried to intervene and pull them apart, but the man was barking and snarling at me now. I could hear Ambus yelp in pain though, prompting me to charge straight at the man blocking my path. He seemed unsteady on his two feet and collapsed readily, allowing me to leap onto the black lab.

I gripped its dragon costume and wrenched it back, but the creature wriggled free at once and leapt on Ambus once more. The green cloth removed, the scattered embers revealed red and black interlocking scales like those of a serpent running down the creatures hide. The animal's human teeth made it a poor match for my husky though, and the two of us were soon able to overpower the creature.

The man had already fled yelping into the darkness by the time I got the two dogs apart.

"Traitor!" the scaled beast howled after its human. "Don't you dare run from me, Wargol!"

With that, the monster sprinted into the night, chasing its human counterpart. I clutched Ambus to me, too afraid to check for her injuries, just holding her and gasping for breath while I listened to the shouting slowly disappear.

"I won't let you go! I need you! Please, I don't want to be alone! Please Wargol, please come back."

Begging, and then screaming, and now softly in the quiet night, I hear the animal crying as a human might, frightened and alone. Or perhaps they have reunited, and it really is the human weeping over how close he came to losing his only companion.

Ambus wasn't seriously injured from the fight, and the dog's human teeth only managed to take a small piece out of one of her ears. She's sleeping at my side as I write this, whimpering slightly in her sleep. I stroked her to comfort her for a long time, but I've stopped since her patchy hair kept coming out in my hand. Since I felt the scales hardening along her skin, and hear whispered words smuggled in amongst her quiet whimpering. I won't leave her here, but she might have to wear the dragon costume herself so she doesn't scare the children.

I don't want forever, but I'm sure as hell not ready to let go yet.

## The Only Time My Father Cried

Other children lived in real houses, with their own bed or even a room with a door on it. There were five of us crowded into the corner of the room, not including my mother and father who slept on mats in the kitchen. But I never once thought other children were better off and I was worse, because I lived where I was loved, and that was all I ever needed.

My father never admitted that we couldn't afford to eat in restaurants. He'd say he tried them before, but none of them knew how to cook properly or had the secret spices like mother had. Father used to laugh at other families who went on trips together, and said we were lucky that we weren't so miserable at home that we had to get away. And when the car broke down and he started getting up early to walk to work with his thermos and lunchpail, the only words I ever heard him say on the matter was how thankful he was we lived somewhere where it didn't rain very often.

Everything always worked out for the best, that's what my father said. We would always have what we needed, and if we didn't have it, then that showed how fortunate we were for needing so little.

I told this to one of my neighbors Mr. Clemens once when I was twelve, and he laughed at me and called my father a liar. Mr. Clemens was a snotty fat old man like bourgeois walrus, and he said my father just told us things to cover up how much of a failure his concession business was. He said my father lied about all kinds of things, and that I didn't know it because I was only twelve. I was furious with him at the time, but I found out my father really was a liar when I got sick.

I knew it must have been bad, because father usually says chicken soup will cure anything, but that it wouldn't be good enough this time. We got a neighbor to drive us across town to a hospital instead, where a doctor poked and prodded at me for a for awhile before going into the other room to talk to my father. I don't remember what any of the medical names were, the only thing that stood out to me was the huge price the doctor said it would all cost: more than he paid for his car. A few minutes later, my father came back in, looking pale and clammy like he was the one who was sick.

"Good news, the hospital worked," father told me, hurrying me out the door. There was a nurse who tried to stop us, but he just gripped my arm tighter and picked up the pace. "You're all better now, and there's nothing more to worry about."

I didn't feel better though. My stomach kept clenching like it was tying itself into a pretzel, and I couldn't sleep at all that night. My parents must have thought I was asleep though, because I heard them frantically whispering behind the kitchen counter. I snuck over to listen, but I was having trouble moving and they weren't talking anymore by the time I got close. Instead I heard soft, muffled crying. I thought one of my brothers or sisters must have gotten sick too, but when I peaked around the counter it was father with tears running down his face. He didn't see me because his back was to the counter, head in his hands, hair gripped in his fists like he wanted to rip it out.

Mom had an arm around his shoulders and was trying to comfort him like she usually did with us. She started saying things like how she could quit her job to stay home with me, or that we could all move in with her parents and live in their yard. And we wouldn't need Christmas presents, or new clothes, and we could get the cheaper canned food, one thing after another, my mother prattling away without my father really hearing any of it. He just kept muttering that everything was going to be fine, but twelve was old enough to know he lied to me in the hospital, and that he was lying again now.

I didn't know what was wrong with me, but I knew I wasn't alright, and that there wasn't anything he could do about it. I didn't blame him for that though. I blamed myself for being such a burden, and I knew it was my responsibility to make things right.

I waited until they fell asleep before collecting my favorite clothes into my school backpack and sneaking out the door. I was going to run away, and I wasn't going to be their problem anymore. I didn't know where to go, so I knocked on Mr. Clemens' door to tell him he was right about my father lying.

Bleary and grumbling in his fuzzy blue bathrobe, Mr. Clemens opened the door and stared at me in confusion. I had a whole speech planned out about how my father tried his best and that it didn't matter if he was a liar, but I was feeling so sick and exhausted from walking over here that I just collapsed and started crying on his doorstep.

## Sleepless Nights

To his credit, Mr. Clemens took me in right away and laid me on a big soft bed. He never once said he told me so, even after I explained everything to him. He just listened very gravely, waggling his mustache as he chewed on his bottom lip.

"You can sleep easy now," Mr. Clemens told me when I finished. "I want you to know I'm not like your father, and when I say I'm going to take care of you and make you better, I really mean it."

I started to automatically defend my father again, but Mr. Clemens cut me off. "It isn't just about you being sick. That man isn't even your real father—everything he's ever told you is a lie. And just you watch, I'm going to prove it."

Mr. Clemens called the hospital and got me the medicine I needed, and I was too afraid to ask many questions. He gave me a place of my own to sleep, and fed me well, and let me use his computer and play games that I never imagined existing before I came here. The only thing he wouldn't let me do was go outside or visit my family, even though I said that I missed them.

"You want to know how much they really care about you?" Mr. Clemens asked. "You were right to think you were only a burden to them. Here, let me show you."

Everyday when he came home from work, Mr. Clemens would show me a video of my family he took from his phone. Sometimes it would be shot through their window, but mostly he captured shots of them spending time in the apartment courtyard where my parents would eat dinner and watch my brothers and sisters playing.

If they really were upset about having me gone, they didn't show any sign. My father especially—the man I thought was moved to tears about my sickness—was always laughing and carrying on like I'd never seen him before.

"Can't you see how relieved he is to be rid of you?" Mr. Clemens made dozens of little remarks like that. "It's because he knows that he was never your real father. A woman as beautiful as your mother, how could she ever love a penniless nobody like him?"

I didn't want to watch the videos and never asked him to elaborate what he meant. I think Mr. Clemens was in love with my mother, but would never say so to me. Instead it was always little negative jabs at my father, at how cruel he was for forgetting me, or how lazy he was for not providing better for us. I'd just let Mr. Clemens talk and say nothing. I didn't feel it was my place to argue or defend my father anymore after what Mr. Clemens had done for me, and truth be told the sight of my father being happy to have me gone crushed my soul a little more everyday.

"It's only a pity your brothers and sisters aren't being so well cared for," Mr. Clemens mused one day after showing me the latest video. "Can you imagine how happy they would be living here instead? Although even this place isn't big enough—if I was the one taking care of them, I'd buy a bigger house and give each of them their own room. And your mother wouldn't have to work anymore—she'd be happy too, don't you think? Oh but it can never happen, not as long as that man who pretended to be your father is holding onto them like that."

It had been a little more than week when Mr. Clemens sat me down at his dining room table and slid a blue vial across to me. There wasn't any prescription label like the medicine he usually got for me, and when I reached for it he put his hand over mine and stopped me.

"This isn't medicine for you. It's medicine for your father."

"My father isn't sick," I replied, not understanding.

"Don't be stupid, boy. Your family is sick, and this is the cure. You remember where he hides the extra key, don't you?"

I nodded, terrified and confused. The big man grinned, releasing my hand to let me hold the blue vial. Even with it closed I could smell a sickly sweet odor seeping out.

"You can put this in his thermos without waking him, can't you? And then come straight back here, never breathing a word about what you've done."

"Why would I do that?" I asked, mesmerized by the strange blue liquid.

As if in reply, I heard my father's laughter playing from the phone in Mr. Clemens pocket.

"So I can save them like I saved you," Mr. Clemens gloated. "Do it tonight. Don't think. Don't ask questions."

I found the key hidden beneath the flowerpot in front of the door. I didn't ask questions that I didn't want to know the answer to. I didn't know what would happen to my father after he drank the blue liquid, but I was angry and didn't care no matter how sick he got. I had to keep telling myself how angry I was as I crept into the room, because otherwise I knew I'd never have the strength to do what I came for.

I had to keep hearing that laughter in my head, and know how happy he was to have me gone. When I unscrewed his metal thermos, packed and ready for an early morning by the door, I had to keep telling myself how happy I'd be when he was gone too, when I got to be with my family again.

I kept repeating those things in my head like a mantra, but it wasn't enough to keep my hands from shaking as I opened the blue vial.

Mr. Clemens would be good to us.

Mr. Clemens would take care of us.

Mr. Clemens would love my mother, and maybe one day she'd learn to love him back, and hold him and comfort him the way she held my father when he cried.

But for all my effort, I couldn't lie to myself enough to stop the shaking. I dropped the metal thermos as I was trying to put the vial in, and it banged and rattled on the ground. I froze in terror, unsure of whether to run or try again, terrified to see my family and wanting more than anything for them to catch me so I could just go home again.

I stayed frozen as the lights came on, and the next thing I knew my father was standing over me, glaring down at the spilled thermos on the ground. And then he was hugging me tightly to him, and so was my mother, and all my brothers and sisters jumping out of their mats in the corner to welcome me home as well.

It turned out that Mr. Clemens had told my father that he was paying to have me treated. My father hadn't been so happy this last week because he thought I ran away—he'd been happy because he thought I was getting better again. And all that stuff about him not being my real father, or him being lazy or a liar—that was just Mr. Clemens jealousy talking.

My father never lied to me when he said everything always worked out for the best, and as long as we had each other, that would always be the only thing we'd need.

## Whispers From My Music Box: Part 1

Mr. Wayland doesn't smile. Instead he presses his mouth into a hard line when something pleases him, which isn't very often. He doesn't care whether or not I call him father, as long as I'm polite. I appreciate how honestly he doesn't love me, and I'd like to think he appreciates me too for not asking it from him. He has a little money set aside from when my parents died, and I can always tell whether or not it's safe to speak to him by calculating whether I'm within my monthly budget.

Mrs. Wayland is more difficult because she pretends. She always says how she and my mother were the best of friends, although I never remember seeing her until the day she took me in. I asked her why she didn't seem sad about losing my mother if they were so close, but she switched gears and decided she was my mother now, which meant there was no reason to be sad. She smiles enough for Mr. Wayland too, but the way her smile trembles if she holds it too long makes it harder to trust.

I remember the first thing I asked on the night they collected me was about my sister.

"If you want to be my mother now, then aren't you Jackie's mother too? Why isn't she coming with us?"

"One is plenty, dear. Your father only had one son, and his father before him, and I think it's a fine tradition to carry on."

"But I had lot's of uncles—"

"I'm talking about your *new father*. My husband," Mrs Wayland replied. I remember her peering at all the pictures we had hanging in our house and never quite facing me directly as we spoke.

"Where is Jackie going to go?"

"Your sister is almost a woman. She can go wherever she likes." Then, as an afterthought—"Staying with friends of hers, I think. You've been the one living with her though, I don't know why you'd expect me to know if you don't."

But Jackie hadn't told me. In fact she hadn't even spoken a word to me since our parents death. I knew my older sister was upstairs in her room even now while Mr. and Mrs. Wayland were ransacking the house, and it made me angry that I had to go talk to them alone. Jackie should have been interviewing them to make sure they were going to be good to me.

I followed Mrs. Wayland from room to room as she inspected the contents. Her expression grew more sour as we went, as though she was expecting to find something that wasn't there. Then Mr. Wayland came down the stairs, shaking his head.

"It's not upstairs either," Mr. Wayland said. Then to me: "Boxes. Small, wooden, nicely polished. Two of them. Any idea?"

"Umm…"

"Jackie doesn't know either," Mr. Wayland sighed. "Never mind, we can always come back and look later. Let's get this one home and let him get some rest, it must have been a long day for him."

"I want to say goodbye to my sister," I insisted, trying to squeeze around Mr. Wayland on the stairs.

"Whatever for?" Mrs. Wayland asked.

"We'll be in the car," Mr. Wayland said. "Fifteen minutes with your things. No more than a suitcase full, and nothing that will make a mess."

I knocked on Jackie's door and waited, afraid that she wouldn't open it at all. The silence on the other side of the door was heavy until small, tinny music notes began to trickle through. I knocked again, then finding it unlocked, pushed through to stare at the rustling curtains and the open window. Jackie was already gone.

"Wherever she wants," I mumbled, distracted by the tinkling music. A smooth polished music box, carved with roses with a small golden key, left conspicuously on her perfectly made bed. I lifted it, realizing there were two identical indentations in the fabric where Jackie must have taken the second box with her.

It then dawned on me that I was leaving my home for good. I had moved before and wasn't overly attached to these peeling white walls or uneven floorboards. But as long as I was here, it still felt like there was a chance that any moment my father would walk through the door, or my mother would call me down to dinner. It was a comfort even knowing Jackie was there, sullen and silent in her room. It wasn't this place I would miss. It was the memories of the people in this place, bound forever to these rooms that I wouldn't see again. Part of me

## Sleepless Nights

was glad Jackie was already gone though, because I would have hated for her to see me cry like that.

"Shhh…"

I caught my breath, thinking that Jackie was still hiding somewhere and must have heard me.

"Still here…" the whispered words slipping from the box between the music notes. They still contained a tinny, ringing texture, but it sounded so much like my sister that I didn't doubt it for a second.

"Still with you…"

The box continued whispering, but now the sound was overwhelmed by the honking outside. I turned off the music, listening again for the whispering, but only hearing the blaring of the horn outside. I hid the music box safely amidst my other possessions and hurried down the stairs to where the Waylands were waiting in their car. I let them drive me away, not caring where as long as I knew I wouldn't be alone.

I knew the Waylands were looking for the boxes, so I didn't dare mention them again. They made several more trips to my old house, but they said I couldn't come because it was going to be sold and I would only get in the way. That was fine with me though, because I had the only treasure worth saving, and I needed the secrecy of solitude to open the music box and be comforted by the whispered words.

"Jackie?" I asked, once I was sure the Waylands were gone.

"I can hear… you too…" the music box replied. There was a lyrical quality to the words, which matched the tempo and the gentle rise and fall of the melody. It was a sad song, one of regret and longing for something so far away that it might not be real at all.

"Did you find a new home?"

"I'm home… how is… the brother?" flowed the music without missing a beat.

I became suddenly curious to open the box and try to see whether the music tape rearranged itself to form her reply in front of my eyes. Too risky for something so precious, I decided. I told Jackie that I had a room to myself and the Waylands were good to me.

"That's because… still looking… the boxes…" The melody was changing subtly, the occasional stuttered note branching off to form rapid anxious patterns before returning to the underlying calm.

"Don't worry, I'm being careful," I said. "I'll keep the box hidden whenever they're around."

The pace of the music kept increasing. Dark chords loomed in the periphery, like heavy clouds before the storm.

"They won't… stop looking…" the music warned. "They'll get… so angry. The pain… the pain…"

"Don't worry about me, I'm safer than you are," I shot back. "Where did you go? When will I see you again?"

The music box clicked loudly as the gears snapped shut. I hurriedly picked up the golden key and wound it back up, but the music which played was the same gentle, sad melody which first graced the instrument.

"Jackie?" I asked swiftly. "The Waylands are good people. Help me find you, Jackie. There's enough space for us to be a family again. I'll just need to pick up a few dollars somewhere, and I'm positive I can convince them to invite you."

But the music only played, the echo of a world that used to be.

## Whispers From My Music Box: Part 2

"Absolutely not."

Mr. Wayland's hand was shaking as it gripped the metal fork. We sat across from each other at the long wooden table, waiting for Mrs. Wayland in the kitchen.

"Why not? Jackie just stays in her room anyway, she won't bother anyone. And she can help Mrs. Wayland with the chores."

"My name is Mother," Mrs. Wayland glided into the room with a broad dish of wilted green Brussel sprouts. "I don't want a child making a mess of my kitchen."

"Jackie isn't a child, you said she was a young woman yourself," I interjected. "But I think she's in trouble and needs our help. I'll buy all her food, and—"

"Why do you think she's in trouble?" Mr. Wayland interrupted.

"She just sounded—"

I was hot and angry and didn't catch my mistake until too late. I choked on the words, then took a long drink of water, my eyes on my plate.

"When did you speak to her?" Mrs. Wayland asked pleasantly.

"Not since you picked me up," I lied hastily, their eyes a mountainous weight upon my shoulders. They seemed to relish my shame as a shark breathing in blood.

"The box." Mr. Wayland said unflinchingly. "Where is it?" The fork in his hand wasn't trembling anymore. It was halfway toward the plate of Brussel sprouts, frozen in the air, his muscles locked in terrifying stillness.

"I don't know!" I heaped the vegetables onto my plate and bore down at them intently. Then when I could no longer bear the quiet, "I miss them, that's all."

"Of course you do, dear," Mrs. Wayland said. "And honestly I wish that your sister was the type of person we could accept in this house. The cold hard truth is that she's a wicked woman who does deplorable things with deplorable people, and I won't have another vulgar word spoken on the topic at this dinner table."

I was completely shocked, without any idea what they were talking about.

"That's not true. Jackie never hurt anyone!"

"God would disagree, but I'm not here to judge," Mrs. Wayland said daintily.

"But why are you lying?"

If my eyes hadn't been glued to my plate, I would have seen the blow before it struck me. I tumbled to the ground, my temple an explosion of pain. Next I knew Mr. Wayland was standing over me, his hand balling up my shirt as he dragged me up toward his face.

"The box. Where's the box, boy?" he asked with single-minded grit.

"That's enough playing around, eat your vegetables," Mrs. Wayland said in a far off misty voice.

"I don't know about any box," I promised.

"I know it will take time to adjust to the civilized type of lifestyle we maintain here, but I would like to think he knows better than to lie or steal from his mother and father," Mrs. Wayland said, distinctly ignoring the way her husband's threatening posture. It was a clear signal that he could do whatever he liked to me without worrying about her interference.

Mr. Wayland hoisted me from the floor and propped me up in my chair. I didn't have much of an appetite after that, but that must not have bothered them as neither of them addressed me for the remainder of the meal.

I waited until after 2 in the morning before taking out the box again. I didn't dare open it inside, so I slipped downstairs and out the back door, kneeling amidst the thorny bushes which sprouted in the snowy yard. Once I was far enough away I turned the golden key and listened for the haunting melody.

The gentle rhythm never came though, and a flurry of loud and frantic notes made me snap the music box shut again. Terrified of being heard, I scrambled over the icy ground, through the thorns and the darkness before I dared open the box again.

"Run… run… run…" Jackie repeated with the swelling music.

So I did. Feeling my way along the wooden fence to the little gate in the back. Then around the house and into the freezing street, not knowing where I was going except to find my sister. I didn't stop when lights turned on behind me. I just ran as fast and as hard as I could, my heart racing in beat with the frenzied notes.

"Run… run… run…"

"Where?" I shouted in exasperation, taking a dark street at random to make myself harder to be found.

"Hide… hide…" There wasn't a moment's hesitation where I distinguished the words from the music box with my own thoughts. I dove between bags of leaves beside the road, piling them up around me to conceal me from the street. The music clicked to a stop just as the glare of headlights glowed malevolently through the cracks in my hiding place. I didn't wind the box again until the lights had passed, pleased to hear a more subdued tone return.

"Run… run…" whispered words, so gentle yet so fearful. I threw the bags of leaves aside and stood to run, slipping on the frosty ground as sudden headlights engulfed me. The Waylands—both in bathrobes—had turned off their headlights and turned the car around after passing me by. I was running again, incredulous shock and disbelief as the car began accelerating toward me.

"Leave me behind." Were the last words I heard from the box.

My body obeyed, flinging the box to the ground as I continued to run. High brick walls along the side of the street made it impossible to get off the road, and there was nothing I could do but run blindly and hope another car would intervene. But instead a screeching sound, and an explosive crash which shook me to my bone. The car had skidded off the road and into a light pole at such a pace as to fold the car around it.

The music box lay smashed on the ground behind me. It occurred to me later that Mr. Wayland might have seen it falling and slammed on the breaks, prompting the car to skid across the icy ground and lose control. I remember a policeman asking me about their deaths, and something at a hospital, but nothing after that was clear. When I think back about that time, all I can remember is the music, how it was being written in real time as a mirror upon my soul, and how it felt listening to something so real that I heard it from the inside-out.

I'm still living in the Waylands house, and it was another month before I saw Jackie again. She'd been living at her girlfriend's house, but moved in with me after she found out what had happened. The most curious thing in talking to her about the situation though was that she didn't believe a word I said about the music boxes.

She had never once spoken into her music box, and she'd never once heard me whisper back in return. I never did learn the truth about the boxes, or what the Waylands wanted them for, but it seemed to me that it must have been my mother inside the box all along. My sister kept the remaining box though, where I hope my father is still watching and keeping her safe through whatever trials she has yet to come.

## Trading My Child

It's not my child just because it grew inside me. Maybe all the shared joys and despairs of motherhood could have taught me to love it with time, but nature made it clear the effort would be wasted. I knew even before it was born that the boy wouldn't be normal.

His nervous system wouldn't develop right, and he was likely to suffer from seizures the moment he was born. His heart would be feeble, his brain wouldn't get enough oxygen, and it would be a miracle if he lived to see his first birthday.

My friend Wallace and his wife were pregnant at the exact same time as me.

## Sleepless Nights

Before I got the diagnosis, I'd spend days with Wallace drafting plans for our children's futures. We'd been friends since elementary school, and it was so much fun to relive our childhood memories while we dreamed about the perfect lives for our children. They were going to be best friends with play dates, sleepovers, and matching outfits that would make everyone think they were twins. We even had schools picked out for them all the way through high school so they'd never have to be apart.

It wasn't fair that Wallace's boy would get to live the life we planned while my boy withered and rotted before my eyes. Not to mention that he married rich, and he could spend all his time with his little boy while I was slowly submerged with medical bills I still didn't know how I'd pay. It took almost a week before I could even bring myself to tell Wallace the news. All that time I'd kept smiling and making plans, lying to him and myself that everything was going to be okay.

Then comes the night when Wallace brought over this book full of ideas to decorate their rooms, and all I could think about was how empty and evil that place would become to me. I started crying right there on her sofa, unable to stop the cold truth from pouring out of my mouth. Wallace cried with me, and we were hugging and holding each other when he whispered in my ear, "Would you prefer to have a different, healthy baby instead?"

"I'd settle for a healthy dog at this point," I said, trying to laugh my way through the tears. It was no use, but neither was feeling sorry for myself.

"I'm talking about Lucas," Wallace said. I knew he was serious then because he pushed me back to arms length to look me in the eye. "Although if you're the one raising him, I don't suppose there's anything wrong with you choosing a different name."

That's when Wallace shared the secret he'd been holding too. His wife had been cheating on him, and he was leaving as soon as he got his financials in order. I tried to hug and console him the way he did with me, but he pushed me back again to speak calmly and clearly.

"No don't, it's okay. Don't you see how this is a blessing in disguise? I don't want to raise a child in a broken marriage, and you don't want to raise one you'll lose so soon. But if we were to trade…"

It didn't take much to convince me. The burden of my boy's illness had been grinding me down to nothing, and I was so relieved that I didn't allow myself to question the decision. I had one more chance to change my mind before the children were born though, when Wallace confided why he wanted my sick boy in the first place.

"It will be our secret, right?" he asked. It was strange watching him pacing nervously, checking and re-checking the windows to make sure we wouldn't be interrupted.

"Always," I promised, not mentioning my own shame at the covert deed.

"Not a word, not to anyone," Wallace insisted. "Especially not my wife. After we've made the switch, then I'll confront her about the cheating."

"You still haven't told her that you know?"

"She'll only deny it, but it won't matter when we have your child. I'll take a DNA test that shows I'm not related to your boy, and she'll know she's been caught without any reason to test her own DNA. Then I'll have cold, hard evidence, and I'll take her for every penny I can get. You have no idea how much easier this is going to make the divorce."

"What about my boy?" I asked, incredulous.

But Wallace only shrugged. "It won't be your boy anymore. Why do you care?" Then he turned to see the expression on my face, and his stance softened. "He's going to get the best treatment money can buy, and his short life will be comfortable and happy. You're going to have a happy life with a healthy boy, and my wife… well, everyone is going to get what they deserve. You're not having second thoughts, are you?"

"No. Only first thoughts that never quite go away."

Wallace moved closer to me, close enough to smell the sticky sweetness of his sweat, and whispered, "But we'll both know you'll be raising my child. And who knows, if your husband isn't providing the kind of life you deserve, I'll always be there to help raise my boy. Maybe we could even…"

I felt the child inside me squirm, and I recoiled from Wallace. "If you still want a child, then you shouldn't trade yours away. My husband and I won't need any help, thank you anyway."

"I'm sorry, I didn't mean to suggest…" Wallace kept trying to get closer to me as he spoke, but I quickly intervened.

"I just need time," I told him. "I don't want to see you until the children are born, do you understand? It would only make your wife suspicious."

Wallace let me go without resisting, and I was fool enough to really believe things were going to work out from there. Our two boys were born only two days apart. It was almost a week before Wallace and I could meet in secret. I could barely force myself to look at my boy the whole time, because I was so afraid that I really would start to love him and couldn't go through with it. But what was a week of agony weighed against a full and happy life ahead?

I waited in the empty parking lot as Wallace's Lexus slid into the space next to me. I gently swayed the precious bundle in my arms while he got out of the car empty handed. I thrust my boy into his arms without a word, and he stowed the child safely in a car seat in the back.

"You're sure your wife won't notice?"

"She's on vacation in Miami." Wallace laughed as he circled the car to retrieve the other boy from the back. "The cross-nurse actually taking care of him might notice, but she'll be paid more not to. Speaking of, you know you only have to ask if you need some money for our child—"

"Angelo is not our child," I insisted sternly.

Wallace pulled a quick, tight smile which vanished immediately upon handing the healthy boy to me.

"Right you are, not a word. Your boy is Angelo, and my boy is Lucas, and that's the way it's always been," Wallace said.

"No, you don't understand." I snatched the boy from him to cradle him protectively against my chest. "Angelo is my child. My real child."

"It's not lying if you believe it." Wallace winked as I climbed into my car. "When will I see you again…?"

But he really didn't understand, because the funny thing was that in that moment I really did believe Angelo was my real child. Wallace was the only person in the world who made that a lie real, and I realized I could never look at him again without digging up something in my mind I wanted to stay buried forever. I didn't say another word to him, and just got in the car and drove away, never intending to acknowledge his existence again.

I lied to myself so ferociously that I completely forgot any of these events occurred at all. The effect was so pronounced that the next time I saw Wallace two years later, I didn't even recognize the man until he startled me with his embrace.

"Thought you got rid of me for good, didn't you?" he whispered in my ear.

"Where is my son?" I asked, for the first time referring to my sick child that I'd completely forgotten bringing into this world.

"Lingering." The word was hard and disappointed. "We worked it out though, you know. My wife and I, we're still together. It's amazing how a shared burden like that can pull people together."

"I'm so happy for you," I said, although I felt nothing. I just wanted him to leave so I could go back lying to myself. I caught Wallace staring at Angelo through the car window, and I hurried to retrieve him to take him inside my house.

"Lucas isn't dying," Wallace said accusingly. "You said he was going to die. That's like breaking the deal."

This was not a conversation I wanted, or was even capable of having. "I don't know what you're talking about," I replied stiffly. My shaking fingers fumbled with Angelo's carseat in my haste. Then a rough hand on my shoulder, yanking me away from the open car door.

"Let me look at my healthy boy," Wallace begged.

I shoved him right back, but not before his hand lashed out at the child. Angelo began to scream, and I snatched him from the car and rushed for my front door.

"We want to trade back!" he shouted after me. "We'll say you took him from us!"

I slowed to a stop, my key in the lock. Unable to turn and reveal the truth

I've buried so long. Angelo was still wailing, and that's when I noticed the small clump of his hair that Wallace had ripped out.

"The DNA test will match my wife and I, not you," Wallace gloated. "You can have your boy back if you want. What's left of him anyway. We just want our boy."

"Your boy is waiting for you at your home," I said through gritted teeth.

"Then find us another two year old, my wife won't know the difference. You've got one week before we call the police."

Angelo is my son, and I'm not giving him up for the world.

But if I could do bury something like that for years without remembering, then maybe there's space for a few more bodies to protect my boy.

## The Smell of Death

It began with a tickling in the back of my nose. A cold coming on, or an allergy, some springtime pollen which would dissipate as the summer progressed. If it stayed as it was, a gentle but persistent nuisance, then I think I would have gotten used to it and not have even noticed before long.

Day by day the pressure of the incessant tickle increased. The air in my apartment took on a greasy quality, an irritation that never quite went away. It was getting warmer though, and I didn't mind keeping the windows open all the time. I bought one of those lemon-scented air fresheners that automatically releases throughout the day and put it beside my bed. The next week I bought two more, for my living room and kitchen, but the malodorous intrusion would always find a way through anyway.

Rotten eggs, burning sulfur, noxious and nauseating. My nose and eyes were softly burning all the time, and it made working from home an absolute nightmare. There was no real escape though, because the smell had so throughly permeated my small place that it began to linger on me wherever I went. I started taking two showers a day, practically bathing in cologne every time I went out.

My building manager told me that sometimes rats will crawl into the air ducts and get caught and die in there. Sometimes there's no way to get at them though, and you just have to wait for them to rot and fade away. I kept calling him to remind him to send someone to look into it, but he was evasive and kept insisting he would have smelled it too if it was as bad as I say. Like fermented fish in a gasoline soup, I told him, and getting worse all the time. I threatened to end my lease early if he didn't get it fixed, and then he started accusing me of making it up just to get out of paying rent.

I was so angry when I got off the phone. I immediately started calling my neighbors in the surrounding apartments. The manager might be able to ignore me, but he couldn't ignore all of us if we complained together. I was shocked when one person after the next told me they didn't smell it though. I gradually realized the smell must really be confined to my room, which seemed like remarkably lousy luck.

I searched the place from top to bottom, opening every cupboard, shining a light into the AC vents, moving the furniture around to look beneath, but never found a single clue. I must have been breathing heavier from the exertion and frustration, because the scent was becoming suffocating. It was like my face was buried in a dead animal, with blood and decaying matter dribbling into my mouth and down my throat with every inhalation.

That's when I began to think my manager might have been right, and that it was all in my head after all. Desperate and exhausted, I decided to go to the doctor to get my nose checked. I could tell by the way the receptionist drew away from me that the cologne wasn't enough to cover the lingering smell. I spent a long time in the little waiting room, and when the doctor opened the door he immediately slammed it shut again, coughing and wheezing in the hallway. That gave me a certain satisfaction as I realized I wasn't just hallucinating the whole thing.

The satisfaction vanished when the doctor returned wearing a face mask. He asked me to remove my shirt, his eyes narrowed as he critically inspected my clean and healthy body.

"I'm glad there's nothing wrong with my nose at least," I said, half-jokingly.

"Your nose is fine. I'm more worried about your eyes," he told me, very seriously.

I started to tell him my eyes were fine, but caught my breath at the sharp sting of him picking at my stomach with a gloved hand. I watched in disgust as a flap of my skin easily peeled away, crumbling into dust like a decaying log.

"The brain can sometimes suppress knowledge that is too traumatic to deal with, but I've never heard of the visual system doing the same. How long did you say your skin has been rotting off?"

Somehow I hadn't noticed except from the smell, although no sooner had he said the words that I noticed how my gray and sagging skin came sloughing off at the slightest touch.

## Forced Equality

My brother isn't better than me. I need you to understand this before you judge what happened to him. He isn't better at school, even though my parents act like he's smarter just for being a few years ahead. And he didn't get a girlfriend first either, because no one believes the stuff he pretended he did with his mystery girl. He isn't even better at basketball. He's just tall, which is basically cheating as far as I'm concerned. But none of that would bother me if it wasn't for his snotty attitude.

This all started at one of our high school games. The score was close, and my brother was selfish enough to suggest everyone pass every ball to him. Didn't matter if he was being blocked, didn't matter if I was open, just trust him because he was on a "lucky streak". I told him it was a stupid idea. It was the beginning of the season and the game basically didn't matter, but my team only cared about winning so they agreed. It pissed me off so much that winning didn't even feel good, because I knew I could have made the same shots if my team gave me the same chance. Then everyone would have been cheering for me instead.

I told my girlfriend Ava about it, and she completely agreed with me. Then she told me about this Equality Club that she was getting into. Missing the first few meetups didn't matter either, because it's the only school club that didn't rank people or exclude them for any reason. Ava went on and on about how hard it was for weirdos and disabled kids to feel accepted and valued. I guess I made a big deal about how the whole society should work that way. I just wanted Ava to know I was a good person, or whatever. Shut up, you've probably done it too. I wasn't that clear with what goes on in the club, but when she invited me I didn't see how I could back out.

The lights were all out in the club room, and the blinds were drawn. I couldn't see much more than silhouettes, but I guess that wasn't good enough because someone handed me a blindfold before they let me in. I heard Ava's voice across the room and felt my way across, bumping into an empty desk every other step along the way.

"It's because one of the members is blind," Ava explained. "We give everyone the opportunity to walk in her shoes to help us understand how hard that would be."

"This is cool. It feels like being in a fort at school."

"It is not cool! Imagine trying to cross the street. You'd never drive. Ever. And say goodbye to ever moving away from your parents or any hope at a normal—oops, I mean like an abled person life. There's no such thing as normal, and we don't use violent words like that which make everyone outside of one narrow definition feel excluded. You know, you take for granted how privileged you really are."

"You're right, you're right, it would suck being blind. I'm really going to appreciate seeing stuff from now on, I swear. Like you, for instance."

It was damn dark, but I'm pretty sure that was the right thing to say.

"We've got all kind of club activities too. A lot of team building stuff, and games, and races, and charity and community work."

She was leading me by the hand now, and that fact was more important than wherever she was taking me. I think she was peeking underneath her blindfold, but I couldn't really point that out if I was supposed to be blind.

"How do you do races where everybody wins?" I asked.

"Duh, there's still a winner. We just make everything equal first. Like if somebody is really fast, we make them spin a few circles and get dizzy first to make it fair. It actually makes it a lot more competitive, and that makes it closer and move fun. Tonight we're going to be splitting up into groups and collecting donations around the neighborhood. Don't worry, you'll get to take the blindfold off first."

It was a fun group of people, and I felt good about myself for raising money to rebuild burned homes. I was nervous when it was my turn to knock on a door, but everyone was clustered around to support me and the old prune who greeted me was bubbling with generosity. Those houses were on the rare side though. Most people wouldn't answer at all, or would try to get rid of us as soon as they could. We'd even catch some peeking out their window and scowling at us without ever opening the door. If they seemed really mean we'd laugh and sing at them to prove they couldn't ruin our good time.

Then we hit a long stretch where every single person seemed angry to see us. These people with their perfect houses and their safe families were the ones acting like victims. Seeing them angry made me even madder, because seriously how dare someone get mad at people working for charity? Yet here they were, stomping and cussing as if the great injustice of the world was forcing them off their couch for a minute to deal with us.

"They only do it because they feel guilty," Ava told me in her lofty and knowing way. "Deep down they're ashamed of themselves for not being willing to help, and so they lash out at us to deflect."

"I don't get what his deal was. He could have just said 'no thanks.' It's not like he didn't have a choice."

"Well he made the wrong choice!" Ava declared bitterly. "And why is it fair that they get to choose, anyway? Did the people who lost their homes get to choose where the fire went?"

Ava really snapped at the next one. A middled aged woman who looked like she still hasn't forgiven her children for being born gave us the middle finger through a window. It was a super fancy house with a big pool on the side too, which only added insult to injury.

Ava shouted and called her a *Karen*, and things went down hill from there. The woman came out of her house, a frilly purse gripped in both hands like it was that child she probably wanted to strangle.

"Out! Out! Before I call the Police!" the woman howled. "Do you know you're standing on private property?"

Ava stepped forward, smiling brightly as though the exchange had never happened. "Good evening, fine lady," she articulated in a particularly British voice. "We are collecting donations to rebuild—"

"I've got a gun in my purse! I want you gone. You understand?"

Ava was trembling in anger all over. I'm just staying out of it, glad she has never looked at me like that. I never expected her hand to strike out and seize hold of the woman's purse handle. Their eyes locked like two bulldogs in love. The Karen gaped incredulously, unable to believe her eyes. One of her hands fluttered to her heart in horror, and Ava took the opportunity to dig in her heels and rip the bag clean away.

Ava ran, and we all ran after her. Feet pounding the pavement, hearts racing through our ears, heaving through the side-splints kind of running. We went about five blocks before Ava stopped for breath, still clutching the woman's purse in a gleeful euphoria.

"It's not fair…" Ava said between gulps of air. "That woman… has everything. These people… have nothing. It's not right at all."

She looks both ways down the street before hunching over the purse and digging her hand inside. She pulled out a wallet, from which she clutched a fistful of cash.

"Give me the credit cards before they're canceled! I can donate on the website!" another said enthusiastically.

A car pulled to a screech in front of us and we all jumped bad. My heart was already going so fast, and for a second I was sure I was about to get arrested until I recognized the familiar scars on my brother's old junker car.

Everyone else was freaking out until my brother got out of the car. They calmed down once they recognized him, although Ava was still as worked up as ever.

"Where have you been? Mom has been worried," my brother told me. "Hop in the car and let's go."

"That was a rotten thing you did at the last game," Ava snapped, her face still as flushed as ever. "Why didn't you ever give your brother a shot?"

"Come on, Ava, you're embarrassing me," I mumbled to her. "We'll give you a ride."

My brother snorted and smirked. "What's the big deal? We won, didn't we?"

Ava dropped the purse to the ground, now thrusting the stubby silver gun she found toward my brother. Her pretty face all twisted with spittle spraying as she spoke.

"It wasn't fair! Make it fair!"

The gun went off and my brother jumped in the same moment. I thought he dodged it at first, but he was only reacting to the bullet blasting through his foot. The others descended on him while he lay on the ground, kicking and laughing. I staggered to help him, every wet impact crushing my stomach.

"You think you're better than your brother? You're better than nobody!" Ava roared.

There was a shock of recognition about what they were doing as some lurched back. They shook all over as I pulled them away from my brother, each terrified by the others and by themselves. Ava was the last to leave, getting in another two solid kicks before she snapped out of it. Her brow furrowed as though coming out of a dream, and her skin grew pale as she watched my brother squirming and limping back into the car.

"You're nobody," she said again, spitting after him. "Come on, babe, we've got a few more neighborhoods to hit tonight. Those houses aren't going to rebuild themselves."

"Coming babe. Later bro, looking forward to our next game," I called after my brother as his car tore down the street. I felt good about my chances this time.

## he Forgotten Trauma

"Get off me. Get away. I don't know where to go."

An old woman, with dark sunken eyes that appeared to be looking inward instead of out. I recognized my neighbor Mrs. Naiko hobbling, swaying back and forth treacherously along the side of the road outside my house. She almost stumbled and pitched herself into the street, but caught herself against my car.

I was climbing out as she muttered past, but I leapt after her to guide her back toward safety.

"You can't walk in the street like that," I told her sternly, knowing the words didn't quite reach her even as I spoke.

"Bah, don't bother me." She waved a hand frantically around her head to chase off imaginary insects before taking a few uneven steps away from me. Her other hand carried an over-stuffed leather bag which she clutched to her chest like she was preparing to wrestle me for it, although its weight was obviously making it harder for her to walk.

"Is there someone I can call to help you out?" I pressed. "Do you know where you live?"

She was still muttering to herself, not looking directly at me. Instead she looked over my shoulder, squinting her cloudy eyes as she tried to focus on something that wasn't there.

"'Course I know, I'm not stupid," she said at last. "But don't you dare take me back. I'm running away."

"Why are you running away?" I asked. It was easy to keep pace with her, even though it seemed like she was trying to lose me.

"Such abuse. Such torture. I can't stand it anymore, I'm not going back," the woman snapped. "I'm going to be fine on my own, don't you worry. See, I've got some biscuits, and a warm sweater, and…" The woman was ripping through her leather bag now, but stopped suddenly with trembling hands. "Oh bother, I've forgotten Mr. Whiffles. Do you think he'll be alright?"

"Mr. Whiffles?"

"My cat!" The woman howled in distress. "I can't leave Mr. Wiffles with that lady."

"Naiko! There you are! What are you doing out here all alone?"

An attractive and professional woman wearing a blue pantsuit came running down the street after us, smiling broadly with relief. "You had us all so worried, mother! What were you thinking, sneaking out of the house like that?"

Mrs. Naiko redoubled her efforts down the street, refusing to even look in her daughter's direction. She was muttering to herself again. "You're lying, Lauren. You didn't worry. Not again. No more blood. I can't take it anymore."

The younger woman called Lauren reached out to seize Naiko by the arm to lead her back the way she came. The old woman tried to swat her away as she had with me, but Lauren took the opportunity to snatch the bulky leather bag away, forcing Naiko to pursue her in an attempt to reclaim it.

"Thank you so much for keeping my grandmother safe," Lauren called to me as they departed. "Her mind isn't what it used to be, and she isn't supposed to leave the house."

"I thought she was your mother?" I called back.

But Lauren wasn't paying attention. She had opened the leather bag and was dumping the entire contents into a trash bin. I didn't see any sweater or biscuits, just crumpled papers, and empty bottles, and broken bits of trash and rubbish raining out.

"My treasures! How could you, you awful, nasty woman? I never want to see you again!" The old woman shrieked, pounding her feeble fists uselessly against the blue pantsuit.

"Sorry! Thanks again!" Lauren smiled cheerfully, waving to me. And then turning to the old woman, she clutched her by the arm and began dragging her toward one of the houses across the street.

"Bloody pins and needles," Mrs. Naiko grunted, although she wasn't fighting anymore. She just trudged along behind Lauren, muttering to herself the whole way. "Hot irons. Sharp knives. But nothing worse than those bloody needles."

The whole ordeal was enormously upsetting for me. I checked in on the house several times that day to always see the old woman glaring down at me from a window on the second floor. On one hand the bag full of trash made me think the old woman really had lost her mind, but then there was the matter of Lauren calling her mother once, and then grandmother next, which could be the sign of a sloppy cover story.

Unable to find peace with either version of events, I was restless that night until I found myself rooting through their trash bin for clues. The leather bag had mostly contained old newspapers with handwritten scribbles in the margins. I opened the flashlight on my phone to read a few of them:

*A burden, not a person.*
*She wants to be rid of me.*

*Punish the wicked girl.*

"Is there something I can help you with?"

I jumped, startled to see Lauren watching me from her doorway. I hurriedly stuffed the newspaper back into her trash bin, feeling a sharp sting in my hand as something sharp pierced through the debris.

"It's about my Aunt, isn't it?" Lauren sighed. She peered over her shoulder, then quietly closed the door and began walking toward me.

There was no hiding what I'd been doing. I turned my light back into the trash to see what I'd cut my finger on as Lauren approached.

"I'm sorry if her behavior bothered you, I know it must be quite a shock to see someone so detached from reality," Lauren said sadly. "I've been doing all I can to take care of her, but I still have to go to work and can't be around to watch her all the time. It's gotten to the point where I think I'll have to put her in a home, don't you think?"

"Yeah, she would be safer in a home," I conceded, still staring into the trash. Staring at the sewing kit cluttered with bloody needles which glinted cruelly beneath my light. There were hundreds of them, each soaked in blood all the way from the tip to the base where they must have been driven deep into the skin.

I slammed the garbage lid down again just as Lauren reached me. Her eyes were cold and narrow when I met them, searching my face as though daring me to mention what I'd found.

"You won't tell anyone, will you?" Lauren asked at last.

I swallowed hard. "Torture," was the only word I could force out.

"Oh, it's not as bad as all that," Lauren said, her lips pressed into a hard line. "They're so small, you can barely feel it by the next morning."

"And the hot irons?"

Lauren flinched. "It would only make it harder on her if other people knew what she was going through. No home would take her if they knew how damaged she really was."

Lauren reached out to squeeze my hand in a gesture of familiarity I didn't feel. I stepped away from her, not taking my light off her, just watching her hands tucked beneath her arms for any sudden movement. I don't know what I was expecting, but my finger was already throbbing from where the needle had sunk in. I couldn't imagine what the old woman must have gone through, but even thinking about it made me sick.

Lauren gave me a tight, faltering smile, then nodded.

"A home then. It's settled. And I'll finally be rid of her for good."

She wished me goodnight and I watched her walk all the way back inside the house. I waited until the door closed before I called the police. I told them everything that had happened, and where to find the bloody needles in the bin. Then I walked back across the street and waited, watching through the window.

There was a lot of shouting when they took Lauren away, but I didn't go outside until everything was quiet again. Mrs. Naiko was alone, digging through the trash bin in the dark.

"Mrs. Naiko? Are you alright?" I asked her.

"Got a light?" The old woman grunted.

I wordlessly turned on my flashlight again, unsure of what to say. She withdrew her sewing kit bristling with bloody needles from the trash.

"Deserved every last one of them," Mrs. Naiko muttered. "What an ungrateful, nasty woman my daughter was, although she couldn't even remember who I was half the time. All I've done for her over the years, and she couldn't even remember? Despicable, lazy, stupid girl."

"What do you mean, she deserved it?" I asked.

"Bah, mind your own business, won't you? Her mind was rotten, and she'd never even remember what I did to her the next day. I was getting so tired of punishing her for forgetting things, but the spoiled child left me no choice."

Then clutching her bloody needles to her chest and scowling, Mrs. Naiko gave me a curt nod.

"Thank you all the same. At least now I have the place to myself and won't need to go anywhere to be rid of her."

## I Am Not My Body's Master

I thought I was going to die when my truck slid off the icy road and into the ravine. The screech of brakes, the roar of lumber exploding from the cargo bed, the terrible stillness as the truck turned in the open air. Then the wave of sound catches up to me, pummels me, rips my soul from my body until everything lies still. Until I couldn't tell if there was anything left of me to save.

I remember lying on my side amidst the broken glass, trying to move one finger, one toe at a time. The pain is slow at first, but gradually the adrenaline drains from my system and is replaced by the suffocating pressure of a thousand sourceless wounds, all blending together into a single painful throb.

I was lucky to only lose my right hand, the surgeon said. It was pulverized almost beyond recognition and they had to cut it off, but not to worry, I'd be back behind the wheel in no time. He talked as though my life's ambition was to drive trucks, but that was only a job to keep me alive, not something to live for. I didn't have any medical questions to ask him, only whether I could take my broken hand home with me in a glass jar.

I'd never play the piano again. That's all I could think about while I politely listened to one person after another congratulate me on pulling through. A lifetime of compromises and missed opportunities, all building toward the day when I could show the world what I was really good for. A lifetime of biding my time and waiting for a chance that would never come.

I stayed in bed for a long time after that. I blamed it on the injuries, but honestly the rest of me was perfectly functional after a couple of days. I used to fall asleep dreaming of a crowded concert hall, an audience hanging in rapture at my every note. I can't even entertain the fantasy anymore.

My dreams have been troubled since the accident, but none disturbed me so much as watching my disembodied hand play the piano without me. At first I kept the glass jar with my hand on my bedside table, but after the second recurrence of that dream, I decided to move it into the closet instead.

That only lasted a few hours before I had to take it out again and look at it again. My lost hand was all I could think about. I even imagined catching glimpses of it out of the corner of my eye: hanging on one of the cupboards, or resting on the piano, or even turning slowly on its own accord in its glass jar. Of course the hand was never really there when I looked closely, but that wasn't enough to shake the phantom presence from my mind.

Then came the day when the glass jar was empty. My first reaction was to check the piano, laughing at myself for even entertaining the thought. I had started drinking lately to help me fall asleep, and the only explanation I could muster was that I must have gotten rid of the thing and forgotten about it. I decided it was for the best and that it was time to move on, but still my thoughts never strayed far from that broken part of me.

To make matters worse, it became harder to convince myself that my imagination was playing tricks on me when I glimpsed my hand in my peripheral vision. Creeping along the counter, or peeking out from under my bed, or always sidling along the upright piano which dominated my small apartment. Whenever I got these visions before I used to check the glass jar and reassure myself that I wasn't losing my mind, but now with it empty there was no haven from these disturbing fancies.

I had to drink more before I could fall asleep after that, but there was nowhere to hide in my dreams. All night I'd hear the piano playing in my sleep, the frenzied pace of the notes growing ever faster until all at once I woke with a discordant crash.

I don't know how long I lay awake listening to the sound of the soft melody which followed. Long enough to be sure I wasn't imagining it; long enough to know that I was utterly alone in my apartment. Lying there on my side listening to the music, I got a vivid flashback of lying amidst the broken glass in my overturned truck.

"Hello? Is someone there?" my voice called out tentatively. It had come from me, but I don't remember ever intending to speak aloud to give credence to my waking nightmare.

The music stopped playing the moment I spoke. Of course, I told myself, that's because you were dreaming and now you're not. I checked the glass jar by my bed again, knowing it would be empty, but still feeling unsettled to find it so.

It wasn't even 4 AM yet, but I didn't want to go back to sleep and risk another dream. I got up and put my bathrobe on, stumbling my way to the kitchen to make myself some coffee.

My sleepy eyes stared at the coffee machine for nearly a minute before I was certain that I hadn't turned it on. The coffee had already started brewing before I'd even turned on the kitchen light.

A rapid progression of chords on the piano had me jump. I lurched into the other room, catching a blur of movement rushing past me back to the kitchen. There was no denying it this time. Broken bone splitting through the skin, fingers twisted back on themselves, I stared at my hand crawling up the kitchen counter like some sort of giant spider. My hand withdrew a mug from the shelf and poured my coffee, pushing it across the counter toward me when I didn't move to accept its gift.

Apparently misreading my confusion, the hand then retrieved a nearly empty bottle of Irish whiskey and poured it into the cup, stirring the contents with its twisted pinky finger. Then pushing it along the counter again, more insistently this time so that some of the liquid sloshed out.

Slowly, tentatively, I reached out to take the offered mug, peering inside.

"If you're intending to poison me…" I said.

The hand leaped backwards, pinky and thumb joining at the front as if covering its mouth in shock. I made a show of taking a long drink, wondering whether the alcohol would help reorient me or drive me further into this pit of madness.

"If you are poisoning me though, couldn't you do it a little faster?" I asked. "I'm tired of waiting."

I set the mug down in front of the hand, and it was quick to scurry away on its fingertips. It soon returned however, this time carrying a small vial of white powder, making no pretense to hide as it poured the contents into my mug. I drank again, and again, as many times as it was refilled and offered to me.

I don't know how long until weariness and the substances I consumed lured me back to bed, but I did not intend to wake again. For the first time since my accident, I felt that my soul had already left my body. The air was filled with a slow, methodical melody as I drifted off to sleep. I just remember breathing relaxed and even to the music, waiting for it to stop to know the hand was creeping away from the piano. I felt each breath leave my body, willing myself not to fight it if I woke with the hand around my neck.

But there was no sign of the hand when I woke. Nothing to remain of the nightmare I endured, except a brand new, steel harmonica submerged in the glass jar beside my bed.

## Museum of Alien Life: Part 1

I was never one of those kids into superheroes or fantasy. Magic spells, undead creatures, monsters from the deep, what a waste of time. By the time you learn the truth about Santa, you're old enough to understand that reality is more mysterious and wonderful for being true than any make-believe story can ever be.

Instead of believing the impossible, I believe the probable. Aliens aren't a story of some forgotten past that no one will ever be able to prove. They're part of our inevitable future. Earth has been beaming out radio waves for over a hundred years, and our signal is only getting stronger as technology advances. Space is too big for something not to be listening, and it's only ever been a matter of time before something responds to our call.

"It's not a matter of waiting. Aliens have already been here for ages," my high school friend Nola told me after class one day.

It was a new school for me after I'd had trouble at the last one (different story), and Nola was about the only other person who talked to me here. He had long shaggy brown hair that was constantly in his eyes, and a really dry sense of humor that never showed up on his blank features. It was almost impossible to tell when he was joking or not, and I remember thinking he was making fun of me at first.

"You believe in that stuff?" I asked, cautious not to make a fool of myself.

"Nah, don't believe. Believing means taking something on faith, but there's plenty of evidence for alien visits. Haven't you ever been to the Museum of Alien Life?"

"So what, they have Bigfoot museums too," I countered. "Bunch of blurry photographs and unreliable stories from drunk farmers. No thank you."

"Nope, this place is the real deal," Nola insisted. "Guy who runs it used to be in government. He got his hands on all sorts of stuff that wasn't supposed to get out."

"Like the government would just let him walk out the door with that stuff?"

"Don't be an idiot. The government couldn't do anything to him without making it look like he's onto something. Besides, he's got other things hidden away outside the museum, and they'd get released if anything happened to him. So the government just ignores him and hope people think he's crazy, but he's not. You in, or nah?"

I don't know why I allowed myself to get my hopes up. The Museum looked exactly like I thought it would, with a tacky little gift shop in the front filled with stuffed green alien toys, "ectoplasmic goo", and decorative stickers and mugs. Nola had this little smirk like he'd just pulled one over on me, but I grabbed a green inflatable martian man and held it up like I'd just found the Holy Grail.

"Oh my god, this is unbelievable," I said in shocked awe. "A real life alien, and it's exactly how I thought it would look! Hope you brought the rope, I think this one's a fighter!"

I beat Nola over the head with the inflatable alien, but he barely reacted. The little smirk on his face slowly faded as he stared over my shoulder. I turned to see a man in his forties wearing a shaggy beard and camouflage. He wore a ragged baseball cap that said "Semper Fi" in gold letters. He pulled back sharply as I turned, and I got the unnerving feeling that he had just been sniffing the back of my head.

"You gonna buy that?" the man asked in a disinterested tone.

"No, sir, Mr. Ackles. We're here for the hunting lesson," Nola said without hesitation.

I thought Nola was just making fun of his camouflage so I started snickering, but I stopped when neither of the others reacted. Mr. Ackles took off his hat and scratched his head, scowling. His hair was buzzed short enough to reveal the horrendous scars around the top of his head like someone had once tried to take the top off with a chainsaw.

"You want to be an alien hunter, son?" Mr. Ackles asked me seriously.

"That's how you get to see the good stuff," Nola whispered in my ear.

"Absolutely," I answered loudly. "I almost caught a squirrel once, and figure I'm ready for aliens now."

Nola elbowed me in the ribs, but I maintained a straight face while the man in camouflage studied me. I caught his nose twitching and quivering again, but he swiftly turned away from us and opened a metal door in the back of the room. It was completely dark inside except for blacklights that made the place look like a cross between a retro arcade and a spaceship.

"Go on then. Have a look around. I'll join you as soon as the others get here."

I followed Nola into the backroom, glancing back to see the museum owner moving to the front window and putting up a "Closed" sign behind the glass. In retrospect I should have been more concerned by that, but the dark room was so enticing and Nola seemed to know what he was doing, and I let my excitement get the better of me.

"You ever see anything like this in your life?" Nola asked earnestly as he pressed up against a glass cabinet. "This stuff came straight from a spaceship."

Honestly it was a long way from the rusted debris I expected. Long shards of white, almost crystalline metal lined the interior shelves. They glowed faintly with their own soft luminescence that didn't seem to be coming from the blacklights inside the case. Farther down, something like a spacesuit was on display for a creature that must have had dozens of arms running down each side of its body. There was also a cracked screen that streamed unfamiliar lettering down in an endless display, two big round cylinders which could have been part of an engine, and cases and cases full of strange hooked and curved tools. They were

## Sleepless Nights

all built from the same strange crystalline metal, and if I looked closely enough, the material seemed to be in a constant fluid state as it sluggishly circulated around the objects.

"Living metal." I jumped at the voice so close behind my shoulder. Mr. Ackles had entered quietly along with three other people. They were difficult to distinguish in the dark room, but one woman wore a white shirt which glowed beneath the blacklight. The other two wore dark clothing: a large man who seemed like a body builder who let himself go, and a lanky fellow wearing a suit with a glowing tie.

"You're looking at the salvage from Percia-8, a vessel which touched down in the Utah desert in 2015," Mr. Ackles said, the words rattling off like a practiced monologue. "Only the booster section of the craft that helped them descend into the atmosphere was recovered, however. The aliens themselves naturally would have detached before landing with a more portable vehicle designed for terrestrial travel."

"Why would they leave their spacesuit behind then?" The lanky man asked, maneuvering past me to inspect the artifact. I caught a heavy wave of cologne as he passed, potent enough to cover up the smell of a corpse.

"Not unusual for the Percia type encounters," Mr. Ackles replied sagely. "The evidence suggests these creatures visit Earth on a one way ticket. You don't discard your booster engines and space equipment unless you plan on staying here."

The woman giggled faintly, prompting Mr. Ackles to pivot on his heel and stick his face a few inches from hers. "Did I say something that amused you, Jessie?"

"No, sir," she replied immediately. "There's nothing funny about alien invaders."

"Spoken like a true hunter," Mr. Ackles said, his toothy smile glowing in the blacklight.

Meanwhile Nola and I had apparently reached the end of the display cases. They were cool to be sure, but nothing I'd call definitive proof yet. I was trying to get Nola's attention to see what to expect next, but he was transfixed staring into the cracked screen with its strange lettering. His brow was furrowed in concentration like he was trying to read the script.

"Now, your most important tool that all alien hunters need to get acquainted with is the gamma detector," Mr. Ackles said.

I turned to watch him producing an electronic device that looked a bit like a large forehead thermometer, large enough that he had to use both hands to support it.

"Your typical alien will have spent months or years in a spacecraft before coming to Earth," Mr. Ackles continued. "We rely on our atmosphere filtering out most of the dangerous gamma rays from stars, but that type of long interstellar transit will leave detectable traces on an organic system. Mind you this won't work on aliens that were born here, or your inorganic robotic type that…"

The machine in his hand began to beep rapidly as his voice trailed off.

"How do you read it?" the large man asked, leaning down to peer at the device.

Nola abruptly grabbed my arm, whispering in my ear. "We should get out of here."

"That's odd… it doesn't usually…" Mr. Ackles turned the device over in his hand, shaking it.

Nola began dragging me insistently toward the door, but I was distracted by the gamma device and wasn't cooperating. Then he gave up and made a dash back the way we came.

"Roger! Bar the door!" Mr. Ackles snapped urgently.

The large man shifted into place immediately, blocking the museum entrance.

"You aren't seriously saying one of us…" Jessie stammered.

"The device is functioning properly," Mr. Ackles gloated with undisguised glee. "I've scanned this room a hundred times, there's no reading from these inorganic devices. What a perfect demonstration of alien hunting, to root out one of our own."

"I really don't care about being an alien hunter enough to spend all day here," Nola protested, making another move for the door.

"No one leaves," Mr. Ackles snarled, waving the device viciously through the air. It would have slammed into Nola if he hadn't scrambled back just in time. "Not until we learn who has been lying to us. Not until the imposter is revealed."

## Museum of Alien Life: Part 2

"It's just a game. A show. Nothing to worry about," Nola said unconvincingly. He'd retreated from the barred door to place his back against the far wall beside me. The tablet containing alien scripture glowed feverishly in the black light beside us, and the steady beeping of the gamma detector made the whole thing feel too real for my comfort.

"Why were you trying to escape so damn bad then, huh?" I whispered out of the side of the mouth.

"This is ridiculous," Jessie protested from across the room. "I thought we were going to learn about actual aliens, not people playing pretend."

"Goodness gracious, my dear. You're absolutely right," Mr. Ackles said in a tilting, sing-song voice quite unlike the gruffness of our initial acquaintance. "Roger, why don't you step aside and let Jessie leave."

"Just like that?" Roger shifted uncomfortably from one foot to the next, not quite leaving the door.

## Sleepless Nights

"You're here to learn from me, aren't you?" Mr. Ackles said, the gruffness returning. "A hunter is a warrior, always balanced on the edge between life and death. The field gives you no luxury of doubt or hesitation—obey your commander and step aside!"

Roger did as he was instructed, and the woman wasted no time hustling to the metal door. She threw it open, only pausing to look back as though incredulous she was actually getting out.

"What sort of stupid strategy is this anyway?" Jessie asked suspiciously. "If I really was an alien, then you'd be pretty lousy hunters."

"When detecting an alien in a group of people," Mr. Ackles lectured, "your first step must be to separate the people one at a time. If you walk out that door and the beeping stops, then the hunt begins."

"You're all a bunch of psychos, you know that right? Aliens aren't even real. Grow up already," Jessie said slamming the metal door behind her.

We all held our breaths for several long seconds, staring at the gamma detector. The sound didn't change however, which seemed to satisfy Mr. Ackles just fine. His smirk grew more pronounced as he turned from the device to study the remaining participants in the room.

"See, that wasn't so bad," Nola whispered to me. "We'll be out of here in no time."

"I don't care for this method," the man in the suit said after a long pause. "If she really was the alien, then she'd know it and she'd have a head start escaping."

"Thank you Clayton, you may be silent," Mr. Ackles replied bitterly. "When it is your turn to teach the class, you can do things your own way."

"Do you two know each other then?" Roger asked. The large man had moved back to block the door, although judging by how often he glanced at it, it seemed like he too was about to make his escape.

"But everyone is trapped in this room," Clayton continued arguing. "Why don't you just stand outside the door with the detector and measure everyone as they exit?"

Mr. Ackles adjusted his cap, the white scar tissue on his head glowing briefly in the blacklight. "You're proposing to leave a known alien alone in a room full of innocents? Besides, the thrill is all in the hunt. If they run, so much the better."

"I'm going next then, yeah?" Roger asked, his voice a stressed calm as though he didn't want to appear too eager.

"You may," Mr. Ackles permitted.

Roger nodded stiffly before slipping out the door. Again we listened, and the beeping continued without a disturbance.

"This is stupid," Clayton complained again. "You're doing it all wrong. You know I'm not an alien, so I should have been the first one out. Then I could have setup a trap or an ambush, so that when the real alien escaped you could signal me to neutralize it immediately."

"This is not my first alien hunt!" Mr. Ackles snapped. "And I'll have you know that I'm perfectly capable of doing my own neutralizing!"

A silver revolver pistol flashed in the blacklight, glowing almost as brightly as Mr. Ackles maniacal grin.

"You don't hunt alien hunters with a gun," Clayton sneered contemptuously. "If I were you—"

"Out! Out this instant!" Mr. Ackles howled, leveling the gun directly at Clayton, who hurried to obey. "And I expect a full apology when I've shot the thing dead!"

The metal door slammed shut, and it was just Nola, myself, and Mr. Ackles left in the room.

"Okay Dad, that's enough," Nola hissed. "You need to step outside and get some fresh air. You're going too far with this game."

"Game?" Mr. Ackles growled. "This is a game to you, boy?"

"You never told me he was your Dad!" I blurted angrily.

"I just wanted to drum up some business for his Museum! I didn't think he'd bring a gun!" Nola whined. "Come on Dad, you know neither of us are aliens. Your gadget is probably just busted, so why don't you calm down and—"

"I know you're not an alien, Nola," Mr. Ackles said slowly. "You may go."

"But neither is—"

"I said you may go!" he shrieked.

"Sorry dude. See you at school... I hope."

Nola dashed for the door. I tried to follow him, but a line of silver light marked the revolver pointed directly at me, freezing me in place. I thought for sure Nola was going to stop and wait for me, but the metal door slammed shut, and suddenly there was just the two of us left.

Beep. Beep. Beep. Beep. Without cessation. Mr. Ackles turned his back on me as he strode to the door himself.

"You must not really think I'm an alien," I exclaimed suddenly, "or you never would have turned your back on me. So this really was all just a show, wasn't it? Wasn't it, Mr. Ackles?"

"I know you're human," he replied, his speech slurring into a sing-song voice again.

"So you'll let me go?"

"After all that trouble to get you alone?"

The flash of silver—but it wasn't the gun. It was the lock sliding into place in the metal door, barring any of the others from coming back in. Another flash—this time his teeth, the grin stretching even wider than it had before. Too wide, with too many teeth for a human mouth to ever contain. He then pushed a button on the gamma detector, carefully setting the machine down on a glass case as the beeping finally fell silent.

"You can try to run, if you want," he said gently. "I wasn't lying when I said I enjoyed the hunt."

Mr. Ackles was still holding the revolver loosely in one hand though, and I was too frozen with fear to make a move. He seemed to understand this, because he set down the revolver next to the gamma detector and stepped away from it.

"Go on now. I'll even give you a head start if you want."

Mr. Ackles removed his hat and began to scratch at his scars. It took a few tries before his finger nails seemed to latch into one of them, and then he began to peel the skin back from his head. I watched in horrified fascination as thin brown appendages seemed to reach up out of his head, squirming along with his human hands to peel the skin further back. They reminded me of all those little arms along the side of the space suit. The activity seemed to be taking his full attention though, and it occurred to me that this might be my last chance to escape.

Maybe I could have run for it then, and he would have laughed at my terror. And maybe Nola and the others would be outside, and we'd all be laughing together at the joke he'd pulled.

But I was too angry to let it go at that. At him for toying with me like that, at Nola for abandoning me so easily, at myself for being afraid. And I wasn't leaving empty handed.

I turned and smashed a fist through the glass cabinet beside me, seizing hold of the alien tablet inside. Mr. Ackles must not have been expecting that, because he nearly tripped over himself lunging for the revolver again. His human hands flopped useless at his side like empty puppets though, and for a moment he seemed lost and unsure of how to work his body.

I charged straight at him then, not flinching as those dozens of brown legs came surging out of the top of his head to flail in every direction. Several of them managed to grab hold of the revolver again, but I held the tablet out like a shield as I fled.

"Put it down!" hissed a dozen intermingled voices, all coming from the gaping hole at the top of Mr. Ackles head. "Don't break it, reckless child!"

He must have been too afraid to damage the tablet, because the shot I was bracing for never came. I fumbled with the lock as the creature continued squirming out of its skin, and then I was through, slamming the door behind me and running with all my might.

Clayton was the only one left in the gift shop, leaning against the counter and incessantly scratching at the top of his head. He seemed amused to see me until he spotted the tablet in my hands, and then his face twisted into the foulest of wrath. I didn't wait or slow though, I was through the doors and running, as far and as fast as I could to get away from the Museum of Alien Life.

I don't know what secrets I'll be able to recover from the tablet, but I do know this: The hunt isn't over yet. In fact it's just beginning, and this time I won't let myself be prey.

## For The Right Price

People who drink alcohol know they're ingesting poison. The only honest justification for this I've heard is that there's something inside of them they're trying to kill.

I guess I must be the opposite, because alcohol never gave me that satisfaction. Instead it feels more like there's something dead inside that I'm trying to bring back to life. I haven't felt much of anything since my divorce, but I was willing to give anything a try to break out of that cold, empty place.

"Maybe something exotic," I told the man leaning against the dirty brick wall at the back of the bar. He had a crumpled baseball cap pulled low over his eyes, but I could tell from his contemptuous sneer that he could sense my desperation. "What are my options, anyway?"

"Depends how much you got," the man said. He tried to keep a straight face, but the edges of his smile kept flickering upward, taunting me with his power over me.

I'd never bought drugs before, but I knew how negotiating worked and I wasn't about to fall for that trap. "I'm asking what you have for sale."

"For the right price, everything."

"A chicken sandwich," I shot back.

"$24.99," he replied without hesitation.

"For a sandwich?"

"Plus the value of my time to retrieve it. Everything is for sale, but a clever client will only buy things they can't get for themselves."

"How much to be happy?" I asked jokingly, trying to catch his eye and get a better read on him.

He seemed to sense this, and obligingly pushed the cap back on his head. His dark eyes were hard, focused, and uncompromising. "You can't afford it, but I can do you the next best thing. I can make your ex wife miserable."

"Yeah…? How much are we talking here…?" I looked around, my guilty conscience playing tricks on me in the shadows.

"$400 to humiliate her in front of her new boyfriend."

"Wait a second, how do you even know—"

"Stop you right there," he interrupted, pulling the hat low again. "Sources and methods are strictly confidential. Bad for business, you understand. Half up front, half after I've shown you proof that I've succeeded."

Without a doubt, the best $400 I ever spent. I don't know what type of high I was expecting walking into that place, but it couldn't compare with the giddy delight seeing the pictures he showed me two days later. I can't imagine how he did it, but it turns out I wasn't the only one my ex was cheating on. The first picture showed her and her new boyfriend sitting together on the couch inside their home. Then a series of sexually vulgar chat conversations she'd been having with two other people. And then pictures of her and her boyfriend screaming at each other in the living room, the pictures as clear as if he'd been standing right beside them. Finally a shot of her, hair a mess, diving into a tub of ice cream with mascara running down her face.

"Thanks, that's exactly what I needed," I said, paying the man the rest of his due.

"Come back tomorrow, and I'll have something else you need," he promised.

I thought I was ready to move on and didn't expect to be back again, but that night I got a call from my ex. Honestly I'm not sure whether it was guilt or a sadistic desire to be a voyeur to her distress that made me answer, but I wish I hadn't. She might not have known for sure I was behind the incident at first, but then she started yelling and threatening me, and before I knew it we were screaming at each other again just like old times. She was going to call my boss—my parents—the police—anything to get back at me. She was going to make up lies and accuse me of the most vile filth imaginable. I was so angry I almost smashed my phone on the counter when I hung up.

I lay awake all night after that, flushed and hot and angry, dreading the prospect of explaining my innocence again and again to those she poisoned against me. It was only the prospect of the man at the bar that got me through those hours, knowing only he could deliver what I needed to escape her for good.

"Make it look like an accident," I said.

"$9,000." He wasn't even making the pretext of hiding his grin.

I ground my teeth together. It was still cheaper than losing my job and having to hire a lawyer.

"And make it hurt," I added, mentally calculating how much I could afford.

"$9,500."

"She is terrified of snakes."

"11,250."

"It has to be today, before she can cause trouble."

"$16,750."

I took a long, deep breath. Was it really worth it? I could get a new car for that, but a new car wouldn't make me happy. A new car wouldn't give me a new life like this would.

And that might have been the end of it, if I hadn't just gotten off the phone with the man. I was expecting a confirmation or an update, but instead he said: "It's actually going to be $18,000 now. Maybe more."

"What changed?" I demanded.

"I sell everything to everyone."

"So what? We had a deal!"

"It isn't a sale anymore. It's an auction, and she's a competitive bidder."

I guess I should have just settled for the chicken sandwich.

## The Newspaper Threatened Me

I never thought horoscopes gave specific predictions. They're supposed to be as vague as possible to fit the widest range of circumstances. Something like "You should be ready for good news", or "Your problems aren't as big as you think they are."

But here's what I read in the paper this morning: "Aries: Your deepest desire today at 171 E Cherub Street, behind the cafe. If you miss your chance to be happy, you'll never find peace again."

It didn't make sense to me, unless the opportunity was to meet a bunch of other Aries all showing up at the same spot. Then again, I have been isolated at home for a long time since he was gone, and maybe meeting a bunch of people with the same sign and similar interests really was a unique opportunity by itself. Who knows, maybe there's even an eccentric billionaire who trusts the stars to show them who to help.

I scanned the rest of the horoscopes, but every other month was as vapid and obscure as always. I had nothing else to do though, so I drove to the address and parked behind the crumbling cafe. The place was closed with boards nailed over the windows, and I thought I might be in the wrong spot at first. I sat in my car for a few minutes in the empty gravel parking lot, waiting for someone else to show up. I was beginning to feel pretty gullible and was getting ready to drive home when a black Sudan parked at the far end of the lot.

I stayed in my car and watched as an elderly lady fighting a losing battle against gravity exited the car. She turned in a slow circle, apparently as confused as I was. I watched as she gingerly knelt to the ground and picked up a handful of pebbles before returning to her car and driving away.

Curious, I exited my car and knelt to inspect the stones. Up close I realized there was a letter painted on each of them with pale red paint. I scooped up a handful of them at random as the other woman had done. I shuffled the stones around my hand, staring at them incredulously as a phrase spontaneously spelled itself out.

*he wont come back*

The stones were lined up in my hand, and while some were slightly out of alignment, the ordering was unambiguous. Besides, the letters were all facing upwards, which seemed strange enough by itself considering how round some of the stones were. I couldn't help but think of Bradley, and how frail he looked in the hospital the last time I had seen him. The red stained bandages around his head—the IV needle in his arm—the bruised and twisted knuckles poking out from under the sheet.

My hand began to tremble, and a few of the stones slipped through my fingers. I threw the rest back on the ground, scattering them as I searched the surrounding earth. Then taking another fistful at random, I shuffled them into a line again, staring at the words that formed.

*dont look again*

I threw the stones down at once, conscious of the red smear left on the palm of my hand. I picked up a single letter "d" stone and noticed that the paint on it was still damp. More than damp—it was even brighter now than it had been a moment before when I first held it. And the longer I looked, the brighter it became, almost as if the paint was welling up from inside the stone.

"Howdy miss. What did yours say?"

I was startled to hear the deep voice so close to me. I'd been so absorbed that I hadn't even noticed the other car pulling into the lot beside me. A short, pudgy middle-aged man with suspicious beady eyes was trying to peer into my hand. I closed my hand protectively over my stone, and he chuckled.

"Here's what I got," he said, showing me his hand.

I looked instinctively at the letters which clearly spelled:

*you were warned*

"What do you suppose that's about?" he whined. "I just shuffled the stones like you did, maybe I did it wrong?"

"Maybe it was meant for someone else," I said, my voice sounding small and distant in my own head.

My last stones told me not to look again, had I already made a mistake? I stood from the ground and retreated back to my car, shaking my head at the absurdity of it all. Of course the warning couldn't have been for me. It's not like the stones could have known I was going to look.

"Ew, disgusting," the pudgy man said, hurling his stones at the ground. "Damn things are bleeding on me. Hey where are you going, miss?"

"Leave me alone. I want to be alone right now," I said as I got in my car and slammed the door. What was that supposed to mean, '*he wont come back*?' I knew Bradley was dead. I wasn't expecting him to come back. It had been hard enough losing him the first time.

I jumped as a red smear slammed into my window.

"Is this some kind of joke to you?" the pudgy man shouted, pounding the glass again with his open palm. "You think I'm stupid or something?"

"Hey leave her alone!" another voice shouted from across the parking lot.

I flinched as he slammed the glass one final time before flipping off the newcomer and walking away. I sat very still, staring directly ahead, trying to convince myself that I hadn't just heard Bradley's voice. It was quiet for a long time, but when I couldn't take it any longer I allowed myself to look into my rear view mirror.

Bradley was standing behind my car, just as I had seen him last. The bandages were wrapped so thickly around his head that only his mouth and and nose were clearly visible. It had to be him though—he was even wearing the same hospital gown, with the loose hanging IV still dangling from his arm. I don't know what gave me the strength to get out of the car then, if not for the weight of regret for all the things I never said to him when I still had the chance.

The other car was exiting the parking lot, and it was just the two of us facing each other now. He couldn't have seen me through the bandages over his eyes, but his head turned to follow my movements as though he could. There was a faint rattle as he turned over a handful of stones, and drops of blood dripped freely between his fingers as they moved.

"What is going on?" I asked, terrified by the helpless confusion in my own voice.

"Do you want to find out?"

Bradley's hand stopped moving, and he opened his fingers. The stones in his hand were bleeding freely now, enough to obscure the letters and make them impossible to read from this distance. I took a hesitant step forward, probing his bandaged face for answers, forcing myself not to look into the stones in his hand.

"They warned me not to look again," I protested.

"They also told you I wouldn't be back, but here I am." Bradley grinned. "I can come back, if you want me to. If you care."

"I do care." The words barely a whisper. "I really did love you. I should have told you before you left that night. I could have stopped you from getting into that car when I knew you weren't okay to drive, but I was so angry… but I never stopped caring."

"Then let the stones tell you how to bring me back." He offered his open palm toward me, inviting me to look.

I closed my eyes and shook my head. "I believe the stones. You won't come back, and I won't look again."

The next few seconds were long and arduous. I heard no sound except the dripping of blood, each drop farther from the last. Then the drops stopped altogether, and I finally allowed myself to open my eyes. The parking lot was empty, and the wind had turned a bitter cold. There were still pale painted letters on the gravel, but no blood and no one to go home with me.

My horoscope told me I would find my deepest desire, and it was right. I got the chance to tell him I loved him, and I would be a fool to wish for more.

## Sleepless Nights

### The Forbidden Room

My hotel room smelled of death. There were dark, damp patches on the ceiling, with muddy smears down the wall where the varnish wept. A musty yellow mold was growing in the bathroom, and there was a ring around the bathtub that looked like someone had tried to cook a stew in it. The ceramic toilet was so cracked on the bottom it might disintegrate if someone sat down too hard.

"Absolutely not." My wife Francis pinched her bandana over her nose, refusing to even step foot in the place.

"You don't really want to keep driving tonight, do you?" I protested. I sat on the bed and tried to be a good sport, but the motion caused a cloud of dust to rise which only spread the odor of mildew.

"I'd rather sleep in the car than be patient zero for whatever we catch from this place," she said unequivocally, backing out into the hall. "What about that room with the balcony we passed by the stairs? I didn't see anyone in there."

"Maybe they are just checking in late. The man at the desk said this was the last room left."

"I should remind you that I'm also your last wife, so you've got to be careful with her. It's after midnight, no one else is showing up tonight. Please, let's just ask?"

Back down the dimly lit stairs, past the beautiful room with the balcony, we found the receptionist still patiently waiting at his desk. His hands were folded in front of him and he was staring at the blank wall opposite him. I held out my arm to hold my wife back, and we both watched the receptionist for several long seconds as he continued staring into nothingness, apparently completely content with his role in life.

"You don't just sit there all night, do you?" I asked, advancing once more.

"Yes, sir. How can I assist?" His little trim black mustache wiggled when he spoke.

"We'd like the room with the balcony, please," my wife said emphatically.

"I'm sorry, madam. That's being held for the owner of the establishment. May I interest you in some incense to help you sleep?" The receptionist produced a small wooden box and tried to offer it to me, but I pushed it away. I had the unnerving impression that he was continuing to look over my shoulder at the blank wall.

"We don't think he'll be using it tonight," I said. Then glancing at my wife, I pulled twenty—then forty dollars from my wallet and slapped it onto the desk, upping to a hundred as I watched his perfectly passive face. "Just for the night. We'll leave it exactly the way we found it."

"The room is held for him regardless." The man snatched the money from the table without looking down at it, sliding it into his pocket as though his hand had a mind of its own. "Please take the incense. I myself find it greatly comforting in times of distress."

I tried to refuse again, but my wife nudged me hard and I accepted the box. Sliding it open, I saw a silver key lying on top of the incense.

"I completely understand. Thank you anyway, have a good night."

The mustache wiggled, which might have been the sign of a smile.

The new room was absolutely magnificent. Thick lustrous rugs, a canopy bed draped in black lace, and black silken sheets that Francis was already melting into. I pulled out a lighter and looked for a place to burn the incense, but my wife tossed the box onto the chest of drawers and drew me into the bed.

"Put that away, I won't have any trouble sleeping here."

We gratefully settled in and pulled the black lace closed around us. I was so tired from a long day of driving that I was ready to fall asleep at once, but as soon as I lay down I caught an awful stench that must have been coming from the moldy room next door.

"Woah, you smell that too?" I asked.

"Mmhmm…" Francis said, stretching luxuriously on the silk. "Like cinnamon cookies. Absolutely delicious."

"What are you talking about? It smells like a big fat corpse rotting in the sun. This isn't any better than the other room."

"Don't be disgusting. It smells perfectly wonderful to me," Francis said.

I tossed and turned for a bit, but the stench was only getting worse and it was starting to make me feel sick. I got up to look for the incense again, but my wife reached out and snatched me by the wrist, pulling me back.

"Enough is enough," she insisted. "We have a long day ahead of us, just go to sleep already."

I tried to settle in again, but it was no use. I tried to breathe through my mouth instead, but it felt like rotten eggs dribbling down the back of my throat every time I inhaled. I blearily pushed myself upright again only to feel the wooden box of incense shoved into my hand.

"Thanks honey," I said. "I don't know how you can't smell that."

"Mm," she grunted sleepily from the bed beside me.

I stared at the box in my hand, which had just been on the chest of drawers. Francis had been beside me the whole time and had never gotten up to retrieve it. I thought I saw shadow pass on the other side of the canopy and tore the black lace aside to look. A suffocating wave of nausea washed over me, my lungs feeling as though they were filling with thick syrupy liquid, tasting the air just as my mouth and nose did. I coughed and gagged, hurriedly lighting a match to burn one of the incense sticks.

Beneath the light of the feeble flame, I saw Francis beside me on the bed, only it wasn't her anymore. Her once pale skin was now rotten and gray, with puckered holes in her cheeks through which I could clearly see her swollen tongue. Bloated, decomposing fingers clutched the blanket to her chin, and the miasma rising from her was so thick that it discolored the air into a greasy smear where it leaked around the blanket.

A sudden, vicious gust of wind from the balcony tore into the room and whipped my light into darkness. I grabbed my wife by the hand and tried to pull her from that reeking bed, but she sleepily protested, waving me off with a strength in sharp discord with her decaying appearance.

"We can't stay here! We have to go back to the other room!" I pleaded.

"The other room is dreadful, and this is so nice. Why don't you want to be with me? Don't you find me beautiful anymore?"

The swollen fingers kept grasping at me, and the sight was too revolting to even look.

"Let me at least light the incense! Please! There's something wrong with this place. We aren't safe. You aren't…"

"For Heaven's sake, enough with that dreadful stuff. If you don't love me, just leave me alone!" the words came feebly, distorted by the weakly flopping tongue as the air escaped through her perforated face.

I tried to light the incense again, but she snatched it from me and hurled it out from the bed. I tried to rouse her, but she fought me off, clawing at my arms and face until I leapt from the bed.

"I will not be treated this way!" howled the voice which was not my wife, but came from her spoiled form. "Sleep in the other room for all I care. And take your damn incense with you if that's all you care about, you're the one who will need it in there."

I should have fought harder to drag her out, but I was so overburden by the stench and the horror that I allowed myself to flee. Down the stairs without getting dressed, all the way to the receptionist who remained placidly staring at the blank wall. His mustache wiggled as I approached, panting and gasping in the clean air as I slammed the wooden box down on his desk. He waited patiently for several seconds for me to catch my breath before he said:

"It looks like you're having a bad dream, sir. Why don't you return to your original room, and see if you don't feel better by the morning."

A little mold didn't seem so bad after all that. I nodded deliriously, turning to stagger back toward the stair without another word.

"And remember to light the incense this time! It really does help," he added cheerfully behind me. "The owner of the establishment was very fond of it before he died."

The incense did help after all, and within seconds of lighting it I found myself drifting off to sleep in the old room. I kept telling myself that it was a bad dream and that everything would be fine by the morning, but that was only the voice of cowardice which refused to face what remained of my wife.

Francis wasn't in the other room in the morning. It was clean and empty, the silken bed perfectly made exactly as I had found it. I questioned the receptionist, but he swore up and down that I checked in last night alone. The only thing I'm sure of that night is that the second room was never empty, and that the owner never left that room, even after his death.

## It Wasn't A Real Hospital

The ambulance said they were taking me to the hospital, but I don't know where I really am.

My eyes were closed from the pain in my chest as they laid me on a stretcher. It was a sharp, hot pain like a knife, but the worst part was that it didn't stay put in the same place. The pain almost seemed to crawl around my insides like I'd swallowed a centipede and it was gnawing its way through me. The paramedics were talking fast, throwing back and forth long and unfamiliar medical terms as they speculated about what might be wrong with me. I had no reason not to trust them when they told me I might have imernoplasia, even though I'd never heard of it before.

"You're in good hands now."

I wanted to believe that so badly that I didn't protest as they carried me inside. Dr. Witman introduced himself to me in the whitewashed hallway while the paramedic inserted an IV into my arm. The curly gray-haired doctor was so patient and kind, chattering with lighthearted enthusiasm about the impressive capabilities of their brand new hospital ward. He told me not to worry about all the plastic sheeting draping along the bare concrete walls in the next room, or the discarded construction equipment along the floor.

"Have you ever experienced anything like this before?" Dr. Whitman asked as he fiddled with my IV bag.

I told him that I hadn't, but I had a family history of heart problems. I don't remember exactly what they were though, but if I could just borrow a phone I'd call my father, and—

But no, Dr. Whitman preferred to run his own tests and not be biased. I told him I'd still like to call my father and let him know what's going on, but he just smiled sadly and shook his head.

"The machines in our new facility are extremely delicate, and they'd have to be recalibrated if you made a call from here. Why don't you give this nice young man your father's number and tell him what you want to say, and I'll personally make sure he gets the message."

My arm radiated icy cold where the IV was implanted, and I was beginning to feel drowsy. I mumbled out the number, staring up at the paramedic with his hands folded behind his back, his head cocked to the side in curiosity.

"Shouldn't he be… writing this down?" I mumbled. But Dr. Whitman just stroked my hair and smiled, and that's all I remember before falling into a deep and timeless sleep.

I wish I could tell you more about the dream I had then, because the haunting images which flitted across my mind's eye felt as real as anything. I remember the hot pain in my chest, as keen and sharp as when I'd been awake. I was lying on a table of sorts, and there were faces peering down at me, but they were so fantastical in their construction that I never doubted that I was still asleep. Dr. Whitman was there, only his mustache had slipped down to the end of his chin, and both of his eyes were vertically aligned on the left side of his face. There were several others too, their features a jigsaw puzzle of faces I had known throughout my life.

One had my father's brown eyes glowering at me from inside large flared nostrils that must have belonged to my middle school English teacher. Another had shaggy gray hair like one of my uncles, although it only ever looked like the back of his head no matter which direction he was turned. Then a hand reached down toward me, and I thought I even recognized my own eyes at the end of the index and middle fingers staring back at me. The eyes seemed to lead the hand down toward my chest, but I slept on, immobile and unable to resist as a silver scalpel pierced the flesh of my sternum.

It was all a macabre blur after that, but hands kept descending down toward me and I had the vague sensation that they were taking turns placing one handful after another of something inside of me. The next thing I remember I was waking up in my own bed at home, my familiar Star Wars posters hanging on the wall across from my bed.

"... I think he's starting to come around," I heard my father's voice say. "How are you feeling, son? Are you still in pain?"

I clenched my eyes and rubbed them, opening again to stare at the man who was not my father. He had my father's eyes—where they were supposed to be, thankfully—but the cheeks were far too shallow and his mouth looked all wrong. I kept rubbing my eyes, unable to tear myself fully from the dream I'd had, the comforting pressure of a hand grounding me in reality. Only it wasn't my father's hand—I can't say I can distinctly conjure my father's hand from memory, but I could tell from the way it held me like I might try to leap up and escape that something was terribly wrong.

"It doesn't hurt anymore," I answered honestly, massaging my bandages wrapped around my chest. "I think I'm going to be okay."

"I don't know what you're talking about," my father's voice said suspiciously. "Of course I'm your father."

I stared hard at him through the cloud of my haze, trying to remember whether I'd ever said that I doubted it.

"It's the medication you're on," he continued defensively. "It might play tricks on your memory, but you mustn't be alarmed. The paramedic called me just like you asked him to, and I picked you up at the hospital and brought you home. Everything has been taken care of, so just relax and try not to fiddle with the bandages. They have to stay in place for you to heal properly."

"What hospital did you pick me up from?" I asked cautiously, watching his brown eyes narrow dangerously at the question.

"What sort of question is that? Don't you want to know about your imernoplasia? I'm sure you have a lot of questions about what caused your attack."

"No, I want to know the address of the hospital," I said. "Why won't you tell me?"

"I see that you're still confused from the medication," my father's voice said. "I'm going to fix you something to eat. I'll be right in the other room, so call if you need anything."

I closed my eyes and pretended to be resting until he left the room. Then I leapt out of bed and ran to the bathroom, slamming the door behind me. I stared at myself in the mirror, gingerly feeling along my bandages to find where the incision was. Right on my sternum, exactly where I had been cut in my dream. I proceeded to unwind the bandages, picking at the stitches that sealed my wound together. It stung dully, and I had the distressing sensation of something else inside my chest picking at the other side of the wound.

I pulled my hand away, but the picking feeling persisted like something was trying to get out of me. I grabbed a pair of nail scissors and cut through the stitches in that location, wincing as my wound sagged slightly open. I stared at my chest in the mirror as a small brown antenna felt its way gingerly out from the wound, seemingly tasting the air before slipping back inside me. My fingers trembled and I winced as I cut the stitches further back, trying to widen the space sufficiently to get a clearer look inside. The hot pain that had first sent me to the hospital was beginning to return though, and after staring at the wound for several seconds I thought the medication was still making me imagine things. I started wrapping the bandages back around me when all at once a small brown insect exploded out through the hole, wriggling free to run down the length of my body and off across the floor.

That's when the bathroom door opened, and I saw the man who was not my father glaring at me.

"You shouldn't have done that," he growled. "Get dressed. We're going back to the hospital to get you stitched up again."

I nodded, numb and afraid to resist what I so clearly didn't understand. I just hope I can go to a real hospital this time.

## Will You Be My Mother When She's Dead?

One of my students has been having trouble at home. I teach at an elementary school, and I'd like to think that I can always tell when one of my children isn't being well taken care of. Being chronically tired is always the first clue. It doesn't matter what the problem is, stressing about it impacts their sleep and shows in their behavior.

Delayed emotional development, or desperately needing affection and approval is another sign. Children need love to grow as much as they do food and water, and if they aren't getting it at home, they're going to try to overcompensate while at school. It's difficult to tell sometimes though, because social withdrawal and becoming numb to a world that only hurts them can be just as indicative of a problem. The child might also become rebellious and angry, fighting back at me or the other students in an attempt to assert some self-control to mask their helplessness.

My first sign that something was wrong was when David started calling me mom. Children get used to associating authority figures with their parents, and it's not unusual for one of them to accidentally call me mom as a reflex. The mistake is immediately recognized, the student is embarrassed as the others laugh, and that's usually the end of it.

"Can we eat lunch outside today, mom?" David asked me one day.

Laughter from the class. A patient smile. "Do you want to try that question again?" I asked.

But David didn't seem the least embarrassed. The little boy with the buzzed hair and taped-up glasses scratched his head as though genuinely bewildered that he'd said anything wrong. "Can we *please* eat lunch outside today, mom?"

The laughter was even louder this time. I didn't want to make a big deal about it in front of everyone though, so I waited until recess when I asked David to stay after the other children had left.

"Okay mom," David said.

"You know that I'm your teacher, not your mother," I said sternly once we were alone.

"No thanks."

"Excuse me?"

"No thank you," he added politely. "I've got enough other teachers. I want you to be my mom."

"But what would your real mother think about that?" I asked.

I silently cursed myself for being insensitive. What if his real mother was dead? But David only shook his little head, staring down at his feet as he said, "She wouldn't mind. She told me she doesn't like being a mother. I told her that's okay, because my teacher likes me, and she can be—"

"No," I interrupted, a bit too sharply. "I mean, of course I like you David, and I'm sure your mother loves you too. But you can only have one mother."

"That's not true!" David protested, red in the face. "Mark had a mom, and then she left and his dad found a new mom. I want a new mom too!"

"Well that's different, that sounds like a step-mom," I said, unsure of how to begin untangling that for him. "I mean, you can only have one mother at a time, and you still have one."

"So will you be my mother when she's dead?" he asked innocently.

I opened and closed my mouth without any sound coming out. Then, "David! I don't ever want to hear you saying something so horrible ever again. And tell you real mother that I'd like to have a word with her."

"That isn't a no…" his voice trailed off expectantly.

I spoke to David's mother on the phone that evening. I tried to broach the subject with her, but I hardly understood a word she said between her thick Eastern-European accent, the booming television, and the loud home full of jostling voices. I'm pretty sure that she promised to spend more time with David though, and I would have thought that was enough if David hadn't spoken into the phone right before I hung up.

"Don't worry, she doesn't know," David whispered conspiratorially.

"Excuse me?"

"She doesn't know, mom. She can't taste it, in her drink."

And then the line went dead. I called again twice, but the ringing must have been drowned out in the loud home. I thought about calling the police, but decided how ridiculous it would be to suspect a nine year old of plotting murder. So I let it go and put it out of my head, like a child pretending something wasn't real just because it was too horrible to imagine.

David didn't come to school the next day, but that was no reason to be suspicious.

Or the next day, prompting me to leave a message for his mother that was never returned.

By the third day I was starting to get really worried. None of the other children knew where he was, and I couldn't stop thinking about what horrible event may have transpired. I didn't think the boy could really get his hands on poison, but what if his mother caught him doing something inappropriate and beat him for it? Or maybe they had a fight, and he ran away from home, and she never reported it because she was glad to have him gone.

I looked up his address in the school directory and decided to stop by after school. The apartment building David lived at looked like it used to be white, but there was so much paint peeling back from the muddy concrete that the building looked like it was enduring the last phase of a deadly disease. I knocked on his door and waited while I listened to a chair being pushed across the floor. Then one, two, three metal locks sliding out of place before the door opened.

David was wearing spider-man pajama bottoms and shoes but no shirt, standing on the chair to reach the higher locks. I was surprised by how quiet it was inside after how loud the phone call had been.

"I've been waiting for you," David said, grinning from ear to ear. His mouth started to form the next word, but I cut him off.

"Don't. Where is your mother?" I demanded.

He only giggled, jumping off the chair to race back into the apartment. I took two steps in, quickly surveying the dirty carpets, the marked walls, the paper plates with crusts of food scattered across the floor. I quietly closed the door behind me, hesitating before I called aloud:

"Mrs. Svobada?"

Giggling from the kitchen on the right. I carefully crossed the floor, flinching as something sharp pierced my thin-soled sandal. I knelt down to pull a thumb tack out of the bottom of the shoe. This close to the floor, I could see hundreds of them scattered throughout the dirty carpet. It then occurred to me that the rusty-red discoloration wasn't just dirt, it was dried blood from where someone had tried to flee over these tacks before.

"Watch where you step," the boy called.

"David, why are these things on the floor? This is dangerous."

"Uh huh," he agreed, peeking around the counter which separated me from the kitchen.

"Where is your—where is Mrs. Svobada?"

"She tried to get away," he whispered, eyes wide and quivering behind his broken glasses. "Don't worry. She isn't my mother anymore."

"David this isn't funny. Who else lives here with you? I heard a lot of voices when I called."

"I turned the TV way up. So no one would hear her."

I'd managed to pick my way through the tacks and was now standing over David in the kitchen. He crouched below the counter, holding a sling-shot taunt and ready. He wasn't aiming at me, but his muscles were locked and tense as he pointed at the ceiling. A stash of ammunition was piled behind him. I gripped the counter for balance, feeling faint and weak when I realized his slingshot was loaded with human teeth.

"No, no no no," I heard myself say as I staggered away from him. And then turning to retreat toward the door, I felt the snap and the whirr of something hurtling past my head. I thought he missed me at first, but then the overhead lightbulb smashed sending the whole apartment into darkness.

I took a hesitant step back toward the door, but a little hand around my ankle caught me by surprise and I went crashing down to my knees. I hunched over, protecting my head from a blow that never came. David wasn't trying to hurt me though, he was just stealing my sandals and throwing them away across the dark kitchen.

"Don't leave me, mom!" he shouted. "I won't let you!"

"I'm not going to run," I said, rising once more to my feet. The idea of crossing back through all those tacks without my shoes was grotesque.

"I don't want anything to happen to you," David pleaded. "I don't want to have to find another mother."

"Okay David, you win. I'm your mother now."

"Really?" His voice cracked. So sweet and hopeful and desperate.

My heart was beating out of my chest as I took a slow, deep breath. "That's right, David. I'm your mother. And as your mother, I want you to go to room. You've been very naughty, and you're in time-out now."

"Yes mom! Okay!" he declared enthusiastically. It was too dark to see anything more than his silhouette as he clambered up onto the counter, then down the other side as he retreated further into the apartment.

"Ten minutes time out!"

"Okay okay!" His voice was muffled, further back. "Then we're going to play together, aren't we mom? After time out, it will be okay again?"

"Yes David. Then we're going to play for as long as you want," I said, pulling out my cell phone and dialing 911. "But I want you to wait the whole ten minutes. I won't be your mother if I catch you trying to leave your room before then."

He was still in his room when the police arrived. I got out of there as fast as I could after that, not having the heart to face him and admit that I had lied to him.

As I left I heard him screaming "Mom! Mom! Make them let go of me, mom!" But I wasn't brave enough to turn around and go back into that place of evil. I found out later that Mrs. Svobada was dead, but I made a point of never finding out exactly how she died. As for David, I don't know what he must have gone through to turn out that way, but I can only hope that whoever takes him in after this does so because they love him, and that he will learn love can only be given freely, and never taken by force.

## I Keep Her Close

A date. A harmless dinner. No big deal, so why did I feel so nervous? Sitting in the restaurant booth waiting for him, I ran through a mental checklist to remind myself of all my best qualities. It wasn't helping though, because I wasn't really insecure for myself. I knew what I was worth. But what was he worth to me?

Relationships haven't been easy for me. Ever since I was a little girl, I told myself I was never going to settle. No matter if all my friends already met someone, no matter how hard it was to walk away and start over, I wasn't going to stop looking until it felt like fate. So what if my whole life I never met someone

## Sleepless Nights

sensitive and loving enough to deserve me? If you want something valuable, you shouldn't be surprised that it's rare.

Sebastian was an entirely new kind of man though. It wasn't just his looks, although he was an actor that the camera couldn't get enough of. It was the quiet strength and confidence he carried when he held my eyes and wouldn't look away. Sebastian wasn't just putting on a macho facade either, because he didn't evade the personal questions.

His mother had died when he was a teenager, and Sebastian wasn't afraid to tell me how much he cried the night she didn't come home. He lost his sister two years later, but he kept visiting her in the hospital every day until the very end. He was even married once, but he didn't do that thing guys usually do where they trash their ex as some sort of demon crawled up from Hell. Sebastian was open and honest about how much he loved her, and how difficult it was when they both realized that didn't mean they loved being together.

"But I don't want to talk about myself all evening," he cut in. The way he said it was so refreshing, not as a deflection, but pure and simple humility. "I'll always keep part of them close to me, but I'm looking for something new now. I want to know more about you."

Then he gently cupped my hand in his, rapturous attention on his face while I talked about everything and nothing. It had been a long time since I opened up like that, but his transparency gave me courage, and I never once felt that I was sharing more than what he genuinely wanted to hear.

I thought it was going to be the perfect night when he invited me home with him. The only warning sign I got was when it was time to pay for the bill. The way he discreetly opened his wallet under the table seemed odd to me, always keeping it out of sight even as he counted out the cash. It's my own fault for thinking he was too good to be true, but I got this intrusive thought that he might have given me a false name, and that he was trying to hide his ID so I didn't know who he really was.

Maybe he was still married. Maybe he was such a brilliant actor that he showed me what I wanted, not what he really was. I tried to push the thought out of my head, but it was eating me up inside. I got my chance to put my mind at ease when we got to his place and he used the bathroom, leaving his wallet in his coat flung across the couch.

I knew I shouldn't have peeked, but I really did feel better seeing his ID and knowing he was exactly who he portrayed himself to be.

I would have felt even better if I hadn't checked the other pocket. If I hadn't found the three little black medicine bags. One containing a stubby big toe with chipped red paint on the nail, another containing a slender pinkie, mottled and spotted with age, and the third finger still wearing its golden wedding ring.

He was taking a risk being honest when he said he always kept part of them close to him. So why shouldn't I take a risk now, when fate has finally delivered the (almost) perfect man?

## Lights in the Deep

Fear was a game for us as children. When Bernard dared me to eat a bug, I'd do it, no matter how many legs or how hard it crunched beneath my teeth. Or jumping from a ledge that I really shouldn't have—I didn't even mind breaking my ankle that summer, because I knew it would be his turn next. And even though he watched me jump first and saw me rolling on the ground in pain, he didn't hesitate to jump right after me.

That's how the game went. Whatever it was, we'd both do it together, and we'd be stronger for it. It wasn't just the rush of adrenaline whenever we did something stupid or dangerous. There was something sadomasochistic about the way we wanted it to hurt, knowing it would be the other person's turn next. We didn't understand that as children though. We just thought it was fun to see how far we could push each other.

We were in the woods together the day the game went too far. Our families had gotten together for a group hike when Bernard had the idea to leave the trail. I didn't want to because I knew how angry my parents would be, but I also knew how angry his parents would be at him, and that made it okay somehow.

"They're going to kill you." I grinned at him.

"I'm not afraid of them," he scoffed. Bernard had a slight overbite, and he always had a trollish little smirk that would have made me want to hit him if we didn't understand each other so well.

At first we only intended to hide off the trail for a while to scare our parents, but after about an hour we still didn't see them or hear them calling. We decided they could have found us if they wanted to, and that they weren't looking on purpose to teach us a lesson. But neither of us liked to lose a game, so we kept going farther on purpose, intent on not going back to the trail until nightfall.

We must have gotten turned around while playing in the woods though, because it was almost dark when we stumbled upon a small lake we hadn't passed on our way there. I thought I saw a soft orange light at the bottom, flickering almost like an underwater flame. I thought there was some kind of treasure hidden in the water. I could tell Bernard was starting to get scared and wanted to go back, but I enjoyed seeing how anxious he was about the fading light and it was my turn to make the next dare.

"We're diving in," I told him matter-of-factly, knowing he would agree to whatever I suggested.

"I hope you drown," he smirked, stripping off his shirt and shoes to test the chilly water.

I held him back before he made the plunge though. "All the way to the bottom, or it doesn't count," I said. "We've got to find out where the light is coming from."

"No problem." And he was gone, kicking and struggling to drag himself under the murky surface.

I watched the flickering glow shift for a few seconds before diving after him. The water was a lot colder than I expected, and the shock of it made me lose most of the air I'd stored. I know he must have gone deeper than me, but I couldn't help but surge back toward the surface to get another breath and try again.

The salty water was making my eyes burn, and I stayed there treading water while I rubbed them. I reached out blindly for the grassy bank to use my shirt to wipe my eyes, but after several flailed attempts I couldn't find the place I'd jumped from. By the time I finally opened my eyes, I couldn't believe what I saw.

The setting sun lanced across the rippling water, unobstructed by the trees that were no longer there. It was just water as far as I could see in every direction, with the waves of the open ocean cresting and falling around me. I couldn't see Bernard anywhere, and my heart felt like it was ricocheting around my rib cage it was going so fast. I screamed and called for him for several seconds, thrashing around in the water as I tried to stay afloat.

My feet couldn't touch the bottom. But more than that, I felt an immense emptiness beneath me as though the water went down forever. But down there somewhere the flickering light was still burning, only now it seemed a thousand times farther away.

I kept screaming until a wave went over my head and pushed me under for a moment, and then I didn't dare open my mouth or waste another mouthful of air again.

Finally Bernard broke from the surface. He was spluttering and coughing, rubbing his eyes just as I had done.

"Don't open your eyes!" I shouted. For the first time I didn't want him to see what I saw—didn't want him to feel the fear I felt. "Go back down! Back to the light!"

But it was no good. Stubborn as always, his eyes flashed open, then stretched wide in terror of the open waters. He was so surprised that he stopped kicking, sinking for a moment before resurfacing with a wild yell.

"Can't go down!" he shouted back. "There's something down there. A monster—the light's coming from a monster!"

"We can't stay here. We have to go back! I dare you to swim down!"

But I could tell by his pale, terrified eyes that my words weren't getting through. I tried to grab him to drag him down with me, but he was flailing so wildly to push me away that we both would have drowned if I stayed with him.

"Down! Down!" I kept shouting.

"It was bait. The light was bait," Bernard blubbered. "I saw the creature. It's huge—in the water with us. Under us. Watching us."

The light was coming closer toward the surface as he spoke. As the last of the sun slipped over the horizon, I saw a gargantuan dark shape slip beneath us, the flickering light following it wherever it went.

"You can't be afraid," I begged him. "I'm going to swim down first, okay? You're going to follow me. It's going to be okay. We're going to come back up in the lake."

But he was too scared to speak. Too scared to do anything but kick and stay afloat.

"Our parents are going to be there," I promised him. "They're going to have warm clothes, and hot chocolate, and they're going to be so relieved to see us they won't even be mad. But you have to swim down toward the light. On the count of three."

Bernard was trembling all over, but he was moving so frantically it couldn't have been from the cold. He desperately shook his head while I counted.

"One."

The dark shape was getting closer. Larger than a whale, more like an underwater island.

"Two."

The light was getting closer. It had to be the way home. If it wasn't, there was no way back.

"Three."

Bernard was still shaking his head when I made the plunge. I think part of me knew he wasn't going to follow me when I kicked my way under, but I was so cold and I had no other choice. I swam as hard and as deep as I could, until my lungs felt like they were going to burst. Until the warm flickering light was so bright I could see it with my eyes closed, and I felt a sudden warmth flood over my body. Then when I couldn't take it anymore, I turned around and launched back up toward the surface.

My eyes weren't burning anymore when I broke the surface. The water wasn't salty—I was back in the murky lake. My feet found the stony ground, and I dragged myself back onto the grassy bank. In the distance I could hear my parents calling for me, and I shouted back with all the air I could find.

The light was gone from the water though. The surface was still, no stirring of a beast, no ocean waves, no bubbles of escaping air. My parents found me before I could go back into the water, and they wouldn't let me dive in again. Bernard's father splashed around in there for a while, but he was only up to his chest at the deepest point.

My friend was gone, still treading water, or worse—taken by the creature that lured us down. That's how it has to be for anyone, I think, if you can't master your fear and face it head on. It was a game for us, and now I play the game of fear every night on my own.

## The Demon In Heaven

I did not fear death, even in my final hours. I can't say that I had no regrets, but I know of no other actions or circumstances in my life which could have led to a greater serenity at the end. At peace with myself and the world around me, I slipped into that final sleep I did not expect to wake from.

I believe I can tell the exact moment when I died because it coincided with a vague sensation of falling in every direction at once. I watched something like a klaideoscrpe of my body being left behind from every angle as the world folded in on itself. Thinner and thinner slices, faster and faster, interweaving together as the intricate dance of life spiraled down into a single point. And then rebounding again, a collapsing universe exploding anew, each fragment of mind unraveling itself into the form I next occupied.

I was young and strong again in my new body, and the verdant garden was bliss to behold. Every luscious plant around me grew in perfect symmetry without the slightest blemish or rot, and the branches of every tree fit perfectly into place with the others as though puzzle pieces locked together. There were animals too, squirrels and deer and wolves and many others walking openly without scurrying or stalking; no displays of fear or hunger for one another. The warmth of the sun and the richness of the air was so nourishing that I never felt the urge to eat or drink in that garden, and so too must the animals have been able to coexist so perfectly.

Some of the creatures spoke to me, or at least they spoke to one another and I found no barrier in understanding them. The birds sang with contentment, and I found the song so much more beautiful than any on Earth where they must have often been warning of danger or defending their territory from rivals. There was one thing that bothered me about the way they spoke to one another though: each knew only their happiness in the moment, and none showed the slightest thought about where they came from or how this place came to be.

I began asking the animals, but though they stopped and listened politely when addressed, they grew agitated when I persisted on the existential questions that drew my curiosity. Their answers were always evasive, suggesting pleasant things that I might do, and when pressed always returning to the single unequivocal rule of this place: I could go anywhere or do anything that I liked, so long as I never sought out the person in charge.

If it was simply a matter of their reverence and respect, then I think I could have accepted such an answer. The way they spoke unsettled me though, seeing such peaceful animals become fearful as they warned me away from such pursuit. Hair rising on the backs of their necks, snarling faces, darting eyes, each utterly terrified by the notion that I would want to meet such a being. It did not make sense to me where such fear could be coming from in a world so far removed from death and pain and want.

I could not rest with the idea of living eternally in terror of some unknown beast that ruled the land. The more they warned me, the more desperate my pursuit became, until I found myself unable to linger for a moment without my curiosity cheapening the pleasures around me. I decided that I was only able to find peace at the end of my life because I knew I had followed my passions without doubt or regret. But if I were to turn aside in this quest, then I could spend forever unhappy in the knowledge that my true nature was to be as cowardly and dull as the animals. What was it to be man if it was not to master oneself and one's surroundings, to do what was impossible for other animals?

All this time I didn't find a single other human, and I convinced myself that I was being put to some type of cosmic test. Perhaps there was one afterlife for the animals, and only once man has proven himself worthy is he able to elevate to an even greater paradise that he has earned. I imagined all the other humans in their mighty palaces looking down at me and laughing to see me scurrying around after the squirrels as I proved myself their equals.

I knew the animals must know more than they pretended to display such fear, but none were willing to tell me what I needed to know freely. That is why I set about making a trap, digging a pit in the soft and fertile earth where I might extract an answer by force. The creatures here were so trusting and stupid that I needed only to ask a badger to come stand by me where the leaves covered the hole for it to willingly oblige. The unsuspecting creature's weight burst through the concealment at once, sending it to tumble down whereupon I immediately sealed it inside with a large stone over the hole.

I hadn't counted on quite how easygoing the creature could be though. It continued to disregard my questions about the creator of this place and showed no fear of me, despite my power over it. Even trapped in the dark hole, the badger slept peacefully at the bottom as though it was its den. Forced to escalate my approach, I used two sticks to start a fire on the end of a leafy branch and thrust this into the hole. Finally I had its attention as the badger whimpered cowered away from the flame, pressing itself flat against the wall as it wailed an answer to my inquiries.

The badger said the ruler of this place lived among us, but I would never find him by looking. I could only act in such a way that made him find me.

It was so gratifying to finally get an answer, even one as enigmatic as this. For the first time I felt like I had power over the animals and was no longer their equal. I allowed the badger to escape, and gathering up as much fuel as I could, I set my burning branch into the foliage and watched it spread. I watched the flame smolder into a roaring fire and relished the thick plumes of black smoke curling into the sky. It would be impossible to witness such a display without knowing a man was dwelling among the animals. The creator would find me, and at last I'd have the answers I sought.

The rich air nourished the flames more than I expected however, and they did not stop at the edge of the fuel I collected. Soon the sparks had leapt into the branches, and from one branch to the next, so perfectly fitted together, the fire raced. The bird song turned to one of panic as they took fight in mass around me, but the animals so long unaccustomed to fear were slow to react. Some even approached the flame to marvel at it before the fire leapt to the surrounding foliage, spreading wider and faster than I ever believed possible.

Soon I stood in the middle of a raging inferno that ravished the pristine land. I couldn't stand the heat and was forced to hide myself in the hole I had dug. On Earth the fire might consume the land and move on or smolder out, but here the immortal trees continued to burn without cessation. There was no escape, and I could do nothing but cower as I watched the animals panic, their multitude of voices joining into a single enduring scream. But these immortal beings were not killed by the flames just as the trees persisted, and before my eyes I watched the still-living creatures melt and disfigure into horrendous shapes of flowing skin and exposed bone.

Despite all this, or perhaps because of it, my plan still came to fruition when the Lord found me cowering in my hole. I don't know how long I spent in his presence, but when it was over I felt myself falling in every direction just as I had when I first died. I watched my body burn from every side, until smoldering to nothing, the explosion of pain gradually subsided into the cold shock of awakening into my next birth.

Reflecting upon these memories now in my next life, it seems as though I was banished from Heaven for my deeds. If I ever received answers to my most pressing curiosities about existence, or the nature of the ruler of that land, then those too must have been stripped from me in punishment. Most keenly I remember the pain of that fire, burns from which still covered my body and whose agony I will take with me for the rest of my life. But even this pain I will endure for as long as I am able, for I now fear death like I never had in my previous life. Like the animals, I fear he who rules that place, for I was the demon in Heaven, and through my actions did I transform it to Hell.

## She Knows Your Death

Most people wish they were rich growing up, but I don't. Because I had magic, and that is so much more important.

All the children of Cantleburry know there's a witch living at the edge of town. We know it by her house, with its dead trees, and rotting planks, and dirty windows that never let any light in. We know it by the way she scowls at us when we pass by, as though wishing torment upon whatever she looks at. But most of all we know it by the way she can predict when someone is going to die.

She got it right about Mrs. Wilson, right down to the day. And Stinson with his throat cut—how else but magic could she have known that was going to happen? She even makes a business out of it, charging people to predict when and how the end will come. The children are her only customers though, because they're the only ones who know the truth about her.

When the children ask how their parents will die, she always makes them pay her first. She tells them to steal something valuable from their parents, and to bring it to her for her to work her magic through. The more valuable it is, she tells us, the stronger their emotional connection to it, and the better read she is able to make.

Every child who cares about their parents at all has to do it. A diamond necklace, an antique heirloom, an original painting off the wall—it doesn't matter what it is. She'll run her gnarled old knuckles over the thing, chanting unfamiliar words as she speaks with the spirit realm.

Then she'll start to ask questions. Where the child lives, how old the parents are, what sort of things they like to do for fun when they're alone. The children will always tell her everything she wants to know, because that's how the magic is done. Then she'll start burning incense and humming, holding the child's hand while she holds the valuable possession, her withered old eyes pinched so tightly that her eyebrows meet her cheeks.

My parents didn't have any valuable things, but I brought a pretty nice dress that looked pretty all the same. The witch didn't spend much time with it before telling me my parents would live a long and happy life. I stayed to watch as she performed the ceremony with others though, telling them what they most wanted and dreaded to hear. I watched so many times that I noticed something funny: if you brought her something poor and shabby, then she'll say your parents will live a hundred years. But if you bring her something really nice, you can be sure that death is right around the corner.

She successfully predicted four deaths before she was arrested. Her name was Alice Mattle, and she was so good at making prophesies because it turned out that she was the one making sure they came true. When I was older, I learned that she used the children to find out who the best targets were, and then murdered them to steal the rest of what they had.

I never stopped thinking about how lucky I was my parents weren't rich, because that would have been the end of them.

Sleepless Nights

## A Borrowed Life

How do you know if you've wasted your life? I think it's the moment you realize that as soon as you're gone, there will be nothing left in the world to show that you existed at all.

I was 47 when I realized this. No kids, no great works or influences. I have chronic pain and fatigue, and never even traveled outside the country. I've just existed, staying alive one day to the next more out of fear of the unknown than any great love of life. I've found amusements, and fleeting pleasures, but nothing transformational or awe inspiring. I've worked odd jobs to cover what disability doesn't, but I've created no lasting value that hasn't already been forgotten by my employers or clients. I've accomplished nothing that anyone else couldn't have done just as well, probably better.

It seems pretty bleak now, but I know it's only going to get worse. When I'm really old and looking back for nostalgia, I'm going to have trouble finding anything to hold onto. No truly passionate affairs, no great pride, not even the depth and meaning of any great loss. Year by year I'll just grow more bitter, resentful of everyone else out living their lives when I know I've squandered mine one hour at a time.

I explained all this to my neighbor Borris, a handsome gangly fellow with shaggy blonde hair. I hadn't intended to be so honest about my life. We were sitting in his yard having a few drinks by his BBQ and he was talking about his kids, and suddenly it all came pouring out of me. I felt pretty embarrassed and couldn't even look him in the face after that. I just stared down at my beer can clenched in my fist, feeling his eyes on me and wondering whether it was pity or something else.

"I hope you've never felt that way," I said at last. It was a lie. What I really hoped was that I wasn't the only one who did.

"No. Never," Borris said, running a hand through his thick hair. "I'm still in love with my wife. I've got great kids, and I know they're going to visit me when I'm old. They'll go on doing good things long after I'm gone. And you know I've done a lot of traveling when I was younger."

"Cool. Wouldn't know what that's like," I said, gripping my beer a little tighter.

Borris stood up and clapped me on the shoulder. "You hold tight though. I think I've got something that will help."

He went inside his house, leaving me to gloomily melt into my chair and wish I hadn't said anything. When he came back he had a large wooden box with dozens of little doors around the perimeter. I half-hoped he collected exotic drugs or something—anything to make me feel more alive. Borris smiled kindly down at me, handing me the box before settling back into his own chair.

"You can borrow it if you want. Just make sure to get it back when you're done—it's very important to me."

There were hand-written labels above each of the little doors, so small I had to bring the box up to my face to read what was inside.

*Mexico.*
*Wedding.*
*Father's funeral.*
*First born.*

I slowly turned the box around, seeing each label apparently describing an event in Borris' life.

"What are these, like souvenirs?" I asked.

Borris chuckled and nodded. "Something like that. Wait until you get home to open them, and tell me if that's not what you were looking for."

Confused but curious, I thanked him and took the wooden box home with me. I don't know why I felt compelled to close all the curtains and lock the door before settling down with the box on my living room floor. Holding the thing just felt like a secret though, and when I was alone with it I even imagined the faintest of whispers leaking out from the little doors.

Pale blue smoke curled out from the first door I opened, the one labeled "Mexico". I took the tiny drawer all the way out of the box, disappointed that it was empty but for the smoke. I must have accidentally inhaled some of it while I was inspecting it though, because I immediately began to feel light-headed and absent, like I was drifting off to sleep.

The next thing I knew I was on the beach feeling the warm sun on my shoulders. Only they weren't my shoulders at all, because I didn't have a snake tattoo winding down my arm. From the wet sand beneath my toes to the lapping waves against my feet, it really felt like my body that was moving on its own without the least input or control from my mind.

I decided that I must be living through Borris' memory, seeing and feeling exactly what he must have experienced that day. Then I felt a firm warm pressure around my wait, and felt myself turning to see Borris' wife embracing me from behind. She wasn't an unattractive woman, with long brown hair wet and plastered against a body that was much younger than the version of her I knew. But there was so much more in her laughing eyes than I had ever felt from looking at her.

"I'm going to remember this feeling forever," I heard myself say with Borris' voice. And more than that, I felt it too, that love and devotion so much deeper than anything I've ever felt in my own life. I wasn't just seeing the beach and feeling her body against me, I was living through all the years he'd wanted her before this moment, and all the life that lay in store for them ahead.

I woke up dazed and gasping on the floor of my living room. The blue smoke had dissipated into the air, and it was just me clutching the empty wooden drawer. I was overwhelmed with despair for the loss and jealousy I felt not having lived so truly myself. I didn't stop to think before ripping open the next box, and the one after that as soon as the smoke had cleared.

One day, one fragment of life, one precious moment at a time, I lived through these experiences that were so much more real than my own. I even enjoyed the painful ones, because in the back of my mind I always knew it wasn't really me who was suffering, and that the depth of the experience made all the other triumphs that much sweeter.

It was deep into the night when I'd finally opened the last door and my head began to clear. I lay there on the floor for a long time trying to catch my breath and remember which memories were my own and which were his.

I don't know why Borris gave me that box. It wasn't to make me feel better. You might have thought I'd feel empathy toward him after living through his life so vividly, but I'd never hated anyone so much in my life. How dare he taunt me like that, showing me what happiness was without any means to achieve my own. I even seethed over how freely he'd given me the box, a sign of his conceit and shamelessness over what should have been his most private secrets.

Panting from my bitterness and anger, I saw my own breath form clouds like frost in the air. Horrified and enthralled, I watched the dark clouds pour from my lungs, swirling down to fill the opened doors below. I don't know what experiences from my own life were draining into that box, but I didn't move away or try to stop it. Instead I deliberately focused on every pain, every humiliation, every despair that I've ever encountered. Let him taste my resentment toward him, let him choke on my hatred, I had nothing to hide. The more I focused on my suffering, the thicker the black smoke poured from my lungs. I didn't stop even when I coughed and hacked through the exertion, not until every drawer throbbed and boiled with the greasy darkness like oil staining the air.

I don't know what I was expecting to happen when I gave him back the box. Some tortured fantasy hoped that he would suffocate in my torment, forgetting himself as I had done when I breathed in his happiness. Somehow I thought these thoughts would destroy him as they had me over my years, and that with him gone I could take his place. His wife, his children, I loved them more deeply than my own family after having lived through him. I wanted them, and I would make them mine, although I didn't know how. But my obsession over my own misery so filled my thoughts that night that I didn't allow myself to think too closely. It was all I could do just to stay alive until the morning when I brought the box back to his door.

"What was it like? Did you feel like you went on a vacation?" he asked blearily into the early morning light. He stood in the door in his underwear, not even bothering to dress himself after I had already seen him so intimately. His smugness, his self-assurance, I abhorred it all.

"To Hell and back," I told him.

I didn't wait for him to discover my gift on his own. I pushed my way inside, flinging open every single door as I went.

Even a life filled with pain might be endured, so long as there is space for healing between the incidents. But here with one hurt after the next all thrown in together, the room immediately became intoxicated with the roiling black smoke. An entire lifetime's worth of injustice and torment, all experienced simultaneously.

Borris looked surprised and confused at first, but within seconds he had fallen to his knees and was gagging for air. I held the box upside-down over his head, letting the black waves roll over him. Then I pressed the box down on top of him when he collapsed to the ground.

I heard a scream, clear and pure, cutting through the darkness of my mind. Borris' wife standing on the stairs, but it wasn't just a woman I knew, not just a neighbor. When she screamed it was my love who suffered, and it cut me more deeply than my own pain ever had. I saw her as I had on the beach, on her wedding, and every passionate night I had experienced from Borris' memories. For that brief moment when her scream cut through the noise, I was aware of what I was doing. Suddenly I was horrified by my raw emotions which flooded the white-washed halls.

"Be still, my love—" I began, cutting myself off as the horrible realization dawned that she barely knew me despite my love for her.

I wrenched the box away from Borris, still billowing with smoke, and I fled. Straight out the door, box clutched to my chest, acrid smoke souring the air as I went.

Now that the doors are closed, now that the smoke has stopped, my head has begun to clear again. I won't be able to erase the memories of that darkness, but I do plan to return the box and apologize one day. One day, but not yet. Not until I've learned how to fill those doors with happiness as he has done, not to erase the pain, but to give it meaning as that which taught me to start again.

## The Wolf and The Raven: Part 1

My name is Sara Claver, and I'm supposed to be at home in Wisconsin working on my dissertation for my biology degree. Instead I'm freezing my ass off in a dive bar in Alaska, almost a week into the hunt for my PhD advisor Robert Olsky. It's not my fault there isn't an internet connection in the remote village he hid away in. I tried to be accommodating by mailing back and forth my paper, but then the letters stopped returning altogether.

"You could have at least called. I don't know how you got your wife to stay in this beastly place." I glared accusingly at him across the table, my arms wrapped around myself for warmth. It was so cold that the glass was frosted inside and out. The gloomy little den felt like it belonged to a wild creature. I couldn't

## Sleepless Nights

imagine why anyone would live here unless they weren't allowed to be anywhere else."

"My wife is always looking out for me. Besides, you were doing fine without me," Dr. Olsky grunted, not looking up from the steaming wooden mug he clutched in both hands. His white and wispy manicured beard had grown immense and unruly in the months since I'd seen him last at the University.

"Two planes, second one was held together by spit and glue," I complained.

Robert chuckled and nodded, taking a long drink. I think he had clam chowder in there.

"Then the bus. Then I had to rent a jeep and navigate that switchback road that a caribou would have gone around. Do you think I would have gone through all that if I didn't need you?"

"I didn't ask you to come here," Dr. Olsky growled, wiping his beard with the back of his arm in a way that I couldn't imagine the dainty professor doing before he left. He looked exactly like the locals now, as much animal as man. But then his dark eyes darted up at me, the same old intelligent twinkle buried deep within the weathered and weary face.

"Why didn't you come back when you were supposed to?" I felt myself growing annoyed at the bitterness in my voice. Here I was like this was all some grand conspiracy against me when it was clear Robert had endured some great suffering in the frozen north. "You should have had enough time to track every wolf in Alaska by now."

"Maybe I've got rabies." Dr. Olsky chuckled again, the muffled sound slowly fading as his thick eyebrows drew together in a thunderous scowl. "The gray wolves are smarter than I am though. They can smell when the land is dying, and they run from it while humans linger. I don't think there are any wolves left here anymore."

"Land is dying? What are you talking about? This place is as far from civilization as you can get. I didn't even know there were forests this thick in North America."

"But did you see any animals on your drive?" Dr. Olsky asked. The pleading was in his voice now, his eyes wide and desperate as his thin neck strained toward me.

"Well, no, not next to the road—"

"But did you see any foot prints? Any ravens or gyrfalcons nesting in the branches? Any hunters or fishermen left? Or was it just... quiet?"

Robert's eyes slid away from me, staring over my shoulder and prompting me to turn. A man dressed in gray and white camouflage was watching us from the end of the bar, his face inscrutable behind his small round spectacles and bushy mustache.

"There's one hunter left," the man said, standing stiffly and moving to join us at our corner table.

"Go home, Hank," Dr. Olsky said wearily. "You too, Sara. Go home, and leave me be."

"He knows where the wolves are going, but he isn't saying," Hank said, clapping Robert on the shoulder with a meaty hand. The professor tried to lean away, but Hank held on. "Aren't you going to introduce me to your daughter, old man?" he added, grinning in my direction.

"Not my daughter, she's one of my students—" Dr. Olsky began.

"Coming all the way to visit your icy ass? Evening sweetheart, my name's Hank Saxton, and I'm the closest thing Robert has to a friend up here. He still won't tell me a damn thing about what's happening to this place though. Ain't that right, buddy?"

Robert Olsky just scowled at the hand on his shoulder until it finally dropped away. "Go home," he repeated softly into his beard. "I won't help you chasing something that doesn't want to be found."

"Won't or can't?" Hank asked, grinning down at Robert who stubbornly refused to look at him. "Maybe your student will find what you missed then. Moose, reindeer, brown bears, dall sheep, musk ox—I'll still see them from time to time, although not as many as I used to. The gray wolves though—this place used to be teeming with them, and I haven't seen one for ages. They aren't just wandering off either, there ain't no tracks leaving this place. What do you say, Sara? I can show you where the wolf lairs used to be, and maybe you can tell me what's been happening to them."

"No!" The clatter of Dr. Olsky's wooden chair spinning to the floor gave me a jolt. He was standing now, mad eyes darting in every direction as though surrounded by invisible foes. "Sara isn't part of this. I forbid you to stay. Leave this place tonight, and tell the University I'm not coming back."

"I put too much effort into getting here to give up that easy," I protested. "Okay Hank, you've got yourself a deal. Tomorrow morning we'll check out the lairs and see what we can find."

"That's more like it." Hank grinned broadly. "Sorry your old man's too embarrassed to admit he can't figure out—"

"I'm coming too," Dr. Olsky interrupted fiercely. "Hell of a trouble you'll get into without me, messing with things you don't understand."

---

"WHAT'S a hunter like you want the wolves back for, anyway? Don't they compete with you for game?" I asked Hank as I drove the jeep the next day. He was sitting up front with me while Robert sat in the back: arms crossed, scowling and muttering to himself.

"What's the fun of hunting something that can't fight back?" Hank asked cheerfully. "I'm in it for the sport and the pelt, not the food, and I take no pride in shooting something in the back."

"We're going too far," Robert grumbled behind us. "We should have parked by now."

"You lost the right to give directions when you made it clear you stopped caring about finding them," Hank shot back. "Keep on going, as far as you can before the trees get too thick."

I pulled off on the side of the trail anyway, trusting Dr. Olsky to know best.

"Fine, I don't mind the walk," Hank said, hopping out of the jeep.

"See the raven watching us?" Dr. Olsky said in a hushed tone.

The large black bird was tilting its head from one side to the other, evidently inspecting us from the branches of a nearby spruce tree.

"Ravens and wolves often hunt together up here," Dr. Olsky continued. "They'll lead the pack on the hunt, helping them find prey from the air, or flushing them out from the underbrush. Then the wolves will share their victory after they've moved in for the kill. Some ravens will even form close personal friendships with individual wolves, forming pairs that stay together for years on end."

Hank circled around the jeep to get his long rifle from the trunk. He plodded resolutely through the trees without waiting for us, apparently sure of where he was going. Dr. Olsky didn't follow though—he was just cocking his head back and forth, watching the raven watch us.

"Do you think there are wolves around then?" I asked nervously. "Or do you think the bird is just hanging around where they used to be?"

The raven leapt off its branch and fluttered into the air briefly before settling back down a little farther away.

"Hold on, Hank. It looks like we're going this way," Dr. Olsky called, moving to follow the raven. His voice was sharp and clear in the frosty air. It was loud enough to make me flinch, but Dr. Olsky just smiled patiently. "Don't worry about the wolves finding us. Trust me, they're all gone."

"A pack used to have a lair around here…" Hank called back reluctantly through the thick trees.

A loud caw resonated from the raven as it fluttered to another tree.

"Come, Hank," Dr. Olsky repeated. "She says you're not welcome there."

"Who says?" Hank asked, pushing through the frosted ferns to join us once more.

I stared uncertainly at Dr. Olsky, unaccustomed to such cryptic statements from the professor. His eyes were locked on the raven though, and he would have left us both behind if we didn't follow him. Then he cupped his hands over his mouth, returning the cawing sound toward the raven.

"He's a doctor, you say?" Hank asked me. I nodded, shrugging to indicate I was as confused about his behavior as he was.

We continued in this manner for some time, the raven always waiting for us to approach before launching off to the next tree. There was snow on the ground, but it wasn't thick enough to make the hiking difficult. More snow filled the branches of the trees, and the farther we went along this trail, the larger and older the trees became. Hank kept quipping that we were going the wrong way, wondering what the point of coming along with us if we didn't listen to him. I reassured him that I trusted Dr. Olsky, although I must admit my faith was shaken as the old man continued cawing back at the raven whenever it spoke to us.

Presently the mighty spruce trees began to grow more weak and sickly, with dead branches replacing the thick green ones behind us. The undergrowth around us was growing thin and dry as well, and this trend continued as we progressed until nothing but dead trees with thin skeletal branches grasped toward the pale yellow sun.

"Is this what you meant by the land dying?" I asked Dr. Olsky.

He turned away from the raven we were following and stared me straight in the face. His neck quivered as though he was about to speak, but no sound came out. Curiously, he cocked his head to the side just as the bird had done, and then a squawking, croaking caw emerged from his throat. Nodding to himself as though satisfied with that answer, he turned away from me again to hurry after the raven.

I was beginning to consider changing my vote of confidence and asking Hank to lead instead when I saw small shapes flitting through the trees in the distance. Weary of the dead landscape and encouraged by any sign of life, I pushed ahead through the dry underbrush to try and identify the creatures. The raven overhead began to caw again—or maybe it was Olsky, I can't be sure—but I was getting tired of both of them and pressed on. I didn't stop until I saw a rustle in the bushes directly ahead of me. The sight so close knocked me back into reality, reminding me how deep into the Alaskan wilderness I really was.

I started scrambling back towards the others at once, but not before the dry brush parted to reveal the largest, most grizzled gray wolf I had ever seen in my life. It's fur was matted and smeared with ancient blood, yellow eyes bore through me with ferocious intensity, and the parted mouth bristled with fangs as long as my fingers. The skin above its nose drew back into a snarl, and the creature leapt forward with such graceful deadly purpose that I knew instantly it would be impossible to run. I felt my body collapsed into a quivering heap without the strength to defend myself or resist in the slightest. Then a gunshot broke the air, so close and so loud that I threw myself to the ground and instinctively covered my head with my hands.

"Sara! Move!" Dr. Olsky shouted above me. Rough hands grasped me under my arms and hurled me to my feet, hauling me back toward where Hank was lying on the ground with his long gun. More dark shapes darting through the

## Sleepless Nights

trees—I counted at least four as we huddled together and watched them circle us.

"Give them another warning shot," Dr. Olsky said firmly. "Don't try to hit one—just give them a good scare."

"First shot wasn't a warning shot," Hank grunted.

"Well you missed then," Dr. Olsky snapped.

I thought he must be right, because the large wolf was still standing exactly where I first saw it, its face still warped into a feral snarl. Then the wolf began to advance, and as it moved I clearly saw the devastating impact where the bullet had entered its body near the shoulder. Instead of bleeding, the wound looked more like someone sank a pickaxe into the ice, exploding open a hole bristling with shards of frozen blood and bone.

Another gunshot—but the creature didn't budge. Then I realized that Hank had fired at a second wolf which was running along our flank. An explosion of broken shards lanced through the air, catching and spinning the light in hundreds of directions as the creature sprinted past. In the brief silence that followed I realized no sound emerged, even from the first snarling wolf still advancing toward us. No whimper of pain, no predatory howl. The deadly emptiness was only broken by the cawing of the raven overhead, long raucous notes echoing through the static moment that never seemed to end.

All at once the wolves turned and fled back through the dead forest. Hank took another shot at one of them when it first began to sprint, but he didn't fire again when it was clear they were all running away. Hank was the first of us to rise after it seemed like they were gone, and he swiftly strode through the trees to where the second wolf had been flanking us.

"Dr. Olsky?" I whispered, barely trusting myself to breathe. "Those are the missing wolves, aren't they? What weren't you telling us?"

The professor looked me in the eye again, and the horrible cawing sound rising in his throat made me start to violently tremble in a way I hadn't even done when the wolf was snarling at me. A moment later Hank returned, holding his long gun in one hand, the other holding up a bristling furry tail over two feet long. He threw the tail down at our feet, and I reeled backward from the rancid odor.

"Rotten through," Hank said, "though it's not as bad as it would have been without the cold. That animal has been dead for a long time."

Dr. Olsky quietly rose, scanning the branches until he found the raven once more. Then without a word the old man began to jog after the bird which promptly took flight as though begging us to follow.

"We're going back to town," Hank said, his voice trembling slightly.

"I'm not leaving Dr. Olsky out here, and I've got the keys," I replied, hurrying to catch up with the professor through the dead trees.

## The Wolf and The Raven: Part 2

I could take the cold. I could take the nauseating stench of rotten meat from the thawing wolf tail slung over my shoulder. I could take the silent isolation of the forest, and the numbing fear of the impossible creatures that had attacked us.

"This was a mistake. We don't belong here," Dr. Olsky said.

What I couldn't take? The hopeless surrender in the professor's voice.

Hands on his knees, panting great clouds of frozen breath, the old man stared up at the raven which leered down at us from the nearby branches.

"What fools we were, to think we could understand the secrets of life." Dr. Olsky continued to stare at the bird, not turning as Hank and I caught up with him beside the frozen pond he'd stopped beside. "You want to know why I never returned to the University? Well there's your answer. I used to think that life was an intricate machine, a complex game that one could learn the rules to. But what point is there in applying reason to that which defies it? Why bother to study what man was not meant to comprehend?"

"You led us away from the caves on purpose, didn't you?" I asked. "Is this what you were afraid we'd find?"

Dr. Olsky nodded uncertainly, although I detected a sense of hesitation as though there was more he wished to say, if only he could overpower his own dread to do so.

"Keys, missy," Hank said, his voice cracking around the edges. "We'll never be able to think this through knowing those creatures are out there watching us. Let's all get back to the bar and have another drink, and see if we can't learn anything from that tail."

"I want to see the caves," I protested. "And what about the raven? Don't you think it's trying to tell us something?"

"She already showed us her intentions when she lured us into her trap," Dr. Olsky dismissed. "Hank is right. We should all leave these woods, and never return." He placed his hands on the small of his back and stretched before turning to trudge through the snow the way we came.

I didn't like that we were giving up that easily, but I was excited to examine the rotten tail. On the way back to town I voiced a range of tentative hypotheses to the professor, ranging from skin-eating bacteria, to pain-blocking mutations, or even chemical reactions to some sort of environmental waste.

"I mean, no one really thinks the wolves were dead, right?" I said, unable to hide the pleading tone from my voice.

Hank insisted on driving this time, and Dr. Olsky in the passenger seat didn't reply. He was slouched low, watching the raven swooping above the graveyard of trees as it followed us down the winding road.

The pervading silence which greeted our entry to town made me feel like we never left the forest. There wasn't a single other car on the road, and I didn't see any lights on inside the houses despite the dark rolling clouds which made the midday noon feel like twilight.

"I've never seen it so dark during the day," I commented.

"Expecting a storm, I reckon," Hank said, shifting uncomfortably in his seat. "We have to generate our own electricity up here, so don't be surprised no one is wasting our diesel early."

"I'm not bothered by the dark," I lied. "So how about that drink then? First round is on me, as thanks for taking me out there."

"Second round is on you too, for getting your ass saved from the wolves," Hank laughed. The sound couldn't persist in the frozen air, breaking and falling away into an uneasy silence.

"The raven is still following us," Dr. Olsky grunted. He was slouched down in his seat so he could get a better angle at the sky.

"Well then it knows where to find us at the pub, but that don't mean it's getting any." Hank forced a broad grin, glancing at me from the corner of his eye. It felt like he was looking for reassurance, which felt ridiculous, especially since I had none to give.

There were lights on inside the bar though, and I was beginning to feel better as we pulled into the parking lot. I was looking forward to some hot chowder and maybe a whiskey to relax, and all my scientific hypotheses for what we'd seen that day were stating to run through my mind again. The events of that morning were already beginning to feel like a bad dream, to the point where I almost found myself laughing when I jumped out of the jeep to charge up the steps to the pub.

I didn't make it two steps before I glimpsed the shadow prowling around the edge of the building. The monstrous shape looked almost like a horse at first, but the matted fur frozen into clumps and spikes left no doubt. The wolf and I stared at each other, neither making a move. I was the first to make a sound.

"Get back in the jeep," I whispered with all the breath I could muster.

"Not before I get myself a big mug of—" Hank's voice stopped abruptly. He must have seen it too.

Slowly, cautiously, I opened the car door and slipped back inside. The wolf turned its head to watch me, and I could see a great hollow place in the side of its neck where all the flesh had been torn away from some ancient wound. Its white spinal cord was clearly visible, glinting in the light from the window.

"Two more," Dr. Olsky said softly. "Either end of the street. Start driving."

"Where?" Hank asked.

The gigantic creature lurking around the pub wall turned away from us to peer inside a window. It didn't even need to get onto its hind legs to be able to look inside. Then it turned toward us once more, settling into a crouch in preparation to spring.

"Doesn't matter. Just go!" Dr. Olsky snapped.

The jeep roared to life, churning through the snow as it spun out of the parking lot. The wolf behind us sprang into action immediately, launching from its crouch to fly down the road at a terrifying pace. The wolves at the ends of the street turned like clockwork, racing between the houses to flank us on either side.

I watched the speedometer in disbelief as we approached 40 MPH as the wolves continued to keep pace with us. The jeep was skidding back and forth on the icy roads, and it didn't seem like we could go much faster without losing control of the vehicle. The thought of the ice spinning us off the road into a ditch, helplessly trapped while the monsters closed in from every side was too much to bear. My heart felt like it was beating out of my chest, but my blood ran cold when Dr. Olsky shouted:

"Stop the car!"

"Are you out of your damn mind?" Hank shouted back. The sound reverberated in the enclosed space, but I don't think I could have heard anything spoken more quietly over the sound of the engine, the skidding tires, and my own pounding blood.

"Two people!" Dr. Olsky replied, pounding on his window hard enough to make it rattle in its frame. "We can't leave them out there!"

Sure enough, an elderly man and a woman in large overcoats were both standing on one of the dark street corners. They were huddled together as though for warmth, seemingly oblivious to the wolves racing to catch up with us.

"Not stopping," Hank shot back. "Not for a hundred miles."

Dr. Olsky reached over and smashed the horn, blaring at the couple as we roared past. They didn't even flinch though, barely moving a muscle as they turned to follow us with their gaze.

"Maybe they're frozen…" I began, but the words caught in my throat as the wolves came barreling toward them. I opened one of the windows despite the cold, sticking my head out to watch behind us. I shouted to them in warning, but I might as well have been speaking another language. In a moment the animals would be on top of them, but the couple just kept looking after us as though the racing wolves weren't even worth a moment of their attention.

The monstrous wolf with its open spine was the first to reach them. It smashed between the couple in its single-minded pursuit of our car. The people swayed out of the way, never once taking their eyes off us as the wolf bound on, unceasing and untiring.

More people were coming out of the dark houses now to line the street and watch us pass. Some were bundled against the cold, others in bathrobes, or even minimally dressed in undergarments despite the frozen air. More wolves had joined in the hunt as well, slinking between the houses or watching us from behind snowy banks with eager and unified fascination.

"They don't mind the cold, don't mind the wolves, Gell," Hank said. "What happened to this place while we were gone?"

"It's like they don't even see them," I agreed, equally mystified. I rolled up my window against the cold, just as the professor was rolling his down to stick his head out the window. "Dr. Olsky? What are you doing?"

"The raven," he replied. "She's still overhead, but she's heading back toward the woods now. I think we should follow her this time, Hank. I think we should let her lead us to the lair."

A long, low howl began to rise from the houses behind us, rapidly spreading and being taken up ahead. The sound chilled me to my core. It might have actually been a relief if it were the ghostly animals who finally made a sound, but heads thrown back, staring into the dark sky as the snow began to fall around them, it was the men and women of the town lining the street who were all howling with one chilling voice.

"Bloody Hell," Hank said, his voice somewhere between terror and reverence.

"What fool I was," Dr. Olsky reiterated, "to think blind ignorance would be enough to shield us from what haunts this place."

## The Wolf and The Raven: Part 3

Hardly a word was spoken between us as we wound through the icy mountain road once more. Hank drove with grim determination while Dr. Olsky made one phone call after another from the backseat. I didn't need to ask to know he was trying to call people he knew in town. The first three attempts only found an answering machine, while the fourth picked up to a guttural, snarling reply like something halfway between a man and a wolf. We all listened to the halting, growling words which were not words for a few seconds before Dr. Olsky ended the call. He did not make a fifth attempt.

"Is your wife alright?" I asked, dreading the answer. Then hurriedly: "At least the wolves weren't attacking people."

"That's because there's no people left to attack," Dr. Olsky replied somberly. "Whatever is happening to the wolves is happening to the people too."

"You're not saying they're all dead, are you?" Hank asked, his eyes alternating between the road and the raven flying overhead.

"They're moving, aren't they? I don't think we'll make any sense of this phenomenon while clinging to such primitive superstitions as life and death. They've become something else entirely."

"We could just keep driving," I ventured meekly. "Never look back. Never speak of it. Or we could call for help, and maybe they could send in the national guard or something."

But Dr. Olsky was shaking his head. "It was one thing when it was just the wolves, but it's spreading. Do you want to see what it's like for a host of armed men to start howling like the devil? No, the raven is looking out for us. She will show us what we need to know, and then we can decide from there."

The storm was growing fiercer by the time the raven stopped. The wind was enough to whip the snow diagonally across the mountain slope, and the dead branches of the looming trees did nothing to protect us from the elements. The raven huddled against a trunk to shield from the wind, croaking feebly with exhaustion as we cautiously exited the jeep.

"Thank you love, you've kept us safe," Dr. Olsky said to the bird, his words dispersed by the wind into the gathering night. And then he cupped his hands and cawed at it, a long harsh sound that set my teeth on edge. The raven launched from the branch at once to settle near a small indentation in the snow on the ground.

"Why do you keep doing that?" I asked, though I was afraid to speculate the reason.

I was almost relieved when Dr. Olsky didn't answer and instead stomped his way to the indentation in the snow where he began to sweep the heel of his boot to clear the ice and snow. A small opening began to form by the time Hank and I joined him. I looked around for the raven, but the bird was nowhere to be seen amidst the spinning eddies of snow. Then glancing back, just in time to see the old professor down on his hands and knees, and then flat onto his stomach as he crawled his way into the narrow opening he had made in the ground.

Hank clutched his rifle to his chest as he dropped to the ground to crawl after him, and I knew I had no choice but to follow. Once I got past the initial claustrophobia of the small opening, it felt good to know the route was too narrow for one of the monstrous wolves to follow us without a good deal of digging. The air was rapidly growing warmer as well, and soon the space began to open wider as the ice and snow around us gave way to rock and frozen mud.

Hank turned on a flashlight up ahead that he was holding with his teeth, and every once in a while he'd glance back to check on me. The next flash of light startled me when it revealed the rock had seamlessly given way to a clean white tiling, like one might find in a hotel bathroom. The space widened considerably after that, and soon the three of us were able to comfortable stand in the widening cave.

"This is no lair," Hank spoke first, his voice cracking from the strain.

I stared incredulously at the padded arm chair in the corner of the room. At the walls lined with shelves, stuffed with musty leather bound books cramming the place from floor to ceiling. Dr. Olsky strode across the room to the lamp beside the chair, and turning it on revealed the extent of the comfortable study. There was a large wooden desk on the opposite end, its surface cluttered with glass jars where floating jaw bones, eyes, and other drifting organs were suspended in a thick yellowish fluid. Some looked like they belonged to animals, while others looked disturbingly familiar to those I encountered within human cadavers during my own studies.

"I told you I never intended you to come here, Sara," Dr. Olsky said as he crossed the room to sit in the wooden chair behind the desk. "I told you not to search for the lair. But you have taken after me too strongly, never knowing when you have gone too far."

Scratching, pawing, sniffing—behind us the way we crawled in. Had the wolves found us already? I saw Hank tense as he heard it as well, and he instinctively swung his rifle toward the sound. Then readjusting, he pointed the gun at Dr. Olsky.

"You've been hiding too much, old man," the hunter growled. "What do you know about this place?"

"I know that the wolves really did live here, once," Dr. Olsky mused, lowering himself to stare into one of the glass jars containing the lower half of a jaw. The teeth were too large and pointed to be human, but neither were they of sufficient length to belong to a wolf.

"I never intended for them to end up like this though," the professor continued with resignation. "I thought I could keep them alive, as I flayed one nerve, one muscle, one layer of tissue at a time until I found the line between life and death. Or replacing one tissue with another, subtly changing one living form to another."

The scratching was growing closer outside. And then a howl, low and throaty, although whether it came from a man or a beast I could not tell.

"But the University kept calling for me to return, and my research was going too slowly," Dr. Olsky sighed. "I thought I could hasten my results by inserting a virus to automate some of my slowest alterations. I never thought it was possible for the humans to begin to change. For my wife…"

"Call them off," Hank pleaded, his rifle swaying between Dr. Olsky and the entrance we crawled through. "Give them the antidote. Whatever it is, make it stop."

But Dr. Olsky only shook his head, a wistful smile tugging at the corners of his white beard. "You too have eaten the meat, and dwelled amidst the cursed. I see you shaking already. Do not fight the transformation. The end is nothing to be feared when the distinction between life and death has been destroyed."

The frozen ground leading into the lair collapsed from the digging in a rush of snow and bitter wind. The gun went off, the reverberating blast magnifying in the enclosed space so that its echoes merged with unearthly howl. The bullet pulverized the jaw of the wolf that made it through first, but its cold yellow eyes never blinked as it continued its lunge.

"Don't fight them!" Dr. Olsky shouted, the tension in his voice making it sound almost like the cawing of the raven once more. "They are your brothers!"

Paws and hands, side-by-side clawing the earth as the wolves and humans from the town swarmed into the small chamber. Clamoring over each other on all fours, the matted fur and filthy winter coats really did seem to flow together, one creature no different than the next. The howls rose in their throats, the timbers weaving and merging into one, the blasphemous ensemble of the living dead.

The gun went off again, and this time it was the professor who staggered back against the wall. He stared down at the bullet in his stomach, gingerly lifting his shirt to inspect the damage. The small neat hole was wedged between two of his ribs, spreading a network of cracks through his body as though he was made of ice. Revealed too was the thick patches of fur and twisted feathers which covered most of the professor's body.

"Death has become us!" Dr. Olsky howled with maniacal glee. "Do not fight your nature!"

There was nothing I could do but press myself to the shelves of books and close my eyes. To bear the wave of howls and screams, belonging to neither man nor beast, the living nor the dead. The frozen bodies piling into the room brought no heat, but rather seemed to drain it from the place until everything, even my thoughts, had grown numb.

And then in the pit of my misery and despair, a sound unlike the others broke through the madding fray. The croaking, cawing of the raven, untainted by the deforming influence. Pure and natural and insistent, the cawing continued as the maelstrom grew still around me. When at last I found the courage to open my eyes I saw the broken and bloody stump of a tail disappearing back up the tunnel. The clean white tiles were ruined with filth and blood, but the den was otherwise empty. Both Hank and Dr. Olsky must have followed the pack back to the surface.

Slowly, carefully, as though afraid each movement would cause my body to shatter, I followed them through the tunnel, into the stillness of the waiting night. The wind had stopped, though the snow was falling harder now. I heard the cawing of the raven again, this time farther off. Then the answer cry of howls as that monstrous pack of animals followed the bird's lead. I don't know for sure, but I think the bird must have been Mrs. Olsky's wife, doing all she could to bring me to this place where I might set things right.

I stood there a long time, watching the snow fill in our tracks. Then retreating back into the profane lair, I let the snow conceal the entrance and seal me away from the world I dare not return to. How could I risk ever going back to civilization, knowing I could spread the curse with me wherever I went?

Let the unnatural pack prowl through the dead trees, let them wander until the wind and the snow grinds them into dust. I will stay, and I will study, hoping that one day I find the secrets that have eluded my professor and reverse the changes. Or learning not, to spend forever here between life and death, my eternal curse to be the ignorance of their difference.

## Sleepless Nights

### What Doesn't Kill You Makes You Stronger

The will to power. That's all my boyfriend Jake ever talked about. Self-discipline, self-mastery, self-overcoming—as though he was his own arch nemesis, a constant battle against himself that could never be won.

I thought it was pretty admirable at first. Okay, well if I'm being honest, his incredible abs were what impressed me first, but it was that underlying spirit and dedication to his workout routine that made them possible. Jake was obsessed with this philosopher named Nietzsche. It was almost like a religion for him, complete with a little shrine of his books and a bobble-head doll that he meditated in front of every morning at 6 AM.

Jake was never satisfied with himself, no matter how hard he tried. He'd hate himself for ever eating a piece of junk food or candy, and he'd immediately force himself to do pushups if he ever slipped up. He was always reading, or studying for med school, or listening to audiobooks in the car, angry at himself if he ever felt like he was wasting his time. We couldn't even watch a movie together without him exercising through it.

"Life isn't supposed to be comfortable," he told me once. "Only weak people want comfort. It's supposed to hurt, and the more you can make it hurt, the stronger you'll become for enduring it."

I tried to be as supportive as I could, but it got pretty difficult at times as I watched how agitated and restless he'd become whenever we spent too much time together. I could see how important all these improvements were to him though, and all my friends were so jealous about how perfect he seemed. If he could try so hard all the time, then who was I to complain or hold him back?

It started getting worse when he took the MCAT admissions test and didn't do as well as he expected. He berated himself constantly, calling himself lazy, and stupid, and weak. I couldn't stand the way he spat the word "weak", like it was some unforgivable sin against God. He started sleeping less, waking up at 4 AM now, and starting every day with an icy cold shower just to prove to himself that he could take it. And whenever I began to question his behavior, however subtly, he'd flash that endearing smile of his and say something like:

"But I'm doing it all because I love you. So I can take care of you, so I'll be good enough for you. Aren't you proud of me for working so hard?"

And of course I'd say I was already proud of him, but it was never enough.

Then came the day when I caught him running a razor blade between his fingers. I screamed to see the blood, and Jake panicked too, like he was embarrassed to be caught like that. He said he was punishing himself for having taken a night off from studying. But he as only doing it because he wanted to train himself to be better, and he only wanted to be better because he loved me so much.

On his knees, blood running between his fingers, he clung onto my legs, repeating over and over how much he loved me. How much he needed me, and how dark the world was without me. He confessed how desperately afraid he was that I'd leave if he didn't get into med school, and he made me promise to keep encouraging him to try harder, no matter what. And if he could put himself through all that discomfort for me, then I must be able to endure it too if I loved him back.

Having him need me like that made me weak, although I'd never admit that to him. So I looked away, and pretended everything was alright. Because he loved me, truly and completely, and if it ever got too bad, that love would be enough to make him stop.

I thought things were going to get better after that. Jake started paying me a lot more attention, constantly being affectionate and cuddling up to me. I kept asking if he felt like he was wasting too much time with me, but he reassured me that I was the most important thing in the world to him. He said then that he didn't even care if he got into med school anymore, as long as he had me, nothing else mattered.

I vividly remember the night I was falling asleep in his arms as he stroked my hair. He was whispering a thousand sweet nothings, how much he loved me, needed me, and then hidden amidst the other words slipped:

"Losing you is going to be the most painful thing in the world."

Half-asleep, I mumbled that he was never going to lose me.

"Shh, no, I will," he whispered. "And it's going to hurt, but that's okay, because it's supposed to. Because what doesn't kill me makes me stronger."

I felt his arms tightening around me, but I was still so sleepy and wasn't quite registering what he was saying.

"I was so weak to think giving up easy things like junk food and warm water would make me strong," he whispered. "I don't need those like I need you though. No, there is no strength like giving up the thing you love most."

I was fully awake now, although I didn't move as his arm tightened around my neck. I couldn't believe what I was hearing. Even when it became harder to breathe, I thought he just loved me so much and didn't realize how physically powerful he had become. By the time I started to kick and squirm it was already too late.

"That's even better, I want you to fight back," Jake whispered, his biceps bulging and trembling as the pressure increased.

I was choking and gasping, but I couldn't physically overpower him, and knowing he wanted me to try made it so much worse. I lay still for as long as I could, until I felt the hot wet tears running down his face land on mine and knew that he was really going to kill me. Then my body started to flail and spasm on its own, a desire to live too deep and powerful to control. My fingers dug into his arm, but he only grinned like he enjoyed the pain. The grip tightened after every shallow breath like a boa constrictor, until my throat had closed down to a pinhole.

"Please..." with the last of my air.

"I want you to beg. I want you to make this as hard on me as you possibly can." His breath was hot as his tears on my face, terror and pain and ecstasy all competing as his features twisted between flickering emotions.

I couldn't breathe. Couldn't get out. No one was going to hear me, or save me. I couldn't fight him, couldn't reason with him. My vision was starting to swim, and I thought I was going to pass out when suddenly his grip slackened just enough for me to draw another breath.

"I said beg!" he almost shouted, spittle flying into my face along with his tears.

"You're wrong! You don't love me!" I gasped.

"I wouldn't do this if I didn't love you more than anything," he snarled.

"You love yourself more, or you'd never do this to me. If you really want to be strong, if you really want to destroy the thing you love most, then destroy yourself and let me go."

I didn't expect it to work, but it did. He started smiling, and then laughing, throwing his head back in a savagely maniacal way. Then he rolled me away from him and, grabbing his keys and wallet, left without another word. But I could hear him laughing all the way down the hall of the apartment building, laughter sick with heaving and coughing as though his whole body convulsed with every cackle.

I rushed up to lock my door the moment he was gone, but he never came back. I don't know what happened to Jake—I made it a point never to look, afraid of what he might have done. I hope that he learned to love himself, but if he didn't, then I hope at least he never again lied and convinced himself that he was capable of loving someone else.

## The Lies of Eyes and Ears

My little boy is in sixth grade, and his teacher is a madman. I admit that I have been pretty busy with work and haven't been paying much attention to what he's been learning, but I was shocked and horrified when he said one day:

"Mom, can we go to Disneyland this week? Because afterward it will be too late."

I asked him why it would be too late, and he casually replied, "Because everyone is going to be dead after that."

He was only repeating what "Mr. Y" had told him in class. Apparently there's some kind of alien purge coming up where they're going to start killing people and using their bodies as puppets. It wasn't just this either—the more questions I started asking, the more ridiculous ideas I found lurking around in my boy's head.

"Oh yeah, the birds are just there to keep an eye on us," he told me. "It's so they know who to keep and who to throw away."

Or—"I didn't think planes were really real. Aren't they just projections on the screen in the sky?"

His homework was no better. Page after page of dutifully copying down the most insane nonsense I've ever heard in my life. Government chemical castrations, secret cities hidden in volcanos, winter storms caused by alien weaponry—all mixed in with actual history and science as though one entry was just as valid as the next. I was absolutely furious. Notebook in hand, I drove down to the school that afternoon to make sure Mr. Y never taught another day in his life.

"Ah. Mhm. I see," the principle mused as I flipped through the notebook in front of him. He had a drooping sort of face with heavy eyelids that were almost closed over his glazed and listless eyes. "Yes yes, I do believe I see the issue."

"You do believe, do you?" I raged. "I want him gone. Today, this instant, now and forever."

"That's a bit of an overreaction, don't you think?" The principle said. I was at a loss for words as he continued, "Your son is a very bright student. Sure there's some misspellings, and he's missing a few pages about the history of the volcanic cities, but the solution to that is more school. Not less."

"I'm talking about getting rid of Mr. Y, not my son," I said in disbelief.

"Oh, I hadn't realized," the principle said with a far-off-misty look. "I'm sorry, but what was the problem then? If you're feeling insecure about not knowing the things in your boy's lesson, then I know some excellent adult education programs—"

I couldn't argue with him. What was the point of trying to reason with someone who had so clearly lost their mind? No wonder teachers like Mr. Y were allowed to stay in the school with a lunatic like that for the principle. I left without another word, intent upon bringing my battle to the school board.

There were seven members of my local school board, but I couldn't get hold of any of them on the phone. I tried calling the city about it, but I just got redirected to something that told me about the public comment period at the board meeting where I was allowed to voice my concerns. Fortunately it was coming up next Tuesday, so I decided to keep my boy home until then so his mind wouldn't be any more polluted than it already was.

I called several other parents, and they were all just as angry and confused as I was. They all promised to be there with me at the board meeting, but come Tuesday I didn't see any of them in that dank little office at the Learning and Support Center.

The seven board members were here though. I wanted to speak right away, but the public comments weren't until the end of the meeting so I had to sit

## Sleepless Nights

through the dreadful affair. Dry old men and women with mean little faces, I thought, although maybe I was being unfair just because I was so anxious to speak.

They talked about cafeteria nutrition, and standardized tests, and all manner of boring day-to-day items. When it was finally my turn, I stepped up behind the podium, nervously watching all those beady little eyes tracking my motions. The content of my remarks were so outlandish compared to their dry and practical matters that I was half-afraid they'd laugh me right of the room.

"Did any of you know that the principle believes in lies?" I began. I explained to them everything that had happened, and to their credit none of them laughed or interrupted in the slightest. They all studied me very seriously, taking notes as I finished with, "… and that's why he needs to be replaced, along with all the teachers who believe this nonsense."

The school board all looked at each other gravely. "I believe there's been a terrible misunderstanding," an elderly lady with tiny spectacles commented at last. "You appear to be referring to a class on how to spot conspiracy theories and propaganda. If your son seriously believes anything about volcanic cities and spying birds, then we will certainly review the class materials and teachers."

"Oh, well that's good. As long as the staff don't really believe it…"

"As for the alien purge at the end of the week," the woman continued sternly, "that date is entirely obsolete and wrong. We've been dead for years already, haven't we?"

In unison, the six other board members all nodded and grunted their acknowledgements. The heavy lids, the glassy eyes—it wasn't just the principle. Now that I was close to them at the podium, they all looked like they were on the edge between sleeping and wakefulness.

"Pardon?" I said, my voice dry and hoarse.

"I do take affront to the word 'puppet' though," one of the men said through flabby, warbling jowls. "I think of the body more like a host, a symbiotic partnership."

"Quite right, for their own good, really," another chimed in.

"Such foolishness they would get up to without our help," another added drowsily. A long line of drool was starting to slip from the corner of his mouth. Before my eyes a tooth slid out along with it, clattering onto the desk in front of him. The elderly lady next to him picked up the tooth with a handkerchief, giving it to him which he accepted gratefully.

"If that is all the public comments, I would like to close the meeting by addressing the parking situation," the old woman said briskly.

As for my boy, he's going to be starting homeschooling for the foreseeable future.

## Flesh Zipper

I still have nightmares about how cleanly the flesh peeled back from the bone. Somehow I think it would have been easier if it had been messier, but I'm getting ahead of myself.

Let me first be clear about the fact that I don't have a sister. I mean that in the most literal way. My mother didn't give birth to a girl. My father didn't sleep with anyone who gave birth to a girl. It was just me, an only child, living with my parents and this girl who pretended to be part of the family.

My parents called Amanda their daughter, but they were lying. I know because it was only me in the house until I was almost seven, and then there was Amanda. My mother pretended she had given birth to Amanda, and that she had lived with us for our entire lives. Never mind that they only had photos of me before I was seven, they swore up and down that I must have been too young to remember her. But I was still so young when she showed up, and I didn't know any better, so I let the lie continue until it was too late to do anything about it.

If my parents had to choose one of us, they'd keep Amanda and get rid of me. She did better in school, had more friends, and played the piano better than me. She was happier, and smiled more, and it suited her more naturally than it did me. Everyone who didn't know her loved her, but I knew she didn't belong, and I hated her for it. And if they knew her secret, they would have hated her too.

My parents pretended not to notice the zipper on the back of Amanda's head. It started near the top of her head, a small golden link of metal with long thing golden teeth running all the way to the base of her skull. It was usually hidden behind her curly brown hair that looked so much like mine no-one would even guess we weren't related. Even when I pulled her hair back and pointed the zipper out, my parents only yelled at me for picking on my sister and told me to leave her alone.

I spent a lot of time wondering what was underneath that zipper. Sometimes I'd think there was a monster under there that put my parents under a spell. That it was just biding its time, hidden from the world, waiting for the moment I let my guard down to pull down the skin and attack. I asked her about it more than once, but she'd only grin and put a finger up to her lips, or wink conspiratorially in acknowledgement without resolution.

I think I could have learned to accept Amanda, zipper and all, if the rest of my school could have accepted me. But it wasn't fair that my friends only seemed to spend time with me as an excuse to be friends with her. Or whenever I was invited somewhere, it was as an afterthought, just "Amanda and her brother", like I wasn't even a person on my own.

It wasn't her fault though. As we got older, the less I hated her, and the more I hated myself for not being good enough. And the more I hated myself, the less effort I put in, forgetting to shower for a week at a time until my parents would basically force me. Every time Amanda got an award in school, or performed a piano recital, or did anything that I couldn't, I'd just hate myself more. It got to the point where I didn't even like leaving the house anymore. Let my parents and Amanda go out and be the perfect family, let them forget I even existed, all the better. At least when I was alone I wasn't feeling myself being constantly compared to her and coming up short.

Until the day when Amanda cornered me in my room and asked me:

"Why don't you just run away, if you hate it here so much?"

I told her that she's the one who should run away, and that I'd be fine once she was gone. I said it as a joke, but ever since I couldn't stop thinking about the idea. If I could just get rid of her, then my family would be whole again. I wouldn't need to keep fighting to be seen, always comparing myself to someone who never belonged here in the first place. It got to the point where I'd spent all day fantasizing about her getting lost in the woods, or hit by a car, or even abducted—anything to get her out of my head and out of my life for good.

I got my chance one day when my family went to the ocean together. I didn't want to go, and when I got there I didn't want to take my shirt off or even get in the water. But Amanda was jumping through the waves, and I could tell by how my parents looked at me how disappointed they were that I would never be carefree and happy like she was.

It was starting to get dark, but Amanda was having so much fun and didn't want to go back yet. My parents decided to leave us at the beach while they picked up some food and came back. I'd been in a dark mood all day and wanted to go sit in the car and not get out again, but I saw the unique opportunity that my ghastly thoughts couldn't steer away from.

The beach was emptying out as it grew dark, and I was alone with Amanda beside the endless ocean. I forced myself to go into the water for the first time that day, wading into the icy chill and hating every moment of it. Hating myself for what I was thinking, hating Amanda for not minding the cold, hating the world for bringing me to this point.

"I know what you're thinking," she told me when I waded out to join her.

I told her she was wrong, because I could barely even admit it to myself. I waited until she turned around to look at the crashing waves to grab her by the hair and force her head under the water. I think she really must have known it was coming though, because she didn't even fight me as I held her down. She just floated there so peacefully, and I don't know why but that made me even angrier.

Holding her beneath the waves by the back of her head, my finger scraped across the golden zipper hidden beneath her hair. I hadn't even thought about it since we were kids, but its presence pierced through my haze of bitterness and anger and filled me with an insatiable curiosity. I dragged her out of the water just long enough to grip the slick metal with my other hand, ripping it down through her skin to reveal the terrible secret she'd been hiding for so long.

The skin parted as cleanly as a wetsuit being stripped off, and I was amazed to see more skin and hair beneath it. And beneath that, a second golden zipper. Again I ripped it down, as well as the zipper after that, and the one deeper. There was blood leaking into the water from somewhere, but I was so intent upon the grizzly task that I couldn't stop stripping away one layer after the next. Hidden beneath each suit of flesh was always another, smaller one. It felt less like I was stripping away layers of skin and more like stripping back the years, until deep within the mess of blood there was only a child remaining.

But I kept pulling away the false skin, one layer at a time, until panting and gasping the final zipper parted the skin to reveal nothing underneath. Strewn around me were the ruins of all those different layers, with nothing at all at the center to reveal the monster I'd been searching for.

I stayed a long time in those icy waters, the layers of skin bobbing around me in the dark like discarded swimwear. I couldn't even imagine going back to shore and joining my parents for dinner, or pretending to help them search up and down the beach for someone they'd never find. Then slowly, carefully so as not to damage it, I took the largest outer layer of skin and stepped into it, my feet sliding all the way down to where her feet had been. And then up over my head, finding the skin fit me more naturally than my own did. All the way until it encompassed me completely, and then reaching behind to zip the golden zipper and seal myself within.

I don't know what became of me in those dark waters, but from that day on people called me Amanda and I didn't correct them. It felt wrong at first, but I liked how they looked at me, and how I looked at myself. My parents never asked what happened to their son, but I don't think that means they never cared about him. They recognized me for who I was, and who I was meant to be all along.

## Sacrifice Given, Sacrifice Taken

The Lord have mercy upon these poor sinners, even when the rest of the world has forgotten their names.

I am a priest, and every Sunday after I have delivered my sermon, I take my bible with me where it is needed most at my local county jail. There I will speak for as long as visitors are permitted to whoever will listen to me. Or for those who are not yet ready to hear the Word, I will sit quietly and be the ears while they pour their hearts to me and to God.

Some will speak confessions, begging forgiveness for what they have done. Others still seethe with anger for what the world has done to them, and I will sit quietly and let them speak until they have expelled their wrath. Hardest to bear

# Sleepless Nights

are those who weep before me as before their own mother, and no matter what they have done, it is my part to love them as their true mother no longer can.

But the strangest of all those I've visited, and always the most eager for my visit, was a man named Edgar Rover. Rather than dwell on mistakes or grievances, Edgar was only interested to speak about one thing: all the good he wishes to do once he is free.

"To serve others is the only path to redemption," I told him.

"To sacrifice myself for others is my only ambition," Edgar agreed. "I will work myself to death for the lowest beggar, and ask nothing in return."

"As the Lord has done, so shall you follow," I told him.

"To sacrifice yourself for your brother," Edgar replied, an eager glint in his eye like a small boy salivating over a cake. "That is the highest good there is, isn't it? And the more it hurts, the better you are for doing it, isn't that right? And if they don't appreciate what you've done for them, so much the better, because only a selfish person would help others to extract gratitude from them."

I had no right to be afraid of the man with the prison glass between us, but there was something about his devotion to the idea that bred a nameless disquiet in my heart. I cursed myself then, thinking at the time I was only feeling guilty for not doing more to sacrifice my own life for those I loved.

I listened to many of Edgar's plans in the weeks that followed. He intended to work at an orphanage, taking nothing as payment besides the barest gruel he needed to survive. He was going to build houses for others, while asking nothing more for his own habitation than something to keep the rain off his head. Even more impressive, when I spoke to the guards they told me that he wasn't even waiting to be released to begin his life of charity. He already shared his food freely with his cellmate, and granted the other prisoners his time in the yard or the library or any other opportunity the guards gave him to be selfless.

It seemed to me a crime to keep such a man behind bars when he could be helping so many people outside. No matter the man he killed before his arrest, I have never seen someone make such a complete spiritual transformation as Edgar Rover had done. That's why I appealed to the authorities to commute his sentence, risking my own status and reputation in the community to guarantee his behavior once he was released.

"The risk I am taking in vouching for you, that is something I give freely without selfish motive," I told Edgar when he received the good news. "You can stay at the church for as long as you need until you can provide for yourself. I will care for you, and watch over you, and sacrifice for you so that you may care and sacrifice for others."

"It is a beautiful thing you have done for me. What a world it would be if we could make them all sacrifice as we have done."

I thought about those words many times in the weeks leading up to Edgar Rover's release. They continued to trouble my sleep all the way up to the night when I woke to the warm fluid dribbling down my face. My first thought was that I had been crying in my sleep, but as I lay there adjusting to the shadows, I continued to feel the warm drops falling down on me from the ceiling.

"If our sacrifice is good, so shall theirs be."

I startled to hear the voice right beside my bed. I lurched away from him, turning on the lamp on my bedside table. I don't know how Edgar got into my house, but he stood there looming over me, an eager sparkle in his eye.

"You help the poor sinners who do not know how to do good on their own."

The dripping continued, red streaks running down my face and splattering across my blankets, although I still didn't understand where it was coming from.

"So you have taught me to do the same, helping others to do good, helping them to sacrifice when they are too weak to do so on their own. So thank you, thank you, for teaching me how to make those sinners whole."

Those were the last words Edgar Rover spoke to me before he left my room. I didn't know the man who was nailed to my ceiling, his arms spread wide, his feet together as a crucifix, twisted horror wracking his dead face. I don't know how Edgar managed to put him up there while I was sleeping, or perhaps he was already there before I went to bed without me noticing. The blood continued to drain down from the figure onto my bed for many hours before I was finally able to get a ladder and bring him down, that leering reminder of the difference between sacrifice given freely and sacrifice demanded from another.

## The Toy Soldier that Saved My Life

If you truly love someone, you can look past the evil they've done. We all have both good and evil in us, but if we choose to focus on the good, then we can nurture it and let it grow. We can sweep the evil under the rug, and let it fade away without recognition or acknowledgement. We can play pretend, and smile through the pain. We can hope, and pray, and that will be enough. At least that's what I told myself whenever it got too bad.

My husband wasn't always a violent man. He was sweet and good when I first met him, even if he did have a temper and break things sometimes. But it was always silly things, like a cup or a bowl, or punching the wall where it wouldn't hurt anyone. The sound of it smashing would break through the mental fog which descended over him, and he always used to laugh at himself for ever getting so worked up.

I haven't seen him laugh in a long time now. Ever since he kicked a dent into the car that we couldn't afford to fix, he's preferred a softer target when he couldn't contain himself anymore. I even thought that I was helping him when he'd lay his hands on me, grabbing my hair or pushing me around. I'd make a big show of falling, hoping that he'd see how strong and in charge he was, and that would make him feel better somehow.

## Sleepless Nights

But my husband never got better on his own, and I didn't know how to help. But he took care of me and my son, and if this is what I had to endure for him to make a good life for us, then I wouldn't flinch or let him down. I thought I could be strong enough for the whole family, and that he would see the resolve behind my quiet suffering, and that would give him strength too. But whatever I decided I could put up with, I could never wish the same for my little boy Wallace.

I didn't believe it the first time my husband hit Wallace. The boy kept tugging and pulling at my husband, trying to get his attention while he worked on his laptop. I told myself it was only an accident when my husband turned so sharply that his elbow connected with Wallace's temple, and the little boy ran howling from the room. But I couldn't keep lying to myself when my husband yelled after him: "Next time you'll leave me alone when I'm working."

I thought I was strong, but as I stood trembling, unable to confront my husband about what he'd done, I knew that I'd been lying to myself about that too. I ran after Wallace without a word, comforting him and praying over him as he cried. Hands clasped together until they were white and shaking, I whispered frantic words of prayer that God would do what I could not and set my husband upon a more righteous path.

"Don't pray to God, he's not here," Wallace sniffled through the tears. I pressed his face against my chest, as much to stop him speaking such evil words as to calm him. But he wriggled free to run across the room and grab a toy soldier from his bed. It was a model of one of those straight British redcoats with impeccable posture, a straight line all the way from its shiny black boots to its tall black hat.

"Here," Wallace said, shoving the toy soldier in my face. "Pray to him instead. He's here, and he can keep us safe."

I was so relieved to see Wallace wasn't crying anymore that I laughed and did what he asked. Then, as serious as can be, I knelt before the toy soldier and I repeated my prayers, hoping for the good in my husband to grow while the evil was destroyed, to be forgiven and forgotten forevermore.

As much as I hate to admit it, I think Wallace was right about God not being in this house. The only thing my husband learned from that encounter was that the more we believed he would truly hurt us, the more we respected him and gave him what he wanted.

"Pick up your damn toys, Wallace," he'd shout, swearing as he stepped on one of the soldiers in the hallway. Wallace used to giggle and laugh and keep playing, but all my husband had to do was raise his hand now for the boy to jump to action like a soldier before the drill sergeant.

"In the kitchen? You play with those on the floor, keep your filthy things out of the kitchen!" My husband yelled when he found the toy soldiers lined up on the counter. I took the blame whenever I could, telling him that Wallace couldn't even reach the counter. I told my husband that I had put them there to wash them and forgot about them, so he threw one of them at me instead. The soldiers were made of metal, and I could feel the cut on my face starting to bleed as I glared at my husband. I wanted him to see the blood and feel sorry for what he'd done, but he only said: "Tell your son I'm breaking them with a hammer next time I find one outside his room."

*Your son.* Those words cut me deeper than anything he could have done to me. Wallace was his son too, but day by day my husband seemed to wish he wasn't.

I sat down with Wallace and begged him to be more careful with his things. The little boy looked me in the eye and listened solemnly, and I thought he understood until he said: "The soldiers need to patrol if they're going to guard the house."

I begged Wallace to keep them in his room, but I could tell it was only upsetting him. "It's not my fault!" Wallace whined. "Why do I keep getting blamed for what the soldiers do?"

I was angry at Wallace for not cooperating. I took all the soldiers away from him and locked them in a cabinet, telling him he could only have them back when he took responsibility for his things. Wallace screamed and cried, but I was afraid of what my husband would do if he caught them out again.

"Please mom! They've got to keep us safe!" Wallace begged, but I didn't give in.

I had the key to the cabinet in the top drawer of my dresser. I knew Wallace didn't know where it was, and couldn't get to it even if he did. I don't know how the toy soldiers were lined up at the end of our bed when I woke up, all six of them standing to attention, apparently guarding me while I slept.

My husband was still sleeping beside me as I quietly got out of bed. I thought I could put them away before he woke up so he'd never know. My hands were shaking when I picked them up though, and I managed to knock one of them over to clunk against the bed as it fell. I stood frozen as my husband shifted, not daring to move or collect the rest of the soldiers until I was sure he was asleep.

"Wallace put them there, didn't he?" my husband grunted from the bed.

"I put them there," I said automatically. "I wanted them to keep us safe." It was the only thing I could think of, and I knew how stupid it sounded the moment I said it.

"You're lying!" he shouted. "Stubbornness, lies, disobedience. What will it take for you and your son to respect me?"

My husband leapt out of bed, intent on waking Wallace up and demanding him to confess what he'd done. As soon as he landed on the floor he howled with pain, collapsing onto the ground beside the metal soldier beneath him. I knew there were only six soldiers though, and I had been sure I had counted all six lined up at the end of the bed. Yet there were only five as I counted again now, the sixth one brandishing a bloody bayonet in my husband's hand.

"Wallace!" my husband screamed, eyes flashing with rage.

"He didn't do it!" I swore, running to the door to block him leaving.

"Then you did this to me!"

I narrowly dodged as the metal soldier flew through the air, drops of blood spraying across the room from where it had impaled his foot. My husband was hobbling after me, but the soldier must have cut him deeply because he was moving slow, and I had enough time to get out of the room and slam the door before he caught up with me.

I pressed my back against the door, terrified and frozen. Maybe I should stay where I was and hold the door shut a long as I could, giving Wallace a chance to run. But it would only be worse for us the longer I resisted him. I know if I was really strong, I would have gone back in the room to apologize, and let him do what he wanted to me as long as he left Wallace alone. But as the door rattled behind me, I was too weak, too afraid to face him. It was all I could do to pin the door shut and plead with him to calm down.

I thought the door was breaking when I heard the loud crack behind me. And then another, and another, popping cracks breaking the early morning air. Any moment he'd be through, the broken shards of the door sinking into my back. Or punching a hole through the door, he'd have his hands around me neck, and then there would be no one left to protect Wallace. No one but the soldiers inside the room.

But the door never broke, and gradually the pressure subsided behind me. I heard my husband lean heavily on the door, and then slide to the ground where he collapsed. I listened to the silence and my beating heart for a long while, unable to open the door and see what had happened. I stayed there until I heard Wallace come out of his room and say: "It's okay mom. They won't let him hurt us."

I found my husband lying on the ground when I opened the door. There was a lot of blood from his foot, but even more flowing freely from his back where a dozen small holes ripped through his t-shirt. If the soldiers weren't all still lining the end of the bed exactly where I'd left them, I would have thought the cracks I'd heard had been them opening fire and shooting my husband dead.

The cabinet where I'd put the soldiers was still locked, the key still in my dresser where I'd left it. I don't know how the soldiers got out, or what really happened in that room while I held the door closed. I just know that I had prayed, and that those prayers had been answered. The evil in my husband has been destroyed, and while I don't know if I can ever forgive him for what he did to us, I know Wallace and I are finally safe to grow.

## Transparent Eyelids

I come to you as one who has lived through Hell. Maybe not literally, but then again maybe so, for I saw the flames closing in around me and felt their heat consume my flesh. I was trapped in the building with six others when the inferno descended upon us. I can't think without hearing their screams, or move without my seared and broken skin exploding into a thousand shards of anguish.

I was the only one of my family to survive that horrible fire. Burned and disfigured as I lay in the hospital, I couldn't have known then that I was only at the beginning of my torment. Worse than the experience itself, worse than the memories or the lingering pain, was the enduring curse of my burned eyelids. Half melted away from when I cowered from those flames, only the thinnest layer of skin remains.

I don't see darkness anymore when I close my eyes. I can still see through my semi-transparent lids, a world of half-light and shadows that I can never hide from. I find myself too sensitive to the light to keep my eyes open much anymore, so I spend most of my time in this ghostly world of shade. Besides, I'm too afraid to open my eyes fully, because I can see things with my eyes closed that I could never see when they were open.

Ever since I was admitted to the hospital after my burns, I could see specters drifting across my vision. My doctor told me that these dark shapes were only the veins in eyelids, and that it was only my trauma and imagination that made them swirl across the room. I know that's not true though, because I don't see them all the time. I only see the shadows moving when someone is about to die.

It isn't that uncommon in the hospital. My attending nurse Mrs. Jacobs tried to make me walk as much as I could during my rehabilitation, and I'd often feel my way along the halls with my eyes closed as I tried to get my body moving. The shadows weren't everywhere, but they clustered thickly around certain rooms and it didn't take long before I made the connection.

"They're going to take her soon," I told Mrs. Jacobs as she accompanied me. We were passing by the room of an elderly woman that was thick with the shades.

"Come on, don't stop here," Mrs. Jacobs said. "There's nobody here but us."

"I can see them," I'd tell her. "They're anxious, maybe hungry. They can't wait for her to die."

The nurse would always try to reassure me or change the subject, but they couldn't hide from me that I was right. That same night the woman was dead, and by the next morning the shadows were gone from around her room.

"This one has a few days left," I said of another patient. "There are only a few shades here, and I can see them stretched out on the floor. They're settling into wait."

There would be more of them every time I passed the room after that. And as the time grew closer for the death, they clustered more tightly around the patient, swaying back and forth, almost dancing in anticipation.

The doctor threatened to have me transferred to the psych ward if I didn't stop talking about the shades. Mrs. Jacobs who spent more time with me knew better though, because she knew how accurate I was in my predictions. Without reading the charts or even meeting the patients, I could predict when someone was going to die better than any of the medical staff could.

I knew Mrs. Jacobs started taking me seriously when I saw her begin to cross herself and pray before she joined me for my walk. She must have thought I didn't see because my eyes were closed, but I could tell how her shadow trembled just to be near me. I thought I was being helpful though, and I didn't let that stop me from pointing out the dancing shades whenever another death was near.

"Only the Devil would know that," she replied after one of my predictions.

"I'm not the Devil. I just have his eyes," I told her.

Mrs. Jacobs didn't come for me the next day. I was told she requested to be transferred to a different wing of the hospital. She must have warned the new nurse about me though, because she was hostile and distrustful toward me from the start. As soon as I pointed out the shades to her, she snapped at me immediately:

"Maybe you're to blame then. How else would you know?"

I told her I was only trying to help, but she left in a huff halfway through my walk and I had to find my way back to my room on my own. It was scary navigating those halls on my own with the shades all around, and it seemed like some of them were turning to watch me pass. That was the first time I got the sense that they were aware of me at all. Then it seemed like they were following me, more all the time as they floated away from their vigils by the other rooms to cluster around my door.

Mrs. Jacobs came by again to check on me, even though I don't think it was part of her official duties. I told her that I thought I was going to die soon, and that I was afraid. She kept insisting that I was as healthy as I was ever going to be though, and seemed intent on getting rid of me. I heard her arguing with the doctor and the other nurse, and then she came back and told me it was time for me to go.

I didn't know how I was going to take care of myself, and I didn't want to leave at first. I was scared about all the shades beginning to gather around me though, and I was tired of being in a place where so many of them converged. I pretended that I was doing better than I really was, and after signing a few papers, I let Mrs. Jacobs help me into a wheelchair and roll me out the front door.

"You do believe I'm telling the truth though, don't you?" I asked her as we went.

"I believe," is all she replied.

"You don't think I'm lying?"

"I believe, but I don't want to hear more. Whatever you see, you keep it to yourself."

I wish she hadn't said that. Especially once I was outside, feeling the cool wind burning against my fragile skin.

"I have to tell someone," I told her.

"Someone else then. God bless, and goodbye," is the last thing Mrs. Jacobs said to me.

If she'd stayed longer, I could have told her about the shades I saw outside. The thousands of them floating across the winter sky over the city, stretching from one end of of the horizon to the other. I would have told her how they danced in the air, with great spiraled nebula of them like a slow-motion hurricane drifting over the towers downtown. I would have told her, but now it's too late, so I have to tell someone else. Not because I think it can be stopped, but because I'm alone, because it hurts to cry, and because I'm afraid of what I see through my transparent eyelids.

## Rebooting A Broken Human

*Is nothing going right for you? Do you lack enjoyment for things you were once passionate about?*
*We can fix you.*
*Are you unhappy with your life? Feeling helpless, or broken-down?*
*We can reboot you.*
*Do the people you care for not care back? Do their eyes glaze over when you're speaking, and they can't wait to turn away?*
*We can make you whole, and they will love you again.*

---

THAT'S what the ad said that I responded to. A Facebook post, full of likes and comments saying how great the service was and how happy they were now.

I'm not going to go into my personal life, but I was in a place where that sounded like something that could do me good. I scheduled an appointment downtown, and thought it was some kind of therapy or counseling or something.

I didn't expect the small white-washed room, smelling sharply of cleaning solution. The smiling woman at the desk wore all white, from her knitted cap down to her long white gloves and white boots with golden buckles. I kept trying to ask exactly what they did there, but she kept giving me papers to sign and asking me medical history questions, and pretty soon I got so distracted that I just fell into a pattern of obedient responses.

I guess that's the real reason I came. When someone tells me to do something, whether it's my boss, or my parents, or any authoritative figure in a clean white uniform, I do what I'm told. I have no power to do otherwise, no agency over my life. I'm terrified of disappointing people or being a nuisance in any way.

Even when the woman escorted me into another room and laid me on the table, I didn't ask her what was going to happen or what exactly it meant for me to be rebooted. She seemed like she was very busy and professional, and I didn't want to waste her time with my ignorance and insecurities.

"The first session is free. You literally have no excuse not to try it," she smiled down at me. I smiled back, not because I wanted to, but because it seemed like the polite thing to do.

I know you think you probably would have resisted by the time she handed me an anesthetic mask, and maybe you would have. But then again if you were the type of person to resist, then you probably wouldn't have been there in the first place.

"It's not surgery, is it?" was the only thing I could muster.

She laughed so cheerfully and disdainfully that I felt like an idiot for asking the question.

"Of course not. This is just to make you more comfortable. You do want to be comfortable, don't you?"

"Yeah, of course."

"And you want to be happy?"

"Who doesn't?"

"Then put the mask on." She smiled down at me. I must have hesitated, because she snapped the rubber band back and put the mask on for me without waiting for a reply. Then she gave me a thumbs up, and I found myself helplessly returning the gesture as the drowsiness overtook my body.

When we woke up, we were sitting in the sterile white room again. We had trouble opening our eyes, but the woman was there to help us to our feet and gently guide us out the door.

"Thank you, I'll be back again next week," I heard myself say.

"Of course you will. You love the results, and can't wait to tell everyone about it," the woman told me as she smiled and waved goodbye.

We remained leaning against the building for a long time until our head began to clear. Then, moving as though on autopilot, we got into our car and were already on the highway by the time we realized we had never intended to get into the car at all.

"I don't feel like driving," I mumbled to myself.

"That's okay, you rest," I replied. "I'll drive you home."

I didn't feel that different, but I felt oddly at peace as my body seemed to know exactly what to do without any conscious effort on my part. I didn't fully register the change until I got home and saw my mother and had to think about how to explain where I'd been. But I didn't have to explain anything, and instead hugged her and said:

"I love you mom. I've got some homework to do, see you at dinner."

My mom was surprised. We both were, and she held on a long time. I hadn't told her I loved her since I was a kid, and I definitely was never eager to do my homework. Of course I did love her, and of course I wanted my homework to be done, but the obligation of love and the effort of work both scared me.

"I don't want to do my homework yet," I said, pulling away in confusion. And then immediately afterward, "But I'm going to do it anyway." Then I was bounding up the stairs toward my room that somehow didn't feel like it belonged to me anymore.

Half of the thoughts in my head didn't belong to me anymore. The other thoughts felt just like mine had, a little voice in my head, but they were coming from someone else. Someone else who wanted what was best for me, and who was making my body do things even when I didn't tell it to.

We can't describe how much that scared us. I was scared, the original me, because I never felt less in control over my own life. The other one was scared too, I could feel it, because I was there with all my darkness and fears and insecurities to drag the both of us down.

"We want to do our homework now," I heard myself say, watching my body pull the books from my bag and lay them on my bed. "We want to get good grades, and go to a good college, and have a happy and successful life."

"No argument there," I replied.

"And you aren't going to stop us."

That's the part I didn't like. It's not like I wanted to stop any of those things from happening, but the way it sounded in my head, it was more like a challenge. A taunt. It wasn't encouraging me to do the right thing, it was telling me I was going to do the right thing and was powerless to do otherwise.

That's when the two of us really began to fight. I tried to close the books on my bed to lie down, and the other one didn't like that. Our hand remained frozen in the air, trembling as the muscles clenched and spasmed as I tried to pull in opposite directions. I thought I'd won when I managed to snatch one of the books off the bed, but then my hand hurled the heavy textbook down onto my foot and made us jump from pain.

"I'll do it again," the other one whispered. "I'll do worse. Stop resisting."

"It hurts you too!" I protested. "It hurts us!"

"I don't care," the other said. "I can take more pain than you."

And as though to prove it, my hand snatched a pencil from my desk and drove the point down toward my hand. The tip only just began to pierce the flesh before I was able to react and hurl it across the room. I stared down at my hand and the broken tip embedded in it, gasping for air. I felt the terrible urge to laugh, but I just kept breathing and focusing on my breath until the urge went away.

"Is everything alright up there?" we heard our mother call from downstairs.

"You aren't my mother!" the other screamed back before I got my wits about me.

"Okay dear, just making sure," my mother called patiently.

"She isn't my mother," the other repeated softly. "It will hurt you more than it hurts me if something happens to her. So do as you're told, and open your books. It's time to study."

We've never been so productive before in our life. Our grades are improving, we're losing weight, and our mother is so happy at how sweet and kind we've become.

But me? I've never felt so broken before.

## Every Day is My Last Day Alive

Yesterday was the day I died. And the day before that, and the day before that, for as long as I can remember. I must have once known how it happened the first time, but there have been so many of the grizzly occurrences, each unique in their misery yet blended together into the never-ending horror of my existence.

I must have been shot at least a dozen times in a dozen places. Sometimes it goes quick, a rush of noise and a gasp of air, and then darkness until I find myself screaming myself awake in my own bed once more. Other times I will linger with the mortal wound for hours, but even then I know relief will come before midnight when the final curtain invariably closes.

I've been hit by cars, and thrown from buildings, and drowned, and burned, and buried alive on two separate occasions. Sometimes it happens in the morning and my day is reset immediately, but most often it will come with the nightfall leaving me to dread the inevitable all day long. It's the waiting I hate most: a whole day of mystery, eyes darting at every gray face and shadow wondering how it will happen and who will bring the final blow.

I've come to recognize the poisoned look that glows from my assassin's eye. It could be anyone, any man or woman or even child who suddenly fixates upon me with an insistent fascination. A glance across the room, a turned head on the street, eager and gleeful as though they've been searching for me their entire life.

If it seems that I'm speaking casually about this curse, it's because I've already navigated the five stages of grief in my own fashion. I began with denial, believing I had suffered through an exceptionally vivid nightmare or hallucinogenic attack. Then comes anger, back when I used to struggle and fight for my life, not knowing how futile it would be.

There's no use trying to bargain or reason with them either. Even if I manage to escape then it will always be another, and another, new heads turning like clockwork until the deed is done. I've even tried to flee the city altogether, losing myself in the wilderness, but never able to get far enough before midnight comes and some hunter or hidden foe will bring me down. More than once death has come at the hands of my own family, an end so horrible that I have long since cut contact with them to avoid.

After bargaining comes depression, a stage I thought I would be in forever. At least a conventional death has a finality to it, and one may learn to accept that when they know there is no other way. But there is no escape for me, no Faustian bargain or divine salvation that can bring an end to this tragedy. I suppose it's possible that I really could be dead, already enduring punishment for a crime in another life I've forgotten long ago. But what justice is there without redemption, what transgression could have earned such a fate? I do not know.

What would you have done to bring meaning to such a life? If you kept the sight of another human being from turning to hatred in your heart, then you would have been stronger than I. Somewhere in the midst of waking and death, the thought occurred to me that there would be no end to this until I was the last man on earth. That freedom meant nothing unless it meant an end to the evil looks cast in my direction. I fantasized endlessly about some apocalyptic event that brought humanity to its knees, and if it meant a thousand more of my own deaths, I would weather that storm until the wind blows empty through the hollow cities with no one left to hurt me. And if it was I who had to bring about that armageddon, then I alone would dither out the rest of my days in solitude and mourning for the price of peace.

I took the first step on that journey the night I took the life of my assailant. An elderly man with a blue bow-tie who brought his cane around my throat from behind. I hadn't intended to kill him when I hurled him to the ground, but the next day I discovered his grieving family and knew that he had remained dead even while I came to life again. It was then I realized that I really could bring death to them all, armed with an eternity and the invulnerability that shedding my own death permitted. One by one, or by the dozens or hundreds, I could wipe this world clean and revel in the ruin I've created. And who is to say they didn't deserve it after the way those innumerable wicked eyes looked at me and saw their victim?

But watching the family grieve, the man holding his crying daughter to his chest, the woman weary and weathered from a long night of tears, I knew I could never carry such a plan to fruition. If their deaths are final while mine is not, then let me go where fear and danger keep mortal men from straying. Let me rush into traffic or burning buildings where one might be saved. Let me take a bullet where another might be spared, or fight the corruption of my city though it costs me my life each time. If I can learn to love those who hate me so, if I can die so that they may live, then that knowledge will give nobility to my soul.

Perhaps one day my good deeds will break my curse, but it's no longer a hope I can bear to entertain. I will turn that which haunts me into a blessing for others, and through their joy I will find peace.

## Crown Of Teeth

Of the three of us who sought out King Aodhan's grave, I'm the last still able to share what we found. I don't blame Lewis for telling us about the burial mound. He was only repeating what his father had told him, and his father before him, a family legend that stretched back into the early days of Celtic lore.

"Buried treasure isn't a thing," I'd argued with him. "How long has this guy been dead?"

"Almost 2,000 years. Aodhan died fighting the Romans, and they couldn't take his treasure with him when they fled to Scotland. It was buried with him to keep it from being stolen."

I wouldn't have taken such whimsical thinking seriously from anyone else. Lewis was a shrewd man though, immaculate and calculating in the extreme. He organized his day into half-hour increments, and kept a journal so precise that it never missed what he had for breakfast or how his digestion faired in the afternoon. I suppose it could have been a trait that ran in the family, but I still didn't believe they had record of a secret treasure.

"Surely someone would have found it by now."

"The Romans didn't know," Lewis insisted, his beady eyes shining behind his spectacles, locked intently on my face, even as I tried to evade them. "There was no written record, and Aodhan's ancestors before me never spoke of it to outsiders. But there were hints of the secret hidden within engravings, and I have traced the location exactly. My brother Sean will be there with his truck, but we need you to borrow the excavator from work. One night is all we need, you'll have it back before anyone notices the next day. Assuming you ever want to work again, after the riches we've split fairly."

It was an adventure in camaraderie more than greed that motivated me. Lewis had been there for me many times before, and it was no great hardship for me to bring the excavator half an hour down the road. Sean was a boisterous fellow who drank and laughed while I went to work at the hillside. He would have played music too if Lewis hadn't forced him to be quieter. It felt more like hanging out with friends than grave robbing, at least until the head of the exactor hit the carved stone. I had to get out and run my hands over it, unable to believe the ancient runes chiseled deep within the hill.

"Don't stop now!" Lewis insisted, ushering me back inside the vehicle. "In and out, no time to waste. Under grass and under stone, Balor sits upon his throne."

"I thought his name was Aodhan?" I asked.

Lewis waved his hands dismissively through the air. "Just the demon who guards the dead. Mystical mumbo jumbo."

"Oh no," Sean complained, red in the face and stumbling as he came to join us. "Oh no no. Nobody said anything about no—"

"That's enough from you," Lewis snatched the bottle of ale from his brother's hand. "You can buy the whole pub when we're finished. Come on, we've never been so close."

I thought it was a shame to crack the beautifully engraved stone with my excavator, but Lewis insisted there was no other way. He had already been more right than I could have expected, so I didn't hesitate to smash the thing and clear the broken shards.

I wasn't expecting a palace or anything. A few golden trinkets would have been cool enough for me. Five feet, ten feet past the engraved stone, and not even so much as a body. Sure maybe there were a few old bones that were turned to dust by the excavator, but gold doesn't rot, and there was no sign of anything like the magnitude of treasure Lewis described.

"Someone must have already gotten to it," I complained.

The horizon was starting to glow, and it was almost morning. Sean had long since fallen asleep in the back of his truck, while Lewis was still on his hands and knees with a flashlight, sifting through the piles of dirt.

"They couldn't have. Not without disturbing the burial stone. We'll try again tomorrow," Lewis conceded at last.

"I plan on sleeping tomorrow," I countered. "It was fun boys, but I don't think—"

I was interrupted by Sean's sudden yelp as he sat bolt-upright in the back of his truck. His hands were clutched around his head as though he'd been struck.

"Well what did you expect, drinking half the night?" Lewis snapped. "Lot of help you were—"

"Get it off! Get it off!" Sean cried, tumbling out of the truck to roll on the ground in agony. We were at his side in a moment, and by the early morning light we saw a strange and macabre crown tightly fastened around his head. The circle was made by a double layer of teeth knitted together with twisted gold wire like braces. The teeth were pointed inward so as to bite into Sean's skin, which was bruised and glistening with blood from the pressure.

"How'd you get the damn thing on in the first place?" Lewis complained as we tried to pry it off.

"I didn't!" Sean swore. "Woke up like this. Ow ow ow, careful now!"

"Damn fool must have found it while he was drinking and forgot," Lewis grumbled. "Come on now, I've got this side. Give it a good pull, we got it."

"Ow! Stop!"

Sean protested, bucking violently against our effort. He lashed out wildly in his pain, lurching back against the side of his truck. The tremendous impact lifted two wheels off the ground before the car slammed back into place. We all stared in disbelief as Sean staggered to his feet. Then carefully, curiously, as though forgetting his pain, Sean stooped to try and lift the vehicle again. With a grunt of effort he lifted the front half of the truck all the way up to his waist before letting it drop back to the ground with a crash.

"Blimey." Lewis gaped.

Sean's eyes were wide and terrified. Without a word he reached up to the crown with both hands, trying to rip the thing from his head. His teeth clenched from the effort and pain, and blood began to pour freely down the sides of his face where the teeth bit into the flesh. Then with a dreadful scream he ripped the crown clean off, blood splattering around him in all directions. The entire scalp of his head peeled off with it, everything above the line around his temple where the crown had rested. Howling in agony, Sean tumbled to the ground where he was still.

Lewis knelt beside his brother, but I didn't dare approach the grizzly sight. Lewis stood after a long pause, whispering the word, "Dead."

"Lewis..."

"What are you waiting for?" he snapped at me, beady eyes glistening with anger and fear. "Put the body in the hole and put some dirt over it. We'll talk about this later."

"What about the crown?" I asked.

The crown was nowhere to be seen though. I know Sean was filled with some sort of inhumane strength in his frenzy, but it hadn't looked like he'd thrown the thing that far at the time. Lewis searched the entire hillside while I filled the dirt back in though, and there was no sign of the cursed object.

"Tomorrow. Talk tomorrow. We could both use some sleep," is all Lewis would say when I tried to talk to him.

Need it or not, I couldn't sleep at all despite tossing and turning for a few hours. I kept messaging Lewis until around midday when he agreed to meet. Not in public though—he wanted to meet outside of town, toward the hillside where we'd been digging.

He didn't speak when he got out of his car. He didn't have to. The pain on his bleary face was more than the anguish of loss. It stemmed too from the crown of teeth biting into his temple.

"Lewis... you didn't," I said at last.

"No, I didn't," he shook his head, giving me a wane smile. "I got a few hours sleep, and found it like this when I woke up."

The teeth weren't as deeply embedded in his skin as they were in Sean however. It was a light imprint where they pressed into him, without any bruising or blood. I reached for it to see if I could help get it off, but Lewis swatted my hand away. The small motion felt like a sledgehammer, and almost knocked me to the ground. In confirmation he stooped down to his car, easily hoisting it off the ground with one hand.

"I don't need your help," he told me coldly. "I'm not going to take it off. My brother died so I could have this, and I'm not going to let that be for nothing."

"Why did you want to meet then?" I asked.

"We had a deal, you and I. Split the treasure, and I'm a man of my word. I wanted you to see for yourself that it's safe now, and to promise you that you can have your turn when I'm done with it."

I shook my head, backing up toward my own car. "I don't want it. I don't want anything from you. You can keep it."

"It doesn't matter what you want," he growled. "When I fell asleep, I had a dream about a monster, and in its mouth were a ring of teeth, just like the ones around my head. It had its jaws around me, and it was biting down, tightening, tightening, real slow like. Its body was wrapped around me, its hands over my hands, its legs entwined with mine. I think that's what's giving me this strength. And I don't want to give that up, even if I could."

"I'm never putting that thing on!" I swore.

"It's getting tighter," Lewis moaned. "I don't know how long I have, but sooner or later it's going to be too much for me to bear. Sooner or later Balor is going to eat me, and then I think it's going to be your turn. I just wanted to warn you, that's all."

And with that Lewis climbed back into his car and drove away. I haven't tried to contact him since. I frantically check my head every time I wakeup, but it's been a few weeks and the crown hasn't appeared yet. With any luck, he'll wear it forever and it will never be my turn.

But I've started to have dreams about that monster, always behind me, turning with me as though it were my shadow. In those dreams I can feel the ring of teeth looming so close behind my head, watching me, poised to crown me king.

## World of Wrath

I'm angry at the world right now. I'm angry at how stupid everyone is. At how shortsighted, and narrow-minded, and unbelievably petty they all are, especially those with power.

The first thing I do when I wakeup is grab my phone and read the latest headlines. There's always something in there to piss me off. I've come to rely on that feeling of boiling blood to wake me up in the morning. Then I'll turn on the news and let it play in the background while I get dressed and make breakfast, hating everything that I hear.

I've lived alone for a long time now, and I like to have something playing all the time just to have some voices around me. Even when I'm working I'll have the news playing in the background, the 24 hour hysteria making me feel like I'm always part of something important.

Sometimes I'll grunt or grumble when I hear something truly horrendous, but this morning I couldn't stop myself from actually yelling at the TV. There was this story playing about these assaults, and one of the news anchors was defending the aggressor because society pushed them to that point. I wish I was there in the room with him to shut him down, but as it was all I could do was scream at the TV until I was red in the face. I don't remember exactly what I said, but it was something along the lines of 'I hope you get attacked next, blathering idiot.'

The next morning when I checked the headlines, my rage was temporarily replaced with a sort of sadistic glee that I wasn't accustomed to feeling. The anchor really had been attacked. He'd been jumped when he was getting out of his car, and his head was smashed against the side until some people nearby were able to intervene.

I didn't think I made it happen or anything. I just thought someone else was thinking the same thing I did, and that he had it coming. The news shows were a lot more entertaining that day, and I hardly did any work as I was glued to people discussing the incident. I kept expecting the rest of the anchors to reach a point of self-awareness as they realized their rhetoric was making the violence worse, but that moment never came. So I found myself getting angry again, yelling and carrying on about how I wish every single one of them got what they deserved.

It took about a week for justice to be delivered. Car accident, cancer diagnosis, fired for sexual harassment. Every single morning when I opened the headlines, I discovered another one of the offenders had been brought down one way or the other. Something had happened to the entire panel that infuriated me, and it was only then that I began to realize my power.

Yelling at the businessmen and watching their industries crumble. Yelling at the politicians and the inevitable scandal to ensue. Screaming my heart out at every evil doer I could find, all to watch the universe play its tricks one after the next. I know horrible things happen all the time, but for the first time in my life I felt like more than a passive observer. It was as though my anger was stirring the entire world into action.

There might have been a brief moment where watching the resolutions on the TV was cathartic, but the calm never lasted. I began to feel that the power I had came with responsibility, and it was my duty to be angry all the time. If I wasn't mad, then justice wasn't being done. Besides, only an evil person could look upon all the evil in the world with indifference.

I didn't try to hide from the anger anymore. I whipped myself into a frenzy, spitting and shouting and carrying on like a madman. And if something didn't happen right away, I'd blame myself for not being mad enough, and the next day I'd swear and stomp all the louder.

International news wasn't enough for me anymore. When I ran out of things to be angry at around the world, I'd turn my attention to the local channels, obsessing over every minor problem around me and hoping the solution would come. And when I saw the fire raging through my downtown near my apartment, I knew it was my obligation to drop everything and scream to make it better.

Even when I smelled the smoke, I didn't turn away. I'd yell at the cars for not getting out of the way of the fire engines fast enough. I'd yell at the firemen for taking too long with the hose. There was still part of me that was present enough to feel the heat and cough on the black smoke, but I can honestly say it didn't even occur to me to try and get out. I was fighting the only way I knew how, ready to go down with the ship if it meant I was doing my part.

I didn't turn away from the TV until the power went out and I heard the hammering on my door. I tried to open it, but I was coughing so badly that I had to crawl along the floor, and I didn't get there before an axe tore out the wood where the lock was. Yellow and black uniforms of the firemen streamed past me, their shouting muffled from their masks. I watched helpless as they barged through my closed kitchen door only to be met with a wave of fire and searing smoke. I managed to reach my phone and kept refreshing the page to see what was going on, because I couldn't understand what I was seeing with my own eyes.

It turns out some idiot started the fire in their kitchen when they forgot the food on the stove. The wind had whipped a spark out through the open window and it had spread from there, engulfing everything downwind while the original fire remained contained in the closed room. I didn't feel angry when they told me about it though. I just felt tired, and sad, and utterly useless. And if someone out there was yelling at me on TV, then I hope they take a deep breath, turn it off, and go do something more productive with their life.

At least I know I need to turn off the news for awhile.

## They Were Human Once

They were human once, those pallid shades cowering deep below the earth. There was once a time when they could walk proudly under the endless sky without hunching and scurrying in fear. Their eyes were peaceful, and curious, not these great pale orbs which glowed in terror from the slightest spark. Muscles once toned have grown thin as twisted wires, their full hair matted with grease, their faces pocked with ruin.

I have to believe we were human once, because I have to believe we can become human again if we ever get out of this place. I have to believe there is still some decency in us, something to give pause before the killing blow lands from the unsuspecting dark. I've since accepted that human isn't something that we are though, it's a way we act out of fear of judgement in our brother's eyes. But there is no restraint or mercy where there are no names, no humanity without light to witness the horrors we subject one another too.

First there were three of us, waking in the dark. We were not afraid because we had each other, lending encouragement and support through hollow words we did not believe. None of us knew how we came to this place, but so long as we could remember ourselves and the lives we once lived, we had faith that this moment was an aberration that we could endure together. We explored these underground passes and laughed with joy to find the clear running stream and the edible fungus that lined its banks. We sang songs and told stories of our lives to pass the time, trusting and loving one another as we sought to know our companions the best we could.

Then there were four of us, and we welcomed the newcomer and promised to keep him safe. We showed him how to navigate the dark passages by feeling along the walls, and how to gather food, and where to sleep where the moisture didn't seep through.

Then five of us, each time waking to find another without knowing where they came from. And so we told our stories again, although each time we spoke about our old lives, the goal subtly shifted from getting to know each other to needing to remind ourself of who we used to be. We began to take parts of the passage as our own, marking the lines between us with our scents.

Then six, then seven, until we became sure that we weren't finding our way here by accident. But we kept pretending all the same, because someone putting us here meant that we weren't waiting to be found. We were already found, but we would not be saved.

Then eight, nine, more it seemed with every wakening, although it became harder to keep track when we stopped sharing our names. To know someone's name was to have power over them, reminding them that their actions are constrained by their humanity. There is freedom in having no name, and in knowing each other only by the strength of our arms and the quickness of our feet.

One of the newcomers wouldn't stop crying, and the sound echoed hauntingly through the stone corridors of our domain. We didn't need words or names to descend upon her and beat her into stillness. We all took pieces of her back to our territory with us, and so I don't know which of us tasted the meat first. But I do know that marked the last point we ever called one another by name.

It was a lesson the newcomers were slow to learn. They would talk and sing and try to get to know one another, but they learned swiftly they would be beaten for speaking the tongue of their old life. We knew our territory and how to survive on our own, but we knew we could never hold it if the others worked together against us. Without words but with common understanding, we came to attack any who spoke to keep them from bonding together, a feral pack that broke each newcomer down as swiftly as they arrived. Besides, it was painful to hear words and names and songs, a reminder of a life that had forsaken us.

The day the electric light turned on should have been salvation. The lightbulb dangling from the ceiling of the tunnel showed that there were wires, and that perhaps they could be followed back to civilization. We all gathered around the edge of shadow, terrified to reveal ourselves fully to the others or ourselves. We prowled along the edge of light, growling and shoving one another, trying to get someone else to investigate first.

One man dared crawl into the light, face pressed into the ground against the searing brightness. He was thin and naked and he trembled with each jerky motion, but he persisted all the way into the room to sit directly under the light. The way he pressed himself to the ground reminded me of a prayer, and when he lifted himself there were tears streaming down his face from the beauty and blinding brightness that was the single bulb. And then howling at his own wretchedness, he leapt from the ground and smashed the thing, unable to bear it any longer.

The room descended into darkness, and chaos immediately followed. It had been a long time since so many of us gathered in one place, and we all descended on the man in blind rage at the blasphemy he had committed against the light. Bodies writhed and churned over one another as they grasped at him, pulling at his skin and hair, ripping fingers from his hands and twisting his body apart from all directions.

"Mom! Make it stop!" I heard him cry.

I often wondered whether he spoke out of a wild fantasy, or whether he recognized his own mother among his assailants. I never dared speak the question aloud though, and do not know if there were any still capable of response even if I did.

No one hid in shame that they were eating him this time, knowing they could not slink away without losing the precious chance to be nourished by one more handful of flesh or warm blood stolen from the still-living victim. But there were so many of us and we were so desperate, and in the dark we didn't care whether we were consuming the original blasphemer or someone else we could overpower.

We didn't even stop to think where the light came from, or at least I didn't. We just kept kicking and biting, bodies squirming over one another, hoisting rocks to smash anything that moved and then shoving it indiscriminately into our mouths before it was consumed by another. And the more who died, the more jealously we fought over their bodies, knowing we could not retreat without their meat being stolen from us.

I don't know how many of us crawled away from that bloody mess. More lights were coming on before we could finish, bright lanterns accompanied by the shouting of human voices. Real humans, standing upright and wearing clothing and calling to one another with words. Some of us fled into the dark, hauling with them as many bodies as they could carry. Myself and others surrendered to the burning light and pressed ourselves against the floor.

The original occupants of that place spent a total of 167 days in the darkness, although I was the only one of the first comers to survive. I heard the words "social experiment" and "terminated authorization", but I couldn't look them in the face or properly understand what was being said to me. The men in suits had a lot of questions, and they seemed confused that I was unable to answer them. I remember them talking amongst themselves, not understanding how I could have forgotten language after less than six months away from civilization.

It wasn't that I had forgotten though. It's just that my brain wouldn't let me hold onto the meaning of words without accepting the knowledge that I was human once, a responsibility too heavy for me to bear.

## To Love A Phantom

I didn't know I loved her until I lost her. When I first met her, I wanted her with a passion, but that single-minded obsession didn't leave room for thoughts. Then we grew accustomed to each other, spending so much time together that we forgot what it was to be alone. We navigated life's inconveniences and problems together, letting petty resentments and doubts cloud what should have been bliss.

I should have known then that was love, but it was just the way things were, and I couldn't imagine life any other way. Even when I was alone the voice in my head belonged to her though, every thought a reflection of hers. Nothing was beautiful until I shared it with her and heard her wonder, no meal tasted much of anything without her exclamations of fulfillment.

She was in the hospital for several days before she slipped into a coma. I hate that I thought she was exaggerating her illness for sympathy and attention at first, but it was only because I wasn't capable of imagining a world without her. And then sitting beside her bed, her eyes closed, her breathing slow, all the thoughts I hadn't allowed myself to think came rushing in at once. I felt like I forgot how to breathe. I held onto her limp hand so hard that I was shaking. It just didn't make sense to me how I could feel so much without her feeling anything when she was a part of me.

"Don't worry, love, I can feel you there," came her whispered words.

Those words should have given me hope, but they terrified me. Her eyes hadn't opened, her slightly parted lips hadn't moved, her pale skin hadn't flushed with life. But I had heard her words as clearly as though she'd spoken. I held onto her hand for dear life, studying her passive face as more whispered words slipped through the air.

"Whatever happens to my body, my spirit will always be with you."

Then I felt her around me as soft as mist. I even saw her standing there, a slight discoloration of the air to mark where her arms were wrapped around me. It was too insubstantial to embrace back, but I felt a distinct difference as she released me and moved through the air to the door.

"I'm going home, why aren't you following?" the spirit said to me. "Don't wait for what is already gone."

Mesmerized as though in a dream, I followed the colored shape of her through the hospital without anyone else seeing her. She kept me company while I ate dinner, and she laughed at how distraught I'd allowed myself to get. If I closed my eyes and listened to her whisper it really didn't feel any different than having her here. When I laid down to sleep I told her that this was enough, her spirit all I'd ever need.

Her spirit became a new normal that I grew accustomed to. She was always waiting for me when I got home, prattling on about the gossip she'd overheard while slipping unnoticed through the world. She made fun of me for wanting to go visit her sleeping body, and it really did feel silly when the soul I loved so much was right beside me. The longer this went on, the realer she felt, especially right when I was drifting off to sleep when I could even feel the warmth of her pressed along the length of my body.

This went on for over a month before I got the call from the hospital that she had woken up. The doctor sounded annoyed at me, and said she'd been trying to reach me for days but hadn't gotten through. It was uncomfortable having the conversation while her spirit was there watching me the whole time, but for some reason I was still excited to tell her the good news.

"No she hasn't," her spirit said the moment I ended the call. "I'm still here."

"But you'll be able to go back to your old life!" I protested, not understanding.

"If you really love me, then prove it. Stay here with me and don't go back to the hospital."

It didn't make any sense to me, but she was insistent, and her presence was so intoxicating that I didn't answer the next two times the hospital called. Her spirit praised me for my loyalty to her each time, but something still felt wrong. I had trouble falling asleep that night, and couldn't stop thinking about how much better it would be to have the real, living body there with me.

The next day I visited the hospital on the way home from work, telling myself I could always pretend I was working late if the spirit was bothered by it.

It was harder than I expected seeing my love's body in the hospital, knowing her spirit was waiting for me back at home. Her body was still looking sickly and weak, and I couldn't stop thinking how much more beautiful her spirit was. The body was happy to see me though, and she kept talking about not being able to

## Sleepless Nights

wait until she got home. Then she leaned into kiss me and I gave into it without thinking.

I spoke to the doctor before I left, and she scowled at me, apparently looking down at me for not being more attentive. The recovery was far from complete, and atrophied muscles would need rehabilitation and help. I couldn't promise when I could come visit again though, and I'm pretty sure the doctor was swearing at me under her breath as I hurried out the door.

I could feel the spirit's anger as soon as I stepped inside my home. The discoloration in the air had a darker hue, and her soft presence had a tense edge like the electricity before a storm.

"You said I'm all you need," the spirit accused me at once.

I was on the defensive immediately. I couldn't lie, but neither could I easily admit or even understand what I'd done wrong.

"You only want me for my body," she accused me, not listened to anything I had to say. "You never loved me for who I really am."

The open windows suddenly closed, their curtains whipping shut. I heard the door lock behind me.

"She needs my help!" I protested. "You need my help! You'll be happier in your own body too, you shouldn't be fighting this."

We had a long talk that night, and eventually she promised to come with me to visit the hospital the next day. I thought things were finally going to go back to normal after that, but that night as I fell asleep the spirit's presence had never felt so tangible. More like smoke than mist, with a bitterness that burned my throat when I breathed her in. I couldn't imagine what she must be going through, so I pretended not to notice, hoping things would be right again after tomorrow.

Her spirit was there waiting for me when I next entered the hospital room. The spirit was in an empty chair with her arms crossed, darkly colored with trails of steam or smoke drifting up off her body to cloud the ceiling of the room.

"I was hoping I'd see you today," the body said.

"She's dying," the spirit spoke over her, so that it was hard to listen to them both at once. "Her body is wasting away."

"Did you have a chance to speak to the doctor?" the body asked tentatively.

"She's just a burden now," the spirit continued bitterly. "You won't love me anymore if you have to deal with her."

I turned helplessly between the two of them, unsure of what to say.

"What are you looking at?" the body pressed, studying the empty chair where the spirit dwelled.

"If you love me..." the spirit began.

"If you really love me..." both of them said aloud in perfect unison. "Then we can get through this together."

"But only if you take care of me," the body said.

"But only if you kill her," the spirit snapped.

I closed my eyes and took a deep breath, smelling the bitterness in the air, but remembering the warmth and joy she used to bring.

"Sooner or later, she'll be gone," the spirit hissed. "But I'll be there forever. You know what has to be done."

"You'll have to leave your job, at least for a while," the body continued.

"I need to be the only thing in your life right now. I need your undivided attention," they both said in unison. "Do you love me? Do you really love me?"

"Of course I love you," I said, not opening my eyes. Not showing any sign of who I was addressing.

The body thought she was the only one there, but I could feel the spirit's anger at my indecision. There was a roar of shattering glass as the window exploded inwards, and an alarm started sounding at the nurses station.

I opened my eyes to see my love's body convulsing as the black smoke poured into her nose and mouth. I was shoved out of the way as two nurses jostled past me to attend to her, and I dared not get close to her while they worked. I thought everything was going to work out, and that the spirit and the body would be joined again. But the longer she seized, and the more frantic the nurses became, the more convinced I was that the spirit was trying to kill the body.

"Please don't hurt her!" I begged.

"I'm sorry, there's nothing we can do," the nurse replied, thinking I was speaking to them.

The other nurse checked his watch. "Time of death…"

The house has never been so quiet, but I know she's still here somewhere. I can tell by how dark the place is even with the lights on, and the acid taste of the air. I don't know if she'll ever overcome her jealousy and doubt, nor do I know if I'll ever be able to love her again after what she's done. Our bitterness is poison to each other, but neither of us are strong enough to leave. Every night I feel her suffocating presence wash over me, and I tell her I love her all the same, too afraid to try to live without her, or to ever be alone.

## Fear the Echo and the Answer

When I was a kid, there was a canyon behind my house my friends and I liked to sneak off to. We weren't supposed to play by it, so of course that automatically made it the coolest place in the world to be. There were four of us who went there as often as we could get away, although the oldest of us never let the others look down or get too close to the edge. Mostly we'd just throw rocks and stuff into it, or take turns shouting rude words and laughing at the reverberating echo.

When I spoke about those memories with my friends years later, they only remembered the games we played and the good times we had. No one else but me remembers how the responding echo never quite matched the sounds we made. They dismissed it as my imagination, and teased me about my childhood

## Sleepless Nights

fantasy. I laughed along with them and didn't mention it again. I know I wasn't making it up though, because I've been back to that canyon by myself many times since then, and I know what I heard.

The delay was always too long, for starters. Echos are just sound waves bouncing off the rock and coming back, and I know how fast the speed of sound is. It always takes this echo a few seconds, and even then the voice doesn't sound the same as the original. Even if it mimics our words, the pitch is all high and strained, and it sounds the same no matter who makes the first call.

If that was all there was, then I might have forgotten about it too. But there were also times when only a part of the sound would come back, and I don't know how an echo could ever explain that. Sometimes when I'm there alone I'll make a game out of treating the canyon like a magic 8 ball, calling down questions and listening for the answer as though it was some kind of prophecy.

"Should I go to school tomorrow?" I called once, and the only part that came back was:

'Go to school, go to school.'

"Should I ask her to the dance?" I tried another time.

'Ask her, ask her,' the canyon replied.

The game stopped being fun around the time I started high school. I couldn't talk about it with my friends knowing how silly they thought it was now, and my parents still didn't like me hanging out there. I got distracted with the daily ordeals and dramas of school life, and years went by without me even thinking about the place. It wasn't until my mom got sick and went to the hospital that I found myself climbing over the familiar rocks again one evening, trying to lose myself in forgetting how much I worried about her.

"Is mom going to get better?" I called.

I put a particular emphasis on last words, and waited the few seconds it took for the reply to come. I thought that I'd hear 'get better, get better', and that would be like a prophecy that would give me something to believe in. I guess I must have been embarrassed to shout as loudly as I had as a kid though, because even straining my ears I couldn't hear so much as a whisper back. Feeling foolish but more determined than ever, I filled my lungs and yelled the question again as loudly as I could.

'No.'

A single word, that same strained voice. It even came back immediately after I called without the usual delay.

"Is she going to die?" I tried again.

A few seconds, and then 'To die, to die," echoing the few words just as it always had before. I shivered even though the sun hadn't gone down yet, unable to comprehend what I was hearing.

"You're lying! Everyone says she's going to be fine!" I shouted as loud as I could not caring who else could hear.

'You're lying…' came the echo… 'to yourself'.

I was angry now. I thought there must be someone down there who was calling back at me. I let myself get closer to the edge than I ever had before, peering right over the steep stony walls to try and spot who might be answering. It was getting dark and I couldn't see anyone, but I did spot a wandering path along the slope that looked like I could climb down.

I knew if I went home now then those words would be the prophecy of what was to come, filling my head and tormenting me more than I already was. I resolved to climb down the slope and find the person taunting me, but the way was steeper than it looked at first. I had to go slow, and I was only about halfway down when it had grown completely dark. I threw out a few taunts and jabs on the way down, telling them to show themselves, but I didn't hear any reply.

I could tell it wasn't safe, but I was so angry that I didn't care, and as the last of the daylight faded I lost my footing and started to slide. I tried grabbing at some bushes to stop my fall, but they were sharp and thorny and I reflexively let go as they ripped my hands. Then I was tumbling freely through the open air, flailing with wild panic before curling into a ball and trying to roll my landing. I still hit hard enough to take my breath away, lodging into a tight crevice in the rock. I cursed and swore as I tried to pull myself out, but my foot was stuck deep in the stone and my ankle hurt whenever I tried to yank it.

"God damn it," I said,

'God damn him.'

I froze as the echo replied instantly nearby. The sound encompassed me in the darkness, and I couldn't tell where it was coming from. All my anger and confidence disappeared the moment I slipped, and I was starting to feel really afraid now. Even if there was someone down here, why did that make me think it was safe? There could be some crazy person living here—who else would be shouting taunts at a kid asking about his sick mother?

"You're just an echo," I said, making sure to whisper it quietly enough that no echo could possibly reply.

'Just an echo', that thin strained voice, so close I could almost feel the breath of it on my neck. And then it began to giggle, a wet gurgling sound like someone laughing while drinking water.

I reached for my phone to get a light, but it must have fallen out of my pocket when I fell. I struggled again to get my ankle unstuck, but it must have either been broken or sprained because the smallest movement sent a shockwave through my body.

The moon was just beginning to rise over the lip of the canyon though, and through the feeble light I saw a shadow rising from the stones around me. At first it seemed like the shape of a man standing up, but it continued to raise itself until it was much taller than any man. There weren't any clear arms and legs either, but instead a rippling waveform along its perimeter as it moved sluggishly over the stones toward me.

I wanted to scream, but I was too terrified of the screaming echo that might descend on me. I held my breath as it approached, and its deathly quiet soon had me convinced that it could only make a sound when I did. It wasn't much, but it was the only control I had in the situation. I stubbornly stared the shadow down as it loomed over me. The form rippled this way and that, circling me, seeming to dare me to speak to it or call for help. The longer I resisted, the smaller it seemed to become though, until gradually the shadow melted back into the stones.

I slowly worked off the shoe of my trapped foot, and then was able to slip away. I crawled out on my hands and knees and started working my way slowly, tortuously back up the stony slope. I made most of the way to the top before accidentally putting too much pressure on my wounded ankle and letting out an involuntary yelp.

Immediately the strained yelp was echoed back at me, so fast and so much more powerful than my own sound had been that I know the thing must have been waiting for me to make a sound all this time. The screech echoed upon itself and amplified in the canyon, mounting to a terrifying crescendo before it gradually faded away.

I didn't look back or make another sound once all the way home. Only then did I get the news that my mothers passing and allow myself to cry.

I've never gone back down into the canyon, but sometimes I'll still go to the edge and call out a question, knowing it's there and it's listening. I don't know what would have happened to me if I made a sound while I was in the canyon, but I know it told me the truth when everyone else lied to me. Even if my friends make fun of me for writing this, even if no one believes me, then I'll know I'm telling the truth too, and that's all that matters in the end.

## The Reincarnation Trap

I thought he was a priest, the long-bearded man wearing a hood who knelt at my deathbed. The man looked so familiar, but if I once knew him then he was obscured through the fog of my age. I heard him muttering prayers, but they could not reach me through my wretchedness and pain. I told him to leave, but he told me that I would be the one to leave first, and his solemness and honesty made me laugh.

I asked the man where I would go, and he said that was up to me. I had lived a good life, he said, and I could freely choose the next form I would inhabit. I thought he was making fun of me, but his voice was so calm and soothing, and I saw no harm in entertaining myself in a fantasy to distract me from my final throes. I told him I thought I could be happy as a dog, so long as it wasn't one of the little ones. And not one of those poor homeless ones either, but a comfortable house dog that has everything given to him.

"You'll be my dog then, and I'll take care of you," the man promised.

I laughed at him, but said that if he could take away this pain and let me be a dog, then I would call him my master.

"And you will go freely into your new form, renouncing all claims of your old body?"

I was ready to let go. I readily agreed, closing my eyes to imagine myself running through a golden field. I felt a sharp sting and opened my eyes again to see him withdrawing the IV line that administered my medication, but I knew I didn't need it anymore.

It was curious to watch him slide the needle over his hand though, rubbing my blood between his fingers. Then he went back to muttering his prayers, but I couldn't hear them over my own labored breathing and I knew the end was soon. But I could smell the field and the sun and the wildflowers. The scent was invigorating, and more powerful than any I had ever experienced.

Despite the delicious scents and my inward preoccupation, I could not turn away as the man let his hood fall to his shoulders to reveal his cracked and blistered skin beneath. At the ridge of horned bone which pierced through the skin of his bald head, or the long fangs which hung from his grinning maw.

"And you will call me your master," he said, gripping my feeble hand with his long fingers, their nails curved and polished talons of bone.

I struggled in vain to free myself from his grip. The powerful scent shifted, and soon my rich blood on his hand was the only thing I could smell. It intoxicated me, filling my lungs so that every breath was choked in blood. Until that too faded, and I found that he was no longer holding me down but was instead stroking me, his gnarled hand warm and comforting as it smoothed out my fur.

I was unsteady at first on my four legs, but it was such a relief to be free of that prison of flesh I once inhabited. The strength and balance I soon found made every movement a joy, and as the scent of blood faded from my nostrils a rich and undiscovered world of flavor and texture blossomed into my awareness.

I was grateful to the man despite his monstrous appearance, which indeed seemed so much less terrifying than it had a moment ago. He called me by my name and I followed him from that hallowed chamber, only pausing at the door to look back at my old body which must now be still in death.

"Do not linger!" my master ordered me, but I could not turn away.

Not only was my old body not dead, it was sitting upright and breathing easily, looking younger and healthier than I had in years. It stripped back the covers and stood on legs that no longer shook, smiling at me from a face that was one my own.

"We had a deal," my master growled, "that body does not belong to you anymore. You have renounced your claim, and it belongs to me."

But I felt cheated and lied to all the same, and I growled back at the monstrous man who had lured me from myself. He muttered and swore at me, snatching at my tail with a clawed hand that I was narrowly able to avoid. I began to bark at him. The monstrous man was furious at this, lunging at me a half-dozen times to try to pin me to the ground. Each time I evaded him though, snarling and biting, finally sinking my teeth into his bony hand and holding on despite the horrid sulfuric taste. He couldn't free itself from my grip, and we heard voices rousing themselves around the house as they reacted to our struggle. The demon appeared frightened by this, and with a vicious slash he used a long talon to sever his own hand that I had ensnared. Then pulling his hood down low once more, he retreated from my chambers as the voices closed in.

I felt arms around me, and saw my old body and felt that familiar scent.

"Thank you," the old body whispered, "for this most precious gift. I would have been his servant too if you had not chased the demon back."

My old body seemed younger by the moment as the wrinkles smoothed from his weathered face. He promised me that the demon would never get its hold of either of us. And when my years were spent and he would still be young, and he would give me my body back to live out the rest of my days again.

I lived a long and happy life as that dog, and I miss him now that I am man again. I know the human I once dwelled beside lives on as my own dog though, and that I will have my turn again as an animal after his years are spent. Always switching places throughout the years as we guard against the demon's return, neither master nor servant, but eternally as each other's closest friend.

## The Never-Ending Cave

"I'm not afraid of the dark," I lied.

"Then turn off your light," my friend James said.

He and his brother Jim exchanged a mischievous grin. First James, then Jim, the lights on their phones snuffing out. Mine was the only light left, its pale radiance woefully insufficient to illuminate the stoney cavern around us.

I don't know why I insisted on going with them when they told me about the cave. Growing up as an only child, I never had the sense that I was missing something until I met Jim and James, two sides of the same coin. Before them I'd never imagined two people could be so perfectly in synch before.

They hardly ever spoke to each other directly, but a shared glance was enough for them to communicate as though they read each other's thoughts. Jim and James were always telling stories about the great adventures they'd had, the two spinning the narrative together so fluidly it was as though they were characters reading from a script. Sometimes the things they said sounded too fantastical to be true, like the one about going over a waterfall together, but it was just as hard to believe that one could make up a story like that while the other joined in to elaborate the lie so seamlessly. I guess I followed them out of jealousy, just wanting to fit in and feel that kind of brotherhood.

"You said you wanted to experience the cave," James prodded impatiently.

"I'm here, aren't I?" I asked defensively.

"Not fully," Jim countered. "As long as you rely on the light, you're just passively reliving the same sensation you do everyday. The cave is experienced through a different kind of sensation, but you'll never feel it as long as you're letting your eyes distract you."

"Who you going to believe, us or your lying eyes?" James agreed eagerly. "Trust us, it'll be like nothing you ever imagined."

"Okay but you better not be trying to pull something funny on me," I grumbled, switching my flashlight off.

I felt what they were talking about the instant the darkness engulfed us. The stone above our heads had just been a ceiling before, like any other room I'd been in. I couldn't sense the enormity of the mountain over my head until the light was off, or hear the thunderous stillness of this secret place. I didn't like the darkness itself, but there was something magical about everything it concealed.

The quiet seemed to grow louder with every passing moment until I could hear my own blood in my veins. Then somewhere deeper into the cave I heard the distant echo of voices. My blood grew louder, and I immediately fumbled for my flashlight again.

"Keep it off," Jim chided.

"You wanted an adventure, didn't you?" James added, an infuriating taunt in his voice. I could read the subtext there—he was saying that he and his brother were brave enough, and that if I wanted to go along with them I had to prove myself too. The fact that I was starting to read them so well made me feel like I really did belong here too, and that gave me enough courage to endure the echoes in the dark.

"Who do you think is down there?" I asked in a tentative whisper.

I could hear the footsteps as the brothers began moving toward the voices, and I followed with one hand tracing along the wall.

"Pirates," Jim said without hesitation.

"Murderers," James said with almost the same breath.

They were still testing me, teasing me. Fine then, I could play along. "Oh good," I said, "I was starting to feel out of place being the only murderer here."

I ran into the back of one of them who had stopped suddenly ahead of me. I couldn't tell who it was until James said: "I wanted the place to ourselves. Let's come back another time when there isn't anyone else here."

He turned abruptly and pushed past me to head back toward the entrance. I automatically started to turn as well, but Jim gripped me by the arm to lead me deeper toward the voices. "Don't you hate it when James makes you feel like a coward? Let's keep going, and then we can get him back by reminding him how he ran away."

"I'm not running," James complained from somewhere in the darkness. "The tourists ruin the whole experience. I'll just be at the entrance waiting for you to figure that out too."

I continued to follow Jim deeper into the cave, the voices getting louder all the while. At first I thought it had been a conversation, but now that the words were becoming clearer it seemed that there was only one person there, apparently complaining about the darkness to himself.

We continued creeping along until it seemed like the other person was right beside us in the dark, and then I couldn't take the suspense anymore. I turned on my flashlight and the beam was blinding after having adjusting without it. The person we discovered was shielding their face with hands covered in dirt and bloody scratches as though he'd been digging.

"Who goes there?" I called triumphantly as though I owned the place.

I was the one who was shocked by what the light revealed though. James was standing there at the far end of the tunnel, grinning sinisterly into the flashlight. I had distinctly heard his voice behind us as he went back toward the entrance, and I can't imagine how he got past us and deeper down the tunnel without being noticed. I sensed that I couldn't let my surprise show without him winning though, and I did my best to keep a straight face.

"There you are. We've been looking everywhere for you," Jim said, moving to embrace his brother. "How long have you been down here?"

"Hours, maybe a day," James croaked, his voice dry and cracked.

I knew they must be playing a trick on me somehow, but I couldn't figure out how and it was making me uneasy.

"Okay, I give, how'd you do it?" I asked. "You couldn't have just slipped around us in the darkness, because we were following a voice down here."

"You wait here, I'm going to grab some water from my pack and be right back," Jim said, hurrying off the way we came toward the cave entrance.

Alone with James, there was no denying it really did look like he'd been down here for a long time. His face was pale and weary, his clothes ragged and dirty, and those cuts on his hands looked real. He couldn't have actually cut himself just to play a joke on me, could he?

"There are two entrances, aren't there?" I said. "You went out and circled back through the other one. This whole place is a loop."

"Yeah, that must be it," James said with a sly smirk. "Come on, let's keep going and see if we meet up with Jim."

Still insistent on playing along and not letting them make a fool of me, I agreed and followed him deeper into the tunnel. The path was starting to get tighter, and we had to stoop so low we were almost on our hands and knees. James didn't make any more requests about me turning off my light though, so that was good enough for me. I tried not to think about how we kept climbing downward, and that if this really was a loop then we would have to come back up at some point.

There were voices again, deeper still into the earth. Definitely two of them this time, apparently having a heated argument with each other. I could still see James crawling ahead of me, but I couldn't shake how much the voices sounded like him and his brother.

"See? I told you he'd find us," Jim's voice said.

I stopped cold in my tracks. Once James got out of the way, I could see the cave widening out ahead of us. Jim and James were both standing there facing me, both looking clean and rested. The other ragged person I'd thought was James was nowhere to be seen.

"That's what you get for trying to chicken out and turn around," James jeered.

"That's not right… I didn't…"

"Heard the voices and ran," Jim agreed calmly. "No use denying it."

"But you were the voices! They were coming from you!" I protested, feeling myself grow quite flustered. It wasn't fair for them to think I was afraid when I had kept going. And if Jim and James were both here, then why did I still hear the voice echoing from deeper in the earth? Laughing, taunting, reverberating from the walls, its pressure weighing down on me as surely as the mountain of earth above my head.

"You can either tell me what's going on or I'm going back," I demanded.

The voice deeper down the tunnel shifted subtly, the laughter turning to tears, and then wails of despair.

"Come on, someone needs our help down there," Jim said, hurrying across the stone chamber to where the path narrowed again. James was right behind him, turning on his phone light as he dropped to his knees.

"I'm not going!" I said desperately. I felt like I was going to regret staying here alone, but listening to that wailing voice I knew I couldn't go on. Because I was listening to the sound of my own voice deeper in the tunnel, strange and echoed as it was.

They didn't stop to argue or convince me, and before I could rethink my decision I suddenly found myself alone. I stood frozen in fear as I listened to what I was sure was my own sobbing. I couldn't stay in this place, but at the same time I was afraid to turn back and become even more lost in this labyrinth. Listening to the sound of that crying was too much to bear though, and it wasn't long before I turned around and started climbing back the way I'd come.

"This way, he's in here."

I shuddered at Jim's voice, and flinched as the bright light emerged around the corner to shine in my face. Not the way they'd gone though—there was no mistaking it. Jim and James had emerged from the path I'd thought led toward the entrance.

I didn't let them speak, knowing it would only confuse me more. I pushed past them and ran, resolving not to stop no matter what I heard or saw until I got above ground again.

"Where are you going?" Jim shouted after me. "I thought you were trying to get out."

"Out's the other way, mate," James called. "You're going deeper."

They were lying, they had to be lying. How could they have come from deeper underground to find me? I hadn't gone far before I stopped suddenly though, realizing I should be climbing in elevation after going down the whole way here. Turning in both directions though, the path descended either way as though I was on the top of some subterranean mountain.

The cave was still again, and my blood was pounding louder than ever. I felt the pressure building and building until I couldn't help but scream, immediately slapping my hands over my mouth when I heard the sound that emerged. That wail escaping my lips—it was exactly the sound that had lured Jim and James away from me just a moment before. It really had been me who had been crying down there, not deeper in the cave, but farther ahead in time.

I hated the sobs that heaved from my body, hating them all the more for hearing them a second time. Did that mean that the ragged and dirty James was also a future version of himself, one that would become trapped down here as well?

I resolved then not to go back for them. No matter what happened, I would keep going straight and I wouldn't stop. I would keep going down, even as my flashlight flickered and dimmed. Even as the voices cried and jeered at me from the darkness. Even as I passed Jim and James over and again, sometimes apart, sometimes together, sometimes in health, other times crawling along bloody stones with the last of their strength. I would keep going and not stop or speak until I was out, and if I never make it out…

Then let this record on my phone help whoever finds me make sense of the madness of this wretched place.

## Brutal Bedtime Stories

## Hell is Heaven to the Demons

Justice isn't blind. If she cannot see, then it's simply because she doesn't care enough to look. She turned away that dark night my sister was attacked, where even the moon and stars must have hidden their faces in shame. From all accounts it was an anonymous act of brutality: an impulsive flight, a brief struggle, the humiliation of rape, and then the lifetime of silent nightmares that must surely follow such depraved violence.

I've heard it's a common story where the lonely roads meet beyond the protective halo of street lamps. For all the virtues we profess, there is a savagery dormant in us waiting only for our fellow man to blink. It is easy to be noble while someone is watching and the fear of judgment may yet steady our course. In solitude the moral compass will lose its bearing, replaced by whichever base instinct can scream louder than our pounding blood.

It is some consolation that I found the one who valued his greed over human dignity. Through the course of these confessions you will see that I am no better than the animal I hunted, so I will waste no time professing my merit now. I buy substances from a man who knew everything that happened in his neighborhood, and like anyone who seeks profit from another's misfortune, he was willing to sell me the name I required.

I found the rapist when he returned to the street my sister suffered upon: pacing and circling like a hungry animal haunting the doorstep of his last meal. He didn't see me coming, and I made no sound nor spoke no word save for the poetry my bullet inscribed in his skull. I should have departed at once, but the satisfaction that his last throes of life promised lured me into complacent voyeurism. I stayed to tell him that my sister sent her love, hoping to purchase her closure with the death rattle rising in his throat. I wasn't expecting repentance, nor did I receive it.

"It wasn't the first time, and it won't be the last," were his final words to reach living ears.

I have no-one to blame but myself and my zealous retribution for failing to notice that he didn't work alone. They were on top of me in moments, wrestling me to the ground and stomping my gun away from my shattered hand. Knives punctured my back and neck, leaving great sucking wounds which inhaled the night air; wounds breathing in place of my lungs which were swiftly filled with blood. There weren't any magnanimous thoughts or profound revelations as the light went out. One moment there was simply light and pain and noise…

And then nothing.

And then nothing.

And then… I opened my eyes to find I was no longer of this world. I knew at once, despite the fact that I was sitting at a quite ordinary wooden desk in a room no larger than janitorial closet. On the desk was a piece of paper, and on the paper was a question, and in that question was written my fate for eternity:

**WELCOME TO HELL. Would you like to:**

*1) Remain* **Human**. *You will be tortured by those who became Demons.*

*2) Become a* **Demon**. *You will torture those who remained Human.*

*P.S. If there aren't enough people to volunteer to remain Human, they will be chosen randomly.*

I do not believe it is within my nature to torture anyone. Even my sister's abuser received death as fast as an executioner's ax. But no more could it be said it is within my nature to receive torture: as unnatural a human construct as can be imagined. But if I had to choose – as I'm sure many of you would have done so far removed from the judgment of both man and God – then I choose to accept my new home and dawn the mantle of Hell I was offered.

I steeled myself against the horrendous transformation I pictured, imagining razor talons growing from my bones to rip holes in the flesh or an entropic decay to wrack my body until my skin ran down my face like candle-wax. No physical transformation came over me though, a phenomenon which I can only account to the Devil's ironic sense of humor. I knew it from the first moment the floor dropped underneath to fling me down into the charnel realm however; I was a Demon now.

And it was Heaven to me. I expected the first time to be harder. The woman was presented to me in perfect physical health. I haven't noticed any discrepancies in age since I've arrived – everyone looks to be their mid-20s here. The room sealed and I was given an hour to work on her. I find it distasteful to dwell on exactly what I did, but I remember rationalizing it cleanly with the knowledge that she was only here because she deserved it. Never mind that I was here too – never mind that it could have been me randomly chosen—never mind that she could have volunteered to suffer like this to spare another. She was in Hell, and it was my job to make sure she knew it.

It wasn't until I'd finished that I learned the second rule to this infernal game. Once the hour of punishment had been completed, the human is offered a choice: they can get revenge on me, or they can accept their pain and continue their journey. Those who refuse the chance to retaliate shall be incrementally elevated, until at last their soul is cleansed and they are set to be reborn on Earth. If however they choose to turn the torture on me instead, I will be nourished by the pain and descend further along the dark road I have chosen. For each blow inflicted upon me, my skin hardens, my muscles tighten, and my power will flourish.

It didn't take long for me to realize how to properly play. The only way for me to progress was to inflict a punishment so foul and induce a hatred so deep in my victim that they choose revenge over the quality of their immortal soul. And progress I must, for untold centuries of this game repeated has refined some Demons into legendary masters of their craft. Those Demons have carved out kingdoms for themselves in this infernal domain, and through their countless successes have transformed themselves into towering behemoths of apocalyptic ability, shattering the landscape with their tread and sending their lessers into groveling servitude. Since the moment I chose to become a Demon the gates of absolution have been closed to me forever. It may be my fate to dwell in this realm, but it was my choice to rule it.

And so I went to work honing my skill. It wasn't enough to simply batter the humans into submission; if I was to force their hand against me I had to get inside their mind, caressing and nurturing their spirit into one of mindless wrath. I learned to expose the subconscious dread lying dormant that even the bravest dare not shed light on. I mastered the art of wetting my brush in nightmares to repaint their memories until all they once knew of life was corrupted by my influence. I promised false salvation, or deceived them into thinking they had escaped, or spoiled their loved ones until they could not contain the anger I imbued within them.

But I didn't stop there. I studied the ancient texts of Demonic lore recounting the torment of dying stars from the beginning of time. I served under the foulest creatures I could find, watching their methods and improving upon their design. Experimentation, research, and endless practice refined my mastery over the subtle art until I could induce a pain so exquisite that Angels would shed their wings for the chance to smite me down. And ever I grew stronger, building a devoted following of my own to gather more humans, ever inventing and facilitating the process of extracting unbearable anguish. My human form twisted into a sentient shadow to reflect the pervasive nature of my approach, each victory making it that much easier to dismantle my prey.

And I loved every second of it. I relished in my progression and thought I could live here until the end of time, prospering and expanding my reign to all corners of the nether realm. Perhaps one day I would supplant the Devil himself, designing my own games to watch the universe fold and decay beneath my guiding hand. And perhaps I would have continued this road forever, had it not been for the fateful encounter where I finally met my match.

A human was pushed into the room with me and the door closed behind. I had an hour to play, but I wanted more. It was the man who murdered my sister: infuriatingly smug and dismissive of my ability to break his spirit. I thought I would enjoy this more than anything, but to my mounting dismay he stubbornly resisted my influence. He remained passive through the acid wash of his nerves. His mind did not falter as I summoned the image of his father's lamentations against him. Every trick, every torment, every mental ravaging left him smirking, until with exasperation I resigned myself to simply goad him into action.

"You must feel cheated. Forced to remain human at the mercy of every lowly criminal who cares to punish you."

"I wasn't forced," he replied. "I made the choice."

"Then you're an idiot who deserves what he gets."

"And what I'll get is freedom. I told you this wasn't the first time, and that it won't be the last," he said. "I've been to Hell so many times that it bores me."

So that was his secret. He had gotten out before. He knew how to play the game. But it didn't matter, because no-one played it like I did.

"So you won't retaliate?" I asked. "No matter what I do?"

He shook his head, the smirk unaltered. "I'm going back to Earth. And when I do, I'm going to remember this like I always do. I'm going to wait until I've grown strong again. And just for this, I'm going to find your sister and I'm going to do it again."

I had almost forgotten about my sister. About the world above, filled with its myriad of joys and sorrows. I missed her in that moment; I missed being alive. And as much as I enjoyed the role I had carved for myself here, I wanted to be back again. The thought that this monster would patiently wait out his trials, cheating the system over and over to return to his life of sin; it made me sick. The tables had turned, and all the hatred I sought to pour into him was rushing into me instead. I wanted nothing more than to flay him down to the core of being and set such a fire in what remained to burn for all of time. But even if somehow I could force his hand against me; even if I broke him so badly that he never escaped; I would still be here forever. And I hated him, and I hated myself, and it was the hardest thing I've ever done to hold onto that hatred and turn it aside.

And harder still to let him walk away. To bide my time, sending the weakest demons in my possession so that he might easily resist their influence. Watching, and waiting, and even helping my sister's attacker elevate through the Hell until the time of his salvation was at hand. It was hard, but it was worth it, because that is when I chose to strike.

I had already learned to infiltrate the mind in my pursuit of torture, and through my mastery I infiltrated the spirit as well. I hid within his soul when his judgment was passed, concealing my hatred within his hatred, tempering my fire with his calculating patience. And when that soul was whisked away, I traveled with it, sleeping so softly within his dreams that even he did not know he bore me as his silent passenger. Until the day when he was born again on Earth, and I with him.

The struggle was violent but brief. It is easy to wrestle an infant's mind from them, and when the child's eyes opened it was I who looked out. He may resist me yet, but I bear with me all the subtle crafts I have honed in Hell, carrying them to Earth where they can be put to better use.

You see Hell is Heaven for the Demons, but all the worst of us have found our way back home.

## Do Not Go Gentle Into That Good Night: Tobias Wade

*Grave men, near death, who see with blinding sight*
 *Blind eyes could blaze like meteors and be gay,*
 *Rage, rage against the dying of the light.*


DYLAN THOMAS SAID THAT. My grandfather. I'd heard the name thrown around the house a lot when I was growing up. It was a point of family pride to be descended from such an acclaimed poet, but it never left much of an impact on me. He'd died before I was even born, time reducing even the most brilliant souls to little more than trivia.

After-all, how could I have known that an archaic poem buried away in some dusty volume was written as a warning for what was yet to come?

My father knew better though. And I had the feeling something more was coming too, but my vague foreboding was answered with nothing but his thundering scowl. For the last week he hadn't talked much. He stopped reading like he used to and barely eats at the table, although sometimes I'll hear him prowling the house in the early hours of the morning.

And always, always of late I feel him watching me. From over his newspaper, or parked outside my friend's house after dropping me off. I even caught him sitting outside my room in the hallway, holding a mirror to get an angle through my partly closed door.

"Just checking if you're ready," he mumbled, seeming momentarily embarrassed.

I didn't reply, but it was getting weird and I would have spoken up if he didn't say something first. "Camping trip before school starts," he'd said. His voice carried the insistent authority of a policeman ordering someone to drop their gun. He didn't ask our opinion like he usually did when making plans. Mom must have sensed it too because she volunteered to start packing without hesitation.

"Don't bother," he told her. "It's just going to be me and the boy."

6 AM the next morning, he was hammering on my door. Time to go. He didn't need to tell me not to ask questions. Those sunken eyes and hard-pressed mouth left no room for argument. He was still wearing the same clothes from yesterday when he got in the car.

I kept quiet while he drove. Stoic silence, heavy silence, suffocating all opportunity for conversation. Every now and then he'd pull off the road a little to get out and look around. It felt like he didn't have any clear destination in mind, and it didn't take long for me to realize he wasn't going anywhere in particular; he just wanted to get away.

When he stopped to use the bathroom and get gas I checked the back to see what kind of gear he brought with us. Nothing in the trunk except a backpack. He brought me a sandwich, and after a brief break we were on the road again. A dirt trail cutting straight through the country finally satisfied him. The mood was so dark that I was half-expecting to be murdered the second we'd passed the last hallmark of civilization.

It was night by the time we'd stopped. The sky was a cosmic masterpiece, untainted by the erosion of electric lights. The scattered maple trees we'd passed along the way had grown denser, and dad didn't have any trouble finding some kindling to start a small fire. We didn't have a tent, or sleeping bags, or even food.

I couldn't take it anymore.

"What's going on, dad? What are we doing here?"

He grunted and stirred the fire. I was pacing with agitation now, the restless energy from a day in the car overflowing into jerky, frustrated movements.

"Why didn't you want mom to come?" I tried.

"It's none of her business. This is between you and me, and my father before him, and his father before that." He looked up at me, the guttering flames reflecting dolefully in his deep eyes.

Before I could press for more, he'd sat down on a rock beside the fire and produced an ancient book from his backpack. He held it more reverently than a mother with her child, caressing the dust from its thick leather binding.

"From New York, back to Wales, and then Ireland before that," he said, handing me the tome. "Come now, take a look."

I stood beside him as we flipped through the thick vellum pages of the manuscript. Every sheet was dedicated to a single entry, each written in a myriad of separate handwritings and styles.

"Five centuries of verse," he told me. "Each generation has inscribed lines for the last five hundred years, going all the way back to someone named Brodie in 1522. You'll notice some of the earlier pieces written in Gaelic, but they've been reliably English since around the 18th century. Tonight you're going to add yours to the end, and maybe if you're lucky, the book will be finished after that."

He flipped past the continuous stream of thought through the ages to the last few entries. My eye immediately caught the name of Dylan Thomas, who in his own hand had printed his famous poem "Do not go gentle into that good night."

I quickly began to scan the next page where my father had written:

*Bloodied, sickened, broken down, we tarry while we may.*
*For though life has wearied us, from death there's no escape.*
*One prayer, one stand, one wild charge, before it is too late,*
*For though dark and dreary thus, there's nothing left to hate.*

But father slammed the book shut and pulled it away before I could read on.

"Wait—show me what you wrote," I pressed. He shook his head, roughly dropping the book that he once cradled. "But how will I know what I'm supposed to write then?" I asked.

He was staring at the fire again, not looking at me even when he finally spoke. "Not long now. You'll know when it's time," he said. "You can't see something like that and not have something to say about it."

I didn't have to wait long, but it was unbearable while it lasted. Every rustling leaf turned to the ominous approach of some nameless horror. A snapping twig was re-imagined into the brittle bones of its latest victim, and even the whispered wind became an unpredictable adversary breathing down my neck.

And always, always, my father's eyes – fixated on me, boring into my skull. His rigid attention sent waves of tension down his face at my slightest movement.

That should have been a clear enough sign of what was to come, but I didn't see it then. I just kept watching the woods, or the fire, or the great empty sky, peering and straining my ears against a world which was deaf to us.

But then in the absence of all other sound I heard what he was waiting for: the catching of my breath. I lifted vain hands in feeble disbelief, clutching at the invisible noose around my neck. I wanted to scream, but I could barely draw enough air to breathe. Dad's eyes lit up as the wheezing gasp involuntarily escaped my closing throat. Each breath came shallower than the last; only a few seconds until they stopped altogether. I was getting dizzy, and with the passing seconds mounted a desperate crescendo of my flailing heart and smoldering lungs.

Dad was solemn as the dead, still sitting a few feet away, his eyes an inferno of reflected flames. He didn't say anything, but he withdrew the paper bag which contained my lunch and tossed it into the fire. Blue ribbons of light danced across the open air, although I don't know whether these were a product of my oxygen starved brain or some covert substance revealing their purpose from the chemical fire.

My body thrashed and revolted against the grasp of some unseen specter, yet my whirling consciousness stubbornly refused to abandon me. I felt my body lifted by the pressure around my neck, pitching me to and fro: a cresting ship on its last voyage. The world bled together like running paint, and the meager fire roared into cascading heights to spit sparks like a thousand falling stars.

The dizziness mounted until I couldn't tell left from right, up from down, living from dying. My legs were numb where they beat the open air; my fingers frozen where they scraped helpless against the unrelenting force. Even if I didn't pass out, it was surely only a matter of time before my neck broke. Past the point of all thoughts and prayers a persistent recollection stormed against the closing dark.

*Do not go gentle into that good night…*

And then another thought that was not my own, coming from within me as though my mind played puppet to its presence. A lighthouse beaming words which carved their way through the midnight of my fading mind. I was struggling again, kicking and biting and clawing at the open air. My wild lashing finally connected with something solid, but the running drool of colors flooded my vision and made it impossible to guess what held me.

Every sense, every muscle, every feral instinct begged for me to close my eyes against the nauseating tumult of color. To let go of the insurmountable force I was thrall to; to find acceptance in defeat, and peace in death. But louder than the diminishing throb of my heart were the words: *Rage, rage against the dying of the light.*

And so I did. I swam through the sea of melting colors, fixating on the black blemish which refused to relinquish my throat. I fought back, tooth and nail sinking into yielding flesh, kicking and screaming as stale air tore through my howling lungs. I lunged after that, digging my fingers into the thing that attacked me until warm wet rivers bubbled over my hands up to the wrist. I wouldn't stop, couldn't stop, pouring all my love for the light and rage against its defiler with one unified assault.

Not until it lay still did I allow myself to fall gasping onto my back. One reluctant star at a time unraveled from the tapestry of madness to find its rightful place in the heavens. My body ached to the core, and were it not for the last utterances of my internal voice still coaxing me back to life, I would have been confident that I had died.

I didn't wake until the next morning. My first shock was that I was alive; my second that my father was not. His body had crumbled beside the ashes of his fire, deep craters gouged into his throat to match the width of my hands. I didn't understand until I had a chance to read the whole book: my unequivocal inheritance.

I wasn't the first, and I won't be the last. My family has been blessed to pursue the secret of the divine spark, and through the years our trials have brought us closer to its unveiling. The voice I heard on the edge of death is the same which inspired my ancestors to write their verse: a further puzzle piece in the enigma of creation. And when the final piece is set to place, then born again is the next God to walk this Earth.

I regret to tell you that such wisdom has exhausted all efforts toward its discovery so far. When we have given up, as my father did and his father before him, it is our place to pass the torch for the child to carry on. Until the day when he too sees his child's mind flare more brightly than his own and knows it is time for them to continue the search in his stead.

I am only writing this now because I have grown so weary of doors without handles and windows looking nowhere. I wish my father had explained this to me before I was thrust upon this quest, but I suppose he thought me too cowardly to end his life and begin my search when such an end was already written by a hundred hands.

That's why I am writing this, my son, so you can make that choice for yourself. And so armed with five centuries of verse, you will listen for that whisper at the end of all light and learn from it what you may. Open the book, when you are ready, and your trial will begin.

## Dogs can Recognize Skinwalkers: Tobias Wade

It's hard to imagine what it's like to lose someone you love before it happens. Of course I've seen it a hundred times in the movies: dramatic affairs for the most part, with lots of screaming and crying and carrying on. The shock, the disbelief, the unconstrained rage; all lashing out at the world for the most ordinary and predictable thing in it.

It wasn't like that after dad disappeared though. He was simply there one day and gone the next, leaving behind nothing but a penetrating dull ache. Weeks of police investigation turned up nothing. It wasn't an act of cruelty which made the world steal him away; it was merely universal indifference. His life was short; his death random and meaningless; and there was nothing left but for the rest of us to carry on.

I got the phone call from mom late at night in my studio apartment. Dad was presumed dead, and the police had officially closed their investigation. I stayed quiet and listened to her all the way through, even though there was nothing left to say after the first line. I thanked her politely for letting me know, and then I hung up. After that I stared at the wall for about an hour, not really thinking anything, just observing idle thoughts as they passed in one side and out the other.

I live in a different state and hadn't even seen him in a couple of months. Eventually I decided that waking up tomorrow wasn't going to be any different than every other day when he was still puttering around the kitchen table a thousand miles away.

But I was wrong. I'd lived alone for years, but my apartment had never felt so empty. I had to keep the TV on all the time just so I wouldn't have to hear the soft gurgle of blood in my veins or listen to the dull monotony of my own breath. I don't know how I never noticed those sounds before, but they were starting to drive me crazy now. I guess I couldn't stop thinking about how fragile my own mortality was, and how pointless my life would have been if it were all to end.

That's why I got a dog. Half-husky, half-coyote, about six months old; I picked her up from the animal shelter where some cowboy was dropping her off. The dog was growling and snarling at him, but she calmed down the instant he left. I figured she must have been abused or something, but she seemed so sweet to everyone else that I decided to take her home with me.

A few days later I got the call that dad wasn't dead. About a month after he'd disappeared, he'd just showed up again. Mom said he just walked in one day and sat down at the breakfast table like nothing had happened. She couldn't get a word out of him about where he'd been, but she was so happy to have him back she didn't even press. He wouldn't tell me anything either, just grunted something about "needing to clear his head". It seemed like a miracle to me too, but I guess I had already spent so much time fixating on death that nothing much changed for me.

I kept the dog anyway and named her Snoots, and from the very first time I called her that her ears pressed flat with excitement and she started wagging up storm. She was really skittish at first, but she hated being alone and would follow me from room to room, even sitting between my legs when I sat on the toilet.

## Sleepless Nights

Snoots was absolutely perfect for me. Her constant attention made me feel like I mattered again. Maybe my life didn't matter in an existential sort of way, and maybe my death wouldn't mean anything on a cosmic scale, but it would mean the world to her. I was warned it might be hard to train her because of the coyote blood, but she learned everything almost immediately. She was so shy that she'd try to walk between my legs when a stranger was nearby, but it felt so good knowing she trusted me.

She did have one bad habit though: unpredictably going off. The first time was a couple months after I got her. We were walking down the sidewalk toward the park when her fur started to bristle and her mouth flared to reveal powerful teeth. Before I knew what was happening, she was snarling and barking and howling at the lady on the other side of the street. The lady started running and Snoots actually lunged at the leash, almost dragging me into the street after her.

As soon as the lady was gone, Snoots was back to normal. I couldn't figure out what happened. She had never even growled at another animal before. The lady didn't have a dog with her, and she wasn't carrying food or anything. She hadn't made the least threatening move. It was so random that I just forgot about it, but that wasn't the only time.

The next time it happened she jumped up from the couch and started snarling at the door. A few seconds later someone knocked and she howled in answer. I looked through the peak-hole, but it was only the pizza guy. I had to drag Snoots into the bathroom and lock her there until he left before she would calm down.

That behavior happened so rarely that I couldn't figure out how to predict or prevent it. I couldn't just keep her isolated, and it was pointless to take her to training when she was usually the sweetest thing in the world. I was terrified that she would randomly attack someone and would be taken away from me though. I kept her daytime walks short after that, only going out early in the morning or late at night when there weren't so many people around.

Another few months went by and I thought her feral side had finally been tamed when it happened again. It was after 9 PM and we were doing a last walk through the park before it closed. I was talking to mom and dad on the phone and wasn't really paying attention to Snoots snuffling along behind. My first warning was when the leash snapped violently taut, ripping the phone from my hand.

I automatically dove to catch my phone. Snoots was dragging so hard she managed to break the leash free from my grasp. I couldn't stop her from charging headlong into the darkness, a guttural snarl rising in her throat. I chased after her, shouting her name, screaming a warning for whoever was out there... but by the time I caught up with her, Snoots was already on top of someone. She had his hand in her mouth, savagely thrashing back and forth like she was trying to rip it off. The guy was trying to push her back, but Snoots kept lunging in at him whenever she lost her grip. By the time I caught up with them she had had her teeth around his neck, ferociously shaking like wild animals do when they're looking for a quick kill.

I got hold of the leash and pulled so hard Snoots practically did a back-flip. The guy was on his feet now, swaying unsteadily. I started to apologize, but the words died in my mouth. His hand was a bloody pulp, severed digits scattered on the ground. The wounds on his neck were even more brutal. A whole sheet of skin was peeled back, hanging in ragged tatters along his shoulder. Part of his spine had ruptured straight through the side where it had been unmistakably broken. Exposed sinew glistened with blood as he slowly worked his neck in a long circle like someone luxuriously stretching after a long nap.

I don't even know how he was still conscious. I wanted to go back for my phone to call for help, but it took all my strength just to keep Snoots from diving back in to finish her prey. The man started fumbling at the ruined tatters of his neck, not taking his eyes off me. I braced myself, half expecting him to attack us right back in retaliation.

He was too focused on his own injuries though. I was trapped in place holding Snoots back, helpless to turn away from what happened next. He grabbed the hanging folds of his skin with his good hand and started to peel it down the remainder of his neck. Then he reached around to his back and started to peel it there too, the whole mess of flesh flopping away like a diver getting out of a wet suit. I watched, transfixed but mortified as he slid out of the rest of his skin and clothing to leave them both in a soggy pile at his feet.

It wasn't exactly muscle underneath. It was more like a second skin, pale-grey and slick with blood, but it was fitted so closely to the structures underneath that it mirrored the muscle's striations and fibers. I didn't have long to stare though. He was running as soon as he was free, leaving behind the whole wet mess he'd shed on the ground.

I ran home with Snoots as fast as I could. I didn't even go back for discarded phone. I kept telling myself it wasn't real until I got back into my apartment, but it was harder to lie to myself while washing the blood off Snoots's face and fur. She was wagging her tail again, looking like her old self until she opened her mouth to let the last severed finger drop onto the floor.

I couldn't be alone after that. Even Snoots wasn't enough company. I talked with mom for a long time to help calm down, although I didn't breathe a word about what happened. She sensed that I was rattled though, and she convinced me to come back home and visit home for a while.

I kept Snoot with me, more afraid of the thing that discarded its skin than how she reacted to it. I have her locked in the car with me where I'm writing this now though. I want to run in and hug mom and tell her how good it is to see her again. I want to ask dad about what happened – why he left, and why he decided to come back.

# Sleepless Nights

I can't get out of the car though. I can't let Snoots out. Not with her snarling since the moment I pulled into mom's driveway. There was only one thing that worked Snoots up like that, and I couldn't lie to myself and say it was something else. The only conclusion I could draw was that dad may have really disappeared, but whatever came back was only pretending to be him.

I left Snoots in the car and knocked on the door. I let out a long breath of relief when mom opened the door. Then a hand fell on her shoulder, and the thing that looked like my dad popped up into view. It made me sick to imagine the bloody-slick grey skin underneath that intimate mask. It was one thing to lose my father, but having to look at him again like this was unbearable.

They invited me in and I sat down, but I couldn't take my eyes off him. The disguise was seamless. His affection genuine. Both of them avoided any mention of his disappearance, and I didn't bring it up either. I had to find some way of breaking the illusion though. I couldn't very well just sic Snoots on him and mangle him in the living room. I had to bide my time and wait until I could get him alone.

I got my chance later that evening. Snoots was out back in the yard, still agitated and restless from his proximity to the creature. Mom was out at the store picking up some things for dinner. I invited "Dad" out to the yard to toss a football around like we used to. I figured we could take him by surprise and get rid of him before mom got back. She'd just think he disappeared again, and if she could accept it once, then hopefully she could accept it again. It was better than letting that thing live inside the house, watching her sleep, just waiting to make its move.

I had one of his hunting knives gripped in my hand. I waited just outside the door. I couldn't wait until Snoots started snarling or he might realize he was caught and get away. I had to strike hard, and fast, and then Snoots could join me and help finish the job. I tried not to think of that thing wearing my father's sweater as anything but a monster. I tried to tell myself it was the thing that had killed and replaced my real father. Anything to make it easier to do the deed before the opportunity was lost.

And then the door opened. He stepped outside, not noticing me pressed against the side of the house. I grabbed him from behind, not wanting to see his face. I plunged the knife into his side, not wanting to let him speak. He pitched forward and I let go of the knife. I still couldn't look at him, so I ran to the yard and opened the gate. Now's the chance! I shouted at Snoots, but she wasn't moving. Her fur was calm. She ran up to lick me and her tail started wagging. I had to drag her out of the yard, thrusting her toward the creature crawling on the ground. Snoots looked back at me, unsure of what to do.

I almost thought I really had gone crazy until at last the fur started to bristle down her back. She bared her fangs, hunching down in preparation to pounce. It wasn't until then that I noticed the sound of tires on the gravel driveway on the other side of the house. Snoots wasn't paying my father any attention. It was my mother she sensed.

Snoots was sprinting around the side of the house and I ran to keep up with her. Mom was just starting to get out of the car with an armful of groceries when the dog sprang. She managed to get the door closed in time, but Snoots wasn't giving up. She beat herself against the window, snarling and slamming herself over and over into the car. Mom was in reverse now, tearing back out of the driveway, out into the street to disappear around the block.

I called the ambulance, but dad didn't look like he was going to last. Snoots came to lick his face, but the blood wouldn't stop and I didn't know what to do. He said he didn't blame me, but every word was getting weaker than the last. I asked him why he left, but I could have already guessed the answer. He'd run when he found out mom had been replaced by one of the Skinwalkers.

"Then why'd you come back?" I had to ask. I needed some closure before he was gone for good this time.

"Because I still loved her," he told me. "And that thing is the closest there is to having her back again."

## Dreams are a Two-Way Window: Tobias Wade

Infinity captured in an hourglass, turn it over and it begins again. That's what dreams are to me. I always romanticized dreams as a window into innumerable secret worlds and forbidden fantasies. It wasn't until I began lucid dreaming that I realized every time I looked out through the window, something else was looking back at me.

The concept of lucid dreaming fascinated me since I first learned about it in my psychology class. I couldn't even believe it was a real phenomenon at first; it seems more like a super power to me.

To create any world or situation with such vivid detail that I become God of my own personal universe. That must be too good to be true, but there it was. Printed clearly in my psychology textbook: a guide how to induce lucid dreams. I even made a photocopy in the library to hang above my bed as a constant reminder to follow these steps until I mastered the elusive and subtle art.

**Step One**: Reality Checks

The textbook recommended I try to push a finger through my opposite hand at least ten times a day. This will habituate the motion and make it more likely for it to occur in my dreams. When I try the check in a dream, the finger is supposed to pass straight through my hand and prove it isn't real. The self-awareness that I'm dreaming is what triggers lucidity.

**Step Two**: Set an Early Alarm

I set it for 2 hours earlier than I usually wake up. When the alarm sounded, my goal is to turn it off *without* opening my eyes to make the next transition smoother. This technique is called "wake induced lucid dreaming".

**Step Three**: Mindfulness

After that I have to try and stay mentally awake while I let the rest of my body go back to sleep. This is known as sleep paralysis because my mind will be awake in a frozen body. It occurs because I've interrupted **REM** sleep where the dreams occur, prompting the body to return there as fast as possible.

It took a few days of practice before things started to click. At first I kept accidentally falling back asleep after my alarm rang. Soon I was able to maintain concentration, but then I started to see some basic colors and shapes, and I got so excited that I fully woke up. The longer I persisted though, the more real the images became.

Shapes morphed into forms and the dappled specks of light grew and twisted into rich tapestries of color. Sometimes it felt like an ordinary dream, but as I continued to practice I learned to prolong my focus until the imagery fully matured.

Less than a week had passed before I was reliably alert enough to perform my reality checks, and after that came absolute freedom. I began with enacting idle sexual fantasies, but the sheer possibility of exploration made it difficult for me to maintain attention on any one creation for long. My favorite dream to spin was where I stood in a dark room with a paint brush that transformed everything it touched. Mountains ripped through the ground and soared at my command, and a single stroke on my eternal canvas brought flocks of birds into flight. Crystalline caverns, riding dragons, alien encounters, and the entire cosmos stitched onto the back of my hand; I raced through my dreams with insatiable wonder and boundless delight.

And I kept getting better too. I invented a dozen more reality checks involving clocks, mirrors, counting fingers – anything to ensure I would always find a way to become aware. My worlds became more intricate, and I was able to cast distinct characters and plots to entertain me. It's not like this was the only thing going on in my life, but it was the best, and every night I couldn't wait to uncover the latest treasure in my mind.

That is, until I discovered I was being watched. As my awareness became more defined I grew cognizant to certain elements in my dream which remained stubbornly beyond my control. It started off as a vague uneasiness which settled upon dreams like a gathering dusk of the spirit. I couldn't make out anything specifically wrong, but I can only describe the feeling as though I was a character in someone else's dream. All I had to do was tear down my canvas and begin again in a new dream though, and the feeling would be gone…

For a little while anyway.

Each successive escape solidified the presence in my mind, and like an intrusive guilty thought it penetrated my next dream. I built castles only to find eyes I never conceived of watching me from cracks in the stone. A flight through the air went sour as the sun turned to watch my aerial maneuvers. On to an undersea adventure, but my paranoia amplified as an eel followed me relentlessly through the water. Reality checks confirmed my dream, but I couldn't banish these watchers. I could only hope to lose them by starting again, although each time they found me swifter than before.

I became so unnerved that I forced myself to wake up. I found myself in a cold sweat, panting in the cool morning air. The first step of my morning ritual was now a full range of reality checks. I allowed myself to relax as I passed each one. Just a bad dream, I told myself. I swatted the fly away which snuck in during the night and prepared myself for just another ordinary day. But once they've found you, the watchers will never let go.

I felt anxious all day; a source-less, gnawing feeling that made me keep checking over my shoulder. I second-guessed the motives of everyone who turned to look at me, and when my psychology professor asked me a question in class I froze like a hunted prey. I had to try and push my finger through my palm, right in front of everyone, just to make sure. The warm pressure of skin against skin snapped me back to reality and I was able to mumble a cohesive enough answer for him to turn away. But if I wasn't dreaming, then why did his eyes swim through his skin so that they continued watching me after he had turned? Even with his back to me, I could still see them peeking out through his shaggy grey hair.

Growing awareness works the same way in this world as it does in dreams. As soon as I became aware of one discrepancy, I began to notice them all. The same fly which had been following me all day continued dancing orbits above my head. Passing gazes lingered on me longer than they used to, and always, always the eyes would return in the most unlikely places.

A dropped notebook on the floor opened to perfect sketch of an eye looking at me. A sip of coffee left the fleeting imprint of something staring at me from the foam. From knots in the trees to chips in the sidewalk, everything was an eye and all of them were directed at me.

I don't know whether it was a relief or a fresh terror that waited for me at home. Stepping into the bathroom, my reflection had completely disappeared. That was the first reality check to fail all day. At least if I was still dreaming then it meant I wasn't going crazy…

I couldn't will myself to wake up anymore though, no more than I could will myself not to see through open eyes. I tried throwing myself into bed, tossing fitfully until I at last slipped into an uneasy slumber. I was hoping that falling asleep in a dream would be enough to make me wake up for real, but it only threw me into a fresh absurdity of dreams that even my awareness could not tame.

Ghastly specters of thought whirled through a mind so saturated with fear that I lost track of right from left; of reality and fabrication. Lips began to accompany the eyes in more varied and tortured forms than my waking imagination could conjure. Faces pressed in around me as though struggling to break free from the suffocating cloth that my dream enveloped them in. More than being watched, I was terrified that they would start to speak to me. I don't know why, but just as I had bottled the divine spark of creation, I knew they now dreamed of me and that I would be slave to their slightest utterance.

Faster I spun, willing myself to wake but holding back for the horror of what I might find there. Through the dreams I raced, new ones forming before the searing lights of the last had even faded from my vision. Worlds collided together into maddening abstraction as men with fish-heads rode on horses across the clouds with lances of lightning. Through the clouds the faces pressed, withered lips peeling back to laugh and grunting in mockery of human speech. Endless possibilities are a double-edged sword. An eternity in Heaven is not the same length as an eternity in Hell.

At least now I know why they're watching. They're looking for a way out, just like you're looking for a way in. They've been doing this for much longer than you have, and whatever trick you think you know, you can count on them knowing it too. I know because for as long as I practiced and prepared myself while awake, I've spent many times over learning from the watchers in my sleep.

I'm awake now. For real this time (I think), although I run through my list of reality checks so compulsively that my palm is bloody and raw where the finger keeps pressing in. This isn't a warning against lucid dreaming though, however it may sound. I've seen how shrewdly the watchers hide, and know they were watching me long before I became aware of their existence. They might not reveal themselves to you before you become lucid, but that only means you can't protect yourself from them until it's too late.

Dreams are a two-way window, and if you aren't brave enough to stare down the face on the other side, they can be a door as well.

## For Sale: Human Head. Condition: Used: Tobias Wade

Best ad I'd seen on craigslist all day. I'd spent the last hour surfing the site for a passive-aggressive gift for my ex-girlfriend's wedding. Was this a possible candidate for gag gift of the year? Well I certainly thought so.

I didn't think it was a real for a second when I texted the user. I just told him what I wanted it for and asked if he had any left. It didn't even have to look that real – just enough for a little jump scare and a good laugh.

Here's the reply I got a few minutes later:
PLENTY LEFT. DO YOU CARE WHOSE?
Screw the fact that he's shipping heads. There's nothing that labels someone crazy like typing in all CAPS. But hey, let's be fair here. Considering I was asking

about buying one, maybe I didn't have a right to condemn his eccentricities. I replied and told him I didn't care, just as long as it wasn't someone I know (I mean come on, he's got to have a sense of humor, right?)

WHO DO YOU KNOW? I'LL CHECK.

I asked for a picture and told him I would let him know if I recognized them. I didn't hear back after that and figured the joke had run its course. Just as well really. Maybe it was petty to try to sabotage the happiest day of her life. Then again, she did sabotage my *entire* life when she decided to wait until I'd finished paying off her college loans to tell me she was seeing someone else …

It wasn't until that evening when I got the next reply.

SHE WILL LOVE THIS ONE. NICE AND FAT. HE DOESN'T NEED IT ANYMORE.

I almost choked on the pizza I was eating. Fat was a generous description of the picture he sent. Bloated would have been more accurate, like it had been sitting out in the sun for a long time. Congealed blood still clung to the base where several inches of spinal chord extended past the tattered flesh of the neck. The nose was gone, replaced with an explosion of sticky cartilage from where a massive force like a shovel had pummeled it in.

I've had a few hours to contemplate my life choices, and now that I was staring at the picture while trying to eat, I knew this was a bad idea. *Sorry not interested*, I replied before blocking the number.

The next morning I woke up to three more pictures sent from a different phone. Each bore a macabre description:

THIS LITTLE LADY WAS A FIGHTER, SO SHE'S A LITTLE MORE KNOCKED AROUND.

MY ONLY OLD MAN. THOSE BLOTCHES ON THE SKIN WERE THERE BEFORE.

IF YOU WANT MINT CONDITION, CHECK OUT THIS GIRL. POISONED. NOT A MARK ON HER.

THERE ARE some things you just have to ask even if you don't want to know the answer. Stuff like "do you love him" and "how long will dad be gone for this time?"

"Where are you getting all these heads from" is another one of those questions. I typed it in, simultaneously eager and afraid for the reply.

I ONLY NEEDED THE BODIES.

I seriously considered reporting this creep to the police, but again I still figured it was just a bad joke that I didn't want to waste more time on. I told him not to contact me again and blocked this number too.

A week later I arrived at the wedding empty handed. Without a date. My ex gave me a tight smile and that half-assed hug which is usually reserved for people with a severe skin condition. She said it was nice of me to be here and thanked me for the present.

Present, what present? She told me someone dropped one off with my name on it. I found it sitting on the table in the reception room; a little brown box about the size of a bowling ball with a flair of red string tied up in a dainty bow. A note was slipped underneath which read:

YOU SEEM TO HAVE TROUBLE DECIDING. HERE'S A FREE DEMO TO TRY OUT. IF YOU AREN'T 100% SATISFIED, YOU CAN EXCHANGE IT WHEN YOU'RE DONE.

So many questions came to mind, like how he found me or what exactly one does to "try out" a head? When I lifted the box up to grab the note I couldn't help but notice the dark sticky stain soaking through the bottom and onto the table. I couldn't exactly leave it there. Shit, what was I thinking? It had my name on it and everything. Most of the people were still arriving and talking outside, so I just grabbed it and made for the door. There was a return address after the "demo period" had expired, so at least I could get rid of it.

I scuttled across the dance room, trying my best to wipe up any errant drips which were soaking through the bottom. I almost made it to the door before I spotted my ex. Quick turn-around, racing for the backdoor instead. More people were flooding in now, including her family and many of her friends who knew me. None of them could have guessed what I was carrying though, so as long as I could make it to the door …

… or at least I could have if backdoor wasn't wired to the fire alarm. The blaring sound shocked me so much I almost dropped the box. It started to open and I caught a glimpse of the bloody pulp inside. It half-flopped out of the box as it tumbled, and I had to scramble to keep it closed. From the shards of splintered bone to the puddle of dried blood around the base, I had no doubt that it was real. By the time I looked up, the whole room was staring at me.

There was only one thing louder than the alarm after-that: my ex's mother screaming *" he's trying to steal the presents!"*

My panic-stricken brain didn't want people to think I was a thief, so I just dropped the box. If I had been able to think *even a little* more clearly I would have realized it was much worse for them to think I was a murderer, but I couldn't deal with that accusing siren or all those disapproving eyes. I dropped it and ran, swearing to myself that it wouldn't matter as long as I never saw any of those people again for the rest of my life.

I did get some messages though. The next day, my ex told me that my present was a big hit. Everyone loved the gag. They thought the head was a symbolic gesture which meant her past romances were dead, and I was so sweet for giving my blessing like that. I guess no-one looked close enough to decide whether or not it was real.

It's the other messages that bother me more though. All CAPS, sent to remind me that:

YOUR FREE TRIAL IS UP. YOU CAN PAY 10,000 TO KEEP THE HEAD, OR SEND ONE BACK IF YOU'RE FINISHED.

Now where the hell am I going to get another head?

## I Buy and Sell Memories: Tobias Wade

You know those people who treat everything like they've just been asked to climb mount Everest? Where every little thing is an insurmountable ordeal, whether it's waking up, taking a shower, or even just going outside? Almost as if the whole world was an elaborate conspiracy designed solely to slightly inconvenience them, god-forbid some effort was actually required to survive.

That was my buddy Craig. What irritated me the most is that he hadn't always been like that. Growing up he read philosophy and filled notebooks with plans about what he was going to do when he grew up, meticulously mapping out possible career paths with their required steps. He graduated high-school with nearly perfect grades, and after he was accepted into MIT, I figured his whole life was pretty much set.

The only thing that could have stopped him from getting what he wanted was getting something he thought he wanted, and her name was Natalie. Controlling, obsessive, jealous, always putting him down for this or chewing him out for that. I have no idea why he stuck with her, but two years later when he dropped out I can only imagine that was the cause.

They broke up soon after, but the damage was already done. Craig was an absolute mess. He couldn't get out of bed without a beer, and every time we talked it was just him bitching about how much he missed Natalie and how worthless he felt without her. I thought it was just going to be a phase and that he'd move on, but the obsession just kept growing in an endless feedback loop.

He couldn't do anything because he felt like shit. He felt like shit because he couldn't do anything. And on and on, doubts feeding doubts. Hating her and loving her, and then hating himself for both. Even though I'd known him since we were kids, I was getting to the point of just giving up on and cutting him out for good. Last week I decided to tell him to his face: one last shot at taking some responsibility for his life.

I hardly recognized the guy who opened the door. Clean shaven and grinning from ear to ear, Craig invited me inside. His apartment was immaculate all the way down to the gleaming grout in his tile floor. His laptop was open to spreadsheets and a color coded calendar. I couldn't believe the transformation. I congratulated him on finally getting past Natalie, but he didn't understand what I was talking about.

"Natalie? Who is Natalie?" he asked.

I thought it was a joke at first, but she was just one piece of the puzzle. He kept talking about high-school like it was yesterday, and how excited he was to start MIT. It didn't take long for me to realize the last two years of his life were completely gone. He seemed obviously better for it though, so I held my tongue in case I accidentally reminded him of something that sent him back into his depressive spiral.

It wasn't until I left when I noticed the business card half-concealed beneath his entry mat. Black card, back and front, with nothing but the words "**I buy and sell memories**" and a phone number.

I wouldn't have believed it if I hadn't just seen the results. It was one thing to discard shameful or destructive memories, but the chance of buying new ones too? Maybe I could remember what it was like to travel the world without any of the expense or inconvenience. Or learn new skills without the effort of practice. My fingers were actually trembling as I dialed the number.

An automated voice guided me through the steps of setting up a free consultation. By the next morning I was in the office building, checking the directories for "Dr. Sinclair". Sure enough, there he was, his office listed as *Cognitive Reconstruction*.

"It's not magic," the beak-nosed doctor told me as I sat down. "My team has mapped a large archive of neuronal patterns which can be replicated with their corresponding electrical signals."

I didn't really understand what that meant, but throughout the session he drove his case home. Folders filled with brain scans, a wall cluttered with degrees, and my own mounting excitement proved an irresistible combination. Within the hour I had signed consent for the treatment.

"We're going to put you under for this part," Dr. Sinclair told me. "The fluctuations of the conscious mind make it impossible to get an accurate reading of baseline activity. Just write down a list of memories you'd like to have when you wake-up."

I did so before reclining on his sofa while he set up the anesthesia mask.

"I'm not going to have to forget anything to make room, am I?" I asked.

"Old telephone numbers, the occasional date or address—nothing but clutter. Deep breaths now."

It seemed too good to be true. I was absolutely euphoric as I inhaled the strawberry scented gas. Dr. Sinclair briefly studied the list I wrote before crumpling it up in his hand.

"These are rubbish," he said, his words distorting like a radio with a weak signal.

The anesthesia was muddling my mind, but a brief surge of panic still flooded my veins. I started to sit up, but he put a hand over the mask and pressed my head firmly back into the couch.

"Most people prefer to hold onto their good memories, mind you," he said. "The ones they sell me tend to be a tad more…*exotic*. Why don't you just relax and let me choose?"

It wouldn't quite be accurate to say I fell asleep then. It was more like I fell awoke, slipping in an and out of consciousness so subtly that I didn't even realize time had passed. One second I was struggling against the mask, and the next I tore it off my face and sat up panting. Only now I was sitting on the sidewalk. The mask lay at my feet, dangling from its severed chords. Dr. Sinclair was nowhere to be seen.

And everything in the world was wrong. The roar of traffic bludgeoned me from the nearby street. I flinched and cowered as my every instinct screamed a warning for the impending collision, even though I was well out of harm's way. Dark clouds had begun rolling in from the sky and I shuddered, imagining some phantasmic presence leering at me from behind them. The eyes of passing strangers cut me with their disdain.

Everything in the world was normal. I was the one who was wrong. In the space of those odd hours on Dr. Sinclair's couch I had lived through the nightmares of a hundred lives. A man like my father had beaten me to within an inch of my life, although I knew he wasn't the father I grew up with. My hand burned as it had when it was torn off by a tractor, even though I could see its perfect vitality at the end of my wrist. I had been shot at, maimed, humiliated, and betrayed a hundred times, and so could I feel the blood of my victims as fresh as the day they were choked to death by hands that were not my own.

I don't know how long I sat there screaming on the sidewalk before someone called the police. I'm vaguely aware of an ambulance picking me up, but my internal world was so much more vibrant and clashed so disorienting with the one I saw that I couldn't keep them straight. The hellish memories were mixed with my own so seamlessly that I couldn't figure out which were true and which were not. Maybe I had done these things, hurt these people. Maybe I deserved to suffer.

But the maddening conflict of a hundred contradictory memories made it impossible to maintain any coherent identity. By the time I got to the hospital, I couldn't have told you my own name. I didn't even know whether I was a man or a woman, having lived distinctly through the most traumatic ordeals of each.

The next time I was able to make sense of the world was within a hospital room. Dr. Sinclair was there as I had seen him last, peering down at me from over a clipboard. His presence was branded into my mind, and I couldn't turn

## Sleepless Nights

away from him to look at who he was talking to on my other side. He was the point of singularity: the one common aspect in all my separate lives. The person I most feared and most needed in the whole world. I had seen him from so many different eyes and known him from so many different minds that all these thoughts conjoined into an amorphous blob of desperate hope.

"Patient exhibiting signs of psychosis, schizophrenia, and multiple personality disorder," Dr. Sinclair was saying. "He is a danger to himself and others, and must not leave this room until I consent. Is that understood?"

"Yes doctor."

"I know he's your friend, so if you'd like to be reassigned—"

"No doctor. I can handle it," Craig said from my other side. "?I just want what's best for him."

"We all do," Dr. Sinclair replied, his voice oozing with compassion. "?I'll check in again at the end of my rounds. Buzz me if he remembers anything about that man."

I turned to Craig as the doctor exited the room. Craig was wearing a white lab coat as well, his own clipboard hanging limp at his side. My mouth twisted with uncertainty, trying to make sense of which language was natural to its shape.

"Get some rest," Craig said. "The Doctor knows best. He's going to make you better again."

"He did this to me," I managed to match my thoughts to English.

"Me too," Craig grinned. "He was my professor at MIT. He told me I was failing, and that I'd be expelled unless I participated in the experiment."

"But the nightmares—"

"Yeah, I guess I missed that part," Craig said. "I just had my last two years erased. I've been relying on him to fill me in on the details."

My words were failing. There was so much pain, and loss, and suffering spinning around my head. No-one should ever be forced to bury their son or endure their loved ones wasting away from cancer. Not once. How was I supposed to survive it dozens of times?

Craig patted my hand as he stood to leave. I was speechless, comprehending but bewildered by the situation I was forced into.

"And besides," Craig said as he passed through the door. "These memories will make you stronger if you can get through them. Stronger than you thought possible. Nothing will be able to hurt you after this."

"And if I can't get through?" I asked.

Craig shrugged. "Then you'll be left behind, same as everyone who can't move on from the past. Same as you were going to do to me."

## Flesh-Eating Sea Bugs: Tobias Wade

I'm sure many of you have read the recent news story about the flesh-eating sea bugs. The guy didn't feel a thing standing in the water, but when he stepped out his feet were savaged into a bloody mess, completely perforated by the creatures.

That may sound bad, but after what I've seen, I know it's going to get a whole lot worse.

If you're like me, then your reaction went something like this.


1) WTF, gross. I don't want to look at that.

2) But... a *bug* did that? Actually that's kind of cool. I want to see it again.

First of all, I live in Australia, so assuming all the killer jellyfish and snakes weren't deterrents enough, I'm pretty sure swimming is off the menu for me.

It did give me another idea though. So far I've been stubbornly refusing to acknowledge my summer break science project (we just get 6 weeks, unlike the States), but class will be starting up again soon and I had to pick something. What could be more fun than studying flesh-eating bugs?

A little research revealed that the perpetrator was probably Lysianassidae, a family of marine amphipods. They're a type of detritivore, which means their diet is primarily comprised of decomposing organic matter. As the unusual case recently demonstrated however, they are perfectly adept at shredding living tissue as well.

I actually live pretty close to the beach where it happened, so I figured I'd just collect a water sample for my display, write a report, post some newspaper clippings on a poster board, and voila. All done.

The only tricky part was that I had to go at night. The beach was temporarily closed for an "Environmental Safety Evaluation", but all accounts online suggested it was an incredibly rare and isolated incident. I figured I wouldn't even find any of them, but just to be safe I was up to my knees in rubber galoshes and didn't wade in very far.

I filled a couple glass vials before I got out of the water, but I couldn't tell much just from eyeballing them. The water was murky, and even though I saw some little critters floating around, they could have been anything. I was all set to hike back to my car when I saw the flashlights scouring the beach.

I wasn't allowed to be here, so my first instinct was to run. There was nowhere to hide on the open sand though, and I figured they'd spot me as soon as I started to move. All I could do was press myself into the sand and hope for the best.

The beam of light passed right over my head. I clenched my eyes shut, praying they'd missed me. "All clear, sir."

"Good." The voice was deep and gravely like it was obscured from years of smoke. "Back the van up here and keep it moving. We're going to be in and out in 10 minutes."

I heard a car pull up nearby in the closed parking lot. I didn't lift my head because I was terrified that any movement would give me away. I had the feeling that these guys weren't supposed to be here either, but that might make it even worse for me if I was found.

It sounded like they were dragging something heavy through the sand. I wanted to look so damn bad. I lifted my head just enough to see a massive dolly piled high with bags like fertilizer. It was being pushed across the sand on mounted skies by four men in dark blue overalls.

"It's going to get a lot more visible when the activating catalyst hits the water," the gravel voice said. He was an old man, long white hair flowing half-way to his ass. "Line up the bags, and don't pour them until they're all open and ready to go. Three minutes tops, make it happen."

The men in overalls pulled long bone-handled knives from their belt and systematically slashed the bags open. I strained from my prone position, but I couldn't see what was inside. Their attention was all diverted though, so this seemed like a good chance to make my escape. I pushed myself up to my hands and knees and started a huddled dash back toward the street.

It must have been close to midnight then. Around 10 seconds later, it felt like noon. A wave of green light overtook me from behind and illuminated the sky into ghastly pale. I stumbled over myself, pitching flat again before looking behind. The men were pouring the bags into the ocean one by one, and where the powder inside met the water an explosive wave of luminescence blasted out like lightning streaking through the waves.

It took my eyes several seconds to adjust before I realized the old man was staring directly at me. Robbed the cover of darkness, I lay stark under his steel gaze. If I had hesitated any longer, I would have been dead.

A loud crack rent the night air and the sand ruptured directly in front of me. Another shot – this time tearing through the air an inch from my shoulder. I was back on my feet, dodging through the palm trees that flourished densely at the end of the beach.

Shouting interspersed the explosions of light behind me. I didn't trust the open road around my car, so I stayed in the thicket until the shouting passed. A few minutes later I heard the roar of the van ripping out of the parking lot. I counted to a hundred before I could breathe evenly again. As far as I could tell, they were gone.

I crept back to the empty beach to try and figure out what the hell happened. The water was still glowing softly green, but it was nothing like the display I'd seen a moment ago. The ocean silently churned and boiled as dark shapes slipped below the surface. Something was feeding on whatever these guys had dumped into the water.

The tracks from the dolly were hastily swept up all the way to the parking lot. It looks like they were in a hurry. Approaching the water, I found a small pile of the powder that had been carelessly spilled onto the beach. I gathered it up in one of my extra vials before hightailing it out of there.

I'm not sure who I could contact and be taken seriously about this, so I resolved to do a little experiment of my own. When I got home I poured my samples of Ocean water into a big mixing bowl and then dumped the powder into the water. Sure enough, there was a bright flash upon contact, although nothing compared with the neon splendor in the ocean. Within about 10 minutes the light had all but completely faded, but even my small sample had begun to boil and churn.

I left the mixture out overnight and went to bed, checking it first thing this morning when I woke up. The bowl was nearly overflowing with squirming dark shapes, each almost four inches long. Rows of razor sharp teeth like needles flashed in the light, and a hundred little legs flailed against the walls of the confined space.

Out of a morbid curiosity I dropped a fried chicken drumstick into the water. One of them attempted to swallow it instantaneously, becoming hopelessly encumbered on the bone. The others wasted no time taking advantage of the opportunity, devouring the helpless creature alive. Within seconds even the chicken bone had completely vanished, and all those beady little eyes were turned to fix on me for their next meal. They didn't get it.

By midday, there were only four of them left. They were eating each other with unrestrained savagery, snapping off the legs of any that swam too close. By evening there was only 3, but they'd grown to almost a foot long. I had to dump them into the bathtub to keep them from getting out. I don't know what I'm going to do with them, but the limited space and meager scraps I'm sustaining them with must limit their growth eventually.

I can only imagine what is going on right now in the vastness of the ocean where they're free to reach their full potential.

## Every Subway Car

### Every Subway Car: Tobias Wade

New York is a complicated city to live in. Here, the only way to fit in is to be different. I've tried being that girl who minds her own business, but keeping out of trouble has only ever invited others to start trouble with me. That's why I'm done being quiet and submissive. If you allow yourself to be constrained by social norms, you're never going to win a race against someone who isn't similarly burdened. And to me, there's nothing quite so liberating as singing.

At the bakery while I cook, through the streaming rivers of huddled faces outside, even on the subway; I'll just start singing whatever comes to mind. Not that self-conscious mumbling to echo music from my headphones either—I throw my shoulders back, open my chest, and really belt it out. People don't care as much as you'd think. Most of them don't even notice. Compared to the guy with a boa constrictor around his neck, or the pair of homeless people having sex against a wall, singing is a pretty harmless quirk. It gives me what I need to feel like I belong.

There was one time when my singing really caught someone's attention though. There were about a dozen other people on the subway, so I started off with a soft song (Hide and Seek by Imogen Heap) to make sure I wasn't bothering anyone. No-one even looked up, except for one guy wearing a black hoodie. I like matching the beat to the steady th-THUMP of the car on its tracks, and I gradually let the song build in volume until I was able to transition to a Celine Dion power house.

They all just sat there. Reading their papers, staring at their phones or their feet—too awkward or self-absorbed to even look my way. Maybe they thought I was a crazy person and didn't want to mess with me. The chemically radiant sunset of my hair probably didn't help with that, but I didn't need their approval.

The guy in the hoodie though—he wouldn't take his eyes off me. I started to give him a little smile, but then a square-potato masquerading as a human being shoved his way between us. By the time he passed, the guy in the hoodie was gone. Whatever, this was my stop anyway.

The next day I saw that black hoodie again though. His back was turned, and he was spray painting something around a concrete drain pipe. It wasn't the vandalism that bothered me – Hell, I like to make my mark as much as the next —it was what he was painting. My face was blazoned across the pipe, all the way down to my shock of flame hair and the nose-ring I always wore. It was absolutely surreal staring into my own giant eyes which might have been beautiful if the situation wasn't so damn unnerving.

Maybe I should just be flattered that I made such an impression on him. I sat down about a dozen feet away and watched him expertly apply a light drizzle of shadow to define my cheekbones. It was a triumphant pose: a Queen surveying her adoring Kingdom on the night of her inauguration. What was this guy's deal, anyway? I hadn't even gotten a clear look at his face. Did he paint all the pretty strangers he sees, or was it just me? I was about to go ask him when I noticed the caption he was now writing below my portrait.

**Kill her**

Well what do you know, look at the time. As laudable as New York's diversity is, that unfortunately includes a large population of absolute maniacs. I quietly stood and backed away from the artist. He must have heard me though, because he immediately spun my way.

"Wait! I need you!" He was running after me now, but I wasn't about to stick around for pleasant conversation. I hightailed for the next three blocks until I reached the subway. For a moment I thought I was overreacting, but the two other paintings I passed along the way told a different story.

**Death**—written under the first one. It was another painting of me, this time from another angle. **Steal her**—the words were splashed right across my face on the next painting. I just wanted to be another invisible face in the crowd now. It was a relief to see the people piling up outside the station. I couldn't hide my red hair, but I don't think my stalker would try something here. Now that there were so many people, I was safe again.

I managed to put it out of my mind for the rest of the day, but I began to get worried when it was time to ride the subway home. I have a defense against fear though, and there's never been a night so black that I couldn't lighten with a song. I sat down at the end of the subway car and just began singing. People filed in and out, odd looks occasionally cast my way, but there wasn't anything they could do to make me stop. As long as I was singing—as long as I was me— somehow that made me safe.

But I didn't make it home before the words choked in my throat. There I was —then another, and another—face after face spray painted along the subway walls. I caught a flash of the words **never grow old**, but I couldn't force myself to look out the window after that.

I turned away, and there he was. He'd just gotten on board and was staring right at me. There were a lot of people getting off now too. Two more stops until I got home—I didn't dare ride with him the whole way. I started shoving my way out with the rest of them, but right before I made it past the door, I felt a hand land on my shoulder.

"Why did you come back for me?" he asked.

"I didn't. I ride the subway every day," I answered.

"Did you see my tribute to you?" he asked. "Is that why you came back?"

I didn't answer. I just pulled away and pushed out the door. I looked back, but I didn't see him get off. Good, maybe he took the hint.

"You know why I did it, don't you?"

I spun. He was right behind me again. The train ground to life, and the crowds were beginning to thin on the platform as the people flooded up the stairs.

"Get away from me," I replied. "Hey! Somebody help me." The uncaring crowd kept moving about their business. Couldn't they see this guy was a creep?

"I just don't think you should be forgotten after you die." he said.

The hand gripped at my shoulder again, but I shook him off. I started walking after the people, but insistent, kneading hands kept clutching onto me.

"Help! Security!" I shouted.

There was a guard barely a dozen feet away. He glanced distractedly in my direction before turning back to his phone. What was wrong with this society? Why didn't anyone care?

"Why are you making this so hard on me?" the man in the hoodie asked. I actually shoved him this time. Hard. He staggered back a half-dozen paces, but then barreled right after me again.

"Hey, cool it over there." The security guard looked up again for a moment, but he didn't make the slightest move to help.

"Can't you see that I love you?" the man in the hoodie howled. "Why won't you stay with me?"

He was there with me every step I took. I couldn't shake him. Another subway car was rumbling into place, and I tried to make my way toward it to get away. Hands were on my back, so I spun and shoved him again. This time he didn't catch himself in time. He dropped his pack as he back-peddled—trying to find his balance, tripping over his own feet. His familiar eyes pleaded an agonizing moment while he seemed to hang in the air before tumbling off the platform —? straight onto the tracks.

The train roared into place. I couldn't look—but I couldn't look away. I saw a pair of hands reaching up over the side before a hideous crack rent the air. I covered my ears and ran, but I couldn't block out the anguished scream. It just kept going and going—rising and falling like a car alarm. I'd thought the train would have killed him on impact, but maybe it just caught one of his legs or something.

Finally. Finally people were starting to notice. The crowd surged to the edge of the platform to watch. Shouting — the security guard trying in vain to hold them all back. Then the train started backing up, and the screaming surged up again. It didn't last long this time though. He must have died as it rolled back over him.

The noise was deafening. The only sign that the man in the hoodie had been there was his backpack still lying on the ground. I should have just left it alone and run, but as long as everyone was distracted, why not? Maybe I wanted a clue as to his obsession, or maybe it was my guilt that begged for closure. Whatever the case was, I couldn't stop myself from opening it and looking inside.

Photographs spilled out. Dozens of them. All of me, although some still showed my unaltered brown hair. He must have been following me for years. I sat on the ground in disbelief while the chaos churned around me.

More photos—these the paintings of my face. Many more than the ones I'd seen—the whole city must be filled with them. So far I must have encountered a random selection, but here they were all assembled in order. As I flipped through the photos, I could clearly read the captions in the sequence they were intended.

LIFE COULDN'T **KILL her** spirit.

**Death** couldn't **steal her** soul.
She's still singing, can you hear it?
From lips that will **never grow old**.

THEN PAPERS-NEWS-PAPER clippings: the obituary of my death standing most prominently on the top. Two years ago in this very subway. I died when a man slipped his knife between my ribs and ran off with my purse, leaving me to bleed out on the ground while people walked past me and did nothing.

But did I know this man? Why couldn't I remember him? Then again, why had he been the only one to notice me? Of all the careless faces that pass me every day, why didn't any of them seem to look my way?

I was so overwhelmed and terrified–I just did the only thing I knew to calm down. I started singing, but no-one noticed me over the riotous commotion. And every time I can't make sense of where I am or where I'm going, I'll just start singing again. Sometimes I'll catch an odd glance or two, but more often I can be as loud as I want and no-one will even know I'm there.

I keep forgetting things, and places, and people. But I'm writing this because I don't want to forget that he loved me, and that maybe I even once loved him. Now that he's dead, I hope he'll be able to look at my face painted all over the city and remember me. Until then, I'll keep riding the subway where he found me last, singing until he finds me again.

## From Rags to Stitches: Tobias Wade

Growing up without a dad, it was so easy to blame him for everything that went wrong. Mom wouldn't have to be gone all the time if he was here. She wouldn't be so stressed and angry. I would have done better in school if someone helped me with my homework. I wouldn't be so alone.

It was hard for me to appreciate how hard Mom worked for my sister and I. All I could see were the other families and how much happier they looked. Walking home from school I'd pass dads teaching their sons how to ride bikes or shoot hoops. I'd just walk faster, pretending I had something to do or someone waiting for me when I got home.

It was hard to keep pretending to the locked door and the dark house. Hard to realize that I mattered when most of my interactions with mom were post-it notes on the fridge.

*Be back at 10. You're the man of the house. Remember to feed your sister*
-Love mom

And then just like that, everything changed. Mom got a new job as a live-in maid with Leroy, a wealthy corporate type living in a big house with extra rooms. His face looked rather like a toad that had been stepped on, and it folded into a vicious scowl whenever he happened across me. Passing my sister or me in the hallway, he'd look the other way and press his body to the far wall as though afraid of contracting a disease.

Mom told us not to take it personally; Leroy didn't like *any* children. At first I couldn't figure out why he invited us to live there at all, but I was 15 then and it didn't take long to translate the leering smiles he gave Mom. He was always watching her when she was cleaning, and it made me sick to be in the same room as them. Even worse, Mom seemed to actually enjoy the attention. She made a show every time she bent over, luxuriously stretching her body when she reached high to dust.

I don't suppose it was my place to fight it though. My little sister Casey was just happy to have mom around all the time, and money was a lot easier now. I still didn't trust Leroy, but I figured mom knew what she was doing and could take care of herself. It wasn't long before Leroy's long looks turned into lingering caresses though. As always, Casey was more optimistic about it than I was.

"He's going to take care of us," Casey said one night. "And if he wants to be our new dad, then Mom is going to make him be nice to us."

"We can't have a new dad because we never had an old dad," I told her. "And Leroy won't want anything to do with us either."

But both of us were wrong: things didn't improve, and they didn't stay the same. They got much worse, much faster than we could have anticipated. Any noise was too much noise for Leroy. I could barely say good morning to Casey at the breakfast table without him slapping us quiet with his newspaper. He wouldn't look away anymore when I caught him fondling mom either. He'd just stare right through me and keep going, taunting me, daring me to say something. Once I'd left a pile of my school books on the dining room table and he just dumped them into the trash without hesitation. It was clear that Casey and I weren't welcome here.

We weren't invisible anymore. We were openly despised. Casey wouldn't speak up though, and mom refused to see it. She kept praising Leroy for taking us in and saying how much better he was than my real father. I wanted to stand up to Leroy, but seeing mom so happy I couldn't bear the guilt of ruining this for her. That's what I told myself at least. It seemed more noble than admitting I was afraid.

"Our life changed pretty fast, didn't it?" Casey would say. "It's easy to forget that Leroy's life changed pretty fast too. It's going to take time for him to learn how to deal with us. We just have to keep being good, and sooner or later he's going to notice."

I told her we were already being good, but she couldn't look me in the eye. "Not good enough," she said.

Casey hugged me and I held on because I knew she was being strong for the both of us now. She flinched at my touch though, and that was when I first

# Sleepless Nights

noticed the bruises on her chest. She pulled away from me and put her finger to her lips. *Don't tell*, her eyes pleaded. *Don't destroy our new life because of me.* That time I couldn't lie to myself anymore. I was the man of the house before Leroy arrived, and it was still my responsibility to protect the family. If anyone hurt us, it was my job to hurt them back.

I couldn't lie to myself. It wasn't for mom or for Casey that I was holding back. I was a coward, pure and simple. And it was my fault what happened next.

Less than a week later, Casey didn't get up to go to school with me. When I got home I found dead in her room. Clothing torn. Black and purple bruises around her neck. Her hair was frayed as though she was dragged across the floor. Cuts and abrasions all along her little body. The only thing that didn't look spoiled was her pure white hands. She hadn't fought back. She'd stayed good, even with that monsters hands around her neck.

And still, I was afraid. More than ever now. I wanted to storm down to his office and break open the door. I wanted to gut the bastard, to scream at him for every silent suffering we took in stride. I wanted to let him bleed out on the floor, take his money, and run somewhere I could protect mom. But I couldn't stop thinking about what he did to Casey, or what it must have felt like to be bludgeoned and dragged; choked and killed. I wasn't as brave as she was.

I went to mom instead. Even if we didn't get revenge, we could still get out. Mom didn't answer when I knocked, but I heard her crying inside. My hand froze on the door knob, terrified that he was with her now. I forced myself to open the door anyway. Thank god, she was alone—sitting on the bed, looking up at me as I entered.

"You already know." It was a statement, not a question.

Mom nodded, stifling back sobs. "I'm so sorry."

"It's not your fault." I sat on the floor in front of her, pressing my face against her legs. "It's his fault. He did this to us."

"You're right," she said, breathing easier now. "His fault."

"But it's not too late for us. We're going to go away now, right? We're going to be good. We'll start a new life."

She hugged me close, her hands running through my hair. "We have gotten away. This IS our new life. Even though it was your father's fault for leaving me with two kids, it's going to be okay. I'm free now."

"Dad? I was talking about Leroy -" I began, but I couldn't get the words out anymore. She was holding me even tighter. I tried to break free but her hands ran down my face to latch around my neck.

"I had to kill her, don't you see?" Mom's words bubbled out with hysterical insistence. "I had to fix your father's mistake. This is the only way Leroy would marry me. I could never force him to raise another man's children."

Maybe I could have struck her in the face, or broken one of her fingers and escaped. Even with her hands around my neck though, I couldn't bring myself to hurt her. My panicked brain couldn't make sense of what was happening. I struggled to get away, but my head was swimming as her fingers dug holes into my neck.

"Leroy has been so good to us," Mom cooed. "I'm so sorry, baby. This is the only thing I can do to make it up to him."

I toppled backward onto the floor and was able to gasp a greedy lungful of air into my lungs. I screamed as loud as my battered throat would allow, the air escaping me like I was vomiting burning gasoline. Then mom fell off the bed onto me, her whole weight landing on my throat. I must have been on the edge of passing out then because I was only aware of brief slivers of broken time like my consciousness was a strobe light.

*The door opening.*
*Leroy standing over me to watch.*
*Mom's hands still around my neck.*
*The door opening again.*
*Casey standing in the doorway. Bruised and beaten as I saw her last.*

And then I passed out for real. When I finally did wake up, I was still lying on the floor with mom on top of me. I pushed her off and struggled to my feet, panting and gasping and spluttering up blood. Leroy was on the floor too. Around both of their necks were the black and purple imprints of little fingers which dug so far into the flesh as to make permanent impressions in the corpse.

I didn't call the police until after I ran back to Casey's room. She was pale and stiff just as I had left her on the bed. The only difference was that her immaculate hands were now stained with dark streaks.

The police later confirmed her fingerprints on both Leroy and my mother. It seems as though they had already gotten married, and without any other living descendants I stood to inherit the house.

It's been four years since then, and I've tried to do my best to make up for what happened. I've given most of Leroy's money away, and I've opened up the extra rooms to foster children without a place to stay. I volunteer every chance I get, and am even taking classes to become a licensed family therapist. I know I should have done more when I had the chance, but I'm doing everything I can now.

I'm writing this because I need to know what is left for me to do. When I lay down to sleep at night, why do I still hear her? It was bad enough when it was just me, but now two of the foster boys have told me they hear it too.

Right before sleep in the broken time between waking and dreams, we all hear the same thing. Some nights it is no more than an intrusive thought that can't be banished. Other times I feel the hot whisper and my throat will start to itch like little fingers brushing the tiny hairs of my neck. Every time the same words, begging, pleading, demanding; I can't tell which.

"Not good enough," she'll say.

And I'll know she was right.

## Two Dead Playing the Elevator Game: Tobias Wade

I just wanted to get home that night. An impromptu board meeting ran late, and I had to stay until almost 9 PM just to take notes. When I finally did get out of there, waiting for the elevator was absolute torture. My heels were killing me, my bra was a dagger in my back, and all I had to show for my hard work was a legal pad full of inane political drivel and off-colored jokes.

Five minutes. *Ten minutes* before the door opened. Inside a pair of giggling teenagers were shoving each other back and forth. One girl, one boy. Baggy hoodies. Ripped jeans. Smelled like they thought marijuana was a perfume. It didn't take a legal secretary to guess they had been playing an elevator game by pushing every button.

I thought about reprimanding them, but the moment I stepped inside they went dead quiet. Maybe they knew they were busted. The building should have been locked by now anyway. I don't even know how they got in here, but at my energy was so depleted that didn't really care.

"Where are you going?" I asked, just to be polite.

The boy started to giggle again for a second. Then stopped. So abruptly I almost thought I was imagining it. It looked like the girl was holding her breath. She hid her face beneath her hair and went to push floor #1.

Not my kids. Not my problem. What *was* my problem is that the elevator was going up instead of down. I moved toward the row of buttons, and the girl fell flat to the floor and scrambled out of my way like I was made of lava. I mashed the highlighted #1, but we were going up quicker than ever.

Faster than it had ever gone before. There was nothing to hold on to, and I had to press myself to the wall to stop from falling over. It was shaking now too, buckling back and forth as it screeched up the cable. The lights flickered, and a cold wind started to whistle through the crack in the doors. It wasn't like a storm or anything though. It was more like all the heat in the elevator was flooding out into the shaft.

Another lurch. The hardest one yet. I fell straight on my ass. The kids playing the elevator game were holding onto each other and managed to remain standing, but even after we'd stopped they kept clinging on as though holding for dear life. The #1 button went dark. #10 turned on. Slowly, ponderously, as though it were struggling against a nearly insurmountable pressure, the door slid open.

I started to stand, then slipped again as one of my heels snapped cleanly off. I took the other shoe off, so frustrated that I just threw it at the kids.

"Now look what you've done. You broke the fucking elevator."

The boy glanced in my direction, but immediately turned away again. They were straining to look outside, but terrified to get close to me. Good, they should be scared. Vandalizing a legal office was as stupid as picking a fight in a police station.

"I want your names, and IDs. Both of you," I snapped. "You will be held responsible for any damages incurred. As far as the trespassing is concerned—"

But they still wouldn't look at me. The boy grabbed the girl by the hand and darted out into the hallway. I couldn't just let them run amok.

"Hey, you can't go in there!" I had to run to keep up now. "That's Mr. Bogle's office. You aren't allowed to -"

Annnnd they were inside. Of course. I patted myself down for my cell phone, but it wasn't there. I must have dropped it when I fell in the elevator. I half-turned back, but the door was already closing. I took a step in that direction, but then I heard something *crash* from the office. I spun again, sprinting down the hallway in my bare feet.

The boy was sitting on Mr. Bogle's desk while the girl stared out the window.

"Look at the sky!" she said. "And how tall the buildings are!"

"Dude, this is crazy," he replied.

Either they were stoned out of their minds or it wasn't just marijuana. They were running their hands over everything, so I wouldn't have been surprised if they were rolling too. The boy was even poking the potted plant like it was some alien creature he'd never seen before.

"That's enough!" I roared. Finally they both looked at me. Then at each other. Then back at me. Did they regret playing this stupid elevator game yet?

"Let's get out of here!" the boy rammed straight through me with his shoulder, sending me spinning back to the ground. The girl was trying to jump over me now, but I managed to grab her by the ankle and drag her down. She thrashed melodramatically on the ground for a few seconds, but before I could get to my feet she planted a kick in my face and broke free.

The door was already closing by the time I got to my feet. They were both inside, staring at me with wide trembling eyes as though they were somehow the victim in all of this. I felt absolutely feral as I lunged at them. I managed to get my fingers in the crack before the elevator closed and the sensor reflected the doors open wide. Half a dozen buttons had already been pushed, glowing like one big middle finger. The final stage of the elevator game had been played.

They were cowering in the corner as I loomed over them, an inferno of retribution burning in my eyes. Fine, let the elevator take the long trip down. That was just longer for them to be trapped in here with me. Now that they couldn't run, the struggle was absolutely pitiful. The boy's throat was almost comically fragile, and I was amazed how little pressure I needed to ram my broken heel through it. The girl was almost gone by the time I got to her, withering to a husk in seconds after the venom from my nails coursed through her leg where I had grabbed her.

I got out of the elevator at the bottom, straightening my dress. I'd found my phone again and fixed my hair, and after snapping the other heel off my shoe, I was able to look almost presentable again.

I thought I could finally go home after that, but it didn't take long to realize that I'd never been further from home in my life. What strange green plants they have here, and the dark blue sky was nothing like the purple and orange we have at home. No wonder they were so surprised by everything in my world. If everyone here is as fragile as those two little ones, then I think I'm going to have a lot of fun here.

## One Death is not Enough: Tobias Wade

Gilles Garnier was less than human. I don't mean he didn't have two hands, or two feet, or opposable thumbs – I mean that his spirit was so vile that his mere existence was an insult to the human race.

That's why he was nicknamed the "Werewolf of Dole," so we could think of him as a beast and pretend that each of us did not possess that same capacity for evil. Whatever he was, the creature was famous for strangling and eating four children in 16th century France before he was burned at the stake in 1572.

But that isn't where his story ends. Even the grotesque agony of burning alive was deemed incomparable to the suffering he caused those children and their families. That's why the secret sect known as "The Order of the Forgotten" was founded that same year, honoring Gilles with their very first sentence.

*ONE LIFE IS enough to be forgotten by Heaven.*
*But one death is not enough to be forgiven by Hell.*

THAT WAS THEIR MOTTO. They would wait until the body (or ashes, in Gilles' case) were buried before retrieving the remains. The Order of the Forgotten was initially established by the alchemists who used their macabre ingredients to trace the soul of the departed until it found its next iteration of reincarnated life.

The records indicate that Gilles Garnier was born again in 1574 under the name of Alisa Hathoway. Once the child was located, she was burned as well, serving as further punishment for the original sin she still carried in bearing Gilles' corrupted soul. Although subsequent judgment from the Order of the Forgotten was later restricted to a maximum of five deaths, the soul of Gilles Garnier was fated to serve as a warning for all those who would lend an ear to the goading darkness.

That is why Gilles was sentenced to an everlasting death. Every single time he was found. Every reincarnated animal, or child, or plant that possessed a shred of his original essence would sooner or later be located, and without fail, burned to ashes. These would then be preserved in order to find next soul on his eternal journey.

Now in 2017, the Order of the Forgotten has spanned six continents and over 140 countries, and they have entrusted me with killing Gilles for the 28th time.

"These ashes have been preserved for twenty years since his last death," Father Alexander told me. We were standing in the choir room of his church, now deserted to the lengthening shadows which grew restless with the deepening night.

"Ordinarily," Alexander continued, "we would have found him again much sooner, but the flames of his last death had spread to a nearby forest which consumed him utterly. His remains were contaminated with other ashes, and for a long while we were afraid that his remaining link would be too weak to trace. Although it has taken longer than usual, we have finally been able to succeed."

I'd never killed anyone before. The thought of carrying out this deed should have been abhorrent to me, but my oath to the Order was enough to reassure me that I was doing the right thing. After all, I had been a lost soul as well, and I was in debt to the father for sparing me from a similar fate. I will never forget that night when he found me when I was 14, camping in the woods with my friends. Through the trees he came, bearing a flaming brand which burned with the rage of an angry God.

"You are a sinner." he told me. And there with his billowing robes, basked in the glory of fire and pierced by the wild intensity of his eyes, I could feel my very soul laid bare to him.

"You have killed in your past lives, and you have fallen from grace." My friends had run, but I stood alone with my back to a tree. I was terrified by him, but somehow dependent as well. He knew me as I did not know myself, and it was not only my existence but my very nature which begged for his absolution.

The roaring fire inches from my face – my hair smoldering into my scalp—the exhilarating rush of my eternal realization. Did I remember the evils that I had caused? No, but I felt them like a weight on my soul, and I knew in that moment that I would do them again if I was not purified by the flame.

"You are forgotten by Heaven, but if you do as I say, you will be remembered before you die."

Six years later, I bow to Father Alexander, still fearful of the depth his probing eyes reach.

"Yes Father," I replied, "I will kill Gilles Garnier again."

Through the maturing night I walked, feeling the bag of ashes warm against my skin as I approach my target. I know he is close, which is why the Father has chosen me to do his bidding. *Don't think of it as killing someone. Think of it as killing*

## Sleepless Nights

*the part of myself which fate has cursed me to carry.* That's what I tried to tell myself at least.

It was exciting to feel the bag continuing to warm as I entered the restaurant. I walked slowly now, each step resounding with the unswayable purpose of one following God's will. The bag of ashes was starting to burn my leg now. Father told me that it will burst into flame when Gilles is beside me, and that I must use it to return him to ashes once more.

"Excuse me, have you been seated?"

I walked straight past the waiter without a second glance. Too old. It had been twenty years since Gilles was burned, so the man I was looking for must be less than that. It can sometimes take years before the soul to return to life, so there were still plenty of options.

"We're very full, so if you don't have a reservation -"

I felt a hand on my shoulder, but one look was enough for the waiter to stumble backward. He saw something in me that I had seen in Father Alexander on the night he found me. Such a glorious purpose cannot be seen and turned aside.

"I'm here to meet someone." I told him. His eyes were masks of uncertainty, so I pointed at a table at the far end of the room. "I'm with them."

The teenage couple sitting there glanced up. The waiter bobbed his head, disappearing with the kind of relief you'd expect from a man climbing out of a shark tank. The bag of ashes was searing my flesh now, and the smell of it mingled with the aromatic atmosphere wafting from the table. I smiled through it all, knowing my redemption was at hand.

"We weren't expecting—" the boy started.

"They never are," I answered, sitting down to join them. He couldn't be more than sixteen, face still riddled with enough pimples to make a constellation. Was it him? Or was it the girl, staring at me with her wide blue eyes that quivered around the edges. What was she afraid of, unless she felt the pressing weight on her soul?

"Sorry, but who are you?" the boy asked. I ignored him, digging the cloth bag from my pocket and dropping it onto the table. Sparks forced their way out like smoldering gunpowder.

"Leave us," I told the boy, "I want a word with your friend."

He half-started to stand, but the girl grabbed his arm and pulled him back into the chair. Her blue eyes narrowed, no longer shaking.

"I'm not his friend, I'm his *girlfriend*," she snapped, as though that made any difference to me. "And you're the one who needs to leave."

She was loud. Too loud. Several tables had turned to stare at me. There was no way to do this quietly here. Not yet.

"My apologies, Gilles." I tested her. She didn't even flinch. And why would she? I didn't remember my past life, so why would I expect her to remember a man who lived hundreds of years ago? I grabbed the cloth bag and excused myself from the table before the waiter could return. As I walked briskly toward the door, I could feel the bag cooling against my skin.

I waited outside for them to emerge, clutching the bag between my hands, desperate for the lingering heat to reaffirm my beliefs. Her soul was corrupt, just as mine was. She must be punished for me to become clean. But how could she be punished for something she never did? How could I be absolved by killing an innocent?

They exited sooner than I expected. Maybe I had ruined the mood. I waited until they left the ring of lights before I fell into step behind them. It didn't matter if I had doubts, because I know God was infallible. If he wanted me to kill, then I would enjoy it knowing I was doing the right thing. The Order of the Forgotten had maintained their charge for hundreds of years, and I wouldn't be weak link in that chain.

The bag was burning again. I watched her say goodbye to the boy in front of her house, hugging him after he seemed too awkward to kiss her. The ashes grew hotter as they held each other close, and then he was gone – walking down the sidewalk. The bag didn't cool down. That was it then. She was the one.

*Dark house. Rustling of keys.* She glanced behind her, eyes fixing on the sparkling bag in my hands. Then on my face. I smiled.

"Hello Gilles Garnier," I said. "Would you like to invite me in?"

She shook her head. Back to the door, she fumbled with the keys in her hands. I threw the ashes at her face, watching them come to life as they approached. She threw her arms up to block, but the ashes scattered in fiery impact. She screamed, and I can't deny the satisfaction of hearing my prey realize its helplessness. The burning ashes clung to her like tar, bursting into incandescent color as brilliant as the brand Father Alexander carried when he found me.

I wasn't killing her. I was just sending her back where she belonged.

Only she didn't burn. The light burst around her in a luminous aura. She wasn't screaming anymore either – just staring at her dazzling body in awe. I didn't understand. I wanted to see her soul being purged! I wanted her to suffer for what she'd done! Father Alexander told me that –

"That's enough." It was Alexander's voice. My eyes were stunned from the light and I couldn't see him, but I heard his footsteps approaching from the street. "Gilles has revealed himself to you. It's time to punish him."

"I'm trying–" I spluttered, but Alexander's hand materialized from the shadows to preface his entrance into the light. The hard lines in his skin made it look as though it were carved from stone.

"I'm talking to Lily," Alexander said. His grave face was fully illuminated now, and I could see that he was staring at the girl. "It is as I told you. You do not have to search for the soul in need of punishment. He will find you."

# Sleepless Nights

My blood was boiling. My chest was tight. I could barely breath, but I forced the words out like hissing steam.

"The ashes. You told me to—"

"I told you the day I met you," Alexander growled. "That you carried a corrupted soul. Each time you return, you are tested again. Not once in five hundred years have you refused to kill, and so not once have you been spared. So are all the souls tested before they are punished again. There is no reason so grand or order so high that can justify the choice you've made to kill an innocent."

The light had all but faded from Lily now. The ashes still sparkled where they rained through the air around her. It had been a trick then. I may not have remembered being Gilles Garnier, but I hadn't refused the chance to kill again either. I turned to run, and neither of them followed me.

But where can I run when it was my nature that I must flee? How can I hide when they have already found me over 200 times? Sooner or later the Order of the Forgotten burn me again, so there is nothing left for me but to wait. To wait and to pray, that next time I will find the strength to make my own choices, not rely on God.

## Imagine a Night: Tobias Wade

*Imagine a night when the space between words becomes like the space between trees: wide enough to wander in.*

– Sarah Thomson.


"THAT POOR GIRL," they'd say. "Imagine that happening right in our neighborhood."

"Do you think she suffered much? It's too dreadful to think about."

"We're all holding a vigil in her honor. You'll be there, of course?"

No, I won't be there. I honestly don't understand why people still feel sorry for my sister Catherine. Once pain has passed, it no longer exists. Once life has passed, pain is no longer possible. Her cold body no longer bleeds, nor do her withered lungs cry out as they must have done from the lonely depths of those tangled woods. Sympathy is wasted on the dead.

All my life I've been the one who was pitied. I was diagnosed at four with spinal muscle atrophy which wasted me away until I was too weak to stand. I underwent constant orthopedic surgeries, physio-therapy, respiratory care, and endless new medications. Never once did I think I would be the one to survive. My older sister had always been there to take care of me though. From helping me shower to pushing my wheelchair, she'd supported me literally and figuratively for as long as I can remember.

Now they treat her like she's the victim, but she isn't anymore. I don't care if you think this is selfish, but mother and I are the only victims now. We're the ones living amidst the ashes of a life which burned so bright and brief: a defiant flare from a dying star. Only our unmeasured pain still lingers in her absence.

"She's in Heaven now," my mother told me. "It's the most wonderful place you can imagine."

"Then why are you still sad?" I'd asked.

"Because she got there first, and we must wait." Mother held me close, although I think it was as much for her own comfort as mine. She didn't want me to see, but I could still feel the suppressed trembling of her body and knew she must be crying. At 14, I was too old to be comforted by her facade. Catherine helped me so much while mom was at work, but now that we're alone, I don't know what we'll do. There's a constant source of restless anticipation as though any second could bring her through the door or break the grim silence with her swelling laughter. It still doesn't seem real that she's gone.

Catherine used to sit and read upon that window seat, now cluttered with the graveyard of her possessions. Or out in the garden, dancing among her sprouting seeds with a triumphant exaltation unmatched by the inauguration of an emperor. She walked in grace, warming each room she entered with boundless vitality. Even now in the heat of summer I shiver to remember what that felt like.

I still talk to her sometimes, but not in the way you might expect. I don't ask her about the night she died, or dwell upon evil thoughts of the creature which devoured everything except her eyes. Instead, I'll break the hungry silence of the night by asking how she lived with such innocent wonder. I'll ask how she was so happy, because sitting alone in the room we shared, it seems that I've forgotten.

"You're such a strong girl," they say. "Your sister would be proud."

"It will get easier. Time heals all wounds."

No, I don't believe that either. Time makes a wound fester and rot, magnifying the pain into brooding despair. If Catherine had somehow crawled from the clutches of the wilds, legs torn to shreds, face mutilated beyond recognition, do you think time would have spared her from pain? Or would life's cruelty compound her injury until isolation and rejection stole what remaining dignity even the beast could not take? Will time ever spare me from the prison of this failing body?

They see me eating, and talking, and forcing a smile through my dried lips. They don't realize that two girls died the night Catherine was attacked. They know that we were close, but do not understand that we were the same. One secret glance between us, and we would see into each other's heart. Half a smile, and we both laughed at an unshared joke. Even now through the veil of death I can see her waiting for me on the other side.

My body lingered for a week after her death, but there was no point in delaying the inevitable. I was calm when I rolled up to the pool last night. The chill waters ebbed and flowed against my feet like an electrical current, but it couldn't disturb the tranquility which ushered my spirit toward her. Catherine was in Heaven now, so what was the point of waiting here in Hell?

It would be only human nature to struggle once I rolled into the pool. The chair would pin me beneath the suffocating water though, and even without it I wouldn't be strong enough to swim. Catherine would have struggled too, but that's over now. When the fluid filled my lungs and my oxygen deprived brain stopped thinking about the world that might have been, we'd be together again.

*One deep breath before the plunge.*

If only I had died and she had lived. Mother could have been happy then.

*One look back at the dark house.*

But not dark enough. I could see mom now, watching me from her bedroom window.

She wasn't calling out. She didn't want to stop me. It didn't matter either way though.

*One way or the other, I was already gone.*

I plunged my chair into the water and sank toward the bottom. The peace didn't last, but I waited as long as I could before letting the first bubbles escape my mouth. The pressure built into a silent scream. My fingers dug into my neck, but I forced myself to let go. The last wave of air leaked from my burning lungs and my head spun. I thought I caught a glimpse of mother looking down at me, but my eyes swelled shut and I couldn't be sure. The water poured into my nose and mouth, filling my chest, flowing and growing and swelling until I knew I would burst.

*It's okay.* I told myself. *This isn't the end. This is just a stopping point on between being alone and together again.*

The water was rushing past me now. I sensed a light penetrating into my closed lids. I felt a surge of upward motion. I tried to open my eyes, but the light was so bright that I couldn't see any more than with them shut. My chair was gone. This was it. The wait was over, and I was being carried to Heaven.

My head burst free from the water and I spluttered in the open air. My eyes were still pressed tight, but I flailed until I felt something solid and gripped on for dear… life? Dear existence, perhaps. The water gently pushed me toward the shore, and I pulled myself hand over trembling hand until solid ground welcomed me.

I vomited a veritable river of water. It felt like I must have drunk half the pool. I couldn't still be there though, because instead of the tiles I felt grass and mud squelching beneath me.

*The rustle of leaves.* The strangled caw of a bird, and then a hooting reply. I wiped my face with dirty hands until a sliver of light broke through my swollen lids. The tangled trees rose around me like specters of the night, and a full moon illuminated the stagnant pool which I'd crawled from. Perhaps I was in the woods behind my house, but I had never seen them by moonlight. Was I dead?

What had my sister been doing, so far out alone? She never went anywhere without me. How did she even get there?

*The crack of a branch.* More rustling, prompting a surge of wild panic from my already erratic heart. And what *was* it that had attacked her that night?

Everyone had assumed that she had simply snuck off into the woods with a boy. Wouldn't she have told me though? I had been so obsessed with my own thoughts and feelings that I hadn't even stopped to wonder what really happened that night. It had just been an accident, too horrible to think about. Or was it?

I took a hesitant step back toward the pool of water, but looking down I could see that it couldn't be more than a few inches deep. It was impossible for me to be here, but I was.

I took another step, my feet scrambling below me. For the first time in my life I was walking, but it wasn't just that. I was walking on all fours. They weren't hands which had pulled me out of the water, but predatory paws like some primordial wolf from an age where tooth and claw were the only rules governing the world.

The *rustling* was getting closer.

"Hello? Is anyone there?"

Catherine! It had to be her! We could be together again, but not like this. Not with the fur bristling down my back or claws churning the wet mud. I felt my mouth involuntarily twist into a snarl. *Run Catherine! You aren't safe with me!* If only she could sense my thoughts now like she used to. Tension washed through my body as I crouched to pounce, and savage instincts flooded my awareness with an undeniable compulsion to feed.

But it wasn't Catherine. It was my mother who stepped through the trees to stand before me. I was so surprised that I couldn't even move. She was wearing a bathrobe I had seen her in when she watched me from her bedroom window and smiling from ear to ear.

"There you are. I've been looking everywhere for you," she said. "Come along, your sister is waiting."

She took a step toward me, but the vibration of an alien growl rose in my throat.

"Don't be silly." Mother didn't seem the least afraid, and her confidence in the face of my terrifying presence was enough to give me pause. "You're in Heaven now, child. You needn't be afraid. For our family, that means returning to who we truly are. The body may be tamed, but the spirit can never be deprived of its true form. Your father has decided your sister was old enough to become herself, although you have decided for yourself."

*This wasn't my Heaven.* This wasn't who I was. This wasn't who Catherine – poor innocent Catherine – was meant to be. The feral rage was building inside me again, but I couldn't let myself attack. What would that accomplish, besides allowing mother to transform as well?

"That's right, you understand now." Mother took a step forward. She loosened her robe, exposing her bare neck. "Go ahead. Do it, and we will be a family again."

The flesh was so soft, and I was so hungry. It was so easy to sink my teeth in and shake the life out of her. The freedom of my body was exhilarating as I flew through the air. I wasn't a cripple anymore. I wasn't in pain, or pitied, or a victim. I wasn't alone anymore. In that moment as the blood ran down my jaws, I knew my mother was right. I was in Heaven.

But how quickly that moment passed, and how silent the woods when her body stopped moving. By the morning I woke alone in the woods, covered in my mother's blood. My hands were my own. My feet were my own. And how my body shook as I pulled myself inch by excruciating inch across the forest floor with my degenerative muscles fighting me the whole way.

It's taken time, but I've pieced together what I think really happened to me. The first time I died, it was when I suffocated in my sleep when my failing lungs could no longer support my dying body. That was the night of my first transformation, when I killed my sister and dragged her into the woods.

The second night I died was in the pool, prompting my second rebirth. But just like the first time, it only lasted through the night. I don't know who my father is or where these powers came from, but it seems as though my mother didn't understand as I do now. My mother and sister did not have the gift, and neither of them are coming back. Every night since then, I flee my dying body and relish in the freedom of the hunt. Every night I die, and every night I taste Heaven again.

# Publisher's Note

Please remember to
**honestly rate the book**!

It's the best way to support me as an author and help new readers discover my work.

## Keep Reading!

Join the Haunted House Book Club and read more stories for free.

**HAUNTED HOUSE**
PUBLISHING

TobiasWade.Com

Printed in Great Britain
by Amazon